D0776811

Preacher's Lake

Also by Lisa Vice

Reckless Driver

Preacher's Lake

Lisa Vice

A DUTTON BOOK

ACKNOWLEDGMENTS
Because no one ever really does it alone, the author wishes to express her gratitude to
Rosemary Ahern, Martha Clark Cummings, Marg Hainer, Jean V. Naggar, and Zoe Vice.

DUTTON
Published by the Penguin Group
Penguin Putnam Inc., 375 Hudson Street, New York, New York 10014, U.S.A.
Penguin Books Ltd, 27 Wrights Lane, London W8 5TZ, England
Penguin Books Australia Ltd, Ringwood, Victoria, Australia
Penguin Books Canada Ltd, 10 Alcorn Avenue, Toronto, Ontario, Canada M4V 3B2
Penguin Books (N.Z.) Ltd, 182–190 Wairau Road, Auckland 10, New Zealand

Penguin Books Ltd, Registered Offices: Harmondsworth, Middlesex, England

First published by Dutton, an imprint of Dutton NAL, a member of
Penguin Putnam Inc.

First Printing, June, 1998
10 9 8 7 6 5 4 3 2 1

Portions of this novel have appeared in somewhat different form in *Love's Shadow*
(Crossing Press), *Common Lives/Lesbian Lives,* and the *Palo Alto Review.*

LIBRARY OF CONGRESS CATALOGING-IN-PUBLICATION DATA:

Vice, Lisa, 1951–
    Preacher's Lake / Lisa Vice.
        p.   cm.
    ISBN 0-525-94436-2 (acid-free paper)
    I. Title.
    PS3572.I253P7 1998   97-42993
    813'.54—dc21   CIP

Printed in the United States of America

For Karen and Paul

Part One

Part One

1

Connie Riley drove over the Swift River Bridge, speeding along the steel grids, her tires humming and splashing as she drove into Preacher's Lake, a town scattered along the rocky coast of Sow's Head Bay as haphazardly as the shattered bits of sea urchin shells strewn across the granite by the gulls. Today, the town looked washed out in the pelting rain, a blur of gray and mist rising up into the hills away from the sea. She sped past the white clapboard church, all boarded up, gloomy and haunted-looking on its knoll of dead grass.

It was spring, the advent of mud season, and the rains had washed out culverts, carving ruts in the dirt roads that crisscrossed the county, ruts where even the most rugged trucks had to be eased out with the crank of a come-along. All week long, folks had been out at night dipping their nets in the rivers, bringing them up full of silvery alewives flapping in the heavy rain. Near the lake, in the woods where there were still patches of snow, trillium bloomed in the spongy moss.

"A godforsaken place," Connie muttered, bumping over frost heaves, skimming puddles that spilled across the road like waves lapping the shore. She turned onto Preacher's Lake Road and headed past the twisted pine trees, scrubby overgrown fields, and dooryards where tar paper covered houses bobbed like dinghies in the sea of mud. Although it was a coastal town, Preacher's Lake had an atmosphere of a place not open to the sea but rather walled in, sunken down, nearly swallowed by storms and winds and the harsh day-to-day effort to make a living out of clay, rock, and bloodworms twelve cents apiece.

Slim Riley was in his shed at the Preacher's Lake landfill. He had the barrel stove stoked and was tipped back in a torn BarcaLounger thumbing through a magazine, his glasses sliding down his nose. He heard the car, but before he could get up, his mother was at the door, beads of water from her rain bonnet dripping down her cheeks.

"Ma!" Slim was surprised to see her. He felt panic—both that she had come with some terrible news and that she would see the magazine that slid to the floor, open to a photo of a blonde in black lacy underwear that revealed more than it covered. Who died? he thought, hitching up his green work pants. All of his clothes were salvaged from the trash and since he was so tall, nearly six foot four, and so thin, nothing fit properly. This particular pair of pants with large patches on both knees was lashed around his waist with a length of clothesline. "C'mon and sit by the fire," he said, shooing an orange tomcat off the easy chair.

"I brung a snack," said his mother. Just as she draped her coat over the chair, the lightbulb dangling from the ceiling flickered. The rain smashed against the windows as if someone were throwing buckets of water against the panes, making them rattle like teeth chattering.

"You shouldn'ta come out in this," Slim said. What he really wanted to say was: What's so important it can't wait till I get home? Instead, he sipped the cocoa she'd brought. He'd learned long ago there was no rushing his mother.

Although Slim was forty years old and twenty years younger than his mother, a stranger glimpsing them might have thought it was the other way around. Slim's pale blue eyes were nearly obscured by the thick lenses of his black-framed glasses and his hair, which hung in matted clumps well past his shoulders, was completely white, tinged green from the soot and dust his work stirred. His mother had sharp green eyes, perky as a kitten's, and brown curls without a hint of gray.

Slim put more wood on the fire even though the shed was quite warm. With his mother there, he felt closed in, as if he had to be careful not to knock over the stacks of books and towering heaps of newspapers and magazines along the walls. The woman in the glossy photo of his magazine looked up, licking her lips. But Slim's mother was busy dabbing her face with a tissue. Then she lit a cigarette.

"Boy, I'll tell you. It's been slow as molasses today." Slim yawned nervously. The way the wind was carrying on, it seemed the shed might collapse. He pictured his mother puffing her cigarette while the splintered boards clattered and fell around her.

Slim had built the shed using construction materials gleaned from the dump. He'd fitted the boards in any which way, not bothering to cut them the same length. He hung things from the ones that jutted out unevenly: buckets filled with rusty metal hasps and hinges, coils of rope, chain, and wire. Every single part of the shed was recycled; even the nails had been pulled and straightened before he hammered them into place. The roof and walls were covered with a patchwork of linoleum, asphalt shingles, roofing paper, and tin cans he pounded flat.

The rain was slowing now, tapping the roof softly. It had been raining the day Slim learned his father died, asleep at the wheel; he'd been on a two-week drunk and drove off the ramp to the bridge. That day, his mother served Slim a complete meal, down to fresh apple pie, before telling him the bad news though the minute he got home he sensed something was wrong. "Sank like a sack of kittens tied to a rock," she had finally said.

A week after the funeral, Slim was at the dump tossing tires on the trash, scattering the rats, burning the rubbish that accumulated in his father's absence. "If you do what nobody else wants to do," Slim's father used to say, "folks'll leave you alone." This had been true so far except for Clarence Cushman, one of the selectmen. He complained about the hens Slim kept, complained about the shed, too, calling it an eyesore that ought to be torn down.

Slim found the chickens one morning after Easter when he was poking around in the trash; there they were in a plastic bag, nearly dead, their feathers dyed blue and green and pink. Now they were prancing across the roof of the old car he used for a coop. Tom, the lone turkey he kept, preened behind the steering wheel.

"Well," his mother sighed and fumbled in her purse for her lipstick and mirror. After she outlined her lips bright red, she pressed them together as if kissing herself, then dabbed a dot of red on each cheek and rubbed it in. Slim leaned forward, afraid he might miss what she was about to say. She tipped back her cup and drank the last of the cocoa. "Carl's asked me to come with him. To Costa Rica. That ex of his is making him pay through the nose. He can't hardly keep his head above water. Gimme, gimme, gimme. He took off this morning. He's halfway there by now. I'm gonna go after."

"After?"

"Yeah. After." She lit another cigarette and held the match until it burned down to her fingertips before she blew it out. "I got to sell the house and everything."

Slim stared at his big hands resting on his knees, the cracks in his

skin stained with grease and soot and years of dirt that wouldn't
come out no matter how hard he scrubbed. He thought of the
expression: Waiting for the other shoe to fall. His mother's words
were like the thump of Carl's work boots when he eased them off
and dropped them onto the floor at night.

After his mother left, Slim watched the seagulls peck the garbage.
Dump ducks, he called them. Or flying rats. He rushed toward them
flapping his arms, his boots slapping the mud like a scarecrow come
to life. But the seagulls, unfazed, went on pecking at the mushy
greens, fighting over bones and soggy bread.

The rain had stopped but the sky was still cloudy and dark as he got
on his front-loader and started to bury the day's trash. They didn't let
him burn it anymore. Rules. Regulations. There was even talk of closing many of the landfills across Maine. No one comes to Vacationland
to see heaps of rotting rubbish, Clarence Cushman said.

"Think. Think," he scolded himself as he worked. He had to
come up with a plan. Maybe he could find a way to buy the house
from his mother. Or talk her out of selling. Something.

When he finished, he sat for a while with his glasses off, staring
ahead. *Dumb,* his teachers used to say when he dipped his bony fingers into the jar of paste and licked them clean. *Slow* they said when
during a game of dodgeball he didn't even try to duck but let the
ball smack his chest. It wasn't until third grade when Miss Walker—
fresh out of college and determined to reach the painfully thin boy
in the back row—discovered he could barely see. When he was fitted with glasses, Slim was so startled by the world made sharp
around him he often slipped his glasses into his shirt pocket and
shrank further into himself, preferring the blurry haze. His view was
hazy now, but he knew the familiar hills were there, the white
church spire rising among the pine trees. He knew how the land
sloped to the sea and beyond, the humped blue shapes of Holiday
Island rose out of the mist.

*   *   *

"I gotta go," Crystal Curtis said in her flat, high-pitched voice. She
and her mother, Janesta, had just dashed across the parking lot,
dodging the puddles, and were settled in the steamy car.

"*Now?* You couldn't go inside? You can't wait till we get home?"

"I gotta go wicked bad," Crystal said, grabbing herself between
the legs. Her stringy brown hair fell over her pale moon-shaped
face.

"Jesus Kee-*reist* Almighty." Janesta punched the cigarette lighter. "You ain't gettin' me back in that welfare office. I'll wait here."

Crystal shook her head. "It's gross. Everybody peein' on the floor and no toilet paper."

"If you pee your pants that'll be gross." Janesta pulled into traffic. "Just hold it, you hear me?" She cursed at the impatient drivers who splashed around her as she made her turn into the Chevron station. "Hold tight," she said. "I got to get the goddamn key. They lock it up like it's the bank vault."

Crystal was already pulling her pants down as she hurried inside, but the hot pee ran down her legs, soaking her socks. She sat on the toilet, dabbing herself with tissue while Janesta lit a cigarette and examined herself in the mirror above the rust-stained sink.

"The rent's overdue. All we got's a jar of mustard and a half loaf of bread at home. And that bag of lobster bodies to pick over. God, I'm sick to death of lobster," Janesta said, fiercely pulling at the skin around her eyes to ease the wrinkles. "I sound like some country song. 'I'm down to my last roll of toilet paper,' " she sang. "But no sir. That ain't any emergency for that bitchy welfare worker. 'You got to budget, Miss Curtis.' '*Mrs.*' I say. *Mrs.* Curtis.' "

At least the damn worker that's been on me about Crystal getting tested wasn't there today, she thought, sucking her stomach in, checking her profile. What the hell can the counselors at the health center tell me about Crystal I don't already know?

"How hard up can you get?" Janesta crouched beside the toilet where Crystal sat winding thick wads of toilet paper around her hand. "Crystal, get me my nail file," Janesta said.

Rummaging through her mother's purse, Crystal became distracted by the squashed tissues, the dusty pennies and flakes of tobacco, the half-used matchbooks and tubes of makeup.

"How do birds get pregnant?" Crystal asked.

"Don't start on that now." Janesta grabbed the purse from her and found the nail file herself, jiggling it in the keyhole of the toilet paper holder while Crystal pumped pink soap into her palms. The bright pink of it pleased her, and she cupped it in her hands, enjoying the way it seeped through her fingers.

"I'm gonna get this cussid thing," Janesta said, yanking on the toilet paper until it came loose and rolled across the filthy floor. "Jackpot," she said. "I'll tell you. It don't pay to be honest. If I'd a never told that welfare lady I was waitin' tables, we'd be high on the hog with hamburgers and pork chops for supper. I don't know what

I was thinkin'. Wash your hands, Crystal. Good God Almighty, that's enough soap. C'mon. Let's go."

"I got to pee again."

"No, you don't. You just think you do."

"No, I do. I had me that other Coke, 'member?"

"Just hurry it up. I'll be out bringin' back the key, OK?"

Crystal was on the toilet when her mother left and was still sitting there when Janesta returned and hollered, "Get outa there!"

"I don't got no paper," Crystal said. "I got stuck."

"What d'you mean, stuck?"

"My hand's stuck," Crystal said. Her fingers were jammed in the metal contraption. She didn't know why she reached in there. She wasn't looking for toilet paper. She could see there wasn't any.

In a few minutes, her mother was back with the key and there was Crystal, her pants around her ankles, one hand trapped. Janesta tried to loosen it, but Crystal screamed as if she were cutting her hand off.

"I can't believe it. I can't fuckin' believe it." She smacked Crystal's face and was immediately sorry when Crystal slumped, limp as a rag doll, her hand still trapped.

"Ma'am?" A man cleared his throat. "There some sort of trouble?" He bent over Crystal, averting his eyes from her naked bottom, his large fingers brushing Crystal's small ones.

"She's stuck all right," he announced. "I coulda swore I put a new roll in there this mornin'."

"1816. That's the year they had no summertime. Brrr," Crystal said and shivered. "God."

"What's that?" The man stared at her then waved his hand in front of her face. The girl's eyes rolled around. "She ain't havin' some kinda fit, is she?" asked the man.

"Fit to be tied," Crystal said, pulling her hand free. She sucked her fingertips, refusing to show her mother.

Janesta had half a mind to get the toilet paper from her car and fling it into the rain. Stalk off like it was no big deal. At the same time, she wanted it. Even if she did end up in the police report like Mary Alice Strong did when she got caught drinking milk at the grocery. "I was thirsty," the report claimed Mary Alice said. "I needed it," Janesta would tell the police. She wanted it with an overwhelming desperation, to take it home and not worry about how long it lasted. She couldn't believe how low she had fallen.

"C'mon, Crystal," Janesta said, heading for the car, pretending not to notice the man reach into his pocket and give Crystal a handful of change. She revved the engine when Crystal got in. "I hope you're proud of yourself, Miss Curious," she said.

As they headed out of town, Crystal gazed longingly at the Pizza Place but did not beg her mother to stop. She slid down in her seat and wiggled her fingers. Satisfied they were OK, she squeezed her eyes shut. When they got to the Swift River Bridge—she could tell without looking because of the way the tires sang—she counted at the top of her voice as fast as she could until they reached the other side. She feared they would fall into the river and be carried out to sea if she didn't do this whenever they crossed the bridge. Janesta had long ago given up trying to convince Crystal the bridge was not about to collapse.

"How much you got?" Janesta asked, pulling into the parking lot of Moody's store.

"What?" Crystal ran the tip of her tongue around and around her lips. Even though she knew her mother hated when she did this, she couldn't help it.

"Count up that money he gave you, now. Run in and get us hot dogs. Get the no names. And ask old lady Moody to charge what's extra. Tell her I'll pay her the first of the month. Get a quart of milk, too." She gave Crystal a shove. "Go on, now."

Crystal waded through a puddle at the bottom of the porch steps then trudged inside to get the groceries.

"You're short two twenty-nine," Mrs. Moody announced. Her voice echoed across the store.

"Barometer's rising," Crystal said, looking at the ceiling. Mrs. Moody was like the flying monkeys in *The Wizard of Oz*. Any minute she would swoop down and fly off with Crystal dangling from her paws. "Weatherman says it's gonna be sunny next week."

"You tell your mother she better get in here next time. Not send you to do her dirty work. You tell her I said so." Mrs. Moody tossed the groceries into a bag. "Nut case," she said bitterly as Crystal pushed past a man stomping mud off his boots at the door.

"Where's the fire?" he called, tipping his cap at Janesta.

* * *

"You-know-who's here." J.T. closed the door to the exam room behind her. She tapped the file folder in her hand and rolled her eyes.

Lizzy looked up from the latest issue of *Monthly Extract*. "It says menstrual blood makes a great plant fertilizer."

"Why do I get the feeling you're avoiding me?" asked J.T.

"Don't tell me. Please, not *her* again." Lizzy fiddled with her stethoscope.

"I got a 'east infection, de-ah." J.T. plodded around the room with her breasts thrust forward. "A burnin' in my wound."

"Lizzy? Can you check my breasts?" Lizzy made her voice a high whine. "Sure, Trudy," she answered herself. "Just haul 'em in here. Unloose that load of flesh, woman. I ain't got all day."

"You love it," J.T. said. "Admit it. You just *love* it."

"Don't start. Shit! Aren't we running late?"

"You have a date or something?"

"No. We both know I haven't had a date since Dennis and I broke up. You'd be the first to know if I did." She raked her fingers through her thick black curls. "I just wanted to get home before dark. I'm still not used to going home to an empty apartment. Did you try to talk you-know-who out of it? Did you tell her she was in here last week? She was, right?"

"Yeah," J.T. said. "Exactly a week ago to the minute. And yes I tried to talk her out of it. But I had to give her a pregnancy test, too. It's the works today."

"Oh please! She probably went through menopause before my period even started. What? Hydie bumps his thing against her while they're sleeping and she's ready to conceive? Oh God! I only took four counseling credits and all we did was tell each other our worst sexual experiences and try not to laugh."

"It's your magic fingers," J.T. said. "She's got a craving." J.T. danced toward the door singing, "Thrill me, chill me." She beckoned to Trudy Hyde who was seated on the large sagging sofa in the waiting room anxiously fingering her bra straps.

"I found a bunch the size of a dry bean under my arm this mornin'," Trudy said, huffing and puffing as she came into Lizzy's office.

"Uh-huh," Lizzy said. "Which side?"

"That'd be the left." Trudy stopped and felt under her arm. "Yes, de-ah. I'm sure it's the left. Can't feel it with my clothes on but I was washin' with my right hand. I found it when I was havin' my bath. I'm right-handed, see. Not that I don't wash with my left, but I do favor my right."

"Last week it was under the right one, you said. But we never did find it. You went for your mammogram last February, it says on your chart." Lizzy peered over the curtain at the puffs of steam rising from the cars in the parking lot as the sun broke through the heavy clouds. "What did the doctor tell you, Trudy?"

"Got breasts made in heaven. Nothing wrong with neither one."

"You were here last week. Do you realize you have been in, let's see . . ." Lizzy started to count the number of visits in the last year.

"I get so worried I can't sleep. You girls are here and it comforts me to know I'm OK. I know you don't mind." Trudy considered telling Lizzy about the magazine article she'd read. People were erasing each other from their family photos—whoever they didn't like, say they got a divorce or had a fight, *poof!* Gone. She couldn't stop seeing life without herself in it. Just a cloud hovering over the counter at the diner. Her empty place at the supper table. However would Hydie and Raymond get along without her? How could she explain all this to Lizzy?

Trudy turned her back modestly and slipped on one of the cotton gowns from the stack folded on the chair. She took her bra off only after the gown was on, reaching up under the hem to retrieve it, before settling herself on the edge of the exam table. She took a deep breath to steady her voice. "You want me lyin' down?"

"OK. Lie down. But first *you* try to find it. All right?" Lizzy tried to hold back the impatience in her voice.

"I'm a lookin' for it," Trudy said. The paper was crackling and ripping underneath her. "I'm fubbin' everything up."

"Don't worry about that. Just find the lump you're worrying about."

"I got it. It's right here. Yes, de-ah. The size of a dry bean, like I said. Jesus Lord in heaven, I hope it's not you-know-what."

"Most lumps are just lumps. But let me feel."

Trudy fell onto her back with a sigh and let Lizzy unsnap her gown. Her breasts were huge with the texture of jellyfish. Both nipples were inverted, like shy children afraid to show their faces to company, a feature that had caused Trudy much anxiety. Once, she told Lizzy she'd tried to nurse her baby, Raymond, how her doctor had hooked them up to some mechanism to try to coax them out, but Trudy had to put Raymond on a bottle and to this day, nearly twenty years later, she worried her son might have had a more normal life if she'd nursed him the way her mother had nursed all her children.

"I don't feel anything, Trudy."

With a puzzled expression on her face, Trudy kneaded her breast roughly, but Lizzy stopped her by gently placing her hand over Trudy's.

"You need to hold your fingers flat. See? Like I'm doing. You don't want to be pinching and pulling at yourself like that. The idea is to get to know your breasts so you recognize normal lumpiness and notice anything unusual. Let me show you again."

Lizzy ran through the entire breast exam, and though she was tired and cranky, she was patient while Trudy practiced on the stuffed model of a breast with its normal and abnormal lumps.

"There," Lizzy said, putting the breast into a drawer when Trudy had finished. "You go home and quit worrying."

*   *   *

Nelly Brown stood at the edge of her newly planted strawberry field kicking at the clods of slick gray clay with her heavy rubber boots. Neat rows of soggy green leaves undulated like slimy pond grass; the entire field was under water. I've still got the other field, she tried to encourage herself. At least I had the foresight to plant it on the south slope. Last spring, she plucked all the blossoms off so the strawberries would be more productive. At least that field was in good shape.

She imagined she heard the old-timers on Preacher's Lake Road laughing, but it was only the wind blowing, the branches of the sugar maple trees creaking, and some big crows, their black feathers glistening, lurking at the edge of the field as if eyeing their potential meals.

Nelly had planted this second field of strawberries in a hurry, certain the rains were finally over, eager to get on with her other tasks, but she prepared the soil too early, disking in the chicken manure while the ground was too wet, and the soil dried hard as cement; now the strawberries were drowning. She tucked her hands into the bib of her overalls. One day, she tried to convince herself, I'll hire half of Preacher's Lake to harvest my crops.

The potato plants with tiny twisted green fruit she'd produced last year would flourish this year. There would be cucumbers, melons, and tomatoes for her to sell from the back of her truck. Lettuces as big as her head, onions renowned for being sweet and mild. She worked hard not to fall into a depression, though lately she felt as hopeless as the strawberries rotting under the murky water.

In the evenings, Nelly read about soil improvement, studying varieties of cover crops until her eyes ached. She had already done several soil tests, sending samples off to the Extension Service, learning her soil was deficient in everything. Undaunted, she dumped rock phosphate onto the ground, disked in lime and blood meal, hauled home crab shells Slim kept aside for her at the dump, plowing it all in. She spread wood ashes across the garden when it was covered with snow and in the summer, she collected hair they swept up at the beauty salons and barbershops in Union City, using it as a side-dressing to keep the deer at bay. She buried all her garbage in holes where she planned to set out tomato plants, having read they thrived on kitchen compost. She knew about companion planting and mulching and spent hours drawing plans for the crops she would harvest, calculating the potential yield.

Nelly clomped across her fields, the soles of her rubber boots slapping and sucking at the wet soil. As soon as she was sure the rains had stopped—she would pay attention to the weather report and wait until the ground formed a crumbly ball the way the pamphlets suggested—as soon as the soil was ready, she would plow under the winter rye. The hay field looked great. The rain did it good. The ground was high with the right drainage, the grass a bright green.

I can try another field of strawberries. Latebearers, she thought, determined not to give up though her back ached and her fingers were so stiff-jointed she could hardly move them. A sliver moon glimmered behind a smear of clouds. The clouds were breaking up, swirling across the evening sky.

If she had someone to share the burdens of the farm—and the pleasures too—it wouldn't be so difficult. "Who would want me?" she asked the moon. And as she had so often before, Fiona appeared, not flimsy and ephemeral the way Nelly'd imagined a ghost would be, but solid and very real. Fiona stood barefoot in the muddy field, her thin blue cotton dress pressed against her brown body, her arms outstretched. Her face hideously bloated.

Nelly turned away, rolled herself a cigarette and smoked, one hand on her hip as she watched the bats flutter through the dusk.

* * *

Michael McDonnough's wife, Kaye, got a part in a Pepsi commercial after a talent scout from New York City spotted her buying nail polish at La Verdierre's. Kaye and their little girl, Aran, strolled hand in hand along Sandy Beach, the sea breeze blowing their long blonde hair away from their freckled blue-eyed faces, and earned more money than Michael made in a year. They put Aran's share in a trust fund. But Kaye took hers and flew to Ireland. I need to think, she told Michael. I've never had options before.

Every evening after supper, Michael sat Aran on a towel on the kitchen counter and washed her with a thick white washcloth. Her face, her neck, her ears. He washed her palms and between her fingers, making her stand up to wash her private places before she soaked her feet in the basin of water he heated for this purpose. His daughter's skin glowed pink in the flickering light from the kerosene lamp.

When Michael and Kaye first decided to build the house, there were plans for running water. Electricity. A telephone, too. Of course they would have these things, there had been no question. Someday a backhoe would dig out the spring down in the woods. It wouldn't take much to lay pipe to the house. It wouldn't take much to dig a septic tank. They would pay Bangor Hydro to put in the poles required to bring the line up through the woods and the phone wires could be strung underneath. But these plans were made before the land was cleared, before the postholes were dug and the sills laid. Before the hospital bills came. Due to the complications of Aran's birth—no effort from the doctor could prevent her from trying to enter the world ass first—Kaye had to have a caesarian to save both their lives. A hysterectomy, too. Still, the bills came every month.

At first, Michael imagined what Kaye's money could have bought, though lately, he preferred his simple life, cooking over a woodstove, trimming the wicks on the lamps, driving home with the two five-gallon containers of water he filled at Cushman's Springs sloshing in the truck.

"So pure it floats." Aran stepped on the bar of Ivory soap to make it sink, smiling for the imaginary cameras always aimed her way. Maybe it's genetic, Michael thought, this obsession about jingles and products for sale. After all, Aran's great grandmother came up with that particular slogan. It won her a car and a year's supply of gasoline when she entered the Ivory Snow contest. Kaye had a newspaper clipping of her dressed in her Sunday best, one foot on the running board of a new Ford.

While other people taught their kids nursery rhymes, Kaye taught Aran the jingles she'd learned growing up. Michael was sure the two of them had something to say or sing about every item on the grocery or drug store shelves. At the moment, Aran was singing a theme song from a soap opera. All day long, Aran watched TV while Mrs. Hatfield, the babysitter, ironed. Aran told Michael she ironed everything. The sheets. The dish towels. Underwear and socks. Once when Michael ran into Mrs. Hatfield at the laundromat, she was folding clothes still wet from the washer. Aran explained she put them in the freezer so when she ironed them, the wrinkles came right out.

Outside, the Rhode Island Reds were pecking at the puddles, their yellow claws stirring the loose soil around the stumps left when Michael cleared the land. The old-timers said the best way to uproot stumps was to bury corn under the roots, then get yourself some pigs. But Michael was planning to hire Alton Poors with his backhoe to yank them out. He claimed he'd give each stump a good shake before he piled it into the woods so Michael wouldn't lose too much topsoil.

After he put Aran in her nightgown and sat her in the rocking chair with a cup of warm milk, Michael read aloud from *Little House in the Big Woods,* pausing to explain what life was like in the old days before TV, when lots of people lived in the woods. When Aran was asleep, Michael got out the whiskey Buster Maddocks gave him in exchange for the repair he did on the cracked cement steps of the hardware store. He poured himself a shot, then went outside and sat on the steps he'd fashioned from split logs, the rough bark still intact. Breathing the smell of the wet trees and mossy soil, he tossed the whiskey back. Like communion wine. When was the last time he knelt at the altar? The Indian tribe he was reading about, the Arapaho, believed the outdoors was a church. "A cathedral of trees," he said observing the dark circle of sky surrounded by trees. Then with table scraps he lured the hens across the scruffy yard and shut them safely in their coop. His rabbits huddled in the corners of their cages, piles of sodden manure steaming underneath. Last week he put Mr. Bunny into Pinky's cage the way old man Poors had instructed. "He'll know what to do," Poors had said. But Pinky hissed and kicked and bit Mr. Bunny until the poor fellow, not knowing if he was coming or going, actually tried to mount her head. Michael reached through the chicken wire to pat Pinky but she stamped her back foot and moved further into the corner, her whiskers twitching.

* * *

All day and well into the evening, it had been raining steadily in Manhattan. The gutters rushed with filthy water and the cars speeding down Second Avenue threw sprays of water onto the sidewalks, making the pedestrians wary as they trudged along, holding their umbrellas like shields. Carol sat by the window watching the lights from the passing traffic smear color on the wet pavement. If she were to paint this scene, she would use pastel shades of ink on silk, let the colors bleed and blur, then sketch in shapes with black ink. She could see the finished painting but could not do the work. She felt old. Washed out. She didn't paint anymore. She didn't make her pieces either.

It seemed to Carol that she had been staring down at the street her whole life, waiting, time ticking by like the clocks in the museum lined up, pendulums swaying. It was Annie's favorite exhibit. She always hurried Carol past the demented-looking Early American children, past Pilate washing his hands, up the marble steps through the room where the ivory oboe with its feather-like reed was displayed, and into the hall of clocks. Annie said the clocks ticking sounded like water falling over rocks, but to Carol it was just ticking; it made her anxious to move on. *Annie.* Carol felt a soft place in her chest crumple and cave in like the ground giving way after a flood.

What am I waiting for? she asked herself. Waiting to get better. Waiting to get over it. Waiting.

"Grief is like a long illness, it takes time to heal," Iris said. Every week, Carol sat in Iris's office trying to be brave, waiting there, too, for some kind of healing. Last time, Iris told her it might never go away. "You get used to feeling it, you find a place for it in your life, you go on with your life anyway," she'd said. "But not talking about it makes it worse."

Carol pulled a wool blanket to her chin and leaned back, letting the memories wash over her like the dark rain streaking down the windows.

It had been raining that night, too. She expected Annie to call, but it was so much later than Annie said. When Carol called Annie, there was only her machine. Things hadn't been going very well between them, they were fighting, but they were working it out. They loved each other. Carol knew this. When the doorbell rang she assumed it was Annie come to surprise her. The policemen were tall and broad-shouldered. One with dark hair slicked back, lips like a rosebud. The other with smooth cheeks like polished stone, rain damp as if he'd been weeping.

"Carol Tierney?" he asked, clearing the gruffness from his throat. The gun in his holster creaked as he stepped into the apartment. "There's been an accident." He explained how her name and address had been found in Annie's wallet. "She died before we got to her. I'm so sorry," he said, as if he had been the bicycle messenger barreling across Prince Street, heading through the dark night the wrong way, as if he were the one who crashed into Annie and sent her flying.

In a recurring nightmare, Carol stands near an old newsstand boarded up and plastered with handbills. In the dream, it is always raining. Annie runs toward her, holding up a newspaper against the rain, smiling although she is drenched. Carol wants to rush toward her, but she can't move. She tries to wave, but it's as if she's glued to the old wooden counter with the boarded up window. She hears a thud and she's back with her grandma, beating dust from the rugs they spread over the clothesline. There's another loud *whump* and Annie is flying overhead, as if she's been shot out of a cannon. She rises until she is part of the rush and tumble of the city, gone.

Annie had been away at one of the workshops she frequently attended, this one dedicated to dancing with her inner child. They hadn't made plans for later because Carol liked to leave things open. She hated feeling tied down. But she missed Annie and though she'd done some sketches, her heart wasn't in her work. She hoped Annie would spend the night when she got home. She did the laundry so there would be clean sheets. She vacuumed—a rarity—and planned what they'd order from the Beacon Deli: cold chicken sandwiches with honey mustard, potato salad, brownies. She left a message on Annie's machine, telling her she loved her, inviting her over. When the intercom buzzed, Carol's heart hammered and raced like it did the first time she kissed Annie.

I won't answer it, Carol thought. It frightened her to have such strong feelings. But by the second buzz, she buzzed back, knowing Mario, the elevator operator, would be in the lobby reading the *Post*. He would tell Annie she was home. Carol waited for the rattle of the elevator rising to the twelfth floor, listening to the woman next door playing "I Love Paris in the Springtime" the way she did every night, sometimes as often as twenty times. She smiled as she unlocked the door, smiled when she pulled it open, the smile plastered stupidly on her face when she saw the policemen, a blur of blue, cheeks wet with rain or tears or both.

Whenever she recalled that night, a flurry of memories ricocheted through her body; she had to move to calm down. Carol slipped on her old sneakers, grabbed her rain gear, and rang for the elevator.

"Good evening," Mario said in his weird voice. He'd confessed to Carol he learned English by watching cartoons in his uncle's apart-

ment for two years before trying his English on the world.
Sometimes he imitated Tweety Bird, but tonight he could tell Carol
was not in the mood. He was silent as the elevator sank slowly and
stopped with a jerk, a few inches below the floor.

"Wash you step," he said, pulling open the squeaky gate.

Carol walked down First Avenue toward the United Nations
where she and Annie used to walk on Sundays. Annie always refused
to watch out for the tourists taking photos. "We'll be part of the
scene," she'd say, marching along, her arm linked with Carol's. All
over the world, people had snapshots and videos with her and
Annie in the background.

A homeless man was getting ready to sleep in the doorway of a
storefront, spreading old papers on the sidewalk. Other than this
man and Carol, and a few cars zipping past, the avenue was
deserted. She headed back toward home, stopping to lean on the
railing at the end of her street. Across the river, the Pepsi-Cola sign
shimmered in the mist. The rain was finally letting up. There was
the smell from the river, thick and oily, and the traffic rushing
beside it, the swish of tires on the wet pavement. The doorman from
the corner near Beekman Place gripped his nightstick as if she
might be a criminal. What a stupid place to live, she thought. Back
in college, she had moved to this neighborhood when her friend
Sam was the super and got her a good deal. Now everything was so
expensive only the very rich could consider moving to another
apartment. I've got to get out of the city, she told herself. Everything
reminds me of Annie.

She passed the restaurant with its red-and-white-checked cafe curtains where they used to go for barbecued chicken on the Friday
nights Carol had off. The last time, Annie tried to break up. Carol
hated remembering they had trouble. She strode up First Avenue
toward Fifty-Seventh Street, deciding to walk west then back again.
Maybe then she could sleep.

Annie had arrived at the restaurant with a shopping bag she
thrust across the table. "Here," she said. "I don't want to see you anymore." "Don't you want to talk about this?" Carol had said, patting
the empty seat. Later, she discovered the bag held a stack of underpants, the *Take Back the Night* T-shirt she slept in at Annie's, and at
the bottom, the plate she'd put Annie's birthday cake on, a
reminder of when the whole thing started.

When she heard Annie was turning thirty, Carol, whose idea of
cooking consisted of fried egg sandwiches and canned corn, baked
Annie a cake using a recipe that called for heavy cream, whipped

egg whites, and six ounces of chocolate. After the cake was sliced
and two pieces each consumed, Annie reached across the table to
touch Carol's hair. "It's as soft as it looks," she said, her eyes dreamy
and so dark Carol felt she had no choice but to kiss her, so she had,
sinking against the cushion of Annie's body.

Before Annie, Carol's idea of a relationship was that at any time
she could walk out and nobody would be that upset by it. But Annie
had wanted her to really be there. She wanted to have what she
called a "happy home" with Carol. She used the word *commitment* as
if it were sacred. Just before Annie died, Carol had started wondering if she wanted some version of this as well.

Carol skirted a flooded gutter and ran across Third Avenue
before the light changed, her sneakers slapping the pavement,
the wind threatening to pull her umbrella inside out. At what
point did Annie know she was about to be hit? Did she try to back
away? Did she try to run out into the street away from the man on
his bicycle? Did she scream and freeze in place? Or was she just
hurrying along and then suddenly flying, the way she did in
Carol's dreams, only instead of rising, she fell, cracking her head
on the granite curbstone, a sickening sound. Did the man on the
bicycle try to help her before he fled into the night? Did he
dream about what happened and contemplate turning himself
in? Did he still careen up and down the streets whatever way he
wished to go?

Every day a pedestrian was killed in New York, Carol had read.
Navigating the streets of New York was like being in a gigantic video
game. Any second, *pow!* She imagined telling Annie this. She could
hear Annie's laugh. They used to hug on the street, not caring
about passersby or their opinion of two women in love daring to
express it.

One of the last times they argued, Annie turned to Carol and
spoke very slowly, her voice thick with defeat. "Loving you is just
another addiction." She had been standing under a mimosa tree.
She looked more beautiful than Carol had ever seen her with the
fluffy pink blossoms framing her dark face, blending with her glossy
curls. Carol hurried home and painted Annie and the tree and the
rosy light, capturing Annie's mood as well as the essence of the city
in early fall, a magical time when good seemed possible. It had been
one of the paintings that got Carol an arts grant.

"It's a gift, the time it buys you," Iris said. And she was right. Carol
didn't have to work. With the grant, her savings, and her low rent,
she could devote herself to her art. But she didn't want to paint. She

didn't want to make her pieces. Since Annie died, she didn't want to do a thing.

The entire time she and Annie were together, they had argued about Carol's need to be alone. "I'm just supposed to wait until you're ready to see me?" Annie would ask, genuinely puzzled. Well, now I'm *really* alone, Carol thought, kicking a can into the gutter, heading into the wind.

While she was gone, Mario had left and Reggie had taken over. "Elevator Operator Extraordinaire," Carol called him, but not to his face, though she was sure he wouldn't mind. Reggie took his job seriously. He made a special sign, a square of wood with the words REGGIE ON BOARD burned into it, that he hung over the elevator bell.

"Nice night, huh?" Reggie said. He whistled softly, staring at the floor numbers as they passed. Even if half the city had been washed away by torrential rains, Carol thought, he'd say the same thing. Reggie stood at the controls, one arm folded against the small of his back, certain of his place in the world. His uniform neatly pressed. His black shoes shining, not a scuff in sight. "You have a good one," he said, lining the elevator up perfectly with her floor. The little white dog that lived beside the elevator flung itself against its door, barking shrilly, its toenails scratching as if to claw its way out.

Carol kicked her soggy shoes off and got a beer from the party-sized refrigerator in what she called her "standing-room-only kitchen." She sat on the bed, clutching Harriet Elephante, the stuffed elephant Annie had given her, part of the campaign to contact Carol's inner child. It was one of the many things they disagreed about. Carol said the idea that everyone had within them sweet innocent children just dying to hug teddy bears was ridiculous. One time, they'd watched a man on TV talking to a group of people who sat in a circle, each clutching a stuffed animal. "Adults!" Carol exclaimed. "Grown-ups with bald heads and size D cups. My inner child is a nasty little brat who'd like to jump on the stage and grab those stuffed animals and stomp on them."

"You'll be OK," Carol whispered to herself as if now she were that sweet child Annie had wanted so badly to find.

*   *   *

Dave sat at the kitchen table in his boxer shorts, his T-shirt tucked into the waistband, eating pistachio nuts. Rita listened to him crack the nuts and slurp the meat out, smacking his lips. He cleared his throat as if he might say something, then scraped his chair back. It was after midnight. Rita knew this because the cuckoo clock in the hallway had just chimed.

Outside, the gutters rushed full of rain that poured onto the sodden grass. Rita was curled on her side on the pull-out sofa bed inches from the kitchen table. She breathed like someone asleep. Otherwise, Dave would start talking. And he wouldn't whisper. He wouldn't even try not to wake up Rainey, Rita's little girl, who was fast asleep beside her, one small brown arm flung across her mother.

When Dave swept the shells into his palm and tossed them into the trash, a few skittered across the floor but he made no effort to pick them up. He slammed the cupboard and stood at the refrigerator drinking from a carton. Rita hoped he was not finishing the milk. What would she give Rainey for breakfast if he did?

"I think we ought to keep our stuff separate. Things'll work out better that way," Dave said when Rita and Rainey first moved in. She had agreed. What choice did she have? It was his place, after all. His and Kathleen's. Though since they'd gotten married, all Kathleen said was, "Yes, honey. Whatever you say." She smiled at him like he was a god.

Kathleen and Rita had been roommates in Boston. They met after Kathleen responded to the sign Rita put up at the laundromat. Her previous roommate had left owing a month's rent. They'd fought over the bathtub ring left after her roommate shaved her legs. The sticky wine she spilled and made no effort to clean up. The long distance calls she claimed she hadn't made. But living with Kathleen had been fun. Five happy months until Dave, her high school sweetheart, turned up begging Kathleen to marry him and move back to Maine.

Now, Rita was living with Kathleen and Dave. What was I thinking? she asked herself for what seemed the millionth time in the last two weeks. How could I come all the way up here like this? And what am I going to do?

Her savings, six hundred dollars minus what she'd already spent, was stuffed in her suitcase, buried under their clothes. She was terrified of spending it. How was she going to get more?

She had read the want ads. Clerk. Waitress. Counter help. Jobs she had done before. But she didn't have a car. She didn't know how to drive. And they were twenty miles from Union City where all the jobs seemed to be. Rapid transit hadn't made it to Preacher's Lake. And she was too scared to hitchhike even though

Dave suggested it. "People do," he said, as if she were crazy to worry. Anyway, what about Rainey? Where would she go while Rita worked? Day care centers hadn't made it to Preacher's Lake either.

"It's going to be so much fun having you. Rainey'll love it," Kathleen had said the day she and Dave drove to Boston to get them. All winter, she'd been writing to Rita, telling her the good things about life in the country, offering details about a woman named Nelly who'd built her own house and had a farm. "She's like you," Kathleen wrote, making Rita sorry she'd ever confessed she was dating Jill, another clerk at the fabric store where she used to work. Rita felt a rush of longing remembering how they'd made out through a double feature of *Mask* and *The Elephant Man.* Jill's hot, surprisingly dry lips in the dark theater. The way they would turn back to the movie, try to concentrate, then seek each other for another embrace.

Rita decided to move to Maine one night when the roof began to leak and water seeped through the light fixture in Rainey's room. It wasn't as if this had never happened before; it had been going on for months, the plaster bulging, the buckets filling with dirty water. But she felt so defeated the last time she woke to the sound of water dripping.

I should have fought the landlord, she thought, fear knotting her stomach. I was crazy to move up here, to quit my job and take Rainey out of day care like it was no big deal.

Yesterday, after supper—Rita walked two miles to the store with Rainey to buy ingredients for chili—Dave announced he had a new job taking photographs of schoolchildren. "We'll travel all over and live in the van," he said. They would leave in a few weeks.

"What about me?" Rita had wanted to say: What about Rainey?

She clenched her teeth, angry again that neither of them had thanked her for the meal, then snuggled Rainey, pressing her cheek against her tangled curls. Is there time to learn to drive? she wondered. Enough money to get a car?

Rainey moaned as Dave shuffled by, bumping the foot of the bed. But she didn't wake. My Sweet Lorrainey, Rainey, Rain, Rita thought and brushed her daughter's cheek in the dark.

Kathleen kept saying blueberry season would come. "You can sign up for that. You can rake berries; Rainey can help. Or you can get a babysitter and work at the freezer in Union City. I did it one year," Kathleen rattled on. "The frozen berries go by on a conveyor belt and you pick out the green ones. The worst is wearing a hair net. And it's cold. But I made a hundred dollars a week." She said it as if a hundred dollars were a thousand.

Now Kathleen seemed intent on fixing Rita up with Nelly. Rita wished she could walk across the road through the thick wet fields, past the ramshackle vacation cabins, and slide down the bluff into the sea, never to be heard from again. But there was Rainey. It wouldn't be fair to Rainey. She had no one else.

2

On the day before his mother left, Slim came home early with a yellow cake mix and a can of chocolate frosting—his mother's favorite—along with ingredients to make spaghetti for her going-away meal. As he closed the door, he overheard her laughing on the phone with a friend.

"I had to sell the damn house out from under him to get rid of him," she said. She was twirling the phone cord around her wrist when Slim walked in. "I hear they got beautiful weather down there," she said, changing the subject. "Anyway, I got me somebody to keep me good and warm."

Slim dumped the cake mix into a bowl, cracked the eggs, and set up the mixer. It had never occurred to him that she wanted him to leave. Hadn't they been happy? If anyone had asked him why he stayed home so long, why he was still home when other men his age had long ago been married, divorced, married again, he would have shrugged. He didn't have an answer. Living with his mother was what he did. Every Friday, he brought home his paycheck and she doled out an allowance like he was still a boy. Over the years, he'd stuffed his extra money into an old sock. It never occurred to him to use it to get his own place. Monday was *Melrose*. Thursday they did the laundry. They had a routine. Even after Carl moved in, Slim never considered leaving.

"You never know. It might come in handy," Slim's mother had said the night before. With a flourish, she handed him a check for five thousand dollars, explaining again that the house sold so quickly because it was in a commercial zone, that she had sold all the furnishings to the Time and Tide shop.

The idea of what was about to happen, his mother fleeing the country like some criminal, had stunned him into a stupor. His car was loaded with his belongings, but the enormity of the change ahead hadn't hit him until now. This is our last supper, he thought, setting the spaghetti water to boil. Tomorrow I'll be eatin' out.

He wouldn't have a kitchen in that furnished room his mother found on Harbor Street. The whole thing seemed so sudden. He had been so busy scrambling, figuring out how to buy the house himself, and then she'd sold it.

They ate their supper while watching *Wheel of Fortune,* same as always, and his mother called out the answers happily, like nothing was different. He looked over at her from time to time, wondering: Is this the last I'll see of her? All he could think of was how happy she was to leave. "I finally got rid of him," she'd said to her friend.

On *Rescue 911,* a kid dove headfirst into shallow water and was never supposed to walk again, but there he was on the TV walking with crutches, smiling happily, like everybody should try what he'd done. "Well, I gotta get a early start tomorrow," his mother said, heading for her room. She didn't offer to do the dishes. "Sleep tight," she said.

Slim watched TV until the news came on. He hated the news and he wasn't in the mood for any of the shows on the other channels. He wasn't going to do the dishes either. Let Time and Tide take them dirty if they wanted them so badly. He lay in bed watching the shadows from the oak tree. He tossed his head back and forth on his pillow, his legs curled so his feet wouldn't bump the footboard of the bed he had been sleeping in since he was a boy—a sagging twin mattress propped on rusty springs, remnants of chewing gum on the bedposts. He pictured himself sleeping on Harbor Street, in a house he had passed by for years without ever considering the room-to-rent sign. He would sleep in a bed that wasn't his, with people whose names he didn't know sleeping in the other rooms behind the brown doors along the narrow hall.

When Carl first moved in with them, his mother would sit on Carl's lap giggling like a schoolgirl. One night while they were watching TV, Slim got up to make popcorn and when he returned, his mother, who was wearing a pair of loose pink shorts, sat on Carl's lap with her legs open so wide Slim could see up between her thighs. She didn't have any underpants on. She was nearly bald there in that space the slit of cloth didn't cover. On the TV, there were gunshots; men cried out as they were hit by bullets. His mother wore black little girl's shoes with straps around the ankles and there were prickly dark hairs on her thin calves.

Slim wanted to shut off the light but he was afraid if he did Carl's hands would creep up those shorts. He wanted to leave, but he felt any attempt to move would make him shatter like the fluorescent bulbs he tossed against the rocks at the dump. Carl and his mother were crunching popcorn, then the bowl was empty, the show was over, and it was bedtime. During the night, when Slim got up to have some milk, he was standing at the refrigerator when he heard them. His mother gasping like she was being strangled. The slap of wet flesh.

"Give it all you got, big boy," his mother said in a voice that made Slim blush. His mother behaving like a teenage slut. Exhaustion washed over him; he could sleep standing like a horse in a stall. Then Carl appeared in the doorway, scratching his hairy paunch, his dick wet and red dangling like some animal on the roadside, mashed and torn. "What are you? Some kinda pervert?" Carl cackled; then, he squeezed Slim's balls so hard he doubled over.

Now, Slim surveyed his room, noticing the wallpaper curling away from the window frames. The pencil lines his mother had drawn on the door to measure him until he was too tall for her to reach. The chair with his clothes laid over the ladder back. His work boots side by side on the scarred wood floor. He had pictured other people sleeping in his room, eating in his kitchen, sitting on his toilet. But he hadn't pictured his house gone, though his whole growing up had been a slow parceling out of the land that had once been a dairy farm his mother's family ran, though the cow pastures were now parking lots and the barn where he'd watched his grandfather milk had long ago been demolished, replaced by a drive-in bank. Tomorrow, his mother would leave to join Carl. Soon, the house would be gone, knocked down and cleared away to make room for another gas station. He wondered if his mother and Carl had been planning this all along.

* * *

It was nearly five o'clock in the morning and Michael was wide awake. He had that dream again. The one where he's holding tight to Kaye's legs as she scoots forward to kiss the Blarney Stone. In the dream, her legs have the texture of fine silk and no matter how hard he tries to hold her, she always slides out from under his grasp at the very moment she pulls herself up to press her lips on the smooth stone.

For Michael, it was almost sacred to wake up in a house he built with his own hands. Where other people saw only a ceiling, he looked through to the rafters he had nailed into place and saw himself high up with the trees swaying in a summer breeze, the ring of his hammer echoing off the hills, the saw scraping across the pine boards. He could still feel the shovel in his hand as he dug the postholes, prying loose the stones he tossed onto a pile for the wall he would build one day.

The house was a post-and-beam construction, situated at the base of a hill, in a bowl surrounded by hemlocks and balsam fir. White birch and poplar. A small place, two rooms up and two down, made for adding on to. Someday they would have a family room with a stone fireplace. The south wall would be all windows. They would have a stereo and a bathroom with the biggest tub he could find. They would laugh when they told about winters they used the pee bucket because it was too cold and the snow too deep to make it to the outhouse. Aran would never take the flick of a light switch for granted the way kids do nowadays, turning on every light in the house without even knowing where electricity comes from.

When he got up, he would make coffee, start the oatmeal. Then Aran would come down the steps, sleepy in her flannel nightgown. He would sit her down with a cup of Ovaltine, slice her an orange, and set the bowls on the table. But before all that, he would wait for the first light to shimmer through the trees. Each day, a little more light, he thought.

Before Aran was born, before they even knew she was a clump of cells multiplying and dividing inside of Kaye, they were planning a trip to Ireland. They took turns reading from the guidebooks Kaye brought home from the library, practicing their brogues as they read about the Lakes of Killarney and Dingle Bay. They hung a map of Ireland in their apartment in Bangor and drew circles around the places they hoped to visit. They got passports, standing the thin blue books up on the dresser beside their wedding photo—Kaye in her grandmother's lace gown, leaning against Michael, his chin resting on the top of her head.

When they got married right out of high school, everyone counted the months, expecting a premature baby, but they were married for years before the day they realized Kaye didn't have the stomach flu. They used their airfare to make a down payment on a piece of land. They named Aran after the islands off the Galway Bay that were to have been their final destination. They named their house Journey's End. Only for Kaye, it was no longer the end of her journey. "I've never seen anything," she said when she left. "I've never been anywhere."

* * *

Rainey Conway knew the sun could turn your skin brown. She had seen the fish belly white of her mother's buttocks—she had seen what her mother called her tan lines—but she knew her own brown skin, which was a different shade entirely, was not the result of the sun.

When she went to Wee Care Day Care, there were other people with brown skin like hers and even darker. Thembie, the teacher who wore her hair in dozens of beaded braids, had skin the color of dark chocolate. Her elbows and knees were an ashy gray. Aisha, the little girl whose cubby was next to Rainey's, was always holding her arm up to Rainey's comparing their skin to see whose was darker. Even though Aisha's skin was lighter than Rainey's, she called herself black. Rainey wondered if she was supposed to call herself black, too. Her mother never said.

There were other children with dark skin. John Almonaur. Paul Parker. Jacky Williams and Doris Brown. They lived in Roxbury, in wood-frame houses with rickety steps up the sides. Rainey watched them climb into the school bus—really an old station wagon driven by a retired teacher. She insisted the children sit with their hands folded on their laps as she maneuvered the car through the streets of Boston to the day care center, known for its effort to integrate, located in a Victorian house on a tree-lined street in Brookline. They all got into the station wagon after Rainey, who, since she was the first one to be picked up, sat in front. Rainey knew she was as different from these children as she was from the ones dropped off in silver Mercedes and glossy maroon BMWs, but she couldn't explain why.

* * *

"What's the matter with you?" Lizzy said. J.T. had her head cradled in her arms. She didn't look up.

"Another positive," she muttered.

"Anybody I know?"

"The Shaw girl. I'm sure it's her father. She's too shy to have a boyfriend. God. She's so skinny I can circle her arm with my thumb and forefinger." J.T. held up one hand to demonstrate.

"Did you ask her?"

"She wouldn't say. Just sat there like she was auditioning for the wax museum. I told her to call us if she needed to talk. I gave her my home phone. I told her she didn't have to go through with it. But I know she will. What *else* can she do? Next time we see her, if at all, she'll be out to here." J.T. began sorting the manila folders strewn all over her desk.

"What is she, sixteen?" Lizzy asked.

"Fourteen. She's supposed to start high school this fall. She'll have to quit school, the whole thing."

"Did you make a referral?"

"Social Services practically camps out in their front yard."

"We can't save everybody. There's only so much we can do."

"Men!" J.T. said, biting into a pencil. "Why can't they pick on somebody their own size? She's still a child!"

"Men," Lizzy groaned. "Speaking of the species, did I tell you? Mark's leaving at the end of the month. We have two more sessions. He's decided he wants to be a carpenter. Isn't that just my luck? I get a therapist who doesn't know what he wants to be."

"I told you to go to a woman therapist but you wouldn't listen. Mark this, Mark that, like he's God. Maybe it's part of his Jesus complex, this carpentry thing."

"Oh, quit it J.T. All men don't have a Jesus complex. You know what? You're heterophobic."

"But I have a straight friend. You. Isn't that enough?"

Lizzy slapped the desk in exasperation. "What is it with everybody today? How many no-shows have we had?"

"Three. And the two o'clock new patient cancelled."

"Nobody's coming in," Lizzy said.

"It's the weather. Everyone wants to go out and play now that the monsoon has ended and the quicksand is drying up."

"Playing," Lizzy sighed. "I can't remember ever playing. All I know is we better order extra pregnancy tests. We'll have a run on 'I missed my period' after everybody was trapped in the rain."

"My pills ran out," J.T. said, imitating one of their clients.

"The last rubber was gone and I couldn't get to town," Lizzy whined. She wrapped the stethoscope around her hand. "Sometimes I think this county could win first prize in the population explosion contest."

That morning she'd done a test for Dawn Hinckley, a beaten down woman who, when she came in the first time muttered with her hand over her mouth, "Roger pulls out," after Lizzy asked what birth control method she used. Her last child was eleven years old, so presumably it had worked, but Lizzy got frantic at the idea, and before Mrs. Hinckley knew it, she'd been talked into an IUD. Now she was pregnant. Baby number five would no doubt be born with its fist clenched around the tiny T-shaped bit of copper that hadn't done its job.

The thing was, of anyone who came to the clinic, of anyone who stuck their feet in the stirrups and told Lizzy they hated the exam, holding their breath till it was over, praying she would find no evidence of a pregnancy, Lizzy was the one who wanted a child the most. What was she doing working in a place where day after day she tried to help women keep from getting pregnant, tried to help them fix up their lives after they did, when she herself would do anything to be a mother?

"Let's finish filing," Lizzy said.

"That bad, huh?" J.T. asked. "I know what you're thinking."

"What?"

"It's about Dennis, right?"

"What makes you think that?" Lizzy reached to twist her wedding ring out of habit, but it wasn't there. She scratched the back of her hand instead. There was a small red patch of skin from all the other times she had done this. She could see Dennis sitting across from her in Hydie's—so smug. He'd planned the whole thing to be public so she wouldn't make a scene. "I feel like a sperm donor," he said. "All you care about is getting pregnant. You don't care about *me*."

"I know it's a strain, honey." When she reached for his hand, he pulled it away and drank his coffee, not looking at her. If she'd had any idea that he was about to leave town with Doris Greeley, she would have smacked the bottom of his cup so hard the hot liquid would've spilled into his lap. How many times had she replayed this scene with this addition? "You're always calculating," he said. "Filling out some chart. I wake up and I can't talk to you till you've taken your temperature. You can't even move because it might not be accurate. God forbid I should want a kiss. We can't make love unless it's the right day 'cause it'll be wasted. My sperm won't be fast enough when the right time comes. And God forbid I'm not in the mood when *that* day hits."

"Oh, Denny. I'm sorry. Why didn't you tell me before?"

"You're only listening now because it's too late. You look at me like all you see is my sperm racing toward your egg. I can't take it anymore, Liz. I don't want to be your husband, let alone some poor kid's father. Besides, we're so much in debt if we had a kid, we'd have to sell it to pay the bills."

This had been right before she got the report from the specialist in Boston, the one who said, "We'll just go in and take one more peek." The one who'd asked her afterwards if she'd consider adoption.

"Yo!" J.T. said. "Earth to Lizzy."

"What?"

"You got this look on your face like your skin was melting or something. Have you found another therapist?"

"Mark's giving me a referral," Lizzy said vaguely. "Some woman named Bonny. He says she's good."

"Look," J.T. said. "Run over to Larry's and get us some cinnamon buns and extra large coffees. The fresh air'll do you good."

"So," J.T. said when Lizzy returned, pretending to fill out a chart. "When was it you decided you were a heterosexual?"

"Hmmm." Lizzy leaned back, sipping her coffee, ready to play the game. "I think it was in second grade. When Lance Zimmerman gave me a chocolate heart on Valentine's Day. It was instant love."

"In love with a boy. Did your parents try to stop this?"

"I kept it a secret as long as I could."

"And when did you act on this obsession? This per-*ver*-sion?" She drew out the last word, shaking her head, clicking her tongue.

"J.T.?" Lizzy said, all seriousness now.

"What?"

"What if you and Betty are the last happy couple on earth?"

"You make it sound like there's been a nuclear war or something." J.T. bit into her cinnamon bun and chewed slowly.

"You two are the only ones—the only couple—I know who are actually happy. Who really like each other. Why's that?"

"I dunno." J.T. shrugged. "Betty says it's because we're so different. I say it's because we're so much alike." She laughed. "It's just one of life's many mysteries. You've gotta not be so scared you clam up and hide your true self, that's all I know. Betty and I were friends for an ice age, back when she was living with Ramona Hunter. Remember her?"

Lizzy hunched her shoulders and sneered, pretending to drink her coffee the way Ramona Hunter might do, slurping noisily.

"Well, we were friends so long we really knew each other. By the time we were lovers, there wasn't a lot left to hide."

"I can't be friends with a man. I don't even know how cars work."

"They talk about other things besides cars."

"Like what?"

"I dunno, honey. You're the one that's straight. You asked me. Friends. That's the secret. You've gotta be friends."

"What about romance?" Lizzy asked.

"See, that's where we differ. You're still waiting for some Prince Charming type from a book. But I think it's extremely romantic to be in bed with somebody I know."

* * *

Most of the fellows in Preacher's Lake Everett Hyde's age or thereabouts had attended the one-room schoolhouse on the hill where the grade school now stood. As kids, they all earned nicknames. And those that were still left, who hadn't died or moved on after being in the service—who didn't mind, as Rip Lawton was fond of saying, going to cities and eating across the table from niggers— were still known by their childhood names.

Everett Hyde—or Hydie as even his wife, Trudy, called him—got his nickname because he always hid behind the outhouse when the teacher, Miss Mosher, rang the bell after recess. Then, Hydie would sneak clear to Preacher's Lake to go fishing. Coalie Brindle had fallen into the ash bin while playing a game of duck duck goose. Rip Lawton was named after a lesson on Washington Irving during which he snored so loudly Miss Mosher grabbed him by the ear and yanked him up to the front of the room where she made him sit, blushing and remorseful, until her attention was elsewhere and he dozed off again, his chin bobbing on his chest. No one could remember Buster's real name and Buster claimed it wasn't a nickname at all. "My dad was Buster, same as me and his daddy 'afore him. Go have a look at the Veterans' Memorial if you don't believe me. You'll see my daddy's name. Buster Maddocks, same as me. It ain't no nickname," he argued when anyone got in the mood to discuss it.

Hydie—who looked like a cowboy singer with his carefully combed wavy gray hair and who, when he dressed up, would put on a cowboy shirt and a string tie—worked most of his life at Union City Cold Storage where, no matter what the weather, he wore his cap with earflaps, his insulated work gloves, a pair of long johns under his clothes, and his red-and-black plaid wool jacket, always ready to take people in to get their frozen food off the pallets where it was stored. He started working there one August during the blueberry harvest when he was in high school, and by the time he retired, he'd saved up enough to open his diner on Route One at the corner of the Preacher's Lake turnoff.

It was a squat building with aluminum siding. A hand-painted wooden sign hammered into the ground said HYDIE'S PLACE. He served a good breakfast, decent home fries and eggs, a breakfast a man could start his day with and not be hungry before noon, and come that time, Hydie had plenty of sandwiches as well as a different hot dinner special every day of the week. Fried chicken and mashed potatoes on Wednesday. Fish cakes and coleslaw on Friday. Beef stew on Saturday. There were always fresh pies Trudy baked displayed behind the counter.

Hydie's was popular with the truckers that passed by as well as with the local men, the regulars, who had nothing better to do than sit in lawn chairs on the porch of Buster's Hardware or stay home and try to ignore their wives. It was not the kind of place where tourists stopped. No fresh-squeezed orange juice, no flaky croissants. The bread came in large plastic bags and the juice tasted of tin. It was not listed in any of the guides to down east they gave away in the Chamber of Commerce offices along the coast.

Hydie designed the place himself and put it together in two weeks with the help of his son, Raymond, who never did learn how to measure. The counter was horseshoe-shaped with the grill off to one side so Hydie could cook while standing facing out. He could see who passed by, watch whoever came in, and talk to the fellows at the counter. On the side wall, he had his deep fryer and the toaster that whirled the bread around a set of red coils like a Ferris wheel. The coffee urns and hot water pots were near the cash register where Trudy was stationed when she was not waiting on anybody.

Trudy did the decorating—she chose the red-and-white paper place mats from the salesman that came by with a color catalog. In her arts and crafts class, she made the welcome signs—over the door a polished wooden slab with the letters burned into it; on the wall above the cash register, two white ducks held a banner in their beaks that said WELCOME FRIENDS. She put together the baskets of dried flowers on each table, each one tied with a plaid ribbon.

She hung the paintings she did with the art teacher from Holiday Island, the one who drove over every Saturday last winter, who told them they were going to behave like real artists and look at everyday objects as if they had never seen them before. And she made cafe curtains with blue pom-poms, but Hydie wouldn't let her hang them because they blocked his view. "I spent most of my life in a freezer," he said. "I aim to look out and see who's driving by."

This afternoon, a half hour before closing, Raymond had already swept the floor spotless. He shook out the rug by the door and he was now standing beside his mother filling the salt and pepper shakers. At the counter, Rip, Coalie, and Buster were having their last cup of coffee, already wondering what was going to be on TV that night.

"That blueberry pie looks awful good," Buster said, stirring a spoonful of sugar into his coffee.

"That mean you'll be wantin' a piece?" Trudy asked.

"I guess it does."

"You guess it or you want it?" She reached for the pencil tucked in her hair and pulled her order book from her apron.

"Just make sure it's a big slice. Got to tide me over till my supper." Buster patted his huge belly. "You know where I get all this muscle from, don't 'cha?" The fellows didn't bother to answer. Buster would tell them whether they said yes or no. "From pushing myself away from the table." He mimed his actions and was busy laughing at his own joke when the bell above the door rang and Slim walked in.

"Well, well, well. Look who's here," Coalie said. "Slim boy, you sit right here by me." He patted the stool beside him and Slim slid into place, ducking to keep from bumping his head on the ceiling fan that spun lopsidedly overhead. He had to spread his knees wide to fit them under the counter, but Coalie was so short, his feet dangled.

"What's the special?" Slim asked. "I'm hungry enough to eat a boiled owl."

"Meatloaf and mashed. We got plenty left. Shall I fix you up a plate?" Trudy glanced at the clock. "We're pretty near to closin', but I don't want you goin' hungry. You miss your mom's cookin'?"

"You could say that." Slim sipped the coffee she put in front of him. "It's bad enough I got to live all cooped up in that measly furnished room. I lie in the gol-darned bed and touch the walls on either side of me." He dipped his fork into the potatoes and gravy. "But I got to eat all my meals out. Even breakfast. Boy, I don't like that. I miss having a fridge. I get hungry in the night, I can't sleep, them stupid headlights'll be shining on the ceiling from them dad-blamed tourists drivin' around half lost—I don't know why in hell they can't get where they're goin' before bedtime—and if I want me a glass of milk, too bad. I could go for a nice bowl of pudding, but nuh-uh. I'm sick to death of the whole thing."

Everyone listened in silence. This was the most Slim had ever said at once in all the time they'd known him. Even way back when he was a boy at the dump with his father, he'd just as soon hide behind the old man, kicking his big feet at the dirt, or run off to sort rusty nails, than say a word. Now, it seemed as if he might never stop.

Trudy shook her head slowly while the fellows clucked their tongues sympathetically and gave each other looks.

"You could get you one of them refrigerators you plug into your cigarette lighter in your car," Buster offered. "I seen that in a catalog. I thought about gettin' me one."

"Yeah. Well. I guess," Slim said. They were silent as he finished the last of his meal.

"You want seconds?" Trudy asked. "It's on the house."

"That'd do me nicely," Slim said. He handed her his empty plate.

"Boy, you got a hollow leg? I eat and eat and it all lands right here." Buster patted his belly. "You eat more'n I do. Where's it go?"

"To my brain," Slim said. "I got a big brain in here to feed." He knocked the top of his head with a clenched fist.

Everyone laughed, but there was a feeling of waiting, as if Slim was about to have another outburst and they would have to wait it out the way they waited out a storm.

"The worst thing is," Slim began. He rocked on his stool, dipping his bread into the gravy and holding it halfway to his mouth. "The worst is, I finish here or I have me a sandwich out at Moody's and sit in my car listenin' to the radio, watchin' the tide. I wait till dark 'cause I don't wanna be in that place in the daylight. Then I drive to Union City and head right straight for home like nothing's changed. You know what I'm gettin' to? I'm pullin' up the driveway before it hits me I don't live there no more."

No one said anything. Hydie was scrubbing down the grill with a wire brush. Raymond and Trudy had finished with the salt and pepper shakers, had filled the sugar jars, and each napkin holder was full.

"It looks like it's that time," Rip said, nodding at the cash register. "You gonna break my pocketbook today?" He winked at Trudy.

"Don't you be flirtin' with my wife," Hydie said.

Rip combed his long white beard with his fingers. "Chin up, my boy. It'll all work out," he said, slapping Slim on the back.

Out on the highway, truckers with their headlights on roared past, heading north with their tankers of oil, their loads of lumber, their freezer trucks full of sides of beef, or south with pulpwood, lobsters, or cans of sardines. While Hydie was locking up, Trudy and Raymond waited in the front seat of the pickup. Coalie headed up Preacher's Lake Road to his trailer on Cozzie's Pond, and Buster went over to check if his son locked up the store for the night. Rip only had to walk a few doors down the road to get home. Slim watched Rip carrying the sack of stale donuts Trudy had given him for his pig. He could see the pig in her pen, her ears alert, her nose waving as if she picked up the scent of her treats. Slim imagined how later, Rip would sit in his easy chair watching TV, waiting for his supper to be served.

Slim sat in his car with his window down; the cool air was fragrant, as if the earth were slowly ripening around him. He placed his hands on the steering wheel and leaned back listening to the traffic swish by. It seemed that everyone had a home to go to, everyone but Slim.

* * *

"Any news?" Mrs. Hatfield asked Michael in a loud whisper, her thick hands cupped around her mouth. She had a permanently startled expression, like a woman who has just realized she left her pocketbook at the grocery store. Her eyebrows were plucked into thin lines. Her lips were smeared with purplish lipstick that leaked into the wrinkles around her mouth.

"No. No news," Michael told her.

On the sagging sofa, Aran sat licking a red lollipop, watching TV with Mrs. Hatfield's son, Bobby. He was practically Michael's age, but she treated him as if he were a ten-year-old. He had the pasty skin of a person who rarely went outside and the dull eyes of someone who thought about no more than what would be on TV next. Though Mrs. Hatfield explained he was an unemployed mechanic, complaining bitterly about how hard it was nowadays to get work, Michael knew it couldn't be true. Someone who fixed things could always find work.

Mrs. Hatfield was the best babysitter he could find. The first one he called had fourteen cats and her house reeked with the stench of their urine. Another woman who put a sign in the window of Moody's watched five two-year-olds in her trailer on Sow's Head Bay. She was enthusiastic about Aran coming. "She'll be a real help," she said.

Michael wished Mrs. Hatfield would take Aran outside. She was right next to the school. He could see children hanging upside down from the monkey bars through her picture window. Watching TV women wearing too much makeup slither across beds all day long was not the kind of activity he had in mind for his daughter.

"You can't expect a female to stay up in the woods without a telephone. Not in this day and age, mister. No sir," Mrs. Hatfield told Michael. "You oughta get one of them double-wides, put it on a lot near the highway."

"You wanna play on the swings?" Michael asked Aran as they headed for the truck. It was getting dark, but the playground was lit by street lamps.

"No, Daddy."

"Why not? I'll push you till your toes touch the sky."

"I'm too tired," she said. "I need some Femiron."

"It's from all that TV you watch. Don't you ever do anything else?"

"Today, me and Bobby played Barbie Beauty Salon. We gave Barbie a shampoo and put curlers in to make her hair puffy all over. Can I get curlers for my hair, Daddy, please?"

"Honey, your hair's so pretty the way it is."

"I never get anything I want." She stared out the window as they bumped along the patched asphalt to where they lived, five miles down Preacher's Lake Road. When they first turned off the highway, there was a house every five hundred feet or so, most of them set back from the road, but the houses grew more sparse as they climbed the hill.

Just before their turnoff onto the dirt road, there were three tar paper shacks where a bunch of skinny kids often stuck out their thumbs, then threw clods of dirt at the truck as it passed. It was ten degrees cooler when they hit the dirt road where the trees grew close. In winter, there were patches of ice in the shadows, but in summer it was a relief to enter the cool shade. Now in late spring, despite the rains and warm spells, there was still snow beneath the trees. The driveway was so muddy and scarred with the ruts Michael's truck had made, he parked off the road, planning to carry Aran down to their house which was set back in the woods where no one could see more than a flicker of light or the smoke from the chimney when they passed by.

A postcard from Kaye was in the mailbox. There had been four so far, all addressed to Aran. This one showed the Shannon River. Michael pictured Kaye walking on the lush thick grass. "Mommy's having a wonderful time, but she misses you," Kaye wrote. "She's looking everywhere to catch a leprechaun."

Michael slid the card into his newspaper. The last time she got a card, Aran had screamed, her shoulders shaking dramatically. "Go away Daddy," she said when he attempted to comfort her.

Tonight, while he made potato soup, he pictured Kaye at an Irish inn, laughing over a mug of foamy beer, eating a bowl of thick Irish stew. A tall man with thick dark hair combed carefully back like a model's, the sleeves of an Irish wool sweater knotted loosely around his shoulders, sat beside her. Kaye was not the kind of woman men could leave alone. Even when he walked down the street with his arm around her, men looked at her and wanted her for themselves.

Michael cut bread for the two of them, grated cheese into their wooden bowls, and ladled the soup over it so the cheese would melt.

"Mm, mm, good. Mm, mm, good. That's what Daddy's soup is, mm, mm, good," Aran sang, making her father laugh at her soup moustache.

After supper, Michael sketched the stone wall he would build along the path and the fence he would put up to keep the deer out of the garden. He could imagine Kaye wearing a straw hat, carrying a basket of fresh vegetables. Later, after he read to Aran and tucked her into bed, he took out the seed catalogs and made a list of what Kaye might plant. Right now, it was impossible to dig into the dirt, it was so full of stumps and tangled roots. But by this time next year, Michael thought, we'll be eating salad from our own land.

As a boy, Michael loved reading *Little House on the Prairie* and *Little House in the Big Woods*. He shared this love with Kaye though she was more a fan of the TV show, dreaming of playing Laura's beautiful sister. All of Laura Ingalls Wilder's books sat on the oak shelf Michael hung in the living room. He read a few pages to Aran every night, though she had little patience for the stories and kept stopping him to ask when the family was going to get a car and why they didn't go to the laundromat. "Gross," she said, when Pa brought home a deer for meat.

On the table, the kerosene lamp flickered and smoked, the wick so uneven it stained the globe with soot. Michael rested his head in his hands and tried to remember what he was doing, living on twenty acres of woods, dreaming of gardens and stone walls. Without Kaye, his life seemed like a farce.

* * *

Nelly stared at Rita with a steady, dark-eyed gaze. Appraising me, Rita thought. As if Nelly were about to purchase her and wanted to be sure Rita had a strong back, that she could carry a sizeable load. Rita half-expected Nelly to ask her to open her mouth so she could examine her teeth.

Rita looked back, of course. She was not shy. She noticed how tall Nelly was and how her short brown hair stood up in cowlicks all over her head like she cut it with nail clippers. While Nelly and Dave discussed chain saws and the best way to sharpen one, Rita promised herself not to do anything as blindly as she did when she moved to Maine to begin with. I'm just having supper with this woman, she vowed. Nothing more.

Kathleen was fussing with the green beans she had picked from her garden last summer, acting as if they were gold she panned from the creek even though they were tough and starchy with thick pink beans inside. There wasn't enough chicken. There was never enough food when Kathleen cooked. Rita suspected Dave snuck in and took extra to eat later. This was why the platter was sparsely filled.

"I'm full," Rita said so Rainey could have the last wing. Just as she was reaching for it, Dave stabbed it with his fork. Rainey looked at Rita helplessly, and Rita patted Rainey's leg. What else could she do? Rita expected Nelly to give Rainey the same appraising looks, but so far she hadn't glanced at her. Rita had never spent this much time with someone who had not spoken to her child.

This supper was Kathleen's fault. She arranged it. Rita'd been hearing about Nelly. How Nelly built her own house. Nelly had an organic farm. Nelly, Nelly, Nelly. "She's a lesbian," Rita whispered when she was washing her face, combing her hair, getting ready for "the big event"—Nelly coming to supper. But of course no one ever came right out and said that. They just said, "I know you two will hit it off." She wondered if they'd do the same thing if she were black. Or Chinese. Soon she'd be meeting all the other people with biracial children. All three of them in the state of Maine. From what she could tell so far, Rainey had integrated the county single-handedly.

Meeting Nelly made Rita feel like a mail-order bride. Nelly sat there as if to say: Come live with me and be happy ever after. Isn't that what you want? So what if we don't know each other?

In a few weeks, Dave and Kathleen would drive across the country. Rita started wondering again if she had time to learn to drive. Dave kept saying he'd teach her, but so far they'd only gone out a few times to the cemetery. He became so upset the last time when Rita ground the gears, he insisted they go home. Rita had been over this so many times, the pattern of her worries had become like a well-trodden path smoothed down by hundreds of feet.

While Dave and Nelly were talking about the flooded field of strawberries at Nelly's, Rita noticed Nelly's thick gnarly fingers, her fingernails, torn and dirt encrusted. The dingy thermal undershirt she wore was soiled at the neck. Nelly looked over at Rita, as if feeling her gaze. She has the eyes of a watcher, Rita thought. Eyes that don't miss a thing. Her gaze was steady, but Rita noticed it was also surprisingly blank.

Rita had been sick of the rattle and whir of the trolleys rushing along the tracks in front of her Boston apartment, leaving soot on the windowsills. Now she wished more than anything she were walking down Commonwealth Avenue to buy Rainey an ice cream. She couldn't imagine kissing Nelly the way she'd kissed Jill. If only Jill hadn't gone back to her girlfriend. They'd be together now.

Nelly didn't have time to stay for the bread pudding Rita made. She had to get an early start in the morning, she said. Something about green manure and a tractor that wouldn't start. But before she went—she had her hand on the doorknob—she turned back and cleared her throat as if to say: Listen up, I ain't gonna repeat myself. Then she asked Rita if she'd care to go to a movie. "I can pick you up at six-thirty," she said, ducking her head, as if the sound of her own voice shamed her.

"That sounds like fun," Kathleen said in a too-happy voice, as if she were the one invited. "Rainey can stay with me. We'll make play dough." Rita didn't have a chance to say yes or no before Nelly was out the door.

"She likes you," Kathleen said. "I knew you'd hit it off."

Rita didn't say anything. Sometimes she was so mad at Kathleen she didn't want to look at her. She ran hot water into the dishpan, squeezing in too much soap, waiting for Dave to complain about waste.

"Don't let the water run like that." Dave reached in front of her and shut the faucet off so abruptly the pipes screeched. "It costs money to heat water. It's not like your landlord is taking care of everything."

Rita didn't say anything to that either. She'd already counted to ten a dozen times since the two of them came home from work. She gritted her teeth, fury pounding in her chest. She'd like to take Dave by both ears and shove his face into the sudsy water. But of course she did no such thing. She washed the plates, stacking them in the drainer. Out in back, Rainey was slouched on a lawn chair. Above her, a flock of swallows swooped across the sky, getting ready to nest for the night in the barn. Rita worried that she might be cold, but when she pushed open the back door to give Rainey her jacket, she was surprised by the warm smell of spring that rose up out of the earth like steam. In the dooryard, daffodils poked out of the flower beds. Beside them, bluebells had already bloomed.

* * *

Carol was the first woman Vivian had ever dated. Sure, she and Jeanne were lovers for years, but they had never actually *dated*. "We found each other in high school," Jeanne would always explain. In retrospect, Vivian worried it sounded as if Jeanne had been on a scavenger hunt. "We saw each other across the cafeteria," Jeanne would sing to the tune of "Some Enchanted Evening."

Instead of dating, there had been arrangements for Vivian to sleep over at Jeanne's house; she had a double bed in her attic room. Her mother, a widow, was often asleep in front of the TV downstairs. They moved to New York City together, taking the train down from Albany, living in the Evangeline Residence, then finding an apartment on the Lower East Side where Vivian still lived—two rooms on the fifth floor of a tenement. Visitors had to phone from the booth on the corner so a key tucked in a sock could be thrown down to unlock the door. As far as their parents knew, they were strictly roommates. Single girls in the city unable to find men was how the story went back home.

When Jeanne went off to live with a lawyer from the firm where she'd been a law clerk, Vivian didn't know what was worse. That Jeanne had left her to live with a man or that she was now alone. This man—John Smith his name was, as if he were a generic man— owned a house in the Virgin Islands. That was where Jeanne was now, no doubt wearing the black bathing suit Vivian had bought for her last summer. Vivian feared she'd spend the rest of her life alone. Then Mary, her colleague at Erasmus High, talked her into going to a SAGE meeting.

"Seniors Active in a Gay Environment?" Vivian said, her eyes wide in disbelief. "This is your idea of fun? I'm not even forty."

"You need to find someone older than you. Someone who can take care of you," Mary said. Mary's new girlfriend, who walked with a cane and wore her long white hair in a braid, was a retired nurse who owned a brownstone in Brooklyn. "I'm ready to kiss my atten- dance records good-bye and be a kept woman." She kissed a folder and threw it onto the heap. She planned to retire when the school year ended. "You won't be sorry," Mary said, handing Vivian a sched- ule of the SAGE meetings.

Vivian had never intended to go, she hated meeting new people, but one Saturday, after dragging herself around Manhattan all day pretending she didn't mind being the only person in New York City who was alone, she made herself go to the SAGE meeting.

A bunch of really old dykes sitting around talking about retire- ment homes, she imagined telling Jeanne. She still caught herself embellishing incidents to make Jeanne laugh. They were planning to have a fund-raising party where everyone dressed butch or femme. They acted like it was innovative. Like they weren't already permanently ensconced in their roles. Jeanne liked it when Vivian used words like *ensconced* and *innovative*. Vivian had a secret collection of build-your-vocabulary books at school. She knew that Jeanne was ashamed of her upstate accent, that she wished Vivian taught something besides Phys Ed and Health. She'd covered her eyes more than once when Vivian launched into a discussion of volleyball techniques at a party.

The two women who led the SAGE meeting sat in the only comfortable chairs, side by side, holding hands, looking at each other adoringly. One wore bright pink lipstick, a tight green sweater that showed her cleavage, and a plaid pleated skirt with nylons and flats. The other had her gray hair cut short like Julius Caesar's and wore jeans and a turtleneck. These two are ready for the party, Vivian thought, looking around.

The room was barely the size of a large closet with one tiny window so caked with soot it was impossible to see through. Vivian felt as if she'd been placed in a cage and was expected to mate while a group of scientists watched and collected data. She couldn't imagine talking to one person there. The only women who were not already paired up seemed slightly demented. One sat muttering to herself, eyeing the contents of the trash can for possible treasures. The other, who had cut her hair so short her scalp looked blue in the dim light, made Vivian shudder.

"Posters?" Julius Caesar asked, nodding at the man with the silk cravat who raised his hand. His lover, who wore red cowboy boots, announced they would post them around the Village.

Abruptly, Vivian scraped back her chair. There was a small stir as she left the meeting, but no one called her back. Out in the hallway, she leaned against the wall, not caring that in doing so she knocked down several flyers from the bulletin board. Downstairs in the foyer, a group of men dressed in denim and leather were filing through, keys and chains jangling as they greeted one another in loud voices. Just as the last man disappeared into a meeting room, Carol entered the building.

I just knew she was the one for me, she planned to tell Jeanne when she got home, describing Carol's rosy cheeks, her thick brown hair streaked with gray, the way her leather jacket ended right where her hips began. Jeanne is not home waiting for you, she felt like shouting. Instead, she ran down the stairs in time to see Carol disappear behind a black door at the back of the building. She didn't even mind squeezing through the men at the Mirth and Girth meeting as she followed her.

Vivian marched into the dimly lit room and sat next to Carol. Carol had unzipped her jacket but she had not taken it off. Carol, who was determined not to go to the bars like in the old days before Annie, was wishing she'd worn sunglasses. She was afraid she would see someone she knew. She was aware of Vivian beside her, her muscular forearms as she unbuttoned her shirt cuffs and rolled up her sleeves. Carol glimpsed Vivian out of the corner of her eye: Short dark hair. Works out. Around my age. Scared but hides it.

Carol turned her attention to the meeting. The topic was Starting Over. SINGLE AND SASSY a sign pronounced. Carol wondered if any of the other women had lovers who died.

"I'm not sure. I really don't know," a small woman with freckles was saying. She had a kerchief tied around her neck and a tear in the knee of her jeans that she worried with one painted fingernail. "I just don't know. I mean. Am I a lesbian if Donna and me aren't together anymore? Am I a lesbian if I'm not having sex with a woman anymore?"

There were a few chuckles. "Honey, half the lesbians in America aren't having sex. Sex isn't everything," a woman by the door said, tipping her chair back, crossing her arms over her ample chest.

"Speak for yourself," a woman in the back bellowed. She was wearing a stretched-out black T-shirt with Mickey Mouse on the front, bent over and peering obscenely through his legs. "I know what I want." She glared around the room as if challenging someone to step forward and take her by the hand.

"Nobody's having sex but the gay boys. We all know this. But that's not our topic tonight." The leader, a tall black woman with a hatchet-shaped face, clutched a red plastic stopwatch and looked anxiously around the room. "Starting over," she said, as if she were imitating Oprah Winfrey reading her cue card after the commercial break. Her deep voice quavered. A woman behind her patted her reassuringly then rubbed her shoulders. The leader closed her eyes and leaned back.

"I don't see why we have to be slaves to the topic. I mean if we wanna talk about sex, then let's talk about sex," said a woman with dyed red hair. She was the one who made her living as a dominatrix. Carol recognized her from one of the twelve-step meetings Annie used to drag her to. Carol turned toward Vivian who winked and rolled her eyes.

"I resent your use of the word *slave*. It belittles the experience of millions of African Americans." The palest blondest thinnest woman Carol had ever seen made this pronouncement, picked up her black fake fur coat, wrapped herself up as if she were headed out into a heavy winter storm, then walked out in a huff. The room was silent for a moment.

"Break time!" a voice called. Before the leader could say a word, women were scraping back their chairs, searching their backpacks, patting their pockets for cigarettes, candy, and change.

Carol stood up and zipped her jacket. "Had enough?" Vivian asked. Carol noticed Vivian's eyes were a light hazel, not dark brown like Annie's. Vivian was all angles where Annie had been curves.

"I need to get out of here," Carol said. Vivian walked beside Carol as if they'd come in together. She wasn't sure what to do next, but she couldn't bear it if Carol left without her. Their shoulders bumped on the way out the door. Carol turned toward Vivian, ready to apologize.

"I'm Vivian." She thrust her hand forward, feeling idiotic but not really caring. I'd like to have sex, she almost added. She grinned her crooked grin. What did she have to lose? "Coffee?" she asked.

"I need something stronger to recover from this," Carol said as they headed crosstown, under the fragrant flowering cherry trees, into the cool spring night.

3

There had been something mechanical about the first night. The candle Vivian lit. The wine she poured. The kisses they took turns initiating. Hands over bare skin reaching shyly, but pretending to be bold. Vivian missed Jeanne. It felt so odd, the thick hair on Carol's legs. Jeanne's had been smooth as a baby's.

Carol went through the motions of lovemaking, experienced enough to realize it would take time to know this woman whose nipple was between her lips. She worried any minute Vivian would jump up and shout, No! Not you! She'd never felt so clumsy as she tried to satisfy another woman. She'd never felt so certain it was a mistake. But she went through the motions. Iris had a theory called "acting as if."

"Act as if everything's OK," she said. "Eventually it will be."

So Carol acted as if she wanted to be with Vivian, as if she didn't want to rush out of the room. Then Vivian surprised her, pressing her face into Carol's hair, letting her warm breath spread over Carol's neck.

"Am I too heavy?" she asked, lowering herself onto Carol at last.

At least I'm not in bed alone, they each thought privately. In the morning, when Carol woke up and Vivian was in the kitchen with the radio on, tuned to 1010 WINS—"All news all the time!" the announcer shouted—Carol decided never to see her again.

But Vivian had persisted, leaving cute messages on Carol's machine until Carol eventually relented. They discovered they both loved eating at Beanie's Burritos, crowded against everybody, practically picking their food off of other people's plates. They both loved the festival feel of the flea market on Sunday afternoons. Squeezing their feet into the old shoes like wacky Cinderellas. Vivian wanted the tan-and-white men's oxfords, even though the toes jutted long past where her own ended. Carol hankered after the rainbow platform sandals that she finally bought, "Just to look at, not to wear."

"So it's not perfect," Carol said to herself. "It's OK for now."

"It's perfect," Vivian said, peering into the mirror, noticing new strands of silver hair above her ears. "Perfect," she said, wondering when Carol would move in.

*   *   *

The dump was open only three days a week, but half the time Slim went there to tinker around, to sort through the clothes and discarded toys to add to his giveaway boxes, to fix up the old bikes for the kids who didn't have one. But this morning, he decided to go fishing at Preacher's Lake. He was sure by now the path was passable. If he was lucky enough to catch anything, he could get Hydie to cook it. He stopped for worms at Moody's, got some Cokes and sandwiches, and headed down the highway, tooting at Hydie's as he turned toward the lake, driving past the dump where seagulls perched on every fence post as still as if they were carved like the ones the fellow at the gift shop made. He could see the blueberry barrens like red moss in the distance. Joe-pye weed bloomed alongside the road and robins flew by with straw in their beaks. The world had gone green overnight. There were new leaves on the trees. The fields were like lush carpets. He pulled beside the old cellar hole where the Seavy place burned flat to the ground and was halfway to the lake when it hit him.

"It was like a lightbulb flickin' on in my head," he told Sal Jones, the realtor, after he drove back to the highway, speeding to Sal's office. "I seen that trailer Lord knows how many times. It never even dawned on me till today. I'd like to buy it. That one your sign's on."

"I got my sign on quite a few places, Slim. Exactly which one would you be talking about?" Sal leaned back in his swivel chair.

"The one on Preacher's Hill. Across from Trudy's mom's place."

"Oh, yeah. Lemme see." He flipped through several file folders.

"I wanna buy it," Slim said. He shifted from foot to foot like a child about to pee his pants.

"Hold your horses," Sal said. "You got to have a look at it." He handed Slim a sheet of paper that described the place then dug around in his top drawer through a tangle of keys. "Here." He held one up. "If you like what you see, we'll sign the papers. But have a look to be sure. It's old and it's sat empty for quite some time."

The trailer was white with a red stripe around the middle. Like a Christmas ribbon, Slim thought. It was propped on cinder blocks at the end of a weedy dirt driveway. He'd often turned around in the driveway and had noticed the way the trailer sat half under an old hemlock tree, tipping precariously at the back as if it might slide off its perch, but he'd never paid attention to the faded FOR SALE sign hammered in the front yard or considered living there. He'd always had a home till now.

Home. The idea of it percolating like a pot of coffee on the back burner. "Home sweet home," he murmured. He watched a robin pull a worm from the patch of dirt in back. Someone was hammering nearby.

"Hey, that's Nelly Brown," he said. "The one the fellas call Farmer Brown from Town." All by herself, she'd put up a house. "I read how in a book," she told Slim when she was at the dump looking for bricks. Slim helped her out with things he'd salvaged. A gas hot plate. A cast-iron sink he'd kept under plastic for years, thinking someday somebody would want it. All her windows and half the lumber. Even that old insulation. She'll be a good neighbor, he decided.

"Welcome home, Slim," he said as he made his way over the scrubby yard. The cinder blocks piled up for steps teetered as he climbed to the door. I'll bring over that sack of mortar I got in back. Make 'em steady, he planned. The door opened with a splooshing sound, like the seal of a freezer door, and it was so flimsy, Slim feared it might come off its hinges. He had to bend over to step inside, but this was not unusual. He always had to pay attention to what he might whack his head on. Standing on his toes, his head just grazed the ceiling. *Home,* he thought again, his heart beating wildly.

The trailer had a main room that was both kitchen and living room, all of it paneled. A green refrigerator. A gas stove, also green, and a green sink so small and shallow Slim felt he might not even be able to wash his hands in it, let alone the dishes. There were cabinets on either side of a narrow window. He cranked it open and bent down to peer outside. A faded red dishrag sat on the trailer hitch.

At the place where the linoleum ended and the rug began, a big rectangle had been cut out of the shaggy yellow and brown rug. Some kind of divider or bar used to be there, Slim decided. He'd make another. He'd have stools to sit on and eat his meals there. He'd put an easy chair in the corner, the TV against the wall. Jerry-rig a woodstove to keep it warm. The heater looked like it would conk out come November.

As he hurried down the hall, the trailer wobbled. He would jack it up and make it level, make it sturdy. Put a skirt around it, batten it down with boughs to keep out drafts. There was a bedroom at the end, slightly bigger than a double bed, cupboards and drawers built into one wall. A bathroom, surprisingly large, with a washer hookup beside the toilet, which like the tub and sink was green. And another bedroom, smaller than the first. "This here's my spare room," he said, making a sweeping motion with his arm, pretending to be Vanna White showing off a prize.

Slim stood sideways in the hallway, measuring the width with his feet, not really concerned with how narrow it was but just from force of habit, measuring the world against his body. Exactly a foot and a half. He could have punched his fingers right through the thin walls, but it didn't matter. He was already planning how he'd fix it up.

He hurried out the door, wondering when he'd be able to move in, doing a mental inventory of furniture he had at the dump. I can stick the chickens out back, he realized. Just haul the car right up here, park her under that tree, and let 'em loose out there to scratch in the dirt. That'll get old Clarence Cushman off my tail.

Across the road, the porch on Trudy's mother's house was half obscured by an old sugar maple tree. The house had once been yellow, but was mostly bare wood with chips of paint like dry mud spattered here and there. He thought the house might be vacant because there was no car in the driveway, but then he spotted a face peering from the window. He waved, eager to be neighborly, but the face didn't wave back. He watched for a minute, still waving. But the girl with the moon face just stared and stared.

*   *   *

Michael started a new contract a few miles from the Swift River Bridge, down by the quarries. "This couple that bought the old Beal place," he told the fellows at Buster's when he stopped for supplies. "He's in the insurance business. Planning to hire out all of the renovations. I'm doing a brick wall with a raised platform for the woodstove."

Michael was beginning to feel he could do these with one hand tied behind his back, but when he had started out, he sweated over every inch of mortar. A mason, he picked up what work he could, mostly by word of mouth though he put an ad in the *Union City Enterprise*. MICHAEL'S MASONRY it said, above Kaye's drawing of a stone fireplace with a cauldron on the hearth. He put in his box number since he didn't have a telephone, but everybody knew to leave a message at Buster's.

"I already put in the foundation. You can't be too careful," he said. "Especially in these old places. The floor joists'll collapse under that extra weight."

Yesterday, he unloaded the brick and sand and was lucky enough to get the bags of mortar covered with plastic before it rained. Today, he was mixing cement in the backyard. The cement had just reached the right consistency when he saw him: a boy about Aran's age with tight red curls, wearing navy blue shorts and a red shirt. Nothing unusual about that. But the thing was, he had a white lace curtain draped over his head and fluttering down his back like wings. He was marching slowly toward Michael, as if he were in a parade. Michael noticed the bunch of dandelions and clover the boy clutched in his hands at the same moment the boy came close enough for Michael to hear the tune he was humming: The Wedding March.

"Derek has wanted to be a bride ever since he started to walk," the woman—who insisted he call her Beth, not Mrs. Wallace—told Michael. He was sitting at the counter, wishing instead he'd gone to his truck to eat the meal he'd brought. Wheat bread smeared with the butter he traded for a dozen eggs with Mrs. Poors who kept a cow. There were thick slabs of yellow cheese, two boiled eggs, and an apple in his lunch pail in the cab of his truck.

"What'll you have? I've got about every kind of Lunch Box. Ham and scalloped potatoes. Cheese and beef. Ravioli. Tic-Tac-Toe." She rose on her toes leaning into the cupboard. A pair of cutoff jeans with thick white fringe slid up her thighs.

"Lunch Box?" Michael said. "Tic-Tac-Toe?"

"Yeah. Like alphabet soup. Only just Xs and Os." She took down a yellow plastic cup with a picture on the label. The noodles were covered with cheese that Michael was sure must glow in the dark.

"I'll take whatever you're having."

There were two glittery slanted cat eyes right above where her nipples pressed the tight cloth of her black T-shirt. Like two ripe blackberries. Michael wanted to suck them through the thin cloth.

Beth slid four yellow cups into the tiny oven on her countertop and pressed a couple of buttons. "Ready in one and a quarter minutes," she said. "Coke OK?"

Michael nodded. How long can I go on like this? he thought.

"We take Derek to this shrink over at the health center. According to Dr. Leonard, Derek's got the Oedipal thing ass backwards. So twice a week I drive him over there so he can plant carrot seeds or whatever they do. The shrink says we all have to talk this over but my husband won't go in there. He calls Derek a little pansy."

A bell rang and she opened the microwave. Back home, Michael baked everything in the cookstove. In warm weather, he used the apple wood he salvaged from clearing up old man Poors' orchard. It made a quick, hot fire and the baking was done before the house heated up. He wondered if Kaye would have stayed home if she'd been able to pop plastic cups into an oven and count the seconds until dinnertime.

Often, he'd come home to find her depressed, the dirty dishes piled up, nothing to eat. It seemed Kaye would never recover from giving birth to Aran. She was born a week after they moved in, when the house was barely a shell, cluttered with tools and stacks of Sheetrock ready to be nailed up and taped, not to mention sanded and painted. The subflooring barely in place. Cupboards to build. Not even any stairs. But Kaye had been lonely in the apartment while Michael devoted every spare minute to building the house.

"Maybe I can help," she said. But before the boxes were unpacked, Kaye started having labor pains. Michael drove to the

Poors' house to call the doctor. "The baby isn't due for another month," he said. "It still hasn't moved into position." But by the end of the week, Kaye was in the hospital hooked to an IV, her stitches aching, and the baby was in an incubator down the hall.

"We had to do a hysterectomy," the doctor explained to Kaye. "We didn't have a choice. You're lucky to be alive. To have a healthy child."

The two of them were stunned by the demands of parenthood, but it was more than that. The doctor mentioned postpartum depression, whispered about early menopause, and handed out prescriptions. But nothing brought relief. Kaye stopped washing her hair. "It's too much trouble to heat water," she complained. She rarely smiled. She grew heavy and thick. The baby became a little girl, but her mother stayed trapped as if she would always be on the sofa reading magazines.

Time after time Michael returned home to find Aran in her nightgown, sprawled on the braided rug coloring everything on the page of her coloring book the same color. One page red, the next page blue. He'd take them out for pizza or, if he had enough cash, they'd dress up and go to the Woodshed for jumbo fried shrimp and margaritas. Sometimes Kaye's mood would stay lifted, like a storm blown out to sea. She'd bake cookies, teach Aran to sew, paint their fingernails bright pink. Then he would come home to find her slumped on the sofa again, crushed as a moth whose wings have been handled.

When Kaye changed, it was like a beauty makeover in one of her magazines. She got her hair trimmed and brushed it till it was shiny. She jogged up and down the hill every morning until her body grew firm. The dark circles under her eyes faded. Her skin glowed. It had glowed for the camera. It wasn't a matter of trick photography. She looked vibrant. Any woman would want to be her. Any child would want to be Aran holding her hand as they sauntered along the water's edge, the waves washing over their feet, smiling as if they shared an important secret. That's the idea, Michael thought. That's what they're *really* selling.

Beth went to the screen door and rang a brass bell. "Derek, honey. Lunchtime," she called. When Derek came in, he sat at the counter eyeing Michael. His dark brown eyes dared Michael to say something about the lace curtain draped around his neck like a stole.

Earlier, when Michael passed through Beth and her husband Bill's bedroom to use the toilet, he paused in front of the dresser where a huge gilt-framed wedding photo nestled in the center of an elaborate ruffled doily. There was Beth in white satin and yards of lace, her luscious breasts pushing the shiny cloth. And there was Bill, looming over her, a football player in a tuxedo. I wouldn't want to tango with him, Michael thought, noticing his beefy hand resting possessively on Beth's shoulder. I don't blame you, Derek my friend, he thought now. If I had to make a choice, I'd rather be her, too.

"I betcha my little girl's your age," Michael said, using the fake voice he reserved for talking to children. Derek blinked.

"She's at the babysitter," he explained to Beth. She reached in front of him to flick on the radio then poured his Coke into a red glass. He could smell the perfume on her wrist. "My wife's in Ireland," he told her, not sure if this meant he was available or already taken.

Kaye was the only woman he had ever slept with. The only one he had done more than kiss. And she'd been the one to put his hand on her breasts. She'd been the one to take his clothes off that first time they made love. He couldn't imagine how to go about making love without Kaye.

Get a grip, he told himself as Beth slid onto a stool beside him, her thigh so close he felt her warm skin through his jeans; or was he imagining it? He could also feel his erection pressing the thick cloth and he was quite sure *that* wasn't just in his mind. He was afraid Beth would see it. Would she like knowing she had this effect on him?

He promised himself that as soon as he put Aran to bed that night, he would touch himself. Why hadn't he been doing this all along? Jesus, man. What're you doing, saving it for Kaye? Following some biblical edict against spilling seed? Still scared of Father O'Donahue?

He shoveled the tasteless food into his mouth, washing it down with the Coke, all the while trying to distract himself from putting his hand on Beth's warm sun-browned leg. After work, he would stop and pick up a six-pack. Get Aran ice cream. And when he put his hands on himself it would be Beth touching him. Not Kaye. That way he wouldn't start to cry.

* * *

Crystal was eating handfuls of Cheez Doodles from the family-size bag Janesta brought home along with a six-pack of Cokes, a loaf of Wonder bread, and a box of Velveeta. "Don't eat it all at once," her mother said, taking a Coke to her room.

Crystal wrapped her arm around her dog, Shotgun, who ate the Cheez Doodles that fell on her lap. She was watching *The Wizard of Oz* on the VCR that Skeeter, her mother's last boyfriend, won at bingo. Dorothy and the Scarecrow were dancing down the yellow brick road. She watched this movie every day and never got tired of it.

Their house had very little furniture. A sagging mustard yellow sofa with a scratched coffee table beside it. The TV on a crate with the VCR underneath. A table and three chairs. The bed and chair in Janesta's room and in Crystal's, a twin bed with a pink comforter and a floor lamp with half-naked women holding up the brass pole. Crystal made blouses out of pink tissues so she wouldn't have to see their breasts. Pink was her favorite color. The house had the feel of a place just moved in to. As if any minute a moving van would pull up and the rest of the furniture would be unloaded.

Crystal tried to keep the house clean. What this meant was she would set up the vacuum cleaner, get out all the attachments, plug it into an outlet by the front door, then leave it out in the middle of the room for her mother to trip over. Or she would sweep the kitchen floor, brushing the crumbs and bits of macaroni, the dog hairs and gray fluffs of dust into a pile before deciding to fix herself a glass of chocolate milk. She hardly ever took that last step with a dustpan. Once, on a sunny day, she sprayed all the windows with Windex but didn't wipe off the smeared glass, so the windows were streaked and the woodwork muddy.

Sometimes Crystal stood on the front porch and sank her fingernails into the soft wood, leaving gouges in the boards. Her mother had never so much as planted a zinnia in the yard. She was always saying she would never have moved out in the middle of nowhere if it hadn't been for Skeeter wanting to be out of town. Crystal missed Skeeter. He always came home with a treat. Ice cream or a pack of balloons. Once a baby doll that went to the bathroom in her diaper and ate special food Crystal stirred up in a bowl. But the doll didn't have any food or diapers left, and her mother refused to buy more.

Crystal wished she could remember her real father. She knew he wasn't Skeeter. Skeeter came along when she was nearly nine years old. She remembered other men before him. Men who kicked their boots off and put their feet up on the table. Men who drank beer at breakfast and smacked her when she cried. Men who smelled like dirty socks and old fish when they grabbed her onto their laps. But no man she called Daddy. When she asked her mother about her father, all Janesta did was light a cigarette and wave her away like she was the smoke.

Through the open door, Crystal watched Janesta peel her clothes off and throw them onto the chair which was already heaped with clothing. Lacy black underpants. Bras with enough metal to set off a detector. Jeans turned half inside out. Tight black pants. A white T-shirt with a spotted leopard on the front. Her red baby doll pajamas. She lay naked across her unmade bed, pulling the pink blanket up from the floor. Feeling Crystal's gaze, she turned and said, "I ain't your private peep show. Shut this damn door. And turn that goddamn movie down. You oughta know it by heart. You're gonna drive me over the deep end one of these days, Crystal. I need me some quiet in here."

Crystal did as she was told, returning to lie on the sofa, one arm around Shotgun, who ate the Cheez Doodles from her hand now that her mother couldn't see. "My name is Crystal Curtis," she whispered. "I am twelve years old. I was borned in Union City. I used to live with my mommy and daddy when I was a tiny little baby. My daddy's name's Frank. We ate potatoes for supper every day. Fried potatoes. Mashed potatoes. Boiled potatoes. Baked potatoes. Homemade french fries. Potato chips 'n dip. You'd like that huh, Shotgun?" She patted the dog vigorously and continued. "My daddy Frank grows 'em. He's got hair the color mine is and the exact same gray eyes like me. Every day he used to say 'Crystal Dawn honey, my little girl. You hungry?' " She looked down at Shotgun and repeated in a deep voice, "You hungry?" The dog flapped his tail lazily and licked her hand. "Then he'd go dig up a mess of potatoes and Mom would give him a kiss and wash 'em up and put 'em on to boil. We always had potatoes on the stove boilin' or fryin' or in the oven bakin' when my daddy Frank was home, you know that Shotgun?" She twirled a strand of hair around her finger and chewed it. On the TV, the Tin Man was being oiled. She heard a car approach and lifted up from the couch to see the man across the road pull into his driveway. She remembered how he waved at her from the old trailer. Did her daddy Frank look like him?

Behind the closed door, Janesta was not sleeping. She was lying on her back smoking, an ashtray balanced on her belly, thinking how when she first met Skeeter she was so turned on half the men in Waukeag County were sniffing after her like she was a dog in heat before she got Skeeter to give her a ride on his motorcycle. She crushed out her cigarette and stared at the cobwebs, remembering her cheek pressed against his leather jacket, her thighs tight around his hips. But it was another motorcycle she really wanted to ride, another black leather jacket she longed for.

In the living room, Crystal raised the volume on the TV and was singing along, but Janesta didn't have the heart to yell at her. At least when she was watching her movie, she had something to do. Besides, Janesta needed to think. In her belly there was a big knot, twisting. She hugged herself, then turned on her side. Feels like a bomb's about to go off, she thought.

When Crystal could no longer smell smoke and was sure her mother was asleep, she lay on the sofa, very still with her eyes shut, and called the dog over in a whisper. "Shotgun?" The dog—an old black Lab going gray around the muzzle—sat near Crystal's face, wagging his tail lazily, the red tip of his penis showing, and began to lick her face, starting with Crystal's cheeks and nose, then licking her forehead and chin and very delicately near her mouth. There was the smell of dried kibble on his hot breath and his stained teeth as his long pink tongue curled and brushed over her face and she lay still, trying not to giggle and then the tickle of it made her face grow tighter. She squeezed her eyes shut, her entire body tense, then slowly relaxed, letting the tension go out of her neck, her lips, her throat and eyes, as if she were receding into the soft cushions all dreamy as Shotgun lapped her face with the delicacy of a cat licking milk from a saucer, his pink tongue rasping from her cheeks to her forehead, curling into her ears and down her jaw. The dog groaned, shifted his old bones, and flopped his tail. Crystal scratched under his collar until his back leg thumped spasmodically, as if Crystal were barely missing the itch, driving him nuts, and he wanted to scratch it himself with his long thick dark nails but he was too busy washing her face, nuzzling her with his lower teeth at the edge of her jaw, growling a little as he licked her ears until she finally gave over to it and screamed with laughter, and the dog jumped up, barking, and ran to the center of the room, chasing his own tail, and her mother yelled from her bedroom for them to pipe down.

* * *

The road down east to Bragdon twisted and curved through several small towns: Watsonville, Cherry Falls, Whitney Harbor. Most with some kind of store or gas station. In between, long stretches of blueberry barrens steaming in the warm sun. Rita knew she ought to turn back. She should never have taken off this way with Rainey in the backseat. She had never driven this far. What if she made a mistake? What if a police officer pulled her over and asked to see her license? What then?

She felt a mixture of power and fear, a sense of "Hey, look at me!" and "Oh my God, what am I doing?" She glanced at Rainey in the rearview mirror. She seemed perfectly content. She read the signs for Rainey: "Betty's Beauty Boot. Daylight Donuts. Grub 'n Grog."

Rita gripped the wheel when cars came up behind her, sped up for the sections of the road where they couldn't pass, slowed down and carefully downshifted when she came to the broken yellow lines to let them pass. She wanted to pull off the road and turn around but was scared she'd lose control of the car. All day long, the moon hung in the clear blue sky. Rainey was singing her favorite song by Squirrel Nutkin. "I've got a tail," she sang. Her mother joined in.

Ahead, Rita saw a bit of congestion and she slowed down, proud of the ease with which she could shift now. It's all a matter of practice, she thought as the car dipped down a hill, over a bridge, and past the sign telling them they were entering Bragdon. Rita was not sure why it had been so important to drive clear up here. Because it's there, she thought. And I've never seen it. The story of my life.

She thought of the town where she grew up. Medora, Indiana. The old men on the bench in front of The Covered Bridge Cafe waiting for their wives to emerge from the Hornets' Nest with their blue-tinted hair whipped like spun sugar around their heads. She bought penny candy from Randy's Market, a grocery stocked with stale crackers and bread, lunch meat and cheese. Soda pop machines for after hours, which came at six, were lined up on the porch where birds' nests dangled from the corrugated tin roof like whiskers. Medora was ringed with cornfields and grain silos, divvied up by railroad tracks. It smelled of burning trash and the plastics plant on the outskirts beside the trailer park. On summer days barefoot girls in shorts and halters rode their bikes up and down hoping for a breeze.

Rita got out of Medora the first chance she had. That was after Gene Simon, a boy from the college in Bloomington, drove into Medora on a hot day in late August. He was sightseeing, he said, and he saw Rita on Randy's porch drinking a Coke. When he offered her a ride, she went without another thought but take me away. They drove clear to Sparksville, speeding along the White River with all the windows down, the radio competing with the locusts that whined and whirred in the corn. They kissed in the graveyard till Rita's lips ached.

Gene said he hoped to become an entrepreneur. Rita did not ask what that was. She leaned against the white upholstery and let him touch her under her blouse. She was amazed that a person could spend his whole life without ever seeing corn grow. That he found it beautiful and commented on the sweet smell of the earth baking in the sun. To Rita, corn was like the air she breathed; she took it for granted. Later, when her mother threatened to throw her out if she didn't quit going with that good-for-nothing city boy who only wanted one thing, Gene gave Rita bus fare to Boston and the name of a girl to stay with. She knew if she stayed in Medora, she would become one more woman with a tired shuffle and a bad perm who pushed a rickety baby stroller along the roadside.

Rita drove slowly down the main street of Bragdon, past the neat brick buildings and the sidewalks glittering in the sun. She eased the car past the five-and-ten and pulled into a huge nearly empty parking lot beside a place called Mary's. Because she felt especially nervous about backing up, she aimed the car so she could pull right out again.

The pie they ordered had a foamy cloud of meringue thicker than the lemon custard. Rainey scooted close to it and touched it with her tongue. Out the window, the Bragdon Falls rushed toward the bridge.

Things aren't so bad. Not really, Rita thought as she took her first bite of pie. We'll be back home before Dave and Kathleen get there. They'll never know. Anyway, Dave left the keys on the counter like he wanted to tempt me.

"Lemon marshmallow fried egg pie," Rainey said. She ate down to the crust, licking it clean, but not biting into it.

"Doing a good job on that pie, ain't the little fella?" the waitress asked. Strangers often mistook Rainey for a boy. Rita had decided that was the way people handled their nervousness about her being mixed race. Anyone who *really* looked knew she was a girl.

"Let's go to Boston," a teenage girl in the next booth said.

"What's in Boston?" the boy across from her asked, sipping his soda.

"Bagel shops with all different kinds of cream cheese. People playing music on the streets. Magicians doing tricks. They got about everything."

People always want to be somewhere they aren't, Rita thought. When she lived in Medora, she just wanted to get out, she didn't care where. When she lived in Boston she wanted to go to the country. Now she lived in Preacher's Lake, but she had to see what was down the road. And now that she was in Bragdon, she was curious about going further to see Meddybemps. She wondered what it would be like to stay in one place. Just stay where you were and make a life right there. Bragdon had called to her like Brigadoon. But it was just a town. There were the usual businesses. It had a church with a white steeple—although it was not boarded up like the one in Preacher's Lake. Of course, Bragdon had its own particular character. But she couldn't know that just passing through. Just stopping in a diner. What had she hoped to find?

Beside them was a family. The children had hot dogs they kept taking out of the roll, examining, then putting back in for another bite. The mother wore a T-shirt that said *How Can a Moral Wrong Be a Civil Right?* She seemed to be smirking at Rita. The youngest was peeling the thick skin off his hot dog with his bottom teeth. "Want dat," he said, banging the tray of his high chair and pointing at his father's french fries. "Want dat!" he repeated but was ignored.

Maybe it's something about when I was a kid, Rita thought. All the things I didn't get. All the times I was ignored. Like that little boy with his hot dog wanting what's on his father's plate. I want to try everything, see everything.

On the way back down the coast, they passed shingled houses with orange and white pot buoys stacked beside lobster traps. They passed trailer after trailer. Rita wondered if someday she could afford a trailer. Last week, she called about two rentals in Union City, thinking she wouldn't need a car if she lived there. "No children," she was told by the first person. "Where d'you work?" the second one asked. Saying she was looking for a job ended the discussion.

Yesterday, Kathleen drove her over to see a camp for rent on Cozzie's Pond. The owner called it The Closet. It was filled with old dresses and women's shoes. There was no water, no bathroom, and it was six miles from Moody's, the nearest store. The murky pond was covered with an oily green scum. Kathleen had been too busy holding the dresses up, stuffing the ones she liked into her backpack, to notice Rita's dismay.

Rita concentrated on the road ahead of her, on the landscape they passed, the tall fir trees with their reddish bark. A herd of cows up close to the fence. She saw a sign pointing to Potter's Bay. No one was behind her. No one approached. Of course, she turned. She wanted to see what was down the crooked road. What was around the bend? What was Potter's Bay? But she panicked when, after driving a few miles, the road grew so narrow it seemed about to end. What if Dave and Kathleen came home early? She slowed down, checking her rearview mirror carefully before she pulled off the road. As soon as she was off the road, she realized she would have to back up in order to turn around. She ground the gears, making a horrible shriek, and the car stalled. When she turned the key in the ignition, the car sounded like an animal taking its last breath. Rita cradled her head against the steering wheel; behind her Rainey began sniffling.

"You OK?" There was a tap on the window. Outside the car was an elderly black woman with a pillbox hat perched on her head. Rita stared in disbelief. Maybe the whole trip was just a dream. Then she rolled down the window, astounded by this woman's presence in the middle of nowhere.

"You look like you could use some help," the woman said. "My husband'll be along in a minute. He'll know what to do. That's a fine-looking girl you got there. I got some apples in the car. Let me get her one."

Sure enough, no sooner had she returned with the apple, than a black man wearing a bright orange hunting cap pulled up in a pickup. Rita explained what happened and got out of the car so he could try it. He shifted into neutral and the car started with one try. Then he put it in reverse and turned the car around for Rita. "Sometimes you kind of panic," he told her. "Get your husband to take a look at it." They waited beside the road as Rita and Rainey drove off, Rainey waving until she could no longer see them.

"That's what you call a miracle," Rita said. "Can you keep a secret, Rainey?"

"I won't tell about the pie," she said and patted her mother's hair.

"Or the drive. You won't tell about that either, will you?"

"No," Rainey said. She was thinking about the man and woman who helped them. Were they her grandparents? she wondered, watching the white puffy clouds float by.

*   *   *

"Back up a minute," Coalie said. "Where'd you say this place was at?" Coalie and his friends were sitting on lawn chairs on the porch of Buster's Hardware when Slim stopped by to tell them the news.

"You up and buy it, just like that?" Rip snapped his fingers. "Don't even ask a fella to give it a look?" Rip, a retired contractor, enjoyed talking about places he thought were on the verge of collapse.

"It's clear up on top of Preacher's Hill. You know, across from Trudy's mom's old place, up by the lake. And yeah, Rip. I just up and bought it. What was there to look at? It's a trailer. If it falls apart, I'll get me another. I could use a hand jackin' up the back, though. It's about to fall off the blocks it's sittin' up on."

Buster took his cap off, rubbed his bald head, and chuckled. The bell on the door tinkled and a young man and woman, both of them blonde and wearing freshly ironed white shorts, emerged from the store. Buster rolled his eyes and wound one finger around in the air beside his ear as they headed for their car. "People from away," he muttered. "It ain't even the Fourth. Used to be they'd come on the Fourth."

Buster had started working at the hardware store with his father when he was a boy. Now he left the business to his son, Binky, who stocked the shelves with all size and manner of baskets and kitchenware. Woks and whisks and tea kettles were displayed where once there were boxes of nuts and bolts and oily lengths of chain. There was even a shelf of ceramic salt and pepper shakers that included a pair of outhouses with quarter moons on the doors, a pink refrigerator and stove set, and a pair of jaunty red lobsters that waved their shiny claws. "Crap" Buster called it, spitting the word from between clenched teeth. He often threatened to take down the sign with his name on it and put up a new sign calling the place BINKY'S DOODADS AND GEWGAWS. "The crap them folks buy," he said. "Half of it imported. You'd never catch me selling that. My store was a man's store."

"Yeah, well, they're buyin' it up," Rip said. He spit a stream of tobacco juice into the dust, wiping the back of his hand across his long white beard. Patches of it were stained brown from the times he drooled.

"The ones with out-of-state plates." Buster took a Mars bar from his pocket and ate it in two bites.

"That's where the money is," Binky said. He was at the screen door sipping coffee from one of his best-selling mugs—a pink pig with a snout that protruded on one side and a curly tail that formed the handle.

"Who asked you?" Buster said. "Why ain't you in there countin' it up if there's so much money?"

"Now tell me, Slim. You up there with Farmer Brown?" Rip asked.

"Yep. She's out in back of me. I seen her workin' her tail off."

"Some tail, wouldn't you say?" Buster laughed and the fellows joined in, tilting their chairs back against the wall.

"You figure she's one of them sex change operations like they got on *Geraldo?*" Coalie asked.

"You watch too much TV," Rip said. "Besides, it's always the man that wants to be the lady. They can take what he don't want off but I never heard of stickin' it onto some female. Anyways, only a female'd build a house without investin' in a level. That place tips like the tower of Pisa. It'll tip right over one of these days."

"Them medical doctors can do about anything," Coalie said "They can fix you up with a new one. I was in the service with a fella that had a whole new zonger made for hisself after he lost it in the war. Some kind of pump makes it go up and down." He clutched his crotch as if he were afraid someone might come and take his away.

"That ain't what Farmer Brown is." Rip patted his beard like it was a cherished pet.

"You never know," Coalie said.

"I know," Rip said. "She's got knockers. I seen 'em. Big ones."

"You better watch your step up on that hill, Slim." Buster chuckled, his belly jiggling. "You got you some kind of he-she-man on the one side and Janesta Curtis across the road."

"Janesta Curtis, now there's one to watch out for. A gal like that goes through fellas like a flock of sheep goes through a new pasture. She's been married, what, three, four times?" Rip adjusted his overalls. "God, it's hot for this time of year." He fanned his face with his cap.

"Frank's the only one I know of. Skeeter and her never got hitched," Buster said with authority.

"Well, all I know, Slim, is you got some kind of Elizabeth Taylor across the road. You better watch your step. Oooh-weee." Coalie shook his hand as if he'd just grabbed a hot pan and made a "ssst" sound through the space in his front teeth.

4

Slim was frying potatoes in bacon grease and beside the potatoes, six of the eggs he had gathered from the hens were sputtering in the cast-iron pan. Since he hauled them up behind the trailer, they had begun producing twice as many eggs. Out his window, he watched Tom, the turkey, fan his feathers on the hood of the car.

"I told Mildred he disappeared," Buster had said when he brought the turkey to the dump. "She was gonna call the sheriff, but I hinted about hungry foxes. I ain't about to whack some poor bird's head off just because it's Thanksgiving."

At the dump, Tom used to follow Slim around, close on his heels like a dog. Whenever Slim stopped, the turkey cocked his ugly head, a mass of mottled red flesh quivering under his beak. But since he'd moved him up to the trailer, Tom was more interested in the hens. Right now Tom was attempting to mate with a hen that ran across the yard, feathers flying.

If Slim could set up the dump the way he wanted, if he could have what he called his Dream Facility, there would be a barn with stalls and pens, cages for the smaller animals. He would get the folks from the veterinary clinic to make displays about animal care. Anyone who took an animal would sign a certificate agreeing to take care of it for life.

Up in back, Nelly was plowing. She was a big broad-shouldered woman. "Big as a man," the fellows down at Buster's said. Slim watched the muscles across her back rippling as she leaned over the steering wheel of her tractor, her skin already tan. He didn't think it was right for a woman to work all day out in the sun the way she did. Wanting to be neighborly, Slim planned to whip up a chocolate cake from one of his box mixes and carry it across the overgrown field that stretched between her place and his. He planned to get to work on it right after breakfast.

Slim buttered four slices of toast and was scooping his eggs and potatoes from the pans when he heard a soft tap on his door. Crystal, wearing a white flannel nightgown, stood on the cinder blocks.

"Mom's getting pizza," she said. Her pale gray eyes darted like nervous flies, returning again and again to land on Slim's plate of food.

"C'mon in. You skip supper last night?"

Crystal nodded and hung her head. She stood at the wobbly card table eating Slim's breakfast while he cooked more. He offered her a seat, but she continued to stand. He poured her some juice and when his meal was ready, sat down at the table.

"I'm gonna build a counter so we can sit up on stools," he said.

"A stool's a poop."

"That's true. But it's also a chair."

"It took me three years to grow three inches," Crystal said. She pressed her back to the refrigerator, measuring herself against it. "I'm almost a teen." Crystal held up her hands, all the fingers spread wide. "I'm this plus this," she said, showing two more fingers. "I got me *Teen* magazine yesterday. It's got all new school clothes. French braid your hair." She walked her fingers across her dark stringy hair. "Mom's takin' me to Bangor school shoppin'."

"That so?" Slim got up to put more toast in.

"You got a girlfriend?" she asked. She asked him this same question every time she came over, which since he'd moved into the trailer across from her was often several times a day.

"Nope. Not yet. Not the last time I looked, anyhow."

"Mom's on the look out for her a boyfriend."

"That so?"

"Least you don't have to worry about your girlfriend gettin' pregnant if you don't have one."

Slim poured another cup of coffee. "That's the truth," he said.

"Weatherman says it hailed something wicked up in Aroostook County. Hailstones big as golf balls smacking people in the head." Crystal licked her finger then ran it over her plate to pick up the crumbs. "Is *balls* a nasty word?" she asked.

*   *   *

It was nearly noon when Janesta Curtis sped up the hill in her big green Buick, the muffler rumbling, the country station blaring so loud Nelly heard it even though she wore earplugs when she drove the tractor. Janesta pulled into her driveway and slammed out of her car. She was a big woman, hefty some would say, who wore clothes that molded to her body, the bright cloth clinging to every one of her curves, and there were plenty of them. Her high heels clicked across the worn wooden porch and through the rooms of her house. When she called Crystal, her voice had the flat unemotional tone of a barmaid in a crowded room ordering three more high-balls for the party at the table by the door. It was a voice that said: I've seen it all and none of it fazes me one bit.

Crystal, whose face was smeared with chocolate, was scooping icing from the can with her finger. She looked up when she heard her mother's car, but she didn't run home the way she had all the other times. She'd be watching TV with Slim, sitting on the sofa eating popcorn, a root beer in one hand, and she'd run out of that trailer as if it were on fire the minute she heard her mother's car. Or she'd be helping him feed the hens and she'd walk across the grass like a robot programmed to move in the direction of her mother's voice. Today, she just kept dipping her finger into the can of icing and licking it clean.

Janesta's heels crunched on the gravel Michael had helped Slim spread on the driveway. She tapped on the door, then pressed her face to the screen, shading her eyes to see into the room. "What'd I tell you, you little shit? You stay to home where you belong. Leave folks alone."

"If it don't rain by Saturday, it'll ruin the blueberry crop," Crystal said.

"She's no trouble to me," Slim said. "I can use the company."

Janesta let herself into the trailer as if she'd been invited. Slim was pleased, but all the same he was backing away from her until he was pressed up against the cupboards. Janesta, in her hot pink blouse with beaded fringe dangling over her breasts, seemed to take up all the space, making Slim feel like a wisp of smoke Janesta could blow away.

Janesta's soft belly pressed the seams of her jeans, the tight blue cloth hugged her thighs. She smelled of smoke and perfume and beer. Sparkling rhinestones ran up the side seams on her pants from the gold zippers at her ankles to the thick fold of flesh at her waist. Where the cloth ended and her bare skin began, there was a tattoo of a winking Cheshire cat. Janesta noticed Slim looking at it. "I'll try about anything once. If I've had me one too many," she said.

"Well, I never," Janesta said and tapped her cigarette into Slim's sink, puckering her lips like she was kissing the air. "I never seen a man workin' on a cake. Not once. You one of them liberated fellas?"

"It's from a box."

"Don't matter. It's a cake, ain't it? And you baked it. You're a man, ain't 'cha?" She slapped herself on the thigh and laughed till Slim blushed clear up to the roots of his white hair.

"Least it looks that way to me." Janesta's eyes brushing over Slim made him feel like fingers were sliding across his skin. He had never been touched by a woman and he decided then, standing in his kitchen with Janesta Curtis, her wild red hair frizzing around her shoulders, that he wouldn't mind finding out what that was all about.

Janesta grabbed Crystal's arm. "You are a sight, sister, lickin' at that icing like a dog. Let's get along home. Leave this fellow to his cake bakin' in peace."

"Hows about havin' a slice? There's coffee, too." Slim held up the percolator, forgetting his plan to bring the cake to Nelly. His hand was shaking as he sliced the cake. Crystal took a bite of hers, then went over to Slim's chair where the orange kitten he had brought home from the dump was dozing. The kitten swatted Crystal's hair, biting it and shaking it like it was a mouse he'd just caught.

"Janesta? Whyn't you give yourself one of them pregnancy tests?" Crystal said.

"Go on with your baby talk." Janesta waved at Crystal. "That's all she talks about. Pregnant ladies. That and the weather." Janesta scraped back her chair. "C'mon Crystal. Let's get along home. I'm about as wore out as an old biddy that's been two-steppin' with a hummybird."

As Slim watched them walk home, he planned the eggplant Parmesan he would make Janesta and Crystal. It was his specialty, what he took to every potluck. He would make green salad. Have ice cream and cake for dessert. Janesta would kick off her shoes and run her foot up Slim's leg the way he had seen his mother do to Carl Strong when Carl tilted back in his chair to wipe a slice of bread across his plate. Janesta would rest her foot in his lap till he reached down and held it warm against him, in that place that ached to be touched.

* * *

Carol counted the windows she could see from her window while lying on the sofa. She was thinking about doing a painting of the windows outside, using her window as a frame, and trying to remember if that had been done already. Should she paint the windows as just that, windows, or add the personal touches: the vase of yellow flowers on a table, the exhibitionist parading back and forth with his equipment dangling, the three pink window shades always pulled down at varying lengths, and the Puerto Rican flag covering a window on the top floor. The post-office building resembled a giant ice cube tray. She could build it as such and the cubes could pop out, bits of people's lives encased in Lucite. The corner of an envelope. A scrap of paper with *arugula* written on it. A black high heel. A lace glove. She would go to the toy store for props.

She was counting again and up to a hundred and sixty-eight when the phone rang. The machine was on, as always. Carol rarely answered it without screening her calls. Especially with Vivian calling so often.

"I just called to say hi," Vivian said. An express train rattled down the subway track and Vivian paused so long Carol thought she'd hung up. "I'll call you later," she shouted, then did hang up.

Carol pushed herself off the sofa. "These old bones," she groaned. She was stiff from lying still for so long. She wished Dougie would call. Yesterday, he'd called and given Carol a detailed description of Boris, his latest fling. "So I'm at the Grand Onion," Dougie said, using his name for the grocery store. "And this gorgeous man. I'm talking hunk, honey, comes right up and pinches my butt while

I'm selecting a bunch of bananas." Hearing about Dougie's escapades always cheered her up, but Dougie would not call now. About this time, he'd be at work, folding the maroon napkins into wine glasses, setting out the silverware. She wished she hadn't let Iris convince her to work part-time so she could devote more time to making art. She tried to concentrate. From her new vantage point, she could see a hundred more windows in the post-office building, like cells in a honeycomb. She could paint the workers dressed in black-and-gold-striped uniforms. But she'd rather go to work. She'd rather spend the evening with Dougie at Noho Nights waiting on tables for what she called "the perfect people"—people who sat under the ceiling fans ignoring the plates of artfully arranged, color-coordinated food set on the marble tables in front of them, men and women with perfect hair and skin, always dressed in black, waiting, it seemed to Carol, to be discovered. Now, she thought, *I've been discovered.* But every time she picked up a paintbrush, she felt inhibited by her success. She imagined the judges whispering: "That's not the one I wanted," the man in the bow tie said. "Isn't she too old to be applying for grants?" a woman who looked alarmingly like Kitty Carlisle asked. "She fit the profile," said a man who slowly pushed his glasses up. "We have our quotas to fill."

Carol studied her painting of Annie. How was she supposed to go on? Then she noticed the time. If she didn't leave right away she would be late for therapy like she had been the last three times. They had spent most of the session discussing it. She didn't want to do that again.

* * *

"What do you think this block is really about?" Iris asked. Carol couldn't believe she had actually started seeing a therapist. She was the last of her friends to go. It made her feel like the last tree in what had once been a forest. Below her, the woodcutters sharpened their axes. *Barbie Does Therapy* she'd call the diorama she would create. Leafy branches would jut from Barbie's head, peeling bark cover her body. She didn't mention this to Iris. Last time they had a big talk about how Carol didn't see anything in her mind's eye anymore, but it wasn't true. She just didn't know how to describe how it felt to see things and not make them. She didn't know how to describe how it felt to live without Annie.

"I'm trying too hard to be perfect. I'm afraid to try because I'll mess up," Carol said. She knew it sounded like something from

Psychology 101. "Since I got the grant I have to be the great *artiste.*"

"Don't you think it has to do with you and Annie?" Iris murmured.

"Annie?"

"Well, from what little you've told me, it sounds like that's a place in your life where you have a lot of pain."

"God. I pay you for this, right?" It was one of Carol's standard lines. A *joke,* Carol insisted. A reflex. "That's too big a topic," she said. "You're going away pretty soon."

When they first started to work together, Iris explained that she would be away for six weeks in the summer. The last two weeks of July were unusual. But her famous August leave was like every other therapist in the city. No wonder everyone tries to get out of here in August, Carol thought. Your chances of being murdered must quadruple then.

"That's just avoidance," Iris said. "We've got plenty of time."

"What's there to say?" Carol asked. Suddenly the rows of corduroy on her black pants seemed immensely interesting. A tear rolled down her cheek but she pretended it wasn't there. Maybe Iris wouldn't see it.

"What are you thinking?"

"That's worse than asking me what I dreamt." Carol stared at her knee as if she found it fascinating. Another tear rolled slowly to her jaw and plopped on her arm.

"The look on your face seems pretty significant to me. Would you mind humoring me?"

Carol hesitated. "I was trying *not* to think. I can't do anything about losing Annie. She's gone forever. I keep obsessing about all the times I *didn't* want to see her. Now, I'll *never* see her again." The tears came faster but she didn't brush them away. "It's like a roadblock. I can't ever get around it. I just stay stuck. I keep thinking how I'll never talk to her again. I'll never get to say I'm sorry."

"Sorry?" Iris said, nodding, her face a picture of sympathy.

"Don't make me play therapist guessing games. Tell me what you're thinking or I'll rip my clothes off and run out of here."

"Promise?" Iris smiled.

"Promise."

"Well, I'm thinking about this other block. This not being able to paint. What you call a visual blank. Remember how you told me that you always saw pictures, always knew when you were about to paint because the image would come into your mind so vividly? How now it's like the TV tube's burned out? These are your words, remember?"

"Yeah." Carol considered the images that were flashing through her mind that very moment, her bare feet pounding the filthy pavement as she ran along Greenwich Avenue, the afternoon sun on her bare skin. She didn't know why she pretended she didn't see any images anymore. Maybe Iris would decide she was cured, then she couldn't come back. But why did she want to come back?

"If you could see your face you'd know why I am always asking you what you're thinking. You don't hide your feelings very well."

"I thought I was supposed to show my feelings here." Carol was crying seriously now. She refused to reach for a tissue even though tears dripped from the tip of her nose. She hated the regulation tissues. She imagined therapists all over the city checking the tissue boxes before the first appointment came.

"Yes," Iris said. "This is a place for you to show your feelings. But it's good to talk about what they are, too." Iris waited, her head resting against her chair. Her legs were long and very white, her stockings so sheer Carol decided she would use this material to paint on. The telephone rang twice, but the machine answered it; the volume was turned down. Would there never be an end to this silence? She wished Iris would ask her what she was thinking now. Iris was watching her, her face placid yet interested. She wondered if that was something they learned in therapy school, that look. If they practiced it in front of the mirror before graduation.

"My friend Dougie's first therapist talked on the phone while he was there. She'd pick up when she got a call and talk right through his time with her. He kept going for three years even though he hated that. Just because she was the first person he told he was gay. Isn't that awful?"

"You changed the subject. I want to talk about you. The way you bring these things up isn't that different from when Doug's therapist picked up the phone. You break the connection. I can tell you're hurting. Of course you miss Annie. Of course you wish she were still alive. And you miss your work. Your work has always helped you and now it's gone, too. Your grief is all mixed up in this inability to express yourself. Isn't there some way the two— Oh, I don't know. You're the artist. You know these things. But isn't there some way you could work out your feelings about Annie *and* make art? Maybe something different from painting and the pieces you described. Some other medium perhaps? Clay?"

"I could make life-sized models of my parents and yank their heads off," Carol said.

"That would be a start."

Carol stared at the wall behind Iris. She knew how rough the cinder block would feel, how cool to her cheek. There were pipes along the ceiling, painted the same shade of beige, and in one corner the large sewer pipe. When the toilet flushed, it rushed right through the room. How Freudian, she thought.

"What are you thinking now?"

Carol shrugged and shook her head. "Yesterday, I bought a half dozen tubes of white and black paint. I couldn't choose any colors. I don't know what it means."

"It's time," Iris said. "We'll have to save that for next week."

Carol sat still, waiting, not getting up like she was supposed to. She wondered what would happen if she refused to leave. Would Iris call the police? Use another office and leave her there? Go home with Carol sitting stonily in the hard gray chair?

Carol felt a weariness that lodged in her bones. In her jaw. In her eyelids which were as heavy as overstuffed suitcases. I'm too old for this, she thought.

"Don't forget. You have my numbers. You can always call," Iris said, standing up. She smoothed her skirt and walked toward the door.

"The patient will now model the therapist's behavior," Carol said.

Iris smiled and patted her shoulder as she left.

*   *   *

"There it is," Nelly said as the truck careened around a curve and climbed to the top of another hill. Rita braced herself against the dashboard and held Rainey back. The old truck bucked and jerked as if any minute the engine would stall. Nelly didn't even wince when she ground the gears, she just thrust the stick shift as if the scraping metallic sound was to be expected.

They sped past a green asphalt-shingled house that looked surprisingly like the one Rita had grown up in. Seeing it, she could feel the rough surface of the shingles, remember how hot they were in the summer sun. She could almost smell the brown mist of her childhood, like a thick fog that enveloped her when she trudged through the back door into the kitchen where bacon fat and vinegar sizzled in a hot skillet of lettuce shrinking and going limp.

"There's Preacher's Mountain. And there's Sugar Hill. You see that? We're almost there. Sugar Hill's the one with the radio tower. See how it's bald and white on top?"

This was the most Nelly had ever said to Rita all at once. Usually she seemed to be quietly brooding. The night at the movies had been a disaster of awkward silences as they drove to Union City to The Ritz, a moldy, smelly theatre on Main Street that was having a Harrison Ford retrospective—that night *Witness*. Afterwards, Rita had hoped they would look in the shop windows. She still hadn't had a good look at the town, but Nelly got into the truck. On the way back to Preacher's Lake, there had been some halting attempts to discuss what they'd seen, mostly from Rita who shouted over the racket the engine made.

"Imagine being that shut off from the world. I wonder how the Amish keep going like that?" She waited for Nelly's response, then not getting one, rushed ahead. "I love the scene where they dance to the car radio." It was very sexy, she thought. How the woman giggled and let herself be twirled. Rita couldn't remember the last time she'd danced.

"I didn't like it." Nelly lit one of her homemade cigarettes. "Except for the barn raising. That'd never happen out here." Nelly's cigarette glowed in the dark truck as they passed the Larry Lobster sign.

Rita peered at the dark river as the tires hummed over the old bridge. "I've never had lobster before," she said.

"I'll make you one," Nelly said. "I get them right off the boat. Then you can see my place, too."

Now, they were almost there. Nelly ground into a lower gear. Rita was being unusually silent, she thought. She had been so talkative after the movie. She glanced at Rita, noticing how her thick wavy hair brushed her shoulders, how shiny it was. She wondered what was on Rita's mind but dared not ask. She didn't want the same question posed to her. Even with the windows down, it was unbearably hot for spring.

"There's Preacher's Mountain again." Nelly's voice cracked ominously. She glanced at Rainey who was studying her toy monkey as if she'd never seen it before. Nelly hadn't bargained on the kid. Kathleen and Dave had made no effort to prepare her. They were very careful not to watch Nelly's reaction to the little girl who closed her eyes and pressed her fingertips over her eyelids when Rita introduced her. Rainey's father was undoubtedly black, though no one mentioned him. The kid makes it so complicated, Nelly thought. Don't I have enough trouble as it is?

"Here we are," Nelly said, bouncing over the ruts in the driveway.

When Rita saw Nelly's house, she wanted to grab Rainey and race back down the hill. *This* was where she lived? *This* was the place Rita had been hearing so much about? It looked like a chicken coop.

"I just put the shingles on," Nelly said. "They're cedar. I got 'em from an old farmhouse that was being torn down. I got plenty more for the addition." She pointed to a pile covered with a blue tarp. She reached out her window, grasped the roof of the cab, and pulled herself out like an athlete doing a chin-up, swinging her long legs out the window and falling to the ground with a thump. The door was bashed in so badly it no longer opened. Nelly had spoken several times about her intentions to fix it. "It's on my list," she said.

"I got the windows from Slim at the dump," Nelly explained, leading the way up the path to a wooden pallet she used for a porch. Something scurried under the house at their approach. "I bought the land when I got back from the Peace Corps. The Philippines," she said before Rita could ask. Inside, the house was dark and cool and smelled of wood ashes.

Two small windows near the ceiling gave the one-room house a lopsided look. Two large square windows with several panes nearly covered one wall. The woodstove sat on bricks in the corner, the stovepipe streaked with creosote. Two old doors hung on opposite walls, and if they hadn't been nailed shut would have opened onto the weedy yard. A long narrow window hung horizontally over the sink.

"Slim gave me this sink," Nelly explained. "It's cast-iron. I have to oil it so it doesn't rust." At one end of the sink was a blistered slab of plywood where chipped dishes drained. At the other, a hand pump.

"This spring I got plumbing." Nelly pumped the handle. The water was rusty at first then ran clear. She gave them each a glass of water as if offering the finest champagne. It tastes of old pipes, Rita thought. Rainey ran her tongue around the rim of the glass, then tipped it out in the sink. Nelly looked disappointed. Children seemed as difficult to understand as the villagers she'd traveled for days to meet, through mud and muck and the thick black night filled with shrieks that echoed from the trees. She had thought the place was abandoned until they came forward, seeming to rise from the ground. Even the old ones with leathery faces seemed small and childlike.

Rita clutched her arms and looked around her, at the insulation

Nelly stapled up and intended to cover with paneling. At the grass poking between the cracks of the pine floorboards beneath which Nelly said she planned to tack more insulation before winter came.

Nelly pumped water into a smoke-blackened pot and set it on the gas burner. She was very tall—an inch too short, she said when people asked, meaning not quite six feet. She took a box from the shelf over the sink, a shelf Rita would have to stand on a chair to reach, and put it in front of Rainey, who took out the different shapes of wood and dutifully made a tower. Nelly took two beers from a cooler.

"I'm gonna get a fridge," she explained, sitting on the bench she built, her dirty work boots thrust in front of her. "As soon as I build a room to put it in." She told Rita again how she planned to add rooms on either side of the house. Right now she slept in a loft bed above the table. A ladder was on the wall but Rita pictured Nelly hoisting herself up the way she hoisted herself out of the truck. She tried to picture herself climbing up after her.

"It was the summer my mom died," Nelly was saying. Rita had no idea what Nelly was talking about. It was as if she had fallen asleep for several minutes. Rainey was on her lap stacking the blocks again. "The big C," Nelly said, taking a long sip of her beer. "It was her dying that got me back up here." Nelly explained how her mother wanted her ashes spread on the farm in Preacher's Lake where she'd been raised. On the farm where Nelly rode the tractor with her grandfather holding her as he let Nelly steer. Where she sat in the kitchen eating the raspberry pies her grandmother made. The farmhouse had been razed and the land divided into lots. Pink and green modular houses sat where the Jersey cows had grazed. On rainy days, the folks who lived in these houses—men and women who drove to Bucksport to mills or down east to the fisheries— could smell the sweet manure scent of the rich soil.

She didn't tell Rita how her father scoffed at her plans. "I'm sorry you weren't born a man. It's not enough you did your Peace Corps thing? A farmer? Don't come crying to me when you spend all your money," he said.

Rainey's tower fell with a clatter, startling Nelly from her thoughts. She got up for another beer, noticing Rita had barely started hers. "My mom left me enough to pay cash for the land. And to live off, too. I used to come here summers," Nelly said. "It sure is different to live here." She stretched, pushing against the bottom of the loft bed. Her arms were thick and muscular. "I figured out how to build this place from a library book." She laughed as if embarrassed at her own foolishness and turned to check the water which was making a rumbling sound but not yet boiling. She lifted the lid, peered into the pot, aware of the spicy scent of almonds, sure of the feel of a warm hand on either side of her waist.

"You never forget me," Fiona whispered. "Never. No matter you try and try. I be there. Ha!" Nelly felt as if her legs were made of wet cardboard and could not possibly hold her up.

"Rainey's got to go," Rita said.

"Go?" Nelly was shocked they wanted to leave. This was the trouble with children, they were wild and demanding. Here she had three lobsters in a bucket, rattling around, a ridiculous extravagance. For what? The kid was ready to go. Spoiled brat, she thought.

"She has to go to the bathroom," Rita said. Nelly could hardly bear to look at her. So small and sturdy, built like Fiona. She would never be able to touch this woman. Why was she thinking of building a room for the child? Building a life? You don't get a life. Remember that?

"It's up in back." Nelly pointed.

Rita and Rainey were gone so long Nelly was convinced they had decided to walk to the highway rather than stay. She watched a goldfinch perched in the apple tree. She chose this spot for the house because of the apple tree, thinking it would be nice when it was in bloom. Right now it was covered with minuscule green apples. "When the leaves are big as a mouse ear, that's when you plant your potatoes," an old guy at Buster's told her. She hoped this year to harvest bushels of potatoes. She stared out her window, smoking.

"We saw a toad." The door slapped shut making Nelly jump. "Rainey tried to catch it. It's pretty here," Rita added.

"I got a lot of work to do. I lost half an acre of strawberries. But I've got some that'll be ready to pick soon. Live and learn. That's my motto," she said, knowing she was talking too fast, sounding crazy. "I want to be all organic." She seemed to be searching Rita's face for an answer. Those eyes, Rita thought. Not afraid to look, but not revealing anything either. Rita flushed bright red from her scrutiny.

"It's time to let somebody love you. Even somebody you're not attracted to," Kathleen had said. Rita didn't like Nelly's thin chapped lips. Even less did she like the look of this so-called house. Thick cobwebs clung to the ceiling and dangled from the light fixture which was filled with hundreds of dead bugs. A bucket of garbage was in the corner, shiny black houseflies crawling lazily over the orange peels and eggshells and coffee grounds.

"It gets lonely out here," Nelly said. She took a slow ragged breath and placed her palms on Rita's shoulders. They were tense and hunched and grew more compressed under Nelly's hands. "The water's ready," she said, her voice cracking as if breaking through thick ice.

Nelly showed Rainey the lobsters, lifting them out from under the seaweed, demonstrating how they waved their claws. Then, Nelly dropped them into the boiling water. The room was silent except for the sounds of the lobsters knocking their hard claws against the sides of the pot. Rainey pressed her face into her mother's lap, sobbing. "Killer," she finally managed to say. The word hung in the air.

Nelly drank the last of her beer, choking a little as she swallowed it too fast. The bottle was damp and her hands felt sticky, as if covered with blood. She wiped them on her jeans, remembering the deer she'd killed last week. Her truck had slammed right into it and the deer, though its back legs were broken, had dragged itself into the woods. She'd hit so many deer, she'd lost count. She lifted the pot lid and stared into the swirling steam. The lobsters were dead now, no longer swishing their tails, their shells turning bright red.

*   *   *

"It's an XY." J.T. shut the door behind her and leaned against it. She wagged her finger. "He's been bad. Now, it's gonna fall off."

Lizzy took the chart from J.T. and glanced at her watch. The night clinic always made her so tired. "He's *it*, right?"

"Uh-huh."

"Is he hideous?"

"You're asking the wrong person." J.T. shrugged. "I'd say he was the average XY. He's kind of dusty."

"Dusty?"

"Like he's been working in a cement factory."

Lizzy slumped in her chair. "Send him in."

The man was average, as J.T. had said. And dusty. His jeans and his scuffed work boots were covered with a fine white dust. He was so nervous he was actually fingering the brim of his hat the way cowboys did when they went courting in old movies. It was a thick leather hat, the brim lashed to the crown with rawhide. Homemade, Lizzy thought.

"I thought you were going to be a man." He ran a hand through his thin brown hair. She noticed the bald spot. Like a baby bird before the feathers come, she thought.

"Sorry. He's only here once a month. His day was yesterday. Why don't you have a seat here," Lizzy said. He sat down with his hat on his knee, staring at the plastic model of a woman's reproductive organs. Visible through the clear plastic was a tiny pink uterus with blue ovaries and green fallopian tubes curled beside it. At the moment, the vagina was filled with spermicidal foam. It had been a busy night. Three new clients who needed an explanation of all the birth control methods. Two pregnancy tests, one positive. And the usual Pap smears and breast checks. The usual pill refills and the terrible itches that embarrassed everyone. Lizzy pushed aside the Pap slides in their cardboard containers and reached for her blood pressure cuff, then put it back down, deciding to save it for later. This guy looked like he was about to have a coronary.

Men rarely came to the clinic even when Bob *was* there. They were as rare as virgins and Lizzy was fond of saying they ought to set off fireworks when either one set foot in the place. There was the occasional teenage boy who slunk in on a dare, his friends circling the clinic while he was inside, the muffler on their car rumbling. He would bite his lip to keep from grinning too widely, his eyes damp with tears of laughter as J.T. unrolled a condom over her hand to show him how strong it was. "Desensitizing" they called it when she got her training. She put a variety of condoms into a paper bag for him, including some red and blue ones she knew would be found blown up and floating down the hallway of the high school the next day. They were certain to get an irate call from the principal whose purpose in life seemed to be trying to shut down the clinic. Every week he wrote a letter to the editor. "I don't believe in teenagers having sex," his last letter began. "Only one size?" the boy would inevitably ask when J.T. handed him the bag, as if part of the dare was to ask that question. "They're all the same," J.T. said, meaning penises, not condoms.

Sometimes a man would come in with his girlfriend. He would sit beside Lizzy, lean forward to see the pink nub hidden among the folds. The woman would lift up from the table, propped on her elbows, and watch the whole thing in the mirror. They always left with their arms around each other.

This man beside her now had a hurt, almost furtive expression in his eyes; he looked like he might cry. Well, let him, Lizzy thought. J.T. always said if more men had a good cry it would lower their testosterone level and we could all get on with life much easier.

"I've never slept with anyone but my wife." He stared at the poster of a pregnant priest. At the bottom it said, IF MEN GOT PREGNANT, ABORTION WOULD BE A SACRAMENT. One of J.T.'s gifts.

"Uh-huh," Lizzy said, thinking, sure, sure. Since Dennis started communicating through lawyers, she had lost her sympathy for men.

"She left me," the man was saying. "She said she needed time to think. Now she's in Ireland. It's been months."

Tell me about it, Lizzy thought. Right now I'm about to enter the peak of my cycle. I'm as ripe as a peach in August and the only thing waiting for me has batteries that have probably run down.

Day after day Lizzy counseled pregnant teenage girls who wept over the news, claiming to have only done it once. Girls who had big moon-faced babies they pushed around the grocery store, their chubby hands reaching. And day after day, Lizzy went home alone.

"I don't know what it is," the man was saying. He crossed his leg over his knee and hung his hat on his toe.

Lizzy looked down at her hands. She felt naked without her wedding ring. Her supervisor, an old-fashioned doctor who believed women should stay home with their mouths shut and their legs open, who said as much more than once, had said her hands were too small to palpate a uterus properly. But Lizzy had graduated at the top of her class. FPNP it said on her name tag. Family Planning Nurse Practitioner.

"Did you use any protection?" she asked the man.

"Protection?" he asked, smoothing his hair with his thickly calloused hand.

"Condoms? You know, rubbers. Spermicide. Anything like that?"

"With my wife, you mean?"

"Wasn't there someone else?"

"No. Nobody but Kaye," he whispered, his upper lip trembling.

"Do you have symptoms?" Lizzy placed her hand near the man who hugged himself, jiggling his leg spasmodically. "You seem really worried," she said, using a technique from school. It sounded fake, but she didn't know what else to say. He was silent for a moment as if various parts of himself had been scattered around the room and he was slowly gathering them up. He nodded, the creases around his thin mouth eased, his pale skin smoothed visibly.

"I keep hoping it'll go away. But it's getting bigger. A lump. Here." He motioned toward his crotch.

"Any soreness or swelling in the groin?"

"No. Not besides the lump. It hurts," he added.

"Discharge?"

"I dunno." He shuddered and seemed to recoil.

"I can check it," Lizzy said. "I know it makes you uncomfortable that I'm a woman. But I've had training with men. Then if you need it, I can refer you to someone."

"Not a priest, I hope?" He laughed nervously.

Lizzy wanted to ask him if he'd been masturbating when he noticed, but instead she took a brief medical history. When she began to take his blood pressure, he made a fist like she was about to draw blood.

"Relax." She tapped his hand. He looked up, grateful. His eyes aren't bad, she thought. Average brown. A moustache would hide the lips. He would be almost handsome. Get rid of that hat. Then she caught herself. What was she doing? Hadn't she just told J.T. she was a divorced spinster? Celibate, she would say if asked her birth control method. It's the only one-hundred-percent foolproof method unless you're the Virgin Mary. Or have messed up innards like mine.

"A little high," she said, releasing the bulb. She felt the glands in his neck and flashed her light down his throat.

"Ah," she said, taking a culture in case he was lying; they so often did.

"Your wife. Is there any chance? Are you worried about STDs?"

"Huh?"

"Any chance you might have contracted VD?" She swirled the swab into the culture and put his name on the label. Michael McDonnough. "A nice Irish name," she said to sound casual. She was nervous about what was coming next.

"Like I said. I've never been with anyone but my wife."

"And her? Has she been with anyone else?"

He looked as if she had slapped him. "I don't know," he said. He remembered Kaye saying she fell in love with him because he was the first man who didn't just want to have sex with her, who actually talked to her, who took her places.

"We'll do some tests. Just to be sure," Lizzy said.

"OK." He sighed. "I guess you never know." Had Kaye snuck off to meet a lover at the Holiday Inn? That talent scout, maybe?

"Let me explain the procedure," Lizzy said. The last man she had cultured got an enormous erection when she inserted the tip of the swab into his urethra and was plainly disappointed it was over so soon.

"I can't do this," Michael said. "I better come back."

Lizzy took a deep breath. She felt a moral obligation to test who-ever came in with a complaint that could possibly be contagious.

"You can do that," she said. "But it won't be for a month. And the test results take a week. If you caught something, you'll want to take care of it. As soon as possible. Get a shot of penicillin, you know?"

"OK. Jesus. This is embarrassing."

"I'll examine you first," she said. "I want to have a look at that lump you found." She turned her back so he could get ready.

"By the time you count to ten, it'll be over," Lizzy said.

Michael was sitting on the exam table, his jeans around his ankles, his penis like a snail curling into its shell. "It's here," he murmured, touching a spot near his pubic bone and wincing.

With her gloved fingers, Lizzy palpated it gently. "I'd say it's folliculitis. It's like an irritated hair follicle, a boil. They *are* painful. Warm soaks help. I can give you some Duracef to help clear it up. I have samples I can give you. I've seen this fairly often. It's nothing to be scared of. Really."

Michael looked so happy Lizzy was afraid he might throw his hat up in the air and whoop. She finished the exam, taking a quick swab, and turned her back while he zipped his pants. "I'll need a blood sample."

He rolled up his sleeve, averting his eyes. Would he feign extreme interest in the spices when she ran into him at the grocery store? Would he stare intently at the back of his hand should she enter the post office when he was in line? She clipped the needle and put the vial of blood in a holder on her desk.

"We'll call you with the results in a week."

"I don't have a phone."

"Then stop in next week. Till then, don't have sex."

"I don't plan on it," he said as he left.

J.T. had taped a note on Lizzy's door that said, "We had to take Alice to the vet." Lizzy was crumpling it up when she heard voices from the waiting room. Not a walk-in, she thought, contemplating sneaking out the back.

"We can't go to Newberry's, honeybun. It's closed. You know that." Michael was tying the shoes of the most beautiful little girl Lizzy had ever seen. Tears raced down her rosy cheeks from her big blue eyes. The mascara she wore left black smudges, giving her a forlorn, haunted look.

"You said I could. Barbie *nee*-eeds an evening gown." She drew the words out, pulling her foot out of his hands and slapping at him.

"Hi." Lizzy leaned against the doorjamb, mentally restraining herself from rushing to wipe away the little girl's tears. "Would you like to see what your tears look like under a microscope?"

"What's that?" She sniffled and looked up, interested.

"A microscope? It's like this special magnifying glass that makes it so you can see things that are so teeny tiny you don't even know they're there otherwise. C'mon. I'll show you."

Michael followed them into Lizzy's office, obviously pleased.

"I'm Lizzy. What's your name?"

"Aran."

"That's a pretty name."

"I'm gonna be a movie star."

"That's a fine ambition." Lizzy caught a teardrop on a slide. "You're certainly pretty enough for that."

"Daddy says so, too."

Lizzy put the slide under the microscope. When she had the tear in focus, she lifted Aran onto a stool to see. She draped her arm around Aran's shoulder. Her body was warm and smelled of talcum powder. Lizzy wanted to hug her, to kiss her ear where it poked through her blonde hair.

Lizzy had fallen in love before. Too many times in fact. This she knew about. But never with a child. The *idea* of a baby, yes. Tiny undershirts in department stores. The soft spot where the pulse beat on the heads of friends' babies. Teddy bears with windup music boxes. Old-fashioned christening gowns. But never a specific baby. Never a child. She felt if she weren't allowed to spend the rest of her life with this little girl, there would be no reason to go on. Already she could imagine brushing her hair. Buying ribbons and barrettes. Sewing dresses with yards of eyelet trim.

There was only one way to get this. She turned to Michael. His hat was perched on his head, not quite large enough to fit. "I'm finished for the night," she said. "Why don't we go get a pizza?"

Aran held out her hands. They each took one, letting her lead them out the door.

5

Slim woke up buzzing with excitement, his body tingling with impatience, his fingers drumming the mattress before his eyes were open. Before the sun could rise and break through the fog, he had eaten a quick breakfast of toast and coffee. There was no time for anything fancy like his special strawberry omelet, no time to go to Hydie's for French toast. He was as eager to get to work as a little boy hurrying downstairs on Christmas morning to see what Santa brought.

In winter, on the days the dump was open, he had the windshield scraped clear before most folks on Preacher's Lake Road ventured out of bed long enough to throw a log on the glowing coals. He was on the road before they had even stuck a tentative toe out of their blankets to ascertain just how bad it was. Whatever chimney smoke there was—many didn't have a stove tight enough to keep a fire overnight—was just a thin wisp in the gray dawn.

By noon he would sort through the overstuffed plastic bags, the greasy brown grocery sacks, the cardboard boxes, and add to the items piled beside the sign he had made from bottle caps glued to a board: TAKE WHAT YOU NEED. He would add to the bins of books and clothes just like his father had done. There would be more dolls with missing arms. Toy trucks with broken wheels. Dented plastic baseball bats. Games with hardly a piece missing. Toasters, frying pans, oven racks. A rusted wheelbarrow beside a blue vinyl chair.

This morning, Slim was ready to leave before Crystal had clicked on the TV. Before Nelly's tractor sputtered to life. He headed for work, his car rolling over the bumps like a boat across choppy waves, his heart racing as he thought of Janesta Curtis. Last night, when her car came in, he looked out his window and watched her light go on. She hadn't lowered the shade. And he hadn't turned away when she pulled her T-shirt over her head. Instead he drew closer to the window, holding his breath not to fog the glass, watching her unzip her jeans and wiggle out of them. Her room was so brightly lit Slim could make out the black lace of her underwear, the sight of which set him trembling. Slim had never been so close to a nearly naked woman before. When Janesta finally unhooked her bra, her breasts bounced like they'd been released from a muzzle. She cupped them in her hands as if to weigh them, then slipped off her panties.

He unlocked the chain across the driveway and was headed down to the shed, still remembering last night, when he saw them. Two sheep. Both with ropes around their necks, tied to a cement block. They looked up at him as if he might be a door-to-door salesman and they'd just as soon slam the door in his face as listen to his spiel.

"Jeezum," Slim said, slapping the steering wheel. Because the dump was situated in an out of the way place, folks from all over thought nothing of sneaking up after hours to dump whatever they couldn't deal with. They threw animals away like broken toys. Once, a beautiful collie with a broken leg he'd taken to the shelter.

Another time, a mutt with no teeth that couldn't eat the food Slim offered him, that whimpered and slunk around, his coat matted with burrs. Slim already had six cats at home and over a dozen at the dump that he fed and got fixed. Still, they came in plastic bags, in boxes, in feed sacks. Never anything as big as sheep, not counting the dead deer the out-of-state hunters dumped after driving around with them tied to the hoods of their cars like trophies.

The sheep were huge. Hay was tangled in their once white wool, now stained with droppings. They bleated when Slim slammed the car door. "Maa? That all you got to say, *maa*? What are you, half cow?" He gazed across the dump, not really seeing the coiled chain, the rusted bedsprings, the chairs with fluffs of stuffing spilling from the sides. His job was to get rid of what folks didn't want, to cover it with fill at the end of the day. But he didn't have the heart to do that with most things, least of all something living. He scratched the ram, reaching through the thick wool until he found the solid surface of skin and bone. The ewe watched, but whenever she moved forward, the ram nudged her away and returned to Slim, letting him scratch his ears.

"What's your problem? Too tough to be lamb chops?" Slim got the Fig Newtons he'd brought for lunch. The ram ate them eagerly, his rough tongue scraping Slim's palm. Slim undid the rope from the cement block. He had heard about rams butting people with their hard heads and could see the nubs where this one's horns had been cut off. He didn't feature being knocked down by a ram, but he had to do something. He held out a Fig Newton and lured the ram toward his car—a twenty-year-old Cadillac with the back-seat removed. When he tossed cookies on the floor, the ram hesitated then stumbled in like an old woman on high heels, the ewe following behind. They stood in back munching cookies as Slim headed up the hill, tooting when he pulled into Nelly's driveway. She was looking under the hood of the truck, a wrench in her hand.

"Got a present for ya," he said. "You want 'em, they're yours."

"Sheep?" Nelly wiped her hands on a rag. "Where'd they come from?"

"Courtesy of the Preacher's Lake landfill, ma'am. What's a farm without sheep?"

"I could tie them in front. I gotta put up a fence one of these days." Using the cookies, they coaxed the sheep from the car. A little brown-skinned girl with curly hair peered at them from the house. In the garden, a small woman wearing a green cap was dig-

ging. Slim looked from the child to the woman to Nelly, but she
offered no explanation.

*   *   *

Carol peered out her window at the man and woman who lived
in the brownstone below her apartment building. Today, they were
planting several flats of brightly colored flowers in expensive red-
wood planters beside two cushioned lawn chairs and a small glass-
topped table. The acoustics were so strange, Carol could hear the
clink of their forks whenever they ate outdoors. The woman, whose
skin was bright pink, wore shorts and a bathing suit top. She raised
her wineglass like the Statue of Liberty's torch. "That bitch," she
said. The man shouted and flung dirt every which way, emphatically
waving a geranium by its stem.

The man who lived at the other end of her hallway was tossing a
ball against her door and Mishka, his little white mop of a dog,
scrambled after it barking. Carol wanted to fling the door open,
grab the dog as he raced toward her, and toss him out onto the roof
garden. And then it all stopped. The couple was no longer fighting.
Flowers were strewn across the rooftop, but they were somewhere
else. The elevator door creaked open, Mario shouted, "Mishka!" as
the man and his dog got on.

Carol missed Annie. She missed her husky voice. She missed her
warm hands. Her easy laugh. The good times they had together,
how they would walk across the Brooklyn Bridge just to be doing it.
Take the F train to Coney Island to eat seafood at Carolina's. Race
through the museum, zooming past the Van Goghs and Monets,
the art flowing by at a dizzying pace. Rubens' fat babies. Renoir's
blushing girls. More portraits of George Washington than Carol
thought necessary. Winslow Homer and the sea. Giant carved
Buddhas. Horns and drums and harps. Christs on crucifixes.
Christ, a fat baby in his mother's arms. Judith with Holofernes's
head. The carved alligator in the Indonesian room that Annie
always had to see before they moved on to the ticking clocks that
she loved so much, as if she had somehow known her time was running out.

Carol could call Vivian. No doubt Vivian would pounce on the
phone during the first ring. Carol felt so alone. Broken. She imagined a mannequin with a frozen smile shattered into lumps of
jagged plaster. The smile still intact. The torso twisted and cracked.
The severed hands. *Broken Heart,* she'd call it. And then a replica of

the same scene. The same frozen smile and severed hands. *Starting Over*, she'd call this one, painting the titles blood red.

*   *   *

After the test results came back, Lizzy was beside herself waiting for Michael to return. All through the clinic, she was convinced she could hear Aran in the waiting room, but the only child was Derek, the little boy who wanted to be a girl, waiting to see Doctor Leonard on the second floor. He got into a frenzied tantrum when his mother encouraged him to look at *Highlights* instead of *Bride*.

Lizzy stayed late, filling in lab sheets, sorting through her drawers, but still no Michael. He knew how to reach her, but he hadn't called. He hadn't stopped by. He'd explained how he was out in the woods, that the phone and electric wires ended a mile before his place, but she had barely paid attention, she was too busy talking to Aran.

"I wanna dye my hair black like Demi Moore," Aran said. "Black like yours is, only not curly. Demi's hair's not curly. Daddy won't let me."

Afterwards, Michael just scooped Aran up and left Lizzy standing beside her car. Lizzy could still feel the girl's warm hand pressing her own. Aran flung her arms around Lizzy's neck when they left, kissing her on both cheeks, crying, "Ta-ta!" in a British accent.

By the time Lizzy closed the clinic, she felt as crushed as an old tube of K-Y jelly. Even J.T. had commented before she left, wondering if Lizzy wanted a blood test to check her iron level. "You look kind of peaked, girl," she said, giving her friend a hug.

Lizzy sat in her car, willing Michael's truck to come down Harbor Street and turn into the parking lot. There was hardly any traffic, let alone a green truck with a beautiful little girl waving from the window. She decided she'd pay him a home visit, something she had only done once when a woman had a positive gonorrhea test and no phone. She remembered the silver trailer with the German shepherd tied to the door, its food and water bowls empty. She'd been afraid to get out of the car and had finally left a note in the bashed-in mailbox.

Tomorrow, she promised herself. Tomorrow. If he doesn't show up, I'll go to his house.

The next day at work, during a brief lull, Lizzy took out the Barbie outfits she had bought. A glittering gold evening gown with matching heels and purse. A white skirt with pleats and a sailor blouse with a tiny sailor hat. A pink nylon negligee. At first she had taken the flannel nightgown with ducks printed on it, but behind it on the rack was the negligee with slippers, each with a puff of pink on the toe. Do I know my girl or what? she thought.

"It's your three-thirty wart treatment," J.T. said, and Lizzy was swept back into her work. By the time the last diaphragm had been fitted, the last demo of foam squirted into the plastic canal, and the last vial of blood spun in the centrifuge, Lizzy was so nervous about visiting Michael and Aran, she was afraid she might break out in hives.

"Let's go to The Quarterdeck. Get chili and beer," she said to J.T.

"What's the occasion?" J.T. asked.

"No occasion."

"Let me call Betty first. Otherwise, she'll worry."

"I'll bring you home a pickled egg," J.T. promised Betty. She watched Lizzy pacing nervously. She looked so strange in her new outfit. She had come back after lunch toting her pants and sweater in a shopping bag, wearing a dress from Alicia's Fashions, stockings, and heels with buckles that fastened thin straps around her ankles. The kind of shoes J.T. thought men designed to keep women from being able to run away.

"What is it with you?" J.T. said when they were seated in a booth with two glasses of beer. "You can't stop grinning."

Lizzy flipped the jukebox selections. Frankie Valli was singing "I've Got You Under My Skin."

"This song always makes me think of scabies," said J.T.

Lizzy giggled and deposited two quarters.

"So what's up, Liz? You're in the best mood I've ever seen you in."

"It's the beer," Lizzy said, clinking her glass against J.T.'s and taking a sip. "You know how it goes to my head."

"You've barely tasted it. It's a man. Am I right or am I right?"

"Wrong."

"A woman? Don't tell me it's a woman!" J.T. was so excited she almost tipped over her glass when she grabbed Lizzy's hand.

"Sort of," Lizzy said. "Relax, will you?" She glanced around the bar to see if anyone noticed the commotion. Ginger Martin, the local masseuse who called herself Miss Ginger, winked. She was dressed in a low-cut leotard and a long flowing skirt that glittered under the dull lights of the bar. She did a little shimmy and tossed her hair. But the men lined up on the bar stools seemed more interested in their drinks. The ceiling fan twirled the smoke-filled air as Frank Sinatra began to sing "Strangers in the Night."

"The Whore of Babylon and the Brazen Hussy make out in the local bar where the town, uh, masseuse hangs out," Lizzy whispered. They always referred to themselves this way when they walked around Union City together. "After dispensing birth control devices to minors, the two lezzies were seen holding hands in a den of ill repute." Lizzy spoke into her clenched fist as if she were holding a microphone. "If we're not careful, we'll make the *Bangor Daily.*"

J.T. lifted her beer to toast Miss Ginger, convinced she was a legitimate masseuse *and* a lesbian, but Lizzy said she was wrong.

"She has more than a drinking problem," Lizzy said.

"You changed the subject," said J.T. "So tell me tell me."

"It's a little girl," Lizzy sighed. "The most beautiful little girl. Motherless, too. She's been abandoned. Don't ask me how anybody could leave a child like that. She's just crying for a woman's love."

J.T. groaned. "Why do I have a feeling this is worse than a man?"

"My biological clock's ticking. It's in my hormones," Lizzy said.

"I'm heading for the big four-oh. Do you hear any alarms clanging?"

"Well, it's true for me. It's out of my control." Lizzy was tempted to show J.T. the doll clothes, but thought better of it. Some things J.T. would never understand. She stared at the photograph of sailors beside their booth thinking how each man had once been somebody's baby.

"Does this child by any chance come equipped with a parental unit or did she arrive fully formed on your doorstep?" J.T. asked.

Lizzy pointed to their empty glasses and signaled the waitress who yawned and looked away. She was a heavy-set woman with permed blonde hair. Shirley, the one who insisted on continuing to use Norplant even though she rarely had sex. "I wanna be ready," she said whenever Lizzy tried to talk her into another method. "You just never know."

"Hello!" J.T. said. "Earth to Lizzy. I asked you a question."

"She has a father."

"Oh, God. A father. The worst kind of man."

"How would you know?"

"I had one, didn't I? Didn't *you?* Why can't you just pick some waif out of an orphanage and be a single mother if that's what you want so bad? Better yet, why can't you get one of those kids you send money to every month. They send you a photo and write you a letter once in a while. Wouldn't that be enough? I thought you swore off men. The ink on your divorce papers isn't even dry yet and you're all swoony."

"It's not just *any* child I want. Oh, you'll never understand."

"Try me."

"It's like we were fated to meet. Like all my life I've been driving down all these roads hurrying to see what's at the end of each one, never really getting anywhere till one day I turn a corner, I go around a curve and come face to face with someone I was meant to find."

"I can see you're too far gone for anything I might have to say."

"You'll like her, too. Wait and see. I know you will."

"At least it's a girl," J.T. said.

*   *   *

Slim had never had a lady friend before. He had never called a woman on the telephone. What if Janesta said, *who?* Slim who? What if she slammed down the phone thinking it was an obscene phone call? He felt like a mouse one of his cats sunk its claws into. As he looked up Janesta's phone number, his clumsy fingers tore the pages. Now he had it memorized—5683—but he still hadn't called. He tried to picture himself walking across the road up onto her porch and inviting her over for supper, asking her the way men on TV do, nonchalantly chewing gum. But imagining himself doing this was like watching a suspenseful show that was interrupted by commercials whenever things got interesting. He could get no further than the idea of heading out the door.

Finally he gave up and leaned against his kitchen sink eating a can of ravioli. He didn't bother to heat it up or put it on a plate. When he finished, he opened another can and ate that, too. Out the window, he saw the two sheep tied to the apple tree in front of Nelly's. Once, he tried to give her a black and white TV he had fixed. But she didn't want it. She just asked if he had any chicken wire. Slim couldn't imagine not having a TV. His was almost always on. Even if he wasn't watching it, it was flickering, the voices talking. Even when he listened to his music, he left the TV on for company.

Slim put on his Luciano Pavarotti tape, then tilted back in his recliner with a can of beer. He kicked off his dusty sneakers and watched the darkness creep down from the hills. The shadows of the trees grew longer until like a slow black wave the night seeped across the fields. Slim felt like Noah watching the floodwaters come, only there was nothing to do but wait till his trailer floated down the hill. The new kitten was curled next to Barney, who had decided to tolerate this attention instead of hissing every time the kitten got close. It seemed to Slim that the world was paired off, ready to go two by two. Even his cats had each other. Mickey and Minnie on the throw rug. Tubby and Lulu in the bedroom. Fireflies flickered in the weeds and stars dotted the western sky, now a purplish bruise behind the spruce trees.

Slim didn't understand what Pavarotti was singing about—he didn't know the stories behind the arias—but ever since he first heard him sing on TV, Slim had been moved by the thick sadness in the man's voice. When he listened to Pavarotti, he felt as if his body were encased in a plaster cast. Pavarotti's voice slid right under that cast like warm honey melting over toast.

*   *   *

Lizzy smelled whiskey on his breath but who was she to talk? It took four glasses of beer for her to get up the nerve to come this far.

"Your results came in today," she said. "I thought you'd like to know you're all right. I would've called but . . ." Her voice trailed off. "I was out this way visiting a friend," she lied. She hoped he didn't ask who. There were about three houses on the road she wouldn't have been terrified to stop in front of and only then if her car had broken down. "I happened to see your sign on the mailbox. I didn't know you were a mason."

"You better turn your headlights off," Michael warned. "You'll wear out the battery." He walked her back to her car.

"Daa-dee," a sleepy voice called from the house. Lizzy felt a pang. "Daddy cakes. Where are you?"

"Right here, sweetheart."

Lizzy stood by her car, her heels sinking into the soft driveway. Michael reached in and clicked off the lights. Around them crickets were chirping. The chickens clucked, and above the house, the thick branches of the hemlock tree swayed. She sensed something in cages, watching, something small scrambling across chicken wire. Michael struck a wooden match on his thumbnail, lifted the globe on the lantern he carried, and lit the wick, his face glowing in the light as he bent to adjust it.

"Why don't you come in for a cup of coffee?" he asked. The lantern lit up the ground at Lizzy's feet. Her shoes seemed flimsy, like they would fall to shreds before she made it into the kitchen where she imagined she would soon be making pancakes.

"Daddy. Daddy," Aran called, her face pressed against the screen of the upstairs window. Lizzy had all she could do not to call out, I'm coming, darling. It's Lizzy. I'm on my way sweetheart.

Michael held her elbow as she picked her way around the stumps and over the rocks and roots in the path.

"I don't usually dress this way," she apologized. She didn't know what had gotten into her, buying this polka-dot dress with the red belt. When she slipped it on and turned to see herself in the three-way mirror, all she could think of was Aran would approve. It seemed like a real mother's dress. The kind of dress women wore to PTA meetings.

"You look pretty," Michael said. He put his hand on the small of her back as she teetered up the steps.

"Gosh," she said, leaning on the cookstove. "You're real pioneers, huh?" There was a kerosene lamp on the table and another one hanging from a beam on the opposite side of the room where there were two rocking chairs and a sofa covered with a plaid blanket. Most of that side of the house was taken up by a huge woodstove, the chrome trim molded into a design of oak leaves and acorns.

"Do you cook on this?" she asked. In her pancake fantasy, she had cooked on a large white gas stove.

"When it's cold. Or when I bake. I have a propane hot plate for summer. Have a seat."

Aran appeared at the top of the stairs.

"We've got company, Aran. Remember Lizzy?"

"Lizzy!" she shrieked, racing down the steps, her bare feet slapping the wood. "Lizzy, Lizzy, Lizzy," she said, rushing into Lizzy's open arms and kissing her on both cheeks.

"I brought you a present," Lizzy said.

"What?" Aran danced around the table clapping.

"I hope you don't mind," Lizzy said to Michael.

He put the kettle on and took down a package of gingersnaps. He was humming as the kettle began to simmer; he couldn't help himself. When was the last time he had seen Aran so happy? It felt good to have a woman in his house.

"No. I don't mind at all," he said, setting cups on the table. "What do you say, pumpkin?" he asked Aran, lifting her up. She laughed her movie star laugh, all breathy, stretching to glimpse herself in the mirror that hung at the foot of the stairs.

"Thank you veddy much, dahlink." She batted her eyes at Lizzy. Then scrambled down from her father's arms to lean against Lizzy's knees.

Lizzy's hands were shaking as she opened the clasp on her purse. "Ta dah," she said, pulling out the evening gown.

"Oh, look. Daddy, look," Aran said, kissing the plastic-covered box. "Lemme go get my Barbie. She'll be *sooo* happy. She's got a date with Ken tomorrow and she doesn't have a thing to wear." She ran up the stairs and as she crossed the room overhead, bits of dirt trickled down.

"I didn't mean to get her so stirred up," Lizzy said, deciding to save the other outfits for another time.

"No. Really. It's OK," Michael said. "She *really* likes you," he added, lowering his voice as if it were a secret.

"Do you think so?"

"I do. I really do. I like you, too," he said. Feeling a little tipsy, he kissed her on the lips. She was careful not to push him away too quickly when she heard Aran begin to descend the steps.

Later that night, after the kerosene had burned low in the lamps and Aran had brushed her teeth, Lizzy listened to Michael's plans.

"Someday, I'll dig out the spring that's back in the woods. I'm sure it's got good water. But first, Alton Poors'll pull the stumps with his backhoe. Eventually, I'll put in a pump. It's not that bad, hauling water. You'd be surprised how many people live without running water in the United States."

When he had walked them both to the outhouse, standing politely off to the side while she peed, and Aran had been tucked in bed and kissed one last time by them both, Lizzy thought she had never been so happy in her life. When Lizzy's dress had been hung beside a row of other dresses in the closet that separated the two rooms upstairs and Michael was lowering himself over her, pushing himself into her, crying out as he rocked the bed, Lizzy let her head fall back on the pillow and remembered the way Aran had slipped the gold high heels onto the doll's feet, her warm sweet breath as she whispered nighty night.

* * *

Janesta groaned and pulled her pillow over her face. She was sinking into the bed, whirling and twirling. Her mouth was as dry as sawdust. Crystal was in the front room watching the weather report.

"Crystal, get in here and bring me a Coke," Janesta said.

Crystal sat stone still on the sofa. While her mother slept, she had been eating brown sugar from the box, spooning out the lumps, sucking them till they melted in her mouth. She feared any minute

Janesta would emerge and see the sugar. Crystal shoved the sugar box between the sofa cushions, down where she stuffed her candy wrappers.

"Sugar makes you hyper," Janesta often said. She was convinced this was the source of Crystal's problem. She wasn't mental the way her last teacher suggested.

"Crystal? I need me a Coke. And bring me some matches, too."

Crystal took a big swig of the Coke then carried it in to her mother. She burped and nudged her mother until Janesta thrust her hand from the covers, blindly reaching for the can, the pillow still over her face. She held the Coke, groaning, and finally sat up and took a tentative sip, then gulped it like someone who had been deprived of water on a desert at last being offered a canteen. She fell back on the bed and pulled the pillow over her face. "What time is it?" she asked.

"The big hand's on the ten. The little hand's on the twelve."

"So tell me. What time is it?"

Crystal felt like a thick black blanket had dropped over her. She rocked from side to side. "Hold still," she muttered, clasping her hands behind her back. "Quit that," she instructed herself.

"I said, what *time* is it? You're twelve goddamned years old and you can't tell time? What the hell do they teach you in school?"

"Time to get up," Crystal said and ran out of the room. When the back door slammed, Janesta groaned. It felt like someone was reaching inside her with a huge pair of tongs, twisting her innards.

"Time to get up," she moaned, wishing she'd come home last night after work. That she hadn't gone to Union City with Bill or Bob or Don or whatever the hell his name was. It had been a slow night in the tips department. Lots of "drive-throughs"—Janesta's name for the tourists, like that couple who ordered a pitcher of beer and a plate of stuffed mushrooms, then left her three pennies, tails up. Janesta swept them onto the floor, feeling superstitious. Then Mr. What's His Name came in.

"You are so hard up," she muttered. So what if he filled her car with gas, this was a hell of a price to pay. "Time to get up," she said, reaching for her cigarettes. "Crystal," she hollered. "I told you to bring me matches." She could tell by the silence that Crystal was not on the front porch or out in the yard. She was probably over at Slim's.

Janesta eased herself up and sat on the edge of her bed, brushing aside the underwear she'd flung on her bedside table, searching for matches to light the cigarette she tucked in the corner of her mouth. She ran her hands over her belly, feeling the extra flesh. Every morning, there was more to her. Her breasts—she was sure of this—had grown an inch overnight. They were heavy and tender. She pulled a T-shirt on, then flopped back on the bed, queasy again.

She could see the man's arm. Bud. That was it. Bud. The thick black hair on his forearms, his sleeves rolled up over his elbows. How he reached for his old-fashioned lighter, flicking it open as soon as Janesta got her cigarette ready. Her body ached from his rough hands.

"Where's old Bud to light my fire now?" She laughed a ragged laugh that set off a coughing spell. Probably back in Augusta with his wife making his breakfast. Probably feeling a bit queasy, too, ol' Bud.

She rolled to her side and used her toes to scoot her jeans closer in order to get the book of matches tucked in the pocket. She propped herself up and as she smoked, using the Coke can for an ashtray, tried to imagine what it would be like with a man like Slim Riley. Yesterday, she'd seen him out hanging his clothes on the line.

"You sure are domestic," she had hollered. He waved shyly, his face bright red. Now he was in his front yard, bending over something he had planted in tires, Crystal beside him talking a mile a minute.

He might smell like old tires, she thought. But he sure is good to Crystal. That's something.

Slim glanced across the road as if he could sense her watching him. But all he could see was the reflection of his trailer in Janesta's window.

She dropped her cigarette butt into the can with a hiss. "You will never learn," she said. She stared at the hot sun heating up the tires on Slim's roof. She yawned and belched; her spit tasted of puke.

"Frank," she said. "You lousy son of a bitch. You ruined me." She could feel her cheek pressed against Frank's leather jacket, her thighs tight around his hips as they leaned into the curves, the motorcycle roaring beneath them, the wind in her hair. "Frank," she said again, a tear trickling down her face before she rubbed it away angrily with the back of her hand.

"He ain't comin' back. You hear me? So get over it. Start takin' care of business," her mother had screamed, tossing the beer cans and empty bourbon bottles into a bag. "You ain't gonna find somebody else carryin' on thisaway. Pissin' and moanin' about how he up and left you. You ain't the first been left high and dry, so get on with it."

Janesta was glad her mother couldn't see her now; she had only memories of her dead mother's disapproval to haunt her.

"Get rid of it," Frank had said when she told him she was pregnant. He was already living with that skinny nurse's aide who probably still held the urine bottle for him. Janesta was shocked when she saw Frank with this woman, surprised she lost him to someone so downright ugly.

"I don't know what I'm competing with here," she said to Frank. He didn't want Janesta taking care of him, didn't want her visiting him all that time he was in the hospital, wouldn't even let her wheel him down the hall.

"I ain't some prize you try to win," he told her, never admitting it was his pride that separated them.

All their time together, they had been so careful, using condoms and foam so religiously Frank claimed making love felt like wearing a raincoat in a champagne bubble storm. And what good had it done to be careful? Getting pregnant seemed like a terrible joke. "You sure?" she had asked J.T., squinting through her puffy eyes. "Positive. It's positive," J.T. said. But she was new at her job then, insecure enough to redo the test. Janesta watched her release a drop of urine onto the square, stirring it, rotating it slowly, only to get the same result.

Janesta had driven over to Holiday Island to get an abortion, imagining it would be like scouring an old pot with food burnt onto the bottom, scrubbing it clean. She lay on the narrow bed staring at the poster of a kitten about to fall from a tree. HANG IN THERE it said. If Frank still loved her, would he be here? Would he pat her thigh, shake his head solemnly, and tell her he loved her even when she cried?

At the last minute, Janesta said, "I changed my mind." It wasn't guilt. Or nothing religious. She was going to hell, hadn't her mother told her that plenty? She wasn't a coward about pain. It was curiosity, the desire to see what she and Frank could make. A little boy with his daddy's bright blue eyes. The spitting image of your daddy, she would tell him, never considering it might be a girl.

Whenever Janesta wanted, she could close her eyes and see Frank. They are at the Rusty Anchor. Willie Nelson on the jukebox, the smell of beer and onion rings, car doors slamming, the cold rush of air when the door swings open. Frank comes toward her carrying their drinks up high so he won't spill them, so sure of himself, gliding through the crowd, Frank in his tight jeans, his hips swiveling, his knife shield hanging from his beaded belt as if it were part of him, his eyes passing over her body like a hot wind off a burning field.

Janesta staggered into the bathroom, and, after throwing up a watery bile, dunked her face in the sink, the cold water dripping down her neck, soaking the front of her T-shirt.

"You never learn," she said to her reflection, surveying the damage. Her tangled hair, her puffy face. Her eyes like two holes burned in a blanket. Her belly brushed the sink, and she could swear something inside her was twisting and turning, pulling her down.

6

The first night she spent at Nelly's, Rita clutched the blanket to her chin, unable to close her eyes with the scratching and scurrying of what Nelly explained was a harmless pack rat adding to its nest under the floorboards. She worried about Rainey, insisting it wasn't all right for her to sleep on the old car seat Nelly used as a sofa until Nelly finally carried the child up to her bed where she slept in the crook of her mother's arm. The first morning when Rita went to the outhouse, a porcupine bristled its quills sending her back to the house screaming, not at all convinced by Nelly's explanation that porcupines did not shoot their quills like arrows, that you'd have to sit on one to get hurt. Rita had wept while Nelly pumped herself glass after glass of water which she drank in quick gulps while Rainey patted her mother's back, moving her tiny hand in circles. Now, Rita and Rainey had moved in with Nelly. And Rita was in the loft bed with a headache.

Nelly pounded the metal fence post into the ground with a sledgehammer clutched close to the head, the pinging sound echoing off the hills. When she just missed her thumb, she swore and wished Rita were there to hold the post steady; then Nelly could swing the sledge with both hands.

That morning, when Nelly leaned over to kiss her, Rita clutched her forehead. "I'm sorry," Rita groaned. "I get these headaches." Her face was very pale, the freckles on her nose dark as cinnamon. "What can I do?" Nelly asked, trying not to feel doomed. "Nothing. I have to lie down. Sometimes I faint." Rainey sat at the table clutching her stuffed monkey, glaring at Nelly with no attempt to disguise the hate in her green eyes. "Well. I have a lot to do," Nelly said. "I guess I'll go do it."

Rita's in the house. In my bed. She has a headache. Nelly repeated the words like a mantra as she pounded the hammer. She considered hopping in the truck. She would head south until she ran out of gas, then get out and walk until she collapsed from exhaustion. Her skin felt too tight, as if the strain of containing all the muscle and blood and bone was finally too much. Rainey was thrashing through the fields like something wild. Nelly hoped she wasn't expected to watch her. She hoped the child did not decide to play in the road.

I have two sheep to take care of, Nelly told herself. One word for every ping of metal on metal. Rita's moved in. She's going to stay. I know it. I know it. I know it. I think I want it. I know I want it. It'll be OK. We'll build the kid a room. It'll be OK when the kid has a room. She pounded the fence post until it seemed sturdy then moved several feet down for the next one. We have two sheep. We will get more. A pig. A pony. The word *we* sounded foreign to her. She said it out loud, picturing Rainey riding bareback, grasping a pony's mane. Her body ached all over from sleeping beside Rita, from the effort not to touch her last night when she lay beside her barely breathing.

"I just want to hold you," Nelly whispered. Then a prickling sensation ran down her spine. Her arms became deer antlers clattering wildly as she wrapped them around Rita. Rita crumpled like an empty wasp nest, dissolving into dust in Nelly's embrace. Nelly heard Fiona's mother scream, a high unearthly sound, saw again how they lifted her from the ground, the front of her dress smeared with dirt. And Cho staring drunkenly, stumbling forward in his ridiculous cowboy boots.

Last night, Nelly coached herself to lean over and kiss Rita. Just one kiss. You can do it, she urged until her chapped lips rasped across Rita's brow. "We don't have to do anything," Nelly had finally said, a sob catching in her throat as she fell back on her pillow and Rita curled away from her, her knees up, rocking. Rainey began to sing the ABC song in a soft whisper. Then the pack rat began its nightly routine.

Nelly stopped hammering. A searing pain spread through her like hot acid; afterwards, a dull ache throbbed in her chest, the memory of Fiona familiar as shrapnel embedded in a war veteran's leg. Fiona, what was it like to tip your head back and swallow? To be so determined the horrible taste couldn't stop you? She saw

Fiona lying across the rumpled bed, the soles of her feet black from her barefoot trek down the path. Nelly had tricked herself into thinking she could be touched again, that it would be a relief, that she could give herself over to the yearning, settle onto Rita's body as if her needs were a swarm of wild bees that had found a new place to hive. Maybe if it wasn't for the kid, she thought. Once I build her a room, we'll have privacy. *Then,* she thought. Nelly gave in to her sense of anticipation, how Rita would pull her close. *Skin,* she thought, letting herself hunger for Rita's touch. She was lost in her thoughts as the sledgehammer came down on her thumb, the steel head crashing against her thumbnail, splitting it down the middle. Dark purple swelled underneath, as if poison were bursting to get out.

*   *   *

Slim sat in a lawn chair behind his trailer, his feet propped on the lobster trap he found washed up on Sow's Head Bay. Several slats, bleached dry as old bone, were splintered where the trap had smacked the rocks during a storm. But the orange bait bag was still intact. He called this the in-between time. The blackflies that descended in thick clouds upon anything that moved had died down enough to venture outdoors. And the mosquitoes hadn't yet taken over.

Slim saw the child in the weeds watching him intently. The first time he had seen her, she and her mother were walking along the highway when he was at Buster's with the fellows. They all watched the woman stop to flick a stone from her flip-flops. The girl's hair sparkled like a halo in the sun. "Christ, lookit that," Rip said. Slim noticed how young the woman was. How her wavy hair fell over her eyes. The girl's skin color was so unusual he couldn't help but look as she stared at the piles of wet black mud the wormers had left along the water's edge. Negro, Slim thought. No, black. That's what they say, *black.* Black didn't describe the color of this girl's skin. Burnt sienna, he thought, like the crayon. As a child, he used to peel the paper from his crayons, gnawing on them, forever surprised they didn't taste the way they looked.

"Now I can lay down and die 'cause I've seen it all," Coalie said. "That's a nigger kid, but it looks just like that woman."

"A mongrel." Rip spit tobacco juice. "What you call a mutt."

"What's this place comin' to?" Buster griped. "First we get a shit-load of tourists that won't go home. Then we get that neighbor of yours, our town homosexual or whatever in hell she is. This town's gettin' too rich for my blood."

Slim hadn't said anything. You can't change people, he knew. You got to let 'em be who they are or else keep your distance. Rip was the worst. Some black fellow had stolen his boots when he was in the service and Rip was still mad about it.

Slim tore open a package of Mallomars and popped one into his mouth, licking the chocolate from his fingers. He felt like he did when he waited for a chickadee to get the nerve to take millet from his hand. If he acted like the girl wasn't there, pretended he had no interest whatsoever, eventually she'd come closer, like a feral cat in January when the windchill hits thirty below, its ribs showing through its matted fur, would crawl toward a pan of meat set at the edge of the woods.

Slim heard a giggle and slowly scanned the rough reddish bark of the hemlock, squinting up into the thick sprawling branches, then turned to study the roof of his trailer as if expecting a head to pop out of one of the tires baking on top of it in the sun. She giggled again and Slim set the package of cookies on his lobster trap and swatted beneath his chair.

"I must be gettin' old. Else my brain's cracked. I'm hearin' things." He smacked above his ears, then lifted his hair, which hung in thick mats like cocker spaniel ears, as if that would help.

Barney, a huge fluffy coon cat, jumped up and sniffed the cookies. "You hear anyone laughin' at us Barney boy? Or is it my 'imagination?" There was a streak of red and the soft flip-flop of rubber sandals as Rainey darted across the yard to hide behind Slim's car.

"Durned if I ain't seein' things. By Jesus, I swear I just spotted somebody runnin' across my yard. But now I don't see no one." The sun was warm on his face and on his back through his flannel shirt. A flock of starlings flew by calling out noisily. A bird wedding, his mother would say. The birds were gallivanting off to spread the word about who got hitched. Slim remembered pulling stalks of rhubarb from the backyard while his mother rolled out pie crust. He hadn't known it would be his last spring with her. She had seemed happy enough then.

"Come out, come out, whoever you are," Slim said. Rainey peered around his car. "Else they'll cart me off to Hopewell for talkin' to myself." He scratched the cat between his ears and offered him a cookie. "Maybe it's a little elf. I'll just shut my eyes, see, and hold out this cookie. I'll squeeze my eyes shut in case it's bashful."

"Boo," she said, taking the cookie from his palm.

Slim could smell the sweet smell of clothes dried in the sun. He opened one eye. She was nibbling the edge of the cookie. "Who've we got here?" he asked. Barney ran across the yard and halfway up the hemlock where he waited, his ears back, his claws sunk into the bark. "I figured you was a tree squeak, only they come out at night," Slim said.

"What's a tree squeak?"

"A little furry animal that lives up in the treetops. Ain't you ever heard 'em squeakin' something wicked?"

"I'm not a tree squeak," Rainey said.

"What are you then? A ghost?"

"I'm a kid."

"You don't look like no billy goat to me. Where's your beard?"

"I'm not a billy goat! I'm a girl."

"Oh, you are, are you?"

"Uh-huh." She finished the cookie, leaving a smear of chocolate around the edge of her mouth.

"There's more where that come from," Slim said, handing her another one. "Well. If you're a girl, then what's your name?"

"Rainey."

"Rainey? It's gonna rain?"

"That's my name. Rainey Conway!"

"Lemme see. I went to school with a Misty Storm. And there's Crystal Dawn Curtis across the road, you know her? But I never met no Rainey. Where you live at Miss Rainey?"

"Boston," she said, kicking her toe in the dirt.

"Beantown did you say?"

"Boston." She smiled and looked down at the ground.

"Where's that?" Slim asked.

Rainey shrugged. Then she pointed across the field to Nelly's.

"Well, if that's Boston, we're neighbors. How d'you do? I'm James Riley. But you can call me Slim. Everybody does." He extended his hand but instead of shaking it, Rainey ran across the field, the weeds rustling around her until they closed over her retreat like a theatre curtain being drawn. It was as if she had never there at all.

* * *

"Say you're not doing this to me." J.T. let her forehead hit the desk with a thunk. She stretched her arms across the papers, clutched the far corners of the desk and began to slowly pound her head against the desk. "Please, tell me this is not happening."

"Oh, c'mon, J.T. You know I need a break. I'll still be here three days. You know I've about had it with this job. I can't keep doing the same thing over and over again every day of my life."

"You know they won't find a replacement. The clinic's already been cut to four days a week. They'll just get Dr. Bob in here. I still haven't recovered from him taking over last time you went on vacation. Oh, God. You're my friend, but I hate you."

"You'll get a headache if you keep that up," Lizzy said.

J.T. continued to hit her head on the desk. Out in the waiting room there was a commotion, but she didn't look up. The people out there were not waiting for her or Lizzy; J.T. had already checked.

"It's that horrible woman with the little boy Dr. Leonard is trying to turn straight," J.T. whispered. One of these days, she'd go out there and shout: Look, lady. You've got a budding drag queen on your hands. Take him to a secondhand store and let him buy whatever he wants. He'll be happier being a woman than you've ever been.

The bathroom door slammed and the little boy said in a shrill voice, "Don't zip my wiener. Don't zip my wiener. Don't zip it."

Lizzy giggled, waiting for J.T. to join her. But it was hopeless. "I'm sorry," she said. "I thought you wanted me to be happy."

When J.T. sat up, there was a red blotch on her forehead. She squinted, made a Dracula mouth with her front teeth poking over her bottom lip, and thrust her pen, pretending to be Dr. Bob in the exam room jabbing the speculum awkwardly into one of his victims. That was how she referred to the patients who got stuck with him.

"I can't find your cervix." She used her gruffest voice to imitate Dr. Bob. "In fact, I can't find your vagina. You *sure* you have one?"

J.T. flung her arms up in exasperation. "And I have to stand there handing him stuff like he's performing surgery. Cleaning the tray after each victim because he can't be bothered to put the speculum in the bucket. He slaps it onto the tray and gets K-Y jelly all over the swabs and Pap sticks. The word *oaf* was invented to describe Dr. Bob." She pronounced *doctor* with disgust. "I can't tell you how many women I have to comfort after they endure the exam. Dr. Bob's a retired pediatrician for crying out loud. Can you picture him and Jane doing it? 'I'm sorry, Jane my dear, but I can't find your vagina tonight,' " J.T. said in her Dr. Bob voice. "And you know how he comes in and takes a shower before anything else. Clients're lined up halfway around the block, and he has to have his shower."

"Bob doesn't have a shower at home. You know that. He and Jane are building that new place," Lizzy said. "I'm gonna be doing that, too. Aran and Michael don't have running water."

"That's so primitive. Are you really gonna move in with him?"

"I'm there all the time anyway. I might as well move in."

"How can you *stand* it? No lights. No TV. No phone."

"Who am I supposed to call?"

"Oh, Lizzy. Are you *sure* this is what you want?"

"I found someone I love. I want to spend time with her."

"Her? With *her*? Excuse me. This Michael man is a *her* now?"

"I meant *him*. I meant I want to spend time with *him*. He's very lonely." Lizzy plucked a dead leaf from the spider plant.

"It's that little girl. You don't even care about this man. You'd better watch it, Lizzy. You'd better think about what you're doing."

Lizzy continued to pull brown leaves off the plant, standing on her tiptoes. She didn't say anything. Last night before bed she had brushed Aran's hair. It was so silky as she tipped her head and let it spill forward. With the lamplight flickering, it was shiny as syrup. Michael glanced up from his newspaper. "You're pretty as a picture," he said in his fake voice. Had he meant Aran or the two of them?

That morning, they had been late because Aran insisted she had to put her face on. She stood on the chair before the mirror and dusted blush onto her cheeks. While Lizzy watched helplessly, Aran daubed blue eye shadow on and flicked sticky globs of black mascara onto her lashes. She had been smearing on pink lipstick when Michael carried her out the door. Lizzy followed in her car, staying close behind despite the dust the truck stirred up. Before the truck pulled into the babysitter's driveway, Aran turned and gave Lizzy a mournful wave.

"I have an appointment," a woman said, rapping on the office door to get their attention. She carried a baby who sucked a bottle filled with Coke. His nose was dripping down his chapped face. The woman coughed a deep rheumy cough. Lizzy knew that as soon as she left, J.T. would insist they both scrub their hands carefully. Then she would rush around the clinic spraying Lysol. J.T. hated the way people spread their flu germs around.

"I'll do the intake," Lizzy said, taking J.T.'s clipboard and leading them into the exam room. It's the least I can do, she told herself as she showed the baby the basket of toys.

* * *

Slim heard Janesta's car revving before she took off. He felt relieved, as if with her gone he could finally relax. He glanced at his watch. In exactly five minutes, Crystal arrived at his door.

"What'll it be today, sister?" he asked, opening his refrigerator.

"I'm not your sister." Crystal put one foot on top of the other, tipping side to side as she struggled for balance.

"OK. What'll it be today, little lady?"

She farted. "Oops," she said.

"Can I get you a Mountain Dew?" He put the kettle on for coffee. Crystal farted again. "Oops."

"You don't get to say oops twice. What you do is yell, 'Canadian geese!' Then everybody thinks it's a bunch of geese making that noise."

"It's thunder," said Crystal.

"I don't hear thunder." Slim looked out the window. The sky was a deep blue, not a cloud in sight.

"Farts're thunder, you jughead." She sat on the sofa with her mouth hanging open. "Shut your fly trap," Crystal said, imitating Janesta.

"I was fixin' to tinker around," Slim said. "Can you gimme a hand?"

In his spare room, Slim had set up a large table to hold his Dream Facility: a model of the ideal landfill. Since there'd been talk of doing away with the Preacher's Lake landfill, and with it, Slim's job, he'd been building his model out of Legos and broken toys from the dump, using matchsticks and toothpicks, Popsicle sticks and colored scraps of paper. When he presented it to the selectmen, instead of closing the dump and making a transfer station, they'd let him create his Dream Facility.

Slim cut scraps of AstroTurf with a razor and fit them onto the board that held the model, gluing them into place.

"What's that?" Crystal asked. When she leaned close, her hair got caught in the bits of fake grass. One piece dangled from the ends.

"I got me new earrings." She tilted her head this way and that.

"Everybody likes grass. It'll be nice and thick with the compost I make. You know, there are some dumps where they make so much compost they sell it and the town makes a profit. We could use fish guts and manure and old hay, even the grass from the cemetery and school yard. Leaves, too. There's always a shitload of leaves."

"Shitload," Crystal said.

"Excuse me. I mean there's always a bunch of leaves."

"Shitload. Pantload. When it rains, it pours. Where you gonna put the babies nobody wants?"

"There ain't none of them. Least not at the dump. Thank the Lord for small favors. But over here, see this barn?"

"That ain't no barn. That's a oatmeal box." She lifted it and peered inside. "Gone," she said, plopping it over a plastic cow.

"That's the barn. See, I painted it red. Barns're red. There'll be a barn and stalls for the animals folks bring in. And cages for the little ones. A kennel for the dogs. The SPCA'll go in on it with me. They never have enough room at their place in Union City. We'll put up displays like the 4-H has at the county fair. Look here." He unfurled a roll of paper. "Here's a picture I drew of the animal area."

"Area," Crystal said, farting again.

"You have baked beans last night?"

"Beans and franks. Underpants," she said. Then she covered her mouth, embarrassed to have said this word in front of Slim.

"See," Slim explained. "The way it is nowadays, nobody wants to hang around at the dump. They just see a smelly dirty place with a bunch of junk. They don't see what you call the potential."

"Potential." Crystal's eyes rolled around. Marble eyes, her mother called it. "Quit that with the marble eyes." Crystal smacked her forehead. "Who was that out back with you?"

"That was Rainey. We got ourselves a new neighbor. She's livin' with Nelly. You know Nelly, right?"

Crystal twisted her arms around her body. "Oooh. She sizzles."

"What d'you mean, sizzles?"

Crystal shivered. "That Nelly smelly sizzles."

"What do I do?" Slim studied Crystal. The blue veins in her temples pulsed faintly.

"You? What d'you do do do?" She stared at the ceiling. "You purr," she said, darting out of the room. She crept across the road as if a monster followed her, twisting her hands nervously.

Slim glued a strip of AstroTurf into place beside the Community Cafe. His Dream Facility would be bustling with activity, like the Mexican plaza he'd seen in *National Geographic*. A place where folks would visit, where a pot of coffee always brewed. There'd be cups with everyone's name on them, not the throwaway Styrofoam that never disintegrated. Newcomers would be given a cup to paint their name on and a peg to hang it on after they washed it out. People would look forward to a trip up the hill, not like now where most everybody pulled up in a cloud of dust, flung their trash into the pit, and raced off like they couldn't get away fast enough.

As he waited for the lawn areas to dry, he sketched the planters he would make from old tires. He'd already made some for his own use, cutting them with the special saw he ordered, and planted tomato seedlings in front of his trailer. When folks asked, he could show them how to make their own. He drew some tomato plants with his red and green markers. But his heart was not really in his Dream Facility. He was not thinking about folks drinking coffee and sharing news. He was not thinking of the old-timers rolling newspapers into starter logs, or the women mending the torn clothes. He was not thinking about the kids climbing on the playground he'd build. He was thinking about Janesta and the coffee cup over the sink stained with her lipstick.

He went out to the kitchen and held it in both hands, then brought it to his lips. It still smelled like her. He caught his reflection in the window and felt so silly he got busy looking to see what was for supper. A pan of dried-up macaroni and cheese. A pound of frozen hamburger. Not enough spaghetti sauce to bother cooking noodles for. He decided he'd drive over to The Woodshed where Crystal said Janesta waited tables. That was probably where Janesta was now. Besides, he told himself, the steak they served was out of this world. Thick, with an edge of crispy fat, the steak was as big around as the plate it came on. So big, in fact, the potatoes and corn that came with it had to be served on a separate platter.

He put on a clean T-shirt, attempted to drag a damp comb through his hair, and slapped on some aftershave from the row of bottles he salvaged from the dump. He would take Janesta's hand and kiss her fingertips. Like one of them suave guys on TV, he thought as he drove down the road.

Slim was so nervous about seeing Janesta, he stopped at Buster's to chat. The CLOSED sign had already been flipped over, but the fellows were still there.

"Say, Slim, how ya been?" Coalie called.

"Doin' nicely," Slim said.

"Don't you guys have nothing better to do?" Buster's son, Binky, said. He looked like his father looked before he got fat and bald.

"I done my work already. Now you get the fun part," Buster said.

"Whee," Binky said. "Fun." He hopped into his pickup, pulling onto the highway without even a glance to see who might be coming.

"Just like a Massachusetts driver, that boy is," Buster said. "Just remember Mildred taught him to drive. I wouldn't a touched that one."

"Tide's in," Coalie said. As if they'd all been waiting for this, they turned toward the cove.

After Janesta put the steaming plates of food in front of Slim, she rested her hand on his shoulder. "Will that do ya?" she asked him. Her hand was cool through the thin cotton T-shirt. Cool like a black stone beside the creek before the dew was off the grass, Slim thought.

"You all set?" She leaned over him, her breast brushing his arm.

He remembered the taste of his mother's lipstick when she kissed him as a boy. He nodded and set to work cutting his steak, chewing the meat slowly, thinking: Now what? Now what do I do?

"They say Janesta Curtis shot the nuts off Skeeter Willis after she found him in bed with some little tart from up in Caribou," Buster had said before Slim drove off. Slim, pretending to be bored, had listened intently. Buster finished his beer with a soft belch. "That crazy kid of hers didn't even look up from watchin' TV. Just acted like it was nothin' going on. Like she was in some Stephen King movie."

"They say he beat the daylights out of her," Coalie added.

"Who? Janesta or the kid?" asked Rip.

"Nobody lays a hand on the likes of Janesta Curtis," Buster said. "That'd be like volunteerin' to do the tango with a bull moose. She'd give you a bloody nose before you'd get a chance to tighten your fingers into a fist. A gal like that don't take shit from nobody."

"She didn't do a thing to Skeeter," Rip said. His version of a story was never like anybody else's. "He did take up with a little bitch from up north. That's the truth. But there wudn't no shootin'. She'd a gone off to jail for that. When she found the two of them in the middle of the love act, right there in her own bed, naked as jay-birds, Skeeter jumped up with that lady friend right behind him and the two of them took off stark naked on Skeeter's Harley. The last Janesta saw was the exhaust outa the back end as they headed for Route One. Now she's all by her lonesome with that retard kid."

"A gal like that can't wait long for it. You better make your move, Slim," Buster had said.

Slim shoved his plate back, unable to finish his meal. He could still hear Coalie laughing. "Get it while it's hot, boy," he'd said, grabbing his crotch.

Janesta moved from table to table delivering pitchers of beer and platters of fried clams. She was squeezed into bright red stretch pants. When she walked away from him, Slim thought her hips looked just like a great big Valentine heart rocking from side to side. He imagined his hands, one on each side, moving up and down like a dinghy tied to a mooring, bobbing on the waves.

7

Rita's thick hair was pinned up off her neck, a red scarf tied over her breasts, the rest of her bare, her skin honey brown and glistening down to her low slung cutoffs. She swung the scythe, its rusted blade hacking at the tangle of weeds in front of the house, so tall in places Rainey once hid from her mother there, barely crouching among the wide burdock leaves, trying not to giggle while her mother called her name.

It was the second Saturday in July and so hot not even a leaf fluttered in the apple tree. Rainey leaned over the edge of the bunk where she slept now, climbing a ladder to her bed, and yanked open the freezer door, cooling her face in the white vapor that rose from the layers of ice. On the bottom bunk, on a sheet of plywood, she kept her things. At one end, a pad of paper and a box of sixty-four crayons with a built-in sharpener. At the other end, her clothes neatly folded.

Slim had helped Nelly set the refrigerator in a niche between Rainey's bed and the doorway. Every night Rainey fell asleep to the hum of the refrigerator and in the morning, the first thing she heard was the sticky whisper of the seal on the door breaking, the jars of mustard and pickles rattling, as Nelly grabbed the milk.

Rainey, who would be five years old two days before kindergarten started, could hear Nelly's tractor down in the field tedding the hay. She could hear her mother cutting the weeds. When she climbed down, she knew there would be a box of Cheerios on the table next to her Miss Piggy bowl and her favorite spoon with the blue handle her mother had received in the mail with a fork and knife that matched. Rainey would not eat if she couldn't use these utensils even if it meant her mother had to pump water and boil it to wash them while supper cooled. Sometimes Nelly slammed her fist on the table and insisted Rita sit down, claiming the kid could eat with her goddamned hands if she got hungry enough. Then Rita would scrape the dirty fork with her thumbnail, rinse it quickly with a pump of water, and hand it to Rainey without a word.

Rainey climbed down and pulled her pajamas off, hanging them on the hook. She dressed herself, proud that she could tie her own sneakers and pull the T-shirt over her head without getting stuck. She loved the way her mother exclaimed over all she could do for herself. Rainey poured her orange juice and didn't spill a drop. When she finished her breakfast, she would play in the tire swing Slim hung in the apple tree. She would clasp her arms around the warm rubber and wait for her mother to finish, twirling around until the whole world tilted and whirled.

Rita seldom cried anymore over what she missed from the city. Like a pioneer, she was making her way in unknown territory. She would learn to bake bread, knit sweaters with wool from their own sheep. Nelly was a stranger, it was true. She was often gruff and had little to say, but the routine of the farm and working the land brought solace.

Rita had planted peas and beans. Dark curly leaves of spinach and lettuces filled a square. Onion shoots and red-veined beet greens sprouted in what seemed like barren soil when she began. Lifeless, Rita often thought when she dug into the thick clay. The shovel scraped rocks and she worked them out, using a crowbar to jimmy the big ones loose. She worked until her back ached as she stooped to break the soil up, the cool clay soothing to her swollen knuckles. She was reviving the land. Spreading seaweed she gathered during low tide. Hauling pine needles down from the woods in feed sacks. Asking for the grass clippings from the golf course and cemetery. Tilling it all in. Now there were a dozen tomato plants with seaweed mulch tucked around their sturdy stems to keep the slugs off and draw heat, rows of corn as high as her knees. And they planned to plant two more acres of strawberries where Nelly had been tilling in manure and cover crops.

Nelly had promised to mow the patch Rita was cutting, swinging the heavy scythe till her shoulders ached. As she hacked away at the witch grass and thistles, swatted the plantain and purple vetch, swinging the scythe as if her hands clutched around the weathered handle were all that mattered, Rita pictured violets in a neat row. An herb garden with rosemary and lavender. Bee balm and summer savory.

Nelly had promised to till the soil, to spread the clover and grass seed that sat in a cloth bag under the table. "Once the hay's in the barn," she kept saying. While Rita devoted herself to the garden, Nelly obsessed about hay. She had hauled in truckloads of manure, spread rock phosphate and fish meal, and this year, as she made her first cutting, she was eager for it to dry, worried that it would rain and be ruined before she could get it under cover. Rita knew it would take Nelly a few minutes to do the job that was taking her all morning. But she also knew she might never get around to it. Like the door of the truck that would not open. The pile of trash she meant to haul to the dump. The insulation she planned to put under the floorboards. Rita knew if she didn't start now they might never have a nice yard. Though the peas should be cultivated, the spinach thinned, the yellow eggs of the cabbage worms brushed from the underside of the broccoli, she wanted something tame when she stepped outside, not the waist-high tangle of weeds that reminded her of her childhood home where the weeds hid the beer bottles her father flung from the porch.

* * *

"This big ol' bird won't let me outa the house," Janesta said.

Slim gripped the phone. She had called him. They were actually talking. He had so many things to say his mind went blank.

"Did you hear me? Hello? Crystal says it's yours."

"That'd be my turkey." His voice came out with a squeak.

"I'm tryin' to get to town. I can't get out my door."

"I'll be right over," Slim said. He'd been trying to get the nerve to call her for so long. Now she had called him. He scooped a can of feed and hurried across the road to find Janesta standing behind the screen door wearing a tight black blouse and red shorts. She did not look happy to see him.

"Buster brought Tom up to the dump. He didn't have the nerve to do him in," Slim said. He waited for Janesta to throw her head back and laugh that deep laugh of hers, the way she'd done that night at The Woodshed. He'd seen her with her arm around a trucker, laughing. But she just scowled.

"Tom?" she said.

"That's his name." Tom fanned his feathers open with a snap and pranced at the foot of the steps, his wattle trembling importantly.

"It's always struttin' season for him. He's after the hens day and night. Half the time they're up a tree hidin' on him."

"That bird liked to scare the bejesus outa me. It came right up here on the porch and tried to bite my feet."

"He's just showin' off. He won't hurt 'cha none." Slim remembered the way Janesta leaned over to pour his coffee at the restaurant. How when she did this, he saw the soft place between her breasts.

"C'mere, ya dumb cluck." He scattered feed on the ground and the turkey rushed over and pecked at it, cocking his head to peer at Janesta.

"He's partial to *fe*-males," Slim said, grinning.

"That's all I need, some bird that's got the hots for me!" Janesta slammed the door before he could say another word. As he lured the turkey back to his yard, Slim decided he had definitely made some progress. He had actually stood in Janesta's yard. They had spoken on the phone. Now that they had done these things, it wouldn't be so hard to do them again. It was time to make a trip to Union City to buy the ingredients for his eggplant Parmesan. Then he'd call Janesta up casual as could be. I'd be mighty pleased if you and Crystal joined me, he'd say.

*   *   *

A Joan Armatrading tape played on the cassette player. She was singing about why it is harder to live than it is to die. Vivian sang along, tapping out the beat on the steering wheel. She had all of Joan Armatrading's tapes. As soon as one clicked off she popped in another, like a chain-smoker who lit a fresh cigarette with the butt of the last.

Joan Armatrading had been singing for nearly six hours, Carol realized, staring at her watch. That's three hundred and sixty minutes. Twenty-one thousand six hundred seconds, she calculated. She had her large bare feet propped up on the dashboard, her bony knees tucked against her chest. "Joan"—as Vivian referred to her, as if they were old friends—was singing as the sun rose through the haze behind the Citicorp Building when Vivian picked Carol up at her apartment. Joan strummed her guitar up the FDR Drive and sang her heart out clear across Connecticut. Joan sang through what there was of New Hampshire and was still going strong as Vivian drove across the bridge into Kittery. Carol had given up praying for the tape to get mangled and jam the machine so they could listen to country radio the way she would have if it had been her car. But Vivian wouldn't let her drive, let alone choose the music. It felt like torture.

"Let's stop here." Vivian pulled into a rest area. A chubby woman with a dachshund in her arms walked toward the grass. "Zap!"

Vivian aimed two fingers at the woman. This was what she did when she saw someone gay or lesbian, claiming she had superior gay-dar.

"Zzzt. Oughta-bes." Vivian nodded at two young men in white shorts leaning under the hood of a white car. Carol ignored her. She was sick of thinking about everyone's sexual preferences. At first it had been fun, now it was boring. Like being with Vivian, she thought.

"I'll wait here," Carol said, going over to lie on a picnic table to watch the sun filtering through the pine trees. She thought about painting what she saw, but Georgia O'Keeffe had done a tree from that angle already. Carol didn't watch Vivian walk away. She didn't have to watch her to know how she looked: her clenched fists at the ends of her muscular arms, the tight black bicycle shorts over her firm legs, the red visor strapped around her forehead, her dark hair cut extra short for the summer. Carol knew the surprised looks and raised eyebrows some of the women would give Vivian when they emerged from the bathroom stalls, how at least one would stop in her tracks—look up at the sign to be sure that it did in fact say LADIES—when she saw Vivian in line.

"What I don't get about you girls," Dougie said after he met Vivian. "I mean, if you like women so much. Excuse me. *Wimmin.* How come half of you look like teenage boys?"

Now here she was waiting for Vivian to take her to some cabin in the Maine woods. Dougie had told her there would be mosquitoes the size of sparrows. That the blackfly was the Maine state bird. How was she supposed to survive without him? And Vivian mentioned back in Connecticut that the cabin had no phone. What had she been thinking? Was it part of her midlife crisis the way Dougie had said? It began to drizzle, but the trees formed a natural umbrella as the rain hit the thick pine needles. She crossed her arms over her chest and shivered.

"Ready?" Vivian peered at Carol over her aviator sunglasses. Seeing Vivian this way reminded Carol of the pictures she had loved as a child, the ones you turned upside down and the woman with the hat became a man with a beard. But Vivian still looked like Vivian upside down.

* * *

"Knock, knock."
"Who's there?"
"Me."
"Me who?"

"Me. Crystal."

"Since when did you start knockin'? The door's open. C'mon in. Look at this," he said, showing her the pictures from an article about a man in New Mexico who made houses out of soda bottles, tires, and cement. "That's what we'll have at the Dream Facility, buildings made out of old tires and cement."

"You got any empty bottles?" Crystal held up a red balloon.

Slim dug around in his recycling bag and offered her an empty catsup bottle. "Will this do?"

"I'm gonna do a spearmint," she said, fitting the balloon over the neck of the bottle. "Now I need a pan of hot water."

Once it was ready, she set the bottle in the water. The balloon began to slowly fill with air.

"That some kind of magic?" Slim asked.

"It's the weather," Crystal said.

"What d'you mean?"

"Hot air rises, you nim wit. Lookit. When I take it out, the balloon'll flop down."

"How come you're so interested in the weather?" Slim asked. Last week, Crystal had shown him her notebook filled with hundreds of figures. For years, it seemed, she'd been recording the high and low temperature of the day.

"How do your brown eyes turn blue?"

"Huh?"

"I said, how do your brown eyes turn blue? Ain't you listenin' to the song on TV?"

Well," Slim said, glancing at the screen. As a medley of lyrics played, the names of the songs scrolled by. "She means she gets sad. Blue means sad."

"Blue's a color, you jughead."

"It's an expression. You ever hear of gettin' the blues?"

Crystal smacked her forehead. "You makin' potatoes for supper?"

"I just might."

"Mom's getting pizza."

"You like eggplant?" he asked.

"What's that?"

"You know, eggplant. See it on my counter? It's mighty tasty."

"I like potatoes. Eggplant? Ugh. Do the chickens make it?"

"No. It grows on a vine. Like a tomato."

"Silly billy. Yummy potatoes're my favorite. Gimme a nice big bowl of mashed potatoes. You got any kids?"

"You asked me that a million times. The answer's still no."

"Tired." Crystal rested her head on the counter Slim was building.

"You're *tired*? Ain't but twelve years old and *tired*? Boy. Wait'll you get my age. Then you'll know what tired is."

"Potatoes're my favorites. Tater Tots and ruffled barbecue chips. Best is mashed. Butter and salt. Gravy. Mm-mm. You like 'em mashed? Mom gets me instant so's I can have 'em whenever I want. Just add hot water and stir it up good with a fork. Shotgun likes 'em too. You got the instant kind?" Crystal rubbed her belly then pressed her face to the sofa. "I'll ask her," she said, her voice muffled by the cushion.

"I can't hear you with your face like that."

"I'll ask her," she shouted, throwing her head back.

"Jeezum. You scared me. Don't shout at a fellow thataway."

"I'll ask her, I'll ask her, I'll ask her."

"What're you talkin' about? Ask who what?"

"Mom to come over for supper. Ain't that what 'cha want?"

"How d'you know that?"

Crystal shrugged and draped the kitten around her neck like a stole.

"You make me feel like I'm on the *Twilight Zone*," he said.

"What 'cha doin' with your countertop?" She fingered the shards of broken crockery Slim had been gluing to the surface.

"I'm makin' what you call a mosaic."

"What for?"

"In my line of work. I see a heck of a lot of broken plates. Look here. This one's got a flower. And here's a little man with a fishin' pole. I'm gonna glue down bottle bottoms for built-in coasters."

"Bottle bottoms. Bottom. Oops! What'd you have for supper last night?"

"Lemme see. Two turkey sandwiches. Potato salad. Ice cream."

"We had mac and cheese. The orange kind. Mom got 'em three for a dollar." The kitten swatted her hair. "You name him yet?"

"How about Tony?

"Tony?"

"You know. Tony the Tiger?"

Crystal picked the cat up and examined it. "Bootie," she said.

"He ain't got boots. He can't be Bootie if he ain't got boots."

"Why not?"

"That'd be weird."

"Weird beard. So?"

"Well." Slim was moving the shards of broken plates around as if fitting together a puzzle. He wondered if Crystal really meant it. Would she invite her mother to come for supper? "You name a cat

Boots if he's got white paws. You could name Mickey Boots for instance."

"Bootie, not Boots."

On the TV a man was painting three apples, talking about the colors he chose and why. Slim imagined people at home painting the exact same picture. Once somebody dumped a load of shag rugs nailed to frames. The rugs had gobs of oil paint smeared on them. Slim had buried them without hesitation. Crystal changed the station. A man crouched beside a white car, a gun in his hand. He ran down an alley and hid behind a row of trash cans, clattering the lids.

"I'll ask in the mornin'. She's not home now. For tomorrow, OK?" she said and ran across the road to her empty house.

* * *

"Mommy misses her honeybunch bunches. I blew you a hundred kisses. Did you catch them?" Michael read Aran Kaye's postcard again.

"My tummy hurts," Aran announced. "I need Pepto Bismol."

"We don't have any," Michael said, patting her head.

"How about a hot-water bottle?" Lizzy tried. But Aran stamped her foot and pushed Lizzy away.

"No!" she screamed. She wouldn't let Lizzy near her.

"It's just a phase," Michael whispered. "She'll get over it. I shouldn't have read her the card." He patted Lizzy clumsily as if she were a baby who refused to burp. She hated the feel of his hands on her. She felt wild inside. Stop touching me! she wanted to scream.

Now Michael was upstairs reading *Cinderella* in the stupid voice he talked to Aran with. Lizzy stared at Kaye's loopy handwriting then threw the card in the cookstove. In a little while, she would cook the supper she and Aran bought that afternoon: hot dogs and pork and beans with the canned corn and applesauce Aran had selected when Lizzy lifted her so she could reach. It's heavenly when it's just the two of us, she thought.

Lizzy heated water and filled the dishpan. She began to wipe down every surface of the kitchen. She scrubbed the propane refrigerator thinking, I am washing away Kaye's fingerprints. She threw away a jar of moldy jam, a half-eaten sandwich, the hard waxy ends of a dark orange cheese. She planned the food she would prepare. Creamed chicken on toast. Spaghetti and meatballs. Apple pie. Oatmeal cookies. She was thinking about taking down the curtain Kaye made to cover the open shelves—a bizarre paisley hemmed by hand with neat, perfectly even stitches. It was strung along a piece of packing twine. No doubt Michael's bright idea. She would have to cut the string. But she could wash the curtain and spread it on the bushes to dry. Someday, she would hang a clothesline so the summer breezes could blow the wrinkles out of Aran's dresses. She smiled happily as she worked, making a place for herself. Then she stopped. She felt like Goldilocks just before the bears came home. Upstairs, Michael was acting out the wicked stepmother refusing to let Cinderella go to the ball. Is that me? Lizzy thought. Wicked?

Lizzy put away the dishes, obviously a wedding present. Fine white china never meant for her hands to touch. Yesterday, with Michael at work, Lizzy had pushed the hangers along the closet rod while Aran napped. Standing before the mirror, she held a black dress up to her body. The dress would fit over hips fuller than Lizzy's. It fell inches below where it was meant to graze the knee. The frilly blouse she held up smelled of Kaye's perfume. Had Lizzy tried it on, the neckline would have dipped to her navel. "You've got a boy's body," Dennis used to tease. "My lad Lizzy."

Fingering Kaye's peasant skirt she could have worn like a dress had made Lizzy feel like a child playing dress up. When she first met Aran and Michael, Kaye had been a ghostly figure that drifted just out of the corner of her eye. But now she had seen Kaye. In all her glory. That was how she thought of it when she found the photograph in the back of the closet. Michael and a woman with Aran's eyes, Aran's sweet pointed chin, her heart-shaped face. The two of them were completely naked. Kaye in all her glory. Michael on his haunches beside Kaye's chair. It was Lizzy's first full view of Michael's naked body; they both undressed furtively in the dark. Even when they had sex—Lizzy refused to call it making love— Michael kept his shirt and socks on. But she wasn't interested in his hairy chest, his gorilla arms, or the belly he was obviously sucking in. She wasn't interested in his ridiculous pose, the shadowy area between his thighs as he crouched, one elbow propped on his knee. It was Kaye who captured Lizzy's attention. She was perfectly proportioned with large perfectly shaped breasts, a slender waist, and smooth rounded hips. Perfect skin and beautiful long hair that fell over her shoulders. Shapely legs that would stride confidently through the door at any moment as she called, "I'm home."

Lizzy left the picture where she'd found it, behind the shotgun and dusty shoes, but she could still feel its presence, like the telltale heart forever beating, as she stepped out the back door. The hens were dipping their wings in the dust, cooing as they burrowed into hollows under the house. The rabbits sat in their cages, waiting. For what, Lizzy didn't know. Behind the house a dark brook rushed over mossy rocks. I can walk away from all this, she told herself. I can walk up to my car right this minute and never turn back. She could almost feel the wind in her hair as she headed toward town; then a voice floated from the treetops.

"Lizzy lovey dovey. Let's play Cinderella. Daddy's the prince."

* * *

"Now what?" Carol asked. She tried not to panic even though Vivian had left the map, along with the directions to the cabin, back in Manhattan. So far, they had found their way all right. She was relieved when they got off the Maine Turnpike, where for long stretches it had been so desolate Carol worried they were the last ones alive. They made it around the Bangor bypass onto Route One, had gone through Union City along the fast-food strip that Vivian called "Anywhere, U.S.A." They had not taken the right fork and gone toward Holiday Island, were not tempted by the turnoff for Adams, and had just been greeted by the waving Larry Lobster sign, before crossing the Swift River on an old bridge that sang with the car's tires. But now they were lost.

"You don't remember what the directions said?" Carol asked.

Vivian chewed her lip. When she stopped playing her cassette player, Carol decided it was a sign that she was thinking hard and would soon know what to do.

"Preacher's Lake, huh? What a weird name." Carol pictured a lake circled with dozens of pulpits, each with a minister behind it waving a Bible. Some wore long black robes that flowed over the sand. Others wore bathing suits, sunglasses, and straw hats.

"You said it, not me." Vivian rolled her eyes. Carol's father was a minister, which Vivian enjoyed teasing her about, calling her the last of the great white Wasps. Only at the moment she was too concerned about being lost to make jokes. If there were a motel nearby, Vivian would check in that minute. In the morning, she would go home and kill her brother. This whole expedition was his fault.

Last Friday, her brother Jeremy called to say he'd been offered a part in an off-off Broadway play. Rehearsals had started. He would not be going to his friend Roger's cabin in Maine as he'd been planning. Roger, Jeremy's roommate from college, had gone to England on a walk through Thomas Hardy land with the new woman he was dating. "Doctor Lit," Jeremy called her. Vivian was sure he called her Doctor Clit to everybody else. "Sissy, believe me. You need a break," he said when she asked him what she and Carol were supposed to do up in the woods. "And you know what to do when you're alone with a woman. Your new honey'll roll over at your feet," he said.

When Vivian called, Carol had laughed and said, "Yeah, sure, I'd love to go." And this after telling Vivian twice she was too busy to have dinner even when Vivian said everyone had to eat. "Time away is just what I need," Carol said.

The day before she and Vivian took off for Maine, Carol withdrew a thousand dollars in traveler's checks. Then she went to Eastern Mountain Sports and charged a new pair of jeans, a wool sweater, and a bright red flannel shirt. After that she headed down to Pearl Paint, shoving her way through the crowds around the Chinese immigrants hawking batteries and clocks on Canal Street. She would do watercolor miniatures, she decided, and bought small blocks of watercolor paper and a watercolor set that fit in her palm, the brush no longer than her index finger.

"Here we are in the wilderness," Vivian said. "Miles from the nearest Howard Johnson's."

"Maybe something's up ahead," Carol said. "Where we can ask."

Vivian gave her a terrified look as a logging truck rumbled past, making the whole car shake.

"OK. Where *I* can ask." One of the things she'd learned about Vivian so far was how frightened she was of talking to strangers. Carol had felt heroic when she entered a sandwich shop and returned with lunch.

They drove in silence, past an old stone farmhouse with a mansard roof. Curving along the coves, dipping over the hills. "Look." Carol pointed at Buster's Hardware. "I'll ask those old geezers. Pull over."

"Hi," Carol said when she got out of the car. She looked from one to the other and smiled uncertainly. These were the kind of men who, back in the city, would be dozing on park benches next to empty Four Roses bottles. They were like the three monkeys: See no evil, hear no evil, speak no evil. Which one was which? She glanced back at Vivian, who nodded nervously as if to say: You're doing good. When she turned back, the men were staring at Vivian as if her car were a UFO burning a crater-sized hole in the parking lot.

"Here's two more," Carol thought the man with the dirty Santa Claus beard said. She was sure she smelled booze.

"Hi," Carol tried again. "Can you help me? We're lost."

"What's that?" Coalie scooted forward until his feet touched the porch. "Lost, you say?" His eyes twinkled with amusement. "Where'd it be you're tryin' to get to?"

"Preacher's Lake. We're looking for Preacher's Lake. I mean the lake, not the town. I know this is the town."

"Girl. You ain't lost. You just ain't went far enough," Rip said. He shot a stream of tobacco juice into the dust. "Besides, you ain't lost so long's you got gas."

At that moment, something crawled across Carol's stomach. It felt like a spider. She flapped her shirt, hoping the spider would fall out.

"Preacher's Lake, you say?" Buster Maddocks asked. Carol noticed how his belly spilled over his thighs. "What you wantin' up that way?"

"Roger Baker has a cabin there. We're friends of a friend of his."

"Ayuh," Coalie said. "I cut pulpwood on Roger Senior's land. That son of his let the place go to hell, excuse my French." Coalie began giving directions. At first Carol thought he spoke another language, his accent was so thick with added "uhs" and "ahs" while the ends of other words seemed to disappear down the front of his overalls.

"Keep right on this road here straightaway," he said. "See now, head on down east. Go right on past the church."

"Go past Rhonda's Resale," Rip added, fumbling with his tobacco.

"Ayuh. Rhonda's Resale. Can't miss all she's got out front."

The spider, instead of falling to the ground as Carol had hoped, was inching its way south via her large loose shorts. She turned her back on the men and pulled the waistband out, peering surreptitiously inside.

"Excuse me!" Carol leapt around shaking the hem of her shorts. "I've got a bee in my pants."

Carol motioned to Vivian to come out. Vivian took her visor off and checked herself in the rearview mirror, running her hand over her hair which looked like an overgrown crew cut. She got out of the car while Carol continued her flapping dance in the dirt.

"There," Buster said. "It's out now. It won't hurt you none."

Carol saw what she was certain was a different bee hovering around her knees. But she could no longer feel the bee crawling across her skin, so she tried to forget it and pay attention to the directions.

Rip couldn't stop staring. When was the last time he'd seen a woman with so much hair on her legs?

"Now. Like I said. Go on past the church. There'll be a turnoff on your right, but don't take it, you'll end up at the landing. Keep on straight for another mile or two and then it's your next left. You can't miss it. There's Hydie's Place. Right there at the corner." Coalie's red mouth glistened as he continued. Forks in the road. A dump. Blacktop to gravel.

"I hope you got all that," Carol said when they were back in the car. "I couldn't understand half of what he said." She peered down her shorts again, but still no bee.

"Excuse me. I've got a bee in my pants," Vivian mimicked Carol.

"I bet I made their day," Carol said. "They'll be talking about this for weeks to come."

They both laughed as they headed up the highway.

"You looked so cute jumping around, doing your little bee dance." Vivian felt a rush of contentment as she reached across the car and placed her warm hand on Carol's knee. Carol wasn't sure if she liked it or not, so she just sat there with Vivian's hand on her knee as they drove past the church. To Carol's surprise, it was boarded up like a condemned house.

"America," Vivian said. "The land of heathens."

They found Hydie's and turned.

"I can't remember if he said to take the fork or not," Vivian said.

"I think he said go straight."

"Do I have to?" Vivian gave Carol a significant look—she raised her eyebrows and pinched her lips in surprise—a look she reserved for her corny jokes, all of which had to do with being gay or sex.

"Just don't expect me to ask *there*." Carol pointed at a trailer where a wheelchair was parked beside a bashed-in mailbox. Four huge barking dogs were chained to a truck set up on blocks.

"Did you see that sign? BEWARE OF OWNER. Where are we?" Vivian said.

"There's the dump. See the gulls? We did something right. Go straight," Carol said when they came to another fork.

"No no no. Don't make me," Vivian groaned. "Anything but that."

They passed an old asphalt-shingled farmhouse with a refrigerator on the porch. A sign said RABBITS FOR SALE. DRESSED OR UNDRESSED.

"They mean stuffed ones in cute little outfits, right?" Vivian said.

They continued along the road, which grew narrower and more curved as they climbed. When they had passed over the railroad tracks, gone up the steep hill, and were high up in the blueberry barrens, the road divided. They had no idea which fork to take.

"Turn around. I'll ask at the first house where there's a car in the driveway," Carol said. They pulled up behind a big green Buick. As Carol headed for the front door, she heard Judy Garland singing "Somewhere Over the Rainbow." She knocked, but there was no answer. She shrugged at Vivian and headed around back thinking maybe someone was in the kitchen, but they couldn't hear with the music blaring.

Vivian got out to follow her, suddenly worried if Carol got out of her sight, she might never see her again. She'd never survive if she had to fend for herself in a place like this. She waited nearby while Carol knocked and peered through the sagging screen.

"Uh-oh," a woman said when Carol called hello. "Yeah?" The woman stuck her head out the door, squinting in the sunlight.

Her hair was such a unique shade of red, Carol thought it had to be natural. Color like that didn't come from the hairdresser. Rusty red with a daub of pink and yellow. When I paint her, I'll concentrate on her hair.

It was at this moment, caught up in her fantasy painting, that the bee, which did not fly free but had instead become trapped in her underwear, chose to sting Carol. The pain was like a hot needle jabbing. But instead of crying out she explained where they wanted to go.

"Bu, bu, bu," Janesta twiddled her lips. "Excuse me. My tongue ain't workin' right." She came out into the yard, swaying on her high heels. Carol saw her as if through a zoom lens as the bee stung her again. While Janesta pointed up the road, explaining where to go, Carol was having all she could do not to yank down her shorts. She had heard bees only stung once, but this one was doing overtime.

An old black Lab rolled in the grass, his coat covered with burrs. He ran to Vivian, jumping up with his paws on her chest.

"Shotgun! Get down!" Janesta hit the dog with her shoe.

"Take that first left and just stay on the dirt till you see another little old road off to the left. You can't miss it. He's got his name on a tree," Janesta said.

"Don't panic or anything," Carol said once they returned to the car. "But that bee was in my pants all that time and it just stung me." She unzipped her shorts. There was the bee. It dropped to the floor, dead.

"You're not gonna have to be rushed to the hospital, are you?"

"No," Carol said, examining the swellings on her skin.

"We don't have to make a detour back to civilization or anything, right?" Vivian asked. It was just her luck, Carol would have to spend the vacation in the hospital.

"No. I just need some mud or baking soda or something."

"You know what they say about bees, don't you?" Vivian made her famous expression.

"Don't tell me," she said. "Don't even say it."

"What?" Vivian acted hurt. "Isn't it funny how a bee likes honey? Buzz, buzz, buzz."

"Quit it," Carol said, but she smiled in spite of herself.

8

Black-and-gold-striped beetles were mating on the cucumber vines, riding each other piggyback. Potato bug larvae clustered on the potato plants; the leaves were pitted and torn from the incessant chewing. Rita and Rainey picked them off; popping them felt like bursting ripe grapes from their skins. Rainey wore a red scarf tied low over her ears and forehead to keep the flies from becoming entangled in her curls.

"Hold still." Rita cupped her palms, ready to slap the fly that hovered over Rainey. "They like you 'cause you're so sweet."

"Icky," Rainey said when her mother showed her the dead fly. Rainey hated being outside. She hated the bugs and the sun which was hot on her skin, making it browner. She was thirsty, too, and her bug bites itched. "I wanna go in." Rainey rested her forehead on her knees and stared at the yellow sneakers her mother bought at the yard sale. "I wanna go color," she said.

"But it's a nice day." Rita was planning how she would hill the potatoes, loosen the soil with a spade and pile it around the stems the way her father used to do. What would he think if he could see her now? "Didn't get too far from the farm, I see, Miss City Girl. Still think you're better than us?" His voice came back to her as if he were standing over her, casting a shadow, the stench of cheap beer in the air.

Rita noticed the girl who stood like an apparition at the edge of the field, chewing a stalk of timothy. Rita waved and called hello but the girl just stared, reminding Rita of the deaf boy down the road when she was growing up, always lost in his own world. She went back to killing bugs, scooting along on her butt tiredly. All her muscles ached.

The Three Steves, she thought. She didn't know why she recalled these men, as if it were a test of her memory. The first Steve worked as a window washer in Cambridge and once won a bet that he could sample every kind of liqueur at Jack's and still balance his washing stick on the tip of his nose. Steve number two had long thick glossy black hair that spilled over his shoulders and blue eyes the color of a wolf's. Shopkeepers often called him Miss. The last Steve had hitchhiked from Santa Cruz to Boston with a German shepherd named Love. He took too much speed and sat under Rita's window singing "Born in the U.S.A." until the neighbors called the police. What would life be like if she had stayed with one of the Steves? Sometimes her life seemed like a movie she was dozing through, waking up when the cymbals clashed or a gun exploded, then dozing off again. Now Nelly. Every night Rita lay beside Nelly still as a corpse. Every morning they fought. This morning, Rainey tipped over her bowl when she slapped a mosquito. Big deal. A few Cheerios. Nelly yanked Rainey from her chair. "You clean this mess," Nelly yelled.

"This stupid house is full of mosquitoes," Rita screamed. "They come right in the cracks. She's covered with bites. Look at her arms." Nelly clenched her fists and stood very still; only a muscle twitched in her jaw. Then she stomped out, slamming the door so hard Rita feared she'd never get it open again.

I wish I never let her touch me, Rita thought as she crushed the potato bugs.

Women took trains across the rough country to homestead with men they had never met, arriving to find barren land, surviving the worst storms. Rita wondered how many went crazy from loneliness, how many cracked under the strain of hard work and life with a stranger. A horrible panic filled her, like the razor-sharp claws of an eagle slashing into her back. To distract herself, she pretended she had a thick straw broom to sweep her fears aside the way she had swept the floor that morning, the straw pulling her worries like the crumbs, dirt, and dead flies she had swept into a neat pile. She thought about Jill. The dark movie theatre, her hand on Rita's neck, the heat of their kisses. Cher on the screen, sexy as ever. Back then, Rita had imagined that being with a woman would transform her life.

The girl at the edge of the field was walking toward them. She wore a white nightgown and flip-flops, the rubber heels worn through. She scanned the sky and announced in a singsong voice, "Weatherman says it's gonna be a scorcher this weekend. Thunderstorms. Lightning, too."

"Really?" said Rita. The girl's eyes darted like silver marbles in a pinball machine. Maybe she's blind, Rita thought, not deaf. "I'm Rita. This is Rainey, my little girl."

"Wicked hot," Crystal said. "What 'cha doin'?"

"Killing potato bugs."

"Oh. Bugs're gross. Bees're the worst."

"What's your name?"

"Crystal Dawn Curtis. I hate bugs." She smacked her forehead.

"Not all bugs're bad," Rita said. "We need bees, you know."

"Bees'll kill you if you're allergic. I saw on *Rescue 911*. You get one hour to get to the hospital or else. When you're dead, you're gone, right?" She turned to Rainey, who nodded. "Gonna be wicked hot," Crystal predicted. "You married?" Her eyes darted from Rainey to Rita, then back to the sky. "Too skinny to be pregnant. I know that."

"No, I'm not married. I live with Nelly. You know her?" Rita pointed to Nelly who sat on the tractor engulfed in a cloud of dust and chaff.

Rainey wondered if her daddy was dead. Maybe this was why she never saw him. "Everybody has a daddy," Paul Parker had told her at the day care center. "Somebody's got to do the nasty with your moms. That's how you get bornded." He jabbed his finger in and out of a hole he made by curling one hand into a loose fist. "Like this," he said.

"Nelly." Crystal stuck her tongue out. Then she ran away, her nightgown fluttering, her flip-flops slapping her heels.

* * *

"The Beauty Hut? You're taking Aran to The Beauty Hut?" J.T. said.

"You know. That new place. Over by The Quarterdeck," Lizzy said.

"I know where it is. I just can't believe you're taking a little kid to get her hair done. Hair spray, curlers, the works?"

"I know it's a little weird, but I figure I'll give her what she wants and then gradually she'll realize how stupid it all is. If I say no, she'll just want it more."

"She's five years old. Aren't you worried about, you know, spoil-ing her? I mean, if she's getting her hair done when she's five, won't she be wanting to drive the car when she's in first grade? Won't she be in here next week trying out birth control methods?"

"Oh, come on, J.T. Don't you know anything? The reason people have kids is so they can ruin someone else's life for a change. Anyhow. Just because you wear your hair exactly the same way you have since second grade doesn't mean all little girls have to do the same thing."

"What's wrong with my hair?" J.T. picked up the mirror Lizzy let women use to see their cervixes. She squinted and fluffed her bangs.

"What's happening with your new therapist?" J.T. asked.

"I quit. She gives me the creeps. She always wears a suit, like it's a business conference. She sits there with her pad like she's taking minutes. Last time she had on a tie."

"Maybe she's a big dyke."

"Well, if she is, she's got a rich conservative girlfriend because the rock she wears on her left hand could be a weapon."

"These straight girls acting butch confuse me," J.T. sighed.

"I miss Mark," Lizzy said. "He was such a good therapist. He really listened. And I never noticed what he was wearing. Did I tell you I saw him yesterday? I went to Buster's Hardware to get some cup hooks, and there he was, buying big sacks of nails. He just nodded at me like I could have been anybody. Like he didn't know my entire life story. I had all I could do not to blurt out the latest chapter."

"Hmm," J.T. said. From what Lizzy had told her, it seemed all Mark *ever* did was nod. "At least that nod didn't cost fifty bucks," she said.

"Very funny. If I don't figure out what I'm doing pretty soon . . ." Lizzy's voice trailed off as a client came in, her sandals scuffing.

"I need some supplies," she muttered, eyes downcast, behaving as if she were hoping to buy illegal drugs.

"OK," J.T. said, leading the woman into the other room.

Lizzy listened to the doors of the supply closet creak open, she heard J.T. snap open a bag, but she wasn't really paying attention. Yesterday, Michael showed her the empty space he'd made in the closet, the wooden pole that no longer held Kaye's clothes. Kaye's shoes and the photograph were also gone. Lizzy felt strangely bereft. "I want you to make yourself at home," Michael had said, rubbing his dark prickly whiskers. He'd gotten carried away and decided to grow a full beard. His face looked like it was covered with soot.

"Your one-thirty's here," J.T. said, patting Lizzy's back softly.

* * *

Nelly hunched over the baler, working at the thick knots of twine. Finally, with a scream of frustration, she slashed the tangled twine with her jackknife, yanking off the shreds of knotted string, flinging it into the wind. She would have to go to Buster's Hardware and ask for help. Let them laugh. She had hay to bale, sheep to feed.

The bales had flopped off the baler in misshapen lumps. Now the twine was tangled. Fortunately it was perfect weather for hay, dry with a breeze, though she worried about the dusty rows of strawberries. If it didn't rain soon the berries would not be sweet or juicy. The peas would not fill their pods. The lettuce would wither. She should set up irrigation but worried the well would run dry.

She could see Rita weeding and killing the potato bugs. Chemicals would do the trick quicker, but she was determined to be organic. NO SPRAY she wrote on signs she hammered by the roadside for when the weed crews came by. All week long, airplanes buzzed overhead, spraying the blueberry barrens. She worried it would drift to her gardens. *Guthion. Malathion.* The words tore into her like bullets. The *smell.* As if her hands were soiled with the thick stink.

Stupid asshole, she scolded herself. Why didn't you know? She punched her thighs and smacked her face as if she could beat the memories away. But Fiona was always there. Nelly could hear the stark cadence of Fiona's voice. "Sorry not good enough," Fiona said, spitting on the ground.

Get it together, Nelly instructed herself. She leaned against the tractor and rolled a cigarette. Don't think about her. She's only in your head. You can make her go away.

Her depression was building, like dark storm clouds gathering, rumbling overhead, ready to soak her to the bone. Don't think about it don't think about it don't think about it, she repeated as she smoked. But she couldn't help herself.

If only Rita would sit beside her, nodding encouragement, her hand on Nelly's arm. Then Nelly would tell her. From beginning to end. Not stopping, no matter what, not stopping. She would make it sound like any other story. Oh, this is what I did back then, she would start. I had this job.

She remembered Cho spraying Malathion gleefully, using an old pump sprayer, no face mask, no protection. "Kill 'em dead," he shouted, inviting her to watch. They thought she was crazy to expect them to weed and kill bugs by hand when a spray did the trick. They pretended they didn't understand English when she brought it up. One day she drew a skull and crossbones in the dirt and lay beside it pretending to be dead.

"It kills the bugs. It kills the fish. It kills the birds. It kills me," she said. They laughed at their teacher; they shook their heads. What kind of crazy woman would lie in the dirt like that?

* * *

Crystal was in her front yard cutting the weeds with scissors.

"By the time you finish that," Slim said. "The place where you started'll be back up to your knees again."

Crystal went on snipping. Behind her, the shades were drawn. It looked to Slim as if the house were covered with eyes, every one of them shut tight. He wondered if Crystal had asked her mom to come over for supper. Yesterday he waited, his ingredients lined up, but Crystal did not come over. Janesta drove off at five and did not come back until after Slim went to bed. It's hopeless, he thought.

"Wanna go fishin'?" he asked Crystal. He was carrying his fishing gear and a can of crawlers.

"You mean me and you?"

"Who else would I be meanin'? You see anybody else I'm talkin' to?"

Crystal looked up and down the road, then back at Slim. "No."

"No, you don't see anyone else or no you don't wanna go?"

"Can't go. Mom says not to leave the yard."

"Well, tell her I say you're invited."

"Can't."

"How come?"

"She says if I wake her up, she's gonna slit my throat from here to here." Crystal drew a finger from one ear to the other and made a slicing sound. She snipped a clump of buttercups.

"We don't want that." Slim glanced at the house. He wondered if Janesta had really shot at Skeeter the way the fellows said she had.

Crystal threw the scissors in the direction of the porch. "OK," she said, wiping her hands on her T-shirt.

"What d'you mean, OK? I ain't about to help you get murdered."

"She don't really mean that. She just says it."

"How d'you know?"

Crystal giggled and tried to do a cartwheel. She ended up sprawled on her back, bits of grass and weeds in her hair. "I know Mr. Toe."

As they walked down the path that wound through the woods to Preacher's Lake, Crystal kept tripping over the tree roots and then her flip-flops came undone and she had to stop and push the knob of rubber back through the hole. She was having trouble with the fishing pole Slim let her carry because the tip kept catching on the alders, but she wouldn't relinquish it.

Along the path, chickadees made their staccato sound. Slim gazed at the blue sky above the trees and took a deep breath. The path to the lake was a half mile through what had once been pasture but now was scrubby woods. Whoever made the trek felt it was worth the effort. The beach had sand white as sugar and there was a gentle drop-off, making it a good place for children if you could get them—and all the things children required to spend any length of time away from home—down to the lake.

Often Slim had the place to himself. Sometimes on weekends the beach would be full of people lounging on blankets, playing Frisbee, throwing each other into the lake. Slim enjoyed watching the families play in the water. The children dammed the stream and built sand castles at the water's edge. Their fathers made campfires and cooked hot dogs and hamburgers. He just wished people wouldn't throw used Pampers on the sand. He wished people wouldn't toss empty cans and bottles in the bushes, drop their candy and potato chip wrappers on the path.

"Don't they think about havin' to look at it next time?" He picked up a Pepsi bottle and dropped it into the bag he always carried down with him. He would never understand people or the way they threw things away. "I was readin' where the top of Mount Everest is one big junk heap. Imagine climbin' all that way and it's like you're at the dump," he said.

Crystal was singing "It Won't Be Long Now." She didn't respond to Slim, but he kept talking anyway.

"Yesterday this lady with New York plates pulls up. She's got New York plates, but a sticker for the dump just the same. She's in her fancy four-wheel drive and sits there like I'm some kind of car hop, waitin' on me to unload a perfectly good easy chair. 'He burnt a hole in it,' she goes, pointin' to this teensy charred spot on the cushion. 'Dropped one of his damn cigarettes.' Jeezum Crow, lady, I wanted to tell her. Whyn't you just flip the cushion over? But I just wait till she drives off and stick that chair in my trunk and bring it home. You have to come over and sit in it," he said. "It's pink. Your favorite."

"Can I sit in it when we come for supper?"

"What d'you mean, come for supper?"

"You forget to get me my mashed potatoes?" She stopped in her tracks, scowling. "You didn't forget, did you?"

"You mean you asked her?"

"Course I did. You crazy nutty butt. You'll be sorry. Weatherman says if it don't rain up north the forest fires'll start."

"So when'll it be?"

"Gonna thunderstorm Saturday or Sunday. Gonna rain cats and dogs," Crystal said, staring at the sky as if expecting the animals themselves to come hurtling toward her. "Or else the fires," she said.

"I mean, when's your mom comin' over?"

"Mom's got Saturday off this week. Saturday's date night for singles. You're a single, right? You got any kids, Slim?"

Slim wanted to pick Crystal up and twirl her around, but she was running down the last stretch of the path, holding the fishing pole like a sword. They settled in a small cove on the far end of the beach so if anybody came down to the lake to swim, they wouldn't scare off the fish.

"Saturday night, you say?" he asked, casting into the shadows.

"I told you told you. Now, quit it." She slapped her hand over her mouth. "Shut your fly trap, Crystal." She leaned against Slim. "If they took all your blood outa you and filled you up with somebody else's blood, would you still be you?" Crystal asked.

"What kind of question is that?"

"I dunno. Would you?"

"How'm I supposed to know? Do I look like Einstein?"

Crystal sighed and hung her head. "I gotta go pee."

"Well, that's what the bushes are made for."

A wild look crossed her face. "I gotta *go!*" She jumped up and disappeared down the path into the woods.

Slim wished she had stayed so he wouldn't have time to think. But Crystal was always rushing off and there was never any talking her out of it. Saturday night. He was afraid to believe it. But Crystal never lied. He would get up early and start frying the eggplant before he went to work. Saturday was the busiest day at the dump, but he could get home early and make the sauce and still have plenty of time to bake a cake.

Across the water, he could see a canoe approach. There were seldom boats on the lake because no motors were allowed, and because the lake was so large, few people discovered the narrow neck, nearly obscured by the thick growth of fir trees, or passed through it to this end where it jutted off from the main lake like the head of a duckling. It was like discovering a secret pond hidden from the main beach. Slim watched the canoe pass in and out of the shadow Preacher's Mountain threw across the water. If he had a boat, he could catch some smallmouth bass. He was positive they were out where the water was deep. But he would settle for a few silvery pike. Even a couple of togue. Anything to get his mind off Janesta.

* * *

Carol was on her knees dipping the paddle into the crystal clear lake water, twirling the end in a maneuver she called sculling. Vivian was in front of her, trailing her hand in the water, thinking. Now. Ask her now. Instead, she sprinkled some water over her shoulder at Carol.

"Don't," Carol said. But Vivian pretended she didn't mean it. However did men get the nerve to propose? It wasn't as if she wanted a lifetime commitment with Carol. But living together would be nice. She'd never get used to living alone.

"Tell me something." Vivian's voice cracked ominously. To hide her nervousness, she shielded her eyes and squinted across the lake. She had lost her nerve. Maybe later, she decided. "Where'd you learn canoeing?" she asked.

"Summer camp," Carol said. "You've really never been in a canoe? Didn't you study boating in Phys Ed school?"

"It wasn't Phys Ed school. It was Hunter College. I specialized in indoor sports." Vivian glanced over her shoulder to give Carol that significant look.

"Anybody can handle a canoe. Even a moron."

"I guess I'm worse than a moron then."

"You just never had a chance. You want to try now?"

"No!" Vivian gripped the sides, making the canoe rock dangerously. She was still not convinced it wouldn't tip over. "Careful, will you?"

"Don't worry. Didn't you go to summer camp?"

"No, I didn't go to summer camp. And I wasn't a Girl Scout either. My mother hated uniforms. Uniforms made her think of Nazis."

"Well, a camp full of girls in Girl Scout green is mighty sexy. Camp Natarswi. Up near Mount Greylock. Picture it: Tents. A bunch of girls out in the woods. It was great."

"What? The woods or the girls?"

"Both," Carol said.

"America," Vivian said. "Here we are in America. If a lake like this was anywhere near Manhattan, every inch of water would be filled."

"Every boat would have a dozen people in it. And every person would have a boom box blaring," Carol added.

"And every inch of that white sandy beach would be swarming with people and their screaming kids."

"Let's go over there, want to?" Carol pointed with the paddle.

"It's pretty shallow," Carol said as they neared the beach. She pushed the paddle into the sandy bottom until the canoe bottom scraped the sand. She stowed the paddle, rolled up her pant legs, and jumped out to steady the boat for Vivian.

"This is incredible," Vivian said. "I've never seen anything like it. Just us and Mother Nature. You ever swim nude?"

"A few times." Carol shrugged. She was not about to do it now. "What about you?" she asked.

"No. Never. Well, this is my big chance. Last one in's a dot dot dot." Vivian unzipped her jeans and slid them down. For some reason she was sure this was what Carol wanted her to do. Shivering a little, she feigned bravado as she yanked her tank top off. She never wore a bra, so only her underpants were left. "Aren't you gonna come in?" Vivian thrust her hips suggestively.

Carol had such mixed feelings about Vivian. It's so easy to touch her, she thought, placing her fingertips on Vivian's dark nipples. But I don't really want to.

Sometimes when they were wrapped in each other's arms, Carol felt as if she were grasping handfuls of air. Other times, she was hyperaware of Vivian's taut skin, the muscles of her neck hard as green apples. She still yearned for Annie. Still longed for her plumpness, the folds of her silky skin. I will miss Annie forever, Carol thought, picturing Annie waving from a boat across the lake, calling good-bye as she disappeared into the shadows.

Kissing Vivian felt as fake as it had at summer camp when Mary Lou Ritter crawled into her bunk and pretended she was Carol's husband, brushing her cold lips over Carol's face until they giggled so much they had to stop. It felt that way now, as if they were playing at making love, just going through the motions.

* * *

Slim was on a log, hidden in the shadows, his mouth hanging open in alarm. First, he had watched Janesta strip naked. Now, he was watching two women kiss. The one who was nearly naked was reaching up under the other one's shirt. Slim was so embarrassed he closed his eyes. When he looked back, the dark-haired one was tossing her underpants into the air. She threw up her arms, twirling on the sand, thrusting her hips, teasing the other one who laughed but backed away from her proffered hand. Slim was witnessing this when a fish yanked on his line with so much force he had to jump up and grab the pole before it was pulled into the lake. The fish was smacking the water with its tail. Vivian was so startled when she saw Slim fighting to land his fish that she ran up the path into the woods, away from the lake, away from the canoe, still naked, her bare feet stumbling over the path.

Slim reeled the fish in but let it go. He just wanted to get out of there. How long would she be able to stay in the woods naked, the bugs feasting on her? He hurried across the beach past Carol who was calling Vivian's name. They both shrugged awkwardly.

"Sorry," Slim muttered, continuing up the path. Then there was Vivian, limping as if every step she took was like walking on hot coals.

"Fuck. Fuck. Fuck," Vivian was saying. "Double fuck," she said when she saw Slim. She crossed her arms over her chest and crashed through the underbrush like a frightened deer.

"I'm sorry," Slim called, as he passed the place where she was hiding. "I really am. I'm sorry."

9

The first thing Raymond did every morning after Hydie unlocked the door and flicked on the lights was lift the red broom from its hook and sweep, checking carefully for any dirt he might have missed when he swept and mopped before closing up the day before. Afterwards, he washed his hands the way Trudy taught him, counting to twenty. Then Trudy brought him breakfast. The rest of the day, he sat in back waiting for his mother to ask for his help, waiting for his dinner, waiting for Hydie to announce, "Closing time." Then Raymond flipped over the sign on the door and swept again.

Today, Hydie's cousin, Levon, was at the counter in mud-stained jeans, his blue John Deere cap pulled low. Perched on a stool with his legs tucked under the counter, his knees jutted like a shorebird's. The counter was so low it seemed balanced on his knees. His rubber boots were caked with mud from the flats where earlier, when the sun was just a rosy streak, Levon dug the bloodworms he sold for bait. Now he stared into his black coffee as if to study his reflection.

"That'd be Coalie Brindle," Levon said, finishing his coffee. Trudy glided over to pour him a refill. When she moved across the diner, her large breasts led the way like the headlights of a semi heading through the narrow streets of a town. Coalie's hands trembled so much he slopped coffee down the front of his shirt.

"Criminy, Coalie," Hydie said. "Can't you have one dry day? Or at least stock up?" Hydie shook his head helplessly. Coalie would drink all the bottles of vanilla extract Moody's had if he wasn't in the mood to drive over the bridge. "That stuff'll kill you," Hydie added.

He sat with his back to the door and tried to guess who walked in. If he got three out of four, he could have coffee on the house. If not, he paid double. "Two more and you owe me," Levon said.

"Here's Etta," Levon said. A tiny woman with her back humped high like a quarterback came in, her heels tapping the linoleum.

"You still on decaf, dear heart?" Trudy called.

"One to go, Hydie," Levon said when the door tinkled again. "Rip Lawton," he announced, full of confidence.

"Nope," Hydie said, flipping pancakes.

"Buster's been and gone. That guy, the mason. What's his name?"

"You'll never guess," Hydie said. "Ain't nobody you'd know."

Levon glanced at the women sliding into a booth by the window. The women that came to Hydie's were usually on their way home from the night shift, on their way to town to cash Social Security checks, or else had a bunch of snotty-nosed brats that got slapped when they spilled their drinks. These two weren't like any women Levon had ever seen.

"That *one's* got a crew cut," Levon whispered, whistling softly. "Here's Rip now," he guessed when the door opened again.

"Too late," Hydie said. "You done guessed too many wrong already."

"That was before this joint turned into a tourist trap." Levon stood up, careful to bend over as he fished for change. Above him, a ceiling fan wobbled like a boomerang about to lurch across the room.

"What is this? The Diane Arbus Diner?" Carol whispered, leaning across the low table. She had to press her feet firmly on the floor to keep from sliding off the narrow bench. The table practically rested on her lap like she was seated at a child's table. "I feel like a giant," she said, hunching over to lean on her elbows for effect.

Vivian was studying the menu. "Don't get your hopes up," she said.

Carol stared at the paintings on the wall. One was of a huge safety pin that filled the canvas. The pin was bright orange on a blue and green striped background. Another was of a corkscrew painted diagonally across a green lawn. The third, Carol was unable to decipher.

"Somebody's deranged idea of art," she said, pointing them out to Vivian who made no comment. She was still mad about the scratches on her legs, about the bug bites she got on her bottom while thrashing around naked in the woods. She acted like it was Carol's fault.

"Coffee, sir?" Trudy said, raising her pot of coffee. She was startled when Vivian said yes. She had been sure she was a man. She laughed as if to hide her mistake.

"It's the boss," Hydie yelled. A short man in a plaid shirt slapped his newspaper on the counter. "Say, Clarence. How ya doin'?"

"My wife's doing poorly," Clarence said.

"Her legs, is it?"

"Yeah. They've got her on crutches. Phlebitis."

"Ain't that what Nixon had?"

"Yeah." Clarence patted his hairpiece. He was in no mood for Tricky Dick jokes. Just because he was involved in politics didn't mean he was crooked. He worked hard to run this town.

"You fellas plan on fixin' them potholes out front?" Hydie asked.

"I'm just a garden variety selectman. I'm not the governor."

"Well, put in a word for me when you're in Augusta, will ya?" Hydie pulled the next order from the clip and studied it, frowning.

"Don't look now, but here comes the *real* giant," Carol whispered. When Vivian turned to see the man coming through the door, she choked on her coffee. She hoped he wouldn't recognize her with her clothes on.

"Slim, my boy. Here's Slim," Hydie announced as if he were introducing a guest on a talk show. Slim slid onto a stool.

"You got any diet fries?" Slim asked Trudy. His pale face blushed scarlet when he saw Vivian and Carol.

"Diet fries?" Trudy laughed. "Now lemme see. I think we're havin' a special on them. Can I get you a small order?"

"Make that a double."

"Double order of diet fries," she hollered at Hydie.

"You're a card, Slim. You know that?" Hydie shook his spatula.

When Slim looked over at Carol and Vivian, his pale face flushed red again. They exchanged nods as if by rote.

"How's work, Linda?" Slim asked a woman who got up to leave. Carol saw a flicker of loneliness in Slim's milky blue eyes. Just a flicker, like a figure glimpsed in a lighted window seconds before the curtain is drawn. Then nothing. Pale blue. Ordinary blue.

"I got drafted for overtime. Mandatory two more hours. It don't matter if you're tired, you can't say no. But I'm glad to make a buck."

Vivian had warned Carol that half the women in Maine wore flannel shirts and looked like lesbians, but Carol was sure this one had to be.

"Zap!" she said. But Vivian just scowled and shook her head.

"I got to get home and take off my steel toes. If I make good time, I'll get a load of wash done before Paul gets up. You know the secret to a happy marriage, don't 'cha Slim?" Linda asked.

"Can't say as I do. I'm a eligible bachelor." Slim had been making jokes about himself for so long he had never really considered what he said. But today, thinking of Janesta, he imagined kneeling at Linda's feet begging: Please. I don't know the secret. Tell me.

"The secret is he gets the bed to hisself all night and I get it all day. So long, everybody."

"You workin' today, Alton?" Hydie asked the man in overalls who waited at the cash register.

"I'm workin' if somebody tells me to."

"Go to work," Slim said.

"See," Alton said, "I got to wait for the bank to open. Gotta borrow me enough to buy me a pocketbook to hold my wages. Clarence, you government fellas got all the dough. Whyn't you lend me money for a pocketbook? Don't charge me none of that interest, neither."

"Next thing, you'll accuse me of taking a bribe," Clarence said.

"He's some kind of politician," Carol explained to Vivian. "Did you notice the rug on his head?"

Vivian glanced at Clarence, then back at Carol. She couldn't believe how close she'd come to asking Carol to move in with her when they got back to the city. Now she would never have the nerve.

"Everybody in this stupid place has a weird hairdo," she said. "How much hair spray do you suppose the waitress uses? Enough to rip a few holes in the ozone layer?"

Carol was on her second cup of coffee when a man came in with a little girl who was completely made up. Blue eye shadow. Dark circles of rouge. Pink glittering lips. Her hair was heaped in a mass of stiff blonde curls. She carried a box of crayons and marched over to the table beside Slim and proceeded to color the place mat.

"Green is the best color. Palmolive Liquid's green. It keeps your hands looking young." She held her hand up for an imaginary camera.

"Say, Mike. Who's that lovely lady you got with you?" Hydie called.

"You know me. I'm Aran." She smiled, showing her dimples.

"I got that foundation poured," Michael told Slim.

"That's a start." Slim was more interested in Aran than talking cement. She drew a large *A* then a backwards *R*.

"The *A*'s a man with two legs," she told Slim.

"Where's his arms?"

"He's like this." She stood up with her arms at her sides. "See?"

"Where's his eyes and nose? Where's his mouth?" Slim asked.

"It's the back of his head, silly. He's walking away."

"Ain't she smart as a whip?" Trudy set a box of Kix on the table.

"It's an eggbeater," Carol whispered loudly to Vivian.

"What?"

"That painting by the door. It's an egg beater. On a checkerboard."

"America," Vivian muttered. "God help me. I'm in America."

Carol had often wondered how it felt to have a nervous breakdown. She imagined it involved tears and muttering about Jesus. Maybe it feels like this, she realized, laughing.

"What's so funny?" Vivian asked, wide-eyed with alarm.

Carol laughed and laughed, her eyes filling with tears. She couldn't stop when Vivian kicked her under the table and threatened to leave. Finally, she dabbed her wet cheeks with her napkin. When she looked up, there was Raymond watching her, grinning broadly, not at all self-conscious. His face glowed with pleasure and curiosity, with the interest only the most simple-minded were unafraid to show.

He looks happier than I will ever be, thought Carol.

* * *

"You sure he *gave* it to you?" Rita asked. "Slim gave you a camera?" She was washing the dishes, her hands wrist deep in the soapy water. Rainey aimed the camera at the soap bubbles.

"Uh-huh." Rainey nodded, then holding very still the way Slim had instructed, she pressed the shutter and slowly advanced the film.

"What happened, exactly?"

"He said, 'You want this?' And then he showed me how. I get to take pictures of whatever I want. Slim said. You send away and they come in the mailbox. He said bring it over when it's all done. He's gonna send away for me. He promised."

"What did you say?"

"I said OK. I can, right?"

"It costs a lot of money, that camera. The film, too. And having it developed. Maybe he just means you can borrow it."

"No, Mom. He said it was mine. He said he found it in the trash good as new. He has one already."

"Oh. Did you say thank you?"

"I dunno." All Rainey remembered was how Slim told her she should check all around the edges to be positive everything she wanted to take a picture of was there. In the frame, he called it.

"Well. I'm gonna talk to him. We'll see what he says. Don't use it anymore till I talk to him, OK?"

"*Mommy*," Rainey said, exasperated.

"I'll go over there after I'm done with these dishes," she said, scouring the cast-iron pan thick with the leavings of the scrambled eggs they had for dinner. The hens had been laying so much there were more eggs than they knew what to do with. In a bucket by the door were three dozen more from this morning. She'd hung a sign by the mailbox, but so far no one had come to buy them.

"I have to wash the eggs first, then I'll go. *We'll* go," Rita said.

Out the window she could see Nelly sitting on a rock pile in the pasture, still as a statue, a heap of laundry at her feet. What was she doing with laundry out in the pasture?

Rita stared and stared before she realized what it was. The ewe. Something was wrong with the ewe. All day yesterday, she'd been bleating pitifully, but neither of them knew what was wrong.

The pamphlets they had consulted focused on the various breeds and admonished them to be prepared before they got their sheep. "Sheep need a clean dry shelter," one pamphlet began and outlined the number of square feet each sheep required. Another stressed diet, insisting on the best forage with supplements for winter. Frustrated, they had decided to wait and see; by nightfall, the ewe seemed normal again. She eagerly ate the grain Rita brought her. But now she was on the ground. Rita ran out to see what was wrong.

"What happened?" Rita asked. The ewe was lying on her side. Gasping, Rita noted with relief. Not dead, though her tongue was lolling out of her mouth as if she might be any minute. The ewe lifted her head, bleated mournfully, then dropped back to the ground. Her eyes, usually a bright coppery gold, barely glistened; a thick film settled over them.

"I dunno. I came out to see if they had water and she was just lying here, panting. I tried to get her to drink, but she won't." Nelly was wiping her hands down the front of her overalls as if they were covered with something sticky. The ram stood off to the side, at what seemed to be a polite distance. Flecks of green foam dotted his mouth.

"It's so hot and she's got all this wool on her. We're supposed to shear them in the spring that one book said."

"Well, we didn't," Nelly said. She had a faraway look in her eyes, as if she didn't even see Rita. "The ram's OK. He's just as wooly."

The ewe bleated again, pitifully, and this time she didn't stop. With each exhalation came a ragged bleat.

"She's so fat," Rita said. "Fatter than he is. Maybe she has worms. One thing I read said they get worms and that bloats them up."

"I dunno." Nelly kicked at the rocks. She'd like to kick the ewe. Kick her head like a rock until she stopped making that awful sound.

"I still think we should shear them."

"We don't have any shears. We have to go to Union City for that or mail order them. I just haven't had time." Nelly shook her head in disgust, stalking off without looking back. She's still angry about the cabbages, Rita thought. The week before, the sheep got loose and ate a row of cabbages. They'd started on the broccoli when Nelly caught them. She had to chase them all over to herd them back through the hole in the fence by herself because Rita and Rainey were having a walk when it happened. Rita had returned to find Nelly punching the ewe, screaming, "You're history, you fuckhead," even though she'd successfully herded her back to the pen. Despite this, Nelly had plans to bring home more sheep. "We need a manure factory," she explained. "That's what they do best. Eat and shit."

One book Rita had consulted explained that a shepherd required the right temperament. She was certain Nelly didn't have this. When Rita came back from the house with her sewing scissors, the ewe was docile, as if the bleating had exhausted her and she didn't protest when Rita began to cut the wool off in big tufts. It was thick, oily and matted. Her hands, slippery with lanolin, cramped around the scissors which grew dull and kept folding the wool instead of cutting it. Despite this, she hacked away at it, determined, sometimes getting a handful at a time.

"Can I take one more picture?" Rainey asked. She liked the look of the clumps of wool scattered like snow around the ewe's body. She liked the look of the bare places where the wool once was. "Please, Mommy. He said it was mine, I promise."

Rita didn't answer. She was gasping, her fingers aching where she clutched the scissor handles, her skin torn and stinging. "I've got to get this wool off, Rainey. It's too hot to have this thick coat on. Imagine if I made you wear your coat today."

The ewe looked stunned as Rita worked over her, taking off heavy hunks of wool tangled with burrs and old hay. She held the tip of the ewe's stubby tail away from her body, snipping where it was stained with droppings. That was when she saw the foamy blood under the ewe's tail. That was when she realized what was wrong.

*   *   *

Every evening when Michael came home from work, he cut a few more trees down, enlarging the clearing, getting ready for the backhoe to come. Lizzy would watch him push each tree over. She would listen for the warning crack before the tree fell with a thunk, and Michael reached down for the chain saw sputtering on the ground to cut one more.

Lizzy made supper and when Michael came in, he kissed her dutifully, lifted Aran high and made her scream with excitement, then sat in his chair, ready to eat. Afterwards, he spread newspaper on the table and sharpened his saw; the file made rasping sounds, and the smell of the oil filled the room, mixing with the leftover smells of supper.

Tonight when Lizzy cleaned up the dishes, she managed to spill lentil soup on the floor, smeared a thick gob of it across her shirt, and had even flipped some into her hair. She was so distracted. Her period was late, she was sure of it. She had checked her calendar again this afternoon. She felt a flutter of excitement, a buzz of hope. All the years with Denny when she had been determined to become pregnant, when she had planned so carefully to make it happen, her period had arrived every twenty-eight days. Almost to the hour, the red stain would appear and disappointment would wash over her. It had never been late. Except once. She could still feel her bare feet in the cold stirrups, the doctor's cold hands on her thighs.

But now? She scraped at the burnt saucepan. She had let the soup boil so hard the lentils were thick and black on the bottom. *Now?* Maybe after all these years she was finally being forgiven. Lizzy slid her hand up under her loose shirt and touched her belly to see if she noticed a new contour. She imagined her hands on a larger mound as the baby changed her shape. She felt a rush of gratitude for Michael; no latex barrier could deter *his* sperm. She felt certain it had been Denny's fault all along, not hers the way the specialists had claimed.

Aran lolled on the sofa, languidly eating the Hershey's Kisses Michael brought home for her, slowly pulling the silver paper off. She looks drugged, Lizzy thought, wanting to fling the candy out the door. She felt so confused about Aran. When they were alone together, Lizzy's love for her was like the brook gurgling behind the house, washing over everything in its path. When Michael was with them, she felt as stagnant as the swamp where the skunk cabbages grew. She wanted to do the right thing for Aran, but Michael was always getting in the way.

When Michael finished, he sat on the sofa and Aran wrapped one chubby arm around his neck to pull him down for what she called a butterfly kiss. She blinked her eyelashes up and down his cheeks. Whenever the three of them were together, Lizzy felt like the chaperone.

If by some miracle I am pregnant, Lizzy decided. I'll leave Michael so fast. She didn't plan to wait around to see if the news brought pleasure or dismay. She would steal off into the night with her secret, her treasure, her blessing.

*   *   *

"So when you gonna give me the fifty-cent tour?" Janesta asked. She reached for a piece of bread to sop up the tomato sauce on her plate. She had just finished her second helping of eggplant Parmesan, but Slim could only pick at his food. He had absolutely no appetite. Crystal, whose plate was strewn with slices of eggplant licked clean, was sitting in the easy chair watching TV with her bowl of mashed potatoes on her lap. She offered Bootie a taste, but the kitten twitched his tail and ran away.

"Pipe that down," Janesta said. "Hey. I'm talkin' to you!"

"What?"

"I said turn it down." Janesta examined the red polish on her fingernails. Then she tapped them on the countertop. She didn't say anything about Slim's mosaic. "Well?" She winked at Slim.

"There ain't much to see. You're already lookin' at half of it." Slim had never shown anyone where he lived before. There had just been Crystal coming to visit and she was content to sit at the counter with cookies and a Coke or to sprawl on the sofa in front of the TV flipping through Slim's comic books, cutting pictures from the stacks of magazines, though sometimes she came into his spare room to watch him work on his Dream Facility.

Janesta stood behind Slim's stool, her belly brushing his back. She shook a cigarette from the pack by her plate, her breast brushing his arm as she leaned to light it from the flame Slim held.

"You a fan of his?" Janesta asked, pointing her cigarette at the painting of Elvis on black velvet tacked on the living room wall.

"My mom gave it to me. Back when my dad died. He had it on the wall over their bed for years and my mom said she couldn't stand to look at it no more," Slim explained. He felt like the word *bed* was echoing around the trailer, bouncing off the thin walls.

Janesta traced Elvis's lips with her red fingernail. Her arm was so close to Slim's face he could feel the heat of her skin and see his breath fluttering the pale red hair on her forearms. He wanted to run his tongue from the crook of her elbow down to her wrist.

"You lead the way," she said. She started humming "Love Me Tender."

Slim felt icy cold, the way he did when during the night he kicked his blankets to the floor then woke up shivering. Janesta was so close he could easily put his arm around her. She would fit there, her head against his shoulder. Janesta didn't seem to notice the effect she was having on him. She held her cigarette to her lips and inhaled deeply, one eye shut. Slim tucked his hands under his armpits.

"Careful you don't blink," he said. "You'll miss half of it."

Janesta stepped across the living room to look at Slim's picture of the waterfall, the one Etta Markum threw out when it stopped working. There was a short in the wire Slim had fixed. He flicked the switch on the side of the frame and they watched the water flow over the rocks from the mill as the mill wheel turned.

"Ain't that something?" Janesta said. "What'll they think up next?"

She stood so close to Slim in the narrow hallway, her hips rubbed across the front of his pants. His penis felt like a horse at the gate, waiting for the gun to go off. She stepped into the bathroom and stood at the sink. Slim hoped he flushed. Living alone the way he did, he often forgot, and he was not one to waste water. But Janesta wasn't looking at the toilet. She was fluffing her hair, combing her fingers through it. She adjusted her shoulder pads then leaned close to the mirror to pluck a loose eyelash from below her eye. Her eyes were dark green rimmed with a thin edge of black. Like a cat's eyes, Slim realized. He looked at his sneakers, the laces undone and tucked into the tongue.

"Make a wish." Janesta held the eyelash on the tip of her finger. "Blow," she said. The curved reddish lash had a dot of black mascara on the tip. Slim stared at the swirl of her fingerprint, at the white scar that cut across the middle as if it had been sliced with a thin wire. He thought about how everyone, all over the world, had a fingerprint that was a little bit different, no two alike.

"You got a wish you want to come true?" Janesta pursed her lips.

The theme song for *Cheers* was playing loudly and Crystal was singing along. Slim blew the lash off Janesta's finger, wishing she would put her finger to his lips, wishing she would lean close to him the way she was leaning close to the mirror, applying fresh lipstick. He wanted her to lean toward him that way so he could reach behind her, press his palms on her back and pull her close till she kissed him. He was dizzy with longing, as if his heart were falling through his chest, bumping his ribs, like a rock thrown down a deep well. He pressed one hand on either side of the door frame to steady himself, intoxicated by the smell of her, so sweet and powdery. Talcum powder had glistened on his mother's arms after her bath when she came out wrapped in a towel. He used to pull his mother's warm clothes from the drier, fold her jeans and blouses, stack the silky underpants. Once, Slim had buried his face in the yellow nightgown she hung on the bathroom door and breathed in the scent still warm from her body.

"You holdin' me prisoner?" Janesta patted his cheek. As she brushed by Slim to squeeze out the door, his body jumped as if it had a mind of its own and would do whatever it wanted no matter how scared Slim might feel. Janesta smelled like flowers. Like toothpaste and the minty menthol of the Kools she smoked.

"What's in here?" She tapped the door of his spare room.

"That's, uh, that's my workroom. Just junk. Stuff I'm aimin' to fix." How could he explain his Dream Facility to Janesta? What if she laughed? Slim wondered if when she unbuttoned his shirt she would have to stand on tiptoe to reach the top button. Would she help him pull the sleeves down his arms? Would she unbuckle his belt? Would he be expected to take her blouse off, to unhitch her bra?

He had never taken his clothes off in front of another person, not since gym class and even then, self-conscious as he was, he showered in his underwear, not caring that the other boys taunted him and eventually ganged up to yank his shorts off yelling, "What you got to hide?"

Janesta went to Slim's room. There was his double bed, a chest of drawers, and a bedside table with a lamp and clock. His clean clothes folded into a plastic wash basket with broken handles.

The next day, when Janesta is in her house across the road and Slim is in his kitchen wondering what to do next, he will remember the feel of her bare hips, the smooth silky cushion of her belly, the big brown nipples she lowered to his face and the way Janesta laughed, but in a nice way. The sound of Crystal's TV show and Janesta's hot whisper as she said, "Don't worry. As long as the TV's on, we can take all night."

But now, as he watched her walk into his room for the first time, he was worrying about the magazine under his bed flipped open to a woman who was naked below a black garter belt, her pubic hair glistening.

"They don't give you a hell of a lot of room to play with in these tin houses, do they?" Janesta sat down on the bed and smoothed the blanket. Slim's hands were trembling so much he had to tuck them into his back pockets. He had a vision of Janesta lying across his bed in her black lace panties, her skin white as cream against his blue blanket.

"This sure is cozy." She patted the bed. Slim could kneel down right where he was standing and bury his face in her lap. But he didn't move.

The next night he will sleep alone, afraid to call her, watching her light go off then lying across his bed, the smell of her billowing up when he pulls back his sheets, and he will hold his penis the way she did, wishing she were on top of him the way she was the night before, her breasts soft against his chest as he pushed at the nylon covering her crotch, trying to push his way through the thin fabric as she groaned and gasped and clutched her thighs around his penis, rocking until he wept with longing, surprising them both with his loud sobs and the big wet tears all over his face, his whole body trembling until Janesta pulled down her underpants and helped him find his way.

Janesta had never been with a man who took his time, who waited long enough to let the longing build up in her the way Slim did. Plenty had turned to her after they got what they wanted and found ways to please her, but she'd never gone first. She figured it had to do with the fact that Slim had no idea what he was after. He reached out like a man trapped in a dark cave feeling his way along. There was no harm letting him think this was the way it was done. She moved up and down over him, squeezing her thighs until she was slippery and so hot she didn't know if she wanted him inside or out and when she came he held her so tightly she was ready to give him whatever he wanted.

But now she was sitting on the scratchy wool blanket, looking at him in the doorway, wondering when was the last time he had taken a bath.

"I got an idea," she said, slowly tapping her foot. "Let's have us a moonlight walk. Down to the lake. What d'you say?"

Slim was taken aback. "What about Crystal?" he finally blurted.

"Oh, I leave her home all the time. She don't care so long as she's got the TV. C'mon. What 'cha waitin' for?" She slapped his bottom like he was a child.

"You comin' in?" Janesta called and beckoned from the lake. She looks like a mermaid rising out of the water, Slim thought. Although the night was warm, his teeth chattered like castanets.

"Farm boys don't swim," he said.

"Riley boys ain't farmers no more. You can't fool me with that. C'mon. It's warm as a bath." She floated into the shadows. Slim couldn't see her at all but he could hear her splashing. He worried she would get a stomach cramp and he'd have to rescue her. That he would drown thrashing in after her.

"You ain't supposed to swim after you eat."

"That's an old wives' tale."

"There might could be somethin' to it."

"I'd like to wash my hair. And I need the soap, Slim. Who's gonna bring it to me?"

A bottle of shampoo, a bar of soap, and two big towels Janesta had stopped at her house for were piled on the sand at Slim's feet.

"I need your help," she said. "Don't you wanna help me?" She was up to her waist in the lake, the moonlight on her breasts. In the shallows, a loon called like a lunatic laughing.

"Folks drown in their bathtubs," Slim said, trying to keep his voice steady, but failing. He longed to rub suds over her. Would she let him wash her breasts? A wave of desire rushed over him so fast he felt the way he had the time he had been fixing a refrigerator and two wires that weren't supposed to touch did.

He took his shoes off, his socks, then pulled his T-shirt off. Was he supposed to go in with his pants on? Janesta had taken all her clothes off, like that woman he saw the other day. Maybe all women liked to do this. His mother never mentioned it. But she hated to swim, with or without a suit. Janesta had slipped her clothes off like it was nothing. Her back was very white in the moonlight. Her hips large and firm. Slim had never been naked in front of a woman. He wanted to tell her to close her eyes the way people do before they give each other a surprise. He almost ran through the woods till he was safe at home. But there he stood, his feet on the cool sand, the night breeze brushing his bare body, the water surprisingly warm. He feared his penis would swell and point, but it hung softly bumping his leg as he waded out to Janesta.

"You forgot the soap, Slim."

"Oh. I did, didn't I?" he said through his chattering teeth.

"Get under. If you're under, you won't be cold. Trust me." She put her hands on his shoulders and pulled him into the water. Then she walked up onto the beach, grabbed the shampoo and soap, bending over as if it were the most natural thing in the world to show Slim this part of herself with the full moon like a spotlight on her hips. When she returned, she sauntered slowly, swinging her hips, her shoulders back. Watching her, Slim thought of the girls who wanted to be Miss America, how they walked down the runway in their bathing suits, turning this way and that, acting like they didn't know that all the audience really wanted was for them to take their clothes off. No one really cared about the speeches they made or the songs they sang.

Now here I am with a naked woman, he thought, certain he had to be dreaming, afraid to move, afraid to break the spell.

"Lie back," Janesta murmured. "Lie back and I'll do you first."

And then, though he could hardly believe it, he did.

10

The sounds of the summer storm reverberated through the trailer, waking Slim at 3 A.M. He got up, ate a bowl of cereal, then crawled back into bed ready for sleep only to become acutely aware of the branches from the hemlock tree scratching the trailer. The smell of freshly cut grass and damp soil drifted through the screens and the rain dripped steadily from the gutters, a staccato beat as he pulled the thick tattered quilt up over his face, a quilt somebody's grandmother had pieced together from old wool coats and corduroy pants, embroidering the edges with colorful thread. But even curled up with the quilt over his head, he couldn't sleep. He couldn't turn off the pictures in his mind. Like watching the reruns of a favorite TV show, he saw Janesta, a mermaid rising from the lake. "Lie back," she said. "Lie back and I'll do you first."

Afterwards, they stood outside the trailer, Janesta leaning against him smoking a cigarette. She smelled like soap and clean hair and something else, a fruity scent, like a bowl of apples in the sun.

"Cleanliness is next to godliness," she teased, her hands moving over his body tenderly, her plump belly bumping him gently.

The pillow Slim balled under his cheek smelled like Janesta. He wanted her beside him. It would be so nice when Janesta moved in, sewing curtains, giving the place her woman's touch. He'd clear out the spare room. Make her a cutting table. Find just the right chair for her. He would do something with the junk he'd been hauling home, the TVs and all he had collected. He had already started on a project with the tires he'd saved and would make money off it soon. Money they could use to make a nice home. Slim flicked on the lamp and took out the booklet he'd sent away for that showed how to make things out of old tires: animal feeders, children's swings, planters. Tires were one thing he had plenty of, and the idea that he could put them to further use, rather than bury them, pleased him no end. They never stayed buried anyway. One good rain and they bobbed to the surface, the water trapped inside, a perfect breeding ground for mosquitoes.

He had already made planters and planted tomatoes in each one. The booklet claimed he would be the first in town to harvest tomatoes due to the fact that the black rubber would draw and hold heat. Tomatoes were heat-loving plants, the booklet said. Slim would come into the trailer with a bucket full of red ripe tomatoes. Janesta would be at the stove, an apron around her waist. She would call him Jimmy and exclaim over the luscious tomatoes. Crystal would be lounging on the sofa watching TV and she would bite into one and laugh when the juice dripped down her blouse. Slim and Janesta would can quart after quart of tomatoes, enough to make sauce all winter long.

Outside, the rain had stopped, but the trees still dripped. As he waited for daylight, Slim became more excited about his future, planning how he would get started on the addition. Not a mud-room like he planned at first, a place to leave boots and coveralls, to pile tire chains, stack cans of leftover paint, store old maga-zines and newspapers. No. He would build that later. First, he was going to build them a family room, put in wall-to-wall carpet. He could picture the three La-Z-Boys around the big color TV he would buy brand new, not a TV salvaged from the dump that gave all the TV stars green faces and purple lips like the one he had now. No more of that. He would order a new TV from Montgomery Ward.

The sun was rising over the misty field, streaking the pale sky pink, when Slim got out of bed feeling energized, thinking how the love of his life was waiting for him across the road. Bootie ran to the kitchen and leapt to the counter where he licked a pool of spilled milk then dove headfirst into the trash. When Slim pulled him out and dropped him to the floor, Bootie raced across the room hunched like a Halloween cat then scurried back and tackled Slim's ankles. The older cats were already outside prowling after the rab-bits that came down from the woods to nibble what they could find at the edge of the yard. When Slim scooped the kitten up, he could feel his heart hammering. Then he began to purr loudly. Holding Bootie like this, feeling tender toward the small animal, he went out to check his tomato plants.

The last time he checked, they had doubled in size. He was keep-ing a chart of their growth, comparing them with one tomato he planted outside of a tire. He was certain they would have grown overnight with the rain, but when he bent over the first plant, his yardstick ready, he discovered something had snapped it away from the root. He hurried to inspect the others and found the same thing. Every single tomato plant was dead, the furry leaves shriveled and pale, withered on the damp dirt he had patted carefully around them. There were no tracks, no paw prints, no hoof marks, not even the silvery trail of a slug. It was as if someone had cut them with scis-sors. Snip. Snip. snip.

* * *

"Well, well. Look who's here. Bright and early. Slim Riley," Rip said. He stuffed a plug of tobacco into his lower lip. Waves of heat shimmered from the wet tar. "What's doin' up in your neck of the woods?"

"Oh. Same old, same old," Slim said. Did the fellows really have no idea he was different? Couldn't they read it on his face, sense it in the way he moved? I'm in love! he nearly shouted. "Sure is some hot out, ain't it?" he said instead.

The tide was out and the air was thick with the fishy smell of the clamflats behind the store. Two seagulls were fighting over a donut in the parking lot, flapping their long wings and running forward to grab it away from each other, their beaks open wide. Slim inspected the flats of tomatoes spread out on wooden pallets. Most of them were spindly; some had blossoms. He wanted healthy ones he could count on to make it.

"You stayin' out of trouble up on that hill?" asked Coalie.

"Not if I can help it." Slim put a flat of tomatoes in his car and went back for more. Better too many than not enough, he decided.

"Say, didn't you lug off some flats already?" Buster said, dunking a donut in his coffee.

"I did. And this mornin' all of 'em was dead. Just layin' in the dirt like chickens with their necks wrung. I don't know what'd do that. Wudn't tracks or nothin'. Don't imagine a coon'd do it. And no deer'd come that close. Besides. Like I said, there wudn't tracks. No sign of nothin'. They're right in front in these tires I filled up with good dirt and hen dressing. Got this book says my tomatoes'll ripen first planted thisaway. I'd sure like to know what done that. Don't even eat 'em. Just snaps 'em off like for spite." Slim wiped his brow with the back of his hand as if the speech he'd just made exhausted him.

"You better load your shotgun and sit up tonight," Rip said.

"I just might do that."

"Hell, Slim. The fella's pullin' your leg," Coalie said. "Sounds like you got cutworms. You got to put collars around them."

"Collars? They ain't dogs, they're tomatoes."

"Go on now, dogs my ass." Coalie laughed. "Collars. Works every time. You take you a piece of cardboard. A matchbook'll do. Wrap it around the stem. Mark my words. You dig around in the dirt and you'll find you a cutworm curled up like a satisfied pecker."

"Like whose pecker? Yours maybe," Buster said, stretching his suspenders away from his shoulders. "A little white worm of a thing. It's the little guys that got the little dingdongs."

"Hell, Buster," Coalie said. "Everybody knows it's us little fellas that got three legs to walk on once we get goin'."

"Shit," Rip said. " 'Fore you know it you'll be havin' a pissin' contest out back like a couple a schoolboys."

Slim smiled halfheartedly. He was not really paying attention. Whenever the subject turned sexual, he took this stance, but inwardly he was cringing. He was the kind of person who turned away from potato bugs riding each other piggyback. Who was embarrassed to find two butterflies end to end. To distract himself, he thought of how he would feel when he drove up with Janesta and Crystal. The fellows would tip their hats at Janesta. Offer Crystal nickels. A family man, they'd call him.

"I said, how's that cat in heat across the road treatin' you?" Buster gulped the last of his coffee and crushed the cup in his fat fist.

"Come again?"

"The Curtis woman. She come for you yet, boy?"

Slim shrugged. How could he explain what had happened to him? They would never understand. All he wanted to do was pay for his plants. He'd tell Binky to add a flat of petunias and get busy making another planter by the mailbox for flowers. He wondered what color Janesta liked. Pink. Purple. Red. He'd get some of each.

When Slim came out of the store, Rip was complaining about the kids that put a firecracker in his mailbox the night before. "Busted the sides right out," he said.

"You better watch out for that firecracker you got across from you, Slim," Coalie said. "Never can tell what she'll light under you."

*   *   *

"I've never looked at what I threw away so many times," Carol said, a banana peel dangling from her hand. "It's coming back to haunt us."

The yard was soggy beneath her flip-flops as she picked up chicken bones and wads of paper towels. Soggy newspaper and coffee filters. Dark crumbly coffee grounds spilled over the potato peels. Strands of bloated spaghetti looked like the worms that were drowning in the puddles. A heel of bread like an old wet sponge was buried in the weeds

Vivian was at the screen door watching Carol. She couldn't believe Carol would rather be outside cleaning up the garbage than in bed with her.

"What kind of animal did this?" Carol asked. "I don't think it ate anything. Just made a mess."

Everything they had thrown out was still intact, just spread all over the yard instead of in the garbage bag. This animal, a raccoon maybe, would write a request if it could: "Next time throw out a few sandwiches. Some Oreos. Leave a little milk in the carton, why don't you?"

Neither of them had ever given much thought to their garbage except during a sanitation strike. Vivian never considered where it went after it was thrown in the truck. She had never taken the ferry to Staten Island or seen the Fresh Kills landfill rising like a mountain along the coast. And Carol lived in a building where she dropped her trash down a chute. It fell twelve floors to the basement where the janitor crushed it in a compactor. If she never got up early, she never saw the large black bags lined up on the curb.

"We can take it to the dump one of these days," Carol said when she came inside to wash her hands. "I put it in the trunk."

"You put garbage in the trunk of my car?"

"No. I put it in the front seat. *Your* seat."

"You don't have to get all snitty about it."

"Look who's talking."

Vivian threw her arms awkwardly around Carol. "Truce," she said. "You want to go down there now?"

"We can't," Carol said, pulling out of her embrace. "It's closed. Last time we drove by, I checked the hours. As long as it's in the trunk, nobody can get at it. I didn't exactly enjoy picking it up, OK?"

"You're the one that's all gung ho on country living," Vivian said, returning to the daybed and the paperback she'd been reading.

"When I live in the country the first thing I'll do is get an animal-proof garbage can, OK?"

Vivian turned another page. She didn't even glance up when Carol announced she was going for a walk. She pretended she didn't even care about being left alone.

*   *   *

The road down from Nelly's farm was so steep in places Rita felt she was riding on the back of some large ancient animal about to blindly nose its way over a cliff. She drove with both hands on the steering wheel, perched on the edge of her seat so she could reach the pedals, craning her neck to see as far forward as possible, riding the brakes downhill though Nelly had cautioned her not to. "Just tap the pedal," Nelly had instructed when she was teaching Rita to drive the truck. "Downshift and tap the brakes. You don't want them to overheat and leave you with nothing."

The lacy pattern the sun made as it filtered through the leaves distorted her vision. She worried some animal would dart across her path. Before she could stop, there would be the *thunk* of a furred body hitting the tire. She saw animals sometimes in her drive along the road. Deer at dusk, twitching their white tails. A red fox with its bushy tail held high like a flag. Brown rabbits that crouched in the grass. Once, an owl swooped low as if to fly into her open window, then rose, its huge wings flapping effortlessly like shirtsleeves on a clothesline.

As Rita guided the truck around the curves, she worried she would meet an oncoming car, or worse another truck, and not be able to pull over in time—in places the road was not wide enough for both to pass. Or she would pull over but the tires of the truck would dip into the deep ruts on the shoulder and the truck would tip over on its side, then turn completely over with Rainey and her strapped in, hanging upside down.

Behind the wheel, gravel pinging the sides of the truck, thick clouds of dust rising like smoke behind her, her stomach seeming to fall out from under her, Rita felt the enormity of what it meant to drive. As the truck bucked and bounced over the frost heaves, she gripped the steering wheel, swerving to miss the worst potholes, all the while thinking she was literally taking her life into her own hands. "Don't think of it," Nelly had said. "Keep your mind on the road."

By the time she reached the foot of the hill where Preacher's Lake Road met the highway, Rita was covered with a thin web of dust. She lingered much longer than necessary to make her turn, waiting until her heart slowed, wiping her palms on her jeans, tucking loose hairs back into her ponytail.

"Here's the church, here's the steeple," Rainey said, her voice barely audible over the truck's roar as she folded her fingers the way her mother had taught her.

Moody's Store was on the highway with a strip of gravel for parking. Even though it meant taking extra space, Rita parked so she could pull out onto the highway when she left. She would rather walk home than back the truck onto Route One. She didn't crawl out the window the way Nelly did. It was too difficult, plus she hated people watching like it was a circus act. Instead, she scooted over to Rainey's side and helped her down from the cab of the truck. Besides, the men in front of Buster's Hardware were already staring. She was used to strangers watching. From the minute Rainey was born, Rita had felt it. The silence in the delivery room as the doctor pulled Rainey from between her legs. The nurse who took the baby away as if something were horribly wrong until Rita had wept to hold her. No one shouted, "It's a girl." No one smiled. The nurse turned her back, fussing with her tray, the soles of her shoes whispering shame shame shame as Rita counted the baby's perfectly formed fingers and toes and the doctor bent between her knees, stitching her up.

Rita grew used to the pursed lips of old Irish ladies on the trolley car, the way they had of looking from her to Rainey and back again without ever meeting Rita's gaze, though she would stare at them, daring them to face her. She grew used to the looks. But she would never get used to feeling as if her life were the property of strangers. Something for them to click their tongues over.

Following her daughter into the store, Rita pushed the familiar anger aside. The men who pulled their caps low over their eyes, who nudged each other with their elbows, were only curious. After all, Rainey was different. They weren't used to people of color. She didn't want to see a threat in the eyes that lingered longer than they should.

Rainey pointed to a box of Cocoa Puffs and looked hopefully at Rita.

"No," Rita said. "Get Cheerios."

Then Rita sent Rainey for a jar of mustard while she waited at the meat counter to get cheese. She couldn't decide if Ralph Moody was ignoring her, hoping she would get brand-name cheese from the dairy case, or if he was unaware that she waited. She glanced at her list again: milk, cheese, cereal, mustard. All they needed since they usually did a big shopping when Nelly drove them in to Union City. Though Rita had her license now, she still never drove over the bridge.

There was a bell on top of the meat case with a sign that said RING FOR SERVICE, but Rita was not about to ring this bell, not with Ralph Moody right there arranging the packages of bacon. She picked up a can of olives and read the label, her face growing hot, her head humming and buzzing the way it did when she tried not to feel anything.

"What'll it be, ma'am?" Ralph asked. Rita couldn't tell. Was he being overly polite? She had seen him joking with other people, but he'd probably known them his whole life.

As they waited to pay for their groceries, a woman in front of them, her bony shoulder blades pressing her thin cotton blouse, was holding a little girl who wore a white hat with red polka dots. The child's pale doughy skin was mottled with a bright red rash circling her mouth. A silvery snake of drool fell from her lower lip.

"Ain't she cute as the devil?" Mrs. Moody grabbed the little girl's foot and gave it a shake. "Bet she'd like a sucker."

The mother adjusted the child's hat.

"Here you go, sweetheart." Mrs. Moody held out a cherry lollipop.

Rainey wondered if she would be allowed to take the candy when it was offered to her.

"Say thank you," the mother said.

"Ta do," the little girl responded.

"She must be teething," Rita said, just wanting to make conversation. Both women acted as if she had not spoken a word.

"That'll be nine fifty-two," Mrs. Moody said, putting Rita's groceries into a bag. Rainey looked up at her, waiting to be offered a candy, mentally practicing saying thank you loud enough for the lady to hear. People were always telling her to speak up.

"Add this, too." Rita rarely bought candy for Rainey. She baked cookies with honey, offered prunes and fresh cherries when other mothers would dole out Twinkies. But now she grabbed a Tootsie Roll Pop.

"Don't open it till we get out in the truck," she told Rainey. "It's not safe to walk with a lollipop in your mouth."

Mrs. Moody didn't hold her hand out to take the money from Rita, and when she made change, counting out loud, the numbers fell like pebbles into a still pond as she snapped the coins onto the counter. Her voice hissed like a hot steam iron smoothing wrinkles from a cotton work shirt.

*   *   *

Slim bent his head to the towel Janesta held and let her dry his hair. Her fingers, strong and efficient, sent shivers down his spine. He put his arms around her soft waist and she let him hug her for a moment before she pulled away.

"Now," she said, draping the damp towel around his shoulders. She stood back, eyeing him with a professional stance, a pink comb in one hand, scissors in her other. "Let's do something about this hair."

Janesta circled Slim, her heels tapping the linoleum. She turned his head this way and that, cupping his chin in her palm. Then rising on tiptoe, her arms stretched overhead, she raked the comb across his scalp till it hit the first thick clump of matted hair. "It's gonna have to be short," she said. "I'll never get through this mess of knots."

She lit a cigarette, squinting at Slim, assessing him. His pale dreamy eyes behind the thick dark-framed glasses. His clean smooth cheeks. She noted the scrubbed quality of his neck and hands. He's been working at it, she thought. Good.

"I'm gonna have to get me a stepladder if you stay up on that stool." She slapped his arm playfully with her comb. "Here. Sit on this chair. You gotta be lower."

Slim did as he was told. When Janesta lifted his glasses off, he reached to unbutton her blouse, surprised by the agility of his fingers, how swiftly they moved.

"Not now." Janesta let him dip his hand inside, let him trace the lace edge of her bra. "Not *now*." She moved away, but not before she let him press his face to her breasts, his cheek cool on her warm skin.

The scissors made snipping sounds and clumps of hair fell, thick and white like Santa's beard, as she cut off the matted whorls, the hair falling about his face, down his chest, whispering onto the newspaper Janesta spread on the floor before she began.

"You have a nice chin," she said, tilting his head to one side, then the other. "It's been hidin' under all this hair. Your eyes, too." She snipped the hair in front, shielding his eyes with her hand. The hair fell in a flurry. Bits of hair sprinkled down his face like ashes clinging to his skin, making him feel like he might sneeze.

A smile hinted around the edges of her mouth as Janesta surveyed her work. She lit another cigarette and took up the comb once more, pulling it through Slim's hair, smoothing it over his scalp, playing with his hair, parting it on one side, down the middle, dipping the comb into a glass of water, the water dripping on his nose, down the back of his neck as she clipped and snipped, shaping his hair, pushing his head forward as she trimmed the edge at his neck, the scissors snipping around the curve of his ears. Slim shivered from the dampness on his newly exposed neck. He felt weightless, as if his hair had been heavy sandbags holding him down and at last he could fly.

Janesta reached around almost hugging Slim as she fluffed his short hair, combing her fingers through it, crimping it against her palms.

"It wants to curl," she said. Finished at last, she placed her hands on his shoulders. Then she tugged him out of the chair, led him to the bathroom where he glanced in the mirror, blushing and confused, startled by the feathery white curls, the wide expanse of his smooth forehead, the angle of his jaw. He splashed water over his face, flicking away the hair that dusted his skin.

"Well?" Janesta asked.

"Thanks," he said, reaching up to touch his hair gently, as if testing a cake to see how hot it was. He let her draw him into the other room where she slipped off her shoes with a sigh and fell back on the pillows, pulling him down to her.

"You're a pretty man, you know that?" she said, waiting for him to begin.

* * *

Nelly placed the lamb in the bottom of the hole she'd dug at the edge of the garden. When it was born, its legs were like jelly, it couldn't stand. Its head flopped like a broken puppet. It would not suckle. The ewe was dying, too. She wouldn't get up. She made a horrible sound. The fellow at the extension office said it wasn't right for a sheep to lamb at this time of year, so hot the way it was. He wanted to know why she'd bred them at the wrong time, but Nelly just hung up. The ewe had been pregnant when they got her.

She wanted to bury the lamb before Rita and Rainey saw it, its small belly like an overripe tomato, its eyes glazed like those of a dead fish. She scooped loose soil over the lamb. It seemed so small and frail with the dirt piling up on its wooly coat.

They had rolled heavy boulders onto Fiona's grave to keep her spirit down. But not heavy enough. Fiona would haunt her forever. Nelly had never told anyone how Fiona had begged to come to the States. She never told anyone how Fiona had stood in Nelly's dooryard weeping, pleading in her halting English, unable to accept Nelly was leaving.

"I loves you. I wifes to you," she said. "Wanna be wife with you." Tears streaming down her face, her shoulders shaking, her hands balled up over her eyes. Her dark hair falling forward, thick and glossy. "Why you no loves me? I makes you loves me. I do. I do." She unclenched her small fists, no longer crushed. Defiant. She stamped the packed earth.

"Shhh!" Nelly hissed. She didn't want to invite Fiona in, she didn't want to give Fiona an opportunity to throw her arms around her. But she didn't want Fiona to make a scene in her dooryard either. Even if no one appeared to be about, someone was always watching, listening. Secrets were impossible.

"I loves you," Fiona screamed and there were murmurs, like wind in the leaves as her words were translated and repeated.

"Come in!" Nelly grabbed Fiona's arm. "Sit down," she said, pointing at the chair. Nelly was dizzy with anxiety, nearly blinded by fear, the erratic rhythm of her heartbeat filling her. Fiona would not sit down.

"Sit down," Nelly said as if scolding a recalcitrant dog. During the first weeks in the classroom, teaching English when she was supposed to help them with farming, she would shout out commands: "Sit! Stand! Smile! Hop!" And then do the activity herself until eventually they would all be doing it, hopping around smiling, sitting, standing back up, practically doing the hokeypokey, laughing at the silly teacher, but humoring her. Fiona had understood best. She latched onto the idea of learning English as if she were drowning, believing it would save her.

"I must be go you." Fiona spit the words out angrily. "To State. I must be go. No leavey me. No *way* leavey me," she said, using the expression Nelly had taught them. "No way!" instead of a simple "no."

"It's not that easy," Nelly said. "Look. I'll write to you. I'll send you a T-shirt." T-shirts from the States were quite popular there. Nelly imagined herself selecting a Mickey Mouse shirt for Fiona.

"I no want!" Fiona shouted. "I no want T-shirt. Want you!"

She pulled her dress over her head in one fluid movement and flung it across the room. Underneath she was completely naked. Her brown skin tight over her sturdy ribs, her belly flat, her nipples like eager puppy noses. "I give this. This." She pointed at herself the way Nelly pointed in the classroom. "You give me T-shirt?"

In the corner, a huge black spider slowly wound her web around a green fly that still struggled. Nelly could taste Fiona's kisses, like fresh almonds, like ripe apricots, the texture of her skin. She could feel her thick hair, unbelievably silky. And she would reach down to find Fiona eager to spread her legs wider. Nelly never should have kissed her back that first time. She never should have kissed her that last night when they were supposed to be saying good-bye. She was going home. That was that. Leaving. Not because of Fiona. No, not because of Fiona. It was just time. Her decision was as resolute as a door bolted shut. A firm no to the life she barely allowed herself to have. Just a fluke, Fiona on top of her warm as fresh bread.

"Don't do this," Nelly said. Her hands were clenched on her hips. An aura around her palpable as a wall. "You deserve better."

"I tell you. You no listen me. My mother. My father. Aunt uncle cousin every family. They fix me marry. To Cho! What I do with Cho, huh? What I do?" She spit with disgust and marched outside, leaving her dress crumpled on the floor like the skin snakes shed.

The next morning Nelly woke to the sound of women screaming, ululating cries echoing through the thick trees, and by noon they had paraded Fiona around for everyone to see, carrying her on a litter made from a blanket and poles. Her tongue so swollen it wouldn't stay in her mouth. Her face distorted, bloated like a rotten fish, her huge head lolling on her dead neck. The skin of her lips blackened and thick and the empty can of pesticide beside her, parading her around for all to see, for all to have their pictures taken with her, grinning in their macabre ways, flinging Fiona's dead arms around their shoulders. They didn't mean to shame Nelly. But she too must look, must have her picture taken, must walk to the burial place, stopping to show Fiona to whomever they passed. Cho in front of her weeping, drunk, vomiting in the weeds. Fiona's mother stony-faced as if marching toward her execution. Her father so drunk he had to be carried by his brothers, hoisted on their shoulders as they plodded along.

* * *

Shotgun was barking furiously. The late afternoon sun streaked through the venetian blinds and fell across the bed where Janesta rested her head on Slim's chest, her hair tickling his chin.

"Shotgun, get down!" Crystal yelled and her mother stirred, sighed lazily, then tucked her head in the crook of Slim's arm and closed her eyes again. They both knew in a few minutes Crystal would be at Slim's door. Slim slipped out from under Janesta, tucking the sheet over her, and got dressed. By the time Crystal arrived he was in the kitchen with the oven turned on high, a cookie sheet of french fries ready to bake.

"Oh my God!" Crystal said when she saw Slim. She clapped her hands over her mouth and stared.

"Don't 'cha like it?" Slim touched the edges of his hair the way women on TV did, turning around to let Crystal see the back.

"God," she said. "You don't even look like you." She stared up at the ceiling, rocking from foot to foot. "Whew, God."

"Who do I look like then?"

"I dunno. Not you." She bit into a frozen french fry. "Mom here?"

"Yeah."

"You guys in bed?"

"Crystal! That's private."

"Can Shotgun come in?" she said. The dog was scratching at the door, whining loudly. Slim opened the door and Shotgun rushed in barking, wiggling his tail, lurching toward the cats where they hunched on the sofa, hissing. Shotgun didn't react to their hostile response. He barked and jumped up, resting his paws on Slim's chest.

"Got any biscuits?" Crystal waited for Slim to hand her the box from his cupboard. She took out a dog biscuit, examined it carefully, then threw it at Shotgun. He caught it with a snap of his jaw, crunching loudly. She repeated this gesture, studying the biscuit, turning it over in her hand, then tossing it to the dog. If Slim didn't distract her, he knew she'd feed the dog until the box was empty.

"Your fries are done," Slim said.

Crystal clicked on the TV and sat beside the cats, her feet propped on the coffee table, the plate of french fries on her lap. When Slim tipped back in his chair, he could see Janesta in bed. She was so still, he knew she must have fallen asleep.

"When we move over here, I gotta bring my VCR," Crystal said, clicking the channels. A litter of puppies ran down a flight of stairs. A baby laughed, ice cream dripping from his chin. When she got to the weather station, Crystal relaxed as she watched the map change color.

"What d'you mean, when you move in? You movin' in with me?"

"You'll be sorry," she said.

"I don't know what you're talkin' about, Crys."

"I gotta have the VCR. I gotta watch *The Wizard of Oz* every day."

"Crystal, whatever you want. Really, I promise. If you move in with me, I'd be thrilled to death. You know I would. I'll try to give you whatever you need."

She turned to Slim, her eyes steady, resting on his for a moment, before they darted from the ceiling to the TV to the floor and back. "I gotta watch it every day. I *got* to."

"That's all right by me, Crystal. That's surely all right by me."

"I was just watchin' it before. Them monkeys. Brother." She shivered. "They gimme the creeps bad."

"I don't remember any monkeys."

"Ugh. Don't make me tell it. They're gross."

"What d'you like so much about it then?"

Crystal shrugged and started flipping the stations again. Canned laughter and the wild music of commercials whizzed past before she paused at a scene of a sheep munching some hay, then flipped to *Bewitched*.

"I like when they get to Oz," she said. "And the Scarecrow. He's cool. And Toto. I wish Shotgun could be in a movie."

Slim tried to remember how the story went, but all he could recall was the Wicked Witch melting. In a little while he would make supper. He would open a can of salmon and mix it with cracker crumbs and egg, shaping the thick patties, frying them in butter. He would let Crystal fix instant potatoes the way she liked. He hoped the two of them would spend the night, Crystal tucked on the sofa bed with the dog flopped across her feet, and Janesta beside him all night long.

11

The backhoe crawled across the clearing like a giant insect attacking stump after stump. Lizzy watched Mr. Poors as he worked the levers, swinging the bucket into place, clamping the teeth onto the stumps. Despite the backhoe's clamor, when it wrenched them free she could hear a ripping sound, the slow tear of the roots, some of which were twined around boulders the backhoe wrestled loose and rolled to the edge of the clearing, nudging them like an elephant with a ball. By the time Mr. Poors drove away, the clearing looked ravaged. The woods reeked of diesel and stripped fir bark and wet earth.

At the edge of the driveway, Lizzy saw a stump the backhoe missed. A small birch tree, one she'd cut down herself. Instead of dying, the stump had sprouted leaves, bushy and thick. She knelt beside it, brushing the leaves with her palms. It's a sign, I'm sure of it, she thought as she drove to work with a small bottle of urine in a paper bag on the seat beside her. Finding that stump made her feel hopeful. Life's not so bad, she thought. Maybe by some miracle I'm really pregnant.

The last doctor she had gone to said the fact that she'd *ever* been pregnant at all was a miracle. The word *miracle* stirred her feelings of guilt. She had been so sure she was right then, certain it was the only choice, grateful it *was* a choice. But sometimes it seemed she had thrown away her only chance at a miracle.

Lizzy was eighteen years old and in her first year of nursing school when she discovered she was pregnant. She was at the top of her class, an honor student on scholarship. Having a baby would put an end to her dreams of success, not to mention what it would do to her parents.

All through Lizzy's growing up, her mother, a dietary aide, had returned home just in time to start supper after which her father, the school janitor, left for work where well into the night he hauled trash to the dumpsters and mopped the floors Lizzy would walk on the next day. Their daughter was going to be a professional, the first in the family to go beyond high school. And then she got pregnant, a secret she had never shared, not even with the boy she had finally given in to, only to get caught. That was how she thought of it, *caught.* As if she had been pilfering a cash register drawer and was on her way to jail.

For years afterwards, she took the pill, never missing one though it made her queasy and depressed. Later she tried an IUD but feared she would bleed to death so she was fitted for a diaphragm and used it religiously. When she was finally ready to have a child, she learned she was infertile, that all those years of protection had been in vain.

As soon as there was a lull in the clinic, Lizzy closed herself in the exam room and did a pregnancy test. She was afraid to watch, she wanted so badly for the bright pink positive sign to emerge. But it turned negative right away. It's still too early, she told herself, letting herself hope.

"Hey. What 'cha doing?" J.T. tapped at the door.

"Oh, nothing," Lizzy said, taking the folder J.T. held.

"This one's forty-six years old. She claims she's too old to need birth control. I read her the riot act," J.T. said.

*   *   *

Sitting on a lawn chair in the shade behind the shed, Slim read an article in the *National Enquirer* about a woman who found a severed head in a flowerpot. He hoped he never found anything like that in his dump. The worst was the dead animals in garbage bags. When he was a kid, they had a graveyard for pets and put up markers with the animal's name and the date it died. But people didn't seem to do this anymore. He had promised Crystal they'd do this when she worried about Shotgun dying some day. They had even selected a burial place.

Now that Janesta and Crystal had moved in, along with Shotgun, the trailer seemed smaller, though they had brought no furniture except for the VCR and TV. Just the fact that there were two more people living in the trailer made it feel so crowded it seemed it might be easier to walk across the room on the tabletops and chair cushions than go around them. Not that he was complaining. He enjoyed breakfast with Crystal, the time when he used to feel most alone. And he loved having Janesta beside him in bed.

Soft shimmering cloth brushed Slim's face when he reached into the closet crammed with Janesta's clothes; T-shirts with tiny mirrors embedded in embroidered circles sparkled when he took his socks from the drawer. Her high heels, all twenty-four pairs in a rainbow of colors, were lined up along the baseboard of his bedroom like targets at a shooting range.

Crystal slept on the pull-out bed. "For now," Slim said, worrying she should have privacy, but Crystal was happy to sleep in the middle of things, thrilled to have a double bed. Shotgun made a place for himself in front of the door and had to be coaxed out of the way anytime someone went in or out. The cats crouched on the chairs and countertop, their eyelids half closed, dozing, surprisingly unfazed by the large dog that groaned and flopped like a sack of bones, that whined when he wanted out, howled loud as a dog hit by a car when he wanted in, a dog that scratched and bit at his fleas until Janesta swatted him with her shoe.

Slim added the newspaper to his stacks and started to fuss with a mixer he'd found. His old one gave off a thick black plume of smoke before it shuddered to a stop in the middle of mixing an angel food cake. This one had a problem with the switch. As he searched for the right screwdriver, Slim thought of how amazing it was that two people fit into his life so easily. The idea of serving them warm cake filled him with such love he felt as if he would rise up over the dump like a helium balloon, grinning, foolish as a clown.

*　　*　　*

"Would you look at that?" Vivian said, scowling at Slim's shed. "The three little pigs wouldn't stand a chance in there." She popped open the trunk.

Carol studied the shed, trying to memorize it for a painting she would do. It looked as if a child had nailed it together, picking the boards randomly from a pile. The roof was a patchwork of gray, blue, black, and green. A sign that said PREACHER'S LAKE LANDFILL was made from broken bottles glued to the shed. The wooden door, like a calico cat, was a medley of leftover paint. A snow shovel and rake hung beside the door next to a barrel that held mop handles and golf clubs. Hubcaps glinted in the late afternoon sun beside a heap of tires. One side of the shed was covered with signs: NO PARKING,

DANGER EXPLOSIVES. The DEER CROSSING sign was pitted with bullet holes. The arrows of several NO PARKING HERE TO CORNER signs pointed at each other.

Everywhere they looked, there was a cat. A huge fluffy orange cat inside a dented drier with a missing door. Two gray kittens under a rusty lawnmower. A black cat with one white paw that made it look like it had just stepped in paint rubbed Carol's legs, meowing loudly. Two coon cats lounged on an old car. A black cat with one ear and a white cat with three legs growled and hissed over a pan of food.

"Forget the house. Look who lives in it!" Vivian whispered through her clenched teeth. "Our friend the voyeur giant."

"He looks like he's had a beauty makeover," Carol whispered back.

Slim could feel himself blush clear to the roots of his white curls. He had never shared a secret with strangers before, but that was what he had to do with these two. It was the kind of secret that you couldn't mention to the person you shared it with. It left him feeling like a bulging sack of garbage, ready to spill open.

"Hey!" He flipped his fingers in a wave. "Got some trash, do ya?"

"Yeah," Carol laughed. "A trunk load."

"You just throw it anywheres over that edge." He pointed to where he meant. "If you got anything worth savin', well, then leave it up by the shed here and I'll see to it. Recyclin' and like that."

"It's just garbage," Carol said. The idea of sorting through it gave her a sinking feeling, especially after they'd been keeping it in the trunk where it baked in the hot sun.

Slim leaned his elbow on the roof of the car. He wanted them to know their secret was safe with him, but he didn't know how to begin.

"Nice day," he started. "The sun finally decided to show its face, huh? I might go fishin' later on. They bite after a spell of rain."

As soon as he said it, he knew he shouldn't have. He could see the dark-haired one raising her arms over her head, her breasts flattened like two fried eggs. Not like Janesta's, he thought.

Carol was unruffled by the allusion to the lake. But then, she'd kept her clothes on. "What do you catch, anyhow?" she asked.

"Cold," Slim said. "But I don't get wet when it rains. I walk between the drops." He grinned until Carol laughed.

"You see anything you want, just help yourself," he said. "Maybe you can use a cat?"

"He's just some eccentric guy," Carol said as they drove away. "He probably doesn't even remember what he saw. Probably doesn't even recognize us. Did you see how thick his glasses were?"

"Did you see that demented smile? Like some jack-o'-lantern with all those missing teeth," Vivian said. "I don't know about you, but I've had enough of this place. I'm tired of roughing it. I'd like to have a hot shower, order Chinese takeout, and sleep in my own bed." Vivian glanced at Carol, then back at the road. We could be happy together, she thought, if Carol wasn't so flighty. It seemed the closer she tried to get to Carol, the more she pulled away.

"I'm just starting to like it," Carol said. "Anyway, I've been thinking. I might try to stay. You know. Spend the rest of the summer up here." She held her breath, waiting for Vivian's reaction.

"You're crazy." Vivian pounded the steering wheel with her fist. "New York in August is crazy."

"What would you do?"

"I dunno. Draw. Take naps."

"I mean, how would you get around? You can't exactly hail a cab. Where would you stay? The cabin's so primitive. That outhouse, God. And you'd be by yourself." What about me, she thought.

Carol was silent. Being by herself was what she wanted more than anything. She was certain if she were left alone out in the country, she would be able to figure out her life and get back to work again. But she had also been considering all the issues Vivian raised. Where there's a will, there's a way, Annie had often said. Carol tried to feel as certain as Annie, as if she believed with all her heart.

"Look," Carol said, pointing to some signs. One said EGGS in a child's scrawly print. Another, STRAWBERRIES. "Let's get some real food. You ever have fresh strawberries?"

Vivian rolled her eyes and Carol was afraid she might claim to be allergic, but she turned into the driveway and pulled up to the end.

*　　*　　*

Rita was in the strawberry field, squatting between the rows of lush green leaves, her nimble fingers plucking the ripe fruit, the tips of her fingers stained red and sticky as she deftly deposited the berries in the green quart baskets lined up on a plank at her feet. Bees buzzed lazily over the white flowers as she carefully parted the leaves. She barely touched the fruit and it fell from the stems. The earth was warm and still steaming from the heat of the day. The last rain made all the difference. What a relief it had been when the clouds rumbled overhead and lightning flashed. The rain had provided a rest from the relentless heat, a break from the work of the gardens, work that called to her like a demanding child who couldn't stand having her mother out of sight.

"Did it go up there?" Rainey asked, pointing at an airplane that droned above them like a large lazy fly.

"What?"

"The baby sheep. Is that where heaven's at?"

"I guess so, Rainey. That's what some people think."

"What's it like?"

"Heaven? Well, nobody really knows. Maybe it's like this. Like a beautiful garden where ripe berries are just waiting to be picked."

Rainey dug her bare toes into the dirt and sighed. Behind her, dozens of white moths fluttered above the broccoli in a delicate dance as they deposited eggs on the underside of the waxy leaves. Soon, there would be green worms that grew big and full of green juices as they ate the leaves, their dark green excrement littered on the broccoli heads. Rita planned to crush the eggs later, when she was done picking berries. And if no one bought the berries by tomorrow evening, she would make jam.

The sun pressed Rita's blue tank top against her back and she could smell her skin warming in the heat, could smell the sun on Rainey's hair as she worked beside her, cautious of the bees but willing to be careful in order to pick the berries she loved. "Two for the basket and one for me," Rita said. Rainey popped a berry into Rita's mouth. The fruit was warm and unbelievably sweet. "We're eating up the profits. Let's fill the baskets then graze till our bellies are full, OK?"

They both worked quickly to fill the baskets, then sat back in the dirt, eating. The crickets hummed in the tall grass at the edge of the garden and a robin sang in the apple tree. A car was making its slow grinding way up the steep hill. It paused, then turned into their driveway, the tires spitting gravel.

"Uh-oh," Rainey said.

Rita wiped her hands on her faded cutoffs. She didn't recognize the car or the woman driving it. The last strangers to pull up were two women who came out to the garden where Rita was weeding the string beans. Flies were stinging her ears and her fingers were crusted with dirt and itching from the spiny-haired leaves of the wild mustard she yanked up. Rita had said "no" politely, but the women were persistent, the heels of their shoes sinking into the soil, a fine damp sweat on the upper lip of the one who held the Bible with the gold-edged pages the way schoolgirls carried their books. The other woman clutched a magazine against her chest like a shield. "Why a Cat Has Nine Lives" it said across the cover. The words *sin* and *redemption* floated like dandelion seeds from their mouths as they peered at Rainey where she sat mashing buttercup petals onto her cheeks. What did these women want? A tearful confession? Instantaneous conversion? Rita just wanted them to go away before they said something to frighten Rainey, who was curious about God.

"We enjoyed these articles," the woman with the magazine said. "There's one about angels. Another about God's plan for us." Finally, as if by prior agreement, the women trudged back to the car where a towheaded boy waited, one sunburned arm dangling out the window as if he longed to touch something real but had been forbidden to open the door.

These two don't look like religious fanatics, Rita thought. She lifted the board she had set the berries on, balancing it on one hip, and headed toward the car where a tall woman with hair streaked with gray waved uncertainly.

You are the most beautiful woman I have ever seen, Carol thought. She wondered what the world would be like if you were allowed to say exactly what you thought whenever you wanted to. As Rita came down the path, the strap of her shirt slid down her tanned arm revealing her smooth bare shoulder. Behind her came a beautiful brown-skinned girl whose curly hair was scooped into an elastic on top of her head. She had her mother's delicate chin and curious green eyes.

"We saw the signs," Vivian said, all business, all New York.

"About the strawberries," Carol added. Her voice faltered, as if she were making a speech, hot lights aimed at her, hundreds of faces turned toward her. But there was only Rita, looking directly at Carol with curiosity. And behind her the beautiful child.

"Howdy do. I'm Lorraine Conway. But you can call me Rainey." Rainey clasped her hands over her belly; it was taut as a drum.

"Who taught you that?" Rita asked, looking at the child with surprise. Rainey hid her face against her mother. Then, somewhat nervously they all introduced themselves. Lovely Rita, Carol thought. And Sweet Lorraine.

"You grew these?" Vivian asked. "You know, like from seeds?"

Rita laughed and shook her head gently.

When you laugh you're even more beautiful, Carol decided.

When Vivian laughed, she sounded like she was choking on a chicken bone. But Rita tucked her chin and made a musical sound.

"Not exactly. We buy them as plants and then they multiply. From runners," Rita said. "I can show you if you like."

Carol was certainly not the first person to be struck by love at first sight. Songs have been written about it, wars fought over it, and many a broken heart and unexpected child the result of that instantaneous flash of love between strangers. But for Carol, seeing Rita carry the strawberries up the path, feeling the rush of love like butterflies trapped in her throat, was the first such experience she had ever known. She had loved Annie in the best way she could. But it had never felt like this.

Carol used to pride herself on being a cynic about love, arguing that it was all propaganda. "Het hype," she called it, claiming it was a system set up to keep people reproducing. Annie had given her a book about lesbians who married each other and hinted that she'd like them to exchange rings. "Why do lesbians have to model themselves after straight people?" Carol ranted. "Who do you know, gay or straight, that you could call happily married?"

Carol, as most of the unsuspecting souls who are shot down by the arrows of fated love, forgot all she had ever said about the subject in that moment she saw Rita. As she watched the coppery light shimmer in Rita's hair, she was acutely aware of a red-winged blackbird singing from the poplar trees. The sound flooded her with longing. All she wanted to do was kneel at Rita's feet and brush the silvery dust from her warm smooth flesh.

* * *

"OK. So strawberries grow from plants, big deal," Vivian said, starting the car and heading down the driveway.

"Zap!" Carol said, mimicking Vivian, pointing with two fingers back at the garden where Rita and Rainey worked. "Superzap!"

"No way."

"What d'you mean, 'no way'?"

"She's got that kid." Vivian paused at the end of the driveway.

"So? You've never heard of a lesbian mother? Join the twentieth century, Viv. It's a trend."

"I've seen plenty of lesbian mothers. But she's not."

"If *she's* not, *I'm* not," Carol said, hugging herself. She was afraid Vivian would be able to tell she had fallen in love, as if a brightly colored aura radiated around her.

"Hey, did you see that?" Carol pointed to the FOR RENT sign on a tree in front of Janesta's house. "That's the house where we went that day we were lost. Go back, OK? I wanna see."

"What? I suppose you're gonna rent it?" Vivian backed up, frowning, trying to humor Carol but wanting to scream. *What about me?*

Carol stepped onto the porch and pressed her face to the window. The front room was large with a wood floor and several tall windows. *My studio,* she planned. Vivian slid her sunglasses on, checking the effect in the rearview mirror as Carol prowled around the back.

"I dunno," Carol said when she returned. She was obviously excited and more certain than she was letting on. "It might be the right place for me. I feel like I could work here." She had already told Vivian that being able to work again was what she wanted most.

"You'll last a month, six weeks tops," Vivian said, sure of herself. *Then she'll come crying to me,* she thought.

"The sign says to ask at Hydie's."

"Hmm," Vivian responded, noncommittal. She pushed a cassette into the tape player and turned the volume up; Joan's voice filled the car.

"It's perfect!" Carol shouted, interrupting Vivian's moment. She hated having her moments interrupted. She snapped the tape out.

"If you ask me, it looks like it's about to slide right off the hill. If the porch doesn't fall off first," Vivian said.

"Oh, half the houses out here look like that. There's a big room I can use for my studio. Hydie's is already closed. But tomorrow, OK?"

As if in answer, Vivian jammed the tape in. The music blared as they entered the woods where dusk had already begun to fall.

* * *

"Holy shit!" Michael said. He clutched Aran as she screamed dramatically, tossing her head as if she were in a science-fiction thriller and the monsters had finally arrived. He was tipsy from the tequila he had at The Quarterdeck to celebrate having the stumps pulled. He closed his eyes and shook his head. But when he looked again, the snakelike shapes still glowed eerily in the clearing.

"It's like those necklaces at the circus," Lizzy murmured.

"Holy shit," Michael repeated and took a few steps backwards as Lizzy strode into the clearing and touched one of the shapes tentatively. It was cool and damp.

"It's a root," she called, twirling it like a sparkler. Aran ran up and grabbed it, flinging it into the air. The two of them scrambled across the rutted ground gathering the phosphorescent roots, tossing them like jugglers with flaming batons, spinning in circles. They held hands and kicked their feet in a cancan dance, waving the roots.

"Daddy, Daddy! We're dancing," Aran cried. She pulled his hand, eager for him to join them, but Michael didn't like to dance. He didn't like to pretend. He just wanted to stand still. The expanse of the clearing loomed: barren and stripped. Michael stood where he was, breathing the night air, awed by what the earth had hidden, and by the mysterious light his dreams had stirred.

12

"Papa-oo-mao-mao," Carol sang as she walked in the moonlight. The dew was like fine lace spread across the blueberry field. All around her insects were humming and scratching. Where do these songs come from anyhow? she wondered. Here I am. Out in the middle of nowhere with songs in my head like I'm some kind of AM radio. "Da-do-dip," she sang and danced a few steps, her sneakers slapping the packed dirt.

"I'm going out to get a moon tan," she told Vivian when she left. Every evening since she'd met Rita, she went down the hill to Rita's house wishing she had the nerve to sneak up and press her nose against the window. Though Vivian claimed there had to be a man in the picture, Carol had yet to see anyone else.

Vivian was back at the cabin with the door locked, refusing to come out at night, scared a deer would chase them and jab them with its antlers though Carol explained how impossible that was. "Well, a bear then," Vivian said and locked the door the minute Carol left as if she feared a bear would grab her in its large paws and toss her around like King Kong with Fay Wray. Carol gave up trying to persuade her to come out. Besides, her solitary walk gave her uninterrupted time to imagine seducing Rita. Carol would comb flecks of hay out of her hair, her fingers gently undoing the tangles. When they hugged, neither would be sure whose heart thumped the loudest.

Carol slapped a mosquito that settled behind her knee. She enjoyed the fantasy. It was a diversion, she knew. The idea of *really* having a relationship was frightening, especially with someone like Rita. She felt so drawn to her, as if they each had a magnet buried in their chests pulling them closer; when they touched, they might never separate. And Rita was so young. Then there was the child. Children made noise, they needed attention, and Carol needed to be alone. Besides, she thought, I'm not capable of having a *real* relationship. Doesn't being with Vivian prove that? A mosquito landed on her forehead and another tickled the back of her hand.

"The thing about a place like this," Vivian often complained, still hoping to talk Carol out of the idea of staying. "Is some insect is always feeding on you. We're their idea of fast food."

Carol stared at the house she wanted to rent. She still hadn't asked at Hydie's. Was she afraid she wouldn't be able to have it, or that she would? "What would you do, Annie?" She didn't even try not to talk to her anymore. "The dead live on, as long as we remember them," Iris always said.

Annie had a theory about life called Divine Appointments. Everything happened in order to bring you closer to a Divine Appointment, which as far as Carol could tell, was like coming to a crossroads in your life. In the church Annie attended when she was growing up, the purpose had involved the opportunity to save a sinner. But to Annie, it meant letting life happen to you, not planning every moment so carefully you were never open to chance. Carol wondered if Annie would approve of her coming to Maine, if she would say Carol was on the road to a Divine Appointment.

The house was bathed in the silvery moonlight. In the morning, the sunlight would stream through the tall windows as she worked. Across the road, Rita's house was dark, with moon shadows playing across the fields. An owl hooted, then an engine chugged up the hill. She leaned against one of the sugar maple trees alongside Rita's driveway so she wouldn't be caught in the headlights. A truck turned in, drew up close to the house, and stopped. Watching Rita carry Rainey into the house reminded Carol of how her father used to carry her to bed. Some nights she pretended to be asleep just to feel her cheek against his smooth shirt.

With an awful sinking sensation Carol saw someone—a woman, she was sure of it—hoisting her lanky body through the window of the truck. Carol was disappointed and confused but also somewhat relieved. The only reason to stay, her most practical voice instructed, is to work.

Carol was about to turn back when Rita returned, walking past the truck, down the driveway, whistling a soft trill. Carol knew she should hurry away. That she might startle Rita, lurking in the shadows the way she was like a peeping Tom. But instead she began walking nonchalantly in Rita's direction.

"Oh!" Rita said, as if she'd bumped right into her.

"Hi. Don't be scared. It's me, Carol. From the other day."

"I didn't expect to see anyone out here."

"I was just walking. The night's so pretty."

"It is, isn't it? Rainey's asleep so I figured I'd get some air. Sometimes the only way she falls asleep is if we take a drive."

"You mean she stays up all night?"

"Not that bad. But she'll just lie in the dark talking to herself till way past her bedtime. It drives Nelly up the wall."

Zap! Carol thought. I was right.

"Huh," Carol said. "I don't know about kids. Warm milk works."

"God. I've warmed gallons of milk. Lullabies. You name it. The kid just won't let go lately. She even walks in her sleep. The other night I found her under the table like she was in a cage."

"That must be nerve-wracking."

"Don't ever have a kid," Rita said, laughing and tossing her hair.

"I'm too old. But I never wanted to anyway. Why did you?"

Rita was silent.

"Oops. Sorry," Carol said. "I didn't mean to be so personal."

"No. That's OK. It just got me thinking. I'm so used to talking to myself in my head. There's nobody else to talk to."

Carol almost blurted, What about this Nelly person? But she held her tongue.

"I got pregnant," Rita said finally. "Elias." She paused, as if savoring his name. "Elias was somebody I hardly knew. He was nice enough. He was sweet, actually. Anyhow, he went back to his wife. He doesn't know about Rainey. See, now you know the story of my life. Aren't you sorry you asked?"

"No. Not at all. So then what happened?" Carol consciously slowed her steps so they wouldn't reach the end of the road too soon.

"I didn't try to get pregnant or anything. It was an accident. But I was so lonely when Elias left, I thought, now I'll have somebody to love who'll love me back. I had no idea how hard it was to be a mother."

"Accidents. Sometimes I wonder how many of us were accidents, don't you?" Carol laughed. "Maybe there wouldn't be a new generation otherwise. I really surprised my parents. My mom was going through menopause when I came along."

"So you're the baby?"

"I'm it. They thought they weren't gonna have any kids at all and then surprise, surprise. The worst part was it was a public admission that they still had sex. My father was a minister. He still is, it's just that he's really old now. They retired and moved to California. See. Now, I'm going on and on. I don't get to talk much either."

"What about—"

"Vivian?"

"Yeah. What about Vivian?"

"Vivian," Carol said, her tone implying that was all she had to say.

The two women were silent as they walked beside the blueberry field.

"It's a blue moon, you know," Rita said.

"What do you mean?"

"Well, every so often there are two full moons in a month. They call that a blue moon. I don't know why."

"Oh," Carol said, noticing the sheen of moonlight on Rita's hair. She shivered despite the warm night.

"Sometimes I'm out walking and I feel like I'm the last person left," Rita said. "I wonder what it'll be like out here in winter."

"Haven't you been here that long?"

"No. The two of us moved up here this spring."

"The two of you?"

"Yeah. Me and Rainey. Nelly was already here. It's Nelly's place. She said last year the power went out for days. Once it was out for a week. Sometimes the road's closed from all the snow. The plows're too busy on the highway to come up here. I'm scared I'll go nuts. Maybe I already am." She pulled a stalk of timothy and shredded the tip.

"What about Nelly?"

"Is she nuts, do you mean?"

"No." Carol laughed. "I mean, you'll be together, right?"

"Nelly." Rita mimicked the tone Carol used to explain Vivian.

"What would you do if you were?"

"Crazy?"

"No. The only one, I mean."

"After I went crazy from loneliness, I'd take off all my clothes and scavenge for berries. Sleep in a tree. I don't know."

"It'd be cold in the winter."

"That's true."

"Speaking of taking your clothes off, Vivian got caught skinny-dipping. By that giant. You know who I mean?"

"Slim? The guy who lives down there?" Rita pointed at the trailer where a light burned in one window. It seemed no one was home.

"Is that where he lives?"

"Yeah. That must've been funny!" Rita said.

"It was kind of funny to see ol' Viv crawling through the woods bare-assed. The worst part was Slim got so freaked out he ended up rushing right past where she was sneaking back to her clothes. 'I'm sorry. I'm sorry,' he goes. 'I didn't mean nothin' by it.' "

"I wouldn't worry about it. Slim gave me the creeps when I first met him. But he's got a heart of gold." She sighed and looked up at Carol. "I'm glad I ran into you," she said.

"You are?"

"Yeah. We don't get many new people out here to talk to, you know."

"Oh," Carol said. Could she be content just hearing Rita's melodious voice? The way it fell an octave in places where other voices rose was a beautiful sound.

"What do you do? I mean, you're from New York, right?" Rita asked.

"Yeah. Well, not originally. I'm from Massachusetts. But I've been living in New York over twenty years. I'm a waitress. When I'm not doing that, I'm an artist. I paint. But mostly I make stuff."

"Stuff?"

"Pieces. Things. Dioramas. I don't know how to talk about it." She stared across the field. "Once I made this kind of wasp's nest. It was for my first show. It was in the East Village, but it was a show. I chewed paper and then when it was all soggy, I molded it into this honeycomb shape and then made a whole bunch of them and stuck them all together. This woman actually bought it. *Spitball,* I called it. She paid five hundred dollars. That was my first sale."

"That's wonderful." Rita looked at Carol with admiration. "I can't imagine being an artist. The artists here mostly paint the same old fishing village and sunset on the shore. I used to live in Boston. I wanted to be a singer. Now, here I am. Ta da!"

They had come to the Y in the road that led down to the cabin. How could Carol just walk away from Rita, past the rushing brook, down through the arch of poplars and firs where bats swooped across the path?

"Well," Rita said. "You should come over sometime. Bring your . . ."

"Vivian and I are just friends. Don't tell her I said that. But I hardly know her. She wants to go back already. She says she's seen enough of America to last a lifetime. She's such a New Yorker she craves carbon monoxide."

"You're going back soon?"

"Actually, I keep thinking. I mean I know this is wild, but what if I stayed? What if I just tried to live without rushing around trying to be somebody in New York? I'm not rich or anything, but I got this grant. If I found something cheap enough . . ." her voice trailed off. "I need a car though. God. Do I talk too much? I talk too much, right? It's just that Vivian and I don't really talk and I miss my friend Dougie. He's a real sweetie. Oh, listen to me."

Rita was laughing and watching Carol with interest.

"Go ahead. Say it. 'You're a blabbermouth, Carol.' "

"No. Really. I like it. I mean, you're not a blabbermouth. You're saying a lot. Nelly hardly talks. 'What's for supper? Got to get oil for the tractor.' All day long I talk to Rainey and I love her, but she's a little girl. So it's good to hear someone say something besides 'why this, why that.' "

"Really?"

"Really."

"So. You say something. Your turn." Carol leaned forward.

"First, I want to say there's that house for rent, across from Slim's. It's a great house. I'd rent it if I could figure out how to make some money. There aren't exactly a lot of jobs here."

"Why would *you* rent it? I mean, aren't you guys together?"

"Oh, I don't know what we are. It's a long story. I'm not very smart, I guess. I made some unfortunate choices. Anyway, I needed help, Nelly offered, and now I'm trapped in this really big mess."

They were silent. Expectant. Rita was aware of a clenching in her belly, like a fist getting tighter. I won't cry, she told herself. I won't cry in front of the first person I talk to. I *won't.* She turned so her face was in the shadows.

Aware of the shift in Rita's mood, Carol crossed her arms around her waist, tucking her hands out of the way to keep from touching this small sturdy woman who stood with her shoulders squared, as if nothing could topple her. This woman who seemed to be crying, yet doing her best to hide it.

"A singer?" Carol said softly. "What do you sing?"

Rita laughed nervously. "You know Bonnie Raitt, right?"

What were you, two years old when she had her first hit? Carol started to say. "I have her latest tape," she said instead.

"You do?"

"Yeah. I love her." I love you too, she almost blurted.

"Someone once said I sang like her."

"Sing me a song now?"

Rita shook her head. She was wiping her cheeks with the backs of her hands. She took a deep breath and threw her head back. In a low deep voice she sang, "She-Rah! Queen of the Universe, She-Rah."

"Anybody ever tell you you were crazy?" Carol asked.

"Me? Me? You make five hundred dollars chewing a giant spitball and I'm the one that's crazy." She laughed.

"At least you're laughing again."

"Yeah."

"So."

"So. If you move here, I'll be your friend," Rita said.

"OK," Carol said. It was a sweet innocent offering, the kind schoolgirls made to each other. A new way to start, she thought. "But now I have to walk you home."

"But I just walked *you* home."

"Then that means I have to walk you home. It's only polite."

"OK. Halfway. But no further."

They headed down the road in the moonlight, their shadows behind them, their arms swinging in rhythm, their shoulders nearly touching.

* * *

They had planned to spend the night at Rest Assured, a motel outside of Bangor, but Crystal started worrying about Shotgun being home alone and Slim had never stayed in a motel, so they drove home even though it was late and everyone was tired. Janesta drove and Crystal leaned against Slim who slouched down, his head resting against the seat. The full moon was huge and almost red in the dark sky. For long stretches, their car was the only one on the road.

Janesta wore a wraparound dress she had bought on the spur of the moment at Alicia's Fashions, charging it, worried any minute sirens would go off and her card would be confiscated. The dress was cream-colored with large red cabbage roses, and she had on her white heels with the tiny gold zippers up the back. Slim dressed for the occasion in clean work pants and a sweatshirt he'd salvaged from the dump that had Smokey the Bear on the front. REMEMBER it said under Smokey's face. Crystal was wearing her favorite pink pants and a pink polo shirt. She shivered in the night air, but she didn't complain.

Janesta was wide awake, but Slim was sleepy and more than a little drunk. The food at Wok and Roll had been delicious, but the two mai tais had been two too many for him. Just as they rounded the curve, the car dipping over the steep hill, a deer loped across the road and Janesta swerved over the fog line to miss it.

"Don't hit it," Crystal yelled.

"It's gone already," Janesta said.

Crystal snuggled against Slim, sighed and pulled his arm around her. "You're like my daddy now, right?" she whispered.

Slim held his breath, waiting for Janesta to explain. But she said nothing. Her window was down and as the cool night air blew through her hair, her perfume filled the car.

"Gimme a cigarette, will ya?" She punched in the lighter.

Crystal fumbled through her purse till she found them. Slim patted Crystal. She seemed fragile as if the slightest touch could break her.

"If that's how you want it, Crys. I'd be proud to be your dad." He gazed at Janesta holding the lighter, the red coils sinister in the dark car. The car seemed as vast as the new parking garage at the airport. Janesta was on a different level. Slim wanted to reach around Crystal to stroke Janesta's arm, but she might as well have been miles away. The car sped uphill and just as they passed the road to Happytown, a doe and two fawns stepped into the road, mesmerized by the headlights.

"Jesus fuckin' Kee-*reist*," Janesta hollered, glancing quickly in the rearview mirror then pulling sharply off the road with a squeal. She turned off the engine. There was the sound of hot metal ticking and the hooves of the deer clicking across the road, disappearing into the night.

"That was a close one," Slim said. "You OK?"

"Yeah. I'm OK."

"Want me to drive?"

"You hate drivin' at night. You claim you can't see."

"Yeah, but you must be kinda tired. Ain't 'cha tired?" He waited. "We did have a big day." He chuckled nervously.

"I ain't lettin' no blind man drive me." The car rumbled to life. She signaled even though there were no other cars on the road. Slim realized she did that just to calm him down.

"We might could stay there." Slim pointed at a VACANCY sign next to a string of cabins trimmed with winking Christmas lights.

"We're almost home. I ain't stoppin' now."

Slim watched the insects fly into the headlights. He'd felt so proud to stand up with Janesta, to say, "I do" and slip the ring onto her finger. To walk down the steps into the bright sunlight with Crystal asking in her loud flat voice if this meant she was going to get some brothers and sisters. Feeling dizzy as the car rushed past the trees, Slim closed his eyes and pictured the trailer full of children, children lounging on the sofa and chairs, sprawled on the rug, perched on the counter, stuffed into the spare room, their faces pressed against the windows like fish in a crowded tank. A buck with antlers that made huge shadows in the headlights loped across the road, its legs tucked under him as if he were flying.

"Did ya see that?" Slim asked.

"What?" Janesta threw her cigarette butt out the window.

"That buck," Slim said. "It looked like it was flyin'."

"Like Rudolph and them," Crystal said and began to sing the song.

"Quit that," Janesta snapped. And just as abruptly as she started to sing, Crystal stopped.

"It's crazy drivin' at night," Slim said. "Anything can happen." He thought of all the dead animals the night produced. Possums squashed and bloody. Raccoons that appeared to be asleep where the impact had flung them. The stench of dead skunks. Once a bull moose the newspaper came out to photograph. The car that hit it had been totaled but no one was hurt. Unless you count the moose, he thought, worried that the car he was barreling down the road in would add to the carnage any minute.

"Let's just pull over," he said. "Wait till daylight."

"Are you crazy?" Janesta turned to study him for so long he was sure the car would veer into one of the pine trees they whipped past.

"Don't you care if you hit anything?"

"Care?"

"We could get hurt," Slim said. "The other day I was readin' where hittin' deer figures in one out of five car crashes here in Maine."

"I ain't hittin' no deer."

"We could. You never know." Slim was upset that they were having an argument. That he wanted one thing and Janesta wanted another and there was nothing he could do about it. All at once the road seemed to be lined with deer, like people watching a parade pass, the deer were lined up, waiting, daring each other to leap to the other side.

"You're not makin' sense," Janesta said with finality.

"Honey," Slim said. That was what Carl had called his mother. "I just don't want my little family to get hurt."

Janesta snorted with contempt and at that moment there was a thump and a yelp. She pulled onto the shoulder, inches from the guardrail. Crystal was crying loud horrible sobs and Slim feared she'd been hurt. He ran his hands over her face, terrified he would find blood.

"A dog," Janesta said.

Slim's hands were trembling as he comforted Crystal, patting her clumsily while Janesta got out of the car. Her heels made a terrible scraping sound on the road as she walked away until the night swallowed her up. Slim was afraid she would keep walking forever, that she would never return. I am the man of the family, he thought. I should be driving. I should be out there with Janesta. But he made no move to go.

Crystal was muttering, "What if it's Shotgun? Shotgun's never ever gonna die, is he? Is he?" She slapped her thighs, then she began to slap herself in the face. "Quit it, Crystal. Quit it," she said in a horrible voice. Slim caught her by the wrists and held her hands.

"Why're you talkin' like that? Shotgun's OK. He's home waitin' on you. Waitin' on his crunchies. I got a whole new box of Milk-Bones and you can give him the whole thing tomorrow if you want. One at a time or all at once. Whichever way you want. OK?"

Janesta slid behind the wheel. "It's dead," she said.

Slim didn't say anything. He didn't want to say I told you so. He didn't offer to go back and see if the dog had tags. Somewhere, a boy was in his backyard calling his dog. The next day, would he be going for Little League practice and see his beloved dog smashed beside the road?

Janesta was driving slower now and Crystal was breathing rhythmically, asleep with her mouth open, her breath warm on Slim's arm.

"Father," he murmured out the window into the passing night. When he was Crystal's age, he would walk up the dusty driveways with his father pulling the little red wagon full of books they'd saved at the dump. He would follow him to the back of the farmhouses where the women who came to the door would take their time selecting one or two, sometimes offering freshly baked cookies and cold glasses of milk. "Father," he whispered again. He liked the sound of it. He could see the word like skywriting floating above him.

They were approaching the bridge now, rushing over the river where his father had drowned. The air was full of the sound of thousands of insects calling, searching for each other in the night.

13

"Well, look who's here," Hydie called as the screen door slapped behind Slim. "Long time no see, buddy."

"Jesus Christ, what in hell happened to your head?" Rip asked. "You get it caught in the lawnmower?"

"Slim, now don't 'cha listen to him," Trudy said. "Your hair looks real nice. Don't he look nice, Hydie?"

"Where you been keepin' yourself? We ain't seen you in I dunno how long," said Buster.

Slim was so flustered, he tucked his hands into his back pockets, then into his front pockets, finally stuffing them under his arms.

"Guess what?" Slim tried to sound casual as he settled onto a stool.

"You look like you done won the lottery 'er something," said Coalie. "Do tell, do tell."

Slim waited until he was sure he had everyone's attention. Until even Buster looked up from his chowder, wiped his mouth with the back of his hand and said, "Looks to me like he's got a shiteatin' grin on his face. That only means one thing."

Raymond was scouring the chowder pot, the hot water running full blast, the pot clattering against the sink. Trudy reached over and shut the faucet off. "Raymond, honey. That's gallons of water going straight down the drain."

"You're lookin' at a happily married man," Slim said.

"A what? A happily what?" Buster pushed himself off the stool with the effort of the very fat for whom the smallest task seemed monumental. He slapped his jowls as if to clear his ears.

"You heard me. Me and Janesta done got ourselves hitched."

"Hitched like a jackass to the plow, I'd say," Coalie said.

"You did what?" Trudy was pouring coffee into Slim's cup. She raised her eyebrows so high her eyes popped like a flounder's.

"Leave the fella alone." Hydie wiped his hands on his apron and extended his hand. "Put 'er here. It happens to the best of us."

"You watch your mouth, Hydie Hyde." Trudy flicked him with her rag.

"We drove to Union City to the courthouse and all," Slim said. "Then we went clear to Bangor and had a look at the airport. We saw us a movie. *Invasion of the Body Snatchers.* Then had Chinese food at that Wok and Roll at the mall. Sweet-and-sour shrimp. You ever eat that?"

"That your honeymoon?" Rip asked. "Wokin' and rollin'?"

"You been snatched good, that's the truth. Snatched by a snatch. Yes, indeedy." Buster shook his head sadly. "Slim. Are you mad? People don't up and marry thataway, not when they're old as you."

"It ain't like I'm some crazy teenager," Slim said. "Don't get me wrong." Here he paused, gathering his thoughts. "It's just. Hell. I dunno. Laugh all you want, I'm happy to have her and Crystal livin' with me. I like knowin' she's up on that hill waitin' on me to come home, knowin' I got me somebody to say good night to after I flick off *Star Trek* and get ready to turn in. You're all married, ain't 'cha?"

"Yeah," Buster said. "I got Mildred like a convict's got his ball and chain. Thirty-five years I been kickin' myself over it."

"Make that thirty-seven years of pure hell for me." Rip grimaced.

Coalie didn't say anything. He and his wife hadn't spoken in over a decade. They even had two newspapers delivered, so they wouldn't have to talk about who was going to read which section when.

"Maybe Slim here's different from you old dogs," Trudy said, sliding a cheeseburger platter in front of Slim.

"Who you callin' an old dog?" Rip said.

"I guess I got the right to know what I been missin'," Slim said.

Coalie sashayed over to Slim, twitching his bony hips in an exaggerated motion. He was chewing on a toothpick and he raised it as if for a toast. "Snatched by a snatch. That's all I got to say."

Buster stared at his empty bowl. "You're one sorry cuss if I ever seen it."

Slim tried to ignore them. He dipped his fries into catsup, planning how tonight he'd make pot roast, heap slices of the tender meat onto their big white plates. He'd reach for the bowl of mashed potatoes he kept warm on the back of the stove and scoop the soft carrots and turnips with the broth from the meat over it all, proud to serve Janesta and Crystal their supper. My family. This is my family, he thought.

* * *

"You know what I can't get over," Buster said after Slim left.

"What?" Hydie stared out the window at a BMW with New Jersey plates. The two people inside appeared to be having an argument.

"I can't get over the three of them in that tin box. Can't you just picture it?" Buster laughed. "All bruised up and down from tryin' to get sideways around each other."

"Look who's talkin'," Trudy said. "I bet you can't even fit in the front door."

"Oh, now. Just gimme a slice of that apple pie. I'm a hungry man."

"You're a fat man," she said. She made no move to get the pie.

"Well, that ain't exactly no secret. Am I gonna get my pie or not?"

"All I know is I'm not gettin' it till you apologize."

"Apologize? For what?"

"For makin' fun of Slim. He's been a lonely bachelor since I don't know when. You go and make fun of him for finally gettin' company."

"Sorry! I just betcha there's something more to it."

Trudy made a show of getting the pie, stabbing at it with a big knife. "I got to put ice cream on this?" she asked.

"What you figure Janesta Curtis's got up her sleeve?" Rip asked.

"Beats me. I betcha five bucks it won't last a week," Coalie said.

"You don't have five bucks to spare."

"I will when my check comes in, Rip."

"When your check comes in. Hell, you might as well be waitin' for your ship to come in, Coalie. You done drank up that check a week ago."

"I'll betcha five bucks." Buster waved the bill. "You're on."

"What I'd like somebody to tell me is why in Sam's hell she and that kid'd move across the road to that dinky trailer. Janesta was in that big house already," Rip said. "What's the rent, Trudy?"

"Fifty dollars a month," Trudy said. "If you ever listened to me, you'd know Janesta's owed me so long it ain't even funny."

"You know Slim and that trailer of his," Hydie said. He poured himself a cup of coffee and another for Trudy. "It's his Shangri-la. You ever seen that HOME SWEET HOME sign he's got in the front yard?"

"All I know," Trudy said. "Is Janesta owes me rent I'll never see. I got to find someone to rent Momma's house. She needs what money it brings in. Who's gonna rent it with winter comin' on?"

"Christ, Trudy. Winter coming on. We ain't done with summer." Rip fingered his beard, lifting it up to examine it for crumbs.

"Them two're gonna be bruised up and down bumpin' into each other in that tin box. Tryin' to get sideways around each other to make it out the door. Bruised up and down." Buster laughed.

"That ain't all they're gonna be." Rip rolled his eyes and smacked his lips as if he were kissing the air.

"Go on now, you old farts. There's a lady present," Hydie said.

"Well, if she ain't heard it by now it's high time she did." Rip leered at Trudy. "Don't Hydie keep you posted on the facts of life?"

Trudy slapped Rip with her order book. "You gonna have anything else or you just takin' up space?"

"I just don't like it," Rip said. "Something's fishy in Denmark."

"That's rotten," Buster said. "It's rotten in Denmark."

"Whatever. It still don't make it right."

"I'll bet five bucks it lasts." Hydie took the money from the cash register and was waving it when Clarence Cushman walked in.

"You giving money away?" he asked, trying to grab it from Hydie.

"It's a bet," Buster said.

"On what?"

"How long Slim Riley and Janesta Curtis're gonna last," Coalie said.

"What're you talking about? You hitting the Boone's Farm again?"

"It's true," Hydie said. "Slim was just in here with the news."

"I just wish he'd clean that dump up. He's got such a mess up there the state inspector's gonna be after me. Rats and what all," Clarence said. He patted his hairpiece and took a seat.

"Give you something to do to earn your keep," Rip said. He was still mad at Clarence because the town selectmen decided to stop plowing the road to his camp. He claimed if Clarence had a camp out there, the road would not only be plowed, it'd be paved with gold.

Trudy went over to the table where the couple from the BMW were slouched over menus. The woman ordered the fish chowder and biscuits.

"That's a smart choice," Trudy said. "You're gonna like that one. The fish comes out of that water you see over yonder."

"I'll have the rump steak," the man said. He pushed his glasses up the bridge of his nose and blinked.

"It's a platter. It comes with peas or carrots. And potatoes."

"Peas," the man said.

"I can get you any kind of potatoes you want."

The man shook his head and handed her the menu. "I'd like some onion rings," he said.

"Onion rings? It don't come with onion rings. I can't substitute. Onion rings are extra. Seventy-five cents an order. The rump steak special's a platter. It comes with potatoes. That's how we fix it."

"That's OK. I'd like the onion rings anyway."

Trudy walked back behind the counter muttering about the way city folks wasted their money. Raymond took down a platter and set it beside where Hydie was stirring a bowl of eggs. The grill sizzled when he poured the eggs on and began scrambling them. He had a game going with Buster. If he had the eggs ready before Clarence ordered them, so that as soon as Clarence announced his order Trudy slid it under his nose, then Buster owed Hydie a pack of cigarettes. But if the eggs weren't ready or Clarence ordered a grilled cheese or a hamburger, Buster got his meal on the house. So far Hydie had accumulated a carton of Lucky Strikes which he lined up on the shelf over the grill. Clarence never seemed a bit surprised at the rapid service.

"Acts like the world revolves around him," Rip said.

"Whyn't you order a BLT once in a while," Buster whined. "They say variety is the spice of life."

Clarence just peered at them, as if momentarily confused, then shook salt over his home fries.

"You can't hardly afford this bet, my friend," Hydie said.

"You could always bribe him," Rip said. "Politicians are always ready to take a bribe."

"Excuse me, gentlemen. But are you talking about me?" Clarence asked. He looked genuinely puzzled.

"What makes you say that?" Rip fluffed his beard.

"You just wait," Buster said. "I'm gonna make a wad on Slim. I'm gonna get rich."

*　*　*

The transmission made a rasping sound—metal against metal—as Carol tried to downshift. Vivian, seated in the back, leaned forward, about to suggest Carol forget it, planning to tell her that the floor was so rusted she could see the road, when the man selling the car scooted over, blocking her view, and started to explain, miming the actions he wanted Carol to perform.

"See," O'Dell said, thrusting his right hand in the air, "it's like I said. You got to shift her into second first. You can't get to first anyways else. On account of the way I fixed her. Like I said.

Shoot on up into second then down to first. Smooth as smooth can be."

Carol felt as if she were driving a tank. Although the speedometer could go clear to a hundred, she doubted she'd ever go faster than thirty on these old country roads. She ignored the faces Vivian was making in the rearview mirror. At least she'd have an excuse to go slow.

"She runs real good. Just needs a new radiator. Like I said. You got a lot of play in the steering but you get used to it, see? Put on the brakes. See how she pulls to the right? You get so's you know it's comin' and act accordingly. I'm tellin' you. She's got four new snow tires. Hell. Them's practically worth the price alone."

O'Dell was asking four hundred dollars for the car though he'd penciled O.B.O. at the bottom of the FOR SALE sign. Carol wondered if three hundred would be a good offer. It's better to start low, she decided. If the car lasts a month it'll be cheaper than a rental.

"She's only had but two owners." O'Dell patted the dashboard as if he were complimenting the car. "Me and my Aunt Tattie. And Aunt Tattie was a schoolteacher. She only drove to work and once in a blue moon up to the Rusty Anchor when she was on a toot. Them's the original miles."

Vivian rolled her eyes and muttered, "Sure, sure."

By the time Carol got to the highway, stalling only once when she failed to "gun her good" as O'Dell instructed, slamming his foot against the floor to show Carol what he meant, Carol knew she had to have the car. She tried the horn to see if it worked.

"Would you take three hundred?" Carol asked.

"You throw in a six-pack and she's yours."

"Really?"

"We got us a deal." O'Dell thrust his hand at her. Carol pulled over so they could shake. O'Dell's palm felt thick as a saddle.

"You're nuts," Vivian said. "If you ask me, you're nuts."

"I didn't ask you, did I?" Carol said, driving over the bridge. She pulled into the parking lot, leaving the car running as she ran in for the beer.

Carol felt liberated as she drove by herself down to Hydie's, "gunnin' her good," the window down, a warm breeze in her hair. "Alone at last," she said, fiddling with the radio knobs but getting only static. She'd have to pull the antenna up. At least I don't have to listen to Joan Armatrading anymore, she thought with relief. When they arrived back at O'Dell's place, Vivian had jumped into her car and raced away, "Save Me" blasting from the tape deck as she headed in the opposite direction, not even waiting to see if Carol followed her to the cabin.

The sound of the car still reverberated in her head when she stepped into Hydie's. It was late in the afternoon and she was the only customer. The place sparkled as if every surface had recently been polished. Her hands trembled from the vibration of the steering wheel. She rubbed them together and slid onto a stool.

"What can I get you?" Trudy asked.

"I'll have a Coke."

Trudy turned and scooped ice into a glass.

"But that's not what I want," Carol added.

Trudy stopped with the glass poised under the spigot. "D'you want this Coke or not?" She frowned. She would never understand these people from away. You'd think they spoke another language. She scratched her scalp with the eraser end of her pencil.

"I *do* want the Coke. Please," Carol said. "But I came to ask about the house for rent. The sign said to ask here."

Trudy set the Coke on the counter and wiped her hands on her apron. "That'd be me you're wantin' to see. Is it for yourself?"

"Yes. For me." Carol pulled the paper from her straw back and forth between her fingers, smoothing out the crinkles.

"Just you?"

"Yeah. Just me."

"Well," Trudy said. "I dunno. All by yourself up there on that dead-end road. It's not in any kind of great shape, but it's furnished. If somethin' goes wrong I can't be runnin' up there to fix it."

"That's OK," Carol said. "I like to fix things."

"The rent's fifty dollars a month. And I ask that you meet Momma. It's only right it bein' her house that she gets to lay eyes on who's livin' in it. She's over to The Manor."

"Fifty dollars?"

"Yessir. That's all I can charge else she loses her Medicaid. That includes water and electric but you pay the gas. It's got a propane heater. And a woodstove. I'd like to sell it but then Momma'd make too much money and have to leave The Manor and Lord knows the way they eat up old folks' money there ain't anywheres else she can go. Anyway, not to tell you my troubles. But that's the deal. You got a job?"

"I'm an artist," Carol said. She was about to explain about the grant and her savings account, quickly calculating how many years she'd be able to live in the house with a rent so low.

"You the one gonna teach them classes over to the high school?"
"What classes?"
"Every winter, an artist comes and teaches us. Over to the high
school, like I said. We used to have this girl from over Holiday Island
come but she's gone and got herself in the family way, expecting
twins. So she won't be over here no time soon. There's a group of
us that come regular. A couple of ladies from Bragdon. There's
Tammy Bridges from over Cherry Falls and Pamela Joy that comes
over from the peninsula. I did *them* last year." Trudy pointed at the
paintings on the wall.
"I wondered about those," Carol said, looking at the huge eggbeater that had seemed so mysterious the first time she saw it.
"Ain't they somethin', huh? We were supposed to paint everyday
things but see 'em in a whole new way."
"I've never taught," Carol said.
"Jenny never did neither before she got to us. They don't have a
bunch of requirements and like that."

* * *

"You've really lost your mind," Vivian said when Carol returned
to the cabin and showed her the keys to the house. She had stopped
by to walk through the rooms on her way back, sitting on the yellow
sofa in the large front room that would be her studio, looking out
the window at Rita's place, remembering the night she and Rita had
walked in the moonlight. "I'll be your friend," Rita had said.
"It's perfect," she said to Vivian, thinking that it would be perfect
to have a beautiful woman across the road to flirt with, who would
visit then go home so Carol could go on with her work.
"You're crazy. First you buy some junk heap of a car. Now you rent
some falling down old house. You're gonna stay all by yourself in the
middle of nowhere? I'm supposed to just drive off and leave you?
Let you ruin your life?"
"I'm a grown-up. Remember?" Carol was making a list of what she
wanted Dougie to send her: her winter clothes and boots; her army
blanket; the portable easel in the back of her closet; her paints and
brushes; the painting of Annie.
Vivian shook her head and groaned. "This is my fault, you know.
If it wasn't for me, you wouldn't be here."
"But I'm glad I'm here. That's what you don't get. I *belong* here."
"With all the other nut cases. You and that O'Dell and the giant
dumpkeeper. Yeah. You're part of the sideshow. You *do* belong here."

What about *us?* Vivian wondered, but didn't say. She looked at the watercolor Carol had painted, tacked to the wall. A child's red rocking chair from the yard sale they'd gone to, nearly obscured by a tall clump of shimmering grass. Beside it, one of the canoes turned upside down on the white sand. Carol said she was rusty and pointed out the imperfections, but the paintings seemed flawless to Vivian. Her only attempt at creativity had been the lumpy mosaic ashtrays she'd put together from a kit she got on her tenth birthday. All I've ever been good at was playing basketball, she thought. Her happiest memories were when she'd been captain of the Lady Bobcats in high school even though it drove her mother nuts, all that go-team-go stuff reminded her of Hitler. Maybe she could start a team at the community center. The Lady Bull Dykes. Make that the *old* Lady Bull Dykes, she thought.

She shuffled over to the daybed and picked up *F Is for Fugitive,* flipping the pages slowly, as if she were concentrating. Carol was at the table, painting again. Even at a time like this, she could paint. She doesn't need me one tiny bit, Vivian thought.

"What about your apartment?" Vivian asked, sure she'd come up with the argument that would make Carol go back home. She'd been looking forward to being with Carol back in the city, even if they didn't live together the way she hoped. There would be movie dates, dinners in Chinatown, tea dances on Sunday afternoons.

"I live within walking distance of the U.N.," Carol said, clinking her paintbrush in the glass of water. "I can sublet in a second."

"I know where you live," Vivian said. She sniffed huffily.

"It's perfect for me here," Carol said. "I can afford it. The house is just right. There's even a possibility of a job."

"It's rained half the time we've been here," Vivian shouted.

"It rains in New York," Carol said, not sure what they were arguing about.

"I didn't drive all the way up here to break up with you," Vivian said, a few tears sneaking out of her eyes.

"I'm sorry, Viv." Carol went over and sat on the edge of the bed. She patted Vivian awkwardly. "I'm really sorry. I just feel like I *have* to do this. It's part of being able to do my work. I just want to try it. I don't mean to hurt you."

Vivian pulled away from Carol, flipping another page, her eyes scanning the words but not really reading. First Jeanne, now Carol. Everyone she loved ended up leaving her. She pictured herself driving back to the city all alone; eating her solitary meals in front of the TV; hanging around the flea market by herself listlessly pawing through other people's discards; moping across the city past the couples making out in doorways; dragging herself over the river to work day after day and returning home to her empty apartment. Then winter would come and the old woman downstairs would cry, "Julio, Julio!" and bang the pipes to summon the super when the heat wouldn't come on, and there Vivian would be, shivering in her queen-sized bed, alone. She imagined Carol, up to her waist in a blizzard, a beatific smile lighting her face, *happy* to be alone, savoring her solitude. How did she stand it? What was her secret? Vivian hated to be alone.

* * *

Nelly and Rita had an unspoken agreement to talk only about their daily lives. The rain that didn't come or that lasted too long. The carrots that needed to be thinned or the row that failed to sprout. The bag of corn almost gone in the shed or the rats nesting in the hay. Over breakfast, they spoke of selling the surplus eggs; Don's Health Food Store in Union City agreed to take a few dozen when they came to town. But though it was only twenty miles away, to Nelly, going to town was like traveling over a mountain range on horseback and should be planned for accordingly, done rarely. It was better to do without.

Thanks to her inheritance, Nelly had all the money she needed. Although she was frugal, making do with less, she was not stingy. There was always a twenty-dollar bill on the table when Rita went to Moody's. She didn't even count the change Rita put in a teapot on the shelf. Nelly said Rita could have whatever profits she made from the eggs or berries. She didn't want Rita to feel trapped because of money, and she recognized the value of the work Rita did.

They were careful not to mention life too far in the future, though talk of winter was inevitable with wood to split, insulation to put up, the harvest to store. Their future together was as uncertain as the life of the farm itself. Both of them knew as though by a sixth sense that the past was a tangle of hurt best left untouched. Rita took on the role of the farm wife, cleaning the house, seeing to the laundry, planning and cooking the meals. She was up at dawn with the kettle on for coffee; she swept the cabin after breakfast and made up the beds. Rainey would be at the table with her crayons or would take a turn washing the dishes while Rita dried and set them on the open shelves.

"The bugs aren't so bad today," Rita would tell her when she came in from feeding the hens. She would take Rainey's kerchief from the nail on the wall, dab on Woodsman's Friend, and tie it around her head. Together they would weed the peas, thin the lettuces, gather the curly green leaves for a lunch salad, pull thin pale carrots they would eat whole. It was a job like any other, and Rita was determined to do it well, enduring Nelly's moods and outbursts—familiar now, almost predictable. I am earning my keep, she told herself, leading Rainey out the door for a walk when Nelly came in muttering, an evil expression on her face. I am a good worker, she reminded herself.

When she worked at the fabric shop in Boston, Rita had always been on time and never left early the way the other girls did. She would unfurl the heaviest of bolts with a matter-of-fact thump and measure whatever the customers required, waiting patiently while they examined their patterns anxiously, offering suggestions when asked. She would cut ten yards of vinyl or a quarter yard of calico, treating both customers the same, and search for the right buttons and thread, zippers and bias tape, not overly solicitous, but there when her expertise was required.

Sewing was something she had shared with her mother. They would drive to Seymour, to Franny's Fabrics, just to look at the rows of fabric bolts on shelves that reached the ceiling, the newest bolts crowded onto the cutting tables, propped against the wall. The remnants on sale tables in back with the upholstery fabrics on heavy tubes. The crisp cottons, the nubby wools, soft flannels and smooth bright satins, all of it a pleasure. Her mother made all her own clothes and taught Rita to do the same, starting her on potholders and dirndl skirts, working her way up to blouses with buttonholes, pants with pleats and pockets. Though she stopped sewing during high school when the pressure to have store-bought crowded out the satisfaction of making her own, Rita never stopped loving the feel of new fabric, the pleasure of ironing the tissue pattern, spreading it onto the cloth, pinning the pieces into place, the scissor blades knocking the table rhythmically.

In the evenings while Nelly studied her pamphlets and books about farming, Rita set up her sewing machine and worked on Rainey's school outfits. Sometimes Nelly watched Rita with Rainey and wondered what kind of man could have turned his back on her. Look who's talking, she admonished herself, repeating her motto: Onward ever onward. She said it to herself whenever the past slipped into focus and she caught herself reliving scenes, replaying them like a record she knew all the words to by heart. Onward ever onward, she instructed herself. Don't stir up the past. So instead of wondering about Rita when she saw her bend over the girl, she focused on Rita's hair parting over her neck, yearning to kiss her there where the hair was feathery and pale. To do so had come to seem like a breach of their silent agreement. But when she didn't kiss Rita, inevitably there was the salty sweet taste of Fiona's skin, Fiona stretched across the bed ready for Nelly, laughing like she'd just won a prize. Onward ever onward, Nelly repeated as she poured another cup of coffee and sliced herself a piece of the rhubarb pie Rita baked.

"We need to pinch the suckers off the tomatoes," Nelly would say, waiting until Rita glanced up from filling the bobbin and gave her a confirming nod.

14

"Well, what d'you think?" Slim held up his latest invention.

"What in hell is it?" Janesta asked.

"Can't you tell?"

Crystal looked up from the TV. "If the wet weather keeps up, the blueberries're gonna rot in Bragdon County," she said.

"A bunch of tin cans tied together, right?" Janesta rolled her eyes.

All the way home, Slim had planned how he would march right over and kiss Janesta even though the last time he tried, she pushed him away. But as soon as he came through the door, he could tell it wasn't a good idea. Something about the way she sat in his chair with her ankles crossed said: *Keep Off!* He felt the way he did as a boy when he'd reached unwittingly into a box of crushed Christmas wrappings and pulled his hand back studded with splinters of broken ornaments.

Janesta lit a cigarette and blew smoke rings as if to further insulate herself from any possible advances. She examined her fingernails. The polish was chipped, but she didn't have the energy to fix them. Though she felt fat and slightly queasy, she reached for the box of Cheez-Its and ate another handful.

"It's like the Tin Man. In Crystal's movie. See, here's the funnel I got up at Buster's for his hat." Slim's tin man made a hollow clanking sound as the cans rattled against each other.

"Tin Man oh man." Crystal got up and danced with the tin man, singing, "If I only had a heart."

"It only cost me for the funnel. The cans're free. Cans I got. String, too," Slim said. He had used various sizes of cans, from an industrial-sized tomato can from the school cafeteria for his chest, to the small one-serving cat food cans for the tin man's elbow and knee joints. He imagined the three of them punching holes in the cans and threading them with string while they sat around after supper, but now he was glad he'd left the supplies in the car.

"What're you supposed to do with it?" Janesta asked.

"I'm gonna sell them at the Christmas fair."

"Why in hell would anybody wanna buy it?"

"It's a wind chime." Slim rattled his tin man for effect. "You hang it on your porch or in a tree or whatever."

"Uh-oh," Crystal said. "They're gettin' a divorce." She pointed at the TV, then curled back up on the sofa with Shotgun's head on her lap.

* * *

"One over two, two over one," Michael repeated as he laid the first stones of his wall into place. John Dority had taught him this rule back when he was a mason's tender, young and green and willing to break his back to push wheelbarrow loads of cement, to shovel yards of gravel, to roll heavy, unwieldy stones end over end to learn the trade. More often than not, the old man rested on the rock pile with his pipe lit, watching Michael struggle alone; he was too old to help.

Old Rockpile John, as he had been known around Preacher's Lake, was a little bandy-legged fellow with his body shaped by the work he gave his life to, his back permanently bent, his head thrusting from his twisted shoulders like a battering ram, his thick, leathery hands. "It's not a matter of strength," he'd say as Michael struggled with a particularly large stone, rolling it up a plank until it was settled in the place John had indicated. "It's know-how. Use your legs. Think before you move."

On days when the foundations they had been contracted to do had been poured, when the brickwork had been pointed and the chimneys topped, John worked on the fieldstone walls that snaked over his land. Michael used to help, eager to learn what he could.

Stonework fascinated him; it was the highest, most difficult part of the stonemason's trade. John's secrets would die with him if he didn't pass them on.

"A builder of stone has got to possess patience," John would say, twisting his neck to peer up at Michael from beneath his bushy brows. "You got to have patience to wait for the right stone. You got to have vision, too. You can't just pile 'em helter-skelter. And don't be wastin' your good flat ones on the bottom. You got to plan 'em out and save you some nice top stones, save you some pieces of gneiss, a slab of granite. Them's the ones'll hold it in place."

So it wouldn't taper as it rose, Michael was careful to see that every stone cast a shadow, considering each one before placing it just so. Envisioning the finished wall as he worked, he planned how it would meander along the path to the house, provide a place to sit and rest with wild roses along one side, be something solid and permanent that no one could take away. He could see the dirt at his feet, too, the trench he had dug, spreading the layer of gravel for drainage. And there, beside the house, waiting to be put to use, the pile of stones he had been collecting for years.

Michael drove the countryside searching for rubble walls half-buried in blackberry brambles and alder thickets, exploring field-stone cellars he stumbled upon in the woods, coming home with slabs of murky green serpentine, chunks of rose quartz. A piece of folded schist from a trip he and Kaye took out to Little Spruce Head Island. Sometimes he found a stone that seemed to be waiting for him beside the road. He seldom came home without a few stones rattling in the truck bed.

A good foundation holds up over time, holds weight, something to build upon, Michael thought as he nudged the stones into place. He liked the heft of stone. The cold dense feel of it under his hands.

In the house, Lizzy and Aran were making a costume. Aran wanted to be a fairy princess and Lizzy had brought home a rhine-stone tiara and yards of sparkling material to fashion a gown. He could hear the old treadle machine thumping when he paused in his work. Since Lizzy moved in, he hardly ever thought of Kaye, except sometimes, she would loom before him as he touched Lizzy under the covers at night. He had rested against Kaye's smooth curves and hollows as against a fluffy pillow, comforted and lulled. With Lizzy, he had to be careful not to jab himself against her sharp hip bones. He would finger the knobs of her spine, touch her bony elbows and wrists, and see the smooth sun-bleached stones on the beach at Corea, hear the tide rocking them, knocking them gently against each other. He would touch her and think: Solid as stone.

Lizzy, in her small steady way, was taking up the space that Kaye had once occupied. Like the wispy clouds overhead, torn apart by the wind, his sense of Kaye was shredding, floating out of sight. Adultery was a sin. And marriage a sacrament. But when was the last time he'd gone to Mass? It had been a gradual falling away until eventually observing his faith was no longer part of his life.

"One over two. Two over one," Michael repeated as he worked, careful to make sure each stone touched every stone around it.

"Daddy," Aran called, breaking into his thoughts. She was waving her magic wand from the steps. Aran was a miniature replica of Kaye, with her upturned nose and her bright blue eyes. She twirled around so he could see the full effect of her gown. The tiara was balanced on her head, and on her feet she wore the pink ballet slippers Lizzy bought. "Your wish is my command, Daddy."

"You look good enough to eat, honey bunny," Michael said as she dashed back into the house to admire herself in the mirror.

All those days and nights he had wished Kaye would come home and fit back into his life as if she had never gone. Now he didn't know if he wanted her to come back. If he could wish for anything, what would it be? A good stonemason sees what's ahead of him, John used to say. But Michael had no idea what lay ahead of him. If only the pieces of his life would fall into place effortlessly, the way the stones John used to select fit, nestling perfectly into place.

* * *

Mrs. Thomas, Trudy's mother, was a hundred and two years old and lived at The Manor, a nursing home on Sow's Head Road. If you can call it living, Carol thought, standing by the old woman's bed. It was crazy to agree to visit her when she rented the house.

"I figure it's only right she gets to lay eyes on her tenants now and then," Trudy said. "Janesta Curtis never once stopped in, but I know a nice lady like you will do what's right."

Mrs. Thomas was propped up in bed while a large woman in a pink smock spooned something green and grainy into the old woman's trembling mouth. She was buried up to her neck in the bed, the white spread tucked under her chin, a towel spread over it to catch what dribbled from her mouth. The old woman waved, moving her hand in the same forlorn gesture Vivian had made as she took off down the hill, heading back to the city, Joan blasting on the tape deck.

"She wants you to come closer," the woman said.

"I can come back later. When she's finished," Carol said.

"No. It's all right. I can do this any time," she said. "My name's Anita, by the way. I'm the CNA that takes care of her. You sit right down here."

As she edged up to the head of the bed, Carol had a strange feeling that she was consulting an oracle. Will I find love and my true work? she could ask.

"I'm the one who's rented your house," she said. "It's a nice house." The old woman stared at her swollen twisted knuckles, then wiggled her fingers as if testing to see if they still worked. Carol heard plastic crackling and realized the old woman was wearing a diaper.

"Once a man, twice a child," Annie used to say, repeating her Jamaican grandmother's words when they watched the old people being wheeled around the park, slipping down in their chairs, dozing.

"I'm from New York City. Trudy sent me. Your daughter. I'd love to stay here this winter. In your house. I hope that's OK."

The old woman began to laugh. Her gray cat's eye glasses slid down her short stubby nose. "Yes," she said, once she'd caught her breath. Her eyes seemed huge behind the thick lenses.

"You mean yes, it's OK with you that I rented it?" Carol leaned forward, both hands on her knees.

"Yes. Whatever the question is, the answer is yes. That's what I say." And with that, she closed her eyes and began to snore.

Carol watched her, uncertain what to do next. On the bedside table there were two cards, one with a drawing of a clown on a unicycle. It was signed "From your secret pal." The other card said, "Thinking of you today and sending love your way," with Trudy's spidery signature. A bluebird held an envelope in its beak.

"D'you wanna go dancin' tonight?" a young girl across the hall asked.

Carol heard an old woman answer "yes." When I get old, Carol decided, I'll start a nursing home for old dykes. We'll have cute girls to take care of us. Shapely young bodies to look at. We'll make them wear miniskirts and short shorts to keep our blood running.

Carol took out her sketchbook and drew the old woman's hands, her pencil dashing across the page as if she were taking notes. She had been getting back in the habit. So far she had sketched the doorway to her front room, an edge of the window frame, and from memory, the contours of Rita's back. She sketched the old woman's face, working to catch the particular quality of her skin, the folds that hung from her cheeks.

"How we doin'?" Anita poked her head into the room. "Oh. We're havin' a catnap, I see."

"Is she always—" Carol shrugged.

"She's a hundred and two after all. It takes a lot of work to stay awake when you're that old. But she's more with it if you come in the morning. Are you her granddaughter?"

"No. Unh-uh. Nothing like that," Carol said, getting up to go.

"Lovely lady," Anita said.

Trudy had told Carol to bring the old lady candy. Something soft, she instructed. She can't chew good. Carol placed the candy on the bedside table. She was barely out the door when she heard Anita tear open the cellophane.

*   *   *

After a dreary spell of rainy days, the clouds started to break up and Nelly decided to go to town. "For chores," she said, tying her boots, checking her wallet, meaning there would be no time for fun. Meaning she wanted to go alone. Rita was glad to see the truck head down the hill, glad for the silence when the racket the truck made passed out of her hearing. Nelly's sullen gloom had settled like a sack of grain on Rita's shoulders. Immediately after she was gone, Rita's spirit, like the rain-sodden grass bent over in the fields outside, lifted. As the sun broke through the clouds, she made a picnic and took Rainey down to the lake.

Rita and Rainey sat at the water's edge, marveling at the golden bits of mica in the sand they patted over their feet. They waded into the lake laughing at the fish that darted through the sparkling water to nibble their toes. Rita helped Rainey lie back, holding her up until she floated on her own. Then they floated side by side, their feet gently paddling, the cool lake water carrying them along the shore.

"Tell me again," Rainey said when they were on their towels in the shade of a birch tree, unwrapping the sandwiches Rita had brought.

"You remember what I explained last time? About baptism?"

Rainey nodded and bit into her sandwich. She smacked her lips appreciatively and reached for a carrot stick.

"And the preacher's name?"

"Reverend Asa Martin!" Rainey said. She loved to say *reverend*. She repeated the word slowly, watching her mother's face.

"You like that word, don't 'cha?" Rita smiled.

Rainey nodded and said the word again.

"Did I ever tell you where it comes from?"

Rainey shook her head and waited. Rita, looking down into Rainey's eyes, so trusting, so curious, wondered how her own mother could have been so certain of her view of God that she used it to frighten Rita.

"It comes from the word *revere*. That means to worship. Remember how the people who came down to be baptized, how it was to show their faith? To show they believed in God? To show they wanted to be part of the same community?" Rita took a deep breath to steady the flutter of nervousness. Whenever they spoke of God she felt as if she were treading water furiously, that she could sink at any minute. She had never spoken of her own faith to another person and it worried her talking to Rainey this way. She didn't want to impose her confusion and doubt about God on Rainey. But at the same time, she had begun to look forward to these talks and the stories she invented about Reverend Martin.

"Yeah," Rainey said. "The reverend dips you backwards in the water and you come up clean."

"You come up clean," Rita said. "I love you, Rainey." She kissed her, grateful for their time alone, out from under Nelly's disapproving shadow.

"Tell me," Rainey said.

"OK. This all happened a long time ago. Before you were born. Before I was born. Long before they had cars or airplanes or radios."

"No lights. No fridgerators."

"That's right. They had horses and buggies. They used candles at night and had springhouses to keep their food cold. They raised cows for milk and butter and grew vegetables like we do only they didn't have tractors. Horses pulled the plows."

"Way back long long ago," Rainey said, arranging herself with her head in her mother's lap. Rita played with Rainey's curls as she talked, gazing across the blue expanse of Preacher's Lake then back down to Rainey who waited patiently for her mother to go on.

"This was back when Preacher's Lake was a big town. What you call a boom town. Boom 'cause things were growing, lots of new people coming and building houses. They had hotels and big dance halls where the people got dressed up to go on Saturday night.

There were ships that came in to a harbor near the bridge we go over when we go to town. The singing bridge," she said, tracing Rainey's jaw with her fingertip. "The ships had great big sails and a crew of men to operate them. Huge blocks of granite were hoisted onto the ships. Some of it had been cut into paving stones. They sailed to the cities, to places like Boston, where we used to live. And New York. The cities were growing, too. You know, Boston didn't have cars or subways either. They had horses, too."

"But what about the lake? What about Reverend Martin?"

"I'm getting to that," Rita said. She considered how it would be if Preacher's Lake were buzzing with activity, the stonecutters and their dynamite, the chink of chisels pounding. Every day, she had crossed the streets in Boston, stepping over granite curb-stones, never once wondering where they had come from. Now, all across Waukeag County, there were abandoned quarries filled with icy water, some rumored to be bottomless. There were cellar holes where houses and barns once stood and old weedy cemeteries with weathered stones that marked the passing of this time.

"What about Reverend Martin?" Rainey said again, patting her mother's hand. "Mom," she said.

"OK. Well, you know what I told you last time? How Reverend Martin waded up to his waist in the lake?"

"Uh-huh." Rainey watched the lake as if she could see the scene her mother described. A man in a dark suit with thick wavy hair takes his shoes and socks off and wades out into the water with his hands held up toward the sky. The white sand is full of people singing; some of the women carry dark parasols to shield themselves from the bright sun. Then one by one, the ones who wish to be baptized wade in after Reverend Martin. Old people and young people, children, too. People who have already been baptized come back again. The water is thick with the women's floating skirts; men with water dripping from their hair and beards; children laughing, splashing, then growing silent.

"Reverential," Rita said, filling in details she made up as she told the story. She had only the librarian's explanation to go on. "It's where folks were baptized," she said once when Rita asked. "We've only got the old-timers' stories to go by. The town records were lost in a fire." On subsequent visits, she had reported more. "They say that's why they call it Preacher's Lake. The town got the name too because Reverend Martin was so well liked."

The last time Rita was there, the librarian approached her

first. "Did I tell you they almost called it Martinsville?" she asked. "But Reverend Martin said 'no sir.' He didn't want that happening on his behalf. 'Call it Preacher's Lake,' he said. And the town folks did."

Rita had repeated the conversation to herself several times since, recalling the librarian's intimate whisper. BETTY WATKINS, her nameplate said. She was the first person from Preacher's Lake who said more to Rita than what was absolutely necessary. It made her feel as if anything were possible now that this stern woman with her no-nonsense attitude had made such an effort.

"They felt reverential," Rita said, tucking Rainey's hair behind her ears, repeating the gesture each time it sprang back. "So the people got really quiet." She put her finger on her lips as if to shush Rainey. "They listened to the leaves rustling in the trees and they heard the birds singing from the bushes. They saw the white puffy clouds in the blue sky. The light was coming through the clouds just like it is now, see how it's coming down? See how the light's reflected in the lake like a mirror? The people felt something special, seeing that light, standing together in the water side by side. They felt something between them, in the water and the sun and Reverend Martin's words, and they knew God was with them. They knew they were blessed." Rita lowered herself onto her towel and pulled Rainey close. "Let's see if we can feel it, too."

The damp sand seeped into their towels, but the sun was warm as they lay together, the light breeze off the lake caressing their skin. Rita couldn't imagine what it would be like to be part of such a group of people, to be accepted and blessed. In the church she attended with her mother, there had only been a feeling of never being good enough.

Lately, Rita had started to pray. "Dear God," she whispered as she walked through the tall grass, as she went through her daily chores, as she lay sleepless in the night. "Please help me," she prayed. Then she didn't know what else to say. "Please," she prayed silently to herself and sometimes out loud when she was sure no one could hear, flooded with that same futility she felt as a child in Sunday School, unable to recite the Ten Commandments, forgetting the Bible verse she had practiced all week long: "The Lord is my shepherd, I shall not want."

"Can I be baptized?" Rainey asked.

"We'd have to find a church first. It's something a preacher does. Reverend Martin's not around anymore, you know."

"I know that. But can I?" Rainey asked.

"Maybe. All the churches are in Union City. We'll have to see."

Rita watched the clouds move across the deep blue sky and shivered. Though the air was warm, the breeze still full of summer, something about the quality of the light shimmering through the leaves of the birch trees across the water told her that summer would soon be over. Like the first trickle of sand before an avalanche, winter was rolling toward them.

15

On the table, several egg cartons were filled with fresh eggs and beside them a misshapen loaf of wheat bread cooled on a rack. Rita was at the sink using a damp rag to wipe the shells of the rest of the brown eggs she took from the bucket on the floor. The day before, in a burst of confidence, she had gone into Hydie's. Rainey hung back, waiting shyly beside the door, but Rita did not let that stop her.

"I thought you might buy some eggs," she said, steadying her voice.

"You want eggs?" Trudy asked, squinching up her face as if she'd just bitten a lemon. "What kind? Scrambled, fried?" Her eyes were drawn to Rainey. Cute as the dickens, she thought, recalling how the fellows had mentioned this little girl with brown skin. "Is this to go?"

"No. I mean. What I'm asking is. Well, I raise chickens. I was hoping you might buy some eggs. For the diner."

Oh," Trudy said. She put down her order book. "Hydie?" she called. "This girl says she's got eggs for sale."

"Eggs you say?" Hydie came over to the counter. Raymond was crunching on a cup of ice, waiting for his father to say it was closing time. It had been a slow afternoon, the last hamburger grilled long before, but it was too soon to start cleaning up.

"The general store across the bridge sells two or three cartons a day," Rita explained. She still hadn't gotten the nerve to ask at Moody's. But if Hydie bought them, she wouldn't need to.

Hydie nodded slowly. FARM FRESH EGGS FROM HAPPY HENS Rita had written with a marker across the top of the carton.

"I can leave you this dozen to try," she said. "They're real good."

"You don't have to convince me," Hydie said. "My dad raised hens on the Waukeag Road. You know where that big old rock sets practically in the middle of the road at that sharp turn? That's where we had our place, back off the road. Nothing like eggs warm from the nest. Trudy, give these girls a piece of your pie," Hydie said, motioning them to the counter. "They say they got happy hens.

"These're jumbo." Hydie whistled under his breath. "I aim to give a good breakfast and these'll make it *de*luxe." He'd agreed to take whatever she brought in.

With the money she earned, Rita planned to buy corduroy to make Rainey some pants and get herself fabric for a blouse. There'd be money left over to add to her savings. She was interrupted by a knock at the door. She brushed her hair away from her eyes and leaned over to see Carol on the stoop.

"Guess who's your new neighbor?" Carol said.

"Really? You decided to stay?" Rita pulled the door open. "C'mon in," she said.

"Yes. I'm all settled in. Bought a car and everything," Carol said, feeling like her hands were fake hams knocking against her sides as she stepped inside. The house was smaller than any she'd ever seen. But very neat. Rita scratched her calf with her bare foot. Let me do that for you, Carol wanted to say. There was a click as Rainey leaned around her doorway, then disappeared.

"A budding photographer?" Carol said.

"Slim gave it to her. She takes pictures of everything. Ask her to show you. Sometimes it takes my breath away, what she sees and how she sees it. Rainey?" She turned to the doorway but the curtain slid closed. "Maybe another time." Rita shrugged. "So how do you like the house?"

"I love it. But I still can't get used to all the space. The kitchen is as big as my apartment. It's so weird to have a separate room to sleep in. A bedroom. It feels sinful."

Rita laughed. "Well, space is something I could use. You want a cup of coffee or something?"

"I've already had my caffeine ration."

Rita handed her a plate of oatmeal cookies. Carol ate one as she peered out the narrow window at the sheep grazing in the pasture.

"I see you got more sheep."

"Six new girls. The ram's in exile. Hear him making all that racket?"

"I wondered what that was." Carol laughed.

The ram was in a pen by himself, bleating pitifully and knocking his head against the shed.

"Some kind of weird serenade he's got, huh?"

"She-Rah!" Carol sang. Rita blushed and turned back to her task.

"I was thinking," Rita said. She paused, as if she could hear something Carol couldn't. "Nelly's going down to Waterville this weekend. For a tractor show," Rita said, looking Carol full in the face, seeming to plead. "Maybe we could do something." As she placed the last clean egg into a carton, there was a thump on the pallet and Nelly came in, clomping heavily in her boots, tracking in a big gob of chicken shit. The toes of her boots were thick and rounded, like Popeye's, Carol thought. She stared at the smear of green on the rough wood floor to avoid Nelly's eyes.

"Nelly? This is Carol," Rita was saying. "She's moved into Janesta's."

"Huh. Hot enough for you?" Nelly asked, pulling off the sweaty kerchief tied cowboy-style around her neck and wiping her face with it. She pumped water and splashed her face. Paulette Bunyan, Carol thought.

"Sure is," Carol said. Nelly's presence seemed to crowd out any possibilities of conversation. "I came over for some eggs," she finally said. It sounded as if she were apologizing. She stared at the loaf of bread. It looked like the cakes her mother used to bake. Submarine cakes, she called them; they always sank in the center.

Nelly pushed back the curtain and stood at the refrigerator drinking orange juice from the bottle. "That's something we've got plenty of."

Rita put a quart of berries, a bushy head of lettuce, and a bunch of carrots in a paper bag with a dozen eggs. "A gift from the Preacher's Lake welcome wagon," she said.

Nelly slammed the door after Carol left. "You're not supposed to give stuff away," she said.

Carol trudged down the driveway under the canopy of trees, moving in and out of the dappled shade, wondering what life was like for Rita. She pictured them sitting down to supper at the end of the day, huddled in the cramped house like Van Gogh's potato eaters. She inhaled deeply, relishing the sweet smells of the sun on the grass, and felt the same way she did when she first saw Rita, as if she were in the presence of someone important. Not just someone she happened to meet while she was on vacation. Not just a pretty woman. But someone she was meant to know. She couldn't wait for the weekend, for the sound of Nelly's truck grinding down the hill.

* * *

"My mom's tall," Crystal said. She held her arms out and turned in a circle. "She's taller than you. But Slim's taller than her."

"Hmm." Carol glanced up from her sketch of the sugar maple tree. The pencil still felt awkward. She wanted to snap it in two, then tear the sketch into confetti to toss on the grass.

"My mom's tall mall fall," Crystal said, circling Carol now.

"You told me that."

"Well, she is. She's quit her job. Slim says he's the provider. No more welfare neither. It's gonna turn wicked cold come Sunday."

"It's really warm today," Carol said. A V of ducks was gliding overhead.

"You married?" Crystal asked.

"No. I told you that last time you asked. People like me don't get married."

"Oh. People like me don't get married neither. You ever been pregnant?"

"No. Never. And I don't plan on it." What was Crystal's obsession with pregnancy all about? Every time she came over, she brought it up. Carol started to work on her sheep sculptures, weaving strips of birch bark around the driftwood she'd pounded into the ground, winding it through the branches she had lashed on like ribs. When she had envisioned working outdoors she hadn't considered it would be a community event.

"How do birds get pregnant?"

"Where d'you get all these questions, anyhow?"

Crystal chewed on a piece of grass, considering Carol's question. "So, how do they?" she finally asked.

"Birds don't exactly get pregnant."

"Where do baby birds come from Miss-know-it-all?"

"Don't they teach you this stuff in school?"

"School, ugh." She spit as if to remove the word from her tongue. "Mrs. Bartlett says I'm a dummy. I get a roarin' in my head. You didn't say where the baby birds come from dumby dumb."

"They lay eggs and sit on them."

"They got boy eggs and girl eggs?"

"I guess you could say that."

"So how do they get pregnant?"

"Pretty much the same way everybody else does."

"But how de dow dow? God. Tell me how."

"You don't let up, do you?" Carol leaned back on her heels. Being with Crystal made Carol feel like she was in a scene from *David and Lisa*. The first time she saw Crystal, she was in front of Slim's trailer sweeping the grass. "Fall in love, did ya?" she called across the road, as if she could read Carol's mind.

"They have these things called vents," Carol said. "You know, where the egg comes out."

"That where the poop comes out?"

"I dunno. Maybe there's a separate hole for that. I've never looked," she said in exasperation. She had this ridiculous feeling that she was telling Crystal something obscene.

"OK. OK. So they got vents, then what?" Crystal asked.

"They lay eggs. Voila! Baby birds."

"Hmp!" Crystal flung herself on the grass. "Peep peep. I'm the baby bird," she said, in case Carol hadn't already guessed.

* * *

Nelly was under the truck, sharp pebbles pressing into her back while the oil drained. There was no reason for her to stay in this position. No need to watch the thick black oil glide like molasses into the pan. But it felt good to be off her feet and out of the sun.

Rita was harvesting what could be salvaged from the rows of peas she'd staked with brush, pulling the plants up and carrying armloads of them to the compost pile. The pale green leaves were covered with silvery dust and dotted with black, mildewed from all the rain. Rainey was in the house, supposedly having a nap. Nelly worried Rainey was turning into an insomniac. She lay on her bunk in the dark, long after her mother had read her several stories, ending always with the one about Sammy Squirrel, a story Nelly knew by heart now, all about how some squirrel went to the city to visit his friend Rudolph Rabbit, but got lost instead. When Rita neared the end of the story, Nelly sometimes caught herself leaning forward, expecting the moment when Rainey giggled with anticipation as Sammy trudged dejectedly back to the bus only to find his friend on the bus already, on his way to visit Sammy.

Each time the book snapped shut, Nelly got up and brushed her teeth, thinking how in a few minutes she would pull Rita close, stroke her thighs until she murmured, "Yes," Rita's breath hot on her face, the fantasy that real, though it was Fiona she remembered. Fiona languid on the bed, her dress hitched under her arms, the hot stillness of the night and the shrieks of birds like spirits reveling. Fiona moaning, demanding in a language Nelly didn't speak, arching her back, her pelvis dancing slowly, offering herself as she would offer an exotic fruit, and Nelly had tasted her again and again.

"Onward ever onward." Like a spring, the words bubbled up out of that part of herself that longed for control. Beyond Rita, Nelly could see Carol on her front porch staring off into the distance. All Nelly knew about her was that she was from the city.

"I came here to escape," she'd said, like she was a criminal who'd made a break from a penitentiary. Nelly didn't like the way she caught Rita looking at Carol earlier, the expression on Rita's face, how her eyes softened. She never looked at Nelly this way. With affection.

Slowly she tapped the wrench on the gravel, clenching it in her fist, and watched the thick oil drip its last drips.

*   *   *

The gulls swooped over the dump, dipping their long graceful wings, scanning the piles of garbage, then flew off with a clatter of wings when a man drove up in a big shiny turquoise truck. FISH his license plate said. He climbed down from the truck, hitching his clean new boots into the metal stirrups beneath the door. He had a copper-colored refrigerator and matching gas stove to throw away. The appliances looked perfectly good, not even a dent or a scratch.

"We're remodeling," he said. "The wife wants something to match her color scheme. Women," he sighed, implying Slim would understand.

Every day, Slim understood women less. All he knew was something was wrong with Janesta. Something was making her moody. Even when he baked a cake or brought her home a carton of cigarettes, she barely pretended to be happy about it. Bringing home this man's cast-off appliances would not do the trick. Janesta was not the kitchen type.

All afternoon, Slim showed the appliances to everybody that came in until a fisherman from Sow's Head Bay loaded them onto his truck shoved up next to the buckets and tangled nets. "My wife'll be tickled to death when I show up with this," he said.

It pleased Slim to see the man drive off with his treasures. If they closed the dump and replaced it with a transfer station, nothing would be reused. It would all be crushed, baled up, carted off to some giant heap where the tourists never went. It seemed like such a waste.

What's the world coming to? he wondered, absently scratching One Eye, a large fluffy black cat with a long plumelike tail that was missing one of his bright topaz-colored eyes. When Slim first saw the cat he was so skinny he could barely stand. Now he preened like a lion, meowing so loudly the gulls glanced up from a chicken carcass they were picking clean.

*   *   *

That evening after supper, Nelly was crouched over a circular from the grocery store, cutting her toenails when there was a knock at the door. "Shit," she said, sensing bad news. When she heard Rita say "sheep," her suspicions were confirmed. She pulled on her boots.

"Carol says they're heading for the woods behind her place," Rita told Nelly. She tied Rainey's sneakers and pulled a sweater on.

"Christ, Christ, Christ," Nelly said. "I just fixed the fucking fence. If it's not one thing, it's another." She headed out the door ahead of them, her heavy-duty flashlight lighting the way.

The flock of sheep were gathered at the edge of the dark woods, their eyes glowing in the flashlight. Carol, who had been handed a bucket of dry corn, rattled it when Nelly gave her a nod. She could tell the sheep wanted to come back down but sensed their hesitation as Nelly thrashed through the underbrush to get around behind them.

"I'll get a stick and herd them towards you guys," she said.

"Sheep, sheep, sheep," Rainey called. "Sheepy sheep."

Carol rattled the corn and watched as a brave one stepped forward, its hoof delicately balanced as if uncertain the ground would hold it. An image of Jesus with a lamb wrapped around his neck flashed in Carol's mind. Too much Sunday School, she told herself, rattling the bucket of corn, watching the sheep move forward, stumbling on the loose rocks, the others following close behind, thumping toward her, the smell of their wool in the air. She moved backwards quickly, her sneakers slipping on the damp grass, watching as Rita and Nelly came up on either side of the sheep, herding them forward to keep them from straying as they headed across the road to the pasture.

When Rita ran ahead to open the gate, the sheep crowded around Carol and Rainey. For a few minutes, the two of them were surrounded by sheep. Their warm oily bodies pressed close, the anxious baa's of anticipation all around them, the hooves shuffling. Carol held out a handful of corn and giggled at their thick scratchy tongues. She was reaching in for another handful for Rainey when one thrust its head into the bucket, nearly pulling it away; it was much stronger than she had imagined. They pressed close, some bleating in a frenzied manner as if to clear their throats, others echoing with angry spits of disgust, as if they recognized they'd been tricked into returning to the place they'd escaped from. All the while Rita fumbled with the knot. When the gate swung open, Carol backed toward it, rattling the bucket of corn, feeling important as the sheep followed her till they rushed stumbling into the pasture, no longer caring about the corn, tearing at the grass, all around them the wet sounds of sheep chewing and munching and pulling on the grass. Carol sat on a rock watching them, their bodies like white puffy clouds in the dark, and Rainey leaned against her knee.

"Stupid sheep," Rainey said, watching Carol as if anticipating a reaction. This was what Nelly had been saying. "Stupid stupid sheep."

A sheep rushed toward Nelly and tried to butt her aside as she mended the broken fence. Nelly swore and grabbed the heavy stick she had used to herd them. She whacked the animal repeatedly on the head.

"Quit it, you stupid fuck," she yelled and hit the sheep again, a resounding smack. The wood cracked against the animal's skull. It stood for a moment stunned, then collapsed on the ground in a heap.

"Oh God," Nelly cried angrily, flinging the stick into the dark.

"What happened?" Rita came over.

"I killed a sheep."

The sheep was lying on its side shapeless as a pile of dirty wool. Like the gray-faced man Carol saw last winter, a bundle of filthy rags collapsed in the doorway of the bank. She had been certain he was dead; then, his red-rimmed eyes fluttered open.

"Is it breathing?" Rita patted the sheep and rubbed her palm across its nose. "It's still breathing. It's just stunned."

Nelly shook her fist at the sky as if every star accused her. "I just can't stand sheep breaking down fences. I'm trying to fix it and this fucking sheep is knocking me out of the way. Sheep're the stupidest fucking animals alive. Let 'em just get lost in the fucking woods for all I care." She stalked off. In a few minutes, they heard the truck zoom down the hill.

"You're OK," Carol told the sheep, smoothing the thick wool. Rainey patted the sheep, too. It shivered like it really might be dying. The other sheep huddled nearby, as if to witness what happened. Carol once heard a story about mustangs, how they circled a mare when it was her time to foal. She wondered if sheep gathered around one of their own when it was about to die, if this was part of how they lived together. She wanted to explain all this, but she didn't say anything. She just crouched over the sheep between Rita and Rainey, feeling somehow to blame.

"Let's try to get her to stand up," Rita said. She and Carol rolled the sheep into a sitting position, then pushed on it until it rose up, staggering before it gained an awkward footing and hobbled away in a rocking gait as if its front legs were useless except as a kind of pivot to rock against. Then it toppled over and lay panting, finally getting up on its own, bleating pitifully, then hobbling off.

"She'll either die or have something wrong with her." Rita sighed. "Alton Poors has two sheep that kept knocking their heads together. One of them ended up blind."

"And Nelly?"

"Nelly. That's exit number four hundred and thirty-eight. She'll get over it. But she'll still have something wrong with her." Rita's laugh lacked sincerity. There was a weariness in her voice. "Anyhow, I've still got to fix this fence. Would you help me?"

Carol held the flashlight and watched Rita twist the thin wires. They were sharp and kept stabbing her fingers. She cried out but continued to twist them until they held. The desire to touch Rita, to brush her hair away from her eyes, jolted Carol as if she'd touched the electric fence.

"I don't think they'll try to get out again tonight, anyway," Rita was saying. "But this should hold." She turned toward Carol, seeming to sense Carol's longing, and hesitated, as if she were about to step into Carol's arms, then she stepped back. "I'd better walk you home," she said. "It's dark, huh?"

"No moon," Rainey said. She curled her fingers and peered at the sky through them as if through an imaginary camera "Good night moon. Good night sheeps." She ran ahead flapping her arms, pretending to be a crow in the circle of light Rita played on her.

The three of them stood awkwardly in Carol's dooryard.

"Don't you want to come in?" Carol asked.

"No. We ought to go," Rita said. But she didn't leave.

"That was an adventure," Carol said.

"Yeah. Boy am I wired. Thanks for your help. They'd be lost in the woods if you hadn't come to get us."

"How about a cup of coffee?"

"That's just what I need. Adrenaline and caffeine. I'll be up for days. Weeks. Months!" Rita said.

"Hot milk? Popcorn? Ice cream?"

"Ice cream," Rainey said, jumping up and down. "Ice cream!"

"Oops. Did I say the wrong thing?" Carol asked.

"The magic word, it sounds like," Rita said.

"Scrabble?" Carol asked, touching Rita's arm lightly. "We could play a game. Relax. My friend Dougie sent me a deluxe Scrabble board for the long winter, but I haven't had a chance to use it."

"Yeah, OK. That sounds like fun. Ice cream and Scrabble."

There was a thick sadness in the air that neither one was willing to talk about as they leaned over the kitchen table, shyly arranging their tiles, setting their words onto the game board. Rainey was curled on the sofa in the corner of the large kitchen, drawing with Carol's pastels.

"You don't mind?" Rita asked.

"Uh-uh. I was on the verge of getting cabin fever already. And it's not even fall yet. I like your company."

Rita's eyes filled with tears. "I'm sorry."

"It's OK. That sheep'll be OK."

"Oh. It's not just the sheep. It's everything." Rita took her bowl to the sink. Rainey had fallen asleep still clutching a crayon. "I can't believe she's asleep. I should get her home."

"Why don't I just get a blanket? She can spend the night. Really. It's OK. I mean it." Carol tucked a blanket around Rainey. "Don't you want to talk?"

"I don't want to dump all my troubles in your lap."

"It's OK. That's what neighbors are for, right?

"No. It's not. I'll figure things out. Is there any more of that ice cream you lured me in here for?"

"More of zee ize cream. Coming right up." She gave them a second helping. "You sure you don't want to talk about it?"

"You talk. Tell me your troubles."

"Well. I'm single. That narrows them down considerably."

Rita laughed.

"But I wasn't always. Annie," she said, nodding at the painting of Annie she'd hung over the table after she unpacked it.

"She's beautiful," Rita said. "It's an incredible painting. I feel like it's a window she's looking out of, not a painting. Did you do it?"

Carol nodded, returning to the Scrabble board. She spelled the word *helpless*.

"That word isn't supposed to mean anything or anything," she said. She had managed to spend all that time with Vivian without ever mentioning Annie. But she knew that wouldn't be possible with

Rita. If she ever got close to anyone again, she would have to tell the story of Annie. It would be a requisite. It made her feel like one of the homeless people in New York clutching a ragged sack, afraid Rita would want what was inside.

"I'd like to hear about her," Rita said.

Carol brushed the back of her hand against the back of Rita's hand, feeling bold, as defiant as she had when she was a child stealing candles from the altar. Later in her room, she had lit them with her stolen matches, let hot wax drip over her hand until her palm was covered. She turned Rita's hand over, examining her palm as if to read her future in the lines.

They heard Nelly's truck approach and come to a stop across the road. Then, like a wolf howling at the moon, Nelly screamed Rita's name. Rainey woke up crying and stumbled toward her mother.

"Some time," Rita said. "We'll talk. We have lots of time."

"Will you be OK?" Carol asked. "You sure you don't wanna stay?"

The frightened expression in Rita's eyes was like the sheep's as it rocked like a hobbyhorse across the pasture before it collapsed.

"She drinks," Rita said, hitching Rainey onto her hip. "She drinks and then she's sorry. It's OK, really." She turned to leave. "Don't forget. She's going away this weekend." Rita smiled. It was the saddest smile Carol had ever seen.

16

"What's that?" Rainey stood on tiptoe, grasping the edges of the pink granite, trying to pull herself up to the sign. "What's it say?"

"Black dikes," Rita said, lifting her. Rainey smoothed her palms across the Plexiglas.

"They spelled it wrong." Carol traced a *Y* over the *I*. Rita blushed, the color rising into her cheeks like seawater sinking into sand. Annie would have laughed at the sign. She would have said at last they'd named a place after her people.

Carol and Annie made a lot of jokes about "their people" since the time they had gone to a reading and the poet, who had long blonde hair, read several poems about waking up in the morning.

Each poem began with the light coming through the window and progressed to the moment when the poet set her bare feet on the rough wood or the slick linoleum or the deep carpet and looked out the window or wiped rain from the windowsill with the hem of her nightgown or stood naked drawing in the steamy glass. In each poem, she described her lover's anatomy. Pale nipples. Fleshy earlobes. Dark tufts of hair. "Her hips are hills. I am moist," she read in her singsong voice. When Carol leaned close to Annie and whispered, "She's an embarrassment to my people," Annie shook with silent laughter, her dark eyes flickering like candle flames in a sudden draft.

"What's it mean?" Rainey traced the letter *B*. "B. B. B."

"Yeah. That's a B. It's about how a long time ago the rock was liquid. Like hot pudding. And it spread into the cracks in the granite. That's the other rock. And then it solidified, you know, like when water turns to ice? See the black stripes in the rocks? It's called basalt."

"Lemme go!" Rainey scurried away. The waves crashed against the granite outcroppings making a thundering sound, sending up a fine white spray that left rainbows above the surf.

"That's far enough," Rita called after her.

"Mommy! Suction cups!" Rainey reached into a tide pool and pulled up a limpet, placing it on the back of her hand, then gathered more until the backs of both hands were covered with the snails.

Carol ran a finger down Rita's forearm, across the downy hairs that shimmered golden in the afternoon sun. Rita blushed again. This time, her cheeks stayed bright red for several seconds. Rita was acutely aware of the space between them, as if it were crackling with electricity. She had never felt this way standing beside another woman. Beside anyone, for that matter.

"Everybody's got a mate," Rita's Aunt Jessie used to say. "But there's some that search the ends of the earth and never meet their match. I got lucky. Uncle Cleon was right next door." Rita hadn't considered Aunt Jessie's story for years, but now, standing beside Carol, she could hear her aunt's voice. "It ain't like a twin, exactly. You can look different as night and day. Black and white. Yellow or red. Look at Cleon with his red hair and me with this mop of black. That ain't what matters. But on the inside. Yes. In here." She rubbed her heart. "In here, you're the same."

Carol ran her finger along the inside of Rita's arm, down to her wrist, then lightly across the pale veins. Standing so close together, the sea breeze in their hair, salt on their lips, made Carol ache to run her palms down Rita's faded jeans, slip her fingers into the back pockets with their frayed seams.

"I saw this TV show once," Carol said. "*20/20.* It was about all these gay people trying to become straight. It was really weird because they had on disguises. False moustaches, wigs. Anyway, at the end they talked about gay and lesbian animals. Something like twenty percent of seagulls are supposedly lesbians."

Rita laughed. "How do they know?"

"They didn't say. They mentioned it during the credits. There was this shot of two seagulls walking down a beach side by side."

"You're kidding me, right?"

"There's a couple now." Carol pointed at two gulls strutting by.

"You know what this land's called?" Rita asked, then answered herself. "Drowned. It's drowned land."

"What's that mean?"

"It's some geological thing, because it was under water. Most of Preacher's Lake was under water once, too, when the glaciers weighed it down. Thousands of feet of ice. I don't really understand it, but the ice melted, the sea rose, and the land rose too because all that weight was gone." She shrugged.

"Drowned is an odd way of putting it. Imagine drowning out here. The sea is so wild."

The wind flipped Rita's hair across her mouth. Carol knew she shouldn't, she was pushing her luck. But she didn't want to be one of those lesbians who longed for a woman but never made a move. I'll take baby steps, she thought. But without saying Mother may I?

She gently pulled the strand of hair away from Rita's mouth and tucked it behind her ear. Rita's hair was warm and silky. Her ear like a pink shell.

Across the expanse of water, a lobster boat headed for the cove. Straight ahead, the sun made a silvery path. As Rita imagined the two of them walking down this path to meet the sky, she patted Carol's thigh as if they were playing tag. Your turn.

"You think it's wild now, you should see it after a storm," Rita said. "The first time I was out here, the waves were huge. They came clear up here. I'd never seen anything like it. Where I come from, there's just miles of cornfields and lazy brown rivers. I stood here laughing. Then I started to weep. I was weeping so hard I could hardly stand up. Rainey was all upset wanting to know what happened. Nelly didn't know what to do. I kept saying, 'It's so incredible.' The next time we came, it was like now. It's tame in comparison. I mean I love it, but I've never seen it that way since."

"That sign said the sea can toss rocks the size of grapefruits up into the woods." Carol pointed at the twisted dwarfed pines across the road. "It can toss around rocks that weigh a ton. Weren't you scared?"

"It wasn't *during* the storm. It was right after. Lots of people come out here after a storm. But I've never been back since then. Nelly's always got some excuse. She's tired. She's got work to do. Work is her middle name. When Nelly's on her deathbed, somebody'll ask, 'What'd you do with your life?' She'll say, 'Work.' They'll say, 'What else?' Nelly'll say, 'What else is there?' "

"Could I ask you a favor?" Carol knew she had asked Rita to talk about Nelly, but now she wished she wouldn't even say her name. "Could you tell me some of the good things? In your relationship with Nelly? I don't want to be mad at somebody I don't even know."

"I'm sorry." What *were* the good things? Rita wondered.

"Don't be. C'mon. It's natural. I'm the one with the problem."

"You can talk about Annie." Rita brushed the seat of her pants.

"Annie. That's so complicated." Carol picked up a handful of pebbles and flung them. If she talked about Annie, she might never stop.

"Well. Vivian, then."

"Vivian! We had a couple things in common. But I didn't plan to spend my life with her. I'm not into changing people. I once had a girlfriend who treated me like I was an old house that needed renovation. She looked at me like she was always thinking, 'What if we put the door over there? White paint would help. But the floors are creaky.' I made this piece about it called *She loves me, she loves me not.*"

"What was her name?"

"Carol."

"You're kidding!"

"No."

"Wasn't that really complicated?"

"It was weird. Definitely weird. Look. I don't want to turn around and do to you what I just asked you *not* to do to me. Only I go on and on about the ones that were so bad that they're over. I shouldn't have brought it up. It's just that I was hoping. I don't know—"

"What if it was over with Nelly. Then could we talk about it?" Rita studied her hands in her lap. Her hair hid her face.

Carol jumped up and walked away, hopping from rock to rock. She felt wild inside, like the sea smacking the rocks, the undertow ready to swallow her up. Ambivalence is your middle name, Annie used to say.

"They're having a race," Rainey said, motioning Carol over to watch the limpets make their minuscule moves toward the tide pool. "Shh. You'll make 'em nervous." She held a finger over her lips. Rita came over and tightened Rainey's shoelaces, yanking them like she was angry or embarrassed. Carol wasn't sure which. Rainey waited passively for her mother to finish.

When they took a walk together along the ledge, it was impossible to talk with the pounding surf. They gave up struggling with the wind in their hair and let it tangle and grow thick with the humid sea air. They formed a team, holding Rainey's hands, swinging her over the deep crevices where the granite split, walking until their knees ached from stepping up and down over the rocks. Afterwards they drove to the Fisherman's Wife, Rainey between them, her head resting lightly against Carol's arm as she looked through her camera at her mother.

"I get the feeling we didn't finish saying something back there," Rita said. Carol drove along, watching the jagged coastline roll by, the white rocks at the edge of a cove, the toylike boats bobbing near the shore. "You know. When we were talking about relationships," Rita said. Her heart was pounding like the echo of the surf in a conch shell.

"Uh-uh. No," Carol said, frightened of Rita's serious tone.

Don't do this again, she counseled herself. Don't mess up your life. Don't mess up Rita's. And Rainey's, she added. A child equals a family equals trouble.

"Not really," she mumbled. Her skin burned as if she had fallen asleep in the sun.

Carol drove along, lost in thought, her car rattling around the curves, past a small farm where pigs sprawled in mud. Underneath the nervous murmuring in Carol's mind, there was a calm feeling. What Annie would have called her source. The place where you *really* know who you are. Your center. Carol's center was saying: Yes!

"Can I ask you something?" Rita said.

"Yeah." Carol slowed to drive through a village with several gray clapboard houses, each one just like the last.

"How did you know?"

"Know? Know what?"

"That you were, you know, a lesbian."

"Oh. Well, that's easy. I have this birthmark. Don't you have one? Two tiny woman symbols intertwined. Some of us have it under our left breast. Some on the back of our knee. Some have it, uh, sort of hidden. It can be anywhere."

"Be serious."

"I am! Here. Lemme check Rainey for you." She pulled off the road and stopped the car. "Say 'ah.' Nope. Lemme see your belly. Nope. How about in here?" She walked her fingers through her hair. Rainey laughed like it was the funniest thing ever.

"I think she's safe," Carol said.

Rita didn't say anything. Carol drove forward, shifting the complicated way O'Dell had taught her. "Is it my imagination or is everyone wearing a sailor hat?" she asked.

"This is the navy base," Rita said.

"Ice cream!" Rainey shouted as they passed a huge wooden strawberry ice cream cone with a face painted on it.

"After we eat some real food," Rita said.

"So, you tell me," Carol said. "How did you know?"

"I never really thought about it at first. I just did what I thought I was supposed to do. There were these men, I went to bed with them. But then, I met someone who was a lesbian and it was like, Oh! That's it. Before that, I thought something was wrong with me. I mean, the men I met were perfectly nice. And then I met Jill."

At the restaurant, they chose a booth in the back and ordered crab rolls and onion rings, a hot dog for Rainey who insisted she sit alone on her side. Because Carol was left-handed and Rita right-handed, they should have changed sides, but didn't, both taking pleasure in their arms bumping softly as they reached for the onion rings or sipped their Cokes.

The fattest man Carol had ever seen was seated beside them. His fleshy jowls hung like heavy drapes, his eyes were like raisins sinking into bread dough. She wished she had the nerve to ask him to pose.

"Chet, my boy," a man in a plaid shirt said, patting the fat man on his shoulder. "My boss went to Hawaii. Not bad for an old-timer."

"Our boy Chet," Carol whispered and rolled her eyes, making Rita giggle. He lifted his bowl of soup and sipped it like a cup of tea. The woman across from him was chattering on, not seeming to take a breath. "Y'oughta take a good look at that picture," she said. "It's adorable. They hung it up by the door so you can see it on your way out. I'm tellin' you, Brother Jerry was somethin' else. When he was preachin', he was paintin'. He'd talk about it up there on the pulpit. He put the gospels into it. I tell you, it put tears in your eyes. They used to have him over here five nights a week. Musta been a hundred people that come to hear him and see him paint. They called him the last Noah. Everybody was ready to be saved back then. Not like now." She paused in her litany and glanced at Carol and Rita, then Rainey, and clicked her tongue. "I tell you I don't know what this world is comin' to. It's gonna take a flood to wash all this trash away."

Carol and Rita turned to face each other at the same time. Carol kissed Rita lightly. Not really the kiss of a friend. But not yet the kiss of a lover.

"Hey," Rainey said. "Hey. I saw you."

The fat man continued to eat, but the woman across from him was so flustered she finally stopped talking and got busy with her coffee, tearing packets of sugar and stirring much more than was necessary.

On the way out, Carol examined the so-called work of art by this Brother Jerry. The perspective was kind of wacky, as if the birds were drunk, tipping off the boulders. The trees had a halo effect; they were outlined with dabs of white and yellow.

"What's that?" Rainey slipped her hand into Carol's.

"It's a painting," Carol said, continuing to look at it, savoring the warmth of her small trusting hand. "Of the sea and everything."

"Oh," Rainey said. "Did you see the sea?" She laughed at her joke as she tugged Carol away. "You said we'd get ice cream. You promised."

"Ice cream it is," Carol said. "If it's OK with your mom."

"Sure," Rita said, smiling at Rainey who had her camera aimed, ready to capture the light on her mother's hair and the sun glinting on the hood of the car.

*   *   *

Michael shoveled rhythmically, scooping sand into the wheelbarrow. He added mortar and held the hose, pouring in enough water to get the right consistency. A job like this one, I can do with my eyes closed, he thought. It gave him time to think. Too much time. He chewed the stem of his pipe as he scraped the hoe back and forth, then began patching the old brickwork, spreading mortar into the cracks where he'd already chipped the broken mortar away. The job was in Meddybemps and he had stayed overnight, camping out beside his truck. He planned to do this until the job was done. Lizzy agreed it was a good idea saying she would love to spend the time alone with Aran.

Michael concentrated on patching the fireplace in front of him, absorbed by the red crumbling bricks, the red dust that mixed with the gray mortar. All across the campground, a half dozen fireplaces had already been patched. And in the lodge, a stone fireplace needed work. A mantel had to be replaced.

"I just want 'em serviceable," the fellow that owned the campground said. "I don't want nobody complainin' their steak fell off the grill 'cause the fireplace's gone to hell." He was paying Michael a flat rate, so the time he took, and the care he gave, was up to him. Today, he aimed for perfection, scraping the point of the trowel just so, enjoying the sound it made and the flecks of mortar that clung to the short hairs on his arms and speckled his scuffed work boots. He paused to scratch his new beard. He tried not to worry about how long the job was taking. Everything was OK at home. He had called Lizzy at work that morning, pushing the coins into the slot, leaning up against the booth with his hand over his ear as trucks barreled past. "Aran's been cooking," she said. "Everything's fine. Don't worry." And then a client came in and she had to get off the phone. Lizzy was a good woman. He couldn't call what he felt for her love, exactly. Fondness. That's what it was. I am fond of you, he might say, if he said such things.

* * *

Janesta opened a new pack of cigarettes. On the TV, the Scarecrow was on fire and Crystal, as usual when she got to this scene, was crying.

"Every goddamn day you see that. How in hell does it still make you cry?"

Crystal didn't respond. The Scarecrow was jumping around slapping at himself. Janesta flipped through one of the magazines Slim brought home. Every single page was either a recipe for something to bake—rich cakes with lavish chocolate icing, gold cakes with way too many eggs—or else a weight-loss diet accompanied by before and after pictures. "How to Make Him Love You" an article offered. She sure didn't need to read that. She scowled at the thin band of gold Slim had slipped onto her finger, acting like he was some goddamn prince with a glass slipper. She tried to yank the ring off, but her fingers were so swollen it was stuck.

Being loved by Slim Riley, being treated like she was precious the way he did, made Janesta feel like she was turning into one of those pods in *Invasion of the Body Snatchers*. Only instead of turning into someone who felt no emotion, she was turning into someone who was itchy with feelings. Bitchy with irritation at him petting her like she was a wild cat, his fingers reaching timorously across her skin like he was afraid she might scratch him but he just couldn't resist the soft fur. His lips on her forehead, the back of her neck, made her body tingle like fingers and toes nearly frostbit do when you come at last into a warm room. Janesta didn't like it one bit. She felt as if her body were betraying her. Soon she would be sewing buttons on Slim's shirts, baking brownies for the PTA, donating her high heels to some rummage sale.

Janesta was surprised to admit it, but she didn't like being loved. It reminded her of Frank. She didn't want that. Not now. Not ever. He was in the past and that was where he was going to stay.

After Frank, Janesta only went with men who treated her roughly, pushing her facedown onto the rug. Men whose calloused hands grabbed onto her just enough to steady themselves. She grew to like the satisfied zip up afterwards, the sound of his car heading down the road. A steak now and then. A movie and supper in town. But a man who knew enough to make himself scarce. A man who did whatever it was men did instead of trying to suffocate her in the name of love.

"But I love you," Slim said a million times a day, even when she slapped his hand away. She didn't want some man who got her slippers for her the second she walked in the door like some trained dog, hovering over her, trying to come up with things she might want, things it hadn't even occurred to her to ask for yet. She tossed the magazine on the floor in disgust and ground her cigarette out in the overflowing ashtray.

"Jesus Kee-*reist* Almighty. Just look at me." Janesta pushed the pouch of her belly, punched at it as if she were kneading bread.

"Huh?" Crystal paused the movie, holding the remote like a gun aimed at the TV. She plucked at her pants, pulling off the cat hairs. Shotgun wagged his tail hopefully as if a treat were forthcoming.

"Nothing!" Janesta adjusted her clothes, pulling her long loose shirt down over her thighs. "I'm going for a drive," she said.

"You gonna get pizza?" Crystal asked.

"Maybe." Janesta sighed heavily. "I dunno. Maybe I just might."

"Slim'll be home in a little while."

"Don't I know that? What're you, my friggin' secretary?"

Crystal shrugged and turned back to the TV, releasing the pause. Dorothy was singing a song. Bootie ran over and stood on his hind legs, tapping his paw against the screen.

17

When Slim woke up he was immediately aware of the empty place in the bed beside him where Janesta slept, next to the edge so she could get up easily during the night to use the bathroom, which she did frequently, grumbling in the dark, shuffling out of the room, returning with a sigh to push the cats aside and curl against Slim who slept with his back pressed against the wall, his chest snuggled against her. He smoothed the sheet and lifted up on one elbow, squinting down the hallway. Bootie crept up and flopped on Janesta's pillow, purring loudly. The night-light glowed in the living room where Crystal sprawled across the pull-out sofa. Slim turned on his back, stretching, scratching the kitten between his ears, waiting for the sound of Janesta's fluffy slippers dusting across the linoleum. Anticipating the moment when he would lift the blanket for her and put his arms around her tentatively lest she jerk away claiming she couldn't breathe with him clinging to her.

He felt very lucky remembering the night before, Janesta in his arms kissing him, saying, "I'm sorry I drove off thataway. Sometimes I got to get out for a bit." He started to glide his big hands along her curves, was about to reach under her and cup her hips, when she held his hands, cradling them between her warm breasts and kissed him again.

Slim heard a soft groan, like the door to the shed creaking on rusted hinges. He waited, alert in the dark, then heard it again.

"Janesta?" he called. " 'Nesta? You all right?" He fumbled for his glasses and stumbled out of the room, his shoulders bumping the walls, making the trailer sway as if a wind blew at it from all sides.

Janesta was sitting on the toilet, grimacing, clutching her belly. Slim had heard about female trouble. He had seen the bloody pads, some wrapped carefully, some coming undone, some with no effort at all to cover them, at the dump. It was like a secret he had known about for most of his life, his mother muttering about a friend coming to visit and just when Slim was sure any minute there would be a knock on the door, coffee perking and a plate of cookies on the table, his mother would get into bed with a hot-water bottle.

"Is it your friend?" he asked Janesta.

"No." She sighed. "It is not my friend." Then she groaned again and began to pant a little, like a dog out in the sun with no water. She refused to meet Slim's gaze.

He still doesn't get it, she thought with disgust. The dumb ox. He doesn't have a clue. She rubbed her belly.

"Maybe it's my appendix." She moaned, thinking: This is pathetic. Why in hell's name can't I tell him?

"I'll warm up the car," he said. "I'll get Crystal up. I'll get you into Union City in twenty minutes flat. D'you have a temperature?" He placed a trembling hand on her forehead, touched the back of her neck. Janesta slapped his hand away but without the usual energy she reserved to say no to his attentions.

* * *

All morning, Carol sat at the table, listlessly making sketches of crumpled pieces of paper, dreamily remembering the taste of sea salt on Rita's lips when she kissed her in the restaurant. She hadn't cared what anyone thought. She just wanted to kiss Rita's beautiful lips. All morning, she'd been hoping Rita would come over. And then what? she wondered, crumpling her sketch and adding it to the pile on the table.

She had woken to the sound of Nelly's tractor, but now it was quiet. She almost wished Crystal would arrive. Anything to distract her. But there were just birds twittering, an airplane droning, a fly buzzing lazily across the room. The refrigerator clicked on, sounding like a semi idling in the kitchen. The whole house seemed to vibrate. In exasperation, she put on her swimsuit, pulled her jeans and sweatshirt over it, and grabbed a towel. "Good-bye," she shouted to the refrigerator when it shuddered to a stop.

Heading down the path to Preacher's Lake, she forced herself to concentrate. "Use your senses," she instructed, feeling like someone just waking from a deep sleep.

There in the woods lay a fallen tree, the trunk nearly obscured by a thick blanket of pale green moss. She envisioned a painting she'd sketch out later, a woman lying on her back, moss growing over her the way it grew over this tree, with only the faintest image of the shape of her body pushing through. Her long hair swirled into the underbrush; reindeer moss and bunchberries grew in the tangle of her curls.

She pulled a stalk of red tip grass and chewed on the sweet end then brushed her cheeks with the feathery seed head. She inhaled deeply, realizing her lungs must be in shock with all the oxygen they were getting.

Yesterday, a postcard arrived from Vivian—the Statue of Liberty wearing mirrored sunglasses. "In case you wondered, I made it back to civilization alive," she'd written. "America" she'd scrawled at the bottom of Carol's address, underlining it several times. If it hadn't been for Vivian, I wouldn't be here, Carol thought. Soon the rest of the things she'd written to ask Dougie for would arrive from New York. As luck would have it, a friend of his sublet her apartment. Like a puzzle with all the pieces falling into place. That was how it felt.

Some trees in the distance had already begun to turn colors and the bright orange against the blue sky was a comforting sight. She meandered along the path thinking about how lucky she was to be in such a place, to have all this free time, to have what she needed to be able to work. Overhead a pair of seagulls circled, calling shrilly. She thought of Annie. She missed her the way she knew she always would. But at the same time, she missed herself. It was as if she'd died, too. But now she was coming back. Across the field, the ripe grass shimmered as if small animals were scurrying at the roots. She turned from the field to go through the woods, careful not to stub her toes on the roots that snaked across the path. Above her, the branches formed a shady arbor; layered under the trees, a mat of dried beech leaves the color of old crumbling lace. She brushed her palms over the cool mossy rocks, tucked some tiny hemlock cones in her pockets. There was the lake ahead of her. Bluish green, a darker shade than the sky; she'd need a touch of red to paint it. She would carry her easel down to the lake. The wild world, the weather, the whole of nature would wake her up.

Just me and the trees, she said to herself, spreading her towel on the sand, shivering despite the warm sun. The mountains were reflected in the wind-rippled water. Paradise, she thought. When was the last time she'd felt so peaceful? When being alone didn't mean lonely? Now it meant something else. She didn't know what. She was waiting, expectant.

* * *

Rainey was in her room blowing the pennywhistle Slim had given her. If she blew with all her might, there would be a shrill blast that made Nelly cringe and clap her hands over her ears. But she didn't puff up her cheeks to make the whistle scream. She blew it half-heartedly, exhaling into the whistle slowly, sounding like a baby bird that had fallen from the nest and called out, hoping to be rescued.

Nelly was flipping through *Uncle Bob's Barter 'n Buy*, determined to find a used posthole digger so they could put up a sturdier fence for the new pasture. The sheep had already escaped so many times she'd lost track. So far, she'd practically killed one whacking its head. They had eaten several broccoli plants, chewing them down to the roots, and trampled a row of corn. One had fallen into a ravine and Alton Poors had to help her haul it out with his come-along. And the mailman had practically run into the flock of them when he was coming up the hill.

"Would you tell her to quit that?" Nelly said, frowning, stabbing the thin paper like she was nailing it to the table.

"Why don't *you* tell her?" Rita calmly turned from her sewing machine, her foot paused on the pedal. Then she whirred forward, the sound blocking out Rainey's whistle as she guided the cloth. She had already made Rainey a new dress for the first day of school, the skirt dotted with strawberries, the bodice a series of neat tucks. Now she was making corduroy pants.

"Is that supposed to mean something?" Nelly asked.

"If you think it does, then it must." Rita lifted the pressure foot and snipped the threads. She held the pants up, examining her work.

"She never listens to me. You know that. I'm the big bad wolf." Nelly grimaced and showed her teeth like they were fangs.

"Maybe she'd listen if you said something besides 'Do this. Don't do that.' Just because she's a kid doesn't mean she's not a person."

"Thank you, Dr. Spock." Nelly tightened her overall straps and gathered her tobacco and papers. Rainey was lying on her bed, her feet against the insulation on the ceiling. She continued her slow whistling moan, oblivious to what was going on in the other room. Rita got up, brushing past Nelly, not bothering to acknowledge her sarcasm.

"Why don't you take your whistle and go outside?" Rita asked.

Rainey shook her head rapidly as if her mother had suggested she walk barefoot across broken glass. Ever since the huge buzzing beelike fly had entangled itself in her curls and bitten her twice behind the ear, she had been staying inside. The bites it left still

burned and itched. Rainey had decided she might never go outdoors again.

"This house is not a sanatorium," Nelly said. "It's not normal on
a perfectly nice day for a kid to be cooped up the way she is." She
looked accusingly at Rita and let the screen door slap shut. She
grabbed Rainey's bicycle and heaved it into the weeds. She was sick
of the girl hanging around the house. Like Nelly's mother had
done, in her room on the sunniest of days, the shades pulled.

Nelly pulled the ax out of the chopping block and split some
pieces of wood, every smack of the ax, every crack of the splitting
wood an attempt to drive her mother out of her mind. But she
could still smell the dusty, mildewed letters in the closet. Feel how
the paper fell apart in her hands as if made of dust, the envelopes
brittle as dried insect wings. Shoes green with mold. Perspiration-
stained dresses on tangled hangers. She was ten years old the first
time they took her mother away with no explanation. Nelly decided
her mother would be happy again if she cleaned her closet. There'd
been a happy woman on the television, waving at her sparkling
appliances. But her mother had been furious.

"What gives you the right to touch my things?" she said, slapping
Nelly hard across the ear. After that, her mother had a lock put on
her door, but she didn't need to go to such an extreme. Nelly never
set foot in her mother's room again, not even after she died.

Nelly chopped the wood, swinging the ax over her head, savoring
the strength in her back, in her arms, swinging it high then slamming the blade down into the wood on the chopping block. It made
a satisfying crack as the wood split and the pieces clattered to the
ground. She took a length of birch and hacked it into kindling.

Usually when Rita and Nelly fought, Rita stayed in the house and
cleaned. She turned the radio up, twisting the dial until a song she
knew was playing, and sang along as if to drown out the singer. She
would clean the house furiously, swatting at the spiderwebs that
appeared overnight, dangling in the corners, sweeping up the chaff
and dirt that fell from their shoes and clothes, taking time to get
between the cracks in the floorboards, mopping afterwards with the
ratty string mop. She would scour the stove top, soak the burners, slap
the throw rugs against the house and spread them to air in the sun.

This week, they fought so often she had already defrosted the
freezer, chipping away at the ice with a screwdriver. She had already
scrubbed and oiled the cast-iron sink and polished the woodstove
with stove black until it gleamed. Dust and dead flies had been
brushed from the windowsills, even the screens had been swept.

Today, after Nelly stomped out, Rita just sat at the table, not even bothering to wipe up the crumbs and coffee spills, resting her head on her sewing machine, steadily inhaling the scent of her own skin, willing the dull ache behind her eyes to dissipate. She began her familiar litany: I have to get a job. I have to get out of here. I can't depend on another living soul. I can't keep going on like this day after day, Nelly's temper like a time bomb ticking. I'll get a job at Hydie's. They must need help. A chambermaid at the Blue Sky Motel. Pick crabmeat. Pack sardines. Rake blueberries. Dig blood-worms. I had a perfectly good job in Boston. I must be crazy. So what if Rainey had never been out of the city. This is a reason to pack up everything? To end up with a stranger who can't even have a conversation without yelling?

She turned the pants she was making right side out and began pinning the waistband. She had wanted to get away from the traffic on Commonwealth Avenue, had yearned to escape the honking horns, the shrill sirens, to wake up to birds and see the night sky without streetlights.

"Well, you got the birds. You got the night," she said. She jumped when the door slapped shut behind her.

"You gotta watch that talking to yourself," Nelly said. She rubbed Rita's shoulders. Last night, when they had bathed in Preacher's Lake, cooling off from their work under the hot sun, Nelly sham-pooed Rita's hair, striving to be gentle, all the while feeling as charged as the air before a thunderstorm. Yes, she congratulated herself, reaching to pull loose the string holding Rita's top over her breasts, daring to imagine Rita would welcome this.

"Don't," Rita said clutching her top. "Nelly. Don't."

"I just want to touch you," Nelly said, the anger hissing, leaking around her attempt to be patient. "What's wrong with that?"

"Not *here*," Rita said, nodding at Rainey who sat at the water's edge. "Not now." She pulled away from Nelly.

"When then? Where?"

Rita didn't answer. She tied her top back on furiously and walked up the beach holding Rainey's hand, not looking back, not waiting for Nelly to catch up. When Nelly got home, Rita was in Rainey's bed reading to her and they had stayed together whispering into the night.

This time, when Nelly rested her hands on Rita's shoulders, Rita willed herself to relax. She let Nelly kiss her. This is my life, she told herself. I will make it work.

"That tickles," she said when Nelly kissed her ear. She wanted her to stop. But she didn't want to fight again, so she endured Nelly's lips on the edge of her face, endured the thick tobacco smell of her breath.

"Rainey?" Nelly said, pulling away from Rita. "You wanna help me?"

Rainey didn't respond. Nelly winked at Rita conspiratorially, as if to say: Watch me woo her.

She looked almost sweet to Rita, her chin trembling ever so slightly, betraying the confidence she pretended to have. Rita felt so confused remembering Carol's kiss, so full of promise. Why had she grown silent as they drove back to Preacher's Lake? Why had she dropped them off with no plans to get together again? I'm with Nelly, she scolded herself. I can make this work. Carol is my friend.

Nelly stood at the foot of Rainey's bunk. She touched Rainey's arm.

"I said you wanna help me out?"

"Help you what?" Rainey stared at the ceiling.

"Drive the tractor."

"You mean it? I can drive?" She turned slowly to look at Nelly. "Really drive? Really really?"

"Really. Would I ask you if I didn't mean it?"

Rainey contemplated this, drumming her whistle against her lip. "So will you or won't you?"

Rainey swung her legs over the side of the bed. "OK," she said.

"Well. Get your shoes on, partner."

Nelly winked at Rita as if to say: See. I'm trying. I want credit.

"Mommy, I'm gonna drive," Rainey said, running out the door.

*   *   *

Slim came back from the cafeteria with a packet of tiny powdered sugar donuts and a Coke for Crystal who sat in the waiting room, her hair tangled from sleep, hanging across her face. Slim set the food on the coffee table and sat down, sipping his coffee.

"Coke's my favorite," Crystal said. " 'Member the time we made us that Coke slush? 'Member that, Slim? How we invented it?"

"I remember." He felt dazed, as if he were still driving, the head-lights bright in the dawn making the world appear layered with gauze. Crystal slurped her Coke and kicked the heels of her pink rubber boots on the floor. Slim had been in such a hurry he couldn't find her sneakers anywhere and Crystal had cried, worried it was the first day of school and he expected her to wear boots and leave home without breakfast.

"It's still summer, Crystal," he'd told her. "But your mom's sick. We got to take her to the hospital. I'll get you some eats once we're there. C'mon," he had urged while Janesta stayed in the bathroom moaning, splashing water around. After Crystal was dressed, he helped Janesta pull her big maroon sweater down over her nightgown.

"We'll wrap the afghan around you," he said. "Can you get up? Lean on me. Use me like a crutch. I can carry you if I have to. Can you get up? I don't wanna hurt you none."

Janesta had clutched her belly, seeming to disappear into the pain. Now she was down the corridor behind closed doors.

"Mr. Riley?" A nurse with large round glasses stood in front of Slim with a clipboard. Slim and Crystal had been playing a magazine game, trying to see who could find the most pictures of dogs, and Crystal was still flipping the glossy paper, tearing the pages in her excitement to beat Slim.

"It's a boy," the nurse said, smiling broadly.

Slim shook his head, wondering: What on earth is wrong with this lady? Ain't it plain as day Crystal's a girl? All that hair she's got. Dressed head to toe in pink the way she is.

"She's a girl," he told the nurse, rubbing his palms on the knees of his torn work pants.

The nurse glanced at Crystal. "I mean the baby. It's a boy."

"The baby?"

"You *are* Mr. Riley?"

"Yeah," Slim said slowly. The elevator rang and he thought: Here's where I wake up. But nothing changed. He was still in the hospital waiting room. There was his car out in the parking lot taking up two spaces. There was his empty coffee cup with the rim chewed. There was Crystal with powdered sugar spilled down her shirt, humming "If I Only Had a Brain." And there was the nurse with a pin that said SUE R.N.

"Mrs. Riley's doing fine," she said.

Slim was confused. Why was this nurse talking about his mother?

"The baby's small. Just a little bitty thing. But doctor says he's going to be just fine. Do you want to see him?"

"The baby?" he said. What baby is that? he wanted to ask. He ran his hands rapidly through his hair until it rose up every which way, electrified. Then he got up so fast he knocked against the coffee table and tipped over Crystal's Coke can. It rolled under the sofa with a clatter.

"Good thing it's empty, huh Slim?" she asked, pulling on his arm, leading him after the nurse. "A tornado can pluck the feathers right off a chicken," Crystal said. "It can yank the wool right off a sheep."

Slim heard her voice as if it were coming from the eye of the storm itself while all around him the room hissed and whirled.

"Is that so?" the nurse asked, blinking rapidly, worried Slim might pass out, his face was so deathly pale. He didn't object when she seated him in a wheelchair and wheeled him slowly down the corridor to Janesta's room.

18

"All I could think was, holy Moses, Rita's gonna kill me. She's falling through the air like she's doing a somersault. Then she's flat on her back screaming bloody murder. I was scared she broke her back till I saw her feet kicking," Nelly told the doctor in the emergency room. The rest of the story was pieced together as Nelly paced beside the stretcher, picking at the torn skin around her fingernails, chewing her nails down to bloody nubs as she explained how Rainey climbed on the back of the tractor. She had been sure Rainey jumped to the ground.

"I felt her jump off, so I started up again. I didn't know she'd just jumped to the tire. When I pulled ahead, the tire must've flipped her off. Flipped her right off in the air," she repeated, flicking open her matchbook and running her fingertips over the match heads, as if each one were a rosary bead.

What Nelly didn't mention was how Rainey screamed as if a gun were pointed at her head when a harmless sweat bee hovered at the edge of her eye. She didn't mention how she grabbed Rainey, shaking her good. "It's a fucking sweat bee. It won't hurt you," she had growled. She didn't mention how she'd smacked Rainey's face or tell how satisfied she'd felt to see her shocked expression when she clutched Rainey's arm, gripping so hard she felt the bone and was ready to snap it like a dry branch.

"Get the fuck off this tractor if you're gonna be a big crybaby about a little sweat bee," she had said.

As the scene replayed in Nelly's mind, the images rushed at her like so many bright lights. "Open the throttle," she could hear herself saying. "Now push the starter." Rainey laughed when the engine fired, pointing happily at the lid flapping on the exhaust. Nelly was happy, too. In charge. Full of hope. Then the flash of blue as the girl twirled through the air, landing like a sack of grain. Rainey sprawled on her back, one arm twisted at her side like it didn't even belong to her, screaming like a wounded animal until Nelly stood over her; then, she sucked back those screams.

"I didn't realize till it was too late," Nelly said to the doctor's white-coated back as she examined Rainey, running her expert hands over her body, murmuring words of comfort, assessing the damage.

"You're gonna be all right," Rita had said to Rainey when they were in the truck, headed for town. "You hurt your arm. But you're gonna be all right."

When Nelly lifted Rainey from the ground and handed her to Rita, the girl's skin had been cold though the hot sun throbbed. She ran to the house and grabbed a blanket she tucked around Rainey, thinking: Sorry so sorry. Too late for that. Then the drive to town. Going much too fast down the bumpy road, the truck bouncing on its worn shocks. Rainey with the elbow of the arm she knew was broken in the palm of her other hand. The pain worse than the time she fell off the slide at day care and had to have stitches in her knee. But worse than the pain was knowing it was all her fault. Nelly would never forgive her or let her drive the tractor again. She would storm around the house, banging the chairs against the table, slamming the door so hard the whole house would shake. Rainey could feel Nelly's rage rising like the waves of heat on the tar road ahead of them. She was afraid to cry, but every time the truck jounced over a bump, Rainey couldn't help but moan.

"I'd like to keep her overnight. Just in case there's a concussion," the doctor explained. In her confusion, Rita focused on the doctor's appearance. Her neatly ironed jeans and perfect, unsmudged white leather sneakers. The white lab coat she wore over her green silk blouse. A stethoscope around her neck like a scarf. A sapphire engagement ring that glittered. "She's had a shock. Her vitals were off when you got here. I don't want to take any chances."

Everyone was being very nice, but cautious, aware of Rita and Rainey, how different they were. A male nurse brought in a tray with bowls of chicken noodle soup and turkey sandwiches on soft white bread.

"I'll come and get you in the morning," Nelly said before leaving. Rita barely acknowledged her, though Nelly rested her palm on the back of Rita's neck as if she had the right to touch her.

* * *

As soon as she slid through the window into her truck, Nelly knew she was not going back to the farm. She didn't care about the sheep and their empty feeders. She didn't care about the hens with their water pans pecked dry. She didn't care if the sky opened up and rained on the cultivator she had left in the field, drenching her toolbox with the lid thrown open. "Let it all rust, I don't care. I hate my life," she muttered, cutting off a bald man in a black car with New York plates. He honked and pulled to a squealing stop as Nelly lunged across his path to park in front of The Quarterdeck.

I hate it, she thought as she downed mug after mug of cheap draft beer. When Ginger Martin sat beside her, her arm brushing Nelly's, giving off her 'I'm available scent,' Nelly thought she might never return to the farm. She would leave Rita and Rainey in the hospital and let them figure it out. Nelly did not care.

Rainey had been so pale, the color draining from her face, her skin gray as ashes. Nelly feared the child might die before they got to the hospital. She had never driven that fast, that recklessly around the curves, leaning forward as if her weight could propel the truck forward faster, her heavy boot flooring the gas pedal, birds veering crazily across their path, drunk on overripe chokecherries. Rainey staring straight ahead, making no sound.

As Nelly drank, she had flashes of her mother when she was young, her bright eyes as she bent over Nelly laughing. How she would twirl Nelly, her strong hands under her arms, confident. And how her mother looked with her fuzz of hair lusterless as threadbare cloth, the skin around her eyes bruised and puffy. The sickbed smell of her rising. And seeping through this image like a pentimento, Fiona with her bloated tongue a dead gray fish lolling from her swollen mouth.

Nelly wasn't going to think about any of this. She bought Ginger a rusty nail. Then another. She kept at the beers, clinking her mug against Ginger's glass, laughing gruffly at Ginger's jokes.

They ate pickled eggs they dipped from the glass jar in front of them, the brine dripping down their arms, and pork rinds from the cellophane bags behind the bar, sucking the salt from their fingers, not watching the TV that flickered in the corner or paying attention to the men who sat on stools cheering.

Nelly offered to take Ginger to the Oyster Shanty and Ginger accepted, though they were so tipsy, they leaned on each other, stumbling out into the street. Ginger lived above the shoe repair shop, the windows of her apartment hung with lace, prisms, and rainbow decals. It was so much easier to stumble upstairs and fall onto the tousled sheets of her unmade bed than to drive across town to eat a meal they would only throw up later.

On the door to the street, a hand-lettered sign advertised MISS GINGER'S MASSAGE. Beneath that, a red valentine heart balanced in the palm of a hand. Whenever people passed Ginger on the streets of Union City, they whispered how she did everything *but*. Dressed in her flaunting way, glittering and feathery, she stood out like a tropical bird among the faded work shirts and blue jeans most folks wore. Ginger sparkled and jingled, as she did now, her earrings tinkling as she clung to Nelly, her hot pink tube top clenched around her breasts, her hair spilling out of the silver barrettes that only partly succeeded at holding her hair off her neck, her white sandals clattering on the sidewalk as they crossed to her doorway and stumbled up the steps.

*   *   *

The first call Carol made once her phone was connected was to her parents. Her mother, really, since her father wouldn't speak to her. Not that the words she and her mother exchanged could actually be called a conversation. But Carol figured they should have her phone number. In case, she thought.

"How's everything?" she asked after explaining where she was and insisting her mother write down the number even though it meant holding on so long Carol was afraid she might never come back.

"Did I tell you the deer are starving?" her mother asked in her quavering voice.

"Yes. You told me that last time."

"All the rabbits and coyotes have bubonic plague," her mother said.

Already, Carol was not listening. She was busy imagining what she really wanted to say: Ma. Guess what? I met this great woman. You know how you cried about never getting to be a grandmother? Well, she's got a little girl.

Carol pictured her mother offering Rainey a plate of cookies.

"Yesterday a golf ball cracked the picture window. Good thing we got golf ball insurance, Daddy said."

Carol continued her own fantasy conversation: Hey, Ma. Remember that commandment? You know, love one another? So it hurts that I'm a lesbian. I'm your daughter. I'm happy being who I am. I like my life. Is that so bad?

Carol's mother continued to talk, not even noticing there were no "uh-huhs" or "reallys?".

"The strangest thing happened yesterday. I went to hang the dish towel on the line and there was a hummingbird trapped in a huge spiderweb between the two pine trees out back. I thought the bird was dead. It just dangled there from one wing. When I broke the web, it started to fall then it flew right up into the tree and sat on a branch. I've never seen a hummingbird stop flying."

When Carol hung up, she felt as if her life were a *Wheel of Fortune* game. Everyone else was getting a new car, but she kept landing on bankrupt.

This is why so many people live in New York, Carol realized, pacing her kitchen, straightening the chairs, putting the dishes away. So after they talk to their mothers, no matter what day of the week, no matter what time, there's always some place to go to forget. I'll go to Hydie's and lose myself in a double cheeseburger, she decided, checking her watch. Too late. Closed. I'll whip over to Moody's and knock myself out with a couple of Twinkies. Party time. Shit. What is this?

Carol took a long hard look at herself. She was turning back into her teenage self, she was sure of it. She had spent the entire day inside and was still wearing her pajamas.

She went into her studio. So far, she had made a table out of an old door and two sawhorses Slim had given her. Piled in the corner were some old dolls he'd been thrilled she'd wanted and a jumble of broken toys. What had she planned to do with them? "Some studio," she muttered.

She had turned her life upside down and still hadn't even bothered to call Iris to try to analyze it. Besides, Iris was at some swanky beach hotel under a colorful umbrella, her feet up, sipping a bright orange drink decorated with a matching umbrella. It was both liberating and terrifying to be out of touch with her therapist.

I'll call it *The Unanalyzed Life*, she decided, picturing Barbie propped under an umbrella like the one she'd put Iris under.

"I need a New York fix," she said when Dougie was on the line after fiddling with his answering machine.

"Is that you?" he asked. "Officially hooked up to Ma Bell?"

"Oh, Dougie, I miss you so much."

"What'd you do, call your mother?"

"How'd you know that?"

"You always get all mushy about how you love me after a hit of Mom."

"You're right. I just had a lovely chat that makes me want to drive off the bridge. But I really do miss you. When're you coming to visit anyhow?"

"I don't do the rural thing," he said. "Besides, I'm busy."

"How's Boris?"

"Boring." He giggled. "He's gone back to his ex. I met someone new. His name's Thom. With a 'th.' "

"Uh-oh. You're not doing pretentious again, are you?" Carol said, lisping, adding several "th" sounds to the word *pretentious.*

"Not at all. The way he explained it, where he grew up there were so many Thomases they all had to accept a variation. He said the 'th' made him feel like royalty. As in queenly."

"Oh, Dougie! So tell me, tell me."

"I'm still in investigative flirting mode, which as you know is a new one for me. I don't know how you gals stand it. So far, he has not once mentioned an ex or a current or done any whining about me putting a cramp in his psychic space."

"Investigative flirting?"

"You know. Lots of eye contact. Standing too close. That kind of thing. To kind of feel him out, so to speak, before I feel him up."

"And?"

"He flirts back quite well. I'm all a tither. We spent the afternoon strolling around the Village holding hands. Then we went to this piano bar on the East Side. We sat right up at the piano having drinks. He treated, which I always enjoy. And he got the piano player to play all these songs about rain. It's been raining for weeks here."

"That sounds like fun," Carol said. "When it rains here, the big excitement is going nightcrawling with Crystal Curtis afterwards."

Carol had written Dougie a letter about the people in Preacher's Lake, including detailed descriptions of Rita and how beautiful she was.

"Wait. I'm not finished. So there we are, at the piano, our knees bumping, sipping our drinks. The piano player's singing "Don't Sleep in the Subway" and "Raindrops Keep Falling on My Head," like that. All of a sudden he bursts into a medley from *West Side Story*. Finger snapping with the Jets, the whole bit. I practically choked on my drink. 'Because I felt like it,' he says when he's finished. And Thom sings along. He's not at all uptight about whether he's cool. I can't remember the last time I had so much fun."

"You deserve it," Carol said. "So, what's next on the agenda?"

"Sex."

"Of course."

"So. How's it going with you and your new flame?"

"I'm scared."

"What's new?"

"She's very beautiful and very intense and she's got a kid. A kid, Dougie. That seems so. I dunno. *So*. You know I like things all easy to manage. I'm set in my ways. I like my time alone."

"You don't have to marry her."

"I know that. Besides. She's attached. I told you about Nelly."

"Yeah. She sounds like something right out of the Wild West."

"We went to the ocean together the other day."

"That's a start. Hold on. I got another call. Back in a jiff."

Carol dragged the telephone across her studio and stood at the large uncurtained window. Across the road, Slim's trailer looked abandoned, not even a cat in the window. Up behind it, Rita's house appeared to be sinking into the earth. Desolate. Like something Andrew Wyeth would paint. When was the last time a car came up the road? She had a spooky sensation that everybody else had been evacuated.

"It was *him*," Dougie said. He made hot and heavy breathing sounds.

"Gosh!" Carol laughed. "I'm honored you still want to talk to me."

"I don't wanna be too eager. Gotta let 'em know you have a life."

"Tell me something. Anything. I feel like I'm on another planet. Tell me about work."

"You don't want to hear about work."

"But I do."

"OK. It's your nickel. Tonight's special is Aztec corn chowder. Grilled peppered lamb with rosemary. Arugula with miso vinaigrette."

"Mm," Carol said. "What about dessert?"

"Oh, the usual. Death by chocolate. Indian pudding. Laurent's framboise something or other. I'm sick of Laurent."

"What's new?"

"No really. He comes cruising through while we're setting up like he's some ice skater at the Olympics. He gives his stupid little bow.

Those horrible suits he wears. Ugh. And that hair of his. I just wanna knock him in the head with a champagne bottle and give him a buzz cut."

Carol laughed. She could picture Dougie with his hands on his hips, dressed head to toe in black, his dark cap of hair glowing under the restaurant lights, his dark eyes glowering at Laurent.

"He's started wearing this snood."

"This what?"

"A snood. You know. Like a bridesmaid. To keep his glorious hair out of the soup. You know like those swami guys with their beards in a hair net? If you ask me, it looks like he's got it in a jockstrap."

"More! More!" Carol said. She sat with her legs slung over the chair, noticing the sunlight on the rough bark of the trees. A chipmunk scurried across the grass, its tail held high.

"Girl, you must be desperate for action. How long are you planning on doing the celibate waiting game thing?"

"You know us girls. We take our time."

"Listen," Dougie said. "Don't be so serious. Have a little fun."

"Fun? Lesbians don't have fun."

"You could always be the first. Oh, hey. I got another call."

"I'm getting off. I've got phone ear."

"Listen, Carol. Just have some fun. Trouble will find you soon enough."

* * *

A thick white cast covered Rainey's left arm from a few inches above her elbow to where it fit around her hand like a glove with the fingers and thumb cut off. At her age, the doctor explained, it would heal quickly. The bone, which had broken neatly in three places, would knit together good as new, and the heavy cast would be off before she knew it. "You just can't go swimming," the doctor had said. "But the days for that are almost gone anyway."

"I'm sorry," Rainey said. She'd spilled cherry Jell-O on her lap.

"It's OK, honey. Do you want me to help you?" Rita asked.

"I'm not a baby," Rainey said, pouting, on the verge of tears.

"I know that. But anybody'd have trouble eating with their other hand. I can't eat with my left hand. You can't eat with your right."

"God's mad at me," Rainey whispered, lying back against the pillows and squeezing her eyes shut tight.

"What? God's what?"

"Mad at me," Rainey said, so fast the words came out strung together: madatme.

"Why do you say that?"

Rainey thumped her cast like a bird flapping its wing.

"God's not like that. God doesn't get mad and give people broken arms."

"You don't know."

"Listen to me, Rainey. This is not your fault. Nelly did something really stupid. Everybody makes mistakes. Sometimes they're really big ones. All we can do is try not to make them again."

"God's stupid."

"Well. You can think that if you want, but if anybody's stupid, it's Nelly. And me. I should've known it was dangerous." Rita checked the clock again. Nelly had not come back the way she promised. Rita went to the window to see if the truck was there. A car like Slim's was near the entrance. But no dusty green truck with a bashed-in door.

"How d'you know? What if there's no God anyhow?" Rainey asked in a belligerent voice, a voice Rita had never heard her use before. She was still pouting. Rita wished she would cry. All through the exam and even when she came out with the plaster cast on her arm, she seemed on the verge of tears, but no tears came. Rita rubbed her back, around and around in small circles the way Rainey liked.

"It itches," Rainey said.

"Where?" Rita began to lightly scratch Rainey's back.

"My arm."

"Oh. We'll ask the doctor about that. She's gonna check you before we go home." *If* we go home, Rita thought.

"You didn't say."

"What? What didn't I say?" Rita took a bite of Rainey's Jell-O. It was bright red. She had thought it would taste like cherries, but it didn't taste like anything.

"How d'you know there's a God anyhow?"

"I dunno. I just feel it. It's hard to explain, Rainey. That's just the way it is. It's kind of like how you feel when you get up in the morning and there are spiderwebs all sparkling with dew on the grass and you feel good in your heart. Or when I tuck you in bed after you've just had your bath. That's what God's like to me."

"I'm not God."

"Well. They say God lives in us."

"Who says?"

"I dunno. The Bible, I guess. I just heard that before."

"What's God look like?"

"Do you know some people believe God's a she? I had a friend once that had a picture of Jesus and Jesus was a black man with thick wooly hair. Not at all like that picture we saw in the library book. Everybody believes different things. Nobody knows. When I was a little girl like you I was sure God was an old man with a long white beard who sat up in the clouds watching me." She didn't say that she had also feared God was just waiting to punish her for all she couldn't do right.

"Did you see him?"

"No. Nobody ever really *sees* God. It's more complicated than that. You know how when you wake up at night and it's pitch dark but you still know where things are?"

"Yeah."

"Well. It's kind of like that. A way you sense things. Like the wind on your face. Some people think God is the trees and birds and the sky. Like that. What do you think?"

Rainey shrugged. She was sure God was mad. That's all she knew. First God made her different from everybody. Then he broke her arm.

"I've got some paper. You wanna draw me a picture of God?"

"I can't."

"You can try. Just remember, God can be one thing today and another tomorrow. Your ideas can change." Rita took the tray from her table and put the paper and pen down.

"I can't draw with my wrong hand."

"Oh. Sorry. I forgot." She pushed the curls off Rainey's forehead and kissed her. "I'm so sorry, sweetie. Maybe you could take a picture of God with your camera when we get back."

"How'm I gonna do that if I can't see God?"

"You can take pictures of things you see that make you feel God's there. Do you suppose you can use your camera with one hand?"

"Maybe," Rainey said. She swung her legs out from under the covers. "I wanna go now," she said.

"Me too. But we have to wait for the doctor. And I have to go sign a bunch of papers. And we have to wait for Nelly."

Rainey was silent, taking in all that her mother said, but noticing at the same time the raised veins on the back of her mother's hand, the crinkled skin on her knuckles, the strawberry birthmark at the edge of her wrist. She would take a picture of this when she got home. And a picture of her monkey, too, with his rubber banana and white rubber shoes. She'd put him in the flower garden and take his portrait.

* * *

Rita signed everywhere there was an X on the forms the counselor helped her fill out. Having no insurance and no income to speak of, she'd been referred to the office of a woman named Angie. She applied for what Angie called "assistance." The way Angie said it, Rita saw all the letters of the word capitalized in large bold print. Angie was very kind and she clicked her tongue sympathetically to reassure Rita.

"The money's there for people that need it," she said in her matter-of-fact way. "Looks to me like you need it. You can't raise a child without health insurance in this day and age.

"The bill," she continued, tapping a pile of paper on her desk. "The bill will be ridiculous. We both know that. Besides," she said tossing her long red hair over her shoulders. "Think of all the taxes you've paid over the years. That's what it's for. You'll be getting some of that back."

Rita nodded slowly. She felt the way she did in dreams when she'd arrive at work in her underwear: exposed, vulnerable, ashamed.

"Your little girl's gonna need her boosters and all. Plus kids get sick. Accidents happen. And what about you? I bet you haven't had a checkup since she was born, am I right?"

Rita shrugged off the question.

"I'm telling you. You go over to that welfare office and get some food stamps and benefits till you're back on your feet. I did it," she confessed, lowering her voice. "My first husband left me with three kids under the age of five and a stack of bills you wouldn't believe. What was I supposed to do? It's not a thing to be ashamed of, though they try to make you feel that way."

"Thanks," Rita said. "I really appreciate what you're saying. It helps. I used to be able to take care of myself."

"You will again, believe me."

Rita sighed, allowing herself to believe there might be a way out of this mess she called her life after all. "Thank you," she said again.

"You are more than welcome," Angie said. "You call me if there's a problem." She handed Rita her card.

"I do have this problem," Rita said shyly. She cleared her throat. "I'm sorry to ask. I didn't have time to do anything but get Rainey to the hospital. I don't have any change to call my—" She paused, unsure what to call Nelly. "My ride," she said finally. "My ride hasn't come."

Angie pointed to the phone on her desk, nearly buried in papers. "Dial nine to get out," she said. "I'll get us some coffees."

Rita called home, but there was no answer. She imagined the empty house, dust motes glistening in the sunlight. The chickens clucking noisily as they laid their eggs. She let it ring a dozen times to give Nelly time to run in, but still there was no answer. She thought she'd call Carol, but just picturing Carol's face, imagining her concern, made Rita feel like a guitar string about to snap. Besides, she didn't know Carol's last name or her phone number or if she *had* a phone. She dialed Slim, but there was no answer. What day was it? she wondered. Was he at the dump? The calendar on the wall was no help.

"Everything OK?" Angie asked, setting a coffee in front of Rita.

"Nobody answers."

"Well, you've still got a wait. By the time this hospital is done with you, you'll be playing with your grandkids. Here's some change," she said, reaching into her desk. "There's a pay phone down the hall."

"I'll pay you back next time I'm in town," Rita said.

"Please!" Angie tossed her hair impatiently. "Don't consider it."

As Rita headed back to Rainey's room, she could hear an old woman cry, "Help! Hurt! Help! Hurt!"

"Where does it hurt, Gracie?" a woman asked.

"Hurt!" the old woman said in her gruff voice.

"Where? Is it your leg? Does your leg hurt?"

"Hurt!" the old woman repeated as if she were exhausted.

"Hey!" a familiar voice said.

Rita turned.

"Slim? What're you doing here? I just tried to call you."

"Did ya hear?"

"Hear what?"

"I'm a dad."

"A dad?"

"Yep!" Slim looked like a little boy who'd just hit his first home run. "Come see him," Slim said, taking Rita by the elbow and steering her through the swinging doors.

Rita squinted to get a better look at the baby swaddled in a white blanket in the last row.

"He weighs six pounds three ounces. He lost an ounce, but the doctor says that's normal. Ain't he somethin'?"

Rita was speechless at first, then she recovered. "That's wonderful, Slim," she said. He was still holding her arm and she patted his hand. "Congratulations," she said.

"Hey," he said. "How'd you know to come? The phone lines already hummin' with gossip?"

"I didn't know," Rita said. "Rainey's here. She broke her arm."

"Oh, Jeezum. That's terrible," Slim said. As he went back to the room with Rita, she explained that she needed a ride home, that Nelly had not shown up the way she'd promised.

"I was just tellin' Crystal we'll go get us a few things. She's down in her mom's room watchin' TV. Lemme just say hello to Rainey. I'll take you back soon as you're ready. You just say the word.

"What's this I hear about my friend?" Slim said. He did one of his magic tricks, taking a quarter from behind Rainey's ear. She giggled, then sniffled like she might cry at last.

"My arm's broke," she said.

"You ain't got no autographs yet," Slim said. "Can I be the first?"

"Autograph?"

"You know. When you get a cast, people sign their names on it. Write you messages and what all. Lemme see if I got a felt tip." He dug into the pockets of his pants and patted his shirt. "Criminey. I got a slew of 'em back home. Soon's you get home, I'll sign it for ya. I got a big surprise for ya, too." He winked at Rita.

"What is it?" Rainey asked, her eyes shining. Rita was relieved to watch her with Slim. She so obviously loved him. She noticed the white patent leather loafers Slim wore on his bare feet. His floppy pants inches above his ankles, his shirt dotted with holes. But with his new haircut, he was almost handsome.

"It ain't gonna be any kind of surprise if I tell you."

Rainey was giggling when the doctor came in.

"Hey," she said. "Who told you it was OK to laugh in a hospital?"

Rainey, looking stricken, began to suck her thumb.

"That was a joke," the doctor said. "Apparently a bad joke. We love it when people laugh here," she added, beginning the exam.

"Just gimme the signal," Slim said, flicking his fingers in an awkward wave. "Just say when you're ready to go."

19

"My friend, she went to this party and got drunk and had sex with a bunch of different boys," the girl sitting across from J.T. said. Her blue eyes reflected the light like shattered marbles. "What if she's pregnant?"

"You sound really worried," J.T. said. She couldn't read the girl's expression, but she was pretty sure the girl was reporting her own behavior, not that of a friend. Did she want approval? Permission? To be told her body was a gift to share only with someone special? The girl hung her head and sat in silence, zipping and unzipping her purse.

"Did this friend of yours use protection?"

The girl looked up, almost defiant. "No. She had condoms but she forgot. She'd been really drinking. They had margaritas at the party."

J.T. thought of the poem Betty read her last night from *Predisposing Characteristics,* a book she got on interlibrary loan because the theme was teenage pregnancy. Some lines came floating back to her: "Promise cuity/Love has got to be out there somewhere/on some street corner/on a Greyhound to a place I have never been." She sighed. How could she possibly help this girl? It was as if her future had already been mapped out long ago. Like the poem said, "Must be the poverty of assembly line futures/hunger Wonder bread can never fill."

"Were you there, too?" she finally asked. The least she could do was try to give this girl information, maybe get her examined.

"No," the girl blushed deeply. "My friend told me. If she's pregnant, how's she supposed to know which boy did it?" She glanced at the poster behind J.T. WHO CAN GET AIDS? the poster asked. Underneath was a mirror.

"She's my best friend." The girl clasped her hands nervously.

"Do you suppose you could get her to come in here?"

A confused expression flashed across the girl's face, then she shrugged. "I dunno," she whispered. "Maybe."

"Do you ever worry about this yourself?" J.T. asked gently, trying to proceed as if this best friend really existed.

"No," the girl said firmly. "I'd never do that. Anyhow, I got a steady boyfriend."

"Well," J.T. said. "Even so, it's still a good idea to protect yourself. Not just from pregnancy. There are diseases, too. Remember how we talked about that last time? Did you read those pamphlets I gave you? You can share them with your friend, too. Remind her that it's important to use condoms. And to come in for an exam."

"Oh," the girl said. "I will." She got up to leave, then sat back down. "Am I due for one of those?" she asked shyly.

J.T. pretended to study her chart. "Yes," she said. "And as a matter of fact, we can squeeze you in right before lunch."

As J.T. and Lizzy were leaving the clinic for lunch, Derek, wearing his lace curtain like a cape, was being hurried up the steps by his mother. He wore a crown festooned with glitter. J.T. gave him a thumbs-up sign.

"Maybe by the time he's ready for his operation it won't be such a big deal," she said. Lizzy didn't respond. Lately, J.T. noticed she always seemed preoccupied, as if her mind were on some important secret.

"A penny for your thoughts," J.T. said as they passed the Wishy Washy.

"I hear the laundromat is going out of business."

"This is what you're worried about?"

"What makes you think I'm worried?"

"You've just been, I dunno, kind of not here."

"Oh," Lizzy said. "I guess I'm just tired."

They turned into J. J. Newberry's and sat at the lunch counter.

"If I had a job here, my life would be so simple," Lizzy said. "Fry the fries. Pour the drinks. Wipe the counters. Pocket the change."

"You'd be bored."

"Maybe bored would be better," she said.

After lunch, they each popped a balloon to try to get a discount on their hot fudge sundaes. Lizzy's was free. She took it as a sign and became more animated, insisting they look at the racks of paperbacks and read aloud from the last pages the way they used to.

"*Love Nest*," J.T. said, selecting a book. "Sounds kinda risqué for Newberry's, don't you think? This bird on the cover looks lecherous."

" 'Karissa pulled the heavy draperies closed and knelt on the hearth to light the fire. Karl, lounging on the sumptuous sofa, sipped his sherry slowly. " 'Twas a glorious, glorious day, n'est-ce pas, ma chère?" he murmured. " 'Twill be a glorious night," Lizzy read.

J.T. made gagging sounds. "This one actually says, 'And they lived happily ever after.' Who reads these?"

"Women that wish it was true."

"That girl before lunch. Do you suppose she reads this crap? I'm really worried about her."

"Look. We do the best we can. We both told her how to protect herself. She knows what to do. But we are not the sex police."

J.T. pretended to wield a pistol.

"Well, we're not. What are we supposed to do? Sit on the bedside table? Yell, 'put that condom on right this minute or else'?"

"I can't believe only one person in the entire county came to my AIDS Awareness meeting. And she had a fetus feet pin on her lapel."

"We're not exactly a high risk area. There's been only one positive diagnosis in the last five years."

"There's always plain old VD." J.T. flipped the pages of a shiny book covered with gaudy flowers. " 'Sondra leaned against Roderick and he held her close,' " she read. " 'Together, anything was possible.' "

"Forget who reads it, who writes it?" Lizzy said. She giggled and held up a book that featured a woman in a large straw hat walking a sheep on a leash through the town square. She considered telling J.T. about missing her period. But then the moment passed.

"That one's so realistic," J.T. said. "As a matter of fact, I meant to bring my sheep to work with me today."

" 'Do I have to keep telling you? Judith, I love you,' " Lizzy read. " 'Darling, I absolutely worship you.' "

She put the book back and gave the rack a twirl as they left. What if her life turned out perfectly, the way it did in these books?

*   *   *

Rita heaved a huge zucchini into the chicken pen. It landed with a dull thud; the chickens didn't even glance up. They were busy plucking the feathers from the hen they had chosen to pick on. She was nearly bald and in a few places, they had drawn blood. Rita shooed them away, but they came slowly back, first one, then another, pecking while the featherless one continued to eat the cracked corn Rita set out.

At first the hens had run over eagerly, squawking excitedly at the new treat, tearing through the green rind. But the one from yesterday was untouched. The sheep didn't even look up when she threw a few into their pasture and the ram, alone in his pen, had actually yawned.

Rita went to the garden to pick the smallest zucchinis she could find, nearly half a bushel. They were prolific plants as a rule, but the problem was compounded because she had planted too many to begin with. She couldn't even give them away. If only they could be stacked like cordwood for the winter. She pulled several onions and added them to the basket, then surveyed her garden. She felt as if she'd given her life to these plants, as if she'd resuscitated the soil. And it was beautiful. The waxy rows of heavenly scented basil beside the feathery dill. Tomatoes ripening on every bushy plant, sweet and juicy. When she reached for one, it fell into her palm, heavy and warm. She wiped it on her shorts and bit into it, sucking the juice hungrily. The lettuces were like bouquets, crisp and curly, red tip and oak leaf with the Boston lettuce, flourishing under the shade cloth. Celery she had wrapped in newspaper to blanch. Pumpkins turning orange sprawled through the rows of sweet corn where the silk spilled from the silvery green husks. Any day now, it would be ready to eat. The tassels quivered as the bees worked the thick pollen. There were even a few watermelons and cantaloupes she had nursed along, tucking black seaweed under the vines to draw the heat and discourage slugs, carefully feeding them manure tea in the evenings. Everything was going to be ready to harvest at once. What broccoli she salvaged from the cabbageworms and the last rampage of the sheep was forming tight green heads, and the Brussels sprouts were up to her shoulders. The late-bearing strawberries were ripening, the crinkled leaves bobbed ever so slightly in the intermittent breeze. At the edge of the field, a row of sunflowers nodded. The sky was hazy, brooding. With any luck, by nightfall it would rain and she wouldn't have to haul the watering cans.

She tensed as a car approached, then realized it was just someone parking to go to the lake. She'd come back from the hospital and found the house empty, with no sign of Nelly, everything just as it was when they left, the light on Rita's sewing machine glowing, the pants still bunched under the pressure foot. It was like returning to the scene of a crime. She almost expected to find yellow police ribbon strung around the house.

It had been over a week with no word from Nelly. With each passing day, Rita became more adept at recognizing different cars: the soft whir of Slim's car like a boat gliding up the hill, the metallic scrape of Carol's old car when she came to a stop, the chug of the mail truck stopping and starting, the rattle of the propane cans in the back of the delivery truck as it climbed the hill. Her whole body ached from listening so intently for the whine of Nelly's truck. What would they say to one another? What would happen next?

The night before, Rita had been unable to sleep, fearful both that Nelly would return and that she never would. She couldn't think either scenario through to any kind of conclusion. She went out to the gardens, wandering up and down, comforting herself as she paced under the moon that tipped like a bowl and spilled its light over the pale green heads of cabbage that shimmered against the dark soil. She bent over the zinnias, savoring their rich spicy scent, fingering their velvety petals. She tried not to worry. Tried to tell herself that if she could get through this night, the morning would be better. She watched the lights at Carol's place, wondering if Carol was painting. Carol had explained that she liked being productive while the rest of the world slept. Rita was flooded with shame at the thought of Carol, at the memory of how she had behaved. Like a puppy, eagerly bounding at Carol's feet, nipping at her ankles, her whole body saying: Touch me touch me! Like a puppy that would lick anybody's hand for attention. It pained her to remember. She tucked a bright pink cosmos behind her ear and sang "Love Has No Pride," mocking herself as she scuffed her toes in the dirt.

*   *   *

Rainey stared at the plywood bottom of the bunk bed where she used to sleep. A spider was weaving a web above her pillow. Her mother said spiders were good bugs, not really bugs at all but something called arachnids. They caught bad bugs like flies. Rainey wasn't sure whether to believe her. She missed being up high where she could see out the window easily. But with her arm broken, it was too difficult to climb the ladder. Her arm ached as if nails were being driven through the bone. Under the cast, too far for her to reach, she had an itch she was certain was an ant or a mosquito or something worse, trapped inside, eating her skin.

Sometimes Rainey heard her mother crying when she thought Rainey was asleep. At the moment, Rita was in the other room, rattling pans, humming to herself. Rainey's eyes followed the grain in the wood, noticing the places where the knots had fallen out and the resinous smears of glue. An apple fell and rolled across the roof.

"Yoo-hoo." Slim shaded his eyes to see through the screen door. "Just came to say hi. You guys OK?" Slim stepped shyly into the room.

"I'm all right." Rita shrugged, lifting her hair off the back of her neck. "Rainey's kind of blue. I think she's sleeping." She didn't bother to lower her voice, hoping Rainey would come out to see Slim.

Rita had just set a dozen canning jars into a pot of boiling water and the zucchini slices and brine were bubbling on the other burner. Her eyes filled with tears that she pretended were from the rising steam when she turned to dab her face with a dish towel.

"I don't know why I had to pick a heat wave to do this in," she said. She pulled her damp T-shirt away from her back. "But I had to do something with all the zucchini."

Slim laughed. "It's a wonder the pigs in this county don't speak Italian from all the zucchinis they eat. I canned us two dozen quarts of tomatoes last evening. And I got I don't know how many more to go."

"That's next on my list," Rita said, glad she had purchased so many canning jars when Buster's had a sale. "Just remind me when winter comes that it was once this hot." Rita wiped up the spills from the brine. The jars were rattling under the rolling boil.

"If there's any way I can help you out, you say the word."

"Thanks, Slim."

"I mean to be a good neighbor."

"So," she said, changing the subject, suddenly overcome by his simple kindness. "What's the news on Janesta and the baby?"

"They're settling in OK. He's a crier. Such a bitty thing. Ain't hardly big as my shoe. Crystal says he oughta sleep in a shoe box not that big old crib I set up. Say, listen. I brought Rainey something."

Rita nodded at Rainey's doorway. Slim knocked and peered around the curtain. She was lying with her back to him, her curls dark against the white pillowcase, her arm in its cast propped on another pillow. "I came visitin'," Slim said. "I brung you a present."

Rainey sat up to watch Slim use the yo-yo he pulled from his pocket.

"It's good to be two-handed," he said, using the yo-yo with his right hand then switching to his left, slipping the loop over his knuckle, demonstrating how to wind the string and when to let it go. "Most folks can only use the one hand. Ain't that a shame? But just think. If I could use both my hands the same, I could be makin' a sandwich with one hand and writin' my grocery list with the other."

As Rita ladled the hot zucchini pickles into the clean jars, the house filled with the scent of vinegar and mustard seed. She tightened the lids and set the jars into the boiling water, careful not to scald herself. She remembered the time Slim arrived at the door with a lopsided cake. His shirt with the buttons missing, sewn together with black thread. His eyes a smudge of blue behind the thick dusty lenses. So what if he was an oddball? Rita thought. Who wasn't? Who cared anyway? Rainey was giggling and had actually gotten out of bed. This was all that mattered.

"Can she come over to make some splits and see her real surprise?" Slim winked. Rainey had still not met the baby.

"Pardon me? You're making what?"

"Splits. Me and Crystal got all the fixings. Cherries. Whip cream. Nanners and nuts. Three kinds of ice cream and I forget how many sauces. Crystal had to have it all. You're welcome, too."

"No. That's OK. You two go ahead. I gotta be a pickle factory."

"If there's any little way I can help out, you just say the word," Slim said.

"There is something—" she started, then paused. She had seen him hugging Crystal, patting her back with his big hands. She wanted to be hugged that way, but it was not something she was brave enough to ask for. Slim fingered the brown bits of onion skin Rita had piled on the compost bucket while he waited for Rainey to get her camera.

"Sometime when you're going to Moody's or town, I could use a ride," Rita said. They were out of milk and though she had powdered milk for emergencies, this and the butter and flour were almost gone as well.

"Gosh, Rita. I can't get it through my thick skull you don't have no wheels with Nelly away. 'Course I'll give you a ride. I'm goin' down later on to pick up some cat food. I go down every day, sometimes more'n once. Anytime, you just gimme a ringy ding or send Rainey over. I can pick stuff up for you, too. You need anything now?"

Rita shook her head. "Later's fine," she said. After they were gone, she pumped water onto a washcloth and held it against the back of her neck, letting the water dribble down her back, then she turned back to the stove and lifted the jars of pickles out with her tongs, setting them on a clean towel to cool.

*   *   *

The sun was already a hot smear in the hazy sky, but Carol was just beginning her breakfast. Wheat toast cut into triangles set on a blue plate. Slices of bright oranges. A white mug of coffee. She had been up till after three working on what she called her "practice painting." Aware that her heart was not completely taken by it, but vowing to go through with it until she reached the end.

Strewn around the studio were projects she had abandoned. A doll buried in a dishpan of mud, twigs, and leaves. An apple carved to resemble Mrs. Thomas, Trudy's mother. A piece of black sandpaper with a bright blue feather, bits of shells Rainey left in the back of the car, a torn grocery list Rita dropped, all of it arranged around the pink handprints Crystal made on newspaper. These attempts were like dirty plates scattered across a table after a meal.

Carol had forced herself to work on the painting, bulldozed through her resistance and whining, through the longing to run across the road to hug Rita, through the desire to hop in her car and drive just to be driving with the windows down. Hour by hour, she gave herself to the work though her hand cramped and her shoulders burned; she did it anyway. Now that she had finished, she was feverish with accomplishment.

The painting was propped on the easel in her studio. She carried her mug of coffee in and scrutinized what she'd done, pacing around the room, observing it from different angles. She had begun with an attempt to recreate a vision she had of herself in a plain wooden chair in a square room, staring at a white wall and above her, at eye level should she stand up on the chair, a square window cut into the thick adobelike wall. On the other side of the wall, Rita sat in an identical chair, staring in the opposite direction. Carol didn't slow herself down worrying over interpretations. Now, in the harsh afternoon light as she studied what she'd done she still didn't know what it was about. But it made her feel peaceful. Serene.

This attempt to capture her vision was not without flaws; she couldn't quite manage the shape of Rita's face. Her chin was much more delicate than the chin Carol had painted. Her eyes were impossible; she could not get the right shade of green. She could not determine what her expression conveyed. When she closed her eyes to picture Rita, she felt just as confused.

In a burst of insight, she had slapped on yellow, red, and blue, mixing shades of orange and green, concerned more with the light dancing on Rita's face than in depicting it exactly. It was as if the painting had painted itself. Her own portrait was transformed into an image of the back of her head, slightly turned in Rita's direction, a nearly transparent white blouse hanging from her shoulders, her hair glowing with flecks of silver in the muted light, mirroring the light on Rita's face. They both sat in exactly the same pose, their elbows curved ever so slightly, their hands resting weightlessly on their laps.

Carol finished her coffee, went back to the kitchen for more, marveling at the bright sun streaking across the floor, the Queen Anne's lace spread across the field in back like a tapestry. She felt a flurry of excitement, like bees buzzing against her ribs. She splashed cold water over her face and hurried back to her studio, set another canvas on the easel, and began.

LABORARE EST ORARE. These words were displayed, the black letters in careful calligraphy, on the wall of her high school art room. Work is prayer. Moving as if in a trance, she pushed dollops of color onto her palette, reaching as if with a sixth sense for the brushes she had carefully cleaned. She gave herself over to the work.

* * *

Rainey loved having the tiny baby curled upon her lap, his little chest rising and falling under the cotton T-shirt tied across his middle, the soft place on his head that beat rhythmically like a heart. She could hardly believe he was real, though she could feel his warm weight. Slim had gotten her settled after their ice cream. Tucked into the corner of the sofa with her feet up, her cast on a pillow, she was able to rest the baby on her lap.

She petted him a little, his curled fists and his reddish fluff of hair. Crystal gave his foot a tickle. The baby screwed up his face and made a mewing sound, like the kittens that stumbled blindly after their mother as she went to her food bowl, one kitten still locked on her teat.

"He's too little for ticklin' yet," Slim said. "Give him time."

He leaned over the sofa and touched the baby's cheek. He turned toward Slim's finger and moved his mouth hungrily. "His bottle's ready."

Slim sat in the middle of the sofa, Rainey and Crystal on either side, and they both watched as the baby worked the bottle, drinking and hiccuping and spitting back half of what he managed to take in.

"Imagine you're so teeny you got to learn to eat," he said, fussing over the baby, wiping his chin with his shirttail and trying again.

Janesta didn't look up from the movie she was watching on TV.

Her face was puffy, and her lips were nearly invisible without lip-stick.

"Uh-oh, hide the carrots," Crystal said, sucking her fist the way the baby sucked his bottle, greedily smacking it against her mouth. She had seen the movie several times and knew what would happen next. A woman in the grocery store listened to the sounds of heavy thumping, wondering what could be approaching.

"Just dial 9-1-1," Crystal yelled.

Later, there were monstrously huge rabbits hunched in the store, stuffing their mouths, loudly crunching everything, empty cans piled up all around them. The woman was nowhere in sight.

"They're having a beer party," Slim said.

Janesta snorted and lit another cigarette.

Rainey was afraid of the movie. She wanted to scream when the men lined up with rifles they fired at the rabbits. There were more rabbits than bullets.

"You scared?" Crystal asked.

Rainey nodded and looked down at her cast.

"Slim, tell her. If she gets real scared, she can dial 9-1-1."

"That's right," he said. He turned the baby on his stomach and patted his back. Rainey cuddled close to Slim, turning away from the TV. But she could still hear the rabbits stampeding down the road, their high eerie cries of excitement, terror, or pain, she wasn't sure which.

*   *   *

Nelly was stretched out beside Ginger on the rumpled bed. The hot sun streamed through the dusty lace curtains, the smell of low tide from the tidal river was thick in the close air. She had tried to get up earlier, determined to get back to her life, but the heat and her hangover sent her staggering back to the bed with a groan. Now, she wasn't sure if she was asleep or awake.

She can see herself sitting on the tractor, the seat like the palm of a hand, holding her. Her knuckles are white, clenching the throttle, and her skin is covered with orange caterpillars, tiny hairless cater-pillars, their wormlike bodies puffing up like water balloons about to burst. They are inching along, crawling all over each other, between her fingers, across her palms, multiplying as she stares transfixed. Her tongue tingles and itches, and she realizes the cater-pillars are on her lips, crawling out of her mouth, and she wants to cry out but no sound comes out of her, just more caterpillars wrig-

gling up from her throat, edging out of the corners of her mouth
and sliding down her chin like drool. Their bodies swell near to
bursting with the bright orange liquid. A liquid that will burn her
skin, that will have a horrible smell when it spills over her. She can
do nothing to stop them. She wants to smash them, to brush them
away, to squash them against her skin, despite the smell and sting
this will cause, but she cannot move.

"Hey, wake up," Ginger said. She gave Nelly a shake. "You were
hollering," she said and yawned, flopping back against the pillows.

"Tell me something," Nelly said, lifting herself slowly on one
elbow. "Do I look all right to you?"

"What do you mean, all right? You look fine. Like you've been
drinking too much that's for damn sure. But fine enough."

"Do you notice anything funny about my head?"

"Your head?"

"Yeah. My head. Here," Nelly pointed.

"No," Ginger said. She ran her fingertips across Nelly's forehead.

"You don't see my third eye bulging?"

"Go back to sleep," Ginger said, turning on her side, flinging the
sheet to the floor.

*   *   *

Rita put one foot in the tire swing and gave herself a push as she
stared into the distance at the faint outline of the hills. The fog was
creeping up from the coast like a thick cloud, but instead of cooling
her off, it added to the oppressive feeling that had been with her all
day, like a thin veneer of varnish covering her from head to toe.
Later, when Rainey came home from Slim's, they would go to the
lake to cool off. She would not even glance at Carol's house. They
would move quickly down the path toward the cool water, their
voices deliberately cheerful. Rainey couldn't go swimming, but she
could wade, she could sit at the water's edge and watch her mother
bathe.

Rita gave herself another push, uprooting a clump of dead grass.
The lawn had failed. It had been too much trouble to keep it
watered, but a few flowers still bloomed at the edge, bright
marigolds next to a mat of purple alyssum. A few straggly nastur-
tiums twined up the side of the house, clinging to the shingles, their
leaves dotted with aphids. Next year, she planned, then paused.
Where would she be next year?

She twirled slowly, hoping for a breeze. The weather had been hot and humid for weeks before Rainey was born, as hot as it was now, the sky white with humidity, the city mired in a collective grouchiness. The pages of Rita's books curled up and the covers wouldn't stay shut. The hot sticky air clung like a sodden rag to her skin, her hair, even the floor of the apartment was damp. Rita's body had ached to get it over with. She felt like a sponge filling up, her legs swollen. She would pee and pee and still she had to go.

She worried about getting to the hospital. No cab would stop when the driver saw her huge belly, or if one did, the cabby would throw her out when she announced her destination. Sometimes she imagined Elias appearing at her door. But in the end, when the first pains came, they were no worse than indigestion, the only difference being they arrived in a distinctive pattern. So she had packed her backpack and walked to the hospital, stopping to rest when the waves of pain washed over her, leaning against the buildings, sitting on what benches she could find.

It had been an easy birth; she felt lucky for that. Rainey had slipped out of her and nuzzled against Rita's breasts. The hardest part had been being on welfare. But what choice did she have? She couldn't go back to work right away with a newborn baby to take care of. Besides, she couldn't possibly pay the hospital bill on the salary she earned.

The idea of resorting to welfare again made Rita feel like a failure. She had counted the money stashed in the teapot. Three hundred and fifty-six dollars and seventy cents, plus what she still had from when she first arrived in Maine, more than enough to get along for a few more months. She had her egg money. And they could eat from the garden.

She sighed and climbed off the swing. As she went about her chores, she remembered the rows of plastic chairs in the welfare office, each seat molded to the supposed shape of someone's backside, certainly not hers. It had been impossible to get comfortable, but if she stood up, someone grabbed her seat and she had to lean against the cement block wall beneath the huge clock that clicked loudly as the second hand jerked across its white face. Had it really been necessary to spend most of the day crowded in those rooms where no fresh air ever stirred, clutching her number, waiting for it to be announced, like cattle in feedlots, everybody pushed up against each other. It had been horrible to sit with the baby on her lap, hour after hour, trying to entertain her with the plastic disks on a chain, changing her diaper in the filthy restroom, clutching the baby awkwardly while she peed, straddling the toilet where the piss-soaked paper towels were strewn across the dirty tiles.

Either the social workers treated Rita with disdain, as if she ought to be married and off in the suburbs pleasing a man, or they treated her with outright hostility, especially the black workers who behaved as if she were diseased. They sucked their teeth while scrutinizing the forms, careful to avoid eye contact. It made Rita feel cut off from both worlds. She could hope for acceptance nowhere. She would always be alone. Except for Rainey. At least there's Rainey, she thought as she walked the perimeter of the pasture, checking the fence for places the sheep might escape, testing the fence posts.

After a particularly awful time dragging Rainey across the city in the sleety snow, sloshing through ankle-deep slush in her sneakers, sitting so long in the unheated waiting room among the sneezing and coughing crowd, she had feared they would both get pneumonia. "I'm ready to go back to work," she announced when it was finally her turn. The worker stared, seemingly astonished by the high color on Rita's cheeks. Then, as if by some miracle, she said, "Let me see what I can do." She arranged for babysitting vouchers. Car fare. Even hinted at the possibility of training and put Rita's name on a waiting list. But Rita ended up back at the fabric shop, forty hours a week. Never mind that she brought home barely enough to live on, it was better than the constant humiliation.

"Please, God," she prayed, "don't make me go through that again." She couldn't imagine in what form her help would come, but wasn't that what faith was all about?

She filled the sheep feeder and watched the yearlings eat, nudging each other aside as if there weren't enough to go around. There was a click and she turned to find Rainey peering through the fence, her camera poised.

"I got you!" she said, giggling like her old self again.

20

"What'd I have yesterday?" Coalie asked, twisting back and forth on a stool, the tips of his rubber boots thumping the plywood.

Trudy was crimping the edges of the blueberry pies she was about to slide into the oven. "Tuna," she said. "You had tuna."

"Gimme turkey today, then."

"Hot or cold?"

"The one with cranberry sauce."

"You get cranberry sauce with either one."

"Oh," Coalie said, rubbing the underside of his bristly chin. "I'll have me the one that won't break my pocketbook, then."

"Cold turkey. Side of cran," Trudy hollered, but Hydie had already begun to prepare the order.

"Mustard?" he asked Coalie.

They all looked up when Slim pushed open the screen door.

"Big boy," Hydie said, saluting. He dropped his knife when he saw the baby strapped into a denim pouch on Slim's chest.

"What in hell's name?" Buster was goggle-eyed with surprise.

Slim waved a box of cigars excitedly. "It's a boy," he said.

"It's a *what?*" Coalie twirled on his stool to face Slim. Wasn't it just the other day Slim was in announcing he and Janesta were married?

The fellows at the counter exchanged glances. Finally Rip lit the end of the cigar Slim handed him, cleared his throat importantly, and said, "Is that what you'd call a premature birth?" He poked Slim's arm playfully and everybody laughed.

"That fox sure seen you comin'," Buster said.

Slim let the fellows laugh; he didn't really mind at all. He loved the baby boy warm against his chest. He loved the stack of diapers in his bedroom. The scent of talcum powder and baby oil that filled the trailer. The warm sweet formula he heated carefully on the stove. He didn't even care that all Janesta did was watch TV day and night, barely saying a word, not wanting to hold or feed the baby, only coming to bed after he'd fallen asleep. Sometimes, she even slept in the living room, tipped back in Slim's chair with a blanket draped over her lap.

Slim was so taken in by the baby he hardly noticed his wife. He fumbled over the baby's wet diapers in the night. He cradled the tiny baby in the crook of his arm as he jabbed the rubber nipple into the boy's hungry mouth. He was so little. By the time Slim managed to get one bottle down him it seemed it was time to start warming the next one. But already, he was growing.

"Gawd, he's ugly," Coalie said, peering at the baby.

"Go on now." Trudy waved him away and stood on tiptoe to have a look. "All babies are ugly at first. He'll fill out. You wait and see. Sit down, Slim. You must be hungry something fierce. It's on the house. You sure he can breathe in that contraption?"

"Yeah, I'm sure. Rita carried Rainey around in one. She says babies like to feel your heartbeat. Don't 'cha remember how the Injuns did like this? Only I got me a papoose in front here where I can keep my eye on him." He patted the baby's back.

"What'll they come up with next? What's his name?" she asked.

"James. James Junior," Slim said with pride.

"Slim Jim," Buster said. "Hey, hows about Slim Jim?"

"It's James. Not Jim or Jimmy. We decided," Slim said.

"OK. OK. Don't get your bowels in an uproar. I was just flappin' my lips," Buster said. He pulled the cellophane off his cigar and lit it, ignoring Trudy's attempt to wave away the smoke.

"You fellas get on outdoors with them smelly cigars," Trudy said. She turned the fans on high. "We got a baby in here."

Coalie dropped a few coins beside his plate.

"On your way out, Rip, don't forget that box I saved Suzie," Trudy said.

"What's it today?" Buster asked.

"You fixin' to eat it before that pig does?" Trudy said.

"Now, now." Buster clucked softly under his breath and pulled a bill from his wallet. "What 'cha makin' now?" he asked.

"These're hamburg cookies," Trudy said. She squirted green and red frosting onto the chocolate mints she'd lined up on a platter. "Lettuce and catsup," she explained, pressing the vanilla wafer 'buns' in place.

"How much you figure Suzie weighs now?" Slim asked. Rip was planning to win some kind of ribbon at the fair. He hoped Suzie would go down in history as the world's largest sow.

"They ain't invented a scale yet that can measure her," Rip said.

"Surely they have. They can do anything now," Slim said.

"Alls I know is we ain't got any kind of scale like that out in these parts," Rip said. "Alls I can tell you is Suzie'd rather flop in the mud than try and heft herself around the barnyard. I got to put the food

right under her nose." He grabbed one of Trudy's hamburger cookies and waved it under Buster's nose.

"I don't exactly like bein' compared to the world's largest pig,"
Buster grumbled.

* * *

Lizzy stared at the cup of yogurt she brought for lunch. It was
apricot-flavored, not the vanilla she craved. Not a single store in
Union City had a cup of vanilla yogurt left. She had purchased and
eaten them all. Her thighs were cramping the way they did before
she got her period. She wished she'd kept a better record the way
she was always telling her patients to do, but she'd quit being so vig-
ilant after Denny left. When it came, it came. But now she wasn't
sure just how many weeks it had been. Her belly was so puffy and
bloated she was surprised she didn't slosh when she moved. She
willed her period to go away, visualizing a tiny fetus firmly attached
to her uterine wall.

Her last negative pregnancy test rested on a copy of *Women and
Contraceptive Health*. The small pink minus sign pointing like an
accusing finger. Every night as she was falling asleep, she pictured
the test coming out positive. Last night, she had dreamt of a giant
red cross painted across the door of her office. Now she feared her
dream was an omen of the blood to come.

When she went out to check the schedule for the afternoon, J.T.
was on the telephone with Betty. They spoke every day. J.T. said she
always looked forward to Betty's call, even if it was only a quick
hello.

"Let's have spinach quiche," J.T. was saying. "I need the folic acid.
I love you, too," she said, making kissing sounds into the receiver.
When she hung up, her cheeks were flushed, her eyes dreamy.

"Lovebirds," Lizzy said. She attempted a smile.

"You didn't come out here to tell me that. What's with you?
You've been moping around all day."

"I think I'm pregnant," Lizzy said, flopping into the client's chair
beside J.T.'s desk. She chewed her bottom lip nervously.

"Don't tell me, you lost your diaphragm? The kids thought it was
some newfangled Frisbee and threw it over the fence? No, wait. Your
best friend told you it never happened the first time?" J.T. lifted her clipboard, her pen poised, ready to play the game. "Lemme see," she continued, studying the "bouquet" made from condom packets attached to
green wire stems. She flicked a red one. "The condom broke?"

Lizzy sighed and her face grew very pale.

J.T., still caught up in the pretense, continued, "Cessation of menses. Nausea in the morning. Hmm."

"No really."

"Really?"

"Yes. As in really."

J.T. dropped the clipboard. "You mean you're telling me you think you're pregnant, *really?*"

Lizzy nodded. Her eyes gleamed with unshed tears.

J.T. patted her knee. "I thought you said it was impossible. You told me the so-called medical establishment had written you off."

Lizzy smiled warily. "I never miss my period and I think I might've missed two. Plus, I feel different."

"Different?"

"Yeah. Like's there's something in me. Something growing." She placed her hands on her stomach. "This morning, I was certain I was getting my period. I had that woozy feeling and I have some cramps, but nothing's happening. Maybe those're my symptoms. And I crave vanilla yogurt."

"Have you done a test?"

"Haven't you noticed them disappearing? Every single day I come in here with my bottle of pee. But it's always negative. That little pink minus sign is driving me wild. I even dreamt my pee turned pink."

"Oh, Lizzy. I don't know what to say."

"Well. You can't exactly say congratulations, can you?" She stared at the new pamphlets still packed in the box beside J.T.'s desk: *No! and Other Methods of Birth Control.*

J.T. doodled on a sheet of yellow paper. "Listen," she said. "I hate to say the dirty word. But shouldn't you see a doctor?"

"I know I should. I just want to wait a little longer. I just want to believe it's possible a tiny bit longer. Is that crazy?"

"If you were a client, you'd send yourself to the Medical Center."

"I know, I know."

"I don't suppose you were using birth control?"

"You know I've used every single birth control method on the market. I am a walking test case for pregnancy prevention. The model user. Then it turns out I'm infertile. That's my method. Infertile. And even then, we used condoms."

"Maybe you're like those women who can't get pregnant, then they adopt a kid and voila! Now that you've got Aran, your body can relax."

"Oh, J.T. I hope so. I really hope so."

"Promise me you'll make an appointment."

"OK," Lizzy said. "I will. But not right this minute."

"You can't right this minute. You've got other plans." J.T. nodded in the direction of the waiting room where a large woman sat in the middle of the sofa plucking at her blouse, scratching at the edge of her bra, fiddling with the straps that slid down her bare arms.

* * *

Carol felt like a bear waking from hibernation, liable to devour anything in her path as she stumbled out into the bright afternoon light. Crystal ran out of the trailer with a towel draped over her head as if she'd been waiting for Carol to emerge, preparing for just this moment.

"What's with the towel?" Carol asked. Her voice sounded odd, it had been so long since she'd spoken. What day was it? Even her wristwatch had stopped marking time. While she was working, she had glanced at it once, out of habit. Later, when she took a break and checked again, it was exactly the same time, 2:22, but definitely evening she knew as she watched the sun set over the fields and the swallows swooping over the golden grass. Now she had no idea what time it really was, but it no longer seemed to matter.

"It keeps the bugs off," said Crystal, tucking the white towel around her face.

"What bugs?" Carol said. "There aren't any bugs today."

"Well, in case." Crystal dashed back across the road and ran into the trailer, slamming the door behind her.

Carol tinkered listlessly with her birch bark sheep. One had tipped to the side and was about to collapse. Another was covered with blotches of purplish bird droppings. *Jackson Pollock Interpreted by Nature* she imagined on some future plaque in a museum. What should she do next? She had planned to jump in her car and head to the grocery store, but it seemed too drastic a contrast to the solitary days she'd spent holed up in her studio. She was too unsteady to drive. Besides, there was still plenty to eat in the fridge. She wanted to visit Rita, to explain where she'd been, to invite her to take a walk. But it seemed awkward to just stroll up the driveway after such a long absence. She noticed a new sign advertising lettuce, carrots, and tomatoes. A rusty red wagon piled with zucchini was beside the mailbox. FREE a sign said. As she pondered what to do, Crystal returned, sauntering across the road.

"I got a baby brother," Crystal said. "He's seventeen inches long."

"Uh-huh," said Carol, worrying this conversation was about to turn into one of Crystal's harangues on pregnancy.

"His hair's red."

"Really?"

"Rainey's hair's darker brown than mine."

"That's true." She hoped Crystal wouldn't expect her to explain the role genetics played in hair color. Her skull might crack with the effort to discuss Mendel and his peas.

"She looks like Rita but Rita's hair's not dark. Her skin's white."

"Mm," Carol murmured. "That's true."

"I'm taller than Rainey." Crystal flapped her towel as a fly approached. "Mom's taller than me. You're taller than me, too. Measure with me."

"What do you mean, measure with you?"

"Back to back. Lemme see how taller you are." Crystal got around behind Carol. Her head fit right between Carol's shoulder blades.

"Yep, you're taller all right."

"I'm older, too."

"Toe to toe." Crystal pushed the toes of her torn sneakers against Carol's. Carol didn't know what she was trying to do. She decided not to ask. "Whew. Golly," Crystal said. She studied the road, staring into the distance, as if she were expecting someone. "Sometimes a storm just blows in outa nowhere," Crystal said.

"There's not a cloud in the sky."

"James got red hair. Like Mom's."

"James?"

"James. My baby brother, you jughead. Ain't you heard me?"

"James," Carol said. She felt as if she were about to fall backwards into a vortex while the world around her faded. It was as if she'd gone to sleep and woken up to a completely different world. Janesta had given birth to a second child and Carol hadn't even known she was pregnant.

*　　*　　*

Rita moved her canning operation outdoors under a shade tree in the back. She built a wood fire in the grill to heat the water and had more wood, split into small pieces, stacked in the grass. The water boiled in the pot, sterilizing the jars, and the steam rose and dissipated into the air instead of clinging to the windows and Rita's skin. She'd dragged a table out under the tree and stood there scalding tomatoes, pulling off the thin skin, gouging the stems from the fruit before she stuffed them into the clean jars she'd already prepared. A few flies buzzed lazily, hovering over her hands, but it was still better to be outdoors, out of the house.

The sheep crowded against the fence, butting each other aside as if hoping to be first in line, watching her with interest, their jaws working. She caught a glimpse of Carol in her yard, talking to Crystal. Then they went inside. How could she live across the road from someone and so rarely see her, especially someone who occupied a great deal of her thoughts? She wished she had the nerve to go over and see her. Why had she become so shy? She lowered the full jars into the boiling water and added more wood to the fire, setting her timer so as not to forget when they would be done.

Yesterday, she and Rainey had gone walking in the woods before supper. She was teaching Rainey to name the trees. Already she recognized the giant-leafed moose maple, the curled bark of the yellow birch. She knew which cones came from a white pine and pointed out the varying lengths of the needles of the hemlock tree. They turned west onto a woods road they had never walked before and in a short while passed a damp place where ghostly white Indian pipe curled up out of the moss. Rainey took a picture of it, aiming her camera carefully while Rita plucked teaberry leaves for them to chew. After a while, the path curved and they came upon a cabin set at the edge of an overgrown clearing. Most of the tar paper had blown off, the bleached slats held a few ragged edges in place against the splintery wood. From the doorway, they surveyed the interior: Moss covered the floor and the soggy brown rag rug, rotten shreds of curtains dangled from rusted rods, a warped white table sat under the window with two blue plates placed, as if in anticipation of a meal, on either side.

"We can't go inside," Rita said when Rainey asked to. "It's too dangerous. The whole place might collapse."

She held Rainey up so she could take a picture and then they walked around back to where several apple trees grew, the gnarly branches twisted and clogged with new shoots. A few pieces of fruit, brown and shriveled, dangled from the leaves where tent caterpillars had woven silky cocoons. At the base of the trees, a huge pile of undigested apples. Bear vomit. Rita glanced around, fearful the bear was nearby, but there was only the thin grass in the clearing dotted with stunted blue spruce trees and a tiger swallowtail flitting by.

There were three huge gray boulders covered with lichen and beyond them, a dump with rusted tin cans and bottles, most of them broken. Beneath a can that crumpled like dust, Rita spied the bottom of a dark blue bottle. She eased it out carefully. It was perfectly shaped, not a crack or chip. Rainey found a cardboard box weathered to a papery gray. Inside were twelve pale blue canning jars with the lids rusty and cracked, filled with blackberries preserved in murky syrup. Rita carried a few of them home, pried the lids off, and buried the fermented berries in a deep hole. She scrubbed the rust and stains from the jars. ATLAS was printed in raised letters on the glass which was mottled with bubbles and imperfections. In the sunlight that streamed through the windows, the old glass was beautiful.

Everywhere Rita turned, there were signs of someone's abandoned hopes. She wondered about the cabin with the plates set on the table. The canning jars in a box under a tree. The shed door with the rusted hasps, the broken-down hutches where rabbits once had their young. What happened to the people who lived there? Where were they now? And would someone someday come upon the house where she and Rainey now lived and step inside, noting the rusty pump, the dusty woodstove with stale ashes in the box? Would they push aside the cobwebs and peer into Rainey's room to find the yellow insulation sagging, stained with rainwater, the striped mattress ticking torn, the stuffing pulled out, material for a rodent's nest? And where would they be when this happened? Where would they have gone?

Trudy told Rita that when her mother was a girl, Nelly's farm was a sheep meadow. "They kept over a hundred sheep at a time. They used to herd them down to the lake to give 'em a good wash before they sheared 'em," Trudy said. "Folks was all livin' up there on that hill back then. Cows and pigs everywhere and kids rollin' their hoops down the road. You name it, all kinds of activity going on. You can't hardly take a walk around there nowadays without trippin' over a cellar hole."

Rita dipped more tomatoes into the pan of boiling water until their skins cracked and pulled away from the fruit, then set to work preparing them for the last set of jars.

Out of the corner of her eye, she saw Carol meandering up the driveway. Her heart thumped excitedly, despite her best efforts to still her feelings, to tamp them down. A smile, unbidden, spread across her face.

* * *

Rainey was sorting through the latest packet of photographs to arrive in the mail. There was one of her foot, the toes curled like periwinkle shells. Another of her mother's back as she reached to pick a bouquet of pink cosmos. Her favorite appeared to be a blurry shadow, but upon closer inspection a bowl full of ripe raspberries took shape. She pushed them back into the envelope when Carol knocked and got up slowly to answer the door. Carol was so startled to see the cast on Rainey's arm she forgot the speech she had prepared on her way over.

"What happened to your arm, Rainey?" she blurted. Again there was the uncanny feeling of waking up from a deep sleep to find an enormous amount of time had passed.

"It's broke."

"I see that." Carol crouched beside her and examined the autographs that decorated the white plaster.

"Everybody signed it," Rainey said. "You can, too."

Slim had written his name in a black scrawl, dotting the "i" with a smiley face. Crystal had used a pink marker, turning the "a" in her name into a heart. "God is love" it said in small neat print with "Mommy" written underneath. "Trudy and Hydie Hyde" it said in formal script.

"You've got quite an assortment of names and messages here," Carol said. "How'd it happen?"

"It was an accident?" Rainey's response sounded like a question.

"An accident?"

"I was driving the tractor," she explained. "Me and Nelly."

"Does it hurt?"

"Not anymore. Wanna see my pictures?"

"I'd love to," Carol said, sitting at the table. At first she felt nervous, as if she had no right to be there without Rita's permission. She felt tongue-tied, afraid she'd have nothing else to say to Rainey as well. She had never spent time with a child. But before she knew it, she was lost in the photos Rainey handed to her, shyly at first, making no effort to explain them, seemingly comfortable with the soft shuffling and Carol's silence. Then with greater confidence, she marched into her room and returned with a shoe box full of photos. A bee nestled on the face of a sunflower. Taken from Rainey's angle, the sunflower filled the frame. Carol almost expected the pollen to drift out of the picture and fall across her face. A white cat perched on the rim of a garbage can, looking back, caught in the act. A carrot poking up out of the soil, a ladybug perched in the greens.

"These are beautiful," said Carol. "Rainey, you have a gift."

Rainey swayed happily in her seat, pleased with the attention. All at once, there was a thump at the door and then as if a cloud had passed over the sun, the expression on Rainey's face changed from

pleasure to dismay. Carol looked over her shoulder, a smile ready
for Rita, eager to spring up and rush over to her. But then she saw
who it was. Nelly was at the door scowling, both hands clenched into
tight fists. As suddenly as she'd appeared, she was gone as if her
image behind the dark screen had only been a mirage.

21

Slim didn't think anything of it when he heard the tractor start up
in the field behind his trailer. And why should he? The rumble of
the motor as it turned over and caught with the choke wide open
was as familiar as the wind rolling down over the hills. The groan of
the gears, then the slow sputter to an even hum as the tractor
moved across the land was as much a part of a typical summer day
as the crows fighting over the blackberries across the road.

Slim was bent over a heap of ratty T-shirts, pawing through his
stretched-out and torn undershorts and various socks, sorting
through Janesta's bras and filmy blouses, separating her brightly
colored tops and pants from Crystal's pale pink clothes, dropping
the baby's clothes into a separate pile as he sorted the laundry. He
had already done the sheets and towels and they were nearly dry. He
hoped to get two more loads done and clipped to the clothesline
before suppertime. The trailer shook as the washer spun and the
rinse water drained into the sink. On the stove, a pot of chili simmered.

Crystal hopped into the kitchen, her striped dress on backwards,
zipped up to her chin where her hands were curled like the rabbit
she pretended to be.

"James in here?" she asked in a high airy voice that floated
through the kitchen, each word like a smoke ring hovering. Slim
wrapped his arm around her eyes till she giggled and pulled it down
around her waist so he would hug her, lifting her up like she was
light as a feather.

"He's right there," Slim said. The baby was in his plastic carrier
on the countertop curling and uncurling his long delicate fingers.
Crystal smoothed his hand onto her palm.

"Mine's still bigger," she said. She held up her hands wanting Slim to measure his with hers. "Yours is bigger," she said.

"Don't James look like a little old man?" Slim asked. He pulled the baby into an upright position and readjusted the straps. Immediately, James began to weep, a sound like air being squeezed from a beach ball. Slim jiggled the baby's foot to distract him, glancing as he did toward Janesta who was seemingly absorbed in a soap opera. It didn't seem right to Slim that she never wanted to hold the baby.

Crystal began looking through the cluttered cupboards to see what cake mixes were left. She held up a box of devil's food cake.

"This one's Rita's favorite. She's gonna need a cake today. We better get started on it, Mr. Fit," she said. "Read me it." She thrust the box in front of Slim, holding it so close he had to back away.

"You read it, Crystal."

"Can't."

"Never say can't. What'd I tell you?"

"Can't," she said, hanging her head.

"You spoil her," Janesta muttered, flicking off the TV impatiently. "I swear. I feel like some rat in a cage trapped in this friggin' place."

"I'm gonna get started on the addition," Slim said. "Before you know it, we'll have us a mudroom to stick stuff in."

"Seein' is believin'," Janesta said. She was sick to death of his talk about mudrooms and family rooms and cleaning out the spare room. Every day he brought home more stuff and still there was nowhere to put it. She tripped over the swing he'd set up for the baby, one of his dump finds. It fell with a thump and she didn't even bother to set it right.

"Be nice to get another foot this way," Slim said, slapping the ceiling. "I been fixin' to get me a giant can opener and go around the edges and lift 'er right off. Get me some headroom."

"You can't get no giant can opener. You jughead," Crystal said.

"I'm gonna go down to Moody's for some more smokes. We need anything?" asked Janesta. She stood with her hands on her hips.

The first time she'd been in his trailer, she'd stood this way and Slim had felt she was taking up all the space. She was still a large, demanding presence, but one he had slowly become accustomed to. Slim got up and hugged her, but she swatted him away and slammed the door.

"Slim, you didn't read me the cakey bo bakey," Crystal whined. "We gotta bake it. I told you Rita's gonna need it."

"What makes you think that?" asked Slim.

Crystal shrugged. "Read me it, Mr. Nitwit," she said.

By the time Slim had finished reading the instructions, Crystal was perched on the stool, the cake already forgotten.

"Nice day," she said, her eyes curiously blank, as if she were an old woman at Moody's making small talk while she waited to pay for her quart of milk. She scuffed her pink slippers on the worn linoleum.

"Crystal, I swear to God, when you act like this you gimme the willies."

"Willy billy willy worm. Telephone bo bone," she said, lifting an imaginary receiver to her ear. "Better answer it. Telephone."

"The phone didn't ring. For pity's sake, Crystal."

Slim tested the formula he'd warmed to see if it was ready for James to drink. Just as he began to feed him, the phone rang. Crystal drifted out of the room, walking lightly, as if she were making a great effort to keep her feet from touching the floor.

"Hello?" Slim said, holding the receiver with one shoulder, managing to feed the baby at the same time. James sucked the bottle contentedly.

"Ruby there?" asked a man with a deep scratchy voice.

"Huh?"

"Who the hell is this? Gimme Ruby, Bub."

"Sorry. Wrong number," Slim told the man and hung up.

All at once, like storm clouds brewing, Slim felt overcome with a sense of helplessness. He would never be able to soothe his angry wife. Crystal would continue to behave strangely. In fact, she seemed to be getting worse, not better, speaking in rhymes the way she did when she was going through a bad spell. He was reminded of last week when he tried to extricate a box of photographs from the closet. Crystal kept asking what he looked like when he was her age and when he went hunting for them, as soon as he opened the door, a plastic baseball bat knocked him on the head, a stack of paperbacks rained down followed by a cigar box full of half-used pencils, some of them badly chewed. Pan lids clattered all around him before he gave up and shoved everything back inside. His life was such a mess, but if he gave into the despair, if he started to cry, it would be like the junk falling from his closet, the tears would spill down his face, drowning everything in the room. He would never be able to mop it up. He shut his eyes, raising his eyebrows so his eyelids were pulled tight, waiting until the tears dissipated. Then he nuzzled James until the baby smiled. Janesta claimed it was only gas. "Babies that little don't know how to smile," she said. But Slim accepted it as a smile nonetheless.

"My little farter," he crooned. The baby smiled again and kicked his legs happily as Slim lowered him into the swing, cranking it up so it would swing him gently back and forth.

That was when they heard the first scream. A shrill sound, so full of despair it broke through the roar of the tractor.

"What the hell?" Slim hurried to the door. Crystal rushed up beside him.

Rita ran across the fields, flailing her arms, her bare feet stirring up clouds of gray dust as she ran tripping and falling, pushing herself back up from the squashed tomatoes, the leafy vines mangled. She stumbled over the pale cabbages that rolled like heads from a guillotine and came to a stop beside the pulverized squash, the hollow stems from the huge crushed leaves reached like fingers for the sky. Rita thrashed through the twisted stalks of corn tossed every which way like so much straw, the long leaves torn and fluttering like ribbons. She cried out, screaming, "Nelly, no!" But her horrified voice carried with it the strains of the already defeated. Her tear-streaked face was smudged with dirt. Blood flowed down her shins from her skinned knees. She stooped, frantically gathering up the cornstalks and held them awkwardly against her chest, the sharp-edged leaves scratching her arms.

Row after row, in every direction, plants were severed from their roots, the wet fruit of the cracked watermelon, the cantaloupe seeds spilled across the seaweed mulch, all of it mashed and the bright leaves blackened by the heavy tires that continued relentlessly grinding across the land with the determination of an advancing army.

Nelly stood at the wheel of the tractor like a cowboy standing in the stirrups, urging a reluctant horse to gallop faster. She was laughing, steering with one hand, her cap shoved far back on her head, her teeth flashing in the white hot sun as she mowed everything in her path, gashing through row upon row of carrots, slicing the celery off at the roots, the tires crunching over the potato plants, burying the potatoes that bubbled up out of the earth. The sharp smell of crushed basil leaves and uprooted onions, the acrid scent of smashed foliage rose like a thick cloud and mingled with the stench of diesel as the tractor zigzagged toward the field where the strawberries ripened in the summer sun, the mower blade rattling alongside the tractor like a greedy arm, grabbing the bright pink row of cosmos, slicing the crinkled leaves of chard, toppling the row of sunflowers, uprooting the Jacob's cattle beans. The vines tangled around the teeth of the mower, as if attempting to stop it, before the mower spit them to the side in ragged clumps. The long steel arm of the mower glinted in the sun, its sharp blades like ravenous sharks' teeth cutting a deep swath across the field, biting into the delicate leaves of the strawberries, chewing the stems away from the roots once so carefully laid in the pockets of earth. The jagged teeth of the mower snagged the plants flinging them helter-skelter, pummeling them into a soupy pulp.

All up and down the back acre, Nelly mowed the strawberry plants. What the mower missed, the tires steamrolled as she circled the field, retracing her tracks. The tractor paused like a giant insect surveying its task, then turned and began crawling toward Rita where she screamed, the horrible sounds tearing out of her like canvas ripping as she blindly hurled rocks and clods of clay. Oblivious of Nelly's approach, Rita sank hopelessly to her knees rocking back and forth, clenching handfuls of mashed berries, the red juice streaming down her arms.

Slim ran out the door, pushing Crystal back, urging her to stay inside with the baby. He had just reached the edge of the ruined garden when he saw Carol heading straight for Rita, ready to yank her from the tractor's path.

Nelly circled away from them, like a bullfighter teasing, laughing still as she watched them over her shoulder. Slim yelled her name and ran toward her, not knowing what else to do. He waved his arms and shouted her name again. Shotgun tore after him barking furiously and ran up to the tractor, trying to bite the tires. Nelly paused for a moment, as stunned as if someone had just thrown a bucket of ice water at her, then she headed in Carol and Rita's direction, as if to mow them down as well. Carol grabbed Rita by the arm, pulling her, yanking desperately, but Rita was rooted in place.

Above them, a flock of swallows swooped low, tucking their wings to their sides as they fell, then rose, fluttering like bats at dusk. As if waking from a trance, Rita yanked her arm from Carol's grip and ran headlong toward Nelly, daring Nelly to knock her down.

In the distance, a siren shrieked and whooped, the foreign sound echoing off the hills, a sound so rare in their part of the world that all over Preacher's Lake people stopped what they were doing to wonder what was going on. Like children playing the statue game, they were stunned by the siren's shrill lament, each one frozen in place. Even the tractor shuddered to a halt.

* * *

Rita heard someone speak her name and repeat it. She stumbled forward, then stopped. The crows had begun feasting, scolding each other with a deep click in their throats, descending on the fruit, rising up with their beaks dripping red. Already the smell of decaying vegetation strewn across the land, the bruised green reek of the gardens that would hang in the air for days, had begun.

"What?" she cried, looking around wildly as if for something to cling to, like a woman fighting to keep her head above water as the raging current of an undertow threatened to drag her down.

Her hair was tangled with grass and leaves, plastered against her dirt-smudged forehead, her eyes were fierce with disbelief. She stood there with her bare torn feet sinking into the rich loam, with her skinned knees where the blood and dirt had already dried, waiting as if she still expected the tractor to lunge forward and plow her down.

"Slim says they're taking her away," Carol said. She spoke slowly, measuring the words. "He says she wants to go."

Carol pointed at the police cars. The sirens were silent, the red lights no longer flashing. Nelly sat in the backseat of the car that rolled slowly down the driveway. In the other one, an officer sat smoking, the harsh radio crackling as he surveyed the damaged farm.

"I've been canning tomatoes," Rita said. She pointed to her canning operation, to the pot of water on the grill no longer boiling, to the fire already gone out.

Slim offered to take Rainey to his place, but she didn't want to go. He hurried home to Crystal, who was at the back door, her face pressed to the screen. "I called," she said. "I called like you said to if I get scared." Behind her, James screamed, waving his fists furiously.

Carol placed one hand on Rita's shoulder, acutely aware of the bony ridge, of the muscles pulled taut. There was nothing she could say. "I'm sorry" would never do. "It will be OK" seemed presumptuous.

"It's all over," Carol finally said.

Rita's breath was ragged, the effort racked her small frame. Carol wanted to hold Rita, to pull her close, fold her body into her arms, brush her disheveled hair back off her face, and kiss her tenderly. She wanted to take her hands, lead her to the house and wash her with a cool cloth. But she just stood there with the clouds of gnats hovering, her hand trembling ever so slightly on Rita's shoulder. Rainey wrapped one arm around Rita's leg and clung to her, gazing up at her mother with such pleading Carol wanted to hold them both. And then the moment for hugging, for comforting words, passed. The policeman hitched his pants up under his enormous belly, adjusted his belt, flung his cigarette butt into the mangled lettuce, and approached. When the shadow of his bulk fell over them, Carol stepped back. She wrapped her arms around her chest. She hugged herself.

Carol didn't know whether Rita accepted her presence as an offer of support or wished she'd go away. She felt like the first witness at the scene of an accident who must continue on her way, leaving the ambulance crew to attend to the injured parties where they lay moaning on stretchers alongside the road. No longer needed, but reluctant to walk away, still caught up in the horror of what she'd observed.

At last, Carol turned away, half expecting Rita to call her back. When she passed the house, the door hung open on its rusty hinges; she hesitated, then went inside where light streamed through the windows. It was like being in a house where someone had recently died.

As if from rote, she went to work. She sliced thick slices of the homemade bread she found on the counter and arranged them on a blue plate. She cut wedges of cheese, sliced two bright red apples into thin sections. She set the kettle to boil, put cups and spoons on the table, then opened a can of frozen lemonade, lifting the heavy glass pitcher down from the shelf. She pumped water, measuring carefully, then stirred it slowly with an old wooden spoon and added ice. She set out tall glasses for the lemonade and surveyed the table as if waiting for the funeral party to return.

"Oh! You scared me," Rita said when she came into the house. She rubbed her eyes with her fists like a child just waking up.

"I—" Carol began. She waved at the plates of food, at the cups and glasses waiting to be filled. The kettle hissed softly on the burner. Finally, Carol poured the lemonade. The liquid sloshing into the glasses, a familiar comforting sound, the pale drink fragrant and cold.

"I feel so terrible," Carol said, certain that if she had never come over, if she had not been sitting at Nelly's table, none of this would have happened. "I don't know what to do."

"I think what I need. I think. What I want to say is. I need to be alone," Rita said, wearily mumbling. She seemed to have just noticed the food arranged as if for a party. She gripped the chair.

Rainey leaned against her, fingering the hem of her mother's shirt, working it like a young child with a favorite blanket will do, gleaning comfort from the soft familiar cloth.

"I'm sorry," Carol said, suddenly flooded with shame, as if she'd been caught going through the dead one's things. She scuffed her chair back, feeling completely dismissed. There was not one thing she could do or say to ever make things right. Their relationship, what there had been of it, was over before it had begun. There would be no more teasing and flirting, no more eager laughter. No more visiting and getting to know each other better.

Carol pushed open the door but was unable to take the last few steps, unable to let it slap shut, unable to hurry down the driveway up which she had so happily come what seemed like a lifetime ago. Had she really approached Rita's house brimming with hope? It seemed so improbable now.

"All that work," Rita said. "All that work, for what?" She drank the lemonade slowly, blotting her lips with her arm. "The weird thing is I feel so calm," she said, turning toward Carol.

Carol nodded, peering at Rita through the mesh of the dark screen as she eased the door shut with a soft click. Still, she did not walk away. The light streaked across the golden hills. A chicken clucked, then others joined it as if in a chorus. She picked flecks of paint from the door frame and waited. I am not fit for human companionship, she told herself. Whoever I get close to, whoever I feel anything for—Rita interrupted her thoughts. She had begun to talk, as if forgetting she'd said she wanted to be alone.

"Sometimes," she said. "Sometimes I get the strangest sensation. I feel so completely doomed. Then I think, from God's perspective, we're no different than the bugs. Why should my size, my supposed intelligence, my ability to pinch hundreds of bugs dead protect me from the same kind of thoughtless, indiscriminate harm?"

Carol was remembering sleeping with Annie, curled side by side beneath the heavy red wool blanket Annie had loved, the warmth and comfort of the bed, Annie's contented sigh, the way she clutched Carol's arm as if to hold her there forever. And all Carol had wanted was to get away, to rise up out of the bed, dress, and go as if fleeing from a burning house.

Carol pushed herself away from the door with the same urgency that she had pushed herself from the warm nest of Annie's bed. She was quickly out of sight.

*   *   *

Mr. Bunny was attempting to mount Pinky but having no success. Stamping her back foot, her nose twitching angrily, Pinky pushed her rear end into the corner of her cage and flattened her ears.

"Maybe the cage is too small," Lizzy said.

"No matter how big the cage is, she'd still hide in the corner," said Michael. He scratched his beard thoughtfully.

"No. I mean to have babies in. Maybe, you know, it's like she doesn't want to breed in captivity. Plus he's in *her* territory."

"Maybe." Michael chewed the end of his unlit pipe.

Aran sat on the stoop with her Barbie and Ken dolls. "Round and round we go-o-o," she sang, twisting the dolls wildly.

Michael reached into Pinky's cage and when he grabbed her by the scruff of her neck, she resisted, as if putting on her brakes, and he had to yank her out of the corner. She hissed and tried to bite him, but he held tight.

"Michael!" Lizzy cried. She did not want to watch this. "I don't think—" she started, but it was too late. Mr. Bunny, seeing his opportunity, had mounted the doe and was pumping furiously. He fell to his side with a sigh. When Michael let go of Pinky, she snapped at the buck, pulling a tuft of fur from his side. He hopped as far away as possible and plucked a strand of hay from her dish.

"I'll keep doing this till she has a litter," Michael said.

"What're you planning to do if she has bunnies, anyhow?" Lizzy asked, standing aside to let Michael deposit Mr. Bunny back in his cage.

"The meat is supposed to taste better than chicken."

"You'd kill them?"

"Yeah. People do," he said. He looked so pathetic to her in that moment, with the bald patch on his scalp burned by the sun, his small dark beady eyes. She hoped her child would not resemble him.

Lizzy glanced at the house where Aran was grinding a naked Ken against a naked Barbie, knocking their pelvises together, twisting the hard plastic furiously. Lizzy felt a pain in her side. At first a sharp twinge, and then a stabbing sensation that made her gasp.

"You OK?" Michael gazed down at her with concern.

"Yeah, I'm OK," she said. The pain in her side felt like a hot knife twisting, flashes of pain spreading down her thighs, across her belly, around to her back, making it difficult to walk, but she was determined to ignore it. She wanted so badly for nothing to be wrong.

* * *

"Time to put the chickens to bed," Rainey announced. She hooked her fingers into the belt loops of Rita's shorts and tugged her mother from the chair. Rita's body was stiff and her feet had gone to sleep.

Swarms of midges hovered around them as they shooed the hens into their coop where they settled on perches, their heads sinking into the ruffled feathers of their plump bodies. As they worked, Rita averted her eyes from the garden. Like a small child who closes her eyes and thinks she has disappeared, if she didn't look, the wreck of her garden would not exist.

The last rays of the sun streamed across the fields and the clouds, streaked with shades of red, shimmered with a rosy golden glow. The light glinted off the windshield of the truck. The green hulk of it. The bashed-in door. So familiar, Rita didn't really see it as she walked past. Once Rita's father punched the wall beside her bed and it had caved in the same way, crumpled like a beer can in a fist. Rita stopped and retraced her steps, peering through the window of the truck. The keys dangled from the ignition, almost too good to be true.

* * *

Carol lined up her brushes, tightening the caps on tubes of paint. The painting on her easel and the others leaning against the wall might as well have been done by a stranger. She wandered aimlessly around the house. When she was a teenager and things got really bad, she would climb her favorite hill to look at the tallest tree that grew on the ridge. She could picture it still, towering above the other trees, a white pine with spreading uneven branches, her symbol of hope. As the trouble with her parents escalated, just seeing the tree often gave her reason to live. She would climb the hill, up and up, until she saw it outlined against the sky. The last time she went to see the tree, heading up the hill as if to visit an old friend, the countryside had resembled a brightly colored crazy quilt with the leaves at their peak. But when her eyes scanned the ridge, the tree was gone.

She had asked all over town what happened. Finally, Stubby

Buzanne, the town drunk, struggled out of his chair at the Corner Store. "I loved that tree myself," he said, sucking his broken teeth. "It's still up there. But a layin' on the ground now. They didn't try to get it out. Them Harrington boys. Just wanted to prove they could cut it down."

Carol wished she could see the tree now. She closed her eyes, picturing the shape she had sketched so often, but she was distracted. Something unusual was going on outside. Cars were approaching in a slow procession, gliding past her house. From the front porch, she watched the cars, the people inside craning their necks, pointing out the open windows, children on their knees staring. Some idled by the roadside as if they wished for a better look but did not have the nerve to approach. Carol wanted to rush up to the cars and pound on the hoods till they roared away. But she didn't move until Janesta drove up with her radio blasting. As she hurried into the trailer, the sound of the TV and the baby's high-pitched wails spilled across the road.

Carol headed slowly across the yard and up the road, away from the cars, remembering the evenings she used to walk down to spy on Rita and that night they walked in the moonlight. Now, she lived across the road. At the edge of the woods, deer stood, glancing nervously about before they began to pick their way delicately through the fields, their rhythmic pace like a sewing machine jogging up and down. Moving as if drawn by the scent of a banquet, the deer headed for the ruined gardens where field mice and skunks already rustled about.

*   *   *

Rainey was tucked in bed with her cast propped on an extra pillow. She watched her mother pull her clothes off and kick them into a pile. The kitchen was steamy and smelled of soap as Rita lowered herself into the washtub and sat with her knees tucked under her chin, filling a cup with water and pouring it over her head, down her back. The washtub handles clanged as she shifted her weight, water slopping over the edges as she lifted her feet out and rested them on the floor, scooting down so more of her body was immersed.

"Mommy? You forgot."

"Forgot what, Rainey?"

"About the bugs."

"There aren't that many skeeters now like before."

"Please? You have to say it," Rainey said.

"Don't let the skeeters bite."

"Pretty please, say it all?" Rainey asked in a small voice.

"Nighty night. Sleep tight. Don't let the skeeters bite."

"I won't." Rainey sighed and closed her eyes.

Rita swabbed her knees, softening the dried blood, gently rinsing them clean. When she was a child, she hated to bathe and sometimes sat on the edge of the tub splashing the water, pretending to wash. Was it the faulty plumbing, the well that threatened to go dry, the cost of heating water, or her father's miserliness? Rita wasn't sure. But every Saturday night was bath night. Because she was the youngest, she bathed last. Her father, who went first, used to lie back smoking cigarettes he doused in the toilet. Her mother followed, sneaking a few cups of clean water to rinse her hair. By the time it was Rita's turn, the water was tepid. Strands of hair floated on the filmy surface. Across the floor, threadbare towels were wadded in soggy heaps.

A breeze wafted through the screen smelling faintly of diesel and with it, the ripe scent of freshly turned earth mixed with a rank new odor, almost palpable: damp, crushed, green.

* * *

"Good-bye for now. I'm glad you called," Iris said before she hung up. "Don't forget. Do something to calm down. Make something to eat."

Always so practical, so therapeutic, Carol thought. But it had helped to tell Iris what had happened, to describe how badly she felt.

"Pain's part of the package," Iris said.

"What am I supposed to do? That's the part I don't get," Carol responded. "I feel so bad about Rita."

"What about you?"

"I didn't just have some maniac destroy everything."

"I can't help Rita. It's you I'm concerned with. Now listen to me, Carol. You need to do something for yourself. It always comes down to that. And I think congratulations are in order."

"Congratulations?"

"You told me you were painting again. That's wonderful news."

"Yeah, well. I'm sure it's not gonna last. Not now."

"It doesn't go away when you have a problem with your neighbor."

"It's not just a problem with my neighbor. I'm trying to tell you. It's more than that. I love her," she said, exasperated. "I love her," she repeated, as if Iris could not possibly understand.

Do I really? Carol thought as she fixed herself a cheese sandwich, cutting it into triangles she arranged on a square pale green plate, placing beside it some carrot and celery sticks. Can I really love anyone? she wondered as she opened a beer. In the cupboard were the candles she had bought for emergencies. This seemed as good an emergency as any other, so she lit one, letting some wax fall onto a saucer to hold the candle steady.

She felt as if she were wrapped in a heavy cloth, rolled up tightly, her arms and legs immobilized, her face covered, too. She pictured Annie in the gaudy satin coffin, so many pleats and tucks. Annie in a white lace dress like some ghoulish bride. She had wanted to kiss her but was afraid. Not of the cold unresponsive flesh, not of Annie dead, but of Annie's mother, who stood at the head of the coffin, the black net of her hat trembling importantly, obscuring her eyes. Instead, Carol had patted Annie's hand where it was folded on her belly over a Bible. It was the last time she touched her. Annie's hand was cold, her rubbery skin loose over stiff muscles. She had almost screamed: I want to kiss her! Instead, she walked blindly down the aisle, Dougie helping her through the crowd of dark curious faces, onto the bright busy street.

Carol could not remember the last time she prayed. She folded her hands in her lap, waiting for the words to come. She could hear her father's voice, blessing the meals of her childhood. She didn't want to sound like him. She didn't say anything.

The thrushes began to trill, the melodious strains of their song trickling down from the trees as the darkness, like a rich thick syrup, seeped out of the forest and spilled across the land.

22

Rita was sound asleep, dreaming. She is in a barn and when she looks up, sunlight streams through a stained-glass window illustrating the Twenty-third Psalm. People are all around her seated in rows. Slim, dressed completely in white, his white hair combed back off his face, paces the center aisle, trying to get them to sing. "I want you to belt it out," he says. "Show me your spirit."

Then he becomes Rita's father, a short, unshaven man who points an accusing finger as if he would just as soon aim a shotgun. "Who in this sorry group can sing?" He sneers, prancing like a rooster assessing his flock. Several people raise their hands, some holding up both arms waving eagerly. Rita wants to be included though her arm is unexplainably heavy as she lifts it. Just as her father turns toward her, her arm falls like a bird shot from the sky. She folds it against her body, palm over her thumping heart. The people begin to sing in perfect harmony, "Praise God from whom all blessings flow."

At ten o'clock, Rita woke up and pulled herself out of the tangled sheets, groggy from the heat and her long sleep. Rainey was sitting cross-legged on her bed. "Hi, Mom," she said. "I had Cheerios."

They went out to release the hens from their coop and gather the day's eggs. The morning was so still, they could hear the flies hum. The ground was bathed in a harsh light. My garden, my garden, Rita thought as she gave the sheep fresh water and grain. She still refused to look. Back inside, Rita set slices of bread under the broiler and made soft-boiled eggs—Rainey's favorite—scooping the warm egg into two bowls she lined with buttered toast cut into squares. It was one of the last days of summer. Dog days. The sky a deep sapphire with wispy clouds blowing out to sea. Most mornings, Rita worked in the garden, and usually she would have been out there already for hours. But now? She poured herself another cup of coffee.

"OK," she said. Rainey looked up, alert as a deer at the sound of a car approaching. Rita patted Rainey's hand. She felt surprisingly calm, a kind of hazy numbness had settled in, as if she were packed in wool. "It's time to clean up the mess," she said.

She remembered disasters of her childhood. The tornado that lifted her Aunt Jessie's trailer and carried it five miles from home, depositing it in a soybean field, unharmed. The neighbor across the road had not been so lucky. His barn had blown to bits, as if dynamite had been set off inside it. Pieces of it were found on the highway in the next county. The roof of his house had risen as easily as the wind takes a man's hat and it lay smashed in the school yard two blocks away. So much broken glass shattered across the rooms they spent days shoveling it out.

Once a window in Rita's room caved in from the pressure of the wind, another time the cellar flooded. She used to pray the whole place would be taken by the terrible winds, as if this were the only way she might escape. When the wind wrenched an old cherry tree up by the roots and thrashed it against the house, Rita pretended she'd been crippled in the crash, dragging herself around town with a limp, leaning on an old branch, feigning an external injury to show how she felt inside.

Rita took a deep breath and peered out the window. There it was, a tangled mess. The wreckage. Crows strutted up and down like generals keeping watch over a battlefield where the wounded lay. Then she saw Slim and Crystal heading up the path. Slim, who had the baby in the pouch on his chest, carried a covered dish. Crystal studied the cake she carried as if expecting any minute it would slide off the plate.

"Say," Slim said. "We figured. Maybe—" He shrugged then offered the casserole, nodding at it as if words were unnecessary.

"It's for you," Crystal said. "Devil's foody food. Like you like. Weatherman says gonna be a early frost." Crystal snuck a bit of icing and licked her finger.

"You wanna play?" Crystal asked Rainey.

"OK," Rainey said. She ran to get her monkey.

"You ever play Body Snatchers?" Crystal threw her head back and rolled it side to side. Rita noticed the pulse beating in her pale throat. How vulnerable the human body is, she thought. So fragile.

"What's that, Body Snatchers?" Rainey asked. She looked at her mother for an explanation, but Rita shrugged.

"C'mon. I'll show-de-bo you." Crystal hopped out the door.

Slim coughed and fiddled with the bowl of eggshells on the counter, breaking them into smaller pieces. He cleared his throat.

"I—" they both said at once.

"Sorry," Slim said. "Go ahead."

"No. You go ahead. What were you gonna say?"

"It's eggplant," he said, nodding at the casserole. "I, well. I just." He pushed his glasses up his nose. He didn't know what to say. He patted the baby, rubbing his back in small circles, around and around. "You name it," he finally blurted. "Just tell me how to help."

"I haven't really looked at it yet. I couldn't bring myself to. I was about to go out there when you guys showed up," Rita said.

The girls were playing under the apple tree, Crystal on her back with her eyes squeezed shut, her arms pressed stiffly to her sides.

"First it eats your brain," she said. "Then you ain't you no more."

"Oh," Rainey said. She squatted to watch a trail of ants. Like a thick black line they marched through the grass toward their sandy hill.

None of it seemed real to Rita. Maybe something had eaten *her* brain. It was as if she were observing someone else's life, how it felt to watch troubled people on the news. "Here's where the tragedy struck," an announcer's voice rang, then the camera panned the scene. She followed Slim through the tangle of stems and leaves and roots, stopping to pick up a tomato, perfectly formed, unblemished, pale green with the stem intact. A row of carrots had lost their fern-like tops but the thick orange roots were still buried in the earth, one or two sheared off a bit, but mostly unharmed. A pumpkin, seemingly perfect at first, had part of its rind torn away. Inside, ants scurried over the dark orange surface beaded with sticky drops like dew.

Slim rocked on his heels, trying to understand how somebody could do such a thing. It reminded him of the story on the news about that man who went into McDonald's and shot everybody. Strangers. He just got mad and killed a bunch of strangers. He patted the baby, comforted by his soft sucking sounds.

"Heck. I dunno where to begin," he said after a while. Rita stood beside him, her arm almost brushing his. He smelled of laundry soap. She felt a rush of affection for this tall skinny man who wanted so badly to do what was right. They were not exactly friends. To have a friend took time. But they were neighbors. Good neighbors. At the moment, it was enough. She shaded her eyes, staring at the bottle green flies that crawled over a slick smear of smashed tomatoes.

"It makes me think of a wreck or something. Like an airplane crash. I keep thinking these guys'll rush up with the jaws of life," Rita said.

Slim held a zucchini plant up, mindful of the spines. "You got you some zukes." Four zucchinis clung to the plant.

"They're indestructible." She tried to laugh but it came out forced.

"Uhm. Well. I dunno if you know it or not. But they took her to the state hospital. Nelly. I told 'em they could call me if they needed to. She was goin' on about how she had some kind of hole in her head. Something about drinkin' pesticide. Not makin' a lot of sense. They say they'll observe her. Or whatever. Treat her. I dunno."

Rita didn't say anything. She didn't know what to say. Across the road, Carol was in her yard, pushing a hand mower up and down.

"Well, captain," Slim said. He saluted and clicked his heels. "I'm reportin' for duty."

"Maybe you could drive your front-loader up here and bury it."

"I might could do that," Slim said.

"I could set the sheep loose. But they'd eat themselves sick."

"You had you some deer in here feedin', looks like." Slim pointed to the hoof prints. "There's still some good stuff here," he added. "What d'you say? I get the kids to help. I get Carol. She's all broke up over it. I talked to her this mornin'."

Rita shivered as if a cold wind were blowing, but the sun was still hot, oppressively so, like a hot iron searing her skin. All around her bees worked, gathering pollen from the blossoms not yet closed. Slim patted her shoulder. "You hold James," he said, offering the baby as he would offer a precious gift. "Lemme get us some boxes. The wheelbarrow. I'll be right back."

Rita sat in the dirt with the baby on her lap. A breeze lifted his pale red hair, and then he made a grunting sound, but continued to sleep. She slowly began rocking the carrots side to side, pushing back the dirt so she could grip them enough to pull them out. It felt like a major accomplishment. She was exhausted and suddenly as oblivious as James to the scene around her until a shadow fell over her. Carol. Her presence was like a vibration in the air.

"Hey," Carol said.

"Hey." Rita stared at the thick soles of Carol's sneakers, at the stains from the cut grass.

"I came to help," Carol said, her voice nearly a whisper. Rita imagined her lips softly brushing her ear. Behind her, the girls chattered like squirrels, running ahead of Slim. Crystal had a box over her head and she tripped and sprawled at Rita's feet.

"I can use help," Rita said. She fanned James with a broccoli leaf using it to keep the sun off his face. White-throated sparrows sang from the bushes and a mourning dove cooed close by. Their spirits are shining, Rita thought, recalling her dream, how she had risen to sing. She had been hearing the same birds her entire life. Even in the city, they sang in the ailanthus trees, haunting and familiar.

Carol lugged a large hubbard squash over to the wheelbarrow. She studied the texture of the nubby rind, the gray twist of the stem, the mottled end where the blossom had fallen off. There were three cabbages beside it, all of them damaged, but the bad parts could be cut away.

"This reminds me of pickin' the dump," Slim said.

"What do you mean?" Carol scratched her arms nervously. Watching her, Rita realized how little she knew about Carol, how much she still wanted to know, and how hard it was going to be for them ever to talk.

"You know. Findin' what you can use. Pickin' out what's still good. One man's trash is the other man's treasure, they say."

"Can I make you guys lunch?" Carol asked. When she glanced

over at Rita and attempted a smile, she was struck by how young Rita seemed, how vulnerable. "I'll go down to Moody's and get stuff."

"No," Rita said. "No. You don't have to do that."

Carol looked hurt as she bent over the mangled potatoes.

"We'll go to my place," Slim said as if there were no question. "I got sandwich fixins ready to go."

"You guys," Rita said, exasperated. "You've done enough."

"When I say the word, you come on over."

Before Rita could protest, Slim was loping across the field. Carol brushed her arm with a feathery dill leaf. She could not help herself. I'm sorry, she wanted to say, but didn't.

"Don't," Rita said. She pulled away. "I can't talk about it." Rita's voice was husky. It seemed she might weep but then the moment passed.

"Do you want me to leave?" Carol asked.

"No," Rita said. "I'm just not ready to talk about it."

*   *   *

Lizzy was on the sofa with a hot-water bottle. She had begun to bleed. It didn't feel unusual. It was her period. Not a miscarriage. Two Tylenols had eased the cramps. Just plain old menstruation. Lizzy remembered how furtively she had looked that word up, her small fingers on the thin paper, her eyes darting to the drawing of the merganser ducks with crested heads. Then no, she had whispered, you're heading in the wrong direction. Men's room. Menstruation. There it was followed by a string of symbols like hieroglyphics. She hadn't paid attention when they were taught the pronunciation symbols. But back then, it was a word to be whispered. She couldn't foresee herself in her white lab coat explaining the process in words anyone could understand. A shedding, she often said, pointing to the illustrations.

She shifted the hot-water bottle and sighed. Aran, sensing her sorrowful mood, wanted to play house. She was the mommy and Lizzy was her child. So far, Lizzy had been served chocolate milk in a red plastic cup and a plate of crackers smeared with jam. Now Aran was attempting to comb Lizzy's hair.

"Lemme sit up, honey," Lizzy said. She felt a little woozy.

"Don't you call your mommy *honey*!" Aran said.

"Mommy, Mommy. Lemme sit up first," Lizzy said, making her voice shrill. It pained her to say *Mommy*. Aran was so precious to her. How had she ever imagined a new baby could replace this beautiful girl she loved so much? How had she ever let herself hope? It was as if she'd been hit over the head, bound and gagged, dragged into a dark building and forced to take drugs. The effects were finally wearing off.

"I gotta work while the weather's good," Michael had said that morning, promising to stop by the clinic to tell J.T. Lizzy wasn't well. As always, Lizzy was glad to see him go. She loved it best when she was alone with Aran.

"Mommy?" Aran said, forgetting who was playing what role. Lizzy swooned. She kissed her and patted the back of her dimpled hand.

"What, honey?" she asked. She could see the postcard propped on the table, a seascape with fishing nets, the latest to arrive, and the first Michael had read to Aran that elicited no response.

"Lizzy?" Aran asked now, pulling away from Lizzy's hug, her blue eyes pleading. This morning she had not put on any makeup—another sign of her recovery from her mother, Lizzy hoped—and her skin seemed delicate as porcelain. Her eyelashes were thick and sandy, startling without the familiar gobs of mascara.

"Yeah?" Lizzy smoothed her hair, tucking it behind her ears.

"Is it OK? I mean. Is it OK can I love you?"

"Of course. Of course it's OK to love me. I love *you,* you know."

"But," Aran said. Then she squirmed out of Lizzy's arms and did a little dance, twirling and kicking, lost in a frenzy of activity.

"I'm still the mommy," she shrieked in her evil stepmother's voice, shaking a scolding finger. "You go to sleep. Or else!" She flounced upstairs and returned carrying a pair of her mother's high heels that she slipped on, scraping across the floor. "Did you hear me?" Aran screamed.

"Yes, Mommy," Lizzy whispered. She lay back on the sofa and adjusted her hot-water bottle. She felt as if her body were becoming one with the lumpy cushions, that by the time Michael returned there would only be a smear of blood on the dark green corduroy to show where she had been. When questioned, Aran would shrug and dance across the room; she would have nothing to say.

*   *   *

"Meat of unknown origins," Carol said. After eating lunch at Slim's, they stood at the end of Rita's driveway. Carol felt hopelessly determined to coax a giggle out of Rita. "At first I thought it was my eyes. That I'd been out in the sun too long and couldn't really *see* it," Carol continued. "All those beige slices piled up."

"Don't forget the pimiento loaf."

"Oh, yeah. The pimiento loaf."

"They got boy birds and girl birds," Crystal told Rainey.

Carol was afraid Crystal might launch into a discussion of bird reproduction, that she would have to explain to Rita where all the details had come from. But that was all Crystal said.

"Thanks again for your help," Rita said. Her back ached, but other than that, she felt nothing. She was like a paper doll, bent too often at the waist; soon, she would fold over and topple.

"It was the least I could do. I feel like—"

Rita held up her hand as if to ward off a blow. Her bottom lip trembled. Carol hurried off, not even saying good-bye, not even promising to return. The cool dark interior of the house pulled her in.

Carol took a shower, scrubbing the dirt from her hands and knees, washing her hair twice, making the water as cold as she could stand it, as if the shock would cleanse her. Then she sat at the table making a list. JACKASS, she wrote. Beneath it, HOW NOT TO BE ONE.

"I will not try to be funny. I will stop making jokes. I will not try to help. I will not ever touch her ever." I am too old for this, she thought, crumpling the paper. She stared off into space, chewing her pencil. When she had lunch at Slim's, he had looked over at Janesta with so much longing it had been painful to witness. Was this how she looked at Rita?

She wrote ART and underlined it twice then began another list: *Sketch two hours a day. See everything through. Write down my dreams. Go for walks. Paint outside. Watercolors. Play.*

HEALTH she wrote on a third page. She sketched a woman lifting a barbell over her head. Beneath it she made a list: *Do stretches. Walk four miles a day. Swim. One Diet Coke is it. One beer. Eat salad.*

She realized as she wrote this last page that she really needed to go shopping. She made a quick list and headed for her car.

I'll take rides in the evenings, she planned as she drove to Union City. I'll drive up and down every road until I know it all. I'll go to the sea. I'll go to the galleries on Holiday Island. She kept on this way, making plans, until she approached the outskirts of Union City. Then there was traffic, something she hadn't dealt with in a long time, and she gave all her attention to driving, mindful of the cars that darted in front of her, that turned without signaling, that changed lanes as if she weren't even there.

She pulled into a parking space, remembering the job Trudy

mentioned. I'll find out about it, she decided. I need to stay busy. Get out in the world.

The grocery store was twice the size of the Food Emporium where she shopped in the city. The aisles were wide with plenty of room to pass, not crammed with people studying the food labels as if no one wanted to get by. She pushed her cart past the paper towels and toilet paper. The Pepto-Bismol and Metamucil and Ex-Lax. Here we are, folks, she imagined a TV announcer's overly excited voice. The whole cycle of the digestive system. Yes indeed! We've got it all.

Carol nearly ran back out through the automatic doors. She wanted to go home. Not to Preacher's Lake, but to the city. Where she belonged. Instead, she grabbed a loaf of oatmeal bread and continued on, selecting two six-packs of Dos Equis. There. I've got my carbohydrates, she told herself, wheeling past the shelves of brightly colored labels, the cans and jars and boxes that seemed to scream: Buy me! Buy me! like so many hands latching onto her as she passed by, wanting to touch her the way fans grabbed for their favorite rock star.

Over by the dairy case, a chubby man in a brown and orange uniform had a woman by the elbow. Apparently she had just eaten a box of donuts and was halfway through a quart of milk.

"No money?" the man said in disbelief. "You got no money?"

The woman's tangled platinum wig tipped on her head. Blotches of chocolate were smeared on her chin.

Back in the sixties, Carol used to steal food. Not because she needed it, but just to be doing it. Her roommate, Cathy, would come home with steaks in her book bag, her school papers stained with blood. Carol's goal had been to steal all the spices, in alphabetical order, and she had just reached for the paprika when she became aware she was being watched. She put the bottle back on the shelf and never stole again.

"I was hungry," the woman said, slurring the words. Carol had spent years training herself not to react to what happened to strangers. Once, when she was new to the city, she tried to rescue a man who was about to fall in the middle of traffic on Broadway. "He's having a heart attack," she had screamed, trying to get other people to help, trying to make the cars stop. Why wasn't someone calling the police? "Lady? Ain't you never seen no junky?" a man asked before pocketing her wallet.

The woman opened her purse and the man reached inside removing a bottle of generic aspirin, a container of Suave shampoo, three lemons, and a jar of Taster's Choice. "OK," the man said. "Is that it?"

The woman tipped the carton of milk back and took a long swallow. When she was finished, she licked her lips slowly. Maybe things were different in a small town, she thought. Maybe she *should* help. The tension was almost palpable as she reached into her pocket for the wad of bills she'd taken from the cash machine, pulled out a twenty and went up to the man.

"Will this take care of it?" she said.

The woman glared at the money as if it were a dog turd.

"I don't need no charity," she said in a gruff voice. "Not from *you.*" She glared at Carol.

"Don't bother," a woman said to Carol. "She wants to get arrested. It means sleeping inside a few nights."

"Sorry," Carol mumbled. The woman who had spoken to her wore a plastic name tag that said. J.T. CARSON. She seemed to be studying Carol with interest, as if she had something more to say, but then she moved on. Zap! Carol thought, but with no enthusiasm. J.T. was such a dykey name. And so what if this J.T. looked like half the lesbians in New York *and* wore a silver labrys on a chain around her neck? Hadn't she met enough lesbians for a while? A Muzak version of "Lovely Rita" blared from the sound system. What next? she thought as she pushed her cart to the checkout where J.T. flashed her a beautiful smile. She was studying a newspaper that claimed aliens had taken over Antarctica.

"Imagine," she said, holding up the front page. There was a photograph of two people that closely resembled the cone heads. They had very wrinkled cones topped with knitted caps.

Don't even think of flirting, Carol scolded herself, though she noted with pleasure the streaks of gray that ran through J.T.'s dark hair, the laugh lines that accented her eyes. *She* would remember the first time the Beatles were on Ed Sullivan.

* * *

"Hey, look who's here," Coalie said. "Hot enough for ya?"

"Mr. Riley," Buster said. "Boy, we heard you had trouble up there on that hill."

"Yeah," Slim said. What had he come down to Buster's for? He was sorry he'd left James at home. He felt so empty-handed without him. A row of wind socks drooped beside the porch. There was not the slightest breeze, even here on the shore.

"What'll it be next? I hear she went after that other one, the one with the kid." Rip said the word *kid* as if it were obscene. He stopped mid-sentence to spit. "I hear she went after her with the chain saw. Like one of them movies they got. Chain saw massacree."

"It wudn't that. Tell him Slim, it wudn't no chain saw," Buster said. He popped a Reese's cup into his mouth whole, chewed it fast, then licked the chocolate from the wrapper.

There was a commotion in the parking lot. "Derek, c'mon," his mother shouted, trying to yank him from the Jeep though he clutched the door handle. "Derek!" she shouted. "Leave that damn curtain and let's go."

Derek screamed as if she were beating him.

"I'd smack 'im one," Buster announced. He patted his pockets, searching for the rest of his candy bar. "It's that damn kid that acts like he's a bride. You seen 'im?" He nodded in their direction.

Rip chuckled. "What the hell's this world a comin' to, you tell me. You got that he-she whatever up there wreckin' her own farm, practically killin' her lady friend. They put 'er in jail, or what?"

"I told you, Rip," Coalie said. "They took her to Hopewell."

"Damn fool name for an asylum," Buster said.

"It's the name of the town. That just happens to be where it's at." Coalie tipped his cap at Derek and his mother as they came up the steps. Derek had the curtain draped around his shoulders.

"Oh yeah, I come down to get a good rake," Slim said.

"You fixin' to get a head start on the leaves?" Rip asked.

"I'm tryin' to help clean up. It's a big mess up there. She wrecked the gardens. It's a shame," he said.

"You'd have to be plumb clear outa your mind to act like she did," Buster said. He belched and wiped his forehead with a stained bandanna. " 'Member when she came in all fit to be tied with that baler bunged up, how she hauled it in like she figured Binky could make sense of it?"

"Hell, Buster. Anybody that'd figure that son a yours could make sense of anything's gotta be nuts, right ol' buddy?" Rip slapped him.

"Say," Slim said. "I got me an idea."

"Uh-oh! Look out, here comes the lightbulb." Coalie pretended to hide his eyes from the glare.

"Listen. It's a mess, like I said. We got most of what's worth savin'. We done went through it. But them berries're stinkin' something awful. And just the whole shebang. Say—maybe Suzie—"

"Suzie? What's Suzie got to do with it?" Rip asked.

"Maybe we could bring her up there and turn her loose. You're always sayin' she'll eat anything. She chewed the ears offa that sheep that got its head stuck in the fence."

"You want me to bring her up there?"

"Why not?"

"Why *not?*" Rip said. He tipped back in his chair, chewing slowly, a bit of tobacco juice dribbling down his beard.

"It'd be the neighborly thing to do," Slim said.

"Jesus Christ. Pretty soon you'll be quotin' the Bible at me."

"You're startin' to sound like my wife. She's always bellyachin' how things ain't right in a town that's got no church," Buster said.

"Do unto others'n all. What d'you say?" Slim said.

"That pig's too fat to go anywheres," Coalie said.

"He's right," Rip said. "I don't know how I'm gonna get her over to the county fair. Ever since I took Buster fishin' my shocks is shot. I can't be haulin' any pig up any hills. I need one of them two-ton jobs."

"Like Michael's got," Buster added. "For haulin' rock and cement and what all. P.S. don't be blamin' your troubles on me. That truck of yours is about to turn to dust, all that rust on it."

"Look who's here," Coalie said. He nodded toward the parking lot where Michael had just pulled up into the shade.

"How's it going, my friend?" Michael said to Derek, cuffing the boy's shoulder. Derek wrapped his curtain over the bottom of his face.

"Now he's one a them Arab females," Rip said.

"We was talkin' about you," Slim said. He told Michael the problem and his plan to bring Suzie up to the farm.

"I hear she drove the truck right into her house. That the little girl's in the hospital," Michael said.

"Naw. That's not what happened. It's just the garden. That's all," Slim said. "The house and everybody's OK. 'Cept for Nelly's in the hospital."

"I'm game," Michael said about the plan.

"Hold on a minute," Rip said. "I didn't even say yes."

"Why wouldn't you? Won't it make that pig a prizewinner for sure? How many pounds you figure she'll pick up eatin' all that stuff?" Slim grinned. He knew he had Rip with that.

*   *   *

Buster tossed a couple of donuts into the back of Michael's truck, but Suzie didn't respond. She sprawled in a hole she'd burrowed, her stubby legs splayed out, her nose inches from her trough.

"A smart one," Buster said.

"Hold your pants on, Buster. She's got to get the scent." Rip waved a donut under Suzie's snout. She snorted, blinking her eyes, and struggled to get to her feet.

"Too bad I don't have any more a them hamburg cookies of Trudy's. Boy, she snarfs them up. There any a Trudy's bismarcks in that sack?"

"Here." Buster dug one out. He began to eat a cruller.

"Maybe if we ever get her in the truck, we can set the two of you loose up there," Rip said, grabbing the sack from Buster and holding it up to Suzie who was on her feet now, swaying a bit from the effort to carry herself. She stepped up out of her hole and slowly followed Rip as he backed toward the truck, rustling the sack, every once in a while dropping a piece of donut to keep Suzie's interest.

"That is one fat sow," Michael said, whistling through his teeth.

Suzie snorted, her huge nostrils dripping and muddy, and slipped in her own manure in her eagerness to get to the donuts. The men had set up a plank they expected her to ascend, thinking they might have to give her a shove or put a rope around her and pull, but she climbed up after the donuts as if she did so every day. She squealed as they tied her to the sides, but once she realized she couldn't escape, she flopped down and finished off the donuts, eating the sack as well.

"Buster, you better ride with Coalie and Slim. We can't have you and Suzie in the same vehicle," Rip said.

"Jesus Christ," Michael said when he saw the garden.

"Let's just get this over with," Rip said, shaking his head sadly.

Michael put the truck into four-wheel drive and plowed ahead, bumping over the field, aiming to get as close as he could.

Rita had fallen asleep; sleep was the only thing to do at a time like this, it seemed, and Rainey was beside her dozing. She woke up when she heard the truck, terrified that Nelly had returned. She clutched Rainey, her heart pounding crazily. And then she heard Slim calling her.

"I brung help," he said. "You're gonna like this, Rainey." Rainey let him lead her out back where the largest pig she had ever seen was descending from the truck, raising her snout a bit.

"Mommy!" Rainey gasped. She pointed at Rip and clasped her hand over her mouth. She looked so frightened, Rita was afraid she might faint.

Rip, observing her reaction, scratched his beard in confusion and said, "Hell's bells. Do I really look bad enough to scare the bejesus outa that little bastard?"

"What is it, Rainey?" Rita knelt beside her. "Rainey, what?"

Rainey just pointed at Rip, her large eyes staring.

"Is it really?" Rainey whispered. "Is it really *him?*" She hid her face against her mother then peeked at Rip before hiding her face again.

"Hey," he said. "I know I'm ugly, but I ain't that bad."

Suzie was nosing through the vegetation, slurping up everything.

"She's a garbage truck on the hoof," Slim said.

"I betcha she'll clean it all up in an hour," Coalie said.

"You can't afford no bets." Rip was looking curiously at the house. So-called house, he thought, shocked to think they lived in it.

Michael crouched beside Rainey. "He won't hurt ya," he said, nodding at Rip. "He ain't a pretty sight, but he won't hurt ya."

"I've got a little girl," Michael said to Rita. He introduced himself and said where he lived. "Maybe one of these days they could play together."

Rainey was still pressed to her mother's side, hiding her face.

"Will you whisper in my ear what it is?" Rita asked her. Rainey nodded. Rita leaned over to hear what Rainey would say.

"Oh," she responded. "Oh, honey. No. That's not him."

"You sure?" Rainey whispered. "You really sure?"

"Positive," Rita said. "C'mon. Let's say hi to him. You'll see."

She tried to lead Rainey over to Rip, but Rainey wouldn't budge.

"What'sa matter?" Rip asked, genuinely puzzled.

"She thinks you're God."

"She thinks I'm *what?*"

"You heard 'er, Rip." Coalie laughed. He held his sides, he was laughing so hard. "That's a good one," he managed to blurt out.

"Well. I been accused a bein' lotsa things. But never God."

"It's your beard, I guess," Rita said. "I told her when I was a kid I thought God was an old man with a long white beard."

"Well, bless her heart." Rip searched through the pockets of his overalls and pulled out a shiny coin. "This here's my good luck charm," he said, offering it to Rainey. Up close, he could see she was cute as a button, just like Trudy had said. So what if her skin's a different color. She'd given him some kind of compliment and he wanted to give her something back.

"Oh, that's OK," Rita said, urging him to keep the money.

"I want 'er to have it. It would please me if she did." Rip tucked the coin into Rainey's hand and closed her fingers over it one by one. Her fingers were smooth and warm. He thought of the brown bread his mother used to steam on the woodstove. "It's got Eisenhower on it." Rip winked. "You hearda him?"

Rainey shook her head. She glanced up at Rip then quickly turned away. Her mother had described long flowing robes, but this man had on overalls. Up close, she could see his beard wasn't pure white at all, but had brown and yellow stains streaked through the fluffy hair. She was disappointed, but relieved too, uncertain just what she'd have to do if she met God face-to-face.

Rainey uncurled her fingers. The coin was very shiny, heavier than any piece of money she'd ever held. Rip's finger trembled as he pointed out the details. He was an old man, this was true. He had a long beard. But he was not God.

"Look here," he said. "See this man? He used to be president. Do you know who the president is?"

Crystal was twirling in circles the way she often did, pretending to be the earth rotating. She stopped in front of Rita and stood perfectly still, even her eyes were steady. "Every cloud's got a silver lining," she said. "You know that, don't 'cha?"

Rita nodded, observing Rip treating Rainey so kindly. She was beginning to feel something good might come out of this disaster. Maybe Crystal was right.

Part Two

23

Mrs. Cunningham sat at her scarred wooden desk holding up a piece of orange construction paper. It was the third week of school, too soon for the children to be decorating the room for Halloween—she knew she was asking for trouble—but last night, her sciatica was acting up so badly she had to have three big glasses of bourbon to even begin to relax and then she'd had such a terrible time waking up this morning.

She meant to grab the folder of autumn leaves, planning how the children would take turns taping them on the walls and windows—during recess, she could line them up and march them out onto the playground to gather real leaves—but she'd picked up the Halloween folder instead. It was too late to do anything about it. She had two more hours to kill.

"Class," she said, smiling, her thin pale lips sinking into her fleshy jowls, her voice high and wavering. "Today we're gonna make us some decorations. Now, won't that be nice?"

Her head was pounding something wicked and the bright morning sunlight made her long to put her head down on the desk and close her bleary eyes. She considered having the children pull out the mats for their ten-minute lie down. But somebody had taught the little Merrill girl how to tell time. Mrs. Cunningham could just hear her announcing, "Lookit. The big hand's on the ten and the little hand's on the ten. It ain't nap time yet," all smug like she'd been planted to keep tabs on the teacher. Mrs. Cunningham heaved herself up with a grunt.

"Irene?" she said and scanned the room.

"My name's Aran. Like the islands. In Ireland." Aran smiled as if she were a queen and they her adoring entourage.

Funny, Mrs. Cunningham thought. Even in kindergarten, you can tell which one'll end up prom queen. And which one'll stay back till he's old enough to drop out, like Bobby Miller picking his nose, staring intently at what he dug out before he flicked it on the floor. She gave Aran a stack of orange paper, instructing her to hand one sheet to each of her classmates.

"One for you." Aran moved around the room. "One for you and one for you," she said, almost dancing up and down the aisles.

She's a cute little thing, Mrs. Cunningham thought, noting the crisp lace trim on her dress, the shiny shoes, the heels that clicked with confidence. Not run down and manure-flecked like some. In the old days, she was careful about dividing up the duties, not wanting to create a teacher's pet. She'd kept elaborate charts of who she asked to do what. Now she just asked the cute ones in clean clothes and didn't worry about it. Lord. All that blonde silky hair, she thought, propping her elbows on the desk. Probably be on the honor roll, too.

When Aran sat down and folded her hands, Mrs. Cunningham studied her carefully, startled to notice two red smudges smeared down her chubby cheeks. She rubbed her eyes, sure they were playing tricks on her. But there it was, plain as the feathers on a chicken's tail. Some kind of rouge. The skin around the girl's eyes was pale blue, her eyelashes heavy with black mascara. Lord have mercy. Just like a little tart. In all her years teaching kindergarten, Mrs. Cunningham had never had to concern herself with the "no makeup" rule. She'd have to pin a note to the girl's dress. She scanned the room again until she found Jennifer Pomroy—a girl with plain brown hair in a neat French braid. Not a speck of makeup on her clean little face.

"Jennifer?" she asked and held up the can of scissors.

Two boys in the back of the room began to have a duel, quacking loudly as they snapped the blunt-ended scissor blades open and closed.

"Boys!" Mrs. Cunningham used her "I-mean-business" voice. "Them two'll get half the town pregnant," she muttered, glancing at her seating chart. Scotty Scott and Dwight Sargent. She'd have to separate them. Put Scotty Scott under her nose where she could keep an eye on him. Last week, when they were making collages with macaroni noodles, Mrs. Cunningham caught him crunching handfuls of macaroni like it was candy. He had belched loudly and reached into the jar to scoop out more. "What d'you say, Scotty?"

she'd asked. His answer was a loud slow fart that made the other students wild with laughter.

"Now children." Mrs. Cunningham stood up and waved her piece of orange paper. Out the window, leaves were flying by and the flagpole clanged. Dark clouds were gathering. She hoped if it stormed it would come once she was safely home, under her afghan on the couch. It was a good day for a hot toddy. For a moment, she contemplated the sheet of orange paper, her scissors poised. Trees and stars for Christmas. Snowflakes in January. What on earth was orange for? At last, it came to her.

"Pin your little eyes up here on what I'm doing. We want to make nice big round circles so we'll have plenty of room for your jack-o'-lantern's face to fit on. We go right around lickety-split and snip off these here corners. See? Like I'm doing? Just curve it right around. One. Two. Three. Four. Here we are. Now, isn't that a nice pumpkin?"

"I live on Pumpkinville Road," Scotty Scott announced, lifting his desktop and letting it fall with a bang that made Mrs. Cunningham's head pound again. She held a shaky hand to her temples and closed her eyes a moment. Then she fumbled through the envelope of black triangles she had cut out during the summer break. Something wet hit her forehead. A spitball. Ignoring the attack, she held up her creation.

"Eyes. Nose. Mouth." She had put the mouth on lopsided.

The children did their best to mimic her, their scissors awkward in their small fingers as they cut misshapen circles. Derek Wallace—the little boy who, to Mrs. Cunningham's puzzled dismay, still came to school every day with a lacy curtain, a filthy thing, draped around his neck, despite the fact that Mrs. Cunningham had written two notes to his mother about it—folded his paper in half and cut out a heart.

"Derek?" Mrs. Cunningham made her way over to his desk. She was not at all aware of how big she seemed to the children, or that Derek was so frightened of her large bosom heaving a few inches from his face he was in danger of wetting his pants. She took the orange heart away from him and snipped it into a small circle.

"We make hearts come Valentine's Day. Then we'll have red paper and special doilies to fancy them up. Who knows when Valentine's Day comes?" She waited expectantly, then, realizing no answer was forthcoming, worked her way around the room, holding up each child's attempt.

"Round, like Mr. O." She pointed to the letters of the alphabet strung across the chalkboard, then snipped the edges to make them smooth.

Jody Havey hadn't begun her pumpkin. Her paper slid to the floor as she leaned forward to pat Rainey's hair. She had been wanting to touch it since the day school started and had at last gotten the nerve to stretch her hand out. It was softer than she'd imagined. Like lamb's wool. Rainey turned and Jody grinned, revealing a chipped front tooth.

"Nigger," Jody whispered. The word, like music, hummed and reverberated in her throat.

Every night after the lights were out, Jody told her older sister, LaDonna, who got to sleep on the outside edge of the bed Jody shared with her and their baby brother, Bubba, about Rainey's skin.

"It's like cinnamon," she'd said. "Like brown-sugar fudge."

She wanted to rub a Kleenex across Rainey's cheeks, down the back of her neck. The color would smear off the way the color smeared off her mother's cheeks when she wiped the cold cream over her face.

"It ain't cinnamon, you idiot." LaDonna kicked her and told her to get over and stay over on her part of the bed. There was already a big wet spot where Bubba lay sucking his fist. "She's a nigger. Niggers've got nigger skin. Don't 'cha know nothin'?"

"Hello nigger," Jody said now, happy to have a name for what looked so soft and warm to her. She kneeled on her chair to get closer to Rainey. Jody's breath smelled of rotten teeth, of sour milk. Bits of sleep were crusted in her eyes. Rainey didn't say anything. She kept cutting around the edge of her orange circle trying to get it just right.

"I like you nigger," Jody said.

Mrs. Cunningham was standing behind the two girls. At the same moment she heard the word she had been dreading since the first day of school, a sharp pain zigzagged from her skull clear down the backs of both legs. Oh, for a drinky wink right this very minute, she thought.

* * *

"Mornin'! Boy, ain't the frost early this year," Trudy exclaimed when Rita came in with her box of eggs, her cheeks red from the cold. "Caught the farmers by surprise. Everybody hopin' to get more outa their gardens before—" She clapped her hand over her mouth, remembering what happened, how Rita's garden had died weeks ago.

"We went swimming last weekend. It was still warm enough," Rita said, deciding to ignore Trudy's embarrassment. She nodded at the fellows.

"Smells like snow," Rip said. That morning he had put on his long johns, announcing he planned to keep them on till the Fourth of July. "Where's that little girl of yours?" he asked.

"School."

"School? Boy, they start 'em young."

"She's five already. It's just half a day. Kindergarten."

"That so?" Rip scratched his beard. His moustache was so long it drooped over his bottom lip and was beaded with coffee.

"You got your wood in?" Hydie slipped an omelette onto a plate.

"Yes," Rita said, taking a stool at the counter. "Stacked and under cover. Ready to go. I built a fire last night." Rita still couldn't believe it was possible for her to walk into Hydie's as if she belonged. Trudy placed a cup of coffee in front of her and reached for the pitcher of milk she knew Rita liked. Then she went to the cash register to count out the money for the eggs.

"I don't know how much longer I'll be able to supply you with eggs," Rita said. "They're slowing up. Everybody says when the days get shorter you can't count on them laying."

"My dad used to hang lightbulbs out in the coop," Hydie offered. "Them commercial folks keep the hens under bright lights night and day."

"That ain't natural," Rip said. "How can they sleep?"

"They give 'em newspapers to read instead," Hydie teased.

"Don't laugh," Coalie said. "I heard how this fella plays music for his chickens. Highbrow stuff. Says they lay up a storm."

"Bet them eggs're square," Buster said. "Say, square eggs'd go over good. Be easier to pack and all."

"With the days gettin' short and all the tourists gone home, we don't serve up that many breakfasts," Trudy said. "Pretty soon it'll be so cold and dark of a morning, we'll just get a few regulars. It'll work out OK. I don't know about you, but I like when winter comes. I get time to start my wreaths and make my Christmas presents."

"Christmas," Buster said. "What about Thanksgiving? You forgot turkey day, woman. When you gonna start makin' pumpkin pies?"

Trudy ignored him. "Say, you wanna help me with wreaths this year?" she asked Rita. "Hydie's got some fella says he's gonna take 'em down to the city to sell. However many I can get together, he'll take."

"Gosh," Rita said. "I'd love to, Trudy. But I don't. I never—"

"Oh, don't worry. It's easy as pie. Raymond helps me."

Raymond, hearing his name, shuffled up and leaned against his mother. He wrapped his arms around her waist and she stroked his cheek.

"I'll get you started," Trudy promised. "It's good money, too."

As Rita drove back up the hill, she replayed the scene in the diner. She had so little contact with people, delivering eggs had become an event. She loved how the place smelled of coffee and sweet rolls fresh from the oven. She thought about making wreaths with Trudy. Today she planned to insulate the underside of the house. All this talk of winter made her anxious. It didn't matter how much wood was stacked in the woodshed if the wind could whip through the cracks in the floor. Already, their feet were so icy cold in the mornings they took turns standing on the small hooked rug to get dressed.

She passed a car that was pulled haphazardly off the road as if it had skidded to a stop. A woman had her face down on the steering wheel. At first, Rita didn't think anything of it. Cars pulled onto the shoulder were not unusual. But as she drove on, the image nagged at her. A woman alone on a country road, far from any houses. What if her car had broken down or was out of gas? What if she had braked to avoid an animal and hurt herself? What if no one else came along the road for a long time? When she was first learning to drive, strangers had stopped for her.

Rita turned around, carefully maneuvering the truck. The car still sat where she'd seen it, the front tires dipping toward the ditch where goldenrod bloomed in the frost-blackened weeds. The woman's dark curls glistened in the sunlight. She still cradled her face in her arms but at the sound of the truck, she looked up, startled, wiping her face frantically.

"You OK?" Rita asked. "I saw you stopped. I thought maybe—"

The woman attempted to smile. Her eyes were very red; her cheeks still damp with tears. Rita thought she might have seen her before, in Moody's shopping with a little girl. She noticed a Barbie doll in a pink gown flung on the backseat like a disappointed bridesmaid.

"I just needed a good cry. Thanks for stopping." The woman began weeping in earnest, but she waved Rita away. "Really, I'm OK."

"Well, if you're sure," Rita said, backing off. "It's good to cry sometimes," she added. "They say it's good for you."

The woman nodded. She kept her face in her hands, as if it

pained her to be seen. Rita considered telling the woman where she lived, offering her phone number, but that seemed too awkward. "Things get better," Rita muttered.

Back home, Rita thought about the woman, about how alone everyone really was, how even when people wanted to help each other, they were still alone. Carol, across the road, a distance that seemed too far to cross. All they had done for weeks was wave at one another as if from opposite sides of a chasm. Nelly in an institution, locked away. Rita was so tired, she felt she could sleep where she stood, like a horse, dozing in the sun.

She stared down at the tar paper Nelly had nailed around the house. Most of the slats and tar paper had been torn away; what remained flapped in the wind. Even though Slim showed her a note Nelly'd written claiming she was never coming back—tell Rita she can stay there forever, the note said—Rita was afraid to count on it. Sometimes, it seemed as if any minute Nelly would appear around the side of the house, whistling, intent on finishing one of her many projects. She half-expected the tractor to sputter to life. After Nelly was taken away, Rita put a bolt on the door. At night, she locked them in, but still she dreamt Nelly returned, that she kicked down the door as if it were made of straw.

The way into the crawl space was under the kitchen window, near the water pipe. Rita could hardly believe she had to slide under there. She'd put on old clothes, a kerchief over her hair, and pulled on Nelly's work gloves. Still, she wished there were some other way to do the job. She spread a sheet of plastic on the cold ground, hoping to be able to keep it under her as she crawled inside. But crawl was the wrong word. She knelt down and flashed the light under the house. Thick spiderwebs and clumps of dust hung from the floor joists and in the corner, the pack rat's nest: a jumble of hay and silvery ribbon, bits of cloth, a crushed Coke can, a fork. If she could go in on her hands and knees, looking ahead of her, it would not be so bad. But there was only one way in. She lay on her back, the flashlight shoved down the arm of her jacket, and shuffled along, wriggling on her back, pushing with her heels until she was under the house in the dim dusty space. She was immediately claustrophobic. But she talked herself into staying where she was. Right above her, through the cracks in the floorboards, she could see into the house.

"My house," she murmured, trying out the idea. In places, there were knotholes she could poke her fingers through. Though she knew it might not be enough, some insulation was better than none.

Later, she would bank the house with bales of hay the way she'd seen people do.

She planned how she would cut the insulation into manageable lengths, roll them up, and bring them under the house to staple into place. She'd fill the staple gun. Put fresh batteries in the flashlight. Go pee. Bring tissues in case she sneezed. She lay there for a moment, trying to foresee other problems. She hoped the pack rat did not return, clutching a gnarly apple in its mouth.

It was slow work, stapling insulation to the underside of the floorboards, holding it in place, attempting to shield her eyes from the bits of dirt and fiberglass that trickled onto her face. She hated being under the house with the spiders and the thick smell of dust. A box of rusty nails was shoved beside the water pipe near a rusty wrench Nelly had forgotten. She would insulate the pipe too, or their water would freeze. It might freeze anyway. Her father used to curse and bang the pipes in his fury the days when they could not flush. Last night, she read Rainey the story of the ant and the grasshopper. She hoped she was not getting ready for winter too late.

*   *   *

Lizzy insisted the doctor let her see it. "I'm a nurse," she said, as if that gave her the right. She wanted to quell forever this notion of a baby blossoming inside her, a baby she would never have.

"It's a cyst," the doctor had informed her after she went to his office for the exam. "It ought to come out. These things can go on for months unnoticed," he said, ushering her to the receptionist. "Sometimes they disappear on their own, sometimes they grow. Yours is growing."

"I thought I was pregnant," Lizzy admitted before she left. She didn't know why she was telling the doctor. He had a reputation for being gentle, but he was so shy, he could not meet her eyes.

Now she had seen it. The blob of tissue, skin riddled with a clump of coarse dark hair, what appeared to be fingernails, and one tiny perfectly formed tooth. She had studied such growths when she was in school. "Dermoid cysts," they were called. She and her classmates had laughed over the tale of the country doctor, who, upon finding one in the body of a young girl, claimed she had swallowed her baby teeth.

So this is what my body can produce, she thought. Exhausted from her ordeal she slumped on the hospital bed and stared out the window. During the night, the wind had blown so many leaves from the trees they were almost bare, the dark branches swaying against the bright blue sky.

Although the procedure was considered minor—it involved making a small incision near her navel and pumping her abdomen with gas—Lizzy wished she could sign up for an extended stay. She wanted to be tucked under the stiffly starched sheets and stare at the television, have trays of Jell-O and Salisbury steak carried in to her at regular intervals. She did not want to be released back into her life.

Lizzy was woozy, even though everyone said she shouldn't be. And then she began to cry. J.T. hugged her, murmuring words of comfort, finally promising to be a surrogate mother if Lizzy would only stop.

"Ha!" Lizzy said, drying her eyes. Still thinking how all the hope had been scraped out of her with the surgeon's knife. "I might take you up on that. Would you do it the regular way or use the old turkey baster?"

"Ugh. Maybe not me. Maybe Betty. She's more maternal."

"Oh, God, J.T. He stuck it in a Baggy. He said he 'caught it' like he was going fishing. 'We didn't want it to burst inside you,' he said. Ugh. Mr. Sensitive. Like it was a boil."

J.T. imitated the doctor, fluttering her eyelids to avoid Lizzy's eyes. When the doctor came in on rounds, Lizzy was laughing and clutching the bandage on her belly, afraid it would pop off.

* * *

"You're wrong, Dougie. I am *not* scared," Carol said. "Just once I'd like to know who it is I'm rolling around with in bed. No more ipso facto relationships. After Vivian, I don't want to wake up beside some stranger and wish astral travel had been perfected. I'm gonna be a celibate girl."

"You? Celibate?" Dougie laughed. "Honey, lemme count the days."

Carol wondered if, technically speaking, she could call herself celibate since she'd been having a more active sex life alone than she'd ever had with a lover. Annie was strictly a "let's do it before we sleep" lover who was usually too tired by the time they went to bed to do more than snuggle up. With Vivian, it was Carol who was never in the mood. The whole process had a cookbook feel. A pinch of this. A teaspoon of that. Sift. Stir. Carol sighed.

"Aha," Dougie said. "At last, a sign of your true feelings."

"What?"

"That sigh. That sigh says it all."

"It's just my body trying to get more oxygen."

"Tell me another one. That's not all your body's trying to get."

"Oh, Dougie. I can live without it, believe me." What surprised her was how infrequently she even *saw* Rita. In New York, she was always running into her friends. That morning, she trudged across the road, determined to invite Rita for supper. As she knocked on Rita's door, she sensed her presence, but the house was empty. Now she had to eat alone.

"My little nun," Dougie said.

"Your turn," she said.

"I'm not finished with you. Listen, don't gimme that Methodist stiff-upper-lip crap. It's human to want it. Lust," he said, drawing the word out. "Hunger."

"I'm not a Methodist."

"Whatever. Denial is denial no matter what your religion. Say, listen, I've gotta get to work. I'll catch you up later."

After she hung up, Carol made herself some toast and sat in the easy chair with her feet on the footstool. She had smeared the toast with extra butter and a gob of blueberry jam. Hunger, Dougie said. That was a word she understood. Outside, yellow leaves were falling like bits of solid sunlight settling on the flattened weeds, piling up in the ditches alongside Preacher's Lake Road. At first, Carol was uneasy about the change in weather, the early nights, the cold air seeping under the door, but then she realized she was looking forward to the winter. She felt dreamy, drowsy, and leaned back in her chair, pulling a blanket over her lap. Vincent, a huge orange cat that had moved in when she did, jumped up and curled into a contented ball on her lap, purring loudly.

Darlene had been Carol's first official girlfriend, after the fiasco with Loretta. Darlene moved in the day after they made love the first time. Carol felt a rush of desire remembering Darlene on her lap that afternoon, her smooth pale skin. Though they had lived together for two years, they had never once made love again. With Rita, if their relationship ever advanced to such a stage, things would be different. I've learned a thing or two, she thought. Age has its benefits.

She wondered how it would begin. Beginning was always the hardest part. Just yesterday, they had passed on the road, Rita headed home as Carol drove to town. They had honked and waved, friendly enough, but that was the closest they'd been in weeks. Carol had to struggle to give up her attempts to arrange the perfect moment.

She was lonely and her phone bill was horrendous, but she was still glad she'd decided to stay. She pushed the cat off her lap and went into her studio. She'd been working on some sketches, shapes mostly, curious mounds like some kind of primitive boat. She didn't understand what they were, but each day she studied them, added to them, sketched them from another angle, with a different crayon, on another type of paper. She wanted to turn them into pieces, but she couldn't decide what materials to use. She pulled a sketch pad out from under the pile of drawings and as she brushed a Conté crayon over the rough paper, she let her mind go. That was one of the best things about her new life, how easy it was to let go, her hand propelled as if from a separate source.

In fourth grade, Carol realized she was a lesbian when all the boys wanted to marry Miss Rivers, the teacher, and she did, too.

"Girls can't marry girls," Mary Vincent, her best friend, had said.

"Why not?"

"They just can't. Nobody does."

"Well, I'm gonna," Carol said. She knew even then it was women she wanted to spend her life with. But it wasn't until after Loretta that she had a name for it. Loretta's parents sent her to Montana to live with an uncle who had a ranch out in the middle of nowhere, just to get her away from Carol. She wrote a letter, urging Carol to date boys, and Carol had tried. But it made her miserable and half of them turned out to be gay. She had just broken up with the last one when her friend Darlene pulled her sweater over her head. She was naked under the sweater. Her skin was smooth as marble. In that moment with her hands on Darlene, Carol realized her passion for Loretta had not been a fluke. "An abomination," her father had called it.

Carol sketched the scene from memory: she and Loretta naked in each other's arms on top of the sleeping bag. Her father peering in through the flaps of the tent. Whoever would have thought her father would come out with a bowl of popcorn for a treat?

"Surprise!" her father had shouted, flashing the light into the tent, then backing away, making a horrible retching sound.

"Doris?" Carol could hear her father as clearly as if he were in the room. "Tell your daughter to get in here or I'll call the police."

Loretta was already dressed, disappearing into the night by the time Carol's mother came tottering toward her as if she were an accident victim and her mother was about to spread an old army blanket over Carol.

Even now, all these years later, the memory of Loretta, the way Carol touched her as if she were the butterflies she'd caught as a child, careful not to brush the dust from their wings, sent her reeling.

24

Aran wore a blue dress with shamrocks dotted across the gathered skirt and a pair of white tights that sagged at her knees. Her mother had sent the dress from Ireland. The yoke was done up with hand-smocking, and it tied at the back in a floppy bow. Aran insisted on wearing it for her visit. She brought along her Barbies in a suitcase that she carried up the path with the determination of a Bible salesman. Rainey was under the apple tree watching her. She had been teasing China Cat, the kitten Slim gave her, by dangling a strand of yarn in front of it. The kitten ran up the tree at Aran's approach.

"You wanna play Barbie?" Aran asked.

Rainey had no idea what that was. She shrugged and scratched her arm. She still felt lucky to have the cast off. She noticed a pack of candy tucked into the pocket of Aran's jacket as she flicked the suitcase open. A doll was nestled on each side and in the center, an array of clothing hung from minuscule hangers.

"I have a camera," Rainey said. "I can take your picture."

"Me and Barbie are famous stars," Aran said. She batted her eyes. "When I grow up I'm gonna be on the cover of *Glamour*."

Rainey came back out with her camera and aimed it carefully. She took the picture Aran wanted her to take—Aran posed with her head back, her eyes closed, Barbie held high like a torch.

"Now I'm gonna take one of your hair."

"It's Hair So New, dahlink," Aran said. "Only her hairdresser knows for sure. Me and my mommy got hair like Cybill Shepherd."

She might as well have been speaking a foreign language for all Rainey understood. She watched Aran busily undressing one of the dolls, deftly undoing the fasteners, tossing the clothes aside and expertly pulling on a striped sweater and a pair of red stretch pants with tiny loops for the doll's feet. She slipped on a pair of white rubber sneakers. While she did this, Rainey aimed the camera at the red satin bow in Aran's hair, focusing on the tangled golden strands twisted around the knot, on the way one loop sagged on the verge of coming loose.

"Ta dah!" Aran said, displaying Barbie's new outfit. "You dress that one." She pointed at the other doll.

Rainey put her camera back inside and by the time she returned, Aran had dressed the other Barbie in a matching outfit that matched the first one's.

"They're twins," Aran announced. "Double your pleasure, double your fun," she sang. She took the candy from her pocket, and unwrapped a bright pink square she stuffed into her mouth. The sweet scent made Rainey's mouth water. "Here," she said, offering the candy to Rainey. "It's a Starburst."

Once, on the playground, Aran had tagged Rainey, but then the teacher blew her whistle and the game had come to a halt. The candy was so sweet Rainey choked a little. Up in back, she could see her mother beside the tractor talking to Aran's father. China Cat gave the Barbie a suspicious sniff then swatted the doll's hair and ran away, making the girls giggle.

"See? You open the throttle, this here. And then press the starter, like so." Michael followed his own instructions. "Easy as pie." But the engine did not turn over. He chewed the stem of his pipe. "This here's your forward and reverse." He patted one of the levers.

Rita stood eye level with the top of the tires, dwarfed by the tractor. She felt as if Michael were attempting to teach her to drive a sixteen-wheeler. She could not imagine swinging herself up onto the seat the way Nelly had done. She could not imagine dragging the plow across the field or mowing hay. In her panic, her concentration floated off. Overhead, huge white clouds drifted along like whales. The day was warm, Indian summer everybody said, and the air smelled of overripe apples rotting in the sun.

"Well, it's been a while," Michael said. "Let's try adjusting the throttle. C'mon. You can do it," he said, addressing the tractor. The motor sounded like a Ferris wheel grinding into motion and the muffler cap clattered, emitting a spume of smoke. The tractor vibrated so much Michael's voice trembled as he shouted, "That's more like it!"

When he brought the pig up, Michael had promised to return and show Rita how to operate the tractor, but still she had been surprised when he pulled up that day while she was struggling to lug the last bale of hay up to bank the house. "Lemme give you a hand with that," he said. Now he had started the tractor. Rita wasn't used to people helping her. She didn't know what she could offer in return.

"You try it," he said, jumping to the ground. "You'll need a step stool to get up there," he laughed, giving her a boost.

"It's now or never," she said.

"Betcha never thought you'd be operating a tractor."

"I can hardly drive the truck," Rita said. "I'm still scared to drive over the bridge."

"Half the folks in Preacher's Lake're scared to cross that bridge. With the tractor you don't have to worry about traffic."

She pushed the starter, and the tractor roared to life. It was like sitting on top of a spinning washing machine.

"There you go," Michael said.

The steering wheel wobbled as she slowly eased forward. She could feel the drag of the plow.

* * *

"It's weird," Michael said that evening at supper. "I always thought they were ugly." He helped himself to another bowl of black bean soup and finished off his glass of beer.

"Who?" Lizzy said. She had not been paying attention. Aran was telling all about the kitten Rainey had, how it had chased after Barbie.

"Can I have a kitty?" she asked. "Please, pretty pretty please? With sugar on top?" She looked from her father to Lizzy and back again.

"We'll see, dumpling," Michael said.

"She can have Fancy Feast in a special dish, right Daddy?"

"Whatever you say, honeybuns." Michael sliced more bread.

"What were you saying?" Lizzy asked Michael. She wondered if she could find a kitten in time for Aran's birthday.

"I was talking about Rita. The one on the farm. Where we went today. She's, you know." He shrugged and eyed Aran, but she seemed preoccupied with lining up her beans along the crack in the table.

"She's gay," he said in a loud whisper.

"Yeah," Lizzy said. She didn't know what he was getting at.

"Well, I thought women like that were ugly. But she's a knockout. It's weird. She has that little girl, too. She's not adopted either. Looks like her only she's, what you call it, mulatto?"

"Gosh, Michael. You sound like a Neanderthal." Lizzy scraped her chair back. Aran took this as an excuse to get up. "J.T.'s a lesbian. She's not ugly. Why do they have to be ugly?"

"I figured they were chicks that couldn't find a guy." He looked genuinely puzzled.

"Chicks?" Lizzy said. "I haven't heard anyone say that in decades."

"OK. Women." A gob of soup slithered down his beard.

"I know they don't have any sexual deviates in *Little House in the Big Woods,* but really." She rolled her eyes.

"Just one teeny tiny little bitty kitty cat?" Aran said as Lizzy helped her wash her hands. Aran gave her a big kiss.

"What I'd like to know," Michael said. "Is what do they do?"

"What d'you mean, what do they do? J.T. works at the clinic. This Rita woman is a farmer. They're teachers, secretaries, doctors." She opened a pack of chocolate chip cookies and gave Aran one.

"No," Michael said, lowering his voice. "I mean in bed."

"Oh, Michael. I can't believe you said that."

"Why not?"

"Why does it have to be so different from what anybody else does?"

"There's the—how should I put this?—lack of equipment."

Lizzy giggled. "You are something else, Michael, you know that? I'm gonna have to get J.T. to set you straight."

"I am straight," he said, proud of his joke. He grinned happily and lit his pipe. Rita had made them sandwiches, trimming off the crusts the way Aran liked. She had tucked a clean dish cloth over Aran's dress and let the girls mix chocolate milk. There was a jar of goldenrod with a ring of yellow pollen on the table. The whole time he was with Rita, helping her with the tractor, helping her plow the garden and sow the winter rye, then later having lunch in her tiny house, all he could think of was that she seemed so normal. A little shy, maybe. But just like anyone else.

* * *

"Look what I got," Slim said, kicking the door shut.

"A cold front's movin' in," Crystal said, sipping her Coke, reluctant to look up from the weather report. Her homework was tossed on the floor with Tubby the cat sprawled on it. Janesta sat in his chair, ignoring him. Nothing was on the stove the way Slim had hoped, the whole way up the hill imagining the steam on the kitchen window as something delicious simmered.

Slim put a box beside the other boxes he'd brought home that week. One by one, he held up each item he unpacked for their inspection. A kelly green sweater with holes in the elbows. Two plaid flannel shirts with missing buttons. "These could be fixed pretty easy," he said, showing off a thick gray wool sweater, misshapen by too many washings. *Made with Mom's Love* the label sewn in the neck said.

"This is your size," Slim told Crystal, folding the sweater on the sofa. Tubby jumped up and began kneading it. "This'll come in handy." He held up an orange enamel pot lid. He rattled a jigsaw puzzle. On top of the box, two tigers lounged side by side. The box was warped, several pieces sure to be missing.

"Look at this," he said, pretending he didn't notice when Janesta flipped the station and raised the volume on the TV. "We can fix this stuff up and bring the rest over to the Salvation Army. This is good stuff," he said. James shrieked, reaching for the doll with its hair half torn off.

"It's crap," Janesta said. "That's why they threw it away." She waved her cigarette at the clothes shoved into a corner, broken toys half-in half-out of boxes. Stacks of magazines and newspapers.

"Just tell me one thing," she said. "Why d'you bring all them friggin' newspapers home? Ain't they supposed to be recycled?"

"I'm gonna make logs. To start fires. I got this special machine that rolls 'em up good. I'll show you after supper."

"No thanks," Janesta said.

"We already ate," Crystal added.

Slim peered into the oven, hoping to find a meal waiting, but it was empty and smelled of something burnt. Barney brushed against his legs, eager for him to fill his bowl. Lulu leapt down from the top of the refrigerator and sidled over to the sink and began to lick the dirty dishwater. He caught the new cat Fraidy's tail in the oven door as he shut it and the cat let out a loud yelp that got Shotgun barking. James began to cry.

"These friggin' cats. Cripes," Janesta said. "Get off me you fat dust mop," she said when Fraidy hopped onto her lap. She went to the bedroom to get as far away from Slim and the baby as she could. On the bed, several more cats were curled up like a living, breathing blanket. She shooed them off and made a show of brushing off the cat hairs.

"I read this article how some lady's makin' yarn outa cat hair," Slim said, leaning in the doorway. He meant it to be a joke. He meant her to laugh and give him a hug, but Janesta only groaned and pulled the pillow over her face. It made Slim lonely when she was like this. It was worse than being alone to have somebody you loved be just inches away and them making it clear they didn't want to be with you.

He shuffled down to his spare room trying to remember just what it was he had once dreamt of doing. Life before Janesta was impossible to comprehend. When was the last time he worked on his Dream Facility? He didn't know anymore if it would ever come to pass. That afternoon, Clarence Cushman came by and Slim tried to talk to him about how the dump could be different.

"They heat half of Paris from incineratin' garbage," Slim said.

"Preacher's Lake ain't gay Paree," Clarence said. Slim wanted him to look at the books he'd been saving, claiming they could have a book sale, but Clarence didn't want to.

"Your job is to bury the trash, not to save it," he said. "The state inspector would have a heart attack if he saw this operation."

THE BOOK SHED Slim had painted across a model building fashioned out of a cereal box. There ought to be a baby shed, too, he thought. A place where people could leave the stuff their kids grew out of. James was growing so fast he could hardly keep up. Slim rearranged the tables where he had envisioned folks having coffee, thinking how people used to congregate at the post office, but now since they'd closed it down, everyone had to cross the bridge to get a stamp.

Little by little, the trailer had been filling up with things Slim meant to fix or give away. Once he started, he couldn't stop. He'd long ago been bitten by the fever that hit every dump keeper, had always scrounged through the trash, piling up things that might be useful, but he'd never brought much home before. Now, with more talk of the dump closing, Slim felt an urgency to rescue what he could.

What would he do if they closed the dump? He tried not to think of it. He wanted to curl up beside Janesta and forget his worries, but James began to cry. Slim put on water for the baby's cereal and threw a frozen hamburger patty on the skillet.

"What'd you have for supper?" he asked Crystal.

"Nachos and Cokes." Crystal was playing a Beatles cassette Slim had brought home from the dump. At least something he brought home was being appreciated.

"That all?"

"Uh-huh." She hung her head.

"You want a burg?"

"Yeah. If you make potatoes with it."

"OK. But you come and feed the dog and give the cats their meat."

Crystal sighed, but she did as Slim asked. Shotgun crunched happily, swatting them with his long thick tail. As the meal cooked, Slim fed the baby. More cereal dribbled down his belly than went inside, but he kicked his feet and cooed.

"How come he sleeps in the bath?" Crystal asked.

"Who?"

"In the song, silly. Didn't you hear it? He says he sleeps in the bathtub."

"I dunno," Slim said. In between giving James bites, Slim sorted through a bag of cotton housedresses, the cloth ragged at the hems and waist. Underneath was a stack of aprons. Nobody wore aprons anymore. No one would ever buy them secondhand. Maybe Rita could use the cloth, he decided. He held one under his chin and did a little dance, pretending to be one of the tomatoes with faces that decorated the front.

"Look here. Ain't this cute? It's good as new."

"Good as new, P-U," Crystal said and kicked it across the floor.

* * *

"I want a pinata," Aran screamed. "I want it! I want it!"

"Sweetie, we just came to the store for milk. You want a Popsicle?"

"I want a pinata. For my party."

"Do you see any pinatas at Moody's? Where am I supposed to get it?"

"Mommy got me one. When I was four. From Mexico," she said. "A donkey. I wanna donkey pinata." She clutched a bag of Hershey's Kisses and another of Smarties. "I want fireballs, too."

"Aran, I'm really sorry," Lizzy said in her sternest voice. "I know you want a pinata. I tell you what. We can make baskets to put the candy in." There were baskets made with paper cups and pipe cleaners in one of the party books. "But I can't get you a pinata."

"I want a pinata!" Aran flung the candy on the floor and threw herself down after it, kicking and screaming, her face an angry red.

Mrs. Moody scowled from the cash register. It was time to close, but these two were going to keep her late. She didn't want to miss

Melrose. "I say give 'er a good whack on her be-hind," she advised, but her words were obscured by Aran's loud wailing.

"We're a long way from Mexico. If I could get you a pinata, I would." Lizzy felt like flinging herself on the floor, too.

"I hate you!" Aran screamed, kicking a bag of candy down the aisle where it landed at Carol's feet.

"Sorry to butt in," Carol said. "I, uh, I couldn't help but overhear. You could always make one."

"Make one?" Lizzy stared with disbelief at the tall woman whose brown hair was streaked with a silvery gray. If she blinked, would she disappear? Even Aran stopped her racket to hear what this woman said.

"It's just paper-mache," Carol said.

"Yeah? I don't know what that is," Lizzy said. "I seem to have missed all the important things in life." Her eyes filled with tears she didn't even try to hide. My life is falling apart, she thought. Who cares?

"It's not hard. You just use newspaper and paste. Flour and water paste's good enough. You just tear it up. Into strips. Then soak it in the paste. It's kinda messy." She shrugged. "I first did it in kindergarten. Then you wrap it around a form and let it dry."

"A form?" Aran was handing her bags of candies and Lizzy accepted them without protest. She wasn't going to risk having another scene.

"A balloon's good. When it dries you pop it and stick in the candies. You tape it shut or put paper-mache on it. Then paint it." As she explained, a hot flash washed over Carol, drenching her with sweat, making everything around her appear fuzzy.

"I'll try that," Lizzy said. "Did you hear that Aran? We can make a nice pinata. Won't that be fun?" Aran raised her arms to be picked up. When Lizzy turned to thank Carol, she was gone. Lizzy looked around the store, but she was nowhere to be seen. Like an apparition, she thought as she paid Mrs. Moody. She was so preoccupied she didn't even notice the nasty way Mrs. Moody flung her purchases into the bag.

* * *

Carol put the batteries she bought into the flashlight and went down the cellar steps. At the bottom, she found the bottles of wine Mrs. Thomas had told her about, covered with dust. The labels were faded, but the corks were sealed tightly with smears of hardened paraffin. Dandelion, elderberry, chokecherry, mead. Mrs. Thomas had made them herself, she had told Carol in one of her moments of clarity.

"Have you sampled my wine?" she asked, her head bobbing on her neck like a doll in the back of a car. There was a bouquet of plastic roses at her bedside and tucked beside her on the pillow a stuffed pink bunny.

"Your wine?" Carol said. Everything felt dreamlike these days. Where am I? she wanted to ask. She had had insomnia all week, staying up until after two in the morning then waking again at five. The night before, she was sure she had only slept ten minutes. Since she was up so early, she had decided to visit the old woman, to see her at her best. She had brought a bag of apples, forgetting Mrs. Thomas had no teeth.

"Yes," Mrs. Thomas said. "Oh yes. The wine." Her whole face lit up and her cheeks flushed. She brought an apple up to her face and sniffed it deeply then launched into a story about planting potatoes. She and a man named Jack—not her husband; Trudy said her father died from appendicitis soon after she was born—had cut the seed potatoes up, making sure there was a good eye in each chunk. "A good eye," she repeated before she dozed off. "Be sure each chunk has a good eye."

Carol carried two bottles of wine up the steps. Elderberry and dandelion. She was not a wine drinker, but Mrs. Thomas had mentioned it helped you sleep, as if she were clairvoyant. Perhaps the wine would cure the symptoms of menopause, too.

"A good night's rest, that's what my wine will give you," she had said, pleating the bedspread with her gnarled fingers.

"I am not an alcoholic," she said, toasting Annie's portrait. "I am just desperate to sleep."

She sat at the table with her feet propped on a chair, and pulled a sketchbook onto her lap. She had done several sketches of Rainey, who had begun to visit Carol in the afternoons, sometimes with a packet of photographs, sometimes with papers from school. Carol wanted to choose one to paint from. If by some miracle she and Annie had been able to decipher the ancient secrets of parthenogenesis, their child would have looked a lot like Rainey, she realized as she flipped through the sketches, turning them this way and that. Because she had never spent time with a child, she felt awkward at first, worried Rainey might throw a tantrum the way the girl in Moody's had done that evening, flinging herself wildly against the floor. But Rainey was easy to be with and full of insights. Annie would have called her an old soul.

Carol sipped the dandelion wine. It smelled like brandy and was a rich golden color, mild and smooth, slightly medicinal, and it was definitely working. She could feel the knots in her neck relax. She paused over a study of Rainey's hair, the soft whorls twisting like eddies in a stream. Annie's hair had been coarse. Her mother claimed it was bad hair, meaning it was impossible to straighten, though Annie had submitted to her treatments for years.

Sometimes in the evenings, Carol would spread a towel across her lap and rub Annie's scalp, dipping her fingers into coconut oil. It was solid, like butter, and smelled good enough to eat. Carol reached down through Annie's thick curls to her scalp, her fingers glistening with oil and the sweet smell of it filled the room as she rubbed and Annie sighed, settling back. The next day Annie's hair would be especially springy when she drew the metal prongs through, raking it into place.

Maybe it was another sign of getting old. Carol wasn't sure. Perhaps it was just spending so much time alone. But lately, these scenes from her past were more real than the table she sat at now. More real than her elbows on the cool enamel surface, than her feet in the wool slippers on the old wood floor.

25

Smoke drifted from the chimney pipe on Rita's roof. If the gray smoke swirling against the gray sky was a signal, Carol could not interpret it. She had the heat on high, the oven on too, but still felt chilled. Her feet were so cold they felt like hunks of half-frozen meat slowly thawing. The damp overcast morning shrouded the house, pressing against the windows. The wind-shield of her car was plastered with yellow leaves and the bark of the dark trees glistened.

Despite her best efforts, Carol daydreamed about Rita all the time. She had longed for other women and been rejected, but this was different. The idea of Rita made her life come into focus. She wanted to be with her not out of lust, as Dougie had suggested, though that was part of it. She could calm down and get on with her life if only Rita would love her. That was how it seemed. But how would they ever get started?

Last night it rained and now it was drizzling. Another day spent inside, she thought, when she heard someone pull into her driveway. The truckload of firewood had arrived. Just in time. Back home, steam was already hissing in the radiators. Here, she had on long johns and wool socks, a wool sweater and down vest, and still she was cold.

"Michael McDonnough," the man said, yanking off his thick work glove to shake hands. "I don't get much call for masonry work when the weather turns," he explained, nodding at the sign on his truck. "So I cut wood. The thing about wood is it warms you three times."

Michael was already tossing wood onto the ground, kicking the larger pieces off the truck. Carol began stacking it in the shed. Michael looked familiar, but she couldn't place where she'd seen him. Moody's or Hydie's. Eventually, she thought, I'll meet everyone in town.

"It warms you once when you cut it, once when you stack it, and then when it's burning in the stove," Michael explained. "You get it going with some of this here birch, it's dry and light. This maple's nice. I got you a good mix. Cured and ready to go. Get it fired up, then put on your oak, your beech," he said, holding up the wood for inspection. "Bedtime, toss on a nice stick of ash and you'll keep a fire all night."

The ash was heavy as stone, Carol noticed, though Michael called it a stick. He was wearing an insulated jumpsuit. Carol wondered if she should get one for herself; maybe then she'd be warm.

Carol had never used a woodstove, but it seemed simple enough. Like lighting a campfire, she decided, crumpling newspaper, adding some smaller pieces of wood and bits of birch bark; then she lit a match.

"Presto," she said, closing the door to the firebox. No sooner had she done this than thick black smoke seeped out the cracks. When she opened the door, the fire was barely smoldering. Then it began to crackle and hiss. When she closed it, the same thing happened. The kitchen was rapidly filling with smoke.

Should she shake a box of baking soda over the fire? Douse it with water? Wouldn't that make more smoke? She could see Slim on his way to the car. She ran out, waving her arms frantically.

"Help!" she screamed, running toward him.

"Oh, Jesus," Slim said. He hurried across the road, the baby in his pouch bouncing on his chest. "What's the matter?"

"I was trying to start the stove," Carol said. "The whole kitchen's filled with smoke. I'm cold," she added and burst into tears. Her cheeks were smeared with soot.

"Here. You hold James. I'll see what I can do," Slim said.

Carol paced the driveway clutching the baby. Although he was dressed in a bulky snowsuit thick as a sleeping bag, he was so small it was like carrying a roast chicken. She didn't know what worried her more: the house burning down or the baby waking up. How could anyone so small possibly stay alive?

She lifted his hood to be sure he was still breathing. His tiny face was wrinkled and red. He looked like Mrs. Thomas with his pale wisps of hair, his eyes squeezed shut as if to close out the world.

"You left the damper down," Slim called. "No big deal."

"The what?"

"The damper. You got the stove shut tight and it can't get no air. The fire's out anyhow. Gimme a sec and I'll show you. I'll get you set up. Don't worry. It's no big deal."

Carol fanned the smoke out of the house with a newspaper. It was cleared by the time Slim returned carrying a red can.

"On a day like today, you might need to give 'er a boost," he said. "Ain't no wind to speak of. OK. See here. What 'cha do is you open the damper on the stovepipe like this. See? Straight up and down. Then this little doohickey on the back. That lets in air, too. You keep that up till it's going good then you can regulate how fast you want her to burn. It takes a while to get the hang of it. Kind of like drivin' a stick shift. You get it just about when you're ready to call it quits." Slim stirred the half-burned wood and added some fresh kindling.

"Here's your ash pan. You'll wanna keep that clean so air can get up through the bottom. Sprinkle it on the path when we get ice. Now on a cloudy day like this here it's hell, excuse my French, to get a fire goin'. Don't tell Smokey the Bear, but I give her a douse of this. Can't hurt none if you're careful, and it gives you a head start." Slim lifted off both stove tops and dribbled kerosene onto the wood.

"Don't spill it, whatever you do. It's best you light her like so, then stand back," he said, demonstrating. The fire whooshed, then rattled and crackled.

"Keep your dampers open till she's goin' good, then you can add more wood and shut her down some. You'll be bakin' pie in no time."

"Thanks, Slim. I don't know what I'd have done without you."

"Heck. Don't mention it. Glad to help a girl out anytime."

"Can I get you a cup of coffee?" she asked.

"No," he said, backing toward the door. "You need anything, you just gimme a ringy ding." He lifted the red can. "I'll leave you this. Just don't forget when you got no wind you got a fight on your hands. Just don't pour it on after it's lit. Jeez. A fella up on Pumpkinville Road did that one winter and that was the end of him."

"You sure I can't get you anything?"

"No thanks. But thanks anyhow. I gotta go. I was headed to the dump. I bring James with me sometimes to give Janesta a break. He's my little helper," he said. " 'Cept he sleeps, mostly. Won't sleep at home, but I set him up in a cardboard box there in my shed and he nods right off. Well. Don't be a stranger. Say, Punkie," he said, noticing the orange cat dozing on the footstool. "He disappeared right after I brung him home from the dump. I wondered where he'd gone off to."

"Is he yours? I figured he was a stray. He moved in when I did."

"Well, don't he look happy? I tell you, cats is one thing I got plenty of. You're welcome to him. He just showed up one day nothing but skin and bones. He was cryin'. A puny thing. He's filled out quite a bit, now."

The cat stretched and opened his eyes. He glanced up, blinked slowly, and rolled onto his back displaying his large fluffy belly.

"You got you a friend." Slim said. "Listen. By the time you hear my car door slam, you'll be ready to put you another log on. Once it's burnin' good, you try experimentin' with them dampers. As soon as you get any smoke, just open 'em up. You'll do just fine," he said. He paused as the school bus made its way up the hill.

"Here comes Rainey," Slim said. " 'Fore you know it, the bus'll be back with Crystal. Jeez, time flies."

Carol watched Slim head across the wet yard, his loose green pants flapping above his muddy shoes, one white sock and one blue sock sliding down his thin white legs. Rainey got off the bus clutching a handful of papers. She ran up to Carol, her rubber boots slapping through the puddles. Rainey stopped just short of her.

"Hi," she said shyly. She offered Carol a drawing of a large red heart with green arms and legs. Two large teeth protruded from the heart's smiling mouth.

"It's the tooth fairy of the heart," Rainey said.

"Very interesting," Carol said, studying the drawing.

"I made it for you," Rainey said, looking over her shoulder. Her mother was calling her home. "I gotta go."

Carol wanted to run after her, up the driveway, into Rita's arms. But she stayed where she was, waving at Rita, pretending that was enough.

* * *

Nelly's clothes were folded inside the benches she'd made, under a lid she had never put hinges on. The hinges were in a jar by the sink. Her unfinished projects were everywhere, as if she had always been called away in the middle of a task. Rita was slowly finishing them. She lined the hinges up along the edge of the bench lid and marked the holes, then slowly tightened each screw into place.

Sometimes it felt as if Nelly waited in the shadows in the corners of the room, her footsteps creaking the floorboards, her faltering voice mingling with the wind that picked up. It stirred the leaves and set the apple tree swaying, the branches scratching the house. "You're the caretaker now," Slim had said when he came by with a list of things Nelly needed. "That's what she told me." Rita liked the sound of the word.

She sorted through Nelly's shirts, checking for rips, for buttons missing, making a pile of the ones that needed mending. The orange-and-gray plaid shirt was nearly threadbare. Nelly'd given it to Rita to wear the first time she came to the farm, helping her slip it over her T-shirt when the night air grew chilly. That first night held her most distinct memories of Nelly. Her first sight of the house, half buried in weeds. A stick of butter slowly melting in a pan, the sweet meat of the lobster tail, and how Nelly showed her to firk out the morsels tucked in the lobster's body.

As she got the clothes ready, Rita thought of Nelly's dirt-stained fingers, thick with calluses, her pale shaggy hair, how tan the back of her neck was where the sun beat down on it. She could see her still, that day she'd stood on the tractor, driving recklessly, destroying it all. Their time together had been brief and fraught with such difficulty. She remembered how Nelly would place a tentative hand on her waist as they stood in the dooryard before bedtime, watching the bright stars. Her hand was heavy and brought no shiver of pleasure. Doomed, she thought. Right from the start.

Rita sighed and got up, prowling around in her stockinged feet, not wanting to disturb Rainey's nap though she slept easily now, as if with Nelly gone she was released from keeping vigil. As she measured rolled oats into a large bowl, poured water from the softly hissing kettle over them, added honey and butter, then set the bowl to cool on the table, a deep sense of peace fell over the house despite the howling wind. It was as if by packing up Nelly's things, Rita was saying good-bye to her. She was finally leaving for good.

The fire burned steadily, warming the room. Rita added another log and began sorting through Nelly's papers. They smelled like her, steeped in tobacco, as if they'd hung in a smokehouse. Feeling like she was about to read her diary, but unable to resist, she snapped the frayed red rubber band off of a stack of letters. They were all addressed to Nelly's mother, written in a childish scrawl on stationery with scalloped edges, folded into pastel envelopes. One held a photo of a child on a wide veranda, unmistakably Nelly, with her dark serious eyes, clutching a floppy-eared puppy that licked her chin. Nelly's bangs were cut inches too short, her T-shirt rucked up from the squirming dog.

The letters were full of pleas, begging her mother to let her keep her dog, Frisky. "I'll be good," she promised, making a list of what that entailed: always doing her homework, washing the dishes, setting the table for every meal. Sweeping the porch and making her own bed. Then, once the dog was gone, the letters contained threats to run away, bitter invectives full of hate and a child's powerless desire for revenge. Rita wondered why Nelly's mother had kept these letters. Why hadn't she been ashamed?

Finally, along with the lists of stocks and bonds, she found the savings book Nelly'd asked for. The balance was $25,624. Rita was shocked there was so much money put aside, but it made her feel a little less guilty that she'd let Nelly pay the hospital bill. As she packed everything into a box, a snapshot fell onto her lap. A small dark woman seated on a bed, her knees drawn up to her chest, her arms wrapped around them. The woman stared out of the photo as if to defy the camera's ability to capture her. It had been crumpled and crushed, a deep crease cut across her face like a scar, but she was beautiful nevertheless. No doubt another love affair that ended badly, Rita thought. But who was she to judge?

She wished, as she had often wished before, that she had a photo of Elias to show Rainey. As she dissolved the yeast and stirred it into the oatmeal mixture, she could picture him, cross-legged on the pale green rug, peeling an orange, his fingers delicately separating the sections. Sometimes, especially when Rainey ate, Rita was startled to see the way she pulled the chicken from the bone or spread butter across a slice of bread, her movements a mirror image of her father's.

She added flour, a little at a time, until the dough pulled together and it became difficult to stir, then scraped it onto the table to let it rest. The first time she'd made bread, she had dumped in all the flour the recipe called for. The dough was dry and would not hold together as she kneaded it roughly, sure she was doing it wrong, but following the steps anyway. The bread that resulted was flat and so coarse she'd fed it to the hens. The next time, worried about repeating her first mistake, she hadn't added enough flour and the dough was a sticky mess, coating her hands, stuck to the table like thick glue; she'd been so disgusted, she scraped it all up and threw it in the trash. But she persisted, taking recipe books from the library, producing a dozen oatmeal buns that were edible but tasted too strongly of molasses and were somewhat doughy and undone. She kept trying despite the loaves that stuck to the pans and broke when she pried them loose, the rolls that cooked too fast, the crust so hard it tore the sides of her mouth. With practice, over time, her bread improved to the point where she could count on the golden perfectly shaped loaves. Making bread had become something she took great pleasure in, that she looked forward to, sometimes craving the process the way she did now because she knew it would relax her.

She cleaned the bowl and rubbed it with oil, wishing there was a recipe she could follow for love, some rules she could apply until what seemed like an impossible mess turned into something beautiful and nourishing, making everyone happy and fulfilled. She pushed the dough with the heels of her hands, sprinkling more flour over it, rocking it gently, turning it, pushing it away from her, pulling it back until she set up a rhythm, leaning into it, putting the weight of her whole body into her hands. She no longer worried about kneading it too much and had come to sense, without watching the clock, just when it was time to stop. This dough would rise slowly, filling the room with its redolent yeastiness, ready to be punched down before supper and shaped into loaves she would pull from the oven, slicing it for their meal while it was still warm.

If there was one thing she'd learned about making bread, it was that you couldn't hurry it along. Perhaps that was true of love as well, she thought, covering the bowl with a tea towel. She could hear the strains of the old Supremes song, "You Can't Hurry Love." The familiar drumbeat played in her mind, and she began to sing, surprised to discover she knew all the words by heart.

26

Snowflakes drifted like pin feathers spilling from a torn pillow, pelting Rita's cheeks, stinging her bare hands, melting as they hit the frost-covered ground. She tossed tools from the truck into a box: a pair of pliers, assorted screwdrivers and wrenches jumbled on the floor. A rusted trowel. A flashlight with corroded batteries. Bungee cords and a chain with an S hook. A heavy red vise sticky with spilled soda. The floor was littered with empty tobacco pouches, matchbooks, burnt matches. The ashtray crammed full of butts. Crushed beer cans under the seat with paper coffee cups, candy bar wrappers, a pair of sneakers encrusted with thick gray mud. Dozens of lists clipped to the visor with a clothespin. A large black crow feather tucked into the rearview mirror. Rita threw away the filthy towel on the torn seat and smoothed an old blanket over it. With a whisk broom, she brushed the floor clean then sprayed and polished the windows.

The truck bed was piled with so much junk she thought at first she would just drive to the dump and shovel it off; then, she got to work sorting it out. China Cat was prowling through it all as if hoping to catch a mouse, when the school bus groaned to the top of the hill. A few minutes later, Rainey ran up the drive, her hood bouncing against her back, her lunch box banging her leg.

"Mommy!" she called all out of breath. "What 'cha doin'?"

"Cleaning up this junk. I'm gonna go over to the dump later."

Rainey liked the dump; Slim always had something to give her.

"It's snowing." Rainey stuck out her tongue to catch the snow. "Can I make a snowman?"

"Not yet, Rainey. We'll need a real big snow first. You eat your lunch?" Rita packed her lunch everyday since Rainey was the first one on the bus and the last one off, arriving well after noon. Rainey nodded and held up a mimeographed paper of some pilgrims in a row. Each face was colored dark green.

"It's the pilgrooms," Rainey explained. "I'm gonna show Carol it."

"Honey, I don't think you oughta go there so much. Carol's busy."

"She said I could. Anytime. Just knock the secret knock."

"Honey, she's working. She's an artist."

"Me too. I'm a artist. Carol said." Rainey ran to get her camera.

"Just for a little bit," Rita called as Rainey ran down the drive.

* * *

"I dunno what's the matter. I'm too pooped to pop. Just a draggin'. Doctor says I gotta watch my cholesterol so I quit eatin' liver. But you know it's liver that builds up your blood good. I must be eye-nemic." Trudy dropped into the chair beside J.T.'s desk.

J.T. didn't try to discourage her. She snapped her rubber gloves on and gave Trudy's finger a jab.

"That cholesterol's in everything nowadays," Trudy continued. "Can't eat no french fries, can't have your bacon cheeseburgers. You'd think ice cream was poison the way they go on about it." She squeezed the cotton ball against her finger while the centrifuge whirred.

"I due yet for my Pap?" Trudy asked hopefully.

"You just had one in July," J.T. said. "It's normal." J.T. read the results of the blood test. "In fact, a little high."

"Oh." Trudy frowned. She seemed reluctant to go. "Say, you live in Preacher's Lake. You hear anything about there's a new preacher comin'?"

"A new preacher? You mean, to open the church again?"

"I guess. Mary Joy was saying Etta Markum heard somethin' about Martha Zimmer donatin' her money to start it up again. Martha Zimmer used to live over on Sow's Head. In that great big old stone house behind all them bushes? Well, that was way before your time. People from New York own it now. They come up for two weeks a summer. That great big house sets empty the rest of the year." Trudy got up to go just as Lizzy came out with a young terrified-looking girl.

"Thanks," the girl muttered, fleeing with her bag of supplies.

"Hi de-ah," Trudy said. She patted Lizzy's hand as if it were a ball of pie dough she was about to shape. "I thought I had the iron-poor blood but your friend here says I'm high on the scale."

"That's good news."

"I guess so," Trudy said. "I dunno why I'm so tired."

"Hydie been taking you out on the town?" J.T. kidded.

Trudy laughed. "Oh go on now."

"Well, you work hard. It must be that," Lizzy told her.

"Yessir," Trudy nodded. Lizzy worried Trudy might decide she needed a breast exam. She tried to think of something to change the subject.

"Hey, Trudy," she said. "You don't know anybody that's got kittens, do you?" So far she had had no luck finding one for Aran's birthday.

"Kittens? You got a mouse problem?" She glanced around the office as if expecting one to scurry by, her purse held ready to slam it.

"No. It's for a present," Lizzy said.

"Yessir, I most certainly do. Slim Riley's got more cats than they got lions in Africa. I know that."

"Kittens, too?"

"Well, when you got so many cats you must have kittens."

"Slim, you say. Who is he?"

"Don't you know Slim? Surely you must. Why, he keeps the dump."

"Oh," Lizzy said. Michael always went to the dump for them.

"Slim lives out at the end of Preacher's Lake Road. In a trailer," Trudy said. "You can't miss it, all the stuff he's got in his yard. Just look for the place with a bunch of tires and cats outside."

*   *   *

"How do the pictures get inside?" Rainey asked. "How do they get *in* the photographs?" She had learned to say "photographs" from Carol. She sat at the table looking at a book of Edward Weston's nudes and vegetables, turning the pages slowly. Carol hoped Rita wouldn't disapprove. This book and Sally Mann's *Immediate Family* were the only collections of photographs she had with her.

"What do you mean, inside?" Carol was working on a watercolor of Rainey, planning to give it to Rita. The oil portrait she started last week seemed too formal to capture her spirit. Too ponderous.

"I mean, you know." Rainey looked up. "I mean, I see it and then it's in the picture. In the photograph. But how come?"

"Oh, you mean, how does the camera work?"

Rainey nodded then began to arrange the still life. She set two brown pears on their sides next to a handful of acorns. She opened a drawer and took out a cheese grater, two forks, and a wooden spoon.

It was a project they'd begun together, taking turns arranging objects to photograph and draw. Carol started doing it with her in preparation for the adult ed class she had agreed to teach. Practice, she thought of it, though she was sure none of the students would be like Rainey. She had read once that truly creative artists know how to create artistic problems, not just solve them. Sure enough, Rainey's arrangement was not like anything Carol could have predicted.

"I read that taking photographs is painting with light," Carol said. "But I can't explain the scientific part. It has something to do with the chemicals on the film, the way the light comes through the lens. Your mom could get you a book at the library. Or I could," she added. Carol had never realized how much children expected adults to know. Crystal came over yesterday demanding that Carol explain how a hurricane was different from a cyclone. Carol's explanation left them both with questions. She might have to invest in an encyclopedia if she stayed.

Rainey carefully wove a chiffon scarf through the spokes of an eggbeater, arranging it as if it were being beaten. Carol thought of Trudy's rendition of an eggbeater. Too bad she hadn't had Rainey as a teacher. "What about the color?" Rainey asked. "How come the camera knows what color to make it?" She held up one of the photographs from her last batch. "How come it knows the ribbon's red?"

Carol put down her brush and looked at the photograph again. It was slightly blurry. Rainey had stood too close to the girl, as if wanting to capture the intricate detail of the girl's hair. But the ribbon was clear and bright red. Rainey leaned against Carol and sighed.

"I dunno, Rainey. I really don't. But we can find out, OK?"

"Mommy's calling."

"Yes, she is, isn't she?"

"We're gonna go to the dump."

"That sounds like fun."

"You won't move it, will you?"

"Your still life? No way. I'll keep it till you come back."

Carol waited until she heard the truck head down the hill and then she raced outside and tossed a bag of trash into her car. So what if it looked arranged? She had to meet up with Rita one of these days. At least this way it would be in public. Slim would be there.

As she pulled into the dump, she saw Slim leaning against Rita's truck. For a second, she thought of backing away, it seemed so obvious what she was doing, but then Slim looked up. He was waving.

"Here's Carol," he said. Rita glanced in her rearview mirror. Rainey waved, peering through the back window as Carol hoisted her trash over the edge of the pit. She decided to ask Slim about his job. She'd been reading in the local paper about plans to do away with most of the landfills in Maine. It would be a way to talk to them both, she thought, turning back, suddenly frozen with fear. Then Rainey ran over and pulled her toward the truck.

"Hey, you guys," Carol said nonchalantly.

"Hi, Carol," Rita said, blushing deeply.

"What's this I hear about closing the landfills? This one, too?"

Slim looked so stricken Carol was sorry she'd brought it up. Why couldn't she talk about the weather like everybody else?

"I dunno yet," Slim muttered. "I'm thinkin' maybe it won't happen here. Not just yet. I mean, we're so small." The more he spoke, the more confident he became, as if he just needed to warm his voice.

"Hey," he said. "You're from New York City. I hear they got the world's biggest dump. Like a mountain of trash. You ever seen it?"

"No," Carol said. "But I have a friend who lives on Staten Island. She says when the wind blows the wrong way it smells like old pickles." Carol glanced at Rita. It was such a relief to be near her.

"Say, Rita," Slim said. "I almost forgot. I been savin' you something."

"So," Carol said as Slim went behind his shed. She smiled at Rita, then inspected the jar of buttons Slim had given Rainey.

"We can put 'em in our still lifes," Rainey said seriously.

"Buried treasure," Slim said. He had wire hoops slung over his forearm, tied together with string. "Wreath hoops. I dunno who tossed 'em, but they're good as new." He set them in the back of the truck.

"Well," Rita said after she thanked Slim. "I got more chores to do. C'mon, Rainey."

"I hope she's not bothering you," Rita said to Carol.

"Bothering me? Not at all. She's a real pleasure," Carol said. "She's welcome anytime." You, too, she almost added. She felt a flurry of hope as she watched them drive away. The encounter had definitely been a step in the right direction.

* * *

The first thing Lizzy did was take the kitten to the vet to be inoculated and checked for worms. Then she brought it to the clinic after hours for a flea bath. It was scratching an awful lot, its back foot working overtime. It was such a tiny thing, its heart fluttering against its thin ribs. It meowed pitifully as she placed it in the sink, dipped warm water into a cup and poured it over the kitten. It submitted to the bath with doleful eyes.

"You poor little thing," she murmured, talking to the kitten as if to a child. "You're just a teeny tiny baby, aren't you?"

It was a cute thing. If it was a tomcat, it'd be a money cat, Slim had said. Something about the mottled color of its fur. Lizzy was so distracted by Slim's trailer and the rags he dressed in, she could hardly pay attention to what he said.

She had recognized the trailer right away from all the junk strewn everywhere. An old wringer washer on its side. Rows of tulip-shaped tires piled with old straw and dead tomato plants, some with green fruit hanging like forgotten ornaments. Bicycles with no tires. A wheelbarrow with ice in the bottom. She had been stepping around a tangle of rusted garden implements, thinking she should just give Aran the stuffed cat she'd found at Mr. Paperback, when Slim opened the door. "Can I help you?" he asked, dipping his head shyly.

Lizzy recognized him. She had noticed Slim loping into Buster's, his long legs like stilts, a baby strapped to his chest. He was so painfully thin he could moonlight as a skeleton for an anatomy class, she thought. Once, they'd spoken at the Shop and Save. She'd seen him wheeling a cart full of sanitary pads and he'd actually confessed he used them to line his boots. "I work outdoors," he had said, as if he owed Lizzy an explanation. "They keep your feet nice and warm."

"I heard you might have kittens. Trudy Hyde mentioned it," Lizzy said. She stuffed her hands in her pockets. She would have to remember to wear mittens, she thought. Kittens, mittens. Her mind went to work repeating the rhyme. It was beginning to spit snow. She was like the kittens in the rhyme, always on the verge of tears.

"Have I got kittens? You bet I do," he said, inviting her in.

Inside was a further jumble. Piles of clothes and books and cooking utensils and in the middle of the floor a beautiful red-headed baby banging a pot with a spoon. Cats sprawled across the furniture. One slept on top of the television. Another hunched on the refrigerator. Lizzy felt like grabbing the baby and rushing to her car. *Forget the kitten: I want that!* The baby smiled so sweetly up at her, reaching with his chubby arms, kicking his feet. They were covered with thick red booties. She imagined slipping them off and kissing each perfect toe.

"That's my boy, James," Slim said proudly. "His mom and sister are down to the store," he added. "Can I get you a Mountain Dew?"

Lizzy politely declined, afraid he might serve her from one of the dirty glasses stacked in his sink. She forced herself not to look at the baby, to stay near the kittens, piled on a blanket by the stove.

"There's three left. I started with six so that's pretty good. Them're all girls. That's Fraidy, the mom." He pointed to a fluffy gray cat with yellow eyes. "You'd be surprised how many cats that're in the family way get tossed."

Lizzy massaged the flea shampoo, following the instructions on the bottle, and checked her watch to leave it on the required time. The kitten shivered. If it could have produced them, Lizzy was sure real tears would fall down its soggy face and drop off the end of its pink nose. It looked up at her and meowed, showing its bright pink tongue. "You're gonna be a birthday gift," she crooned. "You're gonna like that. I promise. But we gotta get you nice and clean." She combed the wet fur, flicking the dead fleas off, then wrapped the kitten in a towel.

Once the kitten was dry, Lizzy tucked it into the wicker carrying case she had bought at the pet store. She had also bought a red collar studded with rhinestones and at the last minute, food and litter. J.T. had agreed to keep the kitten until Aran's birthday. As she headed for her place on the Waukeag Road, the kitten cried the entire way and was mewing pitifully as Lizzy parked under the pine tree that towered over their white frame house. J.T. flicked on the porch light and stood at the door, then Betty appeared beside her. They looked like they belonged on the cover of *Yankee* magazine.

"She sounds like Aran when she's mad," Lizzy told J.T. and Betty when she walked in, explaining how it made such loud shrieks she was sure she'd picked the right one. She already felt fond of the kitten; a little bit of a thing, it had purred so loudly as she toweled it dry.

"Ooh," J.T. said, scooping the kitten from its case. Alice, their ancient dog, looked up from her mat by the stove and thumped her tail.

"What a cutey," Betty said. She offered Lizzy coffee from a pot warming on the cookstove.

"So what're the latest party plans?" J.T. asked. She looked so different at home. It wasn't just her loose jeans and sweater or the sheepskin slippers. Her whole body seemed loose, at ease in a way it never was at work. Cozy, Lizzy thought, looking around the room.

Dried roses hung from the rafters. Under a large window, Betty's quilt frame was set up. The quilt she was working on had been patched in shades of blue.

"Party plans. Ugh," Lizzy said. "I ordered the cake from Larry's. And I just found out you're supposed to give the other kids gifts. It keeps the jealousy quotient down. So I got bubbles and some plastic people and toy jewelry."

"You must be exhausted." Betty put a plate of homemade muffins on the oak table. She was an intense woman, seemingly stern until you got to know her. Her bright violet eyes were like Elizabeth Taylor's, Lizzy always thought. Later, driving home, she imagined J.T. and Betty cuddled in their queen-sized bed under one of Betty's quilts. J.T. said that was her favorite time of day. Lizzy didn't have a favorite time of day. Her day just seemed like so many hours to get through. The snow was coming down faster, collecting on the hood of the car, covering the grass beside the road. She hoped it wouldn't snow on the day of the party. What if no one came?

She ticked off a mental list: Get crepe paper. Cups and plates. Forks and spoons. Pick up the cake. They had already picked out special Barbie napkins and a tablecloth. Michael would drive to Moody's for ice cream at the last minute; the freezer in their gas refrigerator did not even make ice. And there was the pinata. She'd been wishing Aran would forget, but she still talked about it. They'd get to work on it tonight before bed.

*   *   *

"Visiting hours are almost over," the woman said. Slim didn't know if she was a doctor, a nurse, or what. She didn't wear a uniform, but he knew she was something because of the stethoscope draped around her neck. He had to ring a bell to be admitted onto the ward and now she had her hand on the door as if she meant to send him away.

"I'm sorry," he said. "I know I'm here late. I just brought some things. For Nelly Brown."

"We'll have to check it first. This is a locked ward," the woman said, stepping aside so Slim could enter. She locked the door behind him with a key from a crowded ring at the end of a long chain looped around her waist. She accepted the box as if it were about to explode.

"She's in the lounge." She pointed to the end of a brightly lit corridor. "You'll hear the announcement when it's time to leave."

Slim had never been to a mental hospital. It reminded him of the prison he'd seen on TV the night before. The small doorless rooms that opened off the hallway were like cells. No bars, though. In a prison, there'd be bars. At the end of the hall, a TV blared. A *Hill Street Blues* rerun; he recognized the theme song.

The lounge was filled with old furniture, tables strewn with ratty magazines, and a sad-looking group of people, none of whom looked up when he arrived. The room was murky with cigarette smoke, and the windows, he saw, were the unbreakable kind embedded with chicken wire. Nelly was on one of the sofas beside a man who cut pictures from a magazine with the kind of blunt-ended scissors children used. Slim wanted to run away, but just then a commercial came on and as if waking from a trance, Nelly looked up.

"Slim?"

"How ya doin'?" he asked.

With great effort, she heaved herself up off the sofa. She seemed to have weights on her arms and legs, she moved so slowly, as if heavy chains shackled her ankles.

"Let's get outa here," she said.

Slim worried she meant him to help her escape. How on earth are we gonna do that? he wondered.

"Down here," she said, shuffling along. He took extra small steps to pace himself with her. In one of the rooms, an old man in a straight-backed chair stared out the door. His face was so pale and still, Slim worried he might be dead. Nelly led them to a small room set up like a cafe. Here too, the windows were unbreakable and he could see they had locks on them. In the corner, a refrigerator hummed.

"There's juice if you want," Nelly said. "Fruit." She nodded at the refrigerator. Her head seemed as heavy as a bowling ball; if she moved it too far forward she might never be able to yank it back up. She drummed her fingers on the table. "Full of pesticide," she said, drawing out the last word. "Pesticide. D'you know what I mean?" She raised one eyebrow. The skin around her eyes was dark and bruised-looking. Her expression reminded him of the raccoons he would come upon at dusk, wiping out the insides of food cans with their paws.

"Checkers?" asked a girl who was dressed in various shades of purple. She rattled the game hopefully, twirling around. "King me dee dee," she said, then flounced down the hallway shouting, "No de bo bo!"

She reminded Slim of Crystal, all that rhyming and jumping around. Was this the kind of place the teachers were always trying to get Crystal to go to? All their talk about testing, saying special ed wasn't enough. Was this what they had in store? Never, he vowed. Not my Crystal.

"I brung your stuff. Like you asked." Slim didn't know how to explain why he wasn't giving it to her now.

"They confiscate it?" Nelly grinned. For a moment, she looked like her old self, then her face sagged into a slackened shape. "It's the Thorazine," she explained. "They make you take it. Oh God, I still can't sleep. But the quiet room. The quiet room's good."

She worked at rolling a cigarette, carefully folding the paper, tapping on the tobacco, spreading it out just so. Before she could light it, a voice over the intercom announced the end of visiting hours. Slim worried he should offer to come back, but he didn't want to. It was a long drive and besides, the whole thing gave him the heebie-jeebies. What if they mistook him for one of the patients and wouldn't let him out? How would he convince them he was not crazy? He tipped over his chair in his haste to get up.

"Lemme know if you need anything." He patted Nelly clumsily on her back. It felt like a sack stuffed with sawdust. "Just lemme know," he said, hurrying toward the elevator where the woman with the keys waited.

* * *

"But what's it gonna be?" Aran whined. Her hands were covered with paste and newspaper ink. Bits of sticky newspaper hung from her hair. Lizzy layered the last strips of paper-mache onto the lumpy form they had created. Michael was lying on the sofa reading the newspaper.

"Listen to this," he said. "There's this woman. She's in her sixties. She gets this pain and they find this petrified fetus in her. It was in there for at least sixteen years. That's the last time she had s-e-x," he explained, peering over the paper. As soon as he saw the look on Lizzy's face, he realized he should have kept it to himself.

"What're my two favorite ladies doing?" he asked.

Aran pouted, rubbing her hands against the newspaper Lizzy had spread over the table, not even caring that it made her hands dirtier.

"A bomb?" Lizzy said. She held the thing up.

"It looks like an egg," Michael said.

"An egg?" Lizzy frowned. Why did everything everybody said lately relate to fertility?

"Humpty Dumpty," Aran shouted. "It's Humpty Dumpty!"

27

Carol rushed outside, not even stopping for breakfast or coffee. She felt as if she were running away from herself as she hurried to the lake. From one day to the next, her mood could change so completely. One minute to the next, sometimes. The leaves beneath her feet were crunchy with frost. She liked winter; it wasn't that. Hot flashes. Mood changes. Maybe she was losing her mind.

The Change. Could it really be *that*? She was only forty-five. But she noticed every month, just before she ovulated, she felt a terrible despair. She tried to picture one of her tired old eggs making its lonely journey. Then as soon as it landed, like some space shuttle on a mission, she stopped sleeping. Last night she was up at 2 A.M., mopping the floors. She had gone to bed at a decent hour, but just as she closed her eyes, the cat jumped down from the foot of her bed, said, "Mrt!" then went into the kitchen and began crunching his food. As soon as it seemed she might doze off, the refrigerator clicked on. It seemed like the whole house vibrated. By then, she was so alert there was no hope of sleep. She got up and peered at herself in the old mirror over the sink, noting soft peach fuzz sprouting on her cheeks, flicking the flap of skin under her chin. What purpose did these new symptoms of aging serve? Disgusted, she drank two glasses of chokecherry wine, but this time it had not worked.

Dawn found her mixing a batch of paper-mache, inspired by her pinata instructions. Carol had used Elmer's glue and some tissue paper she'd found cleaning the kitchen. Layer upon layer, she smoothed it over a balloon, soothed by the wrapping motion, not making anything in particular, enjoying the glue on her fingers and the balloon squeaking. When she finally fell asleep, she dreamt she was buried in mud, only her head poking up, while all around her soldiers marched. Now she stood on the path watching the wind stir the bare branches. Deeper in the woods, a tree creaked and groaned and a squirrel rustled in the dry leaves. The sky held the promise of more snow.

"Depression is the absence of feeling," Iris always said. If that were the case, then Carol was not depressed. She was riddled with feelings, crying one minute, laughing the next, flooded with ideas for pieces, then stagnant as a murky swamp.

Curling her fingers inside her heavy wool mittens, she shivered and picked up her pace. Her grandfather was a barber who drank himself to death in a room over Sprague's Furniture Store in Worcester. She still had his black cast-iron scissors. Was she headed for the same fate, sipping Mrs. Thomas's wine like a desperate addict? She was lonely and suddenly terrified, out in the middle of nowhere the way she was. Suppose a crazed man leapt from the bushes?

Once in the city, on her way to visit Annie, just such a man had sprung from the tangle of scaffolding she was walking under and rushed toward her, flecks of spittle on his gray lips, his eyes wild with rage. She had never run as fast as she did to escape this man and his horrible guttural sounds. But there was no man in the bushes. Only her thoughts. And underneath them, a weariness lodged in her bones, settled in her jaw.

"Please, God," she said, hugging a beech tree, pressing her cheek against the rough cold bark. Ahead of her, the surface of the lake was wild with frothy wind-whipped waves. Two seagulls circled, flapping their long white wings as if swimming through the turbulent air.

* * *

At Aran's party, the yellow crepe paper they had twisted and draped across the downstairs was already drooping and several balloons they taped to the window frames had popped. The pin-the-wig-on-Barbie game had gone over well. Barbie, with her ever-present smile, beamed from the wall, her blonde flip on slightly askew. The cake sat on a cut-glass pedestal; a doll was shoved into the cake which was iced to resemble a ball gown. Swirls of pink and white icing dotted with red rosebuds, miniature green leaves, and silver balls. The six blue candles had yet to be lit. Michael had gone to Moody's for ice cream. Chocolate chip, Aran insisted. Lizzy hoped he wouldn't end up driving to Union City for that flavor.

Several of the guests were marching noisily around the room, their hats bobbing. Only two of the parents had stayed. Lizzy'd been so scattered at the beginning of the party she just now realized this. There had been an awkward moment when Rita arrived and Lizzy recognized her as the woman who had found her weeping. But then

Michael rushed up saying, "I told you about Rita, she's got the farm." Now Rita was on the sofa talking to Derek's mother whose eyes seemed unusually bright. Jill? Becky? Barb? Lizzy could not recall her name.

A red-haired girl was singing endless verses of "The Old Woman Who Swallowed a Fly." Derek snatched Aran's hat and held it with his own over his chest like breasts. He swayed like a belly dancer when the girl sang about the spider wiggling and jiggling. Aran grabbed two extra hats from the table and did the same, grinding her hips like a stripper. The girl with a chipped front tooth held a hat over her crotch and wiggled it like a penis. Rainey was outside blowing bubbles and another girl—Lizzy had no idea who she was; in fact, she was positive she had never seen her before—was chasing the bubbles, her party shoes slipping on the frozen ground.

"Are we having fun yet?" J.T. said. She wished she could get Rita alone. She'd been hearing about her for months now. But Derek's mother was talking her ear off. Of all things, they were discussing sewing. Betty had told J.T. about meeting Rita at the library, how she lived out by the lake with some woman farmer. And everybody had heard how this woman went crazy and practically destroyed the place. J.T. wished lesbians had secret marks, like the kiss of the good witch that blazed on Dorothy's forehead. Only people who needed to know could see it. It would make getting to know each other much easier.

Lizzy popped the last one of the pigs in blankets into her mouth and began to pick up the crumpled wrapping paper. Aran's kitten, which she had named Miss Kitty, was cowering under the sofa. Lizzy got down on the floor to try to coax it out with a bit of ribbon. It had been received with the same attention her other gifts had brought: "Oh look, how nice!" Aran said over each gift, ripping the paper with gusto, shoving the gift aside hastily, eager to see what was next.

"Is it pinata time?" Lizzy whispered.

"It better be," J.T. said. "They're getting kinda wild."

After some deliberation, they decided to hang the pinata outside; there was just not room to swing the bat in the house.

"All we need is some kid to go home with a black eye," Lizzy said. It dangled from a rope in the hemlock tree. Lizzy gave it a little push.

"You whomp it with the bat," Aran explained. "Then the candy comes out and you grab it. I get to be first 'cause I'm the birthday girl."

She batted the pinata and set it spinning. Humpty Dumpty, with the silly grin they'd painted on his face, swung back and almost smacked Aran. The children lined up dutifully, the way they had learned to in school, each one taking a turn. They whacked and beat at it, growing frenzied with each try. The pinata was hard as stone.

"What'd you make it out of, cement?" J.T. said.

"Some woman at Moody's told me how to do it," Lizzy said.

"Oh. That explains it," J.T. said. The women all laughed.

"Hey, it's only an egg," Derek's mother said. She swayed a little as she took a turn, swinging the bat as if she were striking a baseball. Each woman gave it a good whack, but the pinata did not even crack.

"Well, at least we're getting our exercise," Lizzy said.

"And the kids're burning off some steam," Rita said. It was her idea to hold the pinata still and let the children hit it that way. "But you be careful you don't hit me," she warned Derek whose turn it was.

Just as he gave the pinata a resounding whack, cracking it open, making the candy fly across the ground, a shiny red car appeared at the end of the driveway. Lizzy looked up when she heard the door slam, certain it was Michael and the ice cream at last.

"Mommy!" Aran screamed. She dropped the candy she'd been collecting in the skirt of her dress and ran up to the woman who stood with open arms, ready to receive her hug. Aran slammed into her and she rose, twirling her against her body. Aran gripped her waist with her knees and the two of them laughed and kissed each other.

"My baby girl's all grown up," Kaye said.

"My mommy, my mommy!" Aran shouted. "It's my birthday!"

"I know that darling. I'm your present."

"Oh, Mommy, Mommy, Mommy!" Aran kissed her wildly all over her face.

J.T. placed her hand on Lizzy's arm, as if to restrain her, but Lizzy was frozen, staring with disbelief. "Well," J.T. said. She almost added *finally* but thought better of it. "We'll get through this. Take a deep breath."

"Hi, everybody," Kaye was saying. She waved like a homecoming queen as Aran pulled her by the hand toward the group. Kaye didn't recognize anybody. Where was Michael? she wondered. Who were these women and what were they doing at her house? Had Michael started some kind of harem?

Everything looked so different. The yard cleared of stumps. The stone wall half built, curving up toward the house. And the house itself, bigger than she'd remembered it, half covered with new cedar shakes.

"Mommy's here," Aran said to Lizzy, beaming up at her.

"I see that." Lizzy's voice was surprisingly calm.

"And you're . . . ?" Kaye said, her eyes quizzical. Just as Lizzy was saying her name, Michael arrived.

"Have no fear, the ice cream's here," he shouted, tossing the bag in the air. He stopped with his mouth hanging open when he saw Kaye. She ran to him crying, "Mikey!" and as he hugged her, he gazed over her shoulder to where Lizzy stood, dressed in her blue parka, her dark curls bouncing in the chill wind, her cheeks splotched with red. Aran stuffed a handful of gummy bears into her mouth and watched, mesmerized by the image of her parents, together at last. Then she ran up the hill to hug them both.

J.T. had her arm around Lizzy, to hold her up or hold her back, Michael wasn't sure which. The children chewed their candies, as rooted as the trees surrounding them. An embarrassed silence gathered. All at once, as if the sky were the pinata bursting open, huge flakes of thick feathery snow began to fall all around them.

* * *

"I didn't *leave* you," Kaye said, jerking her arm from Michael's grip. Aran's arms were tight around Kaye's neck. Instead of turning back to the party, Michael had led Kaye down a path through the woods. They were standing beneath a dead pine tree bulleted with woodpecker holes. "I didn't leave you," she said again, nuzzling Aran. "I needed to get away. There's a difference. But you just let some woman move into my house. Michael, we're married for crying out loud." She looked more beautiful than ever with her blue eyes flashing. She stamped her small perfect foot.

"Married people don't need to get away from each other," Michael said. He was acutely aware of Kaye's scent, the perfume she dabbed behind her ears. Did she still dot it behind her knees? He remembered running his tongue over the silky texture of her legs.

"I needed time to think! You knew that!" she said to Michael. The spicy scent wafted from her hair as she tossed it angrily. The memory of her hair sliding across his thighs as she lowered her face over him gave him an erection. He held the ice cream over it so Kaye would not see.

"Lizzy helped me," Michael said.

"Oh, I bet she did." She looked him up and down. "That beard is ridiculous." She wanted to slap him. "You're a fool, you know that?"

"You were gone a long time," he said. "You didn't even write to me.

Don't tell me you didn't sleep with anybody you felt like while you were doing all your thinking. You just up and left," he said, the sobs catching in his throat while overhead a woodpecker knocked. "You didn't think about anyone but Y-O-U. That's all you ever think about."

"I thought we were married. Till death do us part and all that."

"Don't tell me you didn't play around."

"That's not the point. It looks to me like you practically got married to somebody else behind my back." Kaye shifted her hold on Aran. She tried to be in touch with the soul of the moment, as Jarrett, her acting coach, called it.

"Don't just give in to easy tears. Anyone can cry," Jarrett often instructed. "Go deeper. Go *into* the feeling. Experience the soul of the moment."

Kaye leaned back, letting the snow fall on her face. Her arms ached from Aran's weight. She had grown taller, chubbier. Jet lag and exhaustion gave the scene a dreamlike quality. She had gone halfway around the world, had been traveling for nearly two days to return, but arriving home was the strangest part of her journey. Seeing the women gathered in the front yard. *Her* yard. The bright candies spilling. The children's happy shrieks.

"You expect me to just turn my back on all this?" Kaye asked.

"You did that a long time ago." Michael reached for Aran. "Let Daddy hold you," he said. Aran hid her face in her mother's coat.

"What exactly is that supposed to mean?"

"You were gone before you left." Michael began to shiver; he had to clamp his teeth together to keep them from chattering. Kaye, he realized, was like a prize he'd won at the fair, something to put on a shelf for everyone to admire. But Lizzy was different. More complicated, that was for sure. And he still did not know if they loved each other. But she was steady. He could count on her.

All the way home, Kaye had planned her future. She would try out for the theatre company in Union City, be selected for all the lead roles, and come summer, an important agent from New York who was in town vacationing would discover her. From that moment on one door after the other would open. She hadn't decided how Michael would fit into the picture yet, but she was sure Aran would like being a movie star's daughter.

"Some welcome home," Kaye said.

Beads of melted snow dotted Michael's sparse hair. He looked toward the driveway where cars were arriving and taking off.

"Aran is *my* daughter. This is *my* land, too. The house is half mine. Just don't you forget that," she said before tramping back through the woods feeling like the star of a tragedy. Behind a tree, the director was shouting instructions. "Your heart is broken. But wait. Don't cry. Look like you're about to. You want your audience to cry first."

There had been no birthday song, no ritual candle blowing, no plates of cake and ice cream. Like an orchestra after the curtain call, the guests left soon after Kaye arrived. But J.T. was still there, trying to soothe her friend who had retreated into a kind of stupor.

Lizzy hoped to hear angry shouts from the woods. She kept expecting glass to shatter. She wanted to run out and save Aran from witnessing violence. But there was only the soft brush of snow against the windowpanes and the fluffy kitten on her lap kneading her sweater.

"She can't waltz back and expect things to be the same," J.T. said.

"Why not?" asked Lizzy, petting Miss Kitty, smoothing her fur.

When they heard footsteps thumping up the steps, J.T. wiped a circle of steam off the window and peered outside. The red car was idling.

Michael dropped the bag of ice cream into the sink. The entire time they argued with each other in the woods, he'd held it. Now it was all soupy. "She's taking Aran for a couple of days," he said. "I had to say yes." He patted Lizzy, glancing over at J.T. and shrugging helplessly.

"Don't touch me," Lizzy said, pulling away.

He ran upstairs. They heard him opening and closing the drawers of Aran's bureau. He came down carrying a bag of Aran's clothes.

"We'll work this out," he said. The door closed with a click.

"This is *not* happening," Lizzy said. "Tell me it's not." She stroked the kitten and it kneaded faster, purring till its body shook. She pulled the doll from the center of the cake, staring at the knobs of plastic for breasts. "I've been wanting to do this all day," she said.

Michael came in with an armload of wood. He stirred the fire with a poker and added a log to the cookstove, leaning over it, warming his hands. He still trembled with cold. Lizzy moaned and buried her face in her hands. J.T. didn't know what to say. She put water on for tea and wrapped an afghan around Lizzy's shoulders as if she were sick. Lizzy was tapping the cake with the doll's feet, smashing the thick sugary icing.

"It's just a few days. She'll stay at the Holiday Inn then find an apartment. We'll work it out. People get divorced all the time."

"Divorced?" Lizzy said. Why hadn't she thought this through?

J.T. wished she had left. She didn't think she was supposed to witness this. What would Betty do in the same situation? With a rush of love, she imagined Betty at home, reading by the cookstove, her feet propped beside the stove to get warm. Betty would say something soothing, like "this too shall pass" and it would not sound corny or condescending.

"Kaye is her mother, Liz," Michael said. He lit his pipe with a kitchen match, puffing slowly, wishing he could slither through the cracks in the floor and hide out until this whole thing passed over.

* * *

"Hows about we go shoppin'?" Slim said, rubbing his hands together.

Janesta glanced up from the magazine she was flipping through. "You just got a shitload of groceries."

"For clothes, I mean. A spree. What d'you say, Crys? You wanna new winter coat?"

Crystal looked at her mother as if for approval. "A big snowstorm's headed our way. Gonna get wicked cold and colder. Brrr."

"See, that's why you need a new coat. We'll get you one of them ones that keep you warm at forty below. How about that?"

Hydie had told him that when Trudy moped around, he took her shopping. "It usually does the trick," he said. Slim hoped it would work with Janesta. He couldn't remember the last time she'd smiled. James banged his rattle against Shotgun who looked up as if to plead: Make this stop.

"Well?" Slim said. He kissed the top of Janesta's head. Her hair smelled so pretty, all freshly washed. That morning he sat on the toilet lid watching her dry herself from the shower. Her skin was so buttery smooth. "Any little thing your heart desires," he added.

"They don't sell that kind of thing." Janesta slapped him with the magazine. "Quit fussin' over me. Kee-*reist*, gimme room to breathe."

"I'll go warm the car," Slim said. It was snowing already, but too soon to worry about the roads though this might be their last time out for a while. When he came back in, they were ready to go, even the baby was in his snowsuit, his mittens pulled over his tiny hands.

"How may I help you, ma'am," the salesman at Wilson's asked Janesta. It used to be salesmen went wild flirting with her, falling all over themselves to help her try things on. This one made her feel she was old enough to be his mother. As if he thought she was there to pick up a pair of support hose. She was ready to leave before she'd even looked.

"We're just lookin'," Slim said, steering her to the ladies department where a salesgirl fluttered up, offering her services.

"I can't think with all of them on my case every second," Janesta grumbled. " 'May I show you something in your size?' Like they think I'm gonna shoplift."

She looked at herself in the three-way mirror and scowled. She had never been thin or even tried to be. But now she was definitely overweight. Obese. Her life was over. She was ruined.

"You wanna show me something in my size? How about one of them tents downstairs? Maybe that'll fit," she muttered, turning for a side view. Even her neck was fat, and the shape of her face, what Frank had called lovely, was obscured by a blurry puffiness. And where was her waist? How long had it been since she'd had a waist? When was the last time she'd squeezed into her jeans? How was she supposed to fit into anything, big as a house like this?

"Look at me," said Crystal. She had on a bright pink parka, the hood trimmed with white fur. She petted the fur as if it were alive.

"Go see yourself," Slim said. "Turn around. Can you see the back?"

"How come I gotta see the back? Do I got eyes in the back of my head, you jughead?"

"I dunno. You don't have to," he said. "You see anything you want, honey?" Slim murmured to Janesta. "These sweaters are awful pretty. . . ." His voice trailed off. The shopping expedition didn't seem to be working. Janesta looked unhappier than ever. He could feel James squirming in his pouch, then bearing down, grunting as he took a dump. In a few minutes, the salespeople would be wondering about the smell.

"I gotta take him out," Slim said. "It's number two."

Janesta rolled her eyes. She felt like the guy in that movie, *Groundhog Day.* Trapped while the tedious events of her life endlessly repeated; she would never escape. "I'm ready to go."

"You sure? How 'bout this nice red jacket. Boy, that looks warm. Try it on, why don't 'cha?" Slim took it from the hanger and held it out.

"I don't need to try it on. I can tell you exactly what I'd look like. Mrs. Claus."

Slim slipped it over her arms anyway and stood beside her, looking at the two of them in the mirror. Janesta's so pretty, he thought.

"It'd keep you nice and warm," he said.

"You know what we look like?" Janesta put her hands on her hips and frowned. "Jack Sprat and his wife. That's us." She stuffed her purse under her arm and turned on her heel. "I'll be out in the car."

Crystal ran her hands over each item on a circular rack. When she discovered it rotated, she set it spinning and began counting furiously, as if to tally up the items as they went whirling by. She had the stupidest look on her face. As Janesta walked out, it seemed everyone stared at her. And who wouldn't? I'd stare too, she thought, if I saw a bunch of idiots like us come in. They must figure the circus is in town.

28

All up and down Preacher's Lake Road gutted deer hung to cure from the trees beside people's houses. Hunting season was over, gunfire no longer cracked from the woods, and the men who pulled into town dressed in brand new orange hats and camouflage vests were gone, back to the cities and jobs where they sat behind desks in their suits and ties feeling renewed. Instead of asking, "Did you get your deer yet?" talk was of the latest cold front moving in, the hard winter predicted.

"It's called venison," Slim explained to James as they drove down the hill. "It's OK to hunt if you're gonna eat it." James jabbered back happily from his car seat as if in response.

"I can't stop thinkin' about that bear," he said. He was haunted by the dull glint of the bear's fur and the large face twisted in a grimace. He'd arrived at the dump yesterday to find it tossed in the pit, its paws hacked off. "James, my boy," Slim said, pulling into Hydie's. "Your first huntin' season's behind you. We got other concerns, don't we little tyke?"

Slim tapped the snow off his hat and kicked the snow off his boots before pushing open the door of the diner where the woodstove hissed, and the fellows gathered around drinking coffee, eating donuts.

"Gee whillikers," Hydie called. "It's the abominable snowman."

"I'm freezin' my tail off," Slim said. "Boy, got bad news to boot."

"What's that?"

"I got this letter. Makin' it official," Slim said. "About closin' the dump."

"Lemme see." Buster reached out his chubby hand, but Hydie was faster. He read it aloud then propped it on the counter. Buster stared out the window, chewing his donut like a cow chewing her cud.

"There's been talk of this before. All this hoopla about what the state's got up its sleeve in the paper. But don't it sound like a done deal?" Buster said. "Now why ain't we heard it's a done deal till now?"

"They were havin' a slew of meetings, I remember that," Coalie said.

"Yeah. They had a bunch of meetings," Slim said. "I even told them my ideas. You know, what I told you guys? How we can reuse just about everything? Shred up tires for the town roads. Make mulch from the yard waste. They laughed when I said I could make enough compost outa everybody's garbage to fill the dump in for half what they'll pay to have fill carted up there when they close it down. They laughed when I explained about the shredder and showed them pictures of how they're doin' it out in California in windrows. We could get rich makin' compost outa fish guts and paper trash. You can even compost cereal boxes. Imagine that? But they said it was too cold to make compost up here. Acted like experts."

"What'll you do?" Buster reached for another chocolate donut.

Trudy slapped him. "That hand of yours ain't exactly sanitary. All I need's the Board of Health comin' in here seein' you servin' yourself."

"I dunno. That's the thing. I just don't have any idea." Slim pulled his hanky from his pocket and blew his nose. "I guess I could get on at Stimpson's. And I hear they're hirin' at the toothpick factory. But that's down in Wilton. Jeezum, I hate how it smells down there."

"Hell, Slim. It ain't like that dump smells pretty," Rip said.

"It's a smell I'm used to. Can't say I even notice. The thing is, this is my home. But it ain't like there's a whole heck of a lotta jobs around. Ain't nobody quit the lightbulb factory in God knows when. Besides, I like spendin' time with James." He let the boy grab one of his fingers and try to pull it to his mouth. "It's not like it's gonna happen tomorrow. They don't give no D day. It still could take years. I'm gonna try not to worry till they say when."

James was playing peekaboo with Coalie.

"This kid's too cute for his own damn good," Coalie said. "Make him quit bein' so cute. It's breakin' my damn heart."

"You old softy," Rip said. He reread the letter, hoping to find a clue to solve Slim's problem.

Slim felt as crushed as the aluminum cans in the recycling bin. Flat, squashed, hopeless. He would still go to the dump day after day, doing what he had always done, week after week, month after month, and then one day when they got good and ready, they'd lock it up. That would be that. He'd head down the hill wondering what he would find that day, and the dump wouldn't even be there anymore. Clarence Cushman had explained how a chain-link fence would surround what he called "the site." It would have a lock on the gate. Slim wouldn't have the key.

"We'll plant grass and put up a couple of benches and eventually, when it's safe, we'll take down the fence and it'll be just like if the dump was never there. We'll have a park," Clarence Cushman had said.

After Slim left, the men sat watching the cars go by, waving at the ones that tooted, calling out the names of the drivers, passing along gossip they'd heard about certain ones.

"Remember when Bill Watson lost his job?" Buster said. "How he started passin' bad checks? He lost everything."

"Slim ain't the dishonest type," Hydie said.

"What'll he do?" Coalie asked.

"Well, Slim married Janesta Curtis. That shows the boy's got gumption. He'll live through this here," Rip said, tucking his tobacco into his overalls, ready to leave. "He'll live through this, too."

* * *

The chicken was not hard to catch. In fact, she seemed to expect it. While the other hens frantically flapped their wings, attempting to fly away at Rita's approach, sensing something sinister in her determined attitude, the hen she was after waited by the fence, cocking her head, a patient watchfulness. When Rita grabbed her, she clucked, a murmuring sound, and when Rita tucked her under her arm, the hen stretched her feet as if trying to touch the ground with her thick yellow claws.

Now, as Rita held her down on the chopping block where she split firewood, as she twisted the knife she had jabbed toward the back of the chicken's throat, the hen was almost curious. She blinked her eye and made a low muttering sound. But she would not die.

The thin sunlight cast bluish shadows across the snow. It offered no warmth. The hen was warm under Rita's hand, however; she could feel its heart beating, and what feathers there were had an oily sheen. They gave off a familiar smell. The hen's pale skin was pinpointed with dried blood where several patches of feathers had been plucked. This was the reason why Rita had chosen this hen. To put her out of her misery, away from the others and their incessant pecking. The bird was light, almost scrawny. She would sidle over to the pan of corn, then meekly give up her meal when the others fought her away. Rita wondered if she should have chosen one of the plump ones, but she was sure they produced the most eggs. She didn't want to kill a good layer.

The pamphlet she read made the procedure sound easy, but she had never killed anything except catfish she caught as a child. She withdrew the knife and tried again. Was she supposed to jab it further back or straight up through the roof of the mouth? Wasn't that supposed to come later? She tried both, anticipating the promised squawk, but it did not come. She was haunted by tales of chickens running around with their heads severed, spurting blood, but the instructions claimed this did not have to happen. In fact, if done just right, the follicles that held the feathers were supposed to loosen. If the stick was made properly, the feathers would relax and fall out with ease.

Rita pictured the diagram of the chicken's head. Was she supposed to do something else before she "debrained" it as the instructions had said? She felt as if she had stayed up all night studying for an exam and could no longer remember the important points. Done this way, chickens die with no pain, the caption had claimed. She was surely botching it. She gave the knife another twist, shook it lightly, waiting. The hen opened its beak wider, as if to accommodate the knife. But still she would not die.

Rita spread the hen's neck across the chopping block, petting it a little before she drew the knife across, severing its head. She was so caught up in her task, she did not hear Carol's boots crunch across the snow. She did not hear Carol's startled gasp or sense her witnessing this scene. All she could think of was she had to finish and clean up the bloody mess before Rainey came home.

Rita clutched the headless chicken, pinning the wings to its body, holding it firmly as the headless dance reverberated up her arms, and at her feet in the blood-stained snow, the beak opened and closed. When at last it stopped, she dropped the hen and stared at it. This was something she had actually planned, a deliberate act. It seemed so ridiculous. Chicken, after all, was not expensive. And there were potatoes still left to mash; there was a pumpkin for her to make pie. They would gather cranberries from the bog Slim showed her.

Finish what you start, her mother's voice admonished. She wanted to throw the hen in a garbage bag, take it to the dump. She would bury it if the ground weren't frozen. Instead, she knelt beside it and gave the feathers a yank. They held tight, as if the opposite had happened and they were more firmly secured. She would have to scald the thing, spend the morning plucking it.

Carol hurried away before Rita turned around, clutching the hen's feet, a grim look on her face as she headed inside, missing the blur of Carol rushing across the road. Rita put the hen on a newspaper. She washed her hands, working up a thick lather, then set water to boil.

Rita was shaken by what she'd done, but relieved to be at this stage of it. She checked the clock, noting how much time she had before Rainey's school bus. One of Rainey's photographs was tacked to the wall above the table. A still life: a large blue bowl heaped with leaves. A doll with no head. And a perfectly shaped brown pear with a perfect stem. A drawing Carol had done of the same arrangement was tacked beside it. Carol had used a piece of paper exactly the same size as the photograph. Rita didn't know where Rainey got this ability. Certainly not from *her* side of the family. Rita had not even known there was such a thing as art until she moved to Boston. She knew almost nothing about Elias's family. He used to joke that they were the only black people in America to have absolutely no rhythm. He would hum tuneless songs through his nose to demonstrate and dance, tripping over his own feet. "We're businessmen," he had said, seeming embarrassed to reveal he sold real estate. Maybe Rainey's talent is uniquely her own, Rita thought. Maybe she didn't get it from anybody.

When the water was ready, she gripped the bird's feet and plunged it in. There was a horrible smell. The instructions said something about "bleeding" the bird, but she decided that had already been accomplished. She began yanking handfuls of wet feathers, stuffing them into a bag. When she slit the bird open she found a cavity filled with yolks, like a secret cache. Bright yellow yolks fell into the bucket, a trail of them, each slightly smaller, until the last dot of gold.

Rita had killed one of the layers. Maybe that was why the other hens had picked on her. She put the carcass to soak in a pan of ice water. Then she went outside, scooped up the tiny head with the filmy eyes, and shoveled the bloody snow into a garbage bag. She felt like a murderer, removing all traces of evidence. Rainey knew where meat came from, but there was no sense having her witness the grim reality. She would wrap the carcass in plastic. Then one day, as if it were something she got from the store, she would prepare it for a meal. It would be tough. She would have to simmer it all day till the meat fell from the bones. But for Thanksgiving, she would dip into her savings and buy a turkey. The smallest one she could find, perfect, with no history, factory-sealed in its airtight packet.

*   *   *

Carol deftly twisted the wire into a woman's shape. A woman on her hands and knees, her arms like an insect's grubbing in the dirt, her toes pointed downward, balancing the weight. The hair she shaped like onion greens. She covered the form with gauze she dipped into glue, her latest variation of paper-mache. She wound the sticky cloth around the wire then set it beside a tiny woman who sat cross-legged, her head thrown back, fronds waving down her back. *Vegetable Women* she called them. In college she had studied the fin de siècle in Vienna. She was still haunted by Egon Schiele's emaciated subjects, the twisted naked forms he painted in shades of muddy brown. One of his contemporaries, a philosopher whose name she forgot, had actually hypothesized that women were plants.

On the easel behind her, she had painted Rita bent over the hen, her hands clutching the wings. She had never painted anything so quickly, hurrying into the studio with her coat and boots still on. The bloody snow was almost beautiful, the bright red bleeding into the white. The expression of regret on Rita's face.

When Carol first began to paint, she often destroyed her work, slashing it with her palette knife, once stabbing a painting with scissors until it dangled in shreds from the stretcher frame. Dougie had a former boyfriend who made a career of doing this deliberately on stage. Night after night, he would destroy his paintings while reciting incantatory poems. At the end of his show, he would stand amid the ruined paintings holding an empty frame around his face, smiling a hideous smile, his face garishly lit, makeup glimmering under the hot lights, dripping like wet paint from his jowls. She knew she wouldn't let anyone see this painting of Rita, but she would not destroy it either. Not yet anyway. It was like a fragment from a dream she forgot upon waking. Some mystery she would work out.

She twisted the torso of the third vegetable woman, a shape no body could form unless the person had the skills of a contortionist. The hair she molded into shapes like frilly lettuce leaves. For this one, she soaked strips of cloth from the old aprons Slim gave her, tearing them up, fraying the edges before soaking them in the glue and winding them around the wire. One leg was impossibly long and snaked around the woman like a boa coming in for the kill.

* * *

Crystal locked herself in the bathroom and pulled up her sweater. One breast had begun to swell, a puffy pale pink nipple on her left side. She cupped her hand over it, then pressed hard, willing it to disappear. She held very still and counted to a hundred, but when she looked again, it was still there, a hot swollen bud. She yanked down her pants. There was the thick thatch of hair between her legs that seemed to have sprouted overnight. She touched the dark curls, flooded with a queasy mixture of shame and curiosity that set her heart racing. Her mother had hair down there. Crystal had seen her stand in the bathtub to scrub herself with a soapy washrag; she thought of how the hair dripped and glistened with bubbles. She didn't want hair like that. She got the nail scissors from the medicine chest and carefully clipped the hair off until she cut down to her pale skin. The dark curls floated on the toilet water until her mother banged on the door, shouting, "What'd you do, fall in?" and Crystal flushed it away.

* * *

The arrangements were, they would see each other every Saturday and Sunday, but lately they saw each other during the week as well because Kaye got Aran a part in the local production of *South Pacific* and there were rehearsals. Every Saturday morning, Lizzy helped Aran pack her Barbie suitcase—a clean nightgown and underwear, dresses and sweaters with matching tights, all of which were folded carefully but would come home stuffed in dirty wads.

Lizzy stayed upstairs when Kaye arrived, watching out the window as the large flashy gray Buick pulled up, driven by Victor, a man Kaye had found so fast Lizzy was certain a record had been set. A divorced shoe salesman who wore three gold chains around his tanning-parlor brown neck, he was the director of the Union City players and also the male lead. Aran told Lizzy that in the middle of the play he came out wearing a grass skirt and a bra made of coconut shells. She cupped her hands over her own flat chest and demonstrated how Victor danced. Aran played one of his daughters and sang a song in French she practiced after supper, standing on the table, her stage once the plates were cleared. Kaye, of course, was the female lead.

"Mommy's what you call star material," Aran reported. "Victor says. The best part of the whole play's when Mommy and Victor smooch." Aran wanted to demonstrate with Michael but he wouldn't let her.

"You don't kiss your daddy like that," he said.

"Can I give you a butterfly kiss then?"

"No."

Aran pouted, fluttering her eyelashes.

"How about a elephant kiss?" she asked.

"What's that?" Michael shrugged at Lizzy as if to say: I'm helpless, you know.

Lizzy sat in the rocking chair with the kitten curled on her lap. She didn't say anything as Aran pulled the sleeve of her sweater down over her hand and nudged it against Michael.

"That's the trunk, Daddy." She laughed. "Feel it?"

Today, when Kaye came to pick Aran up, Victor came in too and they sat around chatting about the kind of weekend it was going to be. Would it ever stop snowing? Michael poured shots of whiskey and offered them cookies Lizzy had baked.

While they were downstairs, Lizzy lay on the bed. The pillow wrapped around her ears was not enough to drown out Victor's booming voice. Miss Kitty began kneading her hair with her tiny paws. Lizzy pictured Aran clinging to her father's hand. But she would cling the same way to her mother when it was time to come home, shriek and have to be pried off of her.

Lizzy always said her good-byes before Kaye arrived. She insisted Michael find out a time from her so this would be possible, though Kaye seldom arrived when she said she would. She was always at least a half hour late and once two hours. That time Aran had been frantic, convinced her mother was dead. "Her car fell off the bridge," she had cried. "I know it. I know it."

Every Saturday, as she did today, Lizzy waited upstairs, listening for the back door to click shut, for Aran and her mother and Victor to crunch up the snowy path. She refused to watch them go, waiting instead for the slam of the car doors. She waited for Michael to start up the chain saw which he always did after seeing Kaye. She waited for the resounding crack of yet another tree falling. If he kept it up, pretty soon there would be no more trees.

Lizzy could pull on her boots and parka, get her work gloves from the basket beside the door. She knew that Michael would look up from cutting the brush, satisfied to see her approach. That on the score sheet he kept, she would get a bright gold star. Instead, Lizzy pulled the blankets over her face and hummed the song Aran would sing in the play.

She could hear a fire crackling; Michael had doused an old tire with kerosene and was pulling the brush out of the woods to burn. The sun, nearing the edge of the clearing, had already begun to set. Then there would be the long dark night to get through. Supper to make, Michael's heavy sighs, their endless bickering. Then a whole day to survive before Aran returned. Lizzy was not sure she could face one more weekend without Aran. The house was so empty once she was gone.

29

Carol stood on the porch with her hood up, a scarf wrapped around her neck, the drawstring on the new parka she bought in Union City tight around her waist. Her mouth touched the metal zipper. It was so cold out, she hoped it wouldn't freeze to her face. She stomped her feet to keep her blood circulating and curled her fingers into fists inside her mittens. With this weather, she could understand how people were found inches from home, frozen to death. The snow was fierce, filling the air, blurring everything.

At least a dozen times, she had tried to get her nerve up to pay Rita a visit. This time she was going to step off the porch, cross the road, and not turn back. She would say something straightforward and simple like, "I've been thinking about you." Surely Rita would smile her old smile, the way she did before they had locked Nelly up in the mental hospital, and say, "I've been thinking about you, too." Then she'd invite Carol in for cocoa. Carol didn't dare imagine beyond that.

"I can do this," she said aloud. She had been talking to herself so much lately. It was probably part of the cabin fever everyone talked about. When she stepped off the porch, she was surprised that the snow came up over the top of her boots. She considered turning around. The wind whipped the snow into her face making it hard to keep her eyes open. She wondered how Rita and Rainy were managing. Maybe I can say I'm worried about them, she thought. No, no. Just tell the truth.

The truck was parked at the foot of the driveway nearly buried with a thick layer of snow. When was the last time it had been gone? She started up their driveway, wading through the snow, breaking through the frozen layers, noticing the bottoms of her boots were designed to look like tire treads. Then she realized there were no other footprints. There was no path to the house. Maybe she *should* be worried. Maybe something *was* wrong.

Go ahead, she told herself. I'm sure she wants to see you. If nothing else, she's probably bored out of her mind. She needs you as much as you need her.

Annie used to say that a lesbian love affair was when two women sat across the room from each other yearning until one of them got too old to remember why she was sitting there. Is that what you want your life to be like? Carol asked herself.

"No," she said aloud, tucking her face into her scarf. The snow was pelting her, stinging her skin, accumulating on her eyelashes. "I want something different." She trudged along, past the huddle of sheep, their wooly bodies so thick it seemed impossible their skinny legs could hold them up. They reminded her of the bare-legged teenage girls she saw outside the school, dressed in short tight skirts despite the cold. The snow was blowing hard, drifting against Rita's house up to the windows.

"Nelly was insane," Iris had said. "She would have wrecked the place whether you were there or not. What happened is not your fault."

Carol waited outside the door, trembling both from cold and fear, hoping Rita would notice she was there before she had to knock. It seemed eerily quiet, as if no one were inside. But the truck's there, she thought. Then she noticed there was no smoke coming from the chimney pipe. She knocked and heard a stirring inside. Then nothing. She knocked again, then, kicking the snow out of the way, she pushed the door open. The house smelled like the ashes left from a campfire half buried in sand on the beach. The windows were covered with thick frost, beautiful patterns of ice

streaked across the glass. The woodstove was silent and cold, like
something dead in the corner, and the sink was full of dirty dishes,
the water in the dishpan frozen.

"Hey, you guys," Carol said, afraid there would be no answer, that
they had disappeared or else were frozen in their beds. "Anybody
home?"

"Carol?" Rita said from the loft bed.

"What're you doing? You guys out of wood or what?" The house
was so cold her breath was visible.

"No." Rita groaned. Carol could hear her moving overhead, but
she did not appear. "I wrenched my back out. I got up this morning
and when I went to put on my jeans, I fell down."

Carol climbed onto the bench in order to see her. "Why didn't you
call me?" She felt angry, but scared too. What if she hadn't come over?

An array of brightly colored seed catalogs was strewn over the bed
covering them like a patchwork quilt.

"I thought I'd get better," Rita said. "Rainey's keeping me warm."

"We got a bunch of clothes on," Rainey said. Her nose was red
with the cold. "China Cat's schooched down by our feet." She stuck
her hands out and showed Carol the mittens she wore.

Carol started working on the fire. She emptied the ash pan and
gathered an armload of kindling from the woodpile under a tarp
outside. Soon the wood was burning steadily in the stove. The kitten
scrambled down from the loft bed and brushed against her legs,
meowing hopefully. On the gas burner, there was a cast-iron pan
with dried scrambled eggs stuck to the sides and bottom. On the
counter, the garbage for compost was overflowing: a tangerine rind
furry with mold, some carrot peelings turning brown, sprouted
potato eyes. She wondered when they had eaten last. Outside, the
wind howled and hurled snow against the windows, some of it seeping onto the floor.

"I feel warmer already," Rita called.

Rainey began to list what they wore. "I got on my pj's with feets,
my long johns, my sweater Mommy made me. Mom's got on her
sweater and her long johns and her down vest."

"Well, you can start peeling some of it off soon," Carol said. She
was looking in the refrigerator. A few inches of curdled milk. Some
eggs. A half loaf of bread. She noticed some cans of soup on the
shelf. "How about some nice chicken noodle soup?"

"Yummy," Rainey said.

When Carol went to fill the can with water, the pump handle was
limp. It hung there, seemingly broken, not a bit of tension in it.

"It froze," Rita said in a soft voice. "That's how I hurt my back. I was trying to break the ice in the well."

"How were you doing that?"

"I tied this cement block to a rope and flung it down there. It worked at first. I had to do it a few times. Then I could lower the bucket down. There's still some jugs I filled by the sink."

"I'll bring you some water from my place, OK? In fact, why don't you come over there right now? You can stay with me till it warms up."

"We can manage," Rita said. She sounded all huffy. Carol decided to let it go. At least they were talking again, she thought.

"Can you make it down here or do you want to eat in bed?" she asked.

Rita inched her way out of bed, gripping her back with one hand.

"It's not so bad now. Rainey brought me some aspirins a while ago." Rita could not hide a grimace of pain as she crawled down the ladder. She looked so small and forlorn Carol had all she could do not to rush over and hold her. She helped her settle in a chair by the fire and brought her another chair to put her feet on.

"How about a hot-water bottle?"

"I don't have one." Rita struggled to mask the pain.

"I'll bring you that, too," Carol said.

"I don't want you wrenching *your* back helping me."

"I'll pull everything over on the sled. How's that sound?"

"Good." Rita gave her a grateful smile.

When Rainey started climbing down with her toy school bus tucked under one arm, Carol hurried to help her. All she needed was for Rainey to fall and crack her head open.

After their soup, and Carol's trips back with the supplies and out to feed the animals, the house was warm enough for Rainey to play in her room. She was singing a song about the wheels on the bus, pushing her school bus across the bed, bumping it over the rumpled blankets, laughing as China Cat pounced on it. She paused to eat a slice of one of the oranges Carol brought. Carol put another log on the fire and pulled a chair close to Rita.

"It's helping," Rita said. "Thank you." She shifted and the hot-water bottle sloshed as she reached for Carol's hand. Rita held it on her lap, turning it over and back, examining it as if she'd never seen a hand before, then pulled it to her lips and kissed the palm. Her lips were very warm. She kissed the tender places on her wrist.

"I keep having this dream," Rita said. "I had it again last night. In the dream, I have this garden but I forget to take care of it. I don't water it or weed it. It's all dry stalks and a rubble of weeds. Lettuces and radishes flower and go to seed. I don't pick anything when it ripens. The tomatoes just fall off the vines and rot. The poppies dry and their seed heads split open. The marigolds wither. It's not even neglect, really. I just forget it's there. Then one day I go out and discover this beautiful garden in full bloom. Sunflowers thirteen feet tall. Huge Cinderella pumpkins lolling on the dark earth. Humongous eggplants perfectly shaped. Beautiful flowers all brightly colored varieties like I've never seen. All of it planted itself from going to seed."

Rita rested her head on Carol's shoulder. They sat this way, listening to the fire crackling and Rainey's song. This is what I want my life to be like, Carol thought. She felt unbelievably content.

"That's such a hopeful dream," Carol said, pushing Rita's hair behind her ears, resting her hand at the back of Rita's neck. Rita began to cry. Her sobs were like big waves rushing over her. Carol patted her back, waiting until she grew calm.

"You OK?" Carol finally asked.

"I'm sorry," Rita said, pulling away. "For everything. The way I've been. I don't know how to act."

"Shh," Carol murmured, stroking her cheeks.

"It's just I promised myself."

"Promised yourself what?"

"I wouldn't get involved with anybody until I got my life together."

"Gosh. That could take forever."

"That bad, huh?"

Carol chuckled. "I was thinking about myself. If I promised that it would be like sentencing myself to solitary confinement."

"I just want to be able to take care of myself. I don't want to get in a situation again like I had with Nelly."

"Well, I've had a few more years to work at it. All I know is you never really get it together, not how you think you will. You just get used to the way you are. You realize you're not going to change all that much so you try to love yourself anyway. Besides, maybe it gets easier if you let someone love you."

"Maybe," Rita said, turning toward Carol, reaching for a hug. "Maybe it does."

* * *

"The dog ate my diaphragm. Chewed a big ol' hole in it." J.T. crossed her legs and let one loafer dangle from her toe, but Lizzy still didn't notice the condoms she'd stretched over her feet like stockings.

"I ran out of pills. That's my favorite one," Lizzy said. "I mean, really. You take the last one, you have seven days to come in for more. What's the big deal? If they run out of milk, they go to the store, don't they? They never run out of cigarettes, do they?"

"Bud says his sperms ain't no good. So I don't need no pills."

"Johnny won't wear rubbers. He says they hold back his feelings."

"Ha! That's not all they hold back, honey." J.T. scratched her ankle, hoping Lizzy would notice. She loved to make Lizzy laugh. Since Kaye returned, she'd been morose.

"We do the rhythm," Lizzy said.

J.T. stood up and swayed her hips. She snapped her fingers.

"We do the rhythm," she sang, twirling around.

Thick heavy snow fell steadily. Although it was two o'clock, the vehicles that passed with their chains flapping had their headlights on.

"We should just close," Lizzy said, checking the appointment book. "We've had four cancellations and six no-shows. The only one who made it in was Trudy Hyde for her monthly breast check."

"We couldn't find the foam," J.T. said. "I keep it right there beside the bed and it just plumb disappeared."

"What about the 'waiting till I get some protection' method? What about that? Why can nobody wait?" Lizzy asked.

"Romance is a nuisance!" J.T. sang. "Sex! It's just a hex! Relations. They cause frustrations!" J.T. sang the song she'd made up, imitating Heavy D and the Boys.

"What have you got on your feet?" Lizzy giggled, staring at J.T.'s feet. "Is that what I think it is?"

"I thought you'd never notice. They make a great foot protector." She strutted across the room like a fashion model, her hand on one hip.

* * *

When James cried, as he did often—he was prone to ear infections, allergic to various formulas, his tiny bottom covered with an angry red rash—the cries shook his whole body. He would stiffen, gasp as if inhaling his last breath, his fists contracted against his chest, his legs curled up tight, then he would wail. When Slim was home, he would tuck the boy in the pouch against his chest, walk him up and down, counting the six steps it took from the bedroom, starting where the baby's crib was pushed against the wall at the foot of the bed, and walking in a jouncing step to the living room where Janesta sat in the La-Z-Boy smoking and staring at the TV. Slim would hold the boy and whisper over his downy head, marveling at all the noise that came from someone barely bigger than a pillow.

He would pat the baby's bottom, checking for the first sign of dampness. He would wrap the flannel blanket tight until he was like a roast wrapped in white paper ready for the freezer. He would loosen the blankets to let the baby's legs kick free. He tried every-thing he could think of, even letting Crystal hold him and bounce on the bed like it was a trampoline because once this had worked. He would hold the boy up on his shoulder, spread him stomach down across his knees, or cradle him and try to rock him to sleep. Eventually James would nod off but still Slim held him because he woke up the minute he was put in his crib, his voice pitched to an insistent shriek, his bright blue eyes squeezed tight.

When Slim wasn't home, Janesta turned the volume of the TV so high she could barely hear him cry. Out of frustration, she vacu-umed the trailer because the motor whine often made James fall asleep.

"I can't be expected to vacuum this friggin' tin house every god-damn day of the week, every friggin' hour," she said when the baby's wails started in as soon as she switched it off. She tossed the attach-ments into the closet and kicked the door shut with disgust.

"It'd be easier to rake this damn shag rug anyway," she said. "It has got to be at least thirty years old. Maybe I oughta shave it."

Today, she had even vacuumed under the bed, gone over the molding, taken the brush off to vacuum the edges where the wall met the floor, vacuumed the lintels, kicked aside Slim's piles of mag-azines and newspapers, vacuuming behind them, sucking up his old clothes every time she turned around. But as soon as she turned the thing off, the baby shrieked as if he were being pinched.

"Maybe you can just leave it on," Crystal suggested. This was the third snow day in a row Crystal was home from school. She stayed in her nightgown all day with the blankets piled on her, she was so cold. "You don't have to *really* vacuum. Just leave it on."

"Whyn't you say so before? You are a genius, you know that?" Janesta turned the vacuum back on and yanked it down the hallway where she left it in front of the bedroom door.

On TV, a gaunt woman with sunken cheeks stared mournfully into the camera.

"Don't she look like she's been through the wringer?" Janesta said. "This all we got to watch?" The camera panned on five babies, quintuplets dressed in white pajamas, in a row on a blanket. One baby chewed another one's hand. Another kicked its feet, about to cry.

"They're the same!" Crystal said. "Lookit. You can't tell 'em apart. They got the same teeny tiny hands and feet. The same color hair and all. Even the same clothes on." She rocked excitedly, forgetting her mother hated it when she did this.

"Good God almighty, flip that station. It gives me the creeps lookin' at all of them babies. Like havin' a litter," Janesta said.

With the vacuum roaring, the baby screaming, and the TV on high, they didn't hear Slim pull up.

"Hey hey," he said. His cheeks were fiery red from the cold. He dropped an armload of firewood into the wood box with a clatter. "How's my little family? Is that my boy I hear?"

As he tossed a log on the fire, a smattering of red coals singed Barney's tail. He let out a yowl, as if competing with James.

Janesta just sat smoking, staring at the TV. He shrugged off his jacket, kicked his heavy boots off, and went for James. Janesta rarely picked him up, but when she did, James only cried louder, bucking in her arms like the very smell of his mother turned his stomach.

"He'll take to you if you give him half a chance," Slim told Janesta when he came back with the baby cooing in his arms. He put James on Janesta's lap. He sputtered, kicking furiously, pushing his legs against her stomach as if to shove himself onto the floor.

"Just rock him a little. He likes to get his fingers in your hair. Hold him up on your shoulder like this."

"I know how to hold a friggin' baby. This one don't want me to," she said through clenched teeth. "He only wants you. And far as I'm concerned, he's yours."

* * *

The first thing Joe saw when he pulled up in front of the Community Church in Preacher's Lake was the sign: CLOSED ECAUSE NOBODY CARES. The B had fallen down from the signboard and was lying on its side belly up at the bottom of the glass case. He stared at the church, at the windows boarded up, the steeple white against the dark sky, and thought about how it would sound to ring the old cast-iron bell.

"Welcome to Preacher's Lake, Reverend Philbrook," he said, standing up to his knees in the snow that swirled around him like a whirlwind, bits of icy snow tapping his cheeks, clinging to his glasses. He'd been excited to come here, certain that reviving a church that had dwindled to the point where they had closed it down was what he was meant to do. No worry about filling anybody else's shoes. No ready-made congregation that wanted to do what they'd always done. A fresh start. Now he wondered if he'd been delirious when he decided to come all the way up here. He thought of Lot's Wife. "She was called to stand on the edge," he'd said once in a sermon. "Her whole body a prayer."

"Ask, and it shall be given you," he muttered. It was so cold his lungs hurt and already his fingertips were numb. He waded through the snow to the parsonage, a one-story yellow clapboard house. Inside, it smelled just the way he thought it would: a mixture of old toast, damp wallpaper, and dust. A local handyman had gotten the furnace going, the water and utilities turned on. And the key for the church would be hanging from a red ribbon beside the front door, he'd been informed. There it was. Joe shrugged his coat off. He would see the church later. In daylight. From the looks of it, there might be wild animals settling for the night inside.

"The town has been without a pastor for quite some time," Clark, his advisor, had said. "It's in an out-of-the-way coastal town. You ever been up to Maine?" he asked, raising his thick white brows. "By the time the last pastor retired, the congregation had dwindled to the point where there was hardly anyone left in the pews. About twenty people still consider themselves members though I don't know how many on this roster are still alive.

"I imagine most of them go to Union City for church. It's the county seat. They've probably got a lot more going on. You might have lost your flock already." Clark studied the man who sat across from him. He was so short his feet barely touched the floor when he sat in the armchair. But what he lacked in size, he made up for in enthusiasm. Joe had been so earnest, so dedicated right from the start. So unlike his fellow classmates: The serious ones who were earning doctorates, studying the philosophers and planning to teach; the younger ones, most of whom were following in their fathers' footsteps, even the women; the lost souls who thought the work would bring them love; the sharp-witted ones who would have a knack for talking the old ladies into buying them new cars.

"Odd name, Preacher's Lake. I guess there's a story to go with it. Nothing in these papers, though. No church history to speak of. Maybe an early settler named Preacher. The lake is beautiful, I hear."

The church had received an endowment, Clark explained, but it was only good if the church was functioning. The money came from a woman who'd summered there. Not only had she come from a wealthy family, but she had done quite well for herself as an investment banker. She left the church a neat portfolio that would pretty much take care of itself.

"No doubt it'll need some repairs," Clark said. With the interest income, there would be a fair enough salary. Enough to get him started. The rest would have to come from the people. "If the people come," Clark said, noting the delight on Joe's face.

"OK. I'm ready," said Joe. An immense satisfaction filled him, as if he had just eaten a sumptuous meal. His dark eyes were lively behind wire-rimmed glasses, his hair a mass of disheveled curls. He pushed his fingers through it, jabbing at his hair, not in irritation or from nervousness. His thought simply required a physical component.

"That's it? OK? You're sure?"

"Yeah. I've been called. I can feel it." Joe grinned. He thought of the path his life had taken, his drifting from one odd job to another, taking drugs to expand his consciousness while his soul withered. He liked to think God had a good laugh at his stint as a Hare Krishna devotee in orange robes, his head shaved, on a street corner chanting. Years later, when he returned from Guatemala and worked at the car wash in Rapid City, God watched Joe spray dead grasshoppers and butterflies down the drain and took pity on him, at the sorry state he was in, and reached out with a benevolent hand and dropped him at the doorstep of a church where, for the first time in his life, Joe began to feel at home.

The week before he learned of Preacher's Lake, he had gone to preach at the Broadway United Church of Christ in Pittsburgh, an experience that epitomized all he thought was wrong with organized religion. The parishioners of Broadway Church—this was how they referred to themselves as if the mention of Christ's name and the notion of being united in any way embarrassed them—had been smugly self-assured, their faith seemingly as solid as the polished oak pews they sat upon.

Afterwards, when Clark and Joe had prayed, bowing their heads together as they had so often, Joe felt a tight knot in his chest and there were tears caught behind it. A big wash of tears. He was so exhausted with waiting, exhausted with questioning. Perhaps he should have continued to operate the car wash. There were fewer demands. A bird caught in a grill now and then, that was it. He was aware of the warmth of Clark's hands, and of his spirit, like a nimbus radiating. He let the tears wash down his cheeks; he let them fall.

Joe came to Preacher's Lake bursting with convictions, singing hymns as he drove through the storm; now, he felt like an old organ wheezing its last notes. "You're tired," he counseled himself. He heated water for cocoa, using the supplies he'd picked up on the way, and walked around the house sipping from a chipped mug. The floors creaked terribly as he crept through the rooms, noting the falling plaster, the peeling wallpaper, the layers of dust stirred by the drafts.

Joe went back outside and stood in front of the church. "The souls of the righteous are in the hands of God," Clark had said, quoting his favorite verse from the Book of Psalms. Joe remembered Clark's hand on his head as he was ordained, how it felt to be kneeling, surrounded.

He tried to imagine the church in its heyday as he stood there knee-deep in the snow. Weeds taller than he was poked up like morose sentries. The steps, the very symbols of invitation, were buried under huge drifts. Chips of paint had peeled off the clapboards, remnants of birds' nests dangled from the belfry. He hoped the bell hadn't been converted to ring at the push of a button. He imagined pulling the old rope, people coming up the walkway, their hands reaching for his as he greeted them, pansies blooming in the dooryard, the smell of fresh coffee brewing.

A crescent moon hung at the edge of the trees. The first thing I'll do, he told himself, is change that sign. He would search for the right scripture to quote. An old Russian proverb he'd found taped to the wall in his room at seminary came to mind: "Pray to God but row for the shore." That seemed to summarize Joe's pragmatic faith. But in this backwoods community, quoting from Russian would no doubt brand him as a "Commie." Not the best way to start.

I'll shovel the snow, he planned. Then I'll get those boards off the windows. Let there be light! He shuffled through the snow, doing a little soft-shoe to cheer himself, climbing up onto the crusty layer and walking along on top of the snow, then crashing through, stumbling and falling. He rolled onto his back and gazed up at the bright stars.

"Praised be my Lord for our sister the moon, and the stars, which he hath set clear and lovely in the heavens," he said. St. Francis of Assisi. He imagined the circumstances in which St. Francis wrote those beautiful words. Probably ones very similar to his own. The thought encouraged him.

"Bless me," he said to the stars and the sky and the moon. Then he got up, brushed the snow off, and headed inside. Toward home, he told himself, taking a deep breath. He was ready to begin.

30

Janesta exhaled in a reluctant stream as if she had been hoarding the smoke and was doling it out, savoring it as long as she could before her lungs demanded another intake of the nicotine-laced carbon monoxide they were accustomed to. She wished she could ride the swirl of smoke like a child racing downhill on a sled. In the bedroom behind the closed door, so loud he might as well have been sprawled at her feet, James shrieked, baring his angry red gums, his blanket kicked off. With disgust, she sucked on the soggy end of her cigarette, then dropped it into a half-finished cup of coffee.

"Crystal Dawn! Jesus Kee-*reist!* I've had it up to here." Janesta sliced a finger across her throat. "You and that friggin' movie on for the millionth time and that damn baby squallin' like a boar gettin' his you-know-whats whacked off. Turn that movie off N-O-W!"

Janesta popped back the La-Z-Boy and adjusted the afghan. A draft blew in around the edges of the windows, billowing the plastic sealed over them. "Snow and more friggin' snow," she said. She was sick of the snow and sick of staring at the simulated wood paneling, the evenly spaced knotholes and fake wood grain. From force of habit, she began idly counting the plastic daisies that held up the water-stained ceiling panels. The place was definitely closing in on her.

She fingered the flap of skin on her belly. Though James had only weighed six pounds—she had barely eaten while she was pregnant, nibbling on Ritz Crackers, sipping Cokes—he still took up room. Plus the weight she'd put on since, blowing up, every day more flab. She was going to pot. On the TV, a cluster of people out in California tried to shove a beached whale back into the ocean. "That's me. That's what I am," Janesta said.

Crystal flicked the station, stopping briefly to view a woman happily working up a sweat with a contraption that looked like a pogo stick and a giant rubber band.

"If that thing broke, she'd crack her jaw," Janesta muttered. She was not about to do aerobics or sit-ups. She just wanted the fat gone. She wanted to feel like her old self again. To fit into her clothes.

What was happening to her? All she knew was she wanted out. Not that she was about to trudge into the deep snow dragging the kids with her, stripping the three of them naked like that woman last week. Janesta had no intention of ending up on the evening news for everyone to click their tongues over, telling the story over coffee at Hydie's, over beers at The Quarterdeck, pulling their carts nose to nose at the Shop and Save, repeating the story as if they hadn't told it yet, listening as if they hadn't seen it themselves. The woman's husband sat stiffly on the sofa wearing a suit, some kind of businessman, saying, "She had the flu. Our boy had a fever, but he was getting better. I had no idea she'd do such a thing."

Janesta was not about to lie bare-assed in a snowdrift with her kids beside her waiting while the cold came down like a freezer door locking shut. She was not about to have everybody know how desperate she was. Kee-*reist*. There had to be another way out.

Janesta pictured the two of them, mother and son, shivering, their lips turning blue, staring up at the snow falling over them, the flakes melting as they hit bare skin, accumulating until they were half buried. No tomorrow.

"Weatherman says it's thirty-seven below with the windchill," Crystal announced, writing it in her notebook. "It's been colder."

Outside, the snow was steadily falling, all day long snow coming down on top of other snow. A week after Thanksgiving, there'd been the first really big blizzard. Early that year. There was a cold snap and none of it melted. One blizzard after another. Snow piling up foot after foot, some kind of record. Here it was, January, and still snowing. The wind whistled around the trailer, rocking it. Snow was heavy on the tree branches, drifting higher than the mailbox. Thick wet snow that squeaked underfoot. Heavy snow that would send half the men in the county to bed with backaches, others to the hospital with coronaries from shoveling their way out. Snow so thick that if Janesta were to open the door, she could hear it fall, count the facets on each flake. If she fell facedown into it, she would sink for several inches before her nose hit the frozen layer underneath.

Crystal's deep phlegmy cough rattled in her chest. On the coffee table, there was a bowl of soggy Cheerios, a terry cloth bib with dried vomit on the yellow figure of a duck, and a pair of wet pajama bottoms balled up with a soiled diaper. In the garbage can, the urine stench of old diapers mixed with last night's pork chop bones wrapped in greasy aluminum foil that the dog had already chewed. Before he left for work, Slim started to clean up. "Go on, now," Janesta said, shooing him out.

The snowplow was coming up the hill, its chains slapping the road. Twice in one day, and still it was snowing. Wes Tracey, the driver, scooped the snow out of their driveway, and left the plow running while he popped in for a hot cup of coffee. Janesta was still in her housecoat, her hair uncombed.

"That boy's got him a healthy pair of lungs, I'd say," Wes said, nodding toward the bedroom, his eyes wandering to the bare skin where Janesta's housecoat fell open. She made no effort to pull it closed. "Takes after his mom, I'd say."

If Crystal hadn't been on the sofa bed curled in her unwashed sheets, Janesta would have done it right there in the kitchen, Wes still in his snow boots. It wasn't that Slim didn't please her that way. God knows he made her feel things. God knows he loved her, watching over her, offering to take one of his sick days so she wouldn't have both kids to tend to. But the idea of the two of them squeezing around Crystal's bed all day, bumping into each other as they went to the refrigerator or to the bathroom, seemed like the last straw. Janesta had practically pushed him out the door. He tried so goddamned hard to love her, it made her sick. She looked at Wes, his ruddy skin like a sweating cheese, his damp thin hair falling across his shiny forehead, that knowing leer on his face. This was what she had to look forward to?

"All this snow's a poor farmer's fertilizer," Crystal said. "Gonna be good for the crops."

Janesta gave her a look that said: Shut up!

"You seen that one last night?" Wes asked, spooning sugar into his cup. "Where the tarantulas take over that Texas town?" He draped his parka over a kitchen chair, the snow melting and dripping onto the floor.

"Huh-uh." Janesta lit a cigarette on the gas burner.

"There's this scientist over in a foreign country. He dies and they ship him back. When they open up that box, that's it. What little bit I watched I sat there going like this." Wes fanned his hand over Janesta's face. His hand smelled of oil, as if the creases in his palm had soaked it up. Ten minutes with Wes Tracey and she'd have her body under control. But was this really the best she could do? Trysts with married men who stopped by for a quick one the way they stopped by the bar on the way home from work?

"This girl. She goes into the shower and, oh my God. There's a big black hairy spider clinging to the wall. 'Course she don't look up."

"More?" Janesta held up the coffeepot, leaning close to Wes, her breasts brushing his arm. "It's plenty hot."

"I'll bet it is," he said, tweaking one of Janesta's nipples.

Janesta yawned and finished her coffee. "The black widow'll kill you," she said. "She kills her mate after they're done. The scorpions're just as bad. They breed till they die."

"Mm, mm, mm." Wes licked his lips. "What a way to go. You ever wanna do-si-do, you know my address," he said. He tweaked Janesta's nipple again, holding on long enough to feel it swell. She didn't even bother to slap his hand.

After Wes left, Janesta checked the clock. In exactly fifty-three minutes, Slim would lock up at the dump. And James, who had finally cried himself to sleep, would wake up again, his high-pitched shrieks, like the beacon on a lighthouse, would guide Slim home. That baby's got ESP, Janesta thought. Like a dog that runs to the window long before his owner comes home. She could picture it all: Slim rushing to the baby who would sputter like an engine with water in the gas tank, sucking his fists, hungry for the bottle he spit up as soon as Slim got it down him.

"Cryin' like there's no tomorrow. Shit, shit, shit." Janesta crushed her cigarette out, not caring that she scattered ashes onto the table, spilling them onto the rug. Like there's no tomorrow, Janesta thought, and knew all at once, the knowledge as sure as a bullet hitting its mark, there would be no more tomorrows like this. Not if she had any say-so about it. I won't be here when Slim's headlights flash across the room. I'll be gone before he pulls in the driveway. Out on the highway before he tromps in calling, "How's my little family?"

Janesta took a handful of bills from the envelope Slim had taped behind his Elvis picture, what he called his rainy-day fund, and hurried back to the bedroom. She put on jeans, heavy socks, her red sweater. She pulled open drawers and stuffed underwear into her big black purse. James was on his back in his crib, sobbing softly in his sleep. She pulled the quilt over him carefully. Kissed her fingertip, touching it to his chin so lightly she hoped his pale bluish lids would not flutter open in alarm, the siren of his cry would not start up again. But she couldn't resist some token of good-bye.

She watched James sleep, aware of the clock ticking loudly next to the bed where she would never sleep again. She would never curl up against Slim's warm chest. Would never lie with his arm heavy across her waist. Would never again wait for him to bring her coffee in bed on Sundays. Would never have to watch *The Wizard of Oz* again either, she realized, giddy with the thought as the Munchkins' song blared from the living room. Not even for old times' sake. And there would be no more babies.

"I don't want no more surprises," she had told the doctor.

"We'll fix you good," Doc Hastings had shouted over the baby's first cries. She woke up feeling as if she'd been hit by a semi, and there was Slim beside the bed holding a paper cone of daisies.

Janesta knew it wouldn't be enough to sit on a bar stool at the Rusty Anchor. Wouldn't be enough to stumble up the stairs with whoever happened to be at her elbow when she finally had enough to drink. Knew it wouldn't be enough to wake beside a stranger, a man who couldn't remember her name, who would cough and pull his pants up over his unwashed body or who would turn to her, ready for more, calling her "wild thing." Asking her how long she'd been in heat. Who would say he wanted one more ride and climb on her, not caring that she had a hangover, spreading her thighs, holding them open, pulling himself out of her and watching himself plunge back in as if he were alone, doing it all for himself, she was not even there, half asleep underneath him, sweat prickling her back, the sun already sinking, the band already tuning up downstairs. She knew this would not be enough to forget Slim Riley and his lopsided grin, his big gentle hands on her, asking, "Does this feel good? D'you like this?" His love felt like a thick membrane she had to burst through. She would have to fuck every man from Waukeag County clear the hell across Bragdon County up to and over the Canadian line and still it might not be enough to get that trailer out of her blood. It wouldn't be enough till she hit Quebec City. Till she could talk love talk in French with the men she met. Men she wouldn't even tell her name so they didn't have to worry about forgetting it. Maybe then she could forget the baby that grew in her, unwanted as a tumor. Maybe then she could forget the girl everyone whispered about, saying her mother dropped her on her head, calling her crazy. She wouldn't have to watch Crystal turn into a woman, all the while knowing she would always be a little girl. She could wash her hands good of being anybody's mother. Anybody's wife. Maybe by the time she was through, she'd be free of everyone's touch, everyone's whining hunger snatching at her. She'd be clean. She'd never look back.

Janesta stood in the hallway, her bag slung over her shoulder, the baby behind her, Crystal hunched on the bed chewing the hair she twirled around her forefinger. Janesta pressed her palms against the walls on either side of her, as if the trailer were closing in around her. She was watching Crystal, but in her mind she was already flinging snow off her car, scraping a circle in the icy windshield. She was already heading up Route One. The car warming up enough to unfreeze the wipers, the defroster blowing away her frozen breath. Two cartons of cigarettes on the dashboard, the tank full, the radio blasting.

"What d'you say we surprise Slim?" she said, slipping on the red down parka Slim gave her for Christmas. Not her style, but very warm she had to admit. She went back to her room to decide which shoes she could not live without. She tucked her red leather heels, the ones with rhinestone-studded bows, into the pockets of her parka. Crystal watched her mother take her car keys from the nail by the door and pull on her leather gloves.

"What d'you say I go get us some pizzas?" Janesta kissed the top of Crystal's head.

Crystal looked up, alarmed. "Pizza?" she whispered. "Pizza?"

*　　*　　*

Rainey knelt on the chair adding dots of red to the painting she was working on. Carol had already put hers aside. It wasn't finished, she just needed a break. It occurred to her as she watched Rainey that spending time with her was no different than spending time with a friend. Carol's mother behaved as if Carol's arrival had ruined her placid life. One disruption after another, the whole experience drudgery. But Carol savored her time with gentle Rainey.

Today, she put on her Vivaldi cassette. "It's supposed to sound like the four seasons," she explained.

"We can paint the music," Rainey said, moving her brush in rhythm with the violins. From time to time, she got up and danced around the room. Spontaneous, that was what children were. Carol realized this was what upset her mother. She was so rigid, every moment carefully planned.

Since that day she'd gone over and found Rita in bed, the stove unlit, the house smelling like an old wet campfire, Carol had been helping. She went back every day, comforting her, telling her she loved her, and slowly, Rita began to revive. Now she seemed to be flourishing. "I'm like some weed you pull up over and over again," she said. "But no matter what you do to it, throw it on the compost pile, give it to the sheep to eat, next spring, it comes right back."

Rita had answered an ad in the paper and was training to work at the nursing home as a CNA. Five mornings a week while Rainey was in school, she had classes. Every Thursday afternoon, Rainey spent at Carol's while Rita worked at The Manor, practicing her new skills. "At first I took the job because I could get it," Rita said. "Because it was here in town." But it turned out she liked it. She was even talking of nursing school.

Carol stirred the pot of barley soup that bubbled on the stove. Knowing Rita would come to get Rainey when she finished work, she had cooked something to entice her to stay for supper. Today, she made brownies, too. The sweet rich smell of chocolate filled the kitchen.

She imagined Dougie viewing the scene. "*Domestique,*" he would say in a funny French accent. Yesterday, he had called to tell her his latest escapade. Some doctor had picked him up by saying, "Nice buns," when Dougie was in front of the bread section at D'Agostino's. "I meet all the best guys at the grocery store," Dougie said. Carol hoped he'd be as happy with Dr. Love as she was with Rita.

Rainey dipped her brush in the water; the blob of red paint rose then dissipated like smoke. "It's done." Rainey held her picture up, surveying her work.

"How do you know?"

Rainey tilted her head as if to pick up a distant signal. "It just is." She got down from her chair to look at Carol's painting. It was of Annie. Only the top of her face was painted. The rest was sketched in with charcoal Carol had smudged, making her look as if she were fading.

"That's her?" Rainey pointed at the painting of Annie on the wall.

Carol nodded. She got up to take the brownies out of the oven.

"Is she real or your 'magination?" Rainey asked.

"Real."

Carol scraped the frozen steam from the window and peered out. It was snowing again and very windy. Already it was dark. Soon the headlights of the truck would sweep up the drive.

"What's her name?" Rainey asked. She climbed onto her chair to see the painting better.

"Annie."

"Oh," Rainey said. "Annie." Her mother knew a poem about a girl named Annie. She said it to Rainey sometimes, chasing her around the house crying, "The goblins'll get you if'n you don't watch out." Rainey loved it when her mother did this. She loved the shiver of fear just before her mother caught her.

"Where's she at?" Rainey carried the paintbrushes over to the sink.

"She died," Carol said. She was aware of her feet inside her slippers, of her toes wrapped in the thick wool of the red socks Rita had knitted her for Christmas. "No one ever made me anything," she said when she tore the package open. When she cried, Rita laughed and kissed her quickly on the lips. Now they had crossed into some new territory. To Carol, it felt like a long journey they had made by foot, unwieldy bundles in their arms and strapped to their backs. At this point, they were crossing a treacherous stretch. Like walking on the surface of Preacher's Lake, frozen now, with the thick snow she had swept aside to create a glassy place on which to glide.

Rainey chewed her fingernails. She looked at the photograph of her mother that Carol had hung beside the stove. She was holding a zinnia, the stem woven through her fingers.

"Did they all die?" Rainey asked in a small voice, barely a whisper.

"What?" Carol said.

"Did they all die?" Rainey asked again. She seemed fascinated by a strand of yarn that dangled from the sleeve of her sweater.

"What do you mean?"

"I mean all the black people. Did they all die?"

"What makes you think that?"

Rainey pulled the strand of yarn and her sleeve slowly unraveled a bit. "Did they?" she asked.

"No," Carol said. "There are millions of black people."

"Really?" Rainey fixed Carol with a startled stare.

"Whole neighborhoods of black people. Towns and countries where everybody's black. Millions and millions of black people."

"But how come . . ." Rainey's voice trailed off. She buried her face in the cat's thick fur. A vehicle approached, but it passed by and pulled into Slim's. Carol glanced at her watch. Any minute, she thought.

"How come what, Rainey?" Carol put her hands on Rainey's shoulders. Her back was very small, but sturdy like her mother's. Rainey shrugged and scooped the cat up, holding him like a baby.

"How come there's only pictures?"

"What do you mean, only pictures?"

"You know!" Rainey was exasperated. The cat, sensing her charged mood, leapt from her arms and scurried under the sofa.

Rainey pointed at the painting of Annie. She pointed at the one on the table. "In my book at home, in *Peter's Chair,* there's some more."

"Yeah?" Carol said. She wasn't sure what point Rainey was making.

"If there's millions and millions, where'd they all go?" She turned in a slow circle, her arms out to the side, her eyes squeezed shut. She often did this until she became so dizzy she fell down. She liked watching the way everything kept moving while she stayed still.

"Black people are everywhere. Just not here," Carol said.

"How come?" Rainey was on her back, her knees drawn up to her chest, the room tilting and whirling around as she watched.

Carol couldn't imagine how to explain it. She would have to describe where Africa was. She would need to tell about slave ships, cotton plantations, the Civil War. She would have to tell about the migration to the cities, segregation, integration, civil rights.

"I don't know," she finally said.

"You don't?" Rainey stared at her steadily. The wind rattled the windowpanes and the old house trembled as if shivering from the cold.

"Well, I know some of it. But it's a long story," Carol said.

"Will you tell me it?"

"I'll try." Carol sighed heavily. "One of these days, I'll try." The wind was howling so loudly it reminded her of the subway barreling out of the tunnel. The lights flickered, once, twice, and went out.

"Hey," Rainey said. "Hey, what happened?"

Just then the headlights from the truck lit up the room. Rita was at the back door, stamping her feet. Under her jacket, she wore her uniform: pale blue pants and a matching smock. She looked very tired.

"The lights just went out," Carol said. She held a candle up and motioned Rita inside. "I made soup," she said. "And brownies."

Rita smiled. "Is that an invitation?" she asked.

* * *

Janesta's car was gone. Slim could see that when he pulled into the driveway, his headlights shining on the tracks her tires had left in the snow, still clearly visible despite the new snow that was falling.

The baby lay on the floor, chewing a red rubber teething ring. "Ba-ba-ba," he said. He waved his arms excitedly. Usually when Slim came home, James was in his crib crying. And Janesta was sitting in her chair looking extremely bored.

"Where's your mom?" he asked Crystal. His glasses fogged up but he didn't bother to remove them. He kicked off his boots and hung his parka by the door, dropping his hat and gloves near the stove to dry.

"Where's your mom?" he asked again. He tossed a log on the fire.

"Shh!" Crystal said. On the TV, Dorothy and her friends were asleep in the poppies.

Slim wiped his glasses on his shirttail and grabbed the remote key. He put the video on pause.

"Slim!" Crystal was indignant. She stood on her tiptoes, but Slim held it out of reach. "I like that part." She pouted.

"In a minute," he said.

There was a depression in the chair where Janesta always sat. Slim expected it to feel warm, but it didn't feel like anything. Her perfume wafted around him as he pushed the afghan aside.

James flung the rubber ring across the room then attempted to scoot after it. Everybody said he was much too young to be crawling, but there he was, propped up on his hands and knees, rocking back and forth as if by doing so he would gain momentum and soon be on his way.

"She went to get pizza," Crystal announced. She crawled across the floor talking baby talk and retrieved the toy for James. Then she crawled over to Slim and reached for the remote. "Gimme it," she said.

"When'd she go? A minute ago? An hour? She been gone all day?"

"I dunno," Crystal whined. "We had mashed potatoes."

The movie started again and Slim did not stop it. They sat watching it together, Crystal leaning against Slim, clutching the rough cloth of his loose pants. The baby made his babbling sounds, turning his head this way and that, waving his arms as if he were giving an important speech. The wind whistled and howled, rocking the trailer, and the icy snow was like sand hitting the windows. The lights flickered, the TV screen filled with static, then the room grew dark.

* * *

Michael and Lizzy had no idea the power was out since they had no electricity to begin with. The kerosene lamps were lit. They had just finished eating an omelet and the dishes were in the sink. Miss Kitty was sprawled on the floor in front of the woodstove, passed out from the heat. Michael's shadow flickered across the wall when he knelt at Lizzy's feet, burrowing his face in her lap. She stopped rocking the chair, her toes poised, holding it steady.

"Let's go to bed," he murmured.

"It's not even seven o'clock," she said. At seven o'clock, Aran informed her, she and Kaye would watch *Lois and Clark*. The two of them side by side in front of the TV, laughing their identical laughs, turning to look at each other lovingly with their identical blue eyes. She didn't think she could stand it much longer.

Michael nibbled at her jeans, pulling at the seams with his teeth. "Grrrr," he said. He caught hold of her belt loops. The lamplight fell on his bald spot. She could see each hair follicle around it, as if it were distinctly drawn with black ink. She had the urge to grab his thin hair and yank his head up. To scream: No! I can't go on like this. Like superwoman, she would fling Michael across the room as if he were as light as the snow endlessly falling. Then she would fly into Union City, yank the door off Kaye's apartment, and grab Aran up in her arms. Aran would laugh with delight as they zoomed overhead.

Michael stroked her thighs, pushing them apart. He eased her zipper down. Maybe if she didn't react, he would stop. He would get the hint. He would walk over to the sofa, pull the rubber band off the evening paper, snap it open in front of his face. Puzzled at first by his sudden change of heart, he would quickly settle down. But he continued, oblivious to Lizzy's lack of participation.

"C'mon." Michael tugged her out of the chair. His eyes were dreamy with longing. She noticed the bulge in his trousers. She let him lead her upstairs. I am no different from the teenagers at the clinic, she thought. I have no idea how to say no. Or yes, for that matter.

Lizzy often had the feeling that Michael was practicing, perfecting his techniques, preparing to lure Kaye back home with his newfound sexual prowess. Though he kissed her with great care, it felt fake, as if he were trying too hard, and he repeated her name so often she was certain it was not her body he plunged into with a yelp, but Kaye's. It was the idea of Kaye in his arms that set the bed rocking.

Michael paused, a grimace on his face. He bit his lip as he reached down to press himself in some secret place between his legs. He claimed if he did this in time, he could delay his orgasm. He waited, chewing his moustache. He would look this same way if someone held a gun to his head, Lizzy thought. Then he began pumping again.

Lizzy didn't know why it was so important to make the ordeal last longer. That's how she thought of it: the ordeal. Denny confessed once that he listed the names of the presidents, saying them in chronological order, backwards and forwards, to distract himself while they made love. She never admitted she had been busy pretending he was Harrison Ford.

Lizzy didn't know what ran through Michael's mind as he struggled with his performance; perhaps he calculated complex equations or quoted geological facts. She was too busy enticing Tom Cruise to bother with Michael. Ever since Lizzy learned from a magazine she was flipping through at the grocery store that he was extremely short—in fact, Tom Cruise was only a half inch taller than she was—the idea of making love to him made her swoon. A lover whose eyes she could gaze directly into without tipping her head at an awkward angle, without having to lie in bed with her toes bumping his knees or her face being tickled by his chest hairs. In her fantasies, she and Tom Cruise lay in each other's arms, gazing into each other's eyes, their toes entwined, all their parts fitting perfectly. The thought of this could push her over the edge.

She lay beneath Michael, moving in a way she knew would please Tom Cruise, all the while thinking how ironic it was, the two of them, their bodies in such an intimate embrace, working so hard to be somewhere else.

*   *   *

When the lights went out, Slim scooped the baby up, settled him on his lap, and wrapped an arm around Crystal. He felt as if they were stranded on a ship at sea and their survival was up to him.

"What's wrong with me?" Crystal asked. She bumped her head against Slim and began to rock side to side.

"What're you talkin' about?" Slim blew his nose noisily. He thought of the lion wanting to be courageous, wiping his tears with his tail.

"Am I like the Scarecrow?"

"You'll have to say more, sister. I don't know what you mean." Slim was trying furiously to conjure up the sound of Janesta's car approaching, the familiar whine of her fan belt. Any minute, she would be coming through the door carrying a white box. The room would fill with the tantalizing scent of tomato sauce and pepperoni. "I got froufrou beer," she'd say.

"I don't got no brains." Crystal knocked her fist against her head.

"Oh, go on. 'Course you got brains."

She shook her head vigorously and the baby imitated her.

"Look at James," Slim said.

Crystal nodded and the baby nodded, too. It surprised Slim how light the room was; something about the white snow outside made it glow.

"Everybody's got brains," Slim said.

"Not me."

"Even you. It's brains that make you do everything. You couldn't even shake your head if it was empty inside. Besides. The

Scarecrow's always worried about how he's not smart enough, but he's the one that always comes up with the good ideas. Ain't you ever noticed that?"

"Idee-die-die. James needs a new diaper."

"You wouldn't know that if you had no brains."

"He's a stinker," Crystal said.

"You wouldn't smell it without your brains."

"OK." She jumped up and fumbled through the drawer for the flashlight. Shotgun barked, leaping at her feet, trying to catch the light she flashed across the room like a strobe.

Slim pulled a clean diaper from the box on the counter and put the baby on a pile of old clothes that the dog had pulled from one of the bags. He yanked the dirty diaper off and tossed it into the corner, meaning to pick it up later. James kicked his legs, happy to be free.

"We already got pizza." Crystal had the freezer door open and was flashing the light on the stack of pizzas he'd brought home last week.

"See," Slim said, working to keep the tears out of his voice. "You're smart, just like I said. Really, really smart."

*　　*　　*

"What'd you practice today?" Carol asked as she cleared the table.

"Blood pressures, temperatures, and pulses. Mrs. Thomas has such a slow pulse I had to get my supervisor to recheck it. There's such a long wait between each beat, I was afraid I was doing it wrong."

Rita held Rainey's painting, turning it toward the circle of light the candles threw on the table.

"It's the seasons," Rainey explained. In the scene for fall, the tree was covered with red leaves and on the ground, a heap of red leaves nearly buried the trunk. The summer tree was bright green dotted with red apples. In spring, the tree was covered with pink and yellow blossoms. The winter tree was set against a bleak white background, the black branches bare.

"We'd better go," Rita said, scraping back her chair. When she got up, she checked the narcissus bulbs she had given Carol. The long white roots were twined around the pebbles in the glass. The first green shoots had appeared.

"Do you have to?" Carol said. She came around behind Rita and hugged her. It still surprised her that she could do this, and that

Rita turned in the circle of her arms and hugged her back. She sighed deeply.

"We forgot to have brownies," Rainey announced. "Hey, you guys. You guys," she said, trying to get their attention. She grabbed their legs and hugged tightly.

When Rita kissed Carol, her lips were very soft and warm.

"Some other time," Rita said. "Soon."

"Do you really mean that?"

Rita nodded. "I really want that," she said. She leaned forward and kissed Carol again.

*   *   *

Michael snored loudly, one arm flung across Lizzy, pinning her down. She slipped out from under it, pulled her clothes on, and crept downstairs, careful to avoid the places that creaked. She pulled the door open and stared at the wide white expanse. Snow, like layers of meringue drifting in peaks across the clearing, was laden on the tree branches. Untouched, unsoiled, unlike her life, which felt tramped upon, zigzagged with footprints and tire ruts, bird tracks and pee stains the way the snow would be by the end of the day.

She yanked her boots on, zipped her parka up to her chin, and stepped out into it. She hated to ruin the perfection, but she had to be outside. She didn't know if the moon was rising or setting. Lately, she had not been paying attention to things like that. She stumbled forward, scissoring her legs through the deep snow. Soon, it would be morning. She would wash herself at the sink, heating water to pour over her hair, dressing in a clean sweater and pants. She and Michael would have oatmeal and coffee; then, they would drive through the snow to town. That night, he would pick Aran up from Kaye's and bring her home. Lizzy told herself this was all that mattered.

She passed Pinky's cage, thinking at first that a pile of snow had drifted inside, but when she looked more carefully, she saw that two bunnies, each smaller than her hand, were lying side by side, their nearly furless bodies frozen stiff. Pinky was huddled in the nesting box, her chin resting on her ruff. Lizzy wondered if there were more bunnies underneath, protected by her warmth. Had Pinky tried to keep these two alive? Or had she pushed them deliberately out into the cold?

Part Three

31

Crystal waited in the bus shelter Slim made at the end of his driveway, an A-frame built out of slabs from the sawmill. The cold winter wind whipping up the hill made her shiver as she shifted from foot to foot, clutching her Beatles lunch box. Rainey huddled on the bench chewing clumps of snow from her mittens. It was still dark out, though the sky was stained a pale lavender.

"My mom lets me put lotion on her back," Crystal said. Her breath came out in cartoonlike puffs. "She's got a bunch of places she can't get at and I reach up under her sweater and scratch and scratch. She unhitches her bra. 'Ahh,' she goes. Then I scratch where the straps make them dents, you know what I mean? I scratch and scratch like I do when Shotgun wants me to scratch his ears and then he rolls over and cries till I do his belly. I scratch and scratch. Sometimes Mom gets goose bumps on her arms when I put lotion on. 'Rub it 'tween your hands first, Crystal. That's wicked cold,' she says. So I smear it in my hands good, then I rub it in. You seen that show they had last night, that lady about screamed her head off? That was some scary. My mom's getting us pizza. D'you like pizza? My mom's got a little toe she can stick straight out the side of her foot. Only her left foot does that. The other foot's regular. All curled up the way pinky toes are. Me and my mom got the exact same feet only mine're smaller. Her second toe's longer'n her big toe. Same as me. She says that's a sign of something but I disremember what. My pinky toe don't move like hers does, but I can wrap my leg clear around my neck. I can only do my left leg thataway. My mom used to could do that but when you get old the way she is you just can't do some things. My mom's thirty-seven. She goes, 'Just don't make me no grandma 'fore I'm forty.' I'm not plannin' on that. No way. No sir. That's gross."

Rainey leaned forward to watch the school bus come up the hill. When the door whooshed open, she climbed up after Crystal. They were the first ones on and they always sat behind the bus driver, Pearl Whitcomb.

"My mom lets me put lotion on her back," Crystal said.

"That so?" Pearl called, her voice nearly obscured by the motor. Crystal had been telling this same story for days. Pearl was afraid the bus would stall and she would sit there repeating it until her mouth froze mid-sentence. This morning it was so cold she had been afraid the bus wouldn't start. Now she kept her foot heavy on the gas pedal. She had a recurring nightmare that the bus, loaded with children, stalled before they could get to the bottom of Preacher's Lake Road.

"Rub it 'tween your hands first, Crystal, that's mighty cold," Crystal said as they pulled up to where the Jordan boys waited, their bare heads ducked into their collars, their ears flaming red.

* * *

Carol flicked on her turn signal as she approached Moody's. Then on second thought, she kept going, deterred by the idea of Mrs. Moody's stern expression as Carol heaped packages of super tampons and extra-long overnight maxi pads with wings onto the counter. Maybe if she weren't already *having* her period, she could do it. But she hated the notion of public scrutiny: Mrs. Moody—squinting over at Carol's pale puffy face, her lackluster eyes, her dazed shuffle—would take her time putting it all in some flimsy see-through shopping bag. Carol used to laugh when her mother drove to Pittsfield for Carol's supplies. Now she understood. At least the cashier at La Verdierre's would be a stranger.

Carol's mother had ushered her into her bedroom to explain what she called "the workings of the female body." It could have been performance art, Carol thought. Her mother holding up her fist to demonstrate the uterus's size, her voice unnaturally calm, the words dull and overpracticed, her face pink with embarrassment as she demonstrated where the napkin went, holding it between her legs over her gray wool slacks while Carol perched on the end of the bed, watching the reflection of her mother in the vanity mirror, unable to meet her mother's eyes.

Carol had been sure she knew it all anyway. The girls in her class had already been ushered into the auditorium, gathered on the plush seats where just the week before there had been a magic show, this time to see the requisite filmstrip. She just didn't get why all of a sudden they had to improve their posture instead of playing kick ball. For Carol, it came late, the first bleeding. She had plenty of time to grow used to the idea. Time enough not to be yoked by the curse of it. Now the whole business was ending. Going out with a bang, she thought, moaning at the cramps that racked her lower body. In the paper recently she'd read that the average woman had five hundred periods. She wished she'd been keeping track. Who knows, she thought, maybe this is my last hurrah.

* * *

Lizzy did her best to fit into the life Michael and Kaye set up for Aran. She would help Aran pack her things and play games with her as they waited for Kaye to arrive at what she called "the appointed hour" though sometimes what had been promised as early afternoon dragged on into evening, and no amount of Parcheesi or Chutes and Ladders could keep Aran from rushing anxiously to the window every time a car passed down the dirt road. Kaye never apologized or offered an excuse. "Get a phone," she said when Michael complained at Lizzy's urging.

And when it was time for Aran to be brought back home, Lizzy would be there waiting, never knowing for sure when she would hear the car pull up, the door slam, or whether Aran would trudge down the path sobbing or skip toward her with her hands full of gifts.

Lizzy made cupcakes with blue icing. New dresses trimmed with lace. Aran's favorite Beanee Weenies night after night. She played beauty parlor, letting Aran style her hair, the soap bubbles sliding down Lizzy's back, into her eyes. They played movie star; Lizzy took endless photos of Aran perched on the kitchen table with her legs crossed, leaning seductively against the sofa clutching Miss Kitty, who was squirming to get out of the clothes Aran had dressed her in.

Still, Aran showed signs of the distress in her life. She would fling herself on the floor screaming when she couldn't tie her shoelaces and kick the floor with such fury Lizzy couldn't help her, thrashing until she collapsed in exhaustion and the school bus roared down the road without her. She begged for a baby bottle until Michael gave in. In the mornings, her bed was wet. Lizzy tried to interest Aran in new activities: finger painting, paper dolls, a walk down to the lake to slide on the ice. She even bought figure skates and a red velvet skating skirt. But Aran preferred to lie on the sofa refusing to do anything. "No!" she would say, no matter what Lizzy proposed.

In the evenings, she would explode in a torrent of "Why don't we haves?" "Why don't we have a TV like everybody in the whole world has? Why don't we have a flush toilet and a real bathtub and shower? Why don't we have a phone so I can call Mommy up?" She would shout until Michael gave up. With his shoulders sagging, his jaw clenched, he would slam out the door, hurry down the icy path to his truck and take off.

A few days after returning from Kaye's, Aran would become docile and affectionate. Run down the stairs to greet her father when he came home from work. Help Lizzy feed the rabbits without worrying about getting manure on her boots. Placidly roll cookie dough, carefully cutting the stars. Tease Miss Kitty with a ball of yarn. Then it would start again. Lizzy would stand at the window watching Aran walk to Kaye's car, her thumb in her mouth, disconsolately kicking the snow.

*   *   *

Hydie had gone ice fishing, but Trudy had not been in the mood to close up even though the shadows of the bare trees slanting across the snow foretold the coming dark. She looked up from her magazine when Joe walked in, noticing his puffy down-filled jacket with the sleeves too long. He didn't look like a tourist. Besides, it was February. The worst month of the year, as far as she was concerned. A month to be slept through. What's for a tourist to see up here now, she thought as the man sat at the counter. In Rip's seat. Good thing he's already come and gone, she thought. The last time a stranger sat there he complained for weeks, wanting Hydie to put a RESERVED sign on the stool. He'd actually gotten out his kerchief and dusted it, as if the man who'd sat there eating codfish and boiled potatoes had cooties.

"What can I get you?" Trudy asked.

"A cup of coffee would be nice. That pie looks good, too."

Trudy beamed. She was proud of her pies and these last ones had come out especially well, the crusts flaky and perfectly browned.

"Thank you," she said, taking a better look at the man. He was older than she'd thought at first. There was a bit of gray in his dark curls and the creases near his eyes showed his age.

"Visitin' up here?" she asked, serving the blueberry pie he'd selected after she told him the berries had been picked down the road.

"Sorry," he said. He stood up quickly, letting his jacket fall to the floor, and offered his hand. "Where are my manners? I've just been on my own so much lately, I'm practically uncivilized. I'm Joe Philbrook. The new minister. Over at the community church."

"Well, my goodness gracious." Trudy was so excited she had to clasp her hands over her breast to calm herself. "There's been talk of a preacher comin', but I didn't believe my ears. Lord have mercy, Reverend Philbrook, it's good to see you." She pumped his hand. When she finally let go, Joe felt a glow, a hum of hope. Here's one, he thought. He had worried there would be no one the first Sunday he preached.

So far, he'd cleared away the snow and pulled the boards off the windows. But inside, the sanctuary was a mess. Chunks of plaster strewn across the dusty pews, crashed in heaps on the floor. Boxes of hymnals stained with damp, the pages chewed by mice that strolled freely down the threadbare carpet and scampered behind the altar.

"I've been thinking of having a churchwarming," he said, pleased with this woman who watched him eat as if he himself were something delicious.

"Come again?" Trudy patted her thick cone of lacquered hair.

"A churchwarming. You know how when people move into a new house they have housewarmings and invite all their friends and relatives?"

"Yeah. I believe they did that kind of thing when my momma was startin' out. Like a barnraisin', would that be?" She was wondering if she could get this man to visit her mother in the nursing home.

"That's my son," Trudy said when Raymond began to sweep the floor. "Raymond, honey. That floor's already clean. Don't you be disturbin' this gentleman. He's our new preacher."

Raymond leaned the broom against the counter, wiped his hands on his pants, and offered his thin pale hand.

"Pleased to meet you," Joe said.

Raymond giggled and hid his eyes.

"Now what are you sayin' about this churchwarming?" Trudy asked. She had decided long ago to act as if everything Raymond did was perfectly normal. She figured if she behaved this way, other people would too. Even though he was making his goofy sounds, half gagging the way he did when he was nervous, she did not react.

"The church is so drafty, heating it will surely break the budget."

"I'm tellin' you. That's how it first started goin' downhill. Nobody wanted to cough up for oil, especially during that oil crisis. First it was closed for the winters. Then it was closed year-round. We have to go over the bridge to church if we go at all. Hydie—that's my husband. He's off ice fishin' on Preacher's Lake or he'd be happy to meet you. He says, 'Trudy, I'm tired on Sunday. I don't wanna drive any twenty miles there and twenty miles back to go to church with a bunch of strangers.' I'm lucky to get him there Easter and Christmas."

"We could hook up that woodstove in the back room. It's in pretty good shape. But I need somebody to check the chimney."

"That'd be Michael McDonnough. He lives up near Preacher's Hill. He don't have a phone, but if you drive up there you'll see his sign. Or else leave a message at Buster's. He checks in there for work. Hey, I betcha they'd fix you up with the stovepipe. Mildred'll get Binky to donate it. Binky's her and Buster's son. There was a time when she was head of the Ladies Aid Committee. I'll get on the horn and tell her you're here. She don't get around much, 'specially with this nasty weather. Ain't it wicked cold? Say, what about your wife and family?"

"It's just me. I'm single."

"Oh." Trudy squinched up her face and appraised him.

"I would appreciate your help," he said, worried he had disappointed her. That the fact of his aloneness would put her off.

"I don't mean to pry. It don't make a speck of difference. I just never did hear of a pastor without a wife and kids."

"Well, here's one." His eyes took on a sheen of friendliness. Trudy thought she would melt with him looking at her like that.

"It's just a matter of time," she said. "But say, that idea of using wood's a good one. Oil's so high on account of them Arabs hoardin' it. Besides, who knows what shape that old furnace's in. That was put in way back before me and Hydie was married. I ain't fixin' to tell you how long ago that was." She laughed. "You'll need wood. It's hard to get any wood now unless you haul deadwood out yourself."

"That's where the churchwarming idea comes in. I was thinking, you know, how there's always the offering? There's nothing that says it has to be money. If we could get people to bring firewood, then we'd have enough heat to warm ourselves. The children could bring kindling." He rocked on the seat, thrashing at his hair. Trudy almost put her hands over his the way she would if Raymond were doing something annoying when they were alone. Only she was not annoyed. It had just been a while since she'd spent any time with someone who was so excited.

"I'll be there. You can count on me. Wood we got." She nodded at the stove behind him. "I'll get some of the womenfolk over to help you clean up. And I'll tell everybody. We see most everybody in here at one time or another. You just say when, Reverend. I'll bring pies for coffee hour. Coffee, too, if you need it."

* * *

Slim opened the freezer. "Hungry Man or beans and franks?"

"Pizza," Crystal said.

"We don't got no more pizza. Tomorrow, I'll pick some more up." As Slim opened the can of beans, the cats appeared and rubbed against his legs, swishing their tails. "Didn't you feed 'em?" he asked.

"Shh. It's getting good now." Crystal clutched her skirt and held it up to her face, peering over it at the TV show. She was wearing Janesta's red dress again over her long johns, the straps pinned to her shoulders, the bodice flopping. On the counter, there was another note from her teacher. "Crystal's clothes are inappropriate," it said. Slim crumpled it up and tossed it in the direction of the trash he'd been meaning to empty all week. While he was at work, the cats had got into it and there was a mess of empty cans and dirty diapers strewn across the floor. He was so tired and discouraged, but at night he could hardly sleep. The nights were terrible. He'd crawl into bed weary, his eyes aching and itchy from unshed tears and just lie there missing Janesta. The night before, he knelt in front of her shoes. He slipped his hands into each one as if searching for her warmth still lingering there.

On the TV, the hero was speeding toward a warehouse where the killer waited, his gun held ready. Suddenly a woman was smiling, telling about a new cleaning product.

"What'd you have for dinner?" Crystal asked.

"The usual. A ham sandwich."

"We had meat loaf. Dog food with catsup on it if you ask me. God. It was gross." She made gagging sounds. "I had to drink me three Cokes to get the taste outa my mouth when I got to home."

"Three Cokes? I told you one's enough. You'll stay up all night."

"They got acid rain up in Canada," she said. "You know that Slim?"

"Yes. That's not even news, Crystal." He sighed and dropped the hot dogs into boiling water. James was on the floor with a teaspoon and a cup of water that Slim had given him to play with.

"Keep it in the basin like I showed you," he said, putting the cup back in the basin.

"They had this lady on the TV that hung up her clothes on the line and it rained on 'em and before she could get 'em in the house that acid rain took the color right out of 'em. We got any acid rain?"

"I imagine so. Stuff like that's everywhere now."

Slim warmed a jar of baby food and mashed a bowl of beans he put on the tray of the high chair. Lately, James wanted to feed himself, scooping the food into his mouth with his hands.

When Crystal grabbed one of her legs, attempting to wrap it around her neck, James clapped and shrieked as if he were watching a circus act. He fell over on his back, rolling in the piles of clothes. He pulled out a pair of underpants and put them on his head. Shotgun barked happily and licked the baby's face, looking up as if expecting approval.

*   *   *

"The whale just swallowed him up?" Rainey asked.

"Yes. It just swallowed him up," Rita explained.

"But he didn't get hurt?"

"No, see here he is. Here's Jonah. Doesn't he look OK to you?"

Rainey studied the picture. "So how come God did that?"

"I think it was because God wanted Jonah to go to Ninevah, but Jonah didn't want to. He was trying to hide from God."

"Why didn't he wanna go?"

"Well, the people there were different from him. It was a different country. He was scared of them."

"Are people scared of me?"

"No, sweetie. I don't think so."

"But I'm different."

"Yeah, well." Rita sighed. She wished she could explain things better. She wished she could shield Rainey somehow. "We're all different. In big ways and small ways, too. But God loves us all."

"Does God want me to do something?"

"Are you worried about a whale swallowing you up?" Rita gave Rainey a hug. Reading Bible stories was Rita's way of dealing with not taking Rainey to church. They'd driven into Union City a few times, attending the Congregational Church behind the courthouse where the minister, who called himself Pastor Pat, worked hard at telling amusing anecdotes, almost as if he thought his job was to be a stand-up comic. It seemed harmless enough. And it pleased Rainey to go. But one morning during the children's sermon, Pastor Pat asked them to imagine their parents had a video camera on all the time, recording everything they did. He held one up to demonstrate, aiming it at the kids who sat at his feet. "You'd be good then, wouldn't you?" He peered through the camera, then lurched into an explanation of how God was just like that video camera, watching everything. The children were so innocent, so easily harmed, it seemed unfair to instill them with guilt. Rita was relieved to see that Rainey was studying the huge white floppy bow the girl beside her wore instead of following Pastor Pat's sermon. Rita decided that the next Sunday they would sleep late. She would make pancakes shaped like animals, cocoa with marshmallows, anything to skip church.

Rita wanted to be a good mother, but sometimes she felt crushed under the burden of responsibility. Half the time she was worrying about bills, not giving Rainey her full attention. Just coping with the day-to-day necessities was daunting, not to mention the anxiety of being responsible for shaping and guiding another person's life.

"But how can he breathe in there?" Rainey asked. She was still studying the illustrations of her book.

"It's a story, Rainey. It's not like it really happened."

"Did I breathe when I was inside you?" She patted Rita's belly.

"Well, you know how I told you about the umbilical cord? It's attached to the mom and the baby. The baby gets all she needs from that. That's where your belly button comes from, remember?"

Rainey pulled out her copy of *How Babies Are Made*.

"Read me it," she said.

Rita was happy to be finished with Jonah and his troubles. It was much easier to talk about reproduction.

* * *

"They're going to start having services at that church," Lizzy said to Michael. "J.T.'s been talking about going." They were driving home in the dark, Aran asleep with her head on Lizzy's lap, her mouth open, making a wet spot on Lizzy's coat.

"To church," Michael said. "You want to go to church?"

"I didn't say that. You never listen."

"What *did* you say?"

Lizzy was silent. "I'm thinking of moving out," she finally said.

"Because I don't want to go to church?"

"No," she said, exasperated. It was hopeless to try to talk to him about anything. She'd just keep her plans to herself. Already, she'd begun circling possibilities in the paper. She'd driven out on the Joyville Road and seen a log cabin. But it had no running water and gaslights. If she was going to leave, at least she wanted a bathtub.

"You know I'm a Catholic. Lapsed, that is. Church is not for me."

"I'm practically an atheist," she screamed, not even caring that she disturbed Aran who sat up rubbing her eyes.

Michael didn't know what Lizzy wanted. As they bounced along the dirt road, he tried to picture himself at home without Lizzy. Just him and Aran. By himself when Aran went to Kaye's. He didn't like what he saw.

32

"Well, if it ain't the boss," Rip said as Clarence Cushman came into the diner. "Our very own personal private town selectman. Would you be slummin' it Clarence, my boy?"

Ever since Clarence served on a committee that decided to stop graveling the road to Rip's camp yet pave the one that led to his own, Rip was so angry he had been threatening to run for office himself.

Clarence slapped Rip with his rolled-up newspaper. "Good to see you too." He waved at Hydie with his fake politician's flick of the wrist.

"Selectman one day, governor the next," Rip said. "Cushy Cushman."

"So what in hell's goin' on about the dump?" Buster asked. "Slim Riley's all worked up." He remembered the expression on Slim's face whenever he talked about it. Like he'd seen his own ghost, Coalie said.

"We're closing it. The Preacher's Lake landfill's got to go."

"Closin' it? What're folks gonna do with their trash? Fling it out the back door the way my granddad did?"

Clarence looked at Buster as if he had lost his mind. "We're setting up a transfer station," he said deliberately slowing his speech.

"What in Sam's hell's that?"

"We'll close the dump. Put fill over it. Clean it up, monitor it. You know the state's behind this, not me." He smacked his newspaper as if the evidence was printed therein. "As independent as down easters are, folks aren't fighting it. All over the state of Maine, they're going along with it. They closed down the Bragdon dump last spring and so far nobody's so much as thrown a cigarette butt on it." He took a bite of the scrambled eggs Hydie brought him. On Saturday, when Trudy was at her art class, Hydie served.

"Up in Bragdon, they had the dump in an old quarry. Ours here is in a gravel pit. That's lucky. It'll be a heck of a lot easier to cap without a lot of monitoring because there are no brooks running through. Not a lot of groundwater to speak of. What they do is sink wells and test for leakage. You know, pollution and all. We got to protect our resources. We *are* Vacationland," he said.

"What about Slim Riley?" Rip asked.

"What about him?"

"What's he supposed to do?"

"He can get another odd job."

"Keepin' the dump ain't any kind of odd job for Slim Riley. It's what you call his vocation. His calling. Don't he mean a thing to you fellas?" Rip combed his beard furiously, his rheumy eyes flashing.

"I can't really say what'll happen to Slim." Clarence dabbed his mouth. "He'll most likely go on to something else. We'll need someone at the transfer station. But he'd have to apply for the job same as anybody else. And he won't be able to pick the trash and make a mess practically living there the way he does now if he's hired. But it's a job. Two days a week is all we'll need. There's already this young fellow from Lewiston interested. I talked to him when I was in Augusta. He's intelligent. He took some courses. He'd be a real asset."

"A real *ass,* did you say?" Rip shook his fist. "There must be somethin' for Slim to do. Christ, that wife of his up and left. He's got them two kids to take care of and he's soon to be out of work."

"He's worried over Slim. We all are," Hydie said.

"The committee was everyone from professionals to fishermen. It was their decision, not mine. It's all much neater and cleaner. We'll charge by the bag. That'll encourage recycling. No one wants to get stuck paying for what they don't have to. Besides, with recycling you make money." He brushed his hands as if to say: That's the end of it.

"So what happens then?" Buster asked. "The trash still goes somewheres, right?"

"It goes to a receiving station. They truck it out to consolidated landfills. It's all big business now. The garbage business. They got conferences and men with degrees studying up on it. A regular science."

"That's a crock! All I know's it's hurtin' Slim Riley. He's had enough trouble." Rip almost mentioned that Slim had to bring the baby to work. Then he realized Clarence would have a fit if he knew.

"Three hundred and thirty landfills'll close by the deadline," Clarence said. "We're just one out of that many. Cripes, we've been on that site going on fifty years. What'll happen if we keep adding to it? A mountain of garbage with who knows what going on underneath."

"Didn't they build New York City on top of trash?" Hydie asked. "Didn't they have something on the TV the other night about that?"

"Yes sir," Coalie said. "Half the cities're built on swamps they filled with garbage. Everything from apple cores to dead animals as far as I can tell. They flung it in the swamp and waited for it to fill up."

"That was then and this is now. We're smarter. We got more sophisticated means of dealing with our garbage," Clarence said. "Eventually, we'll take the fence down. It'll be landscaped. We could be done by the end of summer. This town's fortunate to own the fifty acres at that site so we can set up the transfer station right there."

"It ain't right. That's all I got to say. How much you figure to make on all this, Clarence?" Rip asked.

Clarence held up his hands as if Rip had pulled a gun. "Like I said, it's happening all over. Read the paper. Hell, call the governor. I'm following orders. I'm taking care of it the best I can. In a few years, you'll thank me. We'll have a park for the kids, swings and all. You won't even remember what it used to be like," he said as he walked out the door, clapping his hat carefully over his head.

"Remember what happened to Vera Smith? After Henry left her with them three kids?" Coalie said.

"She was too damn proud to go on welfare. Them kids pretty near starved to death before they ended up in foster homes," Buster said.

"That won't happen to Slim," Hydie said. "We won't let it."

"All I know is Clarence Cushman's meaner than turkey turd beer," Rip said. He looked out the window. It was snowing sideways now, it seemed, the way the wind was blowing.

*   *   *

Carol stared through the classroom window at the snow-covered fields. She was sorry she had arrived early. It was better to be late. Then the students could worry if she'd show up instead of her thinking no one would. Steam knocked in the radiators and the sun glinted on the snow. Her plan to have them all draw a quick self-portrait now seemed ridiculous. People could never see themselves. They'd probably run to the bathroom for a glance in the mirror. Or squint into their compacts, anxiously rubbing out the noses they tried to shape on the page.

Sophia Friedman, her first art teacher, had made them close their eyes and listen to a tape recording of what sounded like someone flinging a baby against a piano while a street sweeper cleaned up after a parade. When they opened their eyes, they painted, using the colors Sophia had set out for them on their palettes. Carol had loved it. It made her feel like there was a long corridor inside her and someone had flung open all the doors. Anything could happen. But she wasn't sure the Art Can Be Fun class would enjoy such an exercise, even if she had a copy of the tape. She jumped when the steel doors slammed and voices echoed.

"She a real artist," Trudy was saying. "All the way from New York."

Carol stuck her head out the door and waved. Before they had a chance to gossip about her, she wanted them to know she was listening.

"There she is!" Trudy shouted, huffing and puffing as she hurried past the beige lockers, her shoes squeaking on the beige linoleum. Dressed in her beige slacks and beige parka, Trudy appeared as if she were attempting to extricate herself from a thick wad of Silly Putty. It gave Carol vertigo to watch her approach. She focused on the woman at Trudy's side, a large woman swaddled in thick black fur.

"Hi, de-ah," Trudy said. She grabbed her friend's coat sleeve as if she were about to fall on slick ice and needed to steady herself. "This here's Tammy Bridges."

Tammy's smile revealed ill-fitting false teeth she pushed back into place with her thumb. Carol remembered the time she and Annie went to the Smithsonian to see George Washington's wooden teeth. When they asked where they were exhibited, the woman at the desk looked it up in a guide thick as the Manhattan phone book and announced they'd been stolen.

Trudy was staring at her quizzically. Apparently she'd asked Carol a question. Things were not getting off to a good start.

"I'm sorry, Trudy. Did you ask me something?"

"I was askin' you did you hear we got us a preacher here in town?"

"No. I didn't know that."

"We've started havin' services. Tammy here plays the organ."

Carol was distracted by loud laughter in the hallway. Three women hurried up, followed by a fourth who wore a turquoise cap dotted with sequins.

"It's the old gang." Trudy bustled over to greet her friends. She introduced them to Carol who immediately forgot who was who. Was that Ellen or Barbara with the sparkly cap? Did Becky or Pamela say she was the mortician's wife? Suze was the skinny one in red pants. Suze, not Sue. While they were talking, several more people slipped in the door. When everyone had arrived, Carol launched into her planned speech about why art was important. Then, following plan B, she said she wanted them to introduce themselves using a drawing of an object that was meaningful to them.

"It doesn't have to be something you still have," she explained. "It can be a toy you had as a kid. Something you lost that you still remember. Something a loved one gave you. Or something you used this morning. Does everyone have an object they can picture really well?" She tried not to hold her gaze too long on any one person, not wanting to give them a chance to read the terror in her eyes. "OK. Notice what color it is. What shape it is. How it feels when you touch it. What does it smell like? Did you ever give it a lick? How did it taste?"

Tammy giggled and dipped her head. The woman in the turquoise hat shook her head, the sequins tinkling like pebbles falling on sand. The room was so quiet, everyone with their hands folded, focused on Carol.

"When we make art," Carol explained. "We bring our vision to other people by using our senses. If you had a rubber doll whose fingers you chewed, you could paint that doll with the gnawed fingertips. But to do it right, you'd have to remember how the rubber tasted. Was it bitter? How did it feel to touch? Was it crumbly like stale bread? How would you draw it so when we saw it, we'd know this?"

She was losing them, she knew it. Carol missed Rainey. If only she were in the class, it would all make sense. Why hadn't she just asked them to go around and say their names? Then, she could have taught them contour drawing. Sweat trickled down her spine. First she was icy cold. Then she was boiling hot, as if her body radiated. She wished she'd taken her sweater off but it was too late. If she pulled it off now, she would reveal two dark stains at the armpits of her blue shirt.

"OK," Carol said. She walked around to see what supplies they had brought. Everyone had a pad of paper, a box of pastels or crayons. Some had charcoal. In the back of the room, some easels were in a tangled jumble. Next time, they would spread out the easels. They would paint, using the supplies the school provided. But first they had to get to know each other. All at once, it occurred to her. *She* was the only stranger. It made her feel as if she'd barged in on a family reunion. Trudy gave her a little nod, as if to say: Go on, de-ah.

The man who'd introduced himself as Dr. Bob sneered at her over his half-glasses. His huge belly flopped over his lap like bread dough rising over the lip of a bowl. Chris, a young man with peach fuzz on his upper lip, wore a bright orange U.S. Marine Corps T-shirt. He was busy drawing a strand of barbed wire around his wrist.

"This sounds fun." Trudy gave Carol an encouraging smile.

"OK," Carol said. "I want you to picture this object. Close your eyes if you need to. It says something about you. It tells a story. It reveals a secret. It's a self-portrait of your insides. That's what I want you to draw. OK?" she asked. Was it her imagination or was she saying OK an excessive number of times?

"Can it be real?" a woman in the back blurted.

Carol looked up, startled. She nodded.

"I mean, can it be alive?"

"Yes," Carol said. Changing the assignment to fit their needs. Wasn't that a sign of a good teacher? "You can draw something alive."

When it was time to share, Carol urged them to pull their desks into a circle. There was a commotion of scraping, of dropped supplies, spilled purses, and it took so long to settle back down, it seemed that surely it was time for the class to end. She glanced at her watch. Almost an hour to go. "Who'd like to start?" Carol asked. Papers fluttered. A pencil hit the floor and rolled over to Carol's shoe. When she bent to pick it up she nearly overturned her desk.

"I'll go." Trudy waved like a schoolgirl eager to run an errand.

Trudy had drawn a bright red ladder with a stick woman clinging to the top rung, her blue skirt blowing in what appeared to be a fierce wind. At the foot of the ladder, a gigantic white high heel lay on its side. Wine or blood spilled from the shoe and spread across the grass. She had drawn in the individual blades of grass using an otherworldly shade of chartreuse.

"I can't say as I can make any kind of sense out of it. You just got me goin' and this is what I came up with." She pinched her lips tightly as if to prevent another word from leaking out. Carol wasn't sure what to say. She nodded and hoped that was enough. Her own drawing seemed so tame. A bicycle leaning against a clapboard house. She had gotten so caught up in perfecting the spokes of the wheels, she hadn't stopped to think what it meant. Surely they would all realize she didn't have a creative bone in her body when it was her turn to share.

Dr. Bob had drawn a seagull with a fish in its mouth. It had a sinister look in its eye. He had worked carefully on the waves lapping at the shore. His ornate signature sprawled at the edge of the foam. Carol realized he must have drawn this image so often it was like a large cement block that kept his subconscious submerged.

Wanda, who said she was a lobsterman's wife, had drawn a lobster pot and a pile of red shells. "This here yellow bowl's filled with lobster meat. You just can't see it." She dipped her head shyly. "I spent more'n half my life pickin' lobster meat."

"This is my little teddy," the woman with the hat said.

"Your name?" Carol prompted.

"I'm Barbara Richards." She looked around the room as if checking to be sure there were no strangers. "You started it with the doll example. See here, how his eyes are buttons? My momma made him. I tell you, I don't know when's the last time I thought of this bear."

"What'd he smell like?" Suze asked, trying to be helpful.

"Oh, go on now. I slept with him in my crib. You know what he smelled like." Barbara tucked her drawing inside the front leaf of her sketch pad. "Are we gonna learn how to do still lifes? I have never been able to capture a piece of fruit."

"Uhm," Carol said, trying to suppress the mental image of Barbara sneaking up on an apple wielding a spear. "Mostly we're going to try to have some creative experiences. This is supposed to be a beginner's class. We'll work more on expression than technique."

"Well, how'm I supposed to express myself if I don't know how?" Barbara asked. She looked like she might be about to flee the room.

"That's what we'll try to find out together," Carol said. She couldn't believe she'd decided to teach this class. What did she know?

"It's supposed to be fun. I'm havin' fun," Trudy said, as if she could sense Carol's misgivings.

They continued around the circle. There was a cocker spaniel with a blue bow around his neck. A red car with the headlight smashed out: "The first time I got drunk," Suze confessed. A big wooden spoon that Pamela explained her grandmother had used to stir her homemade soups.

"Every single time I use that spoon," Pamela said. "I think of all those soups she made, all those years of her cooking."

Chris was the last to share. His drawing was of a chubby cherub clutching a bright red heart. Across the heart, in ornate script, it said "Snowy." "That's my dog," he explained. After they admired it, he pulled up his T-shirt. "Here's the real thing," he said, showing off the tattoo on his pale bony chest. He beamed proudly as they all leaned in for a closer look.

*   *   *

"Mommy!" Rainey shouted, twisting in her seat to see over her shoulder. Rita braked the truck, swerving to the side, terrified it had not been a chunk of ice falling from the wheel bed, but something they hit. Luckily, there was no one else on the road.

"Rainey, you can't holler at me when I'm driving."

"Sorry," Rainey muttered, kicking her boots against the seat.

"What is it?"

Rainey pointed behind her. Rita wasn't sure what she was supposed to see. There was the old white church perched on its rise, the pine trees beside it burdened with heavy snow. What's wrong with this picture, she thought. Then she realized what it was. The boards had been taken down from the church windows. The clear glass reflected the snowy hills.

*   *   *

Slim was cutting plastic six-pack rings into bits. Ever since the time he found a dead crow with its beak caught in one, he'd made a point of doing this. Today, he was going to bring home some more boxes of clothes he'd saved from the dump. Some of them he'd held onto since his father died. He hated to see it all bulldozed and buried when they closed down the dump.

"Say little tyke," he said to James who was bouncing happily in his seat, his legs dangling, his feet nearly touching the floor. "Did you know fifteen thousand hunks of junk're orbitin' the earth this very minute? Smashed up nose cones? Exploded satellites?"

James made some sounds as if in reply and reached for his bear. When Slim handed it to him, he immediately tossed it on the floor.

"Oh, it's that game, is it?" Slim made the bear fly around James. "It's space debris," he said, zooming the bear up for a kiss.

Slim stretched, checking out the window to see if the snow was letting up. There was so much of it, and still it continued to fall. It seemed the winter would never end. He pretended Janesta was at home, the fire going good, stew bubbling on the stove, Crystal with her normal clothes on doing her homework. He pictured himself curled up under the quilt with Janesta's plump warm buttocks pressing his belly. Now he slept with her nightgown bunched under his cheek. He was startled from his fantasy by a toot outside. Michael pulled up, then got busy tossing his trash. "Don't bother to come out," he hollered when Slim pulled open the door. "I'll be in in a sec."

Slim poured the two of them a cup of tea from the kettle he kept going on the stove. He got out a zwieback for James and filled a bottle with juice. By the time Michael came in, the tea was steeped.

"Boy, isn't it something?" Michael tweaked James's nose. "I'm bundled up three layers and still freezing."

"Boy, I'll tell you. I know how come some folks wear the same clothes all winter," Slim said. "It about hurts to peel 'em off."

"So what's up?" Michael asked, warming his hands over the stove.

"I guess you heard. They're closin' the dump," Slim said.

"That's what I heard. That's too bad. What'll you do?"

"I dunno. Stimpson's is hirin'. They need guys to load the trucks."

"I think about getting on at the sawmill sometimes. I wonder what it'd be like having steady work. But then I think, hell. I don't wanna get to the end of my life and find out I didn't really live it."

They drank their tea, sitting in silence watching the snow fall, propping their feet on a carton of books Trudy had brought in that morning. The shiny covers were decorated with women dressed in long billowing skirts. One gazed into the distance where a man on a white horse approached. Another swooned in the arms of a man who wore a sword.

"How's your little girl?" Slim asked.

"Aran? Oh, she's fine." Michael wiped his face. "She's with her mom today. My wife came back," he added, in case Slim hadn't heard.

"My wife left," Slim said. "All the time folks're leavin' and comin' back, leavin' and comin' back. But me, I never go nowhere."

"I know what you mean," Michael said. He thought about Lizzy's threat to leave. "Sometimes I just get a map out and try to imagine where I could go. You know, Hawaii. Canada. I dunno, France." Michael finished his tea and moved toward the door.

"I ain't never been more'n a hundred miles from home," Slim said. "My mom's down in Costa Rica. Wherever the heck that is." He couldn't remember the last time she answered one of his letters, though he sat down every month and wrote to her. He tried to picture her at the beach with Carl, eating a banana. She told him they grew them down there. He wished he could write to Janesta: "I miss you. The kids are fine. It's still snowing. Please come home." But he had nowhere to send it.

*   *   *

"It was a nightmare," Carol said. She paced the tiny room. The windows were thick with frost and now and then a gust of wind blew into the chimney pipe, making puffs of smoke billow from the stove.

"Oh, c'mon. I'm sure it wasn't that bad," Rita said. "I'm sure they loved it." She wrapped a wool shawl around Carol's shoulders.

"They hated it. No one's gonna come next week. Not one person. Not even Trudy." She sank into a chair moaning.

"Oh, I'm sure you're exaggerating. I always feel that way after I feed one of the old people. Like I can't possibly do it right. They hate me because all they really want is to be able to do it themselves. Then they say thank you and it breaks my heart."

"I am *not* a teacher." Carol sighed and began to set up the Scrabble board. Rita had promised they would have a marathon of Dirty Scrabble to help her recover from her first class.

"How can you say that? You've taught Rainey so much."

"It's the other way around. She's the one teaching me. Aren't 'cha, Rainey?" Rainey snuck up and put her hands over Carol's eyes.

"Guess who?" she said, giggling.

"Is that an owl?" Carol said.

"Who-o-o!" Rainey said. "We're having special homemade chicken pie."

"So much for secrets." Rita opened the oven door to check its progress. Then she came back and sat on Carol's knee. Their flirting had reached a stage Carol called "the rosy glow."

"Sounds wonderful. Smells wonderful, too." She kissed Rita. "Oh, God. I can't believe I told them to remember how the thing they were going to draw *smelled*. That's so inane."

"I wish you'd let me come."

"I'd be more nervous if you were there."

"Wouldn't it help? I could smile and nod and wink at you." Rita mimed the actions she promised to perform, writhing flirtatiously.

"I'd get flustered. Besides, Trudy smiles and nods and winks enough as it is. You have to be over sixty or a boy to attend my class." She described Dr. Bob, saving Chris and his tattoo for last. "I can picture him at age forty with that tattoo, half hidden in a tangle of gray hair. His dog long gone," Carol said.

"You know what?" Rainey said. "Me and mommy saw the church today and the windows are out."

"What do you mean, the windows are out?" Carol asked.

There was a knock on the door. "It's open," Rita called. She set the chicken pie on the table to cool and took plates down from the shelves. The tapping continued, like someone with a wooden mallet was rapping the wood. China Cat rose on her haunches and growled like a dog, her ears flattened.

"Yoo-hoo," Crystal called. When she stepped in, a big gust of snow came with her. She had the hood of her coat pulled low and a scarf tied over her mouth and nose. Only her eyes were visible.

"Cold out," she said, fingering the miniature eggs in a bowl by the sink. "Starter eggs" Rita called them. They were the size of robins' eggs. The new pullets she'd gotten had just begun to lay.

"You're kidding," Carol teased. "We were gonna go swimming."

"Swimmin'? What're you talkin' about? You nuts?"

"Come in. Stay a while," Rita said.

"It's mighty nippy," Crystal said. "Weatherman says it's gonna warm up. Gonna be a early spring. Hey, what 'cha doin'?"

"Playing Scrabble," Rita said.

"Oh, Scrabble. I know that. You married?"

"No," Rita said. "I'm not married." She rolled her eyes at Carol.

"Carol's not married neither," Crystal said.

"I know. We're just two single gals."

"When you gonna get dates?"

"We're kinda having one now," Carol said.

"Oh, go on. This ain't no date."

"How d'you know?"

"You gotta dress up with makeup on for a date." Crystal unzipped her jacket to show off her sweater. One of Janesta's with an array of multicolored beads splashed down the front, it hung to her knees.

"You going on a date?" Rita asked.

"No way. Gross," Crystal said. "Oops." She had broken one of the eggs. Inside, it was only albumen. "No babies in there."

"That's OK," Rita said. "I just kept them to look at."

"Me and Slim're makin' pizzas. I got a magazine that's got a recipe. Slim forgot flour. Hint hint." Crystal held up a measuring cup.

"You need anything else?" Rita asked, after filling the cup.

Crystal shook her head. "We got *The Parent Trap* tonight." She wrapped her scarf back around her face. "I gotta go."

"She's worse than ever with Janesta gone. Poor kid," Rita said after she'd gone. She spelled the word *neck*. "That's sixteen points with dirty double."

"She doesn't do that rhyming thing quite so much, though."

"That's true. Has Slim said anything to you about Janesta leaving?"

"Slim doesn't talk about it much. I was over there the other day. I offered to babysit, but he acted like he couldn't stand the idea of being alone. You should see his place. He's got so much stuff in that trailer he can hardly move. It made me think of those pictures of pioneers with everything they owned strapped onto their wagons."

"There's this man who did a book where he had people take everything out of their houses and pose beside it so he could take their picture," Carol said. "He'd probably enjoy Slim."

A gust of snow slapped the windows. "Do you realize it's snowed every day for six weeks?" Rita said.

"Yes, I've been keeping track." Carol spelled out the word *screw.* "I thought about leaving, you know. Way before Janesta did."

"Really?"

"Yeah. When it first started snowing, I felt so alone."

"Why didn't you?"

"You know." Carol took her hand.

"Are you glad you stayed? Are you feeling better now?" Rita asked. She ruffled Carol's hair affectionately.

"I can think of a way I'd feel even better," Carol said.

"I bet you can." Rita laughed. "Tell me, is *insert* a dirty word?"

"That depends," Carol said.

33

"It was really sweet. The way he told us how he agonized about the message on the signboard. You know, how they put quotes out in front to encourage people to worship there?" J.T. unpacked the new shipment of spermicide.

"In front of the church?" Lizzy asked. She was getting the Pap smears ready to mail to the lab.

"Yeah, you know, whether to go with 'sinners burn in hell' or something along more inspirational lines. Anyway, Joe said he searched and searched for the right thing to say. You know what it was?"

"What?"

"Welcome all."

"That's catchy."

"No, really. It says so much about who he is. About the kind of church he wants to create. *Anybody* is welcome. I bet you don't even have to be Christian."

"I dunno about you and this church thing, J.T. Didn't Trudy

Hyde tell you about it? It seems really weird to me. I mean, don't Christians hate people like you?"

"Not *real* Christians. You know, love one another is big with most."

"Tell Jerry Falwell that."

"Oh, he's just one of the scared ones. He thinks there's not enough to go around. He doesn't believe in loaves and fishes. If heaven is full of people like him, send me to the devil. Anyway, he's cute."

"Who's cute, the devil or Jerry Falwell?"

"Joe, silly. Even Betty thinks so." J.T. slammed the cabinet.

"What does that have to do with anything?"

"He's single."

"Oh. I get it. I'm all tangled up with this married man and you think I should check out some priest."

"Preacher, not priest. There's a difference."

* * *

"You seen in the paper how they're layin' a new tar road up by the Wincompaugh Road?" Rip asked. "Why the hell do they wanna spend up our good tax money on that? Our senator got him a camp up there?"

Slim shook salt into his palm and licked it, hoping to get his nerve up. "Say," he said, as if it had just occurred to him. "You folks wouldn't know what the story is on Crystal's dad, would you?"

"Who wants to know?" Buster asked rattling his newspaper.

"What'll you have, de-ah?" Trudy asked.

While Slim gave his order, he patted James's back.

"Don't forget about church Sunday," Trudy said, setting a Coke in front of Slim. "I promised Reverend Philbrook I'd get more of you in there. We got to build the congregation." She wondered if James had been baptized and was about to ask when Slim began to speak again.

"Anybody gonna answer my question or what? Here I am tryin' to fill his shoes and I don't even know the fella."

"I forgot your potato chips," Trudy said, setting a small bag in front of Slim. "That baby wakes up, I'll feed him some applesauce."

"There ain't no shoes to fill," Hydie said, leaning on a can of lard. "He was gone before the kid was born."

"They say Janesta threw herself down a flight of stairs tryin' to get rid of the baby. She was a mess, that's for damn sure," Coalie said.

"It was that accident," Trudy said.

"I'll tell you what I know of it," Buster said, pausing to slurp the last of his chowder. "Can I get me some seconds? Christ Almighty, the bowl gets smaller every time I'm in here."

"That's just you getting fatter," she said. "Everything looks small when you're big as a house."

"He wudn't nothing like you are," Rip said.

"Hell, he was just a kid," Hydie added, slapping three hamburger patties on the grill. "Barely drinking age. You ain't any kind of man then, I don't care who the heck you think you are. You ain't a man."

"I know that," Slim said. He sipped his Coke, shaking the crushed ice nervously. James stirred in his pouch and made a sucking sound.

"He was one good lookin' bastard," Rip said. "Had a wild streak in him." Rip raised his empty cup at Trudy.

"Folks said he had Micmac blood," Coalie said. "Liked to hunt with a bow and arrow for criminy's sake."

"His momma was the prettiest thing you ever did see," Trudy added dreamily. "Hair down her back all silky and dark. Ain't nobody left of that Curtis family around here exceptin' Crystal."

"Fellas that ride motorcycles are half outa their minds." Buster noted the interest in Slim's eyes. Like a child hearing about Santy Claus, he thought. Before he learns there's no such thing.

"He drove smack dab into a tree. It blowed over in a ice storm and fell across the road. It was up the Quarry Road. Way the hell outa town. They lived in some shack up in the woods." Buster whistled through his teeth. "Any damn fool knows you don't ride a motorcycle on any icy road with weather like that. Bad enough on a summer day, one of them crazy things."

"The way I remember it," Rip said. "There'd been a big storm the night before. Ice all over. Nasty weather. He's lucky to be in that wheelchair. He's alive, ain't he? He'd a died if Janesta wudn't comin' behind him in the car. She comes around the corner and she sees him and that big old tree, wires down on the road every whichaway. Folks with any kind of sense stayed to home."

Buster cleared his throat. "I'll have a piece of that chocolate cream pie when you get a minute."

Hydie wiped his hands on his apron and took a bite out of one of the hamburgers he had fixed. Raymond leaned against his mother and she rubbed his head slowly like his head was a magic lantern; her touch could transform him. Hydie chewed slowly, acutely aware of the silence as he cleared his throat and said, "Frank was not big in the sense department."

"Hell, Slim. You're the only father Crystal ever knowed," Rip said.

Slim considered what Rip said. How easily everyone accepted his role. Why couldn't he? Sometimes he woke up filled with panic.

"You can't get rid of me, kid," he told Crystal when she worried.

He was joking, but he knew she was afraid he would leave her the way everybody else had.

"Her teacher says Crystal oughta be sent away to a special school," Slim said. But what did she know? Crystal'd never want to go far from home like that. Every day Crystal worried if he was going to come home. Sometimes he'd just be out in the yard and she'd run up all out of breath crying about where was he. Just because she wasn't like other kids didn't mean they had a right to send her away somewhere.

"I figure she's had enough comin' and goin' for one kid," Slim said. "I aim to give her a stable life if nothing else."

"You do that, buddy. That's the way," Hydie said, like a coach urging a player to make a risky move. Raymond leaned on Trudy, his head tucked forward, his eyes closed.

"Just give 'em love. That's what I always say. Love'll carry you a far ways," Trudy said. Slim looked so heartbroken as he left, she almost went after him. But what would she say?

"I been thinkin'." Trudy sliced herself a piece of pie.

"Uh-oh," Buster said. "Time for me to go."

Trudy ignored him and continued. "I was readin' this article. I can't remember where. I guess up at the clinic there in the waitin' room, it must've been. Anyhow, it was about this place where folks get rid of stuff without it goin' to the dump. Slim's furnished his whole place on dump pickings. Every one of us has something he fixed up. Maybe we could set up a place where somebody's throwin' away a door or an old washer or whatever and they bring it to Slim. He could do a buy-back center, too. Folks'd as soon take their cans and bottles to a place here than drive over the bridge. He could use the lot behind us. We're not doin' anything with it. What d'you say, Hydie?"

"You might be onto something. But it can't be messy. It can't have a stink. Nobody's gonna come eat here if it stinks out back."

"It won't be garbage. It'll be stuff to reuse. And like I said, the recycling. He can put up a trailer or whatever."

"Shit. You'll be makin' curtains and decoratin' it, I can tell."

"Oh, Hydie Hyde," Trudy said, winking at him with affection. Maybe Slim would do so well he could take Raymond on. Raymond could count and he could clean. He'd do a good job sorting bottles and cans, putting his skills to use. I could die and rest in peace knowing my boy would be all right, she thought, savoring the pie crust. It melted in her mouth.

* * *

They'd spent weeks practicing their new skills on a dummy, turning it on the drawsheet; making the bed while the dummy stared up at the ceiling, inert, or flopped obligingly on its side; washing its vinyl body, patting it dry, uncovering as little as possible, one foot, one hand, one arm at a time. No dummy could ever prepare you for the real thing, Rita thought as she approached Mrs. Melton's bed. She was so tiny and frail her body barely raised the blanket that had been tucked around her. Her skin and hair were as white as the talcum powder Rita set on her bedside table. It was hard to believe she'd earned the nickname the Holy Terror.

"Good morning," Rita murmured, filling the basin with warm water and lowering the bed rail.

"Is that you, Duane?" Mrs. Melton asked, her white lashes fluttering open. "Oh, it's *you*," she said when she saw Rita. She made a spitting sound, groaned, and turned her head away. Her hair was as thin as a delicate hair net and barely covered her scalp which was dotted with age spots, the hard bones of her skull clearly visible.

Gloria, the cleaning woman, was muttering to herself as she gathered the trash, snapping open a fresh plastic bag, her rubber-soled shoes squeaking as she left the room.

"Let there be light," the handyman shouted down to her from the top of his ladder where he was changing the fluorescent bulbs.

All up and down the hallway, the other CNAs spoke in cheerful cajoling voices, as if they were dealing with recalcitrant children.

"C'mon now Mr. Babcock. You wanna get cleaned up for visitin' hours. We gotta shave these whiskers, now. Ain't it a lovely day today?" Mabel said, loud enough for the entire nursing home to hear.

"Ain't that the cutest card? Is it from your grandbaby?" Delores crooned.

"How ya gonna get yourself a boyfriend if you don't brush your teeth?" Janine said as she cranked Miss Basse's bed up.

False voices, Rita thought, though she wished she could think of something to say.

"I suppose you want to wash this old rag," Mrs. Melton said. "This sack of bones has got to be clean though God knows I haven't done a thing to get dirty." She thrust one arm from the covers and grabbed the cloth. "I do my own goddamn face," she said, dabbing at her pale eyes, sponging her dry mouth then dropping the cloth as if the effort exhausted her.

Rita drew the curtain around the bed and began, smoothing the warm cloth over the old woman, washing the length of her arms, gliding the cloth between her long fingers. Her skin, the texture of handmade rice paper, was so delicate it was like trying to wash a ripe peach without tearing it open. She washed her chest, gently soaping the faded scars where her breasts had been, her sunken belly, then her back, turning her slowly to glide the cloth down her knobby spine, very tentatively washing her pale hairless sex. Rita felt she was holding her breath through the entire procedure, waiting for Mrs. Melton to cry out in pain or anger or disgust. But she was silent and Rita could not think of a thing to say. There was only the sound of the cloth being rinsed in the basin, the squirt of lotion Rita warmed in her palms before smoothing it across her flaccid buttocks, down her legs along her calves which were like flaps of skin hanging off her bony shins.

"Thank you for not trying to cheer me up," Mrs. Melton said in her gruff voice when Rita emptied the basin. She crossed her arms over her chest and glowered, a hint of pink rising in her pale cheeks. "I don't suppose I could get you to comb this poor excuse for hair?" she asked.

Rita smiled. "I'd be happy to," she said, carefully untangling her hair with the soft baby brush she found in Mrs. Melton's drawer.

This was a learn-as-you-go kind of job, Rita thought, relaxing a bit as she worked through a knot in the back of Mrs. Melton's hair and tied the ribbon Mrs. Melton indicated she wanted. Like life, she thought. You get better at it as you go along.

* * *

Crystal pulled down her underpants in the wooden stall of the girls' room at school. All around her voices laughing, talking. Girls checking each other's hair, adjusting their slips and kneesocks. And there it was, a thick dark smudge, like the chocolate pudding she'd eaten two helpings of for dessert. There on her white nylon panties, the pudding was coming out of her and she wiped and wiped herself, while a dull ache formed in her belly and nausea swept over her. She broke into a sweat, her body slick, dew under her arms, trickling down her back. Then Becky Milliken kicked the door.

"You fall in in there?" she hollered and the other girls laughed. Jenny Poors leaped up, trying to see over the top. Susan Allen squatted to look under, noting the dirty pink sneakers.

"It's Crystal Curtis," she announced, and the girls began to sing, "Crystal pistol pissed her pants. The piss so hot it made her dance. She danced out of her underpants."

Crystal wiped herself hurriedly one more time and stuffed a wad of toilet paper into her underpants, yanking them up high around her waist.

The next morning brought a bright red circle of blood that soaked the back of her nightgown and smeared the sheets. She woke up afraid she had wet the bed and when she reached down to touch herself her hand came back sticky with blood. She lay on the sofa bed, the blankets up to her chin, her thighs throbbing, and watched the pale gray light seep into the trailer. She was afraid to get up, afraid Slim would find out. She didn't know what he would do. She looked at the room, at the piles of clothes heaped all over. At the stacks of magazines spilling onto the clothes, all the while the wet spreading beneath her, trickling down her thighs. She played a game with herself, counting all the colors she could see, the blues and greens in the plaids and flowered prints. The red-and-white gingham. Yellow and green rickrack; pink and white lace. Powder blue and navy blue, blue green and aqua, she counted them all until she heard Slim cough and James laugh and then they were in the kitchen, Slim stirring sugar into his coffee, feeding James his oatmeal, asking Crystal just how sick she was, his hand on her forehead. Crystal refused to even sit up, moaned about a bellyache, kept the covers pulled tight lest he discover what she was hiding.

After he'd gone to the dump, she scrubbed the stain on the sheets and on her clothes, using the dish scrubber until the cloth was practically worn through and the blood faded. She draped everything in front of the stove to dry. She stuffed her underpants with wads of toilet paper that soaked through so quickly that she searched the trailer, a wild feeling inside of her, desperate for something to use.

Slim brought home huge boxes of Kotex in the winter to stuff into his rubber boots, to keep his feet warm when he had to be out all day, and Crystal thought of the thick white napkins only for this purpose, using them herself sometimes when it was particularly cold, thick pillows under her feet. But there weren't any and she didn't know what to do and the blood rushed out of her. She wiped at the blood but it wouldn't go away. It was shockingly red. Finally she used one of James's Pampers folded in half. Later, she would find some way to get rid of it. If she put it in the trash, Slim might notice, concerned as he was about not wasting anything.

The school nurse had taken the girls in Special Ed to the cafeteria for a film. While the cooks clattered the trays over big chipped sinks,

Crystal watched tiny purple eggs being whisked by what looked to her like an octopus grabbing. The uterus was a bull's head, she decided. The fallopian tubes the horns. The ovaries were smoke pouring out of the bull's ears. Crystal started thinking of the cow up at Alton Poors' farm where Slim sometimes took them to get milk. The cool gallon jug of milk beaded with sweat. Then the nurse passed out pamphlets. Crystal hated the nurse. Whenever she was in the same room with her, her head was filled with the sound of a semi heading up the highway. She couldn't pay attention with the nurse nearby.

Getting her period was like being hit between the eyes. Crystal was stunned by it. So she did what came naturally to anyone surprised by an event over which they had no control and little understanding. She hoped if she pretended it wasn't there, the bleeding would go away. And in a few days, it did.

34

Joe said he wanted them to question all aspects of the service, to actively participate, not passively accept what came their way just because they were in church. To illustrate this, he had inaugurated a new part of the service called "tell it like it is." Anybody that wanted to could stand up and say any little thing that popped into their heads it seemed to Trudy, though she'd understood it was supposed to be about their struggle to have faith.

"Doubts are the ants in the pants of faith. They keep it awake and moving," he told them, quoting from that fellow Frederick Buechner he often referred to. What that had to do with one of the little Jordan boys bringing in some nest the wind blew out of a tree was beyond Trudy. He was telling everyone how there was one tiny blue feather in it. That dirty thing in church, Trudy thought. She patted Raymond's hand while they waited for the boy to tromp up and down showing the nest off.

"A church is a community," Joe said. "It's something we make together. Just like you bring wood so we can keep the fire going, you bring yourself so we can keep the embers of our faith glowing. We need each other to do this work. There are no Christian Lone Rangers." He made circles of his fingers, pretending to peer through a mask.

"I need your help." His voice trembled so much it startled Buster, whose head was sinking into the pillow of his double chin. His wife, Mildred, gave him a warning jab. Buster liked it better when the church was boarded up, when he could whine about not wanting to drive to Union City and Mildred had to be content reading her Bible alone.

"You don't just come in and pay your dues, then get a gold star from God for showing up," Joe said, making them laugh. "I don't just stand up here telling you what's right and wrong and you get to feel good or bad depending on what you've been up to.

"Why do we come then, you might ask? Jesus said, 'For where there are two or three gathered together in my name, there I am in the midst of them.' " *Sum medio eorum,* he thought, spreading his arms as if to gather the congregation closer, pleased to see several people had started sitting near the front. "Jesus also said something else, in words recorded in the *Apocrypha.* And today I've got some help with the reading."

Rainey walked slowly to the front of the church. She looked at her mother, who nodded, then she looked at Joe, and he nodded, too. She held the paper in both hands as if to read the words she had practiced all week until she knew them by heart. Her voice was soft but clear and the congregation sat so quietly, everyone could hear. "And where there is one alone," she said, her voice quavering slightly. She looked at her mother then down at a patch of bright sun on the worn red carpet, deciding when she walked back, she would step into that patch of light. "And where there is one alone," she said again, her small voice rising. "I say I am with him."

Joe watched the child make her careful way back to her seat and lean into her mother's hug. Then he repeated her words. "I like to think of our bodies as our first churches, a house of worship within. When we come together to worship, what we're doing is noticing the church in each other, noticing the Holy Spirit shining in each other's eyes just like the sun is shining through our windows now. We come together to celebrate this presence in our lives and in the lives of other people."

Trudy struggled to catch the drift of what Joe was getting to, but she kept thinking about how cute he was, a living doll. And that little Rainey Conway didn't look big enough to know her ABC's let alone stand up in front of everybody and read. She didn't care what folks said about her color, the girl was a sweetheart. She even came with her mother when they cleaned the church and helped out like everybody else, handling the broom like it wasn't twice her size. Joe was talking about how being together in church was a process of evolving. Something about flowers growing from tiny seeds. Trudy's mind wandered off until she was startled by a loud voice from the back of the church. It was J.T. from the clinic repeating her prayer request, bellowing like some cranky old cow: "Pray for the oppressed lesbians in the world."

Trudy didn't think that was a proper thing to bring up in God's house. People could do whatever they wanted in the privacy of their own homes as far as she was concerned, but did they have to rub her nose in it? Joe kept saying they weren't there to change anyone. They weren't supposed to point any fingers, to stand in judgement of each other. God's love and grace for all. He quoted the scripture about casting the first stone. Still, it made Trudy uncomfortable. Sometimes she wished she hadn't invited J.T. Ever since that first Sunday, J.T. had been making this request. During their silent prayers, Trudy would be so struck by what J.T. said, she could think of nothing else until Joe prayed out loud for all of them, always including a prayer for her mother as Trudy had asked.

Joe went to The Manor every week and visited the old lady even though she slept a good deal of the time. He read her the Bible. He told Trudy that hearing was one of the last things to go.

"You should keep talking to her," he said. Trudy would sit by her mother's bedside, silent at first, finally rattling on about her fear of dying and what would happen to Raymond when she and Hydie were gone.

Now everyone was rising for a hymn. In the bulletin, some of the words to the hymn had been reprinted with changes. "People" substituted for "mankind." Instead of "God the father," "God the mother and father of us all." What'll they think up next, Trudy thought. She sang the real version from the hymnal. She listened when it came time to switch but she couldn't hear anything different. Maybe Joe was going too far with this "we make it together" notion. But it sure did feel good to be in the old church again. Yes, she told herself, it was good to be back.

*   *   *

The afternoon was so still, Michael could hear the snow hit the dry leaves that clung to the beech tree beside the trail. Like a dusting of powder. He stopped to catch his breath, chewing off the icicles on his moustache. It was exhausting to tromp around in the snow like this. Would spring ever come? he wondered. He unbuckled the hatchet from the holster attached to his belt and hacked off some of the dead branches on the spruce trees crowded so close they created a dense thicket no light could penetrate. Wood lot management, the man from the extension had explained, was an important part of land ownership.

Sometimes Michael was overwhelmed by the fact that the land was his. His and Kaye's. But she wasn't really going to put up a log cabin kit the way she'd threatened to, insisting they could each have ten acres, that she would take this rise where he stood now for her house site. Michael could see smoke winding slowly from his chimney through the leafless trees.

The land was all second and third growth. It had been razed once, everything cut to the ground to get at the really big trees; the second time, they went in after pulp. This tangle of trees had sprung up like weeds, a mixture of oak and maple, fir and spruce, hemlock and pine. Here and there a hackmatack or ash. All of it unmanaged for years. Lots of trash wood, what the poplar was called. But Michael liked the gray bark, and in autumn, the way the pale yellow leaves shimmered.

Above him, chickadees called. A chipmunk scurried along a log that had fallen so long ago it crumpled when Michael rested his foot on it. Just off the path was the granite outcropping where he used to lie with Kaye on the thick green moss. He was tired of being angry at her. Tired of all the bickering. Tired of her threats to burn his house down if he didn't agree to her demands. Besides, he missed her. He hated to admit it, but he did.

Last time he'd gone to pick up Aran, he kissed Kaye. It had just happened. She looked so pretty, all made up with her hair tucked into a bun, that blue suit with the red high heels she wore to her job at the bank. She went limp in his arms. But just for a second, as if it were instinctive. Then she slapped his face, her eyes flashing with anger.

"Don't you *ever* try that again," she had said.

You can't just chop a person out of your life like a twisted tree that will never grow tall, Michael thought. You can't just accept whatever springs up in its place.

He could hear the muffled flow of the stream, but the banks were so piled with snow and ice he could barely glimpse the water as it rushed by, chunks of ice whirling in the eddies. He examined a maple tree, noting the red hue, the tight buds. Any day now. Even if it was still snowing, the days were growing longer. He stirred up a partridge that rose with a whir. Then a hare, its fur mottled white and brown, dashed through the woods, a sure sign of spring.

Michael surveyed a clump of fir trees, then hacked away the crooked spindly ones, leaving one in the center where it would grow bushy and tall. He owned the land, he owned the trees, he decided which ones would live. Following the extension officer's advice, he knew the right approach. He wished he could manage his own life this easily.

*   *   *

"How's the seduction going?" Dougie asked.

"Slow."

"Slow is nice."

Carol laughed. "It scares me. How much I like her."

"Well, you should be happy you can feel it."

"I know. But. Oh. It's Annie. My feelings get all jumbled up. I mean, every day I tell myself I should be over it. But it's still there aching like some phantom limb. I still miss her so much. I dream about her almost every night. Then I start thinking how if I love someone else, I'll forget her."

"Listen, I think loving someone else is a great compliment to her."

"Compliment?"

"Yeah. It's like saying: You loved me so well I can love someone else. Don't be down, girl."

"Oh, it's just the weather. If it doesn't stop snowing, I don't know what I'm gonna do. All I ever used to want was time alone with nowhere I had to be. Well, I've got that now. But I feel so trapped. I can't even go for a walk. It's too exhausting to be clomping through it all. I've never seen so much snow," Carol complained. She stared out the window at the wide white expanse. The snow-woman she and Rainey had made was still completely intact in the front yard though the bottom half of her body was nearly buried in drifts and the old string mop they used for a wig was on askew. The branches they used for arms made it look like she was cheering Carol on.

"You sound like you need the deluxe distraction of Dougie Darnell."

"That would be nice."

"OK. You think you've got it bad up there in your idyllic country abode with a beautiful gal to ogle. Picture this: It's a half hour to last call and this woman struts in with two little kids riding pink plastic Big Wheels."

Carol laughed. "You're making this up."

"Would I make up a nightmare like that?"

"It's winter. Why would they have bicycles?"

"It's Manhattan. We just have frozen black goo. Anyway, they arrived in a limo that waited for them outside."

"Go on."

"OK. You get the picture? These Big Wheels in everybody's way. Little brats jumping around in designer clothes. Fur-trimmed boots. One of their little socks costs more than the tips I earned all weekend. 'We'd like a window seat,' Mother goes. Of course every inch of window those monsters can reach gets smeared with their greasy fingerprints, their nasty little nose prints. They even started licking it at one point and Mother's oblivious, sipping her Chivas on the rocks, nibbling her toast points smeared with chèvre. Gross."

"That's a good one," Carol said.

"That's not all. Remember, this is Dougie's deluxe distraction."

"OK. I'm ready."

"So I've got her at *my* station, of course."

"Of course."

"But I've also got these other two. This old dame that's pissed off because the blackened chicken she ordered is black. I'm scared any minute she's gonna pull a pistol. I don't know if she'll shoot the old dude she's with, who appears to be brain dead already, or me. Even though I've already offered to replace the chicken, at *no* extra charge, mind you, with whatever else her picky heart desires.

" 'It's inedible,' she goes. Of course she's just bitten off a juicy morsel and a bit of Laurent's gourmet organic olive oil is dribbling down her chin. But still she goes on with her hissy fit."

"How's the mortician?" Carol asked, referring to a man named Mortimer Morris, a pale ghostlike man who always trembled so badly when he signed his Visa slip, Carol used to worry he'd wither before her eyes.

"Think mortician playing racketball."

"That's a good one."

"No seriously. He comes in with a racket. Can't you see old Morty on the courts?"

"It's hard to imagine."

"He had a date."

"Morty? A date?" Carol screamed.

"Yeah. This gal that ate like a hamster."

"She stuffed her cheeks with food?"

"No, silly girl. She held it up to her mouth with both little weeny hands."

"You'd love some of the characters up here."

"Do me a favor. You love them for me. Uh-oh. Another call."

"You go ahead. I'll call you another time," Carol said, making kissing sounds into the phone. "It was great to talk to you."

"Ciao baby."

* * *

At the end of Slim's driveway were two claw-foot bathtubs his dad had saved, meaning to scrape the paint spots off and sell them to an antiques dealer. Now they were filled with snow. Beside them were a brown kitchen range, three sets of bedsprings, and a green toilet with a cracked tank Slim decided would make a nice planter. Since Trudy had told him her idea for a buy-back center and secondhand shop, he'd been bringing home everything. Saving it. Come spring, he would dismantle the shed, rebuild it in his backyard. Slim lugged the boxes of chain and pedals culled from old bicycles he'd brought home yesterday and piled them beside the washer he'd brought home too, tossing a tarp over it all. That morning, it seemed like the snow was starting to melt, that they might have seen the worst of it, but it was spitting snow again.

"James wants you to keep him company," Crystal hollered from the door.

"He does, does he? How 'bout you?" She nodded. As she turned to go back into the trailer, she tripped on some bags of clothes and went sprawling. By the time Slim got to the door, he could barely get in with the clothes heaped the way they were, strewn across the room like a thick carpet. He crawled in on his hands and knees, making the kids laugh. He whinnied like a horse and tossed his matted hair. They rolled on the floor giggling, flinging the dresses, tossing the hats and gloves.

"Bury me," Crystal shouted, waiting for Slim to pile the coats and sweaters on top of her until only her face poked out.

"Now sit on me," she demanded.

"I can't, I'll squash you." He placed James on her instead. He pushed his face up to Crystal's, a string of drool falling on her cheek.

Slim almost fell as he kicked the clothes away from the woodstove, so he got back down on his hands and knees to toss a log on the fire. He checked the cans he'd set around the brick hearth to be certain they were filled with water, figuring as long as water was in the cans, he didn't have to worry about the clothes catching on fire. Tomorrow, he'd take them to the Salvation Army. He'd clean the place up. Tomorrow, he told himself, stretching out on his back, inviting his kids to snuggle up.

35

Lizzy gripped the handle of the bow saw. It rubbed against the new calluses on the ridges of her palm, forming fresh blisters. It tore away the skin inside her thumbs. She didn't have her gloves on and was too stubborn to drag herself across the icy snow to get them. The wind tossing the branches reminded her of waves endlessly building and crashing. Winter had lasted so long, it seemed permanent. Her feet were so cold they were numb, but she didn't care. She bent over her work, her saw biting into the tree trunk, scraping the bark, the jagged teeth releasing the smell of resin. The damp crumbs of sawdust collected in the blade, slowing her down.

She only cut the trees she could reach both hands around or a little bigger. First she cut a wedge. Then she sliced into the trunk from the other side. Sometimes while she sawed, she pushed the tree in the direction she wanted it to fall. If it was small enough, that push could make it crack and fall without her having to saw all the way through. When Michael's chain saw sputtered to a stop, she looked up.

"You be careful," he warned. "It'll jump back, twist around and hit you. If that blade gets caught, you'll get hurt." He came over beside her and lit his stupid pipe. Lizzy hated the smell of it. She hated the sight of him clenching the stem in his stained little teeth. Why had she never noticed his teeth? Rat's teeth, she thought as he puffed away. Beady reptilian eyes. She was furious about the list she'd found when she was putting his clean socks away. It was all because of that stupid book Kaye had given him for his birthday, *Trailblazing: Maps to Success.* He'd been working on the chapter "Setting Your Sights on the Sensuous."

"I'm a tit man," he wrote in his florid Catholic school script, then circled it as the chapter instructed. Radiating around it like spokes on a wheel he had listed Lizzy's flaws and good points: "Flat chested. Ten-year-old girl's body. Hairy legs. Bony ass. Good sport. Cares about Aran. Hard worker." Well. She could make a list too. Coward was at the top. Then, heartless worm.

Up on the rise behind the house, smoke from the brush party was billowing thick and black. Lizzy was surprised Michael wasn't up there helping Kaye clear the land if he was so generous. She could hear Kaye's friends laughing and mingled with their laughter, Aran's happy voice. She imagined them dressed in stylish outdoor gear, boots from Eddie Bauer, a rainbow display of wool sweaters from J. Crew, all of them moving across the snow like graceful dancers as they tossed the brush onto the smoldering tires. Michael was just going to let Kaye build on the land. It was all right with him that she planned to live a few feet away.

"It won't amount to anything. She'll never build her own place. You forget. I know her," Michael said as if reading her mind.

"I figure this way is the best," Michael said, combing his stupid beard with his fingers, not looking Lizzy in the eye. "I don't want a messy fight. No judge would listen anyway. Look at me. I don't have a regular job. I'm shacked up with you. In a shack, for crying out loud. That's what he'd think of this place. No running water, Lizzy. Jesus. Half the time I'm scared they'll up and take Aran away from the both of us if we let them poke their noses into our lives too far."

Lizzy didn't say anything. She made the last cut and the rush of the falling tree cracked through the underbrush. Michael sawed the limbs off with neat swipes of his chain saw and tossed them into a pile. He sawed the trunk into manageable lengths. The air was so smoky, it was painful to breathe. The woods were hazy with it, as if the branches were draped in dingy gauze. Lizzy gritted her teeth so hard her jaw ached as she moved toward the next tree, so angry she was ready to yank it up and break it in half.

* * *

Slim got down on his hands and knees to fish the phone out from under a pile of balled-up sweaters and old jeans. Ringo, the new coon cat, jumped onto his back and let out a yowl.

"Mr. Curtis?" a woman asked. "Could I speak to Mr. Curtis?"

"Who?"

"Mr. Curtis. I'm looking for a Mr. Curtis." The woman sounded impatient. She raised her voice as if she thought he couldn't hear.

"Sorry. There's no Mr. Curtis here." He couldn't think straight with that cat sinking his claws into his back. He swatted it off. James crawled after it snatching at its tail.

"I'm looking for Crystal Curtis's father."

"Oh, that'd be me. But my name's Riley." He could hear papers flipping and rustling. The woman sighed heavily. Crystal was sitting up in bed, the blankets pulled over her lap, her mother's black angora sweater falling off her shoulders revealing her stained long john top.

"Mr. Curtis. I mean, Mr. Riley. I'm Melissa Brown. I'm the nurse over here at the school. Mr. Riley, Crystal's teacher says the other kids are complaining. Do you have running water?"

"Yeah." He was remembering the TV show where a lady brought her little girl into the emergency room with a burned hand and the police took the child away. "You can't do this to me!" the lady had screamed. Was this Melissa Brown going to take Crystal away from him? And James, too? "We got running water," he said. "Ma'am," he added.

"Mr. Riley, her teacher says she wears odd clothes. Sizes too big for her. It's a distraction in the classroom. It doesn't make for a proper learning environment. She sent home several notes but nothing's changed."

"Notes?" Slim was stalling, trying to figure out what to say.

"Yes. Notes. Didn't you get them?"

"No, ma'am. I didn't get no notes," he said, though he could see the last one crushed into a ball on the counter beside a half-eaten bowl of popcorn. He had meant to do something about it. "I will surely take care of it. I don't mean for Crystal to be causin' no trouble." He almost mentioned how her mother had disappeared, that this might be what was behind Crystal's behavior. But then he worried it would make things worse if this woman knew. Rip had told him since he married Janesta, the kids were as good as his. But he didn't want to take any chances. "I'll see to it. It won't happen no more."

"Mr. Riley? One more thing. Does Crystal know the facts of life?"

"I've did my best explainin'. I'm still workin' on it," he said. A magazine article he had read suggested while he was alone, at work, or driving the car, he talk to himself and pretend he was telling his children where babies came from. As he got ready to answer Crystal's questions, he practiced his speech on James, telling him about love and sperm and the good feelings between two people, but when he brought home the little booklet he'd found, *Now That You're a Woman*, Crystal just flipped through it, hardly even looking at the pictures. She didn't ask any questions.

After he hung up, Slim surveyed the room, taking in the heaps and piles of junk. There were piles of old coats and sweaters, skirts and pants, slips and aprons, so many clothes heaped on the floor, wadded in the corners. The room smelled of cat pee and mothballs, wood smoke and garbage, and the clothes, ripe with the odor of stale sweat, damp wool, and rotten cloth.

Shotgun wagged his tail so hard he fell off the bed into the heaps of clothes piled nearly as high as the mattress on either side of Crystal. He rolled on his back and gave a halfhearted bark, then turned around and around until he settled down, his nose on his paws, his eyes watchful as Slim rummaged around in the kitchen looking for bags. The kitchen wasn't too bad except for the bags of cans, plastic, and bottles to recycle. And the pail of garbage for the compost. Mostly, it was the clothes. Why on earth had he brought home so many clothes?

There had been times in his life when Slim felt himself grow, as if the effort to take on responsibility filled him until he was like the Incredible Hulk bursting out of an ordinary man's body. Large and powerful, ready for anything. He felt that way when he found the trailer, when he married Janesta, when James was first placed in his arms. And he felt this way now with the woman's voice still echoing, a hint of a threat in her tone.

"Ba-ba-ba!" James scooted alongside the stacks of books and magazines, his rear end high in the air, what Crystal called his spider walk. He fell back on his bottom and clapped his hands as if with approval as Slim stuffed the clothes into garbage bags. At first he sorted them into what he was going to save and what he would toss, but soon he just stuffed the clothes in every which way. He couldn't save everything.

Eager to participate in the new game, Crystal gathered armloads of clothes and dumped them into the bags he held open. He tried to notice if she smelled bad, but the smell of the clothes was too strong. First the trailer, he thought. Then I'll tackle Crystal.

"Hey, look at James," Crystal said. The baby had lifted himself upright. He tottered forward a few steps in the space they had cleared, then fell with a laugh.

"Hey, James," Slim said. He scooped the boy up and gave him a kiss. "You're walkin'." The baby squirmed to get down and try again. Using the coffee table for support, he took a few more steps, laughing as Slim and Crystal clapped.

Slim wrapped twine around piles of newspaper and magazines and Crystal helped him carry them to the car and dump them into the trunk.

"Hey, don't it smell like spring out?" Slim said.

Crystal inhaled deeply. "Smells like wood smoke, you jughead."

"Look. There's buds on the maple tree. Don't it make you happy winter's almost gone?"

"It's gonna be a hot summer. Weatherman says a record breaker." She hurried into the house as if to escape from the heat she'd predicted.

Slim carried James around the yard, his boots crunching on the snow. It had a grainy texture, as if it had already begun to melt. He sidestepped the drifts, circled around the junk he'd hauled into the yard, planning how he'd rebuild the shed on his land to store it all in. He stopped to let the baby watch the hens. They were cackling and squawking. James made chortling sounds in response. Tom, the turkey, fanned open his tail feathers and strutted away. Slim walked up to the edge of the field and back around the trailer again, fitting his boots into the tracks he'd made. He'd drive down to the dump in the morning, dump the junk out of his car, and bury the lot of it. It made him feel free to picture this. Maybe that was why people always threw things away. A fresh start.

"Daddy loves you kiddo." He snuggled the baby, kissing his head. James looked puzzled, as if he were trying to understand each word Slim spoke individually, the way someone learning a language trans-lated each word as it was said. "That's a tree," Slim said, letting the baby pat the rough bark. "That's the sky." He pointed up. "There's Rita and Rainey's place. Look at Barney!" He pointed to the cat curled on the roof of his car. James stretched his arms up to pet him. With no wind, it was almost warm. Slim walked around the yard until James's head drooped on Slim's shoulder and the little fingers let go of the clump of Slim's hair he liked to grab onto. James's body asleep lost all its alert tension. He became like a rag doll, his arms and legs dangling. Slim patted the baby's back and thought of Janesta. How she was missing everything. Here her baby was growing up and she didn't even know what he looked like. He took his first steps and she wasn't there to see.

Inside, Crystal was playing "The Fool on the Hill."

"That my theme song?" he asked, but she didn't respond. The TV was on with the sound off. A woman was waving a mop, acting as if it had changed her life. Tomorrow, he thought, I'll take a mop to this place.

The rich fragrance of the spaghetti sauce bubbling on the back burner filled the room. The windows were wet with steam. James was curled up on Crystal's bed, his rump in the air, a cat on either side of him. Maybe Crystal still wore her mother's clothes because her own didn't fit anymore. She was taller now. Heavier. He thought maybe he should go paw through the clothes in his car and find something her size. But he caught himself. No more of that. She'd have new.

"Tell you what," Slim said.

Crystal looked up, chewing the ends of her straggly hair. Slim held up his billfold. "We got plenty of dough. How's about we go on a shoppin' spree before supper?"

"Like on TV?" Crystal loved the local show where people rushed around filling shopping carts at Tony's Supermarket in Bangor, racing along as the time ran out. She loved to list what she'd get.

"Well, kind of. Only you don't have to beat the clock. You can take your sweet time. We'll go to La Verdierre's first."

Crystal turned the sound up on the TV. Patty Duke, looking strained, fragile, and very old, held her chin high in a courtroom and listened to the judge's verdict. It seemed to Slim, every time they turned the TV on this show was playing. One trouble after another this woman had to face. But she was fighting back. Slim would, too.

"Anything you want," Slim said.

"La Verdierre's is a drug store," Crystal complained. "God."

Slim shut the TV off.

"Hey. I was watchin' that."

"I know, but I'm tryin' to tell you something."

Crystal drew her knees under the sweater and rested her forehead on them.

"You probably don't remember this," he said. "But way back when I first met your mom, back before we got married, she taught me something important and I nearly forgot." As he said this, he realized that he had never spoken of Janesta as if she were someone from their past. He always thought of her as if she were right down the hall or on her way up the hill. But now he felt certain she was never coming back. The realization hurt, but it made him feel strong, too. Like growing pains.

The day they tore his old house down, some men in hard hats came and wrapped a big chain around it, hitched the end of the chain to a truck, and let the truck pull. At first it seemed that nothing would happen. Then the house caved in and collapsed into a pile of rubble. That's what nearly happened to me, he thought. I nearly fell to pieces and lost it. But now I get another chance.

"We've been livin' like moles, buried up to our noses in all that crap. In no time, we'd a been bumpin' our heads on the ceiling, sittin' on our heaps of junk."

"I ain't no mole," Crystal said, aiming the remote at the TV. She pressed the power key but it wouldn't come on because Slim stood in the way. Frustrated, she began to pick her nose, cupping her hand around her nose as if doing that made it a secret.

"So like I said. Your mom taught me something I wanna tell you. I used to never wash. Never took a bath. If it was winter, I'd say it was too cold to be takin' my clothes off. In the summer, I'd say what's the point, I'll only get dirty again. I didn't notice how bad I smelled.

I didn't care how I looked. But your mom taught me a person's gotta keep himself clean. It's a kind of courtesy you do for the people around you even if you don't wanna do it for yourself. If you want people to come close to you. If you want a friend to give you a kiss, well you got to shine yourself up good. You wouldn't eat your supper off a dirty old plate now, would you?"

"Yuck. I don't want nobody kissin' me," Crystal said. "Gross."

"That's OK, too. But it's time we got cleaned up. You need some supplies to get you started."

"Can I really get anything?"

"Whatever your heart desires."

"Candy and like that?"

"Yeah. But mostly girl stuff." He'd take her shopping for clothes another day. Doing both at once might be too hard. "You know, bubble bath. Shampoo." Slim pretended to wash his hair, making a mental note to stop at the barbershop.

"OK," Crystal said. She tickled James's belly. He fell over on his side, laughing and grabbing his feet. "But first I gotta watch the *Wizard*. It's time." She looked at Slim as if he might try to stop her.

"OK by me."

"Slim, you know how Dorothy gets hit on the head and all?"

"Yeah. That's how come she has that dream."

"What dream, you jughead?"

"Never mind. What're you askin' me?"

"What happened to me? How come I'm like this?" She smacked her forehead. "How come I'm a koo-koo nutcase?"

"Who says that?"

"Everybody says I got no brains."

"I told you, everybody's got a brain."

"The Scarecrow don't."

"He's a scarecrow. He's only in Dorothy's dream."

"What if I'm in somebody's dream? What'll happen when they wake up? Where will I be?" Her lower lip trembled.

"Well, Crystal. If you're in a dream, then we're in it together."

* * *

Rita warmed a pan of milk, added butter and honey, and beat in two eggs until the mixture became smooth and turned bright yellow. She stirred it into the sponge that had been slowly rising all day in the large pink bowl, adding flour until her wrist ached with the effort to stir the dough. She scraped it onto the table, pressed it with her knuckles, slapping the dough around, then leaned into it with the heels of her hands and set up a rhythm, puffs of flour shimmering around her. She popped the air bubbles with her fingertips and pulled it toward her, putting her whole weight into it as she kneaded, turning and pushing until the dough became a smooth ball.

"Yummy!" Derek shouted eagerly last Communion Sunday, clapping his hands at the approach of the silver tray of bread, excited by the tiny glass cups of grape juice rattling, as if it were a tea party, crying with disappointment when the feast passed over his head.

It had been a tradition to exclude the children. "But we can always change the rules," Joe said. Tomorrow, the children would share Communion for the first time and it would be the bread Rita was making broken on the altar when Joe tore the loaf, crumbs scattering onto the faded red rug.

"It comes from Moody's," Joe told her when he learned she liked to bake. "It's just ordinary bread. I thought you might like to make it." He shrugged in his characteristic way, as if it were no big deal.

An offering, this bread would be, her gift to the community. Despite Joe's reassurance, Rita felt daunted by the responsibility. She carefully cut the dough into pieces and began to roll each one between her palms, stretching it and smoothing it into three long ropes, then proceeding to slowly braid the dough, tucking the ends together and placing it on the oiled pan.

*   *   *

Crystal yanked a cart from the tangle outside of La Verdierre's and pushed it across the icy parking lot, the wheels bumping and squealing over the ruts as she pushed it through the automated doors. A car engine behind her raced as if the accelerator were stuck, but she didn't look over her shoulder. She plodded ahead stolid as an old woman pushing her cart across the white linoleum under the flickering fluorescent lights. Pausing in front of the magazines on racks against the wall, she fingered the glossy covers. High up were the ones with naked women she had watched men reach for and carefully roll into tubes they smacked against their hands nonchalantly as they headed for the cash register. Near the floor were the comic books and crossword puzzles nearly hidden by the Sunday papers, thick and smelling of ink.

"Take your time," Slim said, resting his hand on Crystal's shoulder. "Come get us when you're ready."

Crystal reached in her pocket to finger the bills he gave her.

"Whatever you want," he said.

"Anything?"

"Anything," he said, taking the baby to the toy section.

She dropped a copy of *Teen Beauty* with a smiling blonde on the cover into her cart. She wheeled past the cashier who was counting coins at her station near the door, moving slowly past the glass case of perfumes. The blue and white boxes with red crosses on them. The bright plastic jugs of laundry soap, the buckets and mops, boxes of lightbulbs and bags of sponges. Down to the back of the store where the pharmacist, with his white uniform snapped across one shoulder, leaned on the counter, his pale eyes blinking at the woman in front of him.

"Got this to home and opened up the box but there wudn't no guts to it!" The woman held up a red rubber hot-water bottle. Her voice scolded like a blue jay. "I can't use it like this! There wudn't no guts."

Crystal's hands were sweaty on the handle of the shopping cart. The wheels squeaked like her hair did when, to please Slim, she had washed it in the shower before they left. The front wheel nosed toward the center of the aisle. Crystal jerked it to the side, passing by the alcohol and camphor smells. The baby powder and disposable diapers. Cough medicines and laxatives. Hairbrushes and barrettes on a rack. Fake fingernails and eyelash curlers. The fluorescent lights hummed.

A woman in a blue coat reached over Crystal's head and selected a can of Aquanet. Crystal was afraid if she reached for something there would be an avalanche. The stacks of tiny boxes sealed in cellophane like candies. The pink plastic bottles. The emerald green shampoos. All of it would fall around her. Jolene. Nair. Lady Gillette. She turned to see what was on the other side of the aisle. Soap. Basis and Lava. Lifebuoy and Dove. Neutrogena. Irish Spring. She reached for the box decorated with sudsy soap bubbles, thinking any minute someone in a uniform would shout at her to leave things alone. Don't touch anything! But the woman at the end of the aisle in the pink smock didn't even bother looking up when Crystal put the soap in her cart. She heard her little brother scream happily near the front of the store. Carefully, she reached for a bottle of Pert; her fingers grasped it delicately as if she feared her touch could crush it. She moved cautiously like the arm of a crane swinging carefully to the place she wanted.

Once she made her first selections it was like a stream when the ice broke up in spring and the water rushed forward. There was no stopping her. She chose cherry-flavored lip gloss. Clearasil. White Rain cream rinse. Oil of Olay in a smooth glass bottle, something

her mother used. She chose Ban roll-on for the same reason, recalling how Janesta would raise her arms and stroke the deodorant up
and down. She got Jean Naté powder and perfume in a special package with a bow attached. And she bought sanitary pads, super and
regular, not even caring if anyone saw.

As she wheeled the cart down the aisle, Crystal thought of the
booklet Slim brought home. How it explained about the ripening
eggs. She selected a packet of Midol, then studied the pregnancy
tests. All everyone talked about was eggs. No one ever explained
how the baby got in there. If one got in her, Crystal decided, choos-
ing First Alert, she wanted to be the first to know.

She smiled to herself, checking to make sure the money Slim had
given her was still stashed in her pocket. "Now I'm a woman," she
said, then stopped, slapping her hand over her mouth, worried someone might have overheard, but there was no one around besides
James waving from Slim's arms, attempting to fling himself at Crystal.

"Jamesy!" She reached for him, tucking him into the child seat.
Someday she might have a baby just like her mom did, the egg getting
fertilized and all. But she would never leave any baby she had. No sir.

"Never ever cross my heart," she whispered, kissing James's
hands. "You wanna candy?" she asked him, steering the cart toward
the register, ready to give him whatever he wanted.

36

Perched on her stool at the battered sink, Rainey brushed her
teeth, checking herself in the filmy mirror before shuffling over to
Carol on her pajama-clad feet. She placed her hands on Carol's
knees and rose on tiptoe for a brief peppermint-scented kiss. Carol
had never kissed a child before. It felt like a rare privilege. She patted Rainey's hands and said, "Nighty night, kiddo."

"It was fun, right?" Rainey asked.

"The best fun ever. We'll do it again soon, too."

"We will, right Mommy?"

Rita agreed, picking Rainey up and carrying her to her room.

Now Rainey was in bed with her light out, the curtain pulled across the doorway. Rita washed the dishes and wiped the crumbs from the table, then knelt to prepare the stove, stirring the bed of hot coals with a stick of kindling, then placing a piece of split birch upon them, adding some ash and maple. She wiped her hands on her jeans and smiled at Carol. "I'll let it burn high a bit, then damp it down," she said.

They stood near the stove, their arms around each other as if it were the most natural thing, and then they kissed. Carol smelled the wood smoke and fresh air in Rita's hair. Her breath tasted of chocolate and sugar. Outside, the snow glistened like a carpet of jewels. She remembered how it felt to position herself behind Rita who had Rainey tucked between her legs on the sled. She sat on the end of the sled, wrapping her legs around them, trying to fit her heels into the slot near the rope. "Are you sure I can fit on?" Carol had asked.

Rainey laughed so hard she fell off and rolled like a puppy in the snow. Soon they were all on their backs in the snow. It was almost warm. A cloudless night with no wind. They felt free to lie side by side gazing up at the thousands of stars, making angels in a row. "Angels holding hands," Rainey had said. Then they slid down the hill, over and over again, laughing until their chests ached.

"Will Rainey be OK?" Carol whispered into Rita's hair, breathing in the scent of it again as if it were an elixir.

"OK?"

"Yeah, OK."

Rita, her hands on Carol's waist, looked up as if to memorize every feature of Carol's face. She shrugged and her eyes filled with tears, tears that did not rush down her cheeks but gathered in her eyes, making them even more luminous. It seemed as if Carol was not asking her if they were disturbing Rainey's sleep but if Rainey would survive, if she would grow up and thrive. How could she ever answer such a question?

"We can play the radio," Rita finally whispered. "Sometimes Rainey asks me to play it when she's going to sleep." She eased out of Carol's embrace and fiddled with the dials, turning past stations that crackled and whined, pausing on a slow jazzy saxophone lament, continuing along, deciding against the slide guitar and boy-meets-girl song, flipping past the static of a weather report, "clear tonight and tomorrow," the announcer said. She hesitated on "the revolution's here" then lifted the radio from its shelf, gave it a gentle shake, and turned the dial again. There was a tinkling sound like softly breaking glass followed by Carole King's clear voice spilling into the room.

"Hey, girl," she sang. They moved together as if the song had been their own private request and danced slowly around the room, careful not to bump the furniture, their arms at their sides, holding hands, their bodies pressed together as they swayed to the song.

Without warning, Carol began to weep, but instead of pulling away and hiding her face in shame the way she usually did when caught off guard by her emotions, she leaned closer to Rita, gave her weight over to Rita as if to say: Here, carry me a while. And Rita did, gliding her hands up and down Carol's back, pulling her close, letting the sobs rock against her as if she were a sturdy wall no storm could blow down.

Rita sang along, her voice blending in harmony with Carole King's. "How am I supposed to exist without you?" she sang.

Carol had never heard such a beautiful voice. It seeped into the room like warm honey. She wished Rita would never stop singing. She wished Rita would never stop holding her, too. It felt so good to feel Rita's hips sway, to let her own hips model their movements after Rita's, to just let herself go. Then Rita too began to weep and they stayed this way long after the song ended and another began, holding each other with such gentle care Carol realized that crying with someone was not unlike making love, as good a way to begin as any other.

Later, Rita sat on the white chair beside the table and Carol knelt to untie her boots. The laces were frayed and mended and double knotted, so it took some time for her to ease them apart, loosen the tongue, and slip them off Rita's feet. The whole while, Rita was smiling down at her, beaming actually, her face glowing with pleasure in the dim light.

"Let's go upstairs," she whispered, pointing to the loft bed. She touched Carol's face and gave her another kiss.

"You sure?" Carol murmured.

"Yes. Yes, I'm sure. I'm *really* sure."

They lay on the quilt. It was warmer in the loft bed from the rising heat, but in a little while, Rita warned, it would be quite cold.

"Where are you?" Rita giggled, slipping her hands under the layers Carol wore, searching beneath the thick wool sweater, pushing aside the heavy waffle weave shirt, sliding her hands at last beneath the thin undershirt she wore next to her skin, which was very warm. Rita traced the ridges of Carol's ribs. She reached for Carol with her mouth.

"What about Rainey?" Carol asked, smoothing Rita's hair.

"She's sleeping. I checked."

"I mean, what if she wakes up? What if she hears us?"

"We'll be quiet," Rita whispered. "Very very quiet." Slowly, she unzipped Carol's jeans, with barely a hint of the zipper scraping as if to demonstrate how quiet she could be. Carol was kissing her, planting silent kisses across her forehead, down her temples, pausing over her mouth, so close Rita could taste her warm breath, then Carol kissed her beside her lips and moved down her neck, everywhere but Rita's mouth. Rita moaned.

"No moaning," Carol whispered in her ear. "No moaning allowed."

She slipped Rita's sweater over her head, pulled off her flannel shirt and the T-shirt she wore underneath, unhooking her bra, stopping to admire the candlelight flickering across her skin, across her breasts which were perfectly shaped. She kissed each one tenderly as if she could not believe she was lucky enough to be able to do so.

With Carol's wool sweater scratching her bare skin, Rita could feel herself grow ready, like an intricate flower unfolding, yielding to the touch of a bee. In this moment, she knew only that she wanted Carol to never stop touching her, to never stop kissing her, to never let her go.

"Hey girl," she sang in a voice that was less than a whisper. "Don't go away. I beg you please don't go away."

"I'm not going anywhere," Carol said, kissing her hands, gazing into her sweet face. "Especially if you keep singing to me, I'll do anything."

"Anything?" Rita said, her eyes flashing, teasing Carol.

"Anything," Carol said.

Greedily, Rita slid out of her pants, flung the covers back, and beckoned to Carol. Carol stripped her pants and sweater off, hesitant under Rita's gaze; she was not willing to be naked. Not yet. They lay on their sides, their knees bumping, their bare toes curled together like snails at the edge of a tide pool.

"You feel so good," Carol said.

"*You* feel so good," Rita said.

Carol reached down, brushed her hands across the front of Rita's underpants, making her shiver with anticipation.

"I have wanted and wanted this," Carol said.

"Yes," Rita said. "I know. Me too."

"For how long?"

"Forever."

"That long?"

"Yes, I have wanted you forever." She shivered again and pulled Carol against her, arranging the blankets around them. As Carol stroked the spongy crush of hair beneath the thin cotton cloth, the logs shifted in the stove and there was the hiss of a spark flying. Carol remembered kissing Annie the first time they slept together, and she thought of her when Rita kissed her, nuzzling her nipples playfully through her undershirts. Loving Annie had prepared her for this and it did not feel like a betrayal to put aside thoughts of her, to give herself over to Rita.

At last Rita pulled Carol's long john shirt up, stopping before she pulled it over her head to place her mouth first on one breast then the other, kissing her through the thin cloth of her undershirt, as if she could not decide which breast she loved more and had to taste each one again, lowering her hot mouth over the nipples that bristled against the damp cloth. But when she began to take Carol's shirt off, pulling the undershirt with it, Carol held her hands and said, "No."

"No?"

"No. I need it," she whispered, her voice cracking. "I need to keep something on," she confessed.

"Like this?" Rita asked patiently. "Do you like it like this?" The two shirts were rucked up under her arms.

"I want my arms out," Carol said. She was crying again, the tears falling like there was no end to them.

"It's OK. Really," Rita murmured, gently freeing Carol's arms and arranging the shirt like a cowl around her neck. As she did so, she could feel the tension ease out of Carol's body. She sighed and smiled at Rita, still crying, she laughed a little, too.

"My silly girl," Rita said, brushing the tears from Carol's cheeks so gently Carol felt her heart would break.

They lay together, breathing in sync, their legs entwined. Outside, it had grown very still, so still it seemed as if they could hear the snow begin to melt.

"It's supposed to warm up," Carol said.

"You can't believe everything. Some things you just can't predict."

"Like us?"

"Yeah, like us."

"I started to think it would never happen."

"It? It? Has *it* happened?" Rita laughed.

"Since when did you get so bold?" Carol leaned on her elbow, tracing a line from Rita's chin down between her breasts, circling her belly button and landing at the edge of her underwear. She flicked the elastic gently, then began to explore Rita's body, softly circling, hesitant then determined. At last she stroked the strip of cloth between Rita's legs, urging her thighs apart, until Rita begged her for more, pleaded for her to please go inside and Carol pushed the cloth aside, resting her fingertips at the edge, poised, stopping to take up her kissing again, before gently caressing Rita to the rhythm of their kiss.

Every nerve of Rita's body concentrated on this one place where Carol teased until she was seized by a longing so great she reached down and pushed Carol's fingers inside her, rocking against them, arching her back, opening her legs wider, pushing against her until a shudder ran through her and a pool of hot liquid spilled over her thighs.

"You're so beautiful," Carol cried. Then she touched Rita again, without any guidance this time, pushing against the spongy places inside her, ready for the next release.

* * *

"Mommy!" Rainey called.

Rita pulled the pillow over her face.

"Mommy, it's Sunday," Rainey said.

"How d'you like my little alarm clock?" Rita asked, running her hand down Carol's bare arm.

"Rainey's the greatest kid. But what's the big deal about Sunday?"

"Church," Rita said tentatively.

"Church? You guys go to *church?*"

"Golly, Carol. You're acting like I just told you we shot heroin."

"Mommy, is that Carol?"

"Yes, sweetheart. It's Carol."

"Hi Carol," Rainey called.

"Good morning, Rainey Day."

Rainey giggled. "It's not a rainy day. The snow's melting." Water was gushing down the drainpipe, splashing into the rain barrels outside.

Carol peered out the window. The sun was so bright it was blinding.

"We've gone a few times. It's a wonderful church, too. Joe's great. He's the minister." As she said all this, Rita was pulling her clothes on. Carol remembered how Rita slid down to kiss her beneath the covers, trembling with the memory of the abandon with which she had pushed herself against Rita's mouth.

"What're you thinking?" Rita teased, kneading Carol's hips gently, leaning over to kiss her as if she had done so every morning for years.

"You know."

"I gotta be a mind reader?"

"You *know*," Carol said.

"Mommy," Rainey called again.

"I'm getting up, hold your horses." The house was warm, as if the fire had not gone out. When she opened the door, the snow was shrinking before her eyes. Rivulets of snowmelt streamed down the glassy path.

"It's beautiful out," Rita called. She propped the door open.

"I gotta pee," Rainey whispered.

"Can you use the bucket?"

"Carol will hear me."

"I'll cover my ears," Carol called.

"Promise?"

"Promise."

Rainey made a peeing sound.

"Did you hear that?" she shouted.

"Hear what?"

"Close your ears till I say yes."

"OK," Carol said, snuggling down in the bed, the pillow around her ears. She could hear Rita pumping water to fill the kettle, scratching the match to light the burner. But she could not hear Rainey pee. The snow melting in the gutters was too loud. Could it really be spring?

"Church?" she murmured, noticing the places where her muscles ached, rubbing her arms, rubbing the back of her neck, remembering as she did how good it had felt to rock against Rita, to let their bodies take over. Now church. What had she gotten herself into?

                              *   *   *

"So I go into this bar," Dougie said. "This guy, he comes right up to me and starts holding my hand. What're you doing? I go. He goes, what're you, shy? I go, wait a minute, I don't even have my coat off. He goes, you don't want to hold hands? I go, I don't even know you. So anyway, after a few drinks—his treat—he's coming on pretty strong and he asks me home. You'll never guess who he is."

"Who?" Carol asked. She was suddenly sorry she'd come home and called Dougie. Would it have really been so awful to go to church? She felt miserable. Lonely and confused. Rita acted like it was no big deal, but Carol was sure she was mad. Talking to Dougie wasn't helping. Last night had been wonderful, but now her life was turned upside down.

"Why do I get the feeling I'm wasting a perfectly good story?" Dougie asked. Carol could hear his slippers scuffing the old wood floor as he shuffled over to pour himself a cup of coffee. She could picture him standing on the kitchen side of his studio, his bathrobe falling from his shoulders, his little dog, Ralphie, tripping him as he made his way back to the bed. As if on cue, he shouted, "Ralphie, sit!"

"I'm sorry. I'm just a mess," Carol said.

"So you don't want to know about the rabbinical student I'm dating?"

"The what?" She was sure she had misunderstood. All this talk about religion had jarred her so.

"You heard me. Rabbi. As in Isaac Weiss. I even left my toothbrush at his place. I think it's getting serious."

"I think it's getting serious with Rita, too," Carol said.

"Uh-oh," Dougie sighed. "Is this about the 's' word?"

"Yeah."

"The deed has been done?"

"Yeah," Carol said, giggling in spite of herself.

"I hate to say it's about time or anything. We've been taking bets down at the restaurant."

"Tell me you're kidding."

"I'm kidding. So anyway, do tell."

"I'm not into details the way you are. You know that."

"I'll tell you what the rabbi says when he takes his clothes off."

"Why is everyone so involved with religion?"

"Huh?"

"They went to church."

"Who?"

"Rita and Rainey. They go to church. I knew there had to be something wrong but I didn't figure it out in time. They're Christians."

"God forbid."

"Very funny."

"Well, I found myself a rabbi. You know what he likes to do besides eat in expensive restaurants?"

"Don't tell me, please. I'm in no mood."

"Boy, you're no fun. I'm glad you don't have sex very often if it makes you like this."

"I'm hanging up now," Carol said.

"I promise not to hold a grudge," Dougie said.

*   *   *

"What is love?" Joe was asking when Carol stepped into the church. She was so worried about being late and making a commotion, she waited outside until the organ finished playing before she pushed open the old doors. There she was. In a church, for Christ's sake, she thought, slipping into an empty pew. Near the center of the sanctuary, a woodstove radiated heat, the stovepipe snaking across the room. Rita, her hair tucked into a ponytail, sat near the front, Rainey beside her in the red sweater Rita had made. There was Slim with James looking over his shoulder, holding hands with the woman behind him, showing his new teeth. Trudy Hyde with her hair set in fierce curls. The librarian. With her lover, Carol realized. That woman she had seen in the grocery store.

Joe stepped down from his pulpit and walked up the aisle. He was so short his robes draped the floor and his hands disappeared up the long flapping sleeves. The children began to raise their hands as if they were in school. He knew their names and called on them. Jimmy? Chrissy? Jodie? Carol had never been in a church where children were encouraged to talk. She had never been in a church where the minister walked up and down the aisles either. Where the minister was her age, for that matter. She had always assumed ministers were versions of her father, stoop-shouldered men with noses mottled with broken veins. But even my father was young once, she thought, surprised, as if she had never considered him other than how he was. Old. Grim. Shut down.

"God is love," a little boy in a red velvet suit announced proudly.

"Yes, Derek. God is love." Joe nodded.

"Love is bigger than like," a girl in overalls said.

"Love is bigger than like. You're right about that, Candy. Bobby?"

"Love is your birthday." The boy giggled and covered his mouth with both hands. There was a ripple of laughter in the congregation.

"Yes. Ice cream and cake and presents. That's love all right."

"Yeah!" another boy shouted, not waiting to be called on.

"Tommy?" Joe turned toward him.

"I love my new bike. I got it for my birthday."

"I love my puppy," another child said.

"Your puppy? What's its name?"

"Marshall. We named him after our dog that died. His name was Marshall too but he got hit by a car. So we got another dog but we don't let him run loose."

"Good. Yes. Love is getting another one. Another chance."

"I love this church," Rainey said, then hid her face against her mother. Carol was aware of a rustling. All around her, people were reaching for tissues.

"Where do we feel love?" Joe looked at the adults as well.

"In our hearts," someone murmured.

"In our bellies."

"In our unmentionables."

Joe laughed and clapped his hands. "Yes," he said. "In our unmentionables. Especially unmentionable in church." He clasped his hand over his mouth and people laughed. Carol had never heard laughter in a church before, at least not genuine laughter.

When Joe was back up at the altar, he began telling a story about visiting Guatemala. When he was still floundering around trying to figure out what to do with his life, he explained.

"I was learning Spanish," he said. "Thinking I might work with immigrants. So I figured I'd go and live in a Spanish-speaking country and that's what I did. I boarded with a woman named Marta who had eleven children. She had a long narrow house and she rented out the rooms. She and her children all slept in one room in the front. One of her daughters couldn't walk but she dragged herself up and down the hallway of the house to dust the rooms of the boarders. She had strong, powerful arms. But what I want to tell you about is how one time they took me with them to worship. They were very excited about taking me. I didn't understand everything they said, but I had this feeling I was in for a special treat. We went to the house of Manuel Ramos, the man who sold flavored ices on the streets. And there, in a room at the back of his house, was a mannequin. Something left over from the fifties. The kind of thing you used to see in JCPenney's window when you were a kid. You know, with the hands that screwed on? I don't know how they got a hold of it. Picture a great big Ken doll," he said to the children. "As big as your mom or dad."

Carol was so startled to realize this was his sermon, and that she actually felt like listening to it, that her body tingled as if the organ pipes still reverberated.

"Try to picture him. Painted-on blue eyes and a grim smile. Propped on a chair. Dressed in jeans and a white embroidered shirt with a cowboy hat on his head, a bandanna around his neck. All around him hundreds of candles flickering. The room smelled of melting wax. Saint Simón they called him and worshiped him with such love and devotion. The thing about this mannequin was he had a mouth that opened like Howdy Doody's doll. And the people poured glass after glass of liquor into his mouth, tucked lit cigarettes in his lips. They tried on his hat and had their pictures taken with their arms around his neck, smoking with him. He was a saint to them. Saint Simón. They took turns having him in their homes. It was a real honor to take care of him. Expensive too, because he required so much liquor and tobacco."

There was the murmur of laughter like the wind rippling the pine tree outside. No snoring like in her father's church. No minutes that stretched out forever while she fantasized taking the blouses off every woman in the place, wondering which ones had pale pink nipples, which had dark elongated ones, imagining herself unbuttoning, lifting, unhitching, pulling down, reaching in, until she was beside herself aching for the touch of real flesh while her father's voice droned on. No one had laughed at his sermons even when he did tell a joke because no one was paying attention. But here, the congregation leaned forward, expectant. And Joe looked out at them as if he adored each and every one of them, as if each were his friend. Carol was startled when she realized tears streamed down Joe's face; his cheeks were shimmering. He didn't wipe his tears away, but let them flow as if it were the most natural thing in the world.

"Saint Simón was an honored guest. He was given the best of everything. It was inspiring to see these people tell this mannequin their troubles. To kneel before him and ask for his forgiveness. To plead with him for the things they needed most. I sat in the back of the room watching. And it was here that I began to understand love.

"I was so touched by their ritual. By their devotion. By the hunger we all have to take care of something. To feel taken care of ourselves. By how much we want to give and give. And to receive. At that time I wasn't sure there was a God. I didn't have anything to worship. I was empty inside and needed to be filled, to be fed, like Saint Simón. And that's when I understood how much we want to love. And how hard it is for us to love each other. God gave us this great capacity to love, but we're so afraid to use it. So we lavish love on idols. Our cars. Our pets. Our homes. But that's OK. We need a lot of practice. Because it's so much harder to love another person. All the fear and risk involved. We don't want to be rejected. We don't want to feel vulnerable or silly. We don't want to get hurt. We think we don't know how, so we don't try. But God wants us to love anyway. That's what God is. The love that loves anyway. That part of ourselves that wants to sit in the honored chair. To be carried from house to house like

Saint Simón. To be wined and dined and given the best. And it's that part of ourselves that wants to give, too. That reaches out and offers a helping hand. That strokes a child's head. That pats a friend on the back. That takes a lover in our arms after an argument or just to say hello. That greets a stranger. That makes each person an honored guest, as loved as Saint Simón."

When church was over, Carol hurried out the door. She didn't stay for the coffee hour even though Crystal ran up to her and announced it was the best part of church. Her legs felt as weak as the stems of the seedlings Rita had growing on the windowsill. She would crumple beside the coffee urn and break down. Though she wanted to believe what Joe said—that she would be held in the arms of strangers—she wanted to get out of there, too.

She pushed her way around the people standing in the aisles talking animatedly, crowded around the door, eager to shake hands with Joe. To give him a hug. Rita waved, but Carol didn't stop. The need she felt, the love she wanted to give and get might come tumbling out, groaning and cracking like the ice melting on Preacher's Lake. She wanted to be alone.

Carol was at her table sketching when Rita came to the door. She never used to like having people come over when she worked, but lately it didn't bother her. It's Crystal's fault, she thought. She turned a hermit into a human.

"I saw you in church. What'd you think?" Rita asked.

"I don't think I've ever felt that way before in a group of people. There was everybody you see all the time around town. And they're all trying so hard to be tolerant and kind."

"Yes," Rita said. "It makes me feel like I'm really part of this place. Because we're all trying together. Buster shook Rainey's hand today. Shook mine, too."

Rainey was in the yard taking photographs of reflections in the puddles of melted snow. It was so warm, Carol had the door open.

"It was so beautiful, all of us holding hands when we said the Lord's Prayer," Carol said. "I even liked Communion."

"You didn't believe me when I told you it was something special."

"Church. Oh my God, I'm going to church. All the way there,

that's what I was thinking. Who's that woman? I about fell off the pew when she asked us to pray for oppressed lesbians."

"J.T.? She works at the birth control clinic."

"I was waiting for everyone to whip around and point at her. Nobody even coughed."

"She says the same thing every week. They're getting used to it."

"You know what I realized?" Carol asked.

"What?"

"I lost my faith at the same time my father stopped loving me."

"You don't believe in anything?" Rita looked alarmed.

"It's not that. I mean the whole idea of church, worship and all that. I have never been to church since I left home."

"Why don't you go and talk to Joe about it?"

"What do you mean?"

"You know. Like in have a conversation. C'mon Carol. We're all in there every other week with our troubles. He's our Saint Simón in a way. Only he doesn't drink or smoke. He's funny, too. Why don't you give him a call?"

"But what'll I say?"

"You don't have to say that much. Just tell him you were in church. You'd like to talk. You won't be the first one. You won't be sorry." She put an arm around Carol's shoulders and hugged her gently.

"Are *you* sorry?" Carol whispered.

"Sorry?"

"About last night."

"Why would I be sorry? It felt wonderful." Rita kissed her cheek.

Carol wanted to give her a real kiss. Their faces were so close, she was already swooning. But she hung back, suddenly frightened, the fear rushing through her body like a stream about to flood its banks. Love despite the fear, Joe had encouraged. But he didn't say how. Carol felt as if she were teetering on a tightrope, afraid to make the next move. What if there were no net to catch her fall? Before she could inch forward, Rita stepped back.

37

"Ah-oat," James said. He was sitting on Slim's chest, patting his cheeks. Slim continued to sleep. "Ah-oat," he said, leaning forward to give Slim a wet kiss.

"Out" was his first and only word. He sang it as if the sounds could transport him to the backyard where he loved to play. He would stumble in his high stepping gait after the sparrows scratching beneath the hemlock tree then clap and flap his arms, chasing the turkey, falling down as he tripped over the bumpy ground, pushing himself back up to follow the chickens, turning his head this way and that, imitating their one-eyed scan of the ground, mimicking their clucks. Being outdoors was what James loved most. From the time the boy had given up crawling around the trailer and begun to walk, he had demanded to go out.

It had taken Slim and Crystal months to figure out James's high-pitched screams did not mean he was hungry or wet, sick or lonely or spoiled. He just didn't like being put in a crib. Night after night, the baby's screams bounced off the walls of the trailer as he thrashed his curled fists and wept. No stuffed toy would appease him. No colorful mobile divert his attention. Light off, light on, blankets or not, it didn't matter. The doctor suggested they let the boy cry himself to sleep, he'd get over it, but Slim would sit in the living room, his shoulders hunched, staring at the TV with such a look of despair Crystal was afraid he might decide to follow in her mother's footsteps so she would stand at the baby's crib patting his back, patting his stomach, rocking the crib while James wailed, the cries growing louder and shriller, and sleep for the three of them impossible until she lifted him out and put him in Slim's lap where he would hiccup and sniffle then doze, his face buried against Slim's flannel shirt.

It was Crystal who finally realized that it was the crib James objected to. So they put it aside for another child who would find comfort behind the slatted sides, who would gaze at the lamb decal and coo. James slept on a pillow on the floor beside Slim's bed. He

curled under the kitchen table, nuzzled against Crystal's back on
the sofa bed, or sprawled across the foot of Slim's bed beside the
cats. Now he was wide awake and he wanted to go out. James pushed
his face up close to Slim's.

"Ah-oat," he demanded, repeating the word until Slim sat up.

"Ah-oat," James said, pointing to the window. Outside, the wind
hurled thick sheets of rain against the trailer, rocking it on its pre-
carious perch. It blew the new leaves on the sugar maple trees and
tossed the hemlock branches that smacked against the roof sounding as if someone were circling the trailer, searching for a way in.

"Out?" Slim asked, propping his glasses on his nose to look at the
clock. It was ten after two. "You wanna go *out?*" Slim scratched his
head all over as he looked at the baby. Had he heard him right?

"Ah-oat!" James nodded and smiled, a smile that lit up his whole
face, that to Slim was like watching a light slowly turned brighter by
a dimmer switch until the baby's face glowed. He clapped his hands
and shrieked his happy laugh, reaching to be picked up.

Slim dressed the baby, then pulled a sweater on and slipped on
his work pants from a pile on the chair. He wrapped the boy in blankets and threw a plastic tarp over his head, clutching it around the
two of them as he stepped out into the backyard. He held the boy
against his chest, burying his nose sleepily at the back of his warm
neck, breathing in the sweet fresh smell of him. He wanted Janesta.
He wanted her with all the pain and confusion that wanting
brought. Even knowing he might never see her again, might never
kiss her again, even knowing she didn't want him, he wanted her.
He stood with that knowledge rushing over him like the rain trickling down his back, drenching his collar, dripping down his neck.
His glasses fogged up and the tarp kept slipping off, but he didn't
really care. The rain was almost warm, the sound of it pinging
against the trailer, fluttering through the thick boughs of the hemlock. The smell of it rising from the wet earth was a comfort even as
his sneakers soaked up the water like sponges, even as the water slid
in slow rivulets down his back.

Slim watched James watching the rain. Every once in a while
James whispered, "Ah-out" and shook his little head from side to
side as if they were on the threshold of heaven itself.

*   *   *

Rita was listening to the rain pelt the windowpanes. Carol, sensing her alertness, turned on her side.

"What's wrong?" she whispered.

"It's raining."

"Oh." Carol snuggled closer. "April showers."

"Yeah, but April's almost over. If it keeps up like this, I'll never get to plant."

"Farmers have the worst jobs."

"Why do you say that?" Rita fluffed her pillow and settled back down. One of the things she really liked about Carol was how ready she was to have a conversation, even in the middle of the night.

"Because it's completely unpredictable. Rain or no rain. Heat or cold. Bugs. Whatever." She had a vision of Nelly charging toward them on her tractor, but she decided not to mention that. "You just have to make the best of it." She tucked Rita's hand under her cheek.

"Why are you awake?" Rita asked.

"I feel like I never sleep. Even when I'm sleeping, I'm awake. It's some hormone thing. I don't mind getting older. I just wish my body wasn't falling apart."

"It feels pretty good to me," Rita said, stroking her side.

* * *

Rain tapped on the windows, streaking down the steamy glass. Kaye refused to let the weather get to her. Refused to take it as an omen, to give it any significance. Finally, she got up and ran water in the bathtub, adding bubbles. She slid in up to her chin.

"The beautiful blushing divorcée," she said dramatically. She remembered her wedding day. She'd gotten her period that morning, heavier than usual, terrible cramps. It was a week early. She'd scheduled the wedding to avoid this. All she could think of was what if there was a bright red stain on the back of her white dress.

If that had happened, people could have stopped whispering and counting, marking their calendars because she and Michael decided to marry so suddenly. Now, they were getting divorced. She decided to wear her blue silk dress, the one with a tight bodice, a square neck that showed off her breasts. She'd wear black heels. Stop at Paul's for a bottle of champagne. Why be morose?

She couldn't imagine what Michael saw in Lizzy. She was flat as a board. That unkempt tangle of curls. Kaye had never seen her wear anything but baggy pants and an oversized sweater or shirt. Even on a work day, Lizzy would be in pants, gray or black, a size too big. No lipstick. No earrings. No pizazz.

This is what he wants? He's just with her to spite me, she thought. Once he's free, he'll get rid of her as fast as he can.

Though she really didn't need to, her legs were nearly hairless except for a few places near her ankles, she carefully shaved. She let the water drain and ran the shower, washing her hair, pampering herself. When she moved to the woods, there would be no more luxurious baths.

*   *   *

The house was even darker than usual with the rain falling. Lizzy grumbled, forcing herself to get up. She had clinic today and the schedule was full. A new patient at nine. Then nonstop for the rest of the day, as far as she could tell. Michael was already downstairs. She could smell the fire he'd made in the cookstove to ward off the damp and the fresh coffee he had brewed. Today was the big day.

She wished that she could just leave. She had told Michael she was going to, but still she didn't pack her things. She didn't get in the car and drive off without looking back. She stayed. Poor Aran, she thought. She needs me now more than ever with her crazy parents and their joint custody. Like a shuttle bus, Aran would be shunted from one to the other. Knowing Kaye, there would never be a schedule to count on. And knowing Aran, whenever something went wrong at one house, she would run to the other. At least Kaye hadn't built her house yet. So far, there were only the postholes dug. Right now, they'll be flooded, she thought. Maybe they'll even wash out.

*   *   *

"You figure we oughta start buildin' an ark?" Buster asked. He dipped his last french fry into catsup, and scowled out the window.

"You'll sink the ship if you keep up like you're doin'," Rip said.

"Speakin' of sinkin' ships. I hear she up and killed herself. Drove right smack dab into the river," Buster said.

"Who we talkin' about today?" Hydie asked.

"That crazy farmer broad up on Preacher's Hill. The one that went nuts and wrecked the place."

"It was poison. They undid the straitjacket and she drank some kinda poison. They say your face swells up something awful when you do that. Your tongue turns black." Rip stuck his tongue out for emphasis.

"Oh, she didn't kill herself. She's been let out," Hydie said. "You can ask Slim. She's goin' to some trade school over in Lewiston, gonna be a mechanic."

"Yeah, right. A mechanic," Buster said. "Next thing you'll be tellin' me she's growed a pointed head."

"I hear she got the operation," Coalie said. His eyes were dancing with amusement. "Mr. Bobbitt in reverse."

"Go on now." Trudy slapped him with her order book. "Ain't you got nothing better to do than chew the rag like a bunch of gossipy old hens?"

"She was one long drink of water, I'll say that for her," Rip said.

"Well, I'd have to be mighty thirsty," Buster said. "Trudy, gimme a slice of your rhubarb pie."

"Buster, d'you ever take the nose bag off?" Trudy asked.

"I gotta keep my figure," he said, patting his belly.

* * *

Slim and Rainey were on the sofa looking at Rainey's latest photographs. There was one of James's ear, the soft curl of his red hair around the edge. Another of the sole of James's bare foot, the skin puckered. James with the back of his diaper sagging. A close-up of his belly button. A photo of his hand resting on his knee, his index finger pointing.

"I'm gonna get copies of these," Slim said. He looked carefully at the one of him with the baby on his lap and Crystal leaning against him. "This here's a family portrait," he said.

On the TV, Bill Cosby was tucking his little girl into her bed.

"Am I like them?" Rainey asked Slim.

"Yeah. I guess. Your color, you mean?"

Rainey nodded.

"Yeah," Slim said. "You got brown skin like them."

"What's a nigger?" Rainey asked. Slim had begun to fry hamburger and onions for the chili he was making. With all the grease sizzling, he wasn't sure he'd heard her right.

"Come again?"

"What's a nigger?" Rainey asked, peering at him over the back of the sofa. Slim thought she looked like her heart might break.

"Did somebody call you that?"

She nodded. He turned the burner down, took a package of cookies from the cupboard, and sat beside her. She stared down at her yellow socks sagging around her ankles.

"Look what I got us," Slim said and tore the cellophane open with his teeth. He shook several cookies onto Rainey's lap. They were her favorites. Pink marshmallow with flecks of coconut on top. She ate one, licking off the coconut first, then biting into the marshmallow, eating it down to the cookie underneath.

"Well," Slim started after some thought. "Sometimes folks don't like it when they see somebody different. Ain't no reason for it, usually. Not really. It's just they're backward. They only see some part of you. Not *you.* So they call you a name. Take me, for instance. Folks laugh 'cause I'm so tall and skinny. They call me the trashman like I'm trash. They think I'm not worth a thing 'cause I keep the dump. Crystal gets called a retard 'cause she's different. Folks with white skin don't like it that other folks've got brown skin, so they call 'em niggers. But they're missin' out on a chance to get to know someone. And God help us if we was all the same. Wouldn't that be boring?"

Outside, the sun was shining, but it continued to rain, a gentle patter on the windows. When Slim looked up, there was a rainbow streaking through the clouds. "Lookit that," he said. He grabbed the baby and they hurried outside. A double rainbow arched across the sky. "If we didn't have a bunch of different colors, we'd never see such a pretty thing." He ruffled Rainey's hair.

"Looks like the pot of gold's in the lake or thereabouts," Slim said. James clapped his hands. Rainey held the camera up and clicked the shutter. "We'll have to be sure to get a copy of that for Crystal," Slim said. "She loves a rainbow."

*   *   *

Carol was so nervous as she pulled up in front of the church she had trouble getting the key out of the ignition. He's just a minister, she told herself. A preacher. Your father's a preacher. You spent half your life in church. What is the big deal? But she knew it was a big deal. A divine appointment, Annie would call it. One of those times when you have the opportunity to see yourself differently.

She walked past the church thinking of all the Sundays she had spent sitting in pews. All those Sunday afternoons putting the hymnals right side up. All those Saturdays when she wasn't allowed to play in the yard. Couldn't have a friend over because her father was writing his sermon. He would sit behind the closed door of his study while Carol and her mother crept around the house. Her mother couldn't cook because the smells distracted him. Then he'd emerge on Saturday evening, drink several manhattans, and collapse in his chair. On Sunday morning, the sermon would sound pretty much like all the others.

Daddy. She remembered him pushing her in the swing out in the backyard. Did she love him or hate him? What is love? she heard Joe's voice ask. How would she answer if he asked her?

Joe was sitting on the porch of his house. He wore slippers, a gray sweatshirt like Carol's, and jeans. "Do you want to sit out here?" he asked. "Or go inside?"

Trudy drove by, splashing the puddles, and tooted. Joe waved. "It's more private inside."

"Inside, I guess."

The house reminded Carol of a hippie crash pad. An unmade futon on the living room floor. Boxes of books half unpacked. A huge bowl of crumbling flowers on the table with a white ring where water stained the wood. Joe waved at the rooms where boxes were stacked. "I'm not very good at unpacking," he said. "So far I've been able to keep the church ladies from helping me. I'm afraid some of my books would shock them."

"So," he said when they were seated in two easy chairs in a small room off the kitchen. He pulled his feet up onto his knees in what looked to Carol like a complicated yoga position. She could feel the tears coming already and she didn't understand why.

"I can't believe I've started coming to church," she said finally.

"Sometimes I can't believe I do myself," he said. "My father thinks my being a minister is part of my adolescent rebellion. Only I'm forty years old."

"My father was a minister. Now he's in California. He's ninety years old but he still plays golf."

"That's something," Joe said. He pretended to swing a golf club. "I guess you've done time in church."

"It feels that way. Like I was in prison. But now, I actually look forward to coming to church."

"What brought you here?"

Rita, she wanted to say, but hesitated. "Everyone talks about this church like it's this great movie you don't want to miss. I'm from New York. I mean, that's where I lived before here. I'm really from Massachusetts. Where I grew up. What did you ask me? I feel like I'm just rambling on." Like my mother, she thought. What if part of going through menopause meant she turned into her mother? As if in response, a flash of heat washed over her body.

"What brought you here?"

"Oh. Yeah." She shrugged, not to indicate that she didn't know but to release the tension collecting in her neck and across her back. "It takes a lot of effort not to cry," she said. The tears began to plop on her lap like the big wet raindrops that were hitting the windows now. Despite the rain, the sun was shining brightly.

"Why try not to? I was reading in the paper the other day how scientists have discovered there's this chemical that's released in your blood every time you cry that actually helps you feel better. When you cry, you're healing yourself. It's one of the body's gifts."

Carol cried quietly for a few minutes. "My lover died," she said, surprising herself. She hadn't planned to talk about Annie. "It was an accident. I was waiting to see her and then she was dead. I feel like I still don't know how to live without her. I'm a lesbian," she added, checking Joe's reaction. The expression in his eyes showed only interest.

"To my dad, it was this terrible shame I brought on the family. I might as well have burst into the church and painted a devil on his pulpit. The last time I went home, before they moved, he wouldn't answer the door. He wouldn't let me in. I could see my mother sitting in the living room beside him, both of them staring at the TV while I knocked. I wanted to smash a rock through the window but I didn't. I've lived away from home longer than I lived at home. But it still hurts to be shut out of their lives. I try to talk to my mother on the phone, but we don't really connect. She's so old I don't know if she can hear me. It hurts to know I'll never see them again, but Daddy won't consider it even after all this time. I can't help it if I turned out to be a lesbian. That's who I am. I've always been this way. I even tried dating men for a while but it was horrible."

Carol looked out the window at the pine tree. A drop of water was beaded at the end of each needle. "It's good to talk about it," Carol said. "I miss my therapist."

"There's a lot of really scared people in the church, you know. Men of cloth? Remember that expression? It always makes me think of scarecrows and their rags blowing in the wind."

"My father never acted scared. He had all the answers. 'Rules to live by' he called it. If we just did what he said there'd never be trouble. I can't stop feeling like losing Annie is God's punishment. Because I loved her and I shouldn't have. And anyway, I didn't love her good enough. I'm too selfish to love anybody."

"It's painful to lose a loved one. It's human nature to feel guilty. But the thing is, when you let yourself love again, when you let yourself believe love is possible, it's like you find your beloved in the new person. Look around you. Who can you give your heart to? All around us, all the time, people are crying for love. Dying to be loved. And we get hung up thinking we'll get hurt if we show our feelings, or we'll just have to lose these loved ones all over again. When you feel that pain about Annie, talk about her, even if to yourself. Tell a story about her. Then let it be a reminder you're brimming with love. Take it as a blessing rather than a cross to bear."

"The cross." Carol groaned. "Oh, the cross. Why do we have to have that poor man bleeding on a cross? All through my childhood I thought every time I disobeyed my parents, which was a lot—it's hard, you know, to be the goody-goody minister's kid. Especially when you can't wait to go over to your best friend's house and see if you can convince her to lie on top of you. Every time I did something bad, later I'd think Jesus was paying for it."

"It's unfortunate that we focus on the cross so much as a symbol," Joe said. "Our culture has latched onto it so tightly. But it's there to remind us of the suffering involved. It's not easy to be human. Sometimes I think it'd be better if we focused on the open tomb. The rolling away of that heavy rock. The move on to a higher life."

*   *   *

"She showed up with a bottle of champagne. Wearing a blue dress. Black heels. Dressed to kill. She marched right into the house like she still lived there. I still had my nightgown on." Lizzy gathered the files for the day's appointments. The rain had caused a few cancellations, but still it would be a busy day.

"Devil with a blue dress on," J.T. said.

"Speak of the devil, did you say?" Trudy lumbered into the office, her rubber boots slapping the floor. She pulled her rain bonnet off. "I'm sorry I'm late," she said. "The roads are so wet I had to go real slow."

"Late?" Lizzy said. "We don't have you down."

"You don't?" Trudy dabbed her face with a tissue. "I made the 'pointment yesterday." She lowered her voice and added, "I found this bunch under my arm."

Lizzy rolled her eyes at J.T. "We did have a cancellation," she said. "You go on in and get ready. I'll be there in a minute."

"I know I'm a lot of trouble to you girls," Trudy said, settling onto the exam table.

"Don't worry about it," Lizzy said. She washed her hands, warming them under the faucet. Then she began the exam, searching for the elusive bunch. For Lizzy it was almost a meditation now. At this point in her life, it felt like the only thing she was doing right.

"Nothing to be concerned about here," she said, shifting to Trudy's other side. "Nothing here either," she said when she was done.

"That's surely good news. That sets my mind to rest," Trudy said.

Lizzy stepped out of the exam room so Trudy could get dressed.

"I need a vacation," Lizzy said.

"You're getting your vacation. Don't worry. I'll get it all arranged. I won't schedule anybody for that whole ten days. I'll just do routine checks. Send 'em to the hospital if there's any emergency. Dr. Bob'll be on call." J.T. shuddered at the idea. "I just can't schedule anyone to see him. I've had it with Dr. Bob. Half the women that get stuck seeing him end up driving to the Bangor Clinic afterwards rather than come back here. It's ruining our great reputation."

"Say, Lizzy. When you gonna come visit us at church?" Trudy asked before she left. "J.T. here's a regular. Now, tell me J.T. Didn't that about break your heart in two hearin' Joe talkin' about them poor little Chinese orphan girls the other week?"

*   *   *

All the way home, Carol felt giddy with relief, as if she were twinkling, bubbling. There was a steaminess in the air from the rain. I'm happy, she thought. It felt good to tell someone. A minister who did not judge her. Who didn't flinch.

"So tell me a story," Joe had said, pressing the tips of his fingers together, studying her carefully. "About Annie."

"Annie was very beautiful. She claimed she was fat but she wasn't, not really. She was large but very solid. Her mother had no idea who I was. Annie was black. My friend, Dougie, and I were the only white people at the funeral. We really stood out." She giggled a little. "Especially because I was such a mess, crying so terribly Dougie had to hold me up. Annie never did get around to coming out to her family. Anyway. Sometimes I think how she would have giggled to see her mother's expression that day. She looked so alarmed and kept glancing at the nurses—you know how they have nurses in some Baptist churches?—anyway, it was like her mother was waiting for one of those women in the nurse outfits to take me out of there. Her mother was very dignified. She wore this hat that was like some kind of armor. You knew no wind would ever dare to blow *her* hat off. She kept looking at me like she wanted to give me a good scolding. And I could hear Annie chuckle. She had a nice deep voice. We called it a radio voice. She could have been a disk jockey. I liked to make her laugh."

As Carol turned into her driveway she could hear Annie's chuckle, could see her as she tried to hold it back then let it go. And then Carol knew what the feeling she had was. She was happy, this was true. But she also felt hopeful. It made her smile to feel it, a big smile that came from deep inside her. A belly smile, Rainey would call it.

38

Carol sat quietly with her arms wrapped around her knees, watching the ripples on the surface of Preacher's Lake. Like goose bumps, Rainey said once. She had Rita and Rainey in her head so strongly now. It was as if they were always beside her, even though they were home now, working in the garden. She was taken aback by how often Rita got out of bed and left like it was no big deal. Sometimes she actually got up before Carol and left. There was no hanging around over endless cups of coffee the way Vivian had done. And the strangest thing was she wasn't doing it to please Carol. It was what Rita genuinely wanted. Still, in Carol's mind, it was as if they were woven together in a fine silken web.

Lily pads were bobbing on the surface. Soon the yellow blossoms would open. A bullfrog croaked and a fish jumped in the shadows. She was replaying a conversation she'd had with Rita that morning, analyzing it, positive there was something important she had missed.

"We're not joined at the hip," Rita had said.

"We're not?" Carol smiled stupidly. Once she had said these same words to Annie and Annie had cried.

"No." Rita smoothed her hips. "I don't feel any appendages."

"But if we don't live together, what'll we do?" Carol couldn't believe they were having an argument about not living together. That she had even suggested it to begin with. Sabotage, Iris would call it. If Rita insisted they move in together, she'd have an excuse to break up.

"What's wrong with what we're doing?" Rita looked truly puzzled. She poured milk into her coffee and stirred it slowly. Rainey was playing in the alcove off the kitchen where Carol had put a bed for her so she'd have her own space when they spent the night. She was pretending her crayons were people. "Mr. Green, quit that," she said. "Miss Brown doesn't like it."

"I dunno. I just thought that was part of the package. You know, fall in love, move in." Carol shrugged.

"Start feeling trapped, break up," Rita added.

"But what will we *do?*" Carol yelled. She set her cup into the sink with such force it cracked into two neat pieces.

"Why do we have to *do* anything?" Rita stood up, ready to flee.

"Why am I yelling about this?" Carol paced the kitchen, her shoes making kissing sounds on the linoleum. "All I've ever wanted was to have a girlfriend who didn't want to live with me."

"So why are you so upset?"

"I dunno. I guess I think it means you don't love me."

"Oh, c'mon. Don't say that. You know that's not true."

Rita hugged Carol, soothing her. And then she had taken Rainey and gone home. With no plans to return. It was infuriating. But at the same time, liberating.

"I'm all mixed up," Carol said. She flopped back on the blanket she carried down to the beach, afraid it might be chilly, that she would have to curl up in it for warmth, but the sun was quite bright. It was almost summer. Almost a year since she'd left New York. She thought about the shape her life had taken. She had a beautiful woman to love who loved her back. At least that was how it seemed. And she had a house all to herself. The whole day to herself, too. She could go home and paint, or take a nap, or read. She could even go over to Rita's and help in the garden. What was the problem? Maybe she just didn't know how to be with another person without bickering. Even if they both wanted the same thing. Maybe if I stop wanting so bad to be happy, I'll be happy, she thought. All of a sudden something black and sticky plopped on her bare arm. Startled, she shrieked and brushed it away.

Bird shit. She scowled at the trees, searching for the culprit. Then, on closer inspection, the sticky mass appeared to be a rotten berry, like the mulberries smashed on the streets in Annie's old neighborhood. She studied the trees but didn't see other berries. She was about to squash the thing into the sand when she noticed it moving.

"Oh my God." She cringed. It reminded her of *The Blob.* Then she felt silly. It was just some bug. Carol wanted to crush it, but at the same time she was fascinated, unable to imagine what it could be. And then she saw, as if it were giving birth to itself slowly in front of her eyes, a thick wormlike body with round bubble-shaped eyes begin to emerge.

"Bug eyes," she whispered, still not knowing what it was. The creature struggled to uncurl itself, as if it were glued into a coil, and as it struggled, it grew until it was several inches long. A black thing with wings plastered to its sides. And then an astonishing thing happened. The wings slowly unfurled and these, too, seemed to grow as she watched. The wings glistened and took shape. Like cellophane, the texture, with an intricate network of dark veins like the skeletons of leaves.

"Hey, you're a dragonfly." She laughed, marveling at the delicate wings. The dragonfly perched on the edge of her blanket like an airplane preparing for takeoff; it lingered, the breeze fluttering its wings. Then it was up, off into the air, disappearing over the waterweeds. A miracle, she thought, remembering a game she had played as a child. Challenging God, she called it. Show me. Prove you're there, she would say and then find herself witnessing something miraculous—a rainbow, a baby bird learning to fly—as if God were showing her a piece of handiwork.

The idea for a piece was forming. She could only glimpse it in her peripheral vision but she knew if she waited patiently, if she let it take shape and form the way she had watched the dragonfly, not realizing what it was going to be, if she could keep believing it would come, it would come. She hurried down the path, eager to get to work.

* * *

It was the first day of her vacation, a clear, warm, sunny day, and since both Michael and Kaye were at work, Lizzy had Aran to herself. To please her, Lizzy bought tuna fish sandwiches from Moody's deli case instead of making them at home. She picked up two small bags of potato chips and added them to her basket. She let Aran choose the dessert and drinks, not complaining about the amount of sugar in her selections, even agreeing to the package of marshmallows Aran held up like a prize. She felt the way she used to when she skipped school and walked around the streets of Dorchester, worrying about being caught, as if any minute some giant net would fall over her and her fun would be over.

Aran trudged along the path to Preacher's Lake following Lizzy. She had insisted on wearing her ballet slippers and they were getting dirty. She kept stopping to brush off the toes with a tissue.

"When'll we get there?" she whined. "My feet hurt."

"I thought you liked it down here."

"Daddy always carries me." She crossed her arms over her chest, about to let loose one of her famous screams.

"I can't carry you *and* the lunch, sweetie. Do you wanna rest?"

Aran sat on a lichen-covered boulder plucking at a buttercup. Every freckle on her smooth pale skin stood out in the bright sun. The shadow of her eyelashes fell across her cheeks. Lizzy wanted to scoop her up in her arms and carry her down to the lake like she would a baby, but Aran was too heavy for Lizzy to carry that far.

"Eye shadow?" Aran said, tilting her head coquettishly at Lizzy, offering her yellow-smudged fingers.

"I don't think so, Aran. It might make you sneeze or itchy."

Aran opened the purse she carried and took out a silver compact with her mother's initials on the top. She dabbed her nose with the powder puff and fluttered her eyelashes. "I forgot my mascara."

"Ladies don't usually wear mascara to the lake," Lizzy said. She felt a hopeless sinking sensation, as if any minute the ground would open and swallow her up. Maybe spending the afternoon outdoors was a mistake. Lizzy sat beside her and cradled Aran in her arms. "You are the prettiest girl I have ever seen," she crooned, smoothing Aran's hair. "Do you know some people are so pretty they don't need makeup?"

Aran studied Lizzy, her expression doubtful.

"It's true," Lizzy said. "Even some movie stars. They are *so* gorgeous that when the makeup artist comes to fix them up, he just says, 'Forget it, doll face. No one can improve on what God gave you.' " Lizzy said this with her palm under Aran's chin. "You're absolutely gorgeous, baby. The other stars should be so lucky."

"Dahlink," Aran said, warming to the game. She stood on the boulder and waved her chubby arms. "I am the star!"

She hopped down and raced ahead of Lizzy. "Follow me," she cried, tripping on the roots. She looked as if she wanted to cry out, but she righted herself and continued on, bravely heading toward the beach. A woman was coming up the path. Aran stopped, confused about what to do. She turned back to Lizzy for guidance.

"It's OK sweetie. It's just somebody coming back from the lake." At first, Lizzy mistook her for J.T. They were both tall and broad-shouldered. Something similar in the way they moved. Then Lizzy recognized the woman who'd told her about paper-mache. She wondered if she should remind her or thank her. Just remembering

Aran's birthday made her feel crushed. But the woman was so pre-occupied, she hurried by with hardly a smile.

When they got down to the lake, they waded in the water, Aran clinging to Lizzy, screeching when the fish swam by. After lunch, Lizzy built a fire so Aran could toast the marshmallows. She liked them to be perfectly brown, without a touch of black, and any that did not meet her specifications were tossed into the woods. At first Lizzy said it was a waste, but then she deliberately burned some so Aran wouldn't eat the entire bag. Afterwards, they rested on the pink blanket naming the shapes they could see in the clouds.

"See the elephant?" Lizzy pointed, tipping Aran's head in the direction she wanted her to look.

"See the dove?" Aran said, pointing at an oval cloud.

"A dove? Where are the wings?"

"Dove, silly. One-quarter cleansing cream."

"Oh. It looks like a marshmallow to me."

"Toast me it!"

"I would if I could reach." Lizzy pretended to reach for the cloud.

"There's the princess on her throne," Aran said.

Lizzy cuddled Aran. "You're my princess. Your hair's spun gold."

Aran ran over and threw her Barbie into the lake. "She's having a beauty bath," she announced and crouched at the water's edge swishing her doll back and forth. "She's at the spa."

"It's time to leave," Lizzy said.

"I'm too tired to take one teeny tiny baby step."

"I'll tell you what," Lizzy said. "You get on the blanket and I'll pull you to the path. Would that be fun?"

Aran's face lit up at the idea. "Really?"

"Certainly, mademoiselle. Get on. It's time for your magic carpet ride."

Aran sat in the center of the old pink blanket, waiting. Lizzy realized she had never done this before or else she would be holding on.

"Hold on tight. Grab the sides, Aran," Lizzy instructed. "Ready?"

Aran waved at the trees and the lake as if they were her admirers, then she grabbed the blanket. "Ready to rock 'n roll."

Lizzy pulled her, slowly at first. She was heavy and made an awk-ward bundle to haul, but then the blanket began to slide across the sand almost effortlessly and Lizzy trotted along, pulling faster. Aran laughed, shrieking from genuine pleasure, not as part of an act. Lizzy ran faster, pulling Aran. When Aran fell off the blanket she still giggled, not caring about the sand in her hair or getting dirty.

She jumped back into the center, clung to the sides, and demanded, "More."

Lizzy pulled her up and down the edge of the lake, bumping over the sand, gliding in places, the two of them laughing so hard after a while Lizzy fell herself, tumbling with Aran on the blanket, tickling her, wrestling with her, then jumping up to pull her some more until finally the blanket just gave way and ripped down the center, Aran still clinging to one half, riding along the sand laughing and happy, grinning with pure pleasure, as if the child she really was had finally burst free from the actress she thought she had to be.

*   *   *

"So what're you gonna do?" Buster asked. He ran his finger over his plate to gather the last crumbs of chocolate cake.

"I told you. I'm startin' a resale shop. On the lines of what Rhonda had there on the highway," Slim said. "She's stayin' outa the business after her place burned flat to the ground. It'll have clothes and household stuff and things I fix up. I'll have a shop in back. I'll be a buy-back center, too. You can bring in your bottles and cans and all. It'll be kind of like the dump only without the garbage." Slim spooned mashed potatoes into James's mouth.

"You stick that shed on the highway, Clarence Cushman'll have a fit. 'Folks don't come to Vacationland to see some shack,' he'll say." Rip tucked his beard into his shirt so it wouldn't flop into his stew.

"None of you guys ever listen," Hydie said. "Slim's been in here talkin' about it more'n once. Where you been?"

"Hic! Hic!" Coalie said, pretending to fall off his stool.

"I got a loan to put up a steel shed. It'll be all insulated."

"It ain't good to go into debt. Not when you barely got a pot to piss in," Buster said. He tapped his plate with his fork. "I'll have another slice of that cake and put a dollup of whipped cream on it this time."

"It's a government thing. Low interest," Slim said.

Trudy handed Rip a sack of the blueberry muffins she'd forgotten to put baking powder in. They were flat as pancakes. But that pig of his wouldn't know the difference. She had been so distracted lately, excited about Slim's new place because Raymond was going to be Slim's first employee. One of the conditions of the loan was that he hire someone from the disabled community. My baby, she thought, patting Raymond's cheek. He would just be down the road, but it seemed he was going further than that. She had never spent an entire day away from Raymond since he was born. I guess it's time, she decided. She still had the summer with him. Slim wouldn't get to work until fall. He had bought Alton Poors' old camper and planned to travel all summer with the kids.

"When the hell you goin' again?" Coalie asked.

"In a couple a weeks."

"You be sure to go to Niagara Falls," Rip said. "Me and the wife had our honeymoon there. It's something like you never seen."

"We're headin' south then west. We're not goin' that way."

"You hit it on the way back, then. It's one of the wonders of the world, all that water. You be sure you walk under the falls. The kids'll remember that the rest of their lives."

"You're comin' back, right?" Buster asked.

"This here's my home," Slim said. "No doubt about it."

* * *

By the end of the next day, Lizzy had driven through New Brunswick and was nearing Quebec. It took much longer to get there than she had thought it would, driving along the winding coast. They got lost in Meddybemps, then spent the night in Calais. Now the sun was a pale smear. Lizzy lifted her thick curly hair off her neck and flicked the radio on, looking for something broadcast in English. The sun was sinking into that portion of the day that demarcates afternoon and evening and she sighed, a sigh of relief and anxiety, as she pulled up to the border and the man in a beige uniform leaned out of his booth.

"Hello," he said, his accent a mixture of Scottish brogue and down east Maine. "Nice day. Summer's finally here, huh?" He waved them on. Aran was fast asleep, her head lolling against the seat. Lizzy reached across to be sure the lock was punched down. She'd meant to go home yesterday. Home, where Aran's things were packed for her visit with Kaye, the freshly washed dresses that had dried on the line folded into a suitcase. Aran had packed her Barbie with all her outfits on the miniature plastic hangers in the carrying case. But instead of turning onto the dirt road when they left the lake, Lizzy had just kept going. Now in the twilight, deer were under the trees, their jaws working. Lights flickered on in the houses they passed. People were home from work, the houses warm with the smells of supper. It was cooler now that the sun was going down. She pulled off the road to roll up the windows.

"Do you wanna lie in back?" she asked and Aran nodded sleepily, then let Lizzy lift her up and tuck the pink blanket around her. "We'll stop at another motel soon. That'll be fun, huh?"

The only other time Lizzy drove up here was when she and Dennis were taking a vacation on the Gaspé Peninsula during the first year of their marriage. The hardest year, everyone said. They bought a tent from L.L. Bean. A Coleman lantern. Neither of them had ever camped. They set the tent up on a slope and kept sliding down into their sleeping bags, their feet cramped against the zippered bottoms. Lizzy kept dreaming she was falling off ladders, sinking into quicksand. During the night, the wind picked up and the tent flapped so much it felt like they were on a sailboat tipping into a roiling sea. "Frost in August," Dennis had complained bitterly as if this were Lizzy's fault. In the morning, he swore as he tried to get a fire going, finally giving up, throwing the coffee water onto the smoking wood, yanking the tent poles up and shoving the fluttering nylon into the trunk, not caring about the tangled mess. "That was the worst fucking night of my life," he'd said. "Now you expect me to stand around freezing my balls off making coffee?"

Lizzy wondered if she would ever forget the disdain in his voice, the way he yelled at her as if he hated her. Had he ever loved her? Had she ever *really* been loved at all? She slowed as she headed toward the lights in the distance, and the promise of a town.

*   *   *

Carol stirred up a mixture of plaster of paris, dirt, clay, and sand. Mud, she called it. Before her was a large form she had fashioned from chicken wire and stuffed with twigs and dry leaves. She scooped the mud in both hands and began to slap it on the form, mixing some of the leaves and twigs in with it. At first she'd thought of it as a boat she could get into; she would hollow out the center. Then it seemed more like a giant milkweed pod. The image of the dragonfly flashed in her mind. It had formed like magic, right before her eyes from the sticky black glob she had almost squashed. She wished she knew the words for the process it had undergone, some kind of metamorphosis.

"Sarcophagus," she said. She liked the sound of the word, the way it felt on her tongue. She mixed more mud. She would need a wheelbarrow to mix it in, or at least a washtub, not this beat-up spaghetti pot. It just wasn't big enough. She could tell there were going to be several pieces. She loved the mixing and the feel and smell of the mud, the way it dried into shapes she hadn't expected. She would ask Rita for hay, build one stuffed with golden stalks.

She wondered what it would feel like to lie very still and have Rita cover her with the mud. It would harden to her shape. But then she would need some way to escape, to leave the mold of her body in the mud without destroying it. She was sure Rita would be willing to try it. She patted the mud in place, shaping it.

She envisioned an army blanket soaked in mud, spread over a form wrapped with barbed wire. She could smell the old wet wool mixed with the thick spicy mud. She would gather clay from out back, soak shreds of canvas and gauze in paint the color of dried blood, wrap it around another form. She could see the forms arranged around the studio, lumpy, misshapen, unmistakably human.

* * *

Pizza. Groceries. Gas. The glare of streetlights humming and buzzing. The first stars were out. But no motel. Lizzy smacked the steering wheel with her palm as she drove through the town. Four beauty parlors on the main drag but no motel. She should have stopped at the last town. But she'd pushed on. Now her shoulders were burning, a throbbing ache pulsed behind her eyes. Then she saw it. The red neon arrow flickered as if it might go out any minute. Rooms. Cabins. A hand-painted sign with a floodlight shining on it in the front yard of a weathered farmhouse that listed to the side. A barn in back like a house of cards. One wrong move and the whole thing would come apart. To the north, dark, bruised-looking clouds were gathering.

"They'll be open another hour," the woman who took her money had said about the grocery store. She handed Lizzy a key and smiled, revealing crooked, coffee-stained teeth. *Instant Asshole* her T-shirt said. *Add alcohol and wait.* In the room beside them, a teenage boy sat in a wheelchair parked a few inches from the TV.

"Howard Johnson's we ain't," the woman said. "But I expect you'll be comfortable." Her laugh had the harsh staccato of machine-gun fire. Her arms were long and white like the stems of exotic flowers.

"Come a long way, did ya?"

"That we did." Lizzy could tell the woman was hoping for more specific details, but she didn't offer them.

Once they were in their room, Lizzy sliced bananas into the plastic cups provided by the motel along with some cereal and milk she

had bought. Aran said little, but she perked up when Lizzy suggested they watch TV before bed. *Attack of the 50-Foot Woman* was on.
Aran snuggled close to Lizzy and giggled as Daryl Hannah, playing
the giant woman, stomped her foot and the people around her
bounced in the air. Oh, God. What am I doing? Lizzy thought. The
enormity of what she'd done began to sink in. Would the police
come after her? Would photos of Aran show up on their morning
milk cartons? And what was Lizzy going to tell Aran when she asked
for her parents?

"Isn't this fun, Lizzy?" Aran said. She seemed wide awake.

"Aren't you getting sleepy?"

Lizzy pretended to watch TV, but the sight of the huge beautiful
woman cowering in the barn was depressing. She stared at the fake
knotty pine with its evenly spaced knotholes. On the wall, two prints
of identical sad-faced clowns were hung. I'll rent an apartment in
Rivière du Loup, she planned, picturing them on a hill watching
ships come down the St. Lawrence. I'll get work at the hospital.
Nurses can always get work. There's no way I'm ever going to have
a child except to take this one. Take this one and hold on for dear
life, she thought, curling around Aran.

Lizzy fell asleep this way with the TV on, all the lights blazing, and
dreamt she found a baby in her car. *Untouched by Human Hands* it said
on the baby's shirt. The car was rolling downhill and Lizzy had to run
to catch it. She managed to jump in and put on the brakes, but the
car careened backwards. She yanked on the emergency brake, but it
came off in her hand. Finally, she grabbed the baby and leapt out the
door. The baby had thick black hair. Suddenly she was walking down
a path lit by paper lanterns decorated with intricate designs. Voices
murmured, but she couldn't understand a word they said.

*   *   *

Just after sunrise, Slim drove down to the dump one last time
with James tucked in his car seat. He tried to convince Crystal to
come along by promising her a treat at Hydie's afterwards, but she
said no.

"I need you to help me say good-bye," Slim said. "In a couple
hours, it'll be gone."

"Good-bye." Crystal settled on the sofa, the remote poised.

As he drove down the familiar road, he tried to picture the dump
a flat place, all the debris buried and the ground smooth under the
loads of gravel and fill. And when he couldn't see this, he pictured

himself driving the camper with Crystal and the baby beside him, traveling high up off the road where they could see everything good. He couldn't wait to get to New Mexico to see the buildings that man had made from tires and cement. He made some with bottles and cans as well. Ever since he'd read about it in a magazine he found at the dump, Slim had been eager to see them. He didn't worry anymore if buying the camper had been the right thing to do. He was glad they were going.

"You wanna take a trip, James?"

James clapped his hands. "Ah-oat," he said.

Slim was looking forward to the day the baby began to really talk. But by then he would be a little boy, not a baby anymore. Life is change. That's what the preacher said.

It startled Slim when he pulled up and the shed was not there even though he had torn it down and carted it home weeks ago and was already rebuilding it in the backyard. He carried James to the pit and they peered over at the rusted car parts, the candy wrappers blowing.

"It don't matter if they set it up like a park. It don't matter if they plant grass. Put up a playground. Everybody'll still know it's where the dump used to be at. Even if they bury these here tires," he explained to the baby, settling him inside a stack of tires so he could look over the top. James stared at him as if to study how he moved his mouth. "Even when they're livin' on the moon, these tires'll still be tires. They'll be under dirt, but they'll be exactly the same."

A breeze from the coast mingled the odor of sea wrack and wet clam mud with the familiar smell of decomposing garbage and tires soaking up the sun. Seagulls dipped and soared, plucking up banana peels, their loud shrieks filling the air. Where would the gulls be tomorrow? And the next day? And the day after that? Slim wondered. Would they return, hopeful, expectant, perch on the fence posts, swirl through the open sky? Or would they know somehow there was no reason to come back?

One of these days, if Janesta comes back, she'll be some surprised, he thought. She'll drive up the road, see where the dump used to be at, and instead find a park. He wondered what it would look like when he got back at the end of summer. Would the grass already be growing by then?

Slim heard the rumble of the dump trucks grinding up the hill and watched the yellow steel glint in the sun as the trucks passed by on the lower road. By the end of the day, the dump would be gone.

39

In the morning, Aran and Lizzy headed north, behind the workers who sipped from mugs as they drove toward factories and shipyards. As they neared the St. Lawrence, the bright blue water made everything seem fresh and full of possibility. Aran sat up, as if noticing for the first time that they were traveling in a place she had never been.

"What's that say?" she asked as they passed a large billboard.

"*Poisson*. That's the French word for fish. Can you say it?"

"Why don't they just call it fish?"

"Well, they have their own words for things. *Bonjour*. That means hello. *Très bien*. That's good."

"Say Barbie in French." She shook the doll in Lizzy's face.

"Not in my face while I'm driving, sweetums."

When they stopped at a diner, Aran chattered nonstop, flirting with the waitress who pinched her cheek. "This is so funny fun," she said, nibbling her donut, batting her eyelashes as if everyone in the place were watching her.

Lizzy tasted her oatmeal. It was the instant kind, thin, gray, and watery. The cook might as well have soaked the cereal box in hot water and served that instead. The real thing took time and effort. Like a family, she thought. Whatever made her think she could step into Aran and Michael's lives and instantly have a family? She checked her watch. Back in Preacher's Lake, Michael would be heating water, looking out the window at the hens scratching in their coop, shaking kibble into Miss Kitty's cut-glass bowl. Had they already formed a search party, scouring the woods? No, her car was missing. He'd be waiting, alert for the sound of it bumping along the road, desperate for the sight of his little girl. Suddenly, she remembered. When they were arguing the night before she left, she'd told Michael about the apartment she was renting. She'd yelled she was going to start spending time there. *That's* where he thought she was now. And Aran? What about Aran? Where was she supposed to be? With *Kaye*?

"Nobody even knows she's gone," Lizzy exclaimed.

"*Café?*" The waitress held a coffeepot poised over Lizzy's cup.

"Where we going, Lizzy?" Aran asked when they were back in the car.

"Home."

"We're going home, Barbie," Aran said, pressing the doll to the window.

* * *

"Maybe it's already too late. But I'd still like to try to find it," Carol said, trying to sound hopeful. After all, this had been her idea. They had been tramping through the woods all morning, up the hill, through the shade of the tall hemlocks and groves of white birches, the air rich with the scent of balsam fir. They had followed the woods road, even when it seemed to disappear into a patch of ferns, and still they hadn't found the tree with the blue cross painted on it or the huge mossy boulder Mrs. Thomas had spoken of that marked the place to turn.

"She made it sound like I *had* to go," Carol said. Her voice was tinged with despair. "Trudy told me Mrs. Thomas was looking for it when they found her out in the woods. She had twigs in her hair. She was all disoriented and had a big bruise on her cheek. That was right before they put her in the nursing home."

The last time Mrs. Thomas had spoken had been to Carol. Just before Carol left, Mrs. Thomas closed her eyes and went to sleep. She'd been sleeping ever since. Rita said it was not unusual. This was how she'd go, just drifting off into her dreams. But it made her last words seem like her dying wish.

Rainey dawdled behind them, taking pictures, picking up various cones and bits of bark. Then she ran up to show them a pinecone that a squirrel had stripped of seeds.

"I don't mind if we keep looking," Rita said. She plucked an inchworm off Carol's shirt and showed it to Rainey. "But I think we should have our lunch. Aren't you tired? Rainey's tired, aren't you kiddo? And I'm starving." She spread the blanket on a grassy clearing.

"Sometimes Lake," Rainey said, biting into her cheese sandwich. She wore a red cap Rita had doused with Woodsman's Friend, and so far the bugs had not really bothered her, though a few midges hovered.

"The Sometimes Lake. That's what she called it," Carol said waving away the bugs around Rainey. " 'Sometimes it's there, sometimes it's not,' she said. Then she closed her eyes." Carol unwrapped the waxed paper from her sandwich. "I know it's right around here. She said follow the woods road till you get to a Y and then it's over the rise. That's where the blue mark should be." She pointed at a gnarly oak tree. "It's in some kind of basin. It's from snowmelt or a spring. She said once she went looking for it and all she found were some damp mossy rocks."

"Well, things've changed since Mrs. Thomas was out walking in the woods. Or else her memory's gone foggy," Rita said.

"The thing is, she was so *clear* about it. She looked right at me. Not like her usual falling asleep in the middle of saying something. She was practically *perky*."

"Mrs. Thomas, *perky*? C'mon. You forget, I take care of her."

"I'm telling you, she was perky. I wouldn't make that up. She made it seem like it was buried treasure or something."

When they were done eating, they curled up together for a nap, they were so worn out and drowsy. The last few days had been hot and dry, so there were no mosquitoes to speak of, making rest possible. Carol was glad of this for Rainey's sake, but she worried it meant that the lake had dried up already. They would never find it.

When they woke up, the sun was slipping below the tree line, the light filtering through the thick leaves.

"I think we came that way," Rita said, pointing toward a grove of beech trees.

"I don't know. Wasn't it from there?" Carol pointed in a different direction. "We were heading toward that oak tree, remember? I just don't know what happened to the path."

"Oh, God. We're lost. Just like Hansel and Gretel only we didn't even try to leave a trail," Rita said.

"Remember how the birds eat up all the crumbs?" Rainey said.

"Which way do *you* think we should go?" Carol asked Rainey.

Rainey shrugged. "We climbed the hill," she said. She picked at a gob of pine resin that oozed from the reddish bark.

"She's right," Rita said. "As long as we go downhill, we'll find our way back."

"But where's the path? How'd the path just disappear? Who came and took the path?" Carol wanted to sound lighthearted, but really she was scared. She imagined them lost all night in the dark woods. She should have just come on her own. Why had it been so important to go looking for this stupid lake anyway? Stumbling after some old lady's fantasy.

"It didn't disappear. We just can't remember where it is," Rita said. She smiled bravely.

"Mommy, Carol, look!" Rainey called. She had wandered off through a patch of ferns to have a closer look at a huge red mushroom.

"Rainey! Don't you go off without us," Rita cried.

"C'mere. It's here, you guys. The Sometimes Lake is right here."

Carol and Rita hurried after her. There, surrounded by a circle of beech trees, was a large shallow lake. Its surface reflected the white puffy clouds that floated across the sky. The bottom was lined with a thick mat of fallen beech leaves, a pale carpet over soft mud. The wind rustling the leaves sounded like a large animal breathing. They watched the reflection of the leaves dancing in the sunlight.

"I didn't believe it was here." Rita put her arm around Carol.

"I did and I didn't," Carol said. "She was just so adamant about it. I'd never seen her like that."

Rainey crouched at the water's edge and dipped her hands in it. "It's warm," she said. Water spiders skittered across the surface. "You guys," she whispered, and pointed.

There was a toad, its body half-submerged in the leaves and mud. A leaf floated by, twirling a bit, and the toad blinked.

"Why's it like that? What's it doing?" Rainey wanted to know.

"Maybe it's ready to duck if something grabs it," Carol said.

"Maybe it wants to disguise itself so if something nice to eat comes along, it'll be ready to pounce," Rita said.

They watched the toad for a while, but it didn't make a move except to blink. It seemed to be staring at the lake the same way they were, with a mixture of awe and disbelief.

"Wait a minute," Carol said. "Look."

Ringing the lake, as far as they could see, hundreds of toads poked up out of the leaves and mud.

* * *

"It's a perfect day," Slim said. He put James in his backpack and grabbed his fishing gear. Crystal was on the sofa, singing "Good Day Sunshine." She didn't want to go to the lake.

The water was as smooth as glass. Like a picture postcard, Slim thought, thankful to live in such a place. He felt lucky. He had so much, though most of it had once belonged to somebody else. Even his wife and kids. *Janesta.* Missing her was an ache he carried, familiar as his heartbeat. "She stood right there, up to her waist in that water," he explained to James. The baby chattered back as if they were having a real conversation. Her wet skin had stuck to his chest as she wrapped her arms around him. Did she ever think of him? Days, weeks, months had gone by with no word. The sheriff said if a grown woman left of her own free will, there was nothing he could do.

As Slim watched the baby playing in the sand, he realized with a start that James had Janesta's hands. The same long thin fingers. A baby's hands, yes. But Janesta's hands, too.

Slim baited the hook and cast out into the lake. He didn't have to wait long before the line went taut and he was reeling in a ten-inch perch, the silvery fish glistening, slapping its tail. James shouted in appreciation and as soon as Slim got the fish off the hook and dropped it into the bucket, he let James try to pat it.

"Fish," Slim said. "That's our supper."

The fish smacked the bucket, splashing them both in the face. At first James didn't know whether to laugh or cry, but when he saw Slim grinning, he wiped at his face and reached in again.

"Fish for supper tonight, little tyke," he told James as he unhitched the hook from the mouth of another fish that was even bigger than the first. "He's nearly as big as you," Slim joked, holding the fish up to James as it smacked its tail in the sand.

By the time the YMCA Camp arrived, the children running noisily up the path, waiting at the water's edge for the counselor to blow his whistle so they could race into the water like wild horses, Slim had four good-sized fish in the bucket swimming in circles. "Guess we better call it a day, old buddy," he said.

James dozed as they started up the path, his head bumping against Slim's back, and Slim stepped carefully, not wanting to disturb him. He used to have to work so hard to get James to fall asleep, once holding him for three hours straight, not moving though his arms grew stiff and his knees ached, scared to breathe for fear it would disturb the baby.

Halfway home, Slim stopped to feel the sun full in his face. I don't have everything, he thought, wishing, though he knew it was impossible, Janesta's car would be in the driveway when he came out of the woods. I don't have her. But I got two kids. Me, the father of two kids. That's a heck of a lot more'n I ever thought I'd get.

James woke up and waved at the crows overhead, their blue-black wings glistening. He bounced happily, imitating their harsh cries.

*   *   *

"Are you sure?" Rita asked Carol as they were clearing the dishes after supper. The fields looked misty in the evening light. A firefly blinked, and then another one followed.

"Yeah, I'm sure," Carol said. She kissed Rita. "I want you to see. I *need* you to."

Despite her reassurance, Rita was afraid to go into the studio. What if she didn't know what to say? What if she just stared and her mind went blank? Was Carol going to show her the paintings she kept turned to the wall? Whatever it was, Rita knew it was important to Carol. A breakthrough she called it.

Rita had seen plenty of Carol's work. The sketches of Rita she had dashed off while they ate breakfast, and the more careful studies she worked on after Rita was gone. One, a painting of Rita in the center of a lush garden beneath a canopy of bright blue morning glories. She seemed to be growing from the earth herself. Carol had painted Rainey in a myriad of poses: in her swing, playing with China Cat, asleep on the sofa. There were several sketches of Slim, Crystal, and James. The wire sculptures she called *Vegetable Women* with their twisted forms covered with cloth and paper-mache. One had legs like carrots. Another had hair like lettuce. Some looked like ordinary women and then you realized their fingers were shaped like roots, their hips like summer squashes.

"The first time I went to a museum," Rita said as she poured the kettle of hot water over the dishes so they could soak. "I was twenty years old and this friend asked me to go with her. It was a Stieglitz exhibit. I had no idea who he was. I didn't know photographs could be art. The only time I'd ever seen anything like a painting was those big-eyed kids. Remember those? My mom got me one from Mammoth Mart."

"Hey, I didn't think you were even born when those were popular," Carol teased, pulling her away from the sink.

"Ha ha, very funny. Anyway, fads came *really* late to Indiana. So, there I was in a museum, all worried about what to say about what I was looking at. I noticed this woman staring intently at this photograph, so I moved up beside her to have a look. And she was arranging her hair! She could see her reflection in the glass."

"Don't be nervous. I just want to show them to you. You don't have to say a thing. I just want you to be with me looking at them."

The studio was dim in the evening light that filtered through the trees shading the house. Rita could make out several large forms on the floor. When Carol turned on the light, Rita felt a catch in her throat, then it was as if she'd been punched in the solar plexus.

"Oh, God, they're bodies," she cried, turning away. She was sorry she'd spoken. The forms just seemed so real, as if Carol had spent her nights alone exhuming the graveyard. It took her a few minutes to gather herself. She could hear Carol breathing steadily beside her. She stroked her arm then turned and let herself be held as she observed the pieces.

"I don't know why I'm crying," Rita said.

"That's the best compliment."

"It is?"

"Yeah. Really." Carol's voice was husky with unshed tears.

The largest form was swaddled in muddy blankets, wrapped with barbed wire pulled tight like a cinch. Beside it was another form shaped from muddy clay with bits of red wool and frayed baling twine tied around it. In the cavity of its torso sprouted a bundle of sweet fern. A third one had thin sun-bleached branches, some twisted spirals of driftwood. The white wood smeared with mud and chicken feathers looked like bones. In the hollow where her belly should have been sat a bowl of paper ashes.

"This one's not finished," Carol said. On the table was a small form swaddled in strips of mud-soaked calico surrounded by the *Vegetable Women* as if they were keeping watch.

"Can I touch them?" Rita asked.

"Sure."

Rita knelt and placed her hands on the piece with the sweet fern. It was surprisingly solid. It smelled of earth and hay. She sat on the floor and patted the place beside her. When Carol settled, she leaned against her. "I'm amazed at all I'm feeling," Rita said. "First, I wanted to just run out of here. I felt shocked. Like I was in the presence of, I dunno, something awful. Something forbidden. Now that I've calmed down and really looked at them, they seem vibrant. Very alive. I just want to sit with them for a while. Is that OK?"

They sat together as the last rays of the sun streamed through the room. Sometimes Rita was certain she could hear a low moan. Other times a soft laugh. Outside, Rainey and Crystal were running across the grass. It pleased Carol to have them close by. My family, she thought, and tried not to panic.

Rita gingerly touched the barbed wire that encircled the large form. Her fingers came away dusted with dry clay that she rubbed into her palms. "This one makes me think of Annie," Rita said. "She's in these pieces, isn't she?"

Carol nodded. "I keep thinking about what Joe said. About heaven. I keep thinking how Annie'd really like you and Rainey."

Heaven, Joe had said, was to him like walking along a road on a perfect day. You turn a corner and you're face-to-face with an old friend or loved one you haven't seen for years. You pick right up where you left off. You walk together and there are more familiar faces coming toward you, people you have missed so long and hard it never stops hurting. And they're there in your arms again.

"You guys," Rainey shouted. She pressed her face to the screen. "We're doing cartwheels. Come and see." Crystal kicked her feet up and flopped on the ground, then attempted to walk on her hands. Rainey ran over, grabbed her feet and held them, walking her across the yard like she was steering a wheelbarrow while Rita and Carol clapped.

Carol had never wanted to have a child, had no desire to be someone's mother. But now, to her surprise, she realized she wouldn't mind being Rainey's father. A protector. A provider. She knew Annie would be pleased.

40

The apartment was brightly lit as if spotlights were aimed at all the windows. Lizzy had pulled the shades, but it didn't make any difference. Like a prison yard, she thought, peering out at the parking lot of the post office behind her apartment. Why did they need so many lights? She hung her beach towel over the bedroom window and even then she could see the huge strawberries splashed across the gaudy wallpaper. She would get busy in the morning peeling it off, she planned. Then get some kind of heavy-duty curtains.

Lizzy tossed and turned, punching the pillow she'd picked up at K mart. It was so bouncy it seemed to push her head away. The new sheets were rough against her skin. The apartment had come furnished, but she'd needed things. Her old stuff from her marriage to Denny was still in storage. And she didn't have the heart to go through all that.

I'll have a yard sale, she decided, turning on her side, away from the window where the bright light leaked around the edges of the towel. She felt as if she were waiting for something, but she didn't know what.

Michael had followed her around as she shoved her clothes and things into paper bags. "Don't you think we should talk about this?" he asked. But he hadn't seemed all that upset. Not really. Maybe he wasn't capable of being upset. Like the dense gray slate he planned to put on the kitchen floor. Impermeable.

When Lizzy closed her eyes, she could see the tar road unfurling, the stream of yellow lines rushing toward her, still hear the whir of the semis whooshing past leaving her caught momentarily in their wake. Aran had wrapped her arms tightly around Lizzy's neck in a stranglehold good-bye. Lizzy missed her. As she struggled to get comfortable on the saggy bed, Lizzy realized she also missed Miss Kitty. Every night the kitten scaled the bedspread, scrambled up onto the bed, and curled beside Lizzy, purring loudly. She wished she could feel Miss Kitty's warm body settle against her.

At 5 A.M. a loud crashing sound tore into her dream that she was on the highway, about to collide with an oncoming truck. Lizzy had no idea where she was. Then she stumbled into the kitchen and looked out the window. A huge woman, her arms and legs distorted like an oversculpted bodybuilder, had unlatched a steel ramp and dropped it against the cement loading dock. She was carting sacks of mail off a truck. The lights still blazed, but they seemed insignificant in the morning light.

Lizzy looked around her kitchen. The cupboards, painted white, were so high she would need a stepladder to reach most of them. They were covered with so many layers of paint, not one door shut. The table was wobbly. When she sat down her coffee slopped over the sides of her cup. In the bathroom, the toilet was running and all the faucets leaked. Modern living, she thought.

As she made some toast, she pictured an orange kitten lapping milk from a saucer by the stove. Still missing Miss Kitty who curled on her lap while she ate, she imagined a black cat on the cushion of the other chair. She would brush them and feed them and play with them. They wouldn't expect any more. She remembered the variety of cats that had gathered in Slim's trailer. Surely, he would be happy to give away a couple more. As soon as it was a decent hour, she decided, she would drive out to Slim's.

* * *

After the sermon, Joe ended with his favorite scripture: "Let us therefore come boldly unto the throne of grace, that we may obtain mercy, and find grace to help in time of need." He loved the word *boldly*, the fearlessness of that approach. He waited to see if anyone had anything to share. Outside, a pair of white-throated sparrows whistled. He could see them perched on a wire. The sun spilled onto the faded red cushions and streaked across the worn strip of red carpet. He gazed gratefully at the pitcher of wildflowers on the altar. "Expect the unexpected," Clark used to say when Joe felt discouraged, reminding him of the disciples pulling in their net full of fish. Joe was glad he had waited for the right call. He couldn't imagine serving any other church.

In a few minutes, they would sing together. He would say the benediction, then they would troop out to their cars and form a procession to the lake. But now he bowed his head and waited, the smooth black cloth brushing the backs of his hands.

Trudy pushed herself up out of the pew and plucked at her skirt. "I'm not one to talk in church," she started. "But—" She paused as if she'd forgotten what she wanted to say. Raymond leaned forward and hugged her around the hips. "Sometimes it's the little ones that got the most to give. I look at these here children in our congregation. I used to think we'd never have another Sunday School. Now I'm teachin' it. It sure does my heart good to see their little faces. Today, we made lambs outa cotton balls. We're all God's little lambs, I told 'em. As you know, I've been just sick over my mother. She's been sleepin' now for so long. They don't figure she'll wake up. It don't matter if the person's lived one year or a hundred and three, you still don't want 'em to go. You just don't. And it's not like I didn't know it was comin'. We've all been waitin' for her to go. It'll be the end of her sufferin', folks say, though we did our best to see she was comfortable. Oh, listen to me goin' on. What I'm tryin' to spit out here is how happy I am seein' these kids. Thinkin' about their lives ahead of them does me good."

Sitting between her mother and Carol, Rainey was playing with the lamb she had made. The plastic eyes she had glued on rolled as she walked it across her lap. She was wearing the new white dress her mother had sewn, the hem trimmed with a ring of embroidered monkeys. She still couldn't decide if she was going to wade into the water wearing it or not. Just in case, she'd put her bathing suit on underneath. Rita had gotten up early to slice the chickens she'd roasted and pack the cooler for the picnic they were going to have. Rainey's stomach growled and Carol smiled down at her and her mother patted her hand. Carol was going to be her godmother and Slim her godfather. Rainey couldn't wait until they were all down at the lake. Patches of sun played over her skirt and she moved her hands in and out of the light and fingered the brown thread of the monkeys. Some of them were linked together by their tails. Others held hands as they marched along. Would she feel different? she wondered. Or would she still be the same?

Slim rose to his feet and shifted the baby to his hip. "I been thinkin'," he said. "I been thinkin' about this whole idea of forgive-

ness. I mean, how Jesus forgives us. I ain't never been one for religion. This is the most church I ever had. My mom used to say it was
the waste of a day off, goin' to church when you could be sleepin'
in. I started comin' because I figured it'd be good for my kids. And
I like gatherin' together the way we do. I can't say as I can make a
whole lot of sense out of it, but I'm gonna take them Bible classes
in the fall. Anyways, what I wanna say is I know some of you got
hard feelings towards Janesta. You think she did me wrong. But
lemme tell you. There's not a day that goes by when I don't thank
the good Lord for puttin' her in my life. I never knew what love
was. I had no idea how it felt. I didn't know you could love somebody so bad you'd act a fool. I never knew how it felt to have a broken heart, neither. Like to hurt so bad you don't want to keep on
breathin'. I never knew any of that before Janesta. I was just a day-
to-day kind of fella and Janesta came along and said, 'Here. Here's
some life. With all its mess. Take a big hunk of it.' And I'm glad she
did. 'Here's two kids for you to love,' she said. And I've did my best.

"The thing is, that love don't up and go away. When you love, it
don't go away. The people go. But the love stays. Right here." Slim
patted his chest. "And I ain't one bit sorry to feel it."

A rustling moved through the congregation, but no one else
stood up. It was as if Slim had spoken for them all. Joe nodded at
the organist who played the opening strains of "On Eagles' Wings."
He lifted his hands, watching his congregation rise, fumbling for
the proper page, an incongruous group of people if there ever was
one, he thought. Brought together by the common love of a place
and their own faltering path toward God.

*   *   *

Rita, Rainey, and Carol were the first to arrive. They waited by the
path until Slim and the kids caught up, then began to make their
way down to the lake carrying bags and coolers.

"We brung potato salad and potato chips," Crystal said. "Slim
made eggplant. Gross." She wanted to know what Carol and Rita
had brought and they had repeated it twice by the time they got to
the edge of the woods. They stopped at the field of wildflowers, a
bright swath of purple, yellow, and pink.

"That's where it used to be at," Slim said, pointing to a spruce
tree that towered in the field. "The old church. You can still see
some of the old cornerstones if you dig around."

A warm breeze was blowing and when they got to the lake, they spread blankets and Slim set the baby on one. He promptly pushed himself up, leaning on a cooler for support. They could hear voices coming through the woods. Hydie, Trudy, and Raymond arrived, Trudy with two of her raspberry pies. Raymond toted a large thermos of lemonade.

"I brung the hamburgs, hot dogs, and buns," Hydie said. "I just hope Buster remembers the charcoal and grill."

Joe came up the beach in his cutoffs and flip-flops, carrying a bowl of salad. And then everyone was there, gathering in clusters, waiting. "I guess I have to start," Joe said.

"You're the preacher," Slim said. James bounced in his arms, reaching out as if he wanted to hug everyone.

"We live in an evolving world. A revolving world. A changing world. A becoming world," Joe began. "Our universe is not static. It cannot stand still. And God is part of that becoming and expanding and changing. Within us and outside of us, ever-present, always there." He looked out over his congregation, gathered on the sand. This is what I studied all those years for, he told himself.

"I've thought a lot about this day," Joe said. "As you know, this is my first baptism. But with your help, we'll do it. Rainey and James will be baptized into the holy spirit of our community, to be watched over, to receive the gift of our guidance. OK, here we go."

Joe took Rainey's hand and waded out into the water. Rainey's white dress billowed for a moment just like she had imagined it would, then it soaked up the water and pressed against her skin. Slim, carrying James, waded in beside them. He winked at Rainey. The first time Slim had waded into this lake, he'd had no idea what he was headed for, he just stumbled out after Janesta. Like James, taking his first steps, everything was new.

Rainey slipped her hand into Slim's. He was not her father. She knew this. Yet she could love Slim anyway. Besides, he would be her godfather. Her mother had said that was really special. The baby clapped and reached down as if he wanted to be put in the water. Was he her brother now? And Crystal her sister? Crystal waded into the water, almost up to her knees, then turned back to the shore where she was busy drying her feet. We're a family, Rainey decided. She couldn't stop smiling. The sun was very warm. It made bright golden patterns on the surface of the lake. Silvery perch darted through the water tickling her feet.

Then Joe began to speak the ancient words, blessing them, telling them that in God's name they were born anew. On the shore, Rainey could see her mother and Carol, their arms around each other's waists. Trudy was behind Raymond, both hands on his shoulders, and Hydie behind her in the same pose. Rip and his wife waded at the water's edge, as if thinking of joining them. And then it was over. The drops of water had trickled through her hair, slid down her nose, and were gone before they hit her chest.

*   *   *

There were twenty or so people and enough food for three times as many, Lizzy thought. Someone had carted down a folding table and it was laden with bread and cheese. Roasted chickens and salads. Papers cups beside a huge container of Kool-Aid. Plates of cookies were spread out beside a chocolate layer cake and two pies. At one end, a tray of sandwiches—egg salad, ham, and tuna cut into neat triangles—stacked like a pyramid. It seemed nobody had the nerve to take one, worried if they did, the whole thing would collapse.

Lizzy scanned the beach looking for J.T. and Betty. She had seen their car with the others parked by the road when she'd gone to Slim's. She imagined they'd come down for a swim. When she saw Trudy Hyde, she ducked behind the old man with a beard she'd often seen on the porch at Buster's. Because she'd never seen him anywhere else, he looked out of place with his pants rolled up, wading in the lake. She wondered what was going on. Why were they all down here? Was it somebody's birthday? Buster and Hydie were standing over a bed of charcoal, seemingly oblivious of the thick smoke rising from the grilled meat. There was Rainey's mother. Lizzy couldn't remember her name. She was talking to the tall woman whose hair was streaked with silver. "Paper-mache gal," Lizzy called her. The day she'd seen her on the path as she and Aran walked to the lake seemed like years ago. Now Aran was home, where she belonged, and Lizzy had moved to the apartment. My hovel, she thought, feeling sorry for herself.

"Lizzy!" J.T. called. She hurried up and gave her a kiss. "I'm so glad you're here," she said, as if she'd been expecting her. "How's your vacation going?"

Lizzy had forgotten she was on vacation. She let J.T. lead her over to the table. She poured her some lemonade and got her a plate. "What's going on?" Lizzy asked. "I mean, what is this?"

"We had a baptism. Rainey, remember Rita's little girl?" she pointed. "And James, Slim's baby. We figured we'd have coffee hour down here and then it turned into a picnic. How'd you find us?"

"I was out here," Lizzy said. She didn't explain about heading to Slim's on a quest for kittens. "I saw your car," she said, and shrugged.

"So," J.T. said. "What's happening? You look kinda freaked out."

"I tried to steal Aran," Lizzy said, waving a fly from the salad.

"You what?"

"I just started driving. I was in Quebec when I turned back. The weirdest thing was nobody knew I had her. We were gone for days and nobody even knew. Michael assumed she was with Kaye. Kaye didn't even notice. They have such a wacky mixed-up schedule about who's going to have her they didn't even know *I* had her. She could've been ready to graduate from high school before they noticed."

"Didn't Michael notice *you* were gone?"

"No. I told him I was gonna move out. I don't know what got into me. I just took that apartment over behind the post office. I figured, what the hell." She clasped her hand over her mouth. "Sorry. I forgot I was with the church crowd."

"We talk about hell," J.T. said. "C'mon. Here's Joe."

J.T. led Lizzy up to a man with dark curls who was jabbing emphatically as he talked to Carol. Carol was nodding and smiling. "I hear you. I just don't agree with you," she said.

"Joe, I have someone I want you to meet." J.T. nudged Lizzy forward.

They stood eye to eye, shaking hands. His hand was small, almost the size of her own, Lizzy realized. Unusual in a man.

"The same, the same," Crystal said. She tugged on Joe's sleeve and plucked at Lizzy's shorts. "Toe to toe," she added.

Lizzy didn't know who Crystal was or what she was talking about. But so far, she liked Joe. His hand was very warm; he still hadn't let go of hers. He held it as if he had some plan for it that he hadn't figured out yet. From time to time, he patted it as if to remind her he hadn't forgotten. He pressed it between both of his hands and continued talking to the people around him, introducing Lizzy as if he'd known her for years. Lizzy couldn't really pay attention to what people were saying. Her heart was fluttering wildly. It's too soon to get involved with someone new, she cautioned herself.

"Hello, de-ah," Trudy said, making her way across the beach. "It's good to see you join us at last."

"Trudy," Carol said. "Did I tell you my good news?"

"What de-ah? You fixin' on gettin' married?" Trudy said.

"Not in this lifetime," Carol said. She gave J.T. a significant look. J.T. winked, then rolled her eyes. "This gallery in New York wants to show my new pieces. My vegetable women."

"Your what?" Trudy asked.

"My vegetable women. These sculptures I made."

"I gotta come by one of these days and have a look at them before you're all famous and too busy for the likes of me."

Carol almost invited her to stop by the house afterwards, but felt suddenly shy at the idea of Trudy in her studio, her mouth gaping, for once with nothing to say.

Crystal dragged Slim up to Lizzy and Joe. Joe was pressing Lizzy's hand against his stomach now. She felt alarmed but did not pull her hand away.

"How'd that birthday cat work out?" Slim asked. His baby boy was toddling around, holding onto people's legs for balance.

"Fine," Lizzy said. "I was thinking I might like another one."

Joe tucked her hand into the crook of his arm, as if trying out various places to find where it best belonged. Why wasn't she yanking her hand away? Lizzy wondered, realizing she liked it. She felt strangely soothed. If nothing else, it felt good to stand shoulder to shoulder with someone her own size. J.T. winked at her.

"See," Crystal said. "Slim, I told you. They're the same." She wanted Joe and Lizzy to stand with their backs together so she could prove they were the same height. She wouldn't stop asking until they agreed. Reluctantly, Joe let go of Lizzy's hand.

"Toe to toe," Crystal said. She pointed at their feet. She wanted them to stand toe to toe. As they did, Joe put his hands on Lizzy's waist and dipped his knees.

"Shall we dance?" He laughed.

Everyone moved aside to make room for them as they waltzed across the sand.

41

"This is it?" Bev asked. The car purred to a stop.

Nelly nodded. She climbed out slowly, careful not to slam the door. She didn't want to make noise. Crickets chirped in the timothy that grew alongside the drive. The strawberry fields had been planted in buckwheat. Not a bad idea, she thought.

"Some operation," Bev said. She got out and leaned on the car.

"Yeah. It used to be. . . . Well, I won't go into that."

"Good plan."

"That's Slim's. That trailer over there." She pointed. A small blue butterfly hovered over a dandelion at her feet.

Nelly had imagined Rita would come to the door when she arrived. She had pictured her standing in a rectangle of light, a defiant look on her face, Rainey behind her silently brooding. Yet when she stepped up onto the pallet, the door was still closed. She knocked, noticing that the weather-beaten door had been given several coats of fresh red paint. Cheerful, she thought. The new screen on the door was stapled neatly in place. She was trembling, but that was nothing new. Sometimes she shook so much she had to lie down and be wrapped in blankets. The doctors said with time it would go away. She knocked again and shrugged at Bev who was making her way through a field of daisies, the hem of her long skirt bunched in her hands.

"No one's home," Nelly said. She shielded her eyes, scanning the back field. It had been planted in oats, silvery green stalks of grass that shimmered. Oats're good, she thought. The garden was a small square at the edge of the field surrounded by zinnias and portulaca, the bright flowers bobbing in the breeze. Rows of onions, lettuce, tomatoes, carrots. Potatoes, cabbage, green beans. Sweet corn and squash. Sunflowers. Basil, dill, and parsley. All of it carefully cultivated. A kneeling angel, cast in cement, was set at the edge.

"Over there," Bev said, pointing toward the pasture where Rita was surrounded by sheep. She'd been about to feed them when a small rapping sound carried on the breeze made her turn toward the house. She wanted to flee, to run up into the woods or across the road to the lake. Anything to get away. She was glad Rainey'd gone over to Slim's to play. Nelly raised her hand and waved once. The sheep crowded around Rita, bleating pitifully, bumping each other, knocking her legs with their hard heads, butting the bucket of grain until she shooed them back and spilled the grain into their feeder.

"They look good," Nelly said. She was on the other side of the fence nervously chewing her bottom lip.

Shattered, Rita thought. She looks shattered. Like a china plate smashed into hundreds of pieces, impossible to mend. "Yes," she said. She was finding it hard to stand there. All this time she'd been terrified of Nelly's return, and now here she was. What was she going to do? Rita felt like she'd been caught trespassing.

"This is Bev," Nelly said.

"I'm her keeper," Bev said, punching Nelly lightly in the arm. "I keep 'er in line." She was small and very round. She barked her words, punctuating what she said with a sharp laugh.

"So, they made it through the winter," Nelly said. The sheep chewed hungrily, pushing each other out of the way to reach the food. You did too, she wanted to say. You look good, too. But she knew that was off base. "Out of line!" Bev yelled when someone in the group home said something inappropriate. "People need their boundaries," she would say.

"Alton Poors helped me shear them. His wife Lucy's gonna spin the wool if I give her half. She'll show me how to dye it with wildflowers."

"Hey, that sounds good," Nelly said. For a moment, she looked like her old self, then her face crumpled and she grew very pale. She was trembling like the leaves in the poplar trees swaying ever so slightly, her loose pants flapping in the breeze.

"You all right?" Rita asked. "Would you like a drink or something?"

"I gave that up."

"I mean water or lemonade."

"I know. I was making a joke. Heh-heh," she said. "Bad joke."

"Bad joke," Bev agreed. They both laughed like this too was a joke.

Nelly wrapped her arms around herself as if to keep from blowing away. She was much taller than Rita had remembered, and so thin. But it wasn't that. Something else was different. Rita tried not to stare. She tried to be casual. It was Nelly's eyes, she realized. They had always been so flat, like mirrored sunglasses, revealing nothing. Now, they were soft, like a doe's.

"We'd like that lemonade," Bev said.

"The garden looks good," Nelly said as they walked toward the house.

"I decided to keep it small. Manageable."

"Manageable. That's good," Nelly said.

"Keep it simple," Bev said.

"Keep it simple. That's what we say in AA," Nelly explained. "I'm in AA now."

"Oh. That's good." Rita didn't know what to say. She pictured Nelly staggering into the cabin reeking of beer. The time Nelly smashed her fist through the window, both of them surprised there was no blood. Then she vomited in the sink and passed out on the floor.

"You built this place?" Bev asked. "We can't even get her to hang a picture at the home."

"I live in a group home," Nelly explained. "Me and five other crazies. Bev's our den mother." She smoothed the worn table with her palms while Rita got their drinks. "You fixed the benches," she said. "And the floor. I see you insulated it."

"Yeah. The winter, you know. It was a bad one."

Rita wanted to know what was going to happen next. When was Nelly going to return? Just when she was finally getting her life together, they would have to move.

"I think I'll just sit outside on that rock. You holler if you need me," Bev said. She looked at Rita when she said this.

"No regrets," Nelly said after Bev had gone outside. She turned her glass in her hands and took a quick sip.

"What do you mean?"

"That's this poem I learned. Julia, this woman in the group home, used to teach English. She reads me her favorite stuff."

"Oh." A fly was knocking against the screen, searching for a way out, buzzing loudly. She unlatched the screen and shooed it away.

"Out of love, no regrets—though the goodness be wasted forever. Out of love, no regrets, though the return be never," Nelly recited. "Langston Hughes. When I heard it, I thought of us." Nelly was trembling so much the lemonade slopped on the table when she set the glass down. She tucked her hands in her pockets. "I get the shakes," she said. "A side effect. I'm on all kinds of medication."

"Is it helping?"

"Yeah." She nodded slowly. "Yeah, it is. It makes the voices get softer. Sometimes they stop."

"That's good." Rita felt she had learned more about Nelly in the last few minutes than she had the whole time they lived together. Regrets? She had some, sure. Mostly about Rainey. She hated to see her hurt. And Nelly had hurt her. That was something you could never fix, not really. Time healed wounds and all that jazz had some truth. But hurt was hurt. It found a place in your life and settled there.

"Listen, the reason I came out here—" Nelly started.

"I'll leave whenever you say," Rita interrupted. She didn't want Nelly to think for a minute they would get back together.

"No, please. Listen. I came out here to tell you. I want you to stay. I don't want to come back. I really don't. I just had to see it. Kind of like revisiting the scene of the crime. I know I did something unforgivable. I can't take that back. In AA, we talk about making amends. That's what I want to do. Make amends."

Rita crushed one of the eggshells she'd dried in the oven, intending to feed them to the hens. She could see Bev wandering around the garden with her hands clasped behind her back. Nelly was crying now, gulping sobs that wrenched her body. She held up her hands as if to ward off any attempt at comfort. "I'm sorry," she gasped.

"Do you want me to get Bev?"

"No. No. I'll be all right. Just gimme a minute." Rita pumped water onto a clean washcloth and handed it to Nelly, who sucked it for a moment, then dabbed her face. Her skin was very pale with two red blotches under her eyes. Rita remembered how dark her tan was before, as if she'd been a different person back then. She had feared Nelly so long, now here she was, shattered, almost helpless.

"So the thing is," Nelly began. She cleared her throat. Her hands were twitching like fresh fish when you salt them before they hit the pan. "I want to give you this place. I have to wait till I'm well," she said, rushing along. "I gotta be considered in my right mind to do anything legal. But I want you to have it. You and Rainey," she said. "The house, the land, the truck. The whole shebang."

Rita started to protest. "No, I insist," Nelly said. "I don't want to come back here. You love it. That's plain to see. So why shouldn't you have it?"

"I could pay you."

"I don't need money," Nelly said. "I just need to feel I did something good here. That it's not all poisoned, that dream I had."

Rita was crying now, too, the tears running down her cheeks.

"You don't have to say anything. If you want, you can sell it. I just think it belongs to you. It's the least I can do."

Rita heard voices out the window. Rainey and Crystal were playing Body Snatchers again. "Don't close your eyes," Rainey shouted. "Crystal, no. They'll get you." She pulled Crystal's arm, trying to yank her off the ground. Then they noticed Bev and stopped.

"Weatherman says expect sun showers," Crystal said.

"Is that so?" Bev looked up at the sky.

"Well, I better go," Nelly said, "I'll be in touch." She offered her hand. Before Rita could take it, Rainey was at the door.

"Mommy! Somebody's—" She stopped when she saw Nelly. Her mouth was frozen in a small round circle. "Oh," she said.

Nelly was panting as if she'd just climbed to the top of a steep hill. Rita was relieved to see Bev appear at the door behind Rainey.

"So," Bev said. "Everything OK in here?"

"Yeah," Nelly said, her teeth chattering. "I-I-I," she began, but could not finish. She sank down onto the bench.

"Deep breaths," Bev said. "Remember oxygen?"

Nelly nodded. Rainey stood between her mother and Nelly as if to protect her.

"It's OK, Rainey," Rita murmured. She fluffed her curls. Bev was massaging Nelly's shoulders rapidly, as if pumping life back into her.

"We ready to go now?" Bev asked, jangling her keys.

Nelly nodded again. She turned away from Rainey and Rita and wiped her face on her forearm. "Ready," she said.

* * *

"Last time we had a circus they set up over by the bridge," Trudy said. She waited by the entrance to the big top clutching Raymond's hand. "A couple of mangy ponies, an old monkey, and two clowns is all it was. I think they were tryin' to get money for beer. Not like this here, no sir. This is really something, ain't it, Raymond honey?" Raymond slurped the snow cone she'd bought him. His lips and teeth were bright red.

"You know what I realized on the way over here?" Rita said.

"What's that, de-ah?"

"I've never seen the circus," Rita said. "I went once with a school group. We took the bus to Indianapolis. But I got lost. I spent the whole time looking for my classmates. All I remember is being in a big panic. All those strangers. I'd never seen so many strangers before."

"I didn't know you was from Indianapolis."

"I'm not. I lived a ways from Indianapolis," Rita explained.

"You hold tight to your momma's hand," Trudy warned Rainey.

Under an awning, some men were hitching up ponies for the pony rides. And on the other side were two elephants named Debby and Dora. Rita was reading the sign to Rainey, about how they were baby elephants.

"Imagine. Big as a house, just about, and babies," Trudy exclaimed.

Carol was in line waiting to buy lemonade and popcorn. A brown pygmy goat made a beeline for Rainey and nudged her hand, waiting to be petted. The silver bell on its collar jingled as Rainey scratched its rough coat. She pretended to let her stuffed monkey ride its back.

"You gonna ride one of them elephants?" Trudy asked her.

Rainey shrugged. She wasn't sure. They were such big animals. She would be up so high. What if she fell? What if it was like the time she rode the tractor with Nelly and broke her arm?

The one-ring circus was set up in a grassy field across from the school, under a yellow-and-blue-striped tent. Inside, the wooden bleachers were set in a semicircle around the ring. A three-piece band was tuning up. There was a man on keyboard, a woman who played a trumpet, and another man who sat amidst an array of drums and cymbals. The keyboard seemed to be set on "circus," judging from the calliope beat of "Yankee Doodle Dandy."

"Look, there's Slim," Rita said.

Rainey ran over to greet him. James was attempting to pull himself onto the seat. "He's a acrobat," Slim announced.

"He's so precocious," Rita said as James tottered over to her.

"He's what? Pre-what?"

"Precocious. What I mean is, he's growing up so fast, already walking and all. Rainey didn't start walking until she was fifteen months old. She was too busy studying everything to move around. But James acts like he's *got* to be on the move."

As if on cue, James stumbled away, reaching for Crystal's balloon. It was blue, covered with white stars. Slim caught the back of his suspenders and held on. The baby sat down with a plop and pulled at the grass, mesmerized by an ant that crawled across the back of his hand. They all moved down to make room for Trudy and Raymond.

"Look. There's J.T. and Betty," Trudy waved. "Boy, just about everybody's here, seems like. The whole town turns out for a circus." Even Rip and Coalie were there with their grandchildren, seated on the top row beside Buster who was eating a wad of blue cotton candy. "Hydie's gonna be sorry he kept the diner open. But he just hates to think somebody might show up for a cup of coffee or a hot dinner and find we're closed. He hates to disappoint anybody."

"We got here just in time," Carol said, returning with the snacks as the ringmaster dashed into the ring.

"Ladies and gentlemen," he said and tipped his top hat. He had a low, mellifluous voice and he drew out every sound as if playing an instrument. Crystal whacked her balloon against Raymond, making him giggle uncontrollably. James stood a few feet in front of Slim, his little feet planted in the mashed grass. When the music began, he danced, waving his arms like a conductor, bouncing up and down, turning to look at them and clap his hands.

"The Fantabulous Fabulas!" the ringmaster intoned. A woman dressed in a gold lamé leotard and a man in a matching suit dashed into the ring. Immediately, the man began cracking a whip, snapping a long sheet of paper the woman held until there was only a tiny square left.

"Is that toilet paper?" Crystal asked.

"I dunno." Slim put his arm around her. Everything was happening so fast Slim felt he could barely get used to what was going on before something else started up. As soon as the man swatted the last bit of paper, the woman backed against a red board they had watched one of the helpers hose down before the circus began. It glistened like fresh blood as the man started hurling knives at her. They landed around the periphery of her body, stabbing into the wood with a thwack. A clown with a garish grin painted on his face rushed into the ring and put a black hood over the man's head. As the drum rolled, he began to take several paces backwards. Then the clown handed him an ax. He flung it at his wife, then another one, again and again. Each time the axes smacked the board around her body, there was a loud crack and the acrid smell of gunpowder. Rita screamed the first time the gun went off, startling herself. Rainey clutched Carol and Rita's hands. As the last ax was hurled, the woman dashed away, the ax just missing her. The audience cheered.

"I can do that," Crystal said.

"You better never try," Slim said.

Two clowns were juggling bowling pins and balls of various sizes while the ring was cleared. "I can do that," Crystal said.

"*That* you can try," Slim said. "But not with anything breakable."

During the clown act, several men hurried through the bleachers with trays of sodas hung on straps around their necks. "My treat," Slim said. He'd sold all the appliances he had saved at the dump to a scrap dealer from Meddybemps, so he was feeling rich.

"And now, ladies and gentlemen," the ringmaster announced. "It's time for the Amazing Amanda!" A small brown-skinned woman dressed in a red spangled leotard bounded into the ring as if she'd been shot from a cannon. Rainey gasped and clapped her hand over her mouth. She was transfixed as the Amazing Amanda approached a thick rope dangling from the top of the tent. Very slowly, she slid off her red slippers and gave them to the ringmaster who set a pair of red clogs in the center of the ring, ready for Amanda to step into afterward. She ascended the rope, hand over hand, rising effortlessly until she was high at the top.

"That's the trapeze," Rita explained.

Amanda swung back and forth just like Rainey did on the swings at school, pumping her legs to go faster, pointing her toes. Her thick curls were pulled back into a braid, secured up the back of her head. Her skin was the same warm shade of brown as Rainey's. She glowed as if her skin were dusted with glitter, as if bits of her sparkling costume sprinkled onto her arms and legs. Rainey was so excited she stood in her seat between Carol and Rita.

"Annie wanted to be in the circus when she was a kid," Carol said. "She wanted to be a tightrope walker. But her mom said no black people would ever do such a thing. Guess this proves she was wrong."

Amanda was swinging higher, then she let go and twirled through the air, grabbing the trapeze at the last possible second. She blew kisses to the audience, then hung upside down from one leg.

"The A*maz*ing A*man*da will now do the Awe-In*spir*ing Jaws of *I*ron!" The ringmaster's voice boomed as the band struck up a version of "I Had the Time of My Life." Amanda rigged a special attachment to the trapeze she clenched in her teeth and hung there for a moment before she began to spin, at first slowly twirling, then faster and faster until she was like a top, a blur of red and brown whirling.

"Amazing Amanda! The Human Helicopter." The audience clapped and stamped their feet. James, thinking it was all for him, raised his arms and twirled a bit then tottered over to Slim.

"I don't want her to get a bellyache," Rita said when the clowns came through with cotton candy and Cracker Jacks. A couple of clowns carried bouquets of balloons. Carol gave Rainey a dollar to get one.

During intermission, Joe walked in arm-in-arm with Lizzy. They were dazed by the dim interior after being out in the bright sunlight and paused for a moment to get their bearings. Then they began weaving their way through the people heading outside for a quick smoke.

"Yoo-hoo, over here," Trudy called. "Them two look like a set of salt and pepper shakers, don't they?" She beamed proudly at Joe and Lizzy as if she'd just made them in one of her ceramics classes.

Lizzy saw Aran across the ring on the top rung of the bleachers sitting between Michael and Kaye. She leaned against Joe and sighed. As soon as Lizzy moved out, Kaye moved back in. Lizzy wondered if a divorce could be annulled. She studied them as if she were a social scientist. The happy family, she thought, surprised that it didn't hurt. Not that she expected to care that Michael and Kaye got back together. But seeing Aran with them. She had assumed that would be hard. They looked like they belonged together. Three peas in a pod, Trudy would say. J.T. whistled through her fingers and Lizzy searched the crowd until she saw her waving. Then she settled against Joe, taking popcorn from the sack he held. They had been up all night telling each other the stories of their lives. And still it felt like they had so much to say. "*You're* a treasure," Joe whispered in her ear after the ringmaster introduced the next act, claiming he was a world-renowned treasure.

Lothar the Lad from Beyond tossed his long brown hair like it was a mane. He stretched his arms beseechingly, his lithe body moving with the ease of a well-practiced dancer, his head thrown back, his face covered with a white mask. The spotlight glimmered on his skintight silver jumpsuit. "Gay people have always been in the circus," Carol said. "You're accepted no matter who you are."

"I don't get it," Crystal shouted. "Why's he holding that thing?"

"That's a cube," Slim explained. The man held a cube-shaped object fashioned from plastic pipe. "See. He's acting like it's got solid walls. Like he's trapped inside. He's feeling his way around."

"What a jughead," Crystal said. "It's air, not a wall. God."

Raymond was strumming the pink plastic electric guitar his mother bought him during intermission, making frenzied whirring noises as he plucked the imaginary strings. He was more involved with the band and his own music-making than he was with the circus acts.

When two elephants were led into the ring, the crowd went wild, as if they'd been waiting for this. "Is that Debby and Dora?" Rainey asked. She held her monkey up so it could see, too.

"They seem bigger, don't they?" Rita said. "Maybe it's their moms."

"Everyone likes to see the trained animals act like people," Carol explained. Their skin hanging off their bodies made them look like they were wearing pajamas several sizes too big. Carol felt a little sad to watch them. They looked so defeated with their long-suffering expressions.

"They're from Africa, right?" Rainey asked. "Like my monkey?"

Carol nodded. She had never seen Rainey so enthralled. The elephants were so large and cumbersome it took several seconds for Carol to realize they were about to lie down. They rolled over like dogs playing dead. Then they sat on their haunches and waved their front feet, their trunks swaying back and forth.

"Hey, I know that song," Crystal yelled.

"What?" Slim tried to calm her. He wished he hadn't bought her that second Coke, she was getting so hyper.

"That's 'Norwegian Wood' you nimwit." She sang along.

"She's right," Rita said, laughing softly. She felt sad and happy and grateful, all mixed up in one. She was surrounded by people who loved her. She had a place in their lives. And Preacher's Lake was her home. She never had to leave unless she decided to go. She squeezed Carol's hand and put her arm around Rainey.

Excalibur, an Appaloosa with a red-plumed headdress and fancy silver-trimmed saddle, was doing complicated dressage. Mrs. Fabula, who wore a matching headdress, rode him around the ring. For his finale, Excalibur climbed slowly up onto a small low table.

"Why's he standin' on that coffee table?" Crystal shouted. "Ain't he gonna break it? Hey, get offa there, horse! Why's he doin' that?"

"It's his trick," Slim said.

The clowns returned in different costumes. This time one of them was pretending to be a carpenter while the other one was attempting to play a fiddle. As soon as he got going on a song, the other clown would start hammering. They pretended to have an argument, then the fiddler began again. He played a few strains from "Turkey in the Straw" before the carpenter began sawing a piece of wood, interrupting the music. At one point, he whirred an electric saw and the man on the fiddle seemed to imitate him. Then they settled down and played, "He's Got the Whole World in His Hands" with the one clown twanging his saw along with the fiddle.

"That's me and Crystal," Slim said. "That's just like us."

During this act, The Fantabulous Fabulas and The Amazing Amanda were circling the bleachers selling programs with their photo on the glossy cover. Carol led Rainey over to buy one.

"What's your name, honey?" Amanda asked Rainey. Her skin shimmered with a fine sheen and her eyes were dark and warm. Rainey looked up at the beautiful woman. She seemed like a princess. There were so many things Rainey wanted to say but she didn't say a thing.

"You really *are* amazing," Carol said, hoping for Rainey's sake to keep her attention longer. She could tell the woman was in a hurry to sell programs. She blew Rainey a kiss and hurried off, her red clogs stirring up puffs of dust.

The Fantabulous Fabulas were back in the ring, this time as King and Queen of the Reptiles. They had a large trunk from which they began to unpack an assortment of pythons, each one larger and longer than the last until they called for Amanda's help. They opened a large black trunk and the three of them lifted out a huge pale pink python.

"Ladies and Gentlemen. The King of the Amazon! A hundred and sixty pounds of muscle!" the ringmaster shouted. Its body was lumpy, as if it had just swallowed dozens of mice. They called for a volunteer to come have his picture taken with the snakes.

"You can't give me five hundred dollars to touch no snake," Crystal said. "Yick!"

"How about a million dollars?" Slim pretended to slither his hand.

Crystal slapped it away. "Nope, not even a zillion. Gross."

After the performers gave their last bows, Lizzy laced her fingers through Joe's and they followed the crowd out. People were lining up at the edge of the ring to have their pictures taken with one of the snakes. Just before they exited through the flap, Joe pulled her aside.

"Look," he said. Lizzy turned around and there were Michael and Kaye, seated on two folding chairs in the ring, Aran already posed on Michael's lap. Mr. Fabula was wrapping a long glossy python around their necks, resting the tail on Kaye's cleavage.

"Smile!" Mr. Fabula commanded, and they did as the camera flashed.

"Creep," Joe said.

"Which one?" Lizzy asked, looking at the happy threesome. How had she ever been so deluded?

"That's the word origin for serpent. *Serpere*. Creep."

"Oh," Lizzy said. She was still worried he'd say something biblical and scare her off. But so far, he seemed totally down to earth.

"Only a real creep would mess up a chance to have paradise," he said as they headed out of the tent.

"I'm afraid I'll get seasick," Rita said as they waited in line for the elephant ride.

"I betcha my legs're too long," Slim said. "But James here wants to go."

Joe and Lizzy offered to take Rainey and James. As they climbed to the top of the platform and waited their turn, Lizzy was comforted to learn from the sign that these two elephants were orphans, that they would have died in the wild if they hadn't been adopted by the circus. She held James in her arms, pretending he belonged there, that he was hers. Just for this one second, she admonished herself as Joe helped them onto the special seat.

At first Rainey was afraid and would not open her eyes. Joe circled his arms around her. "Wave at everybody. I won't let you fall," he said, and she believed him. She opened her eyes and waved at the crowd. Then she saw Slim waving back, her mother and Carol, too. She waved, wondering if this was how they had all looked to Amazing Amanda as she swung so high above them. Below her, the crowd was a swirl of smiling faces.

* * *

Slim finished washing James and started dabbing powder over his bottom, getting him ready for bed. "We got a big day ahead of us tomorrow," he said. "You oughta be gettin' ready for bed soon, Crystal."

"It's still daytime, you jughead. The sun's still out. And I gotta watch my movie," she said. "I missed it when we were at the circus."

"Get your nightgown on first," he said. "It'll be dark before you know it." She hurried to the bathroom to get ready, brushing her teeth because she knew that made Slim happy, washing her face and neck and behind her ears, too.

"How's Mom gonna find us if we're gone?" Crystal asked when she was settled on the sofa with Bootie, who curled up in the last rays of sunlight that fell across the blanket.

"You got a point there," Slim said. "You figure we oughta just sit tight and wait for her?"

"I dunno." Crystal was trying to juggle the tube socks Slim had rolled into balls for her. She couldn't even catch one let alone keep all three in the air.

"It's just a vacation," Slim said. "Like I told you. I'm fixin' on bringin' us home. I figure we have to go just so we learn that."

"Learn what?"

"That we can come back." He tossed a sock at her and instead of trying to catch it, she ducked.

"Oh, Mr. Moe."

"Remember how I told you? I'm startin' a business. Slim's Second Time Around. You're gonna come over there after school and help me."

"School. Gross. I hate school."

"You don't have to go to school till we get back home."

"Where we gonna go?" She lifted the baby into the air. "James's doing his airplane act," she said. The baby let out a happy scream.

"You know," Slim said.

"Tell me."

"You still wanna see Mount Trashmore, right?"

"What're you talkin' about?" Crystal asked.

"Mount Trashmore. Remember how I told you? They built it outa trash they piled up right there on Virginia Beach. A sixty-eight foot man-made mountain peak that's got a great big playground on top. We'll go up there and fly us a kite."

"You go fly a kite, mister," Crystal said.

"And we're gonna go to Wellesley, Massachusetts, where they have a dump kind of like my Dream Facility was gonna be. Remember how I told you they been recyclin' goin' on twenty years? They got quite a operation."

"That all we're gonna do? Look at a bunch of dumpy dumps?"

"No. We're gonna go to Kansas, remember?"

"That's where Dorothy's at, right?"

"She ain't there no more, Crystal. I told you that."

"Why not?"

"Well, sometimes people go away and they never come back. They die or they get a new job or they find someone else to love and they just stay where they are. And sometimes they were never there to begin with. It was just a story. Does that make any kind of sense to you?"

"You jughead. Just a story. God."

"We're going to the Rocky Mountains. I showed you on the map."

"Rocky Raccoon," Crystal said. "But how're we gonna get back?"

"Remember how Dorothy gets back? Remember what she says?"

"There's no place like home." Crystal clicked her heels together. "I ain't got no ruby slippers, you nutty butt. You can't do your sneakers like that." Shotgun playfully bit one of her toes.

"Well, you got other things."

"What things?" She dug under the cushion for the remote. "It's time," she said, aiming it at the VCR.

"Hold off a sec. We're still talkin'. You always got a home. It's right here." He tapped her forehead. "And here." He tapped her chest over her heart. "No matter where we go, you'll carry it with you."

"What d'you mean, carry it? I ain't gonna carry no trailer."

Slim didn't know how else to explain it. He played patty-cake with James. Finally he said, "If me and James and Shotgun are there, it'll be home. Wherever we are, that's your home base."

"Ollie ollie in free. Home base. Can I watch it now? It's time."

"Yeah, go ahead." Slim got up and looked out the window. Several of his cats were lounging on the camper. Carol was pushing Rainey in her tire swing, helping her twirl around. He was glad to have them for neighbors, happy to know they'd be looking in on his place, feeding the animals while he was gone. The evening primroses had opened by the back door, bright yellow blossoms in the falling light. Slim thought of the day Nelly destroyed the farm. How awful it had been. How he worried Rita would never recover. And that day he came home to find Janesta gone. How devastated he was. He used to believe missing her would kill him. Sometimes it seemed like he'd made up all those sad days. And the happy days, too. That it was all something he'd dreamed the way Dorothy had.

"Slim?"

"What, Crys?" When he turned back to her, the trailer was dark, like a cellar they'd been huddling in. When they were on the road, they would spend more time outdoors, he decided. They would take walks every day. Cook hamburgs over a campfire. Watch the stars. The other night, the Milky Way was like a ladder to heaven, he could have climbed it rung by rung.

"You still didn't say how she's gonna find us."

Slim sighed. "You got any ideas about that?"

Crystal paused the video and thought about it, scratching her head.

"We can tie a string to the doorknob and keep the rest in the camper. Then all she's gotta do is follow the string."

"That'd be some giant ball of string. I don't think we could come up with enough string to get all the way to Union City, let alone where we're gonna go. We're goin' a lot further than that."

"Oh." She thought some more, chewing her hair. "I know."

"What?"

"Leave her a note."

"That sounds good. We can tape it to the door."

Her movie came back on and as she settled down to watch, Slim got busy making their lunch for the first day of the trip. He smeared mustard onto hamburger buns and stacked on the lunch meat and cheese.

"Toto come back," Dorothy screamed.

Crystal paused the video again. "Slim?"

"What, kiddo?"

"If you wasn't you, would you be somebody else?"

"I guess so."

"D'you think you'd know you was you?"

"Lemme get this straight. I'm me, but I ain't me. I'm somebody else. But while I'm somebody else, do I know I'm me?"

Crystal nodded, waiting.

"That is one big thought, sister."

"Well, do you?"

"I tell you one thing. I'd know *you* anywhere."

"Even if I was a boy? Or if I was real fat or had purple hair?"

"Yes, Crystal. I believe I would."

Satisfied, she started the movie again, settling back onto her pillows, ready for the story she knew so well.

* * *

Rainey and Carol's laughter drifted through the screens with the warm breeze as they raced through the fields chasing the fireflies that winked in the tall grass. The sun was low in the sky, tinging the scattered clouds above the hills pale pink. Rita noticed the leaves on the poplars shimmering in the soft silvery light as she pinched bread dough from the bowl on the table, shaping round balls between her floured palms. Nestling the pockets of dough into a pie plate she covered it with a dish towel and left it to rise.

A woodpecker, hanging upside down in the apple tree, pecked insects from the leaves. Plump robins hopped across the grass searching for worms while dozens of sparrows gathered for the night in the row of sugar maples, the cacophony of their calls echoing. It was Rita's favorite time of day, evening, not yet dark, the crickets like monks ceaselessly chanting as the thrushes began to trill from the edge of the woods.

This is my house, Rita thought. My land. My trees. My grass. She sprinkled fresh rosemary and thyme onto the onions sizzling in hot olive oil and chopped a handful of parsley. All of the vegetables in the soup she was making for their late supper she had grown herself, even the jar of tomatoes she pried open and emptied into a bowl. It was the last one left from that hot summer day when she canned them out under the trees. As she squeezed the richly scented fruit between her fingers, she remembered Nelly's words. I know I did something unforgivable, Nelly had said, the pain clearly visible in the curve of her shoulders, her fingers knotted on her lap. Forgiveness is hard work, Joe often said. We forget we're doing it for ourselves, not for the person who harmed us.

Rita sighed as she added chunks of squash to the soup and slowly stirred it. The hurt was still there, like a torn muscle in her chest not yet healed. But it was shifting, moving aside, like rocks coming to the surface of the garden, making room for something new.

She left the soup to simmer and went outside. A breeze passed over her carrying with it the faint scent of the cedar shingles, still warm from the sun. On the horizon, feathery lavender-hued clouds hovered, streaked with the golden light of the disappearing sun. She remembered herself as a teenager, could see the girl she'd been, her bony shoulder blades like clipped wings poking through the hair that fell to her waist, her eyes on the worn path as she trudged into the woods one summer day, determined to swallow the painkillers she'd taken from her mother's drawer. She had perched on an old hickory stump, crying, feeling hopeless, unable to imagine any good coming into her life. Then hundreds of mosquitoes descended, swarming over her, stinging her ears, biting her ankles, like fire at the edge of her eyes and lips, entangled in her hair, attacking her scalp, hot needles prickling down her back until she jumped up, swatting at herself, actually laughing as she ran for the shelter of home.

Today a magical quality hung over her. But it was not only today. It was the events of her life unfolding the way they had. Nelly giving her the land, the house, whoever would have thought? Once she had been so rootless, so scattered. Now, she felt like a child who finally had permission to stay up late to see the end of the movie instead of being sent to bed midway through. She could stay and see how things turned out.

She brushed her hands over the clumps of thyme she had planted in the front yard; the pink buds were starting to open. Beside the rosemary, tarragon, and sage, a few bees still worked the bright blue borage flowers nodding from their sturdy stems. Morning glories trailed up the lattice Slim had fastened to the side of the house, the twisted blossoms like umbrellas ready to unfurl at dawn. This fall, she decided, I'll plant tulips and daffodils. Crocuses and bluebells. A peony bush and bearded iris. Set paving stones to make a path to the door.

She breathed deeply, aware of her bare feet planted firmly on the fragrant thyme that cascaded over the path like a thick carpet, of the swallows overhead, dipping and swirling, bright flashes of blue, of her body brimming with life. She waved at Rainey and Carol as they ran toward her.

"Look!" Rainey said, pointing behind the house. Rita turned and there was the moon rising above Preacher's Mountain, a huge orange bowl of light.

• A NOTE ON THE TYPE •

The typeface used in this book is a version of Baskerville, originally designed by John Baskerville (1706–1775) and considered to be one of the first "transitional" typefaces between the
"old style" of the continental humanist printers and the "modern" style of the nineteenth century. With a determination
bordering on the eccentric to produce the finest possible
printing, Baskerville set out at age forty-five and with no previous experience to become a typefounder and printer (his
first fourteen letters took him two years). Besides the letter
forms, his innovations included an improved printing press,
smoother paper, and better inks, all of which made Baskerville decidedly uncompetitive as a businessman. Franklin,
Beaumarchais, and Bodoni were among his admirers, but his
typeface had to wait for the twentieth century to achieve its due.